GOING GREY

KAREN TRAVISS

This is a work of fiction. All the characters, organisations, companies, locations, countries, objects, situations, and events portrayed in this novel are either products of the author's imagination or are used fictitiously. Any resemblance to people living or dead is coincidental.

Published by Karen Traviss
www.karentraviss.com

ISBN-13: 978-1499713046
ISBN-10: 1499713045

Cover photography: Tereshchenko Dmitry/Shutterstock.com

DEDICATION

To the memory of SPC T. Jocic and SPC T. Fisher, US Army, killed in action in Zhari District, Afghanistan in 2012, and to their friend SPC J. Bakerink, who keeps their memory alive.

ACKNOWLEDGEMENTS

My grateful thanks go to Ray Ramirez, for firearms and technical advice, and for steadfast friendship; Jeanne Marie Coleman, for technical advice on police procedure; Sean Baggaley, IT genius and smart marketeer, for cover and formatting support; Anthony Serena; Jim Gilmer; Martin Welsford; Mary Pletsch; Bryan Boult, patient beta tester, for his uncanny ability to zero in on plot holes; and Alasdair McLean, inexhaustible source for perception and cognition research.

I would also like to thank those who provided technical advice but preferred not to be named for professional reasons, including private military contractors currently working in the industry, and scientists in the fields of transgenics and fertility.

I couldn't have written this book without the generous input of all those mentioned above. Any errors in this book are entirely mine.

Karen Traviss
May 2014

PROLOGUE

DUNLOP RANCH, NORTH OF ATHEL RIDGE, WASHINGTON: NOVEMBER, THREE YEARS AGO.

The world's full of mirrors.

They're everywhere. You probably don't notice, but then you're not trying to avoid them like I am.

I don't mean the regular variety. There's just two in the house and I don't use them. I mean all the shiny surfaces that spit your reflection back at you when you're not expecting it. Today it's the water trough in the top field. I need to break the ice for the sheep. I've got seconds to step back before the surface settles and shows me how I look today.

The sheep crowd around the pickup, expecting hay and pellets, so I flap the door a few times to get them to back off and give me room to climb out. They're Jacob sheep — biblical-looking, cranky, and hard to herd. The ram's got six curly horns and letterbox-slit pupils like the Devil. But his name's Roger, not very Satanic at all. He blocks my way and stares at me, head tilted on one side.

"What's the problem, buddy?" Roger knows when I'm having a bad day. I think he can smell it, like those dogs that sense when their owner's about to have a seizure. "Come on, move it."

Roger backs off, looking baffled, but then sheep often do. When I stab my hunting knife into the ice, the chunks tilt and sink. I pull back before the water gets a chance to become another mirror.

Here's my problem. Sometimes I don't recognise myself.

I don't mean the split second that everyone says they get now and again, when a store window catches you unaware, or that distracted second when you're brushing your teeth. I mean that I really see a *stranger*, someone else, someone *different,* and I never go back to the way I was. A week, a month, a year or two later, I risk looking in the shaving mirror, the fold-up one I've learned not to need, and I might look different again.

It's not real. It can't be. So there's only one explanation: I'm crazy.

I've looked in medical books, and all I know is that it isn't dysmorphia, and it isn't prosopagnosia. They don't fit at all. This is my own special kind of crazy. Dunlop's Syndrome. Maybe it'll get its own Latin name one day.

When I hit a bad patch, my face and scalp start to feel wind-burned for a few moments, like the skin's pulling tight. Then I look in a mirror, and I'm not me. But what's *me,* anyway? I can't remember. I just get used to the new face and that's me until the next time it happens.

So Gran doesn't allow shiny surfaces in the house. Blinds cover the windows. There's no glass in the picture frames. The bathroom mirror folds away. Even the photo of her dad and his helicopter, the one on the bookcase, is under a sheet of matt acrylic.

The sheep seem happy, so I head back to the house. There's not a lot to do around the ranch in the winter apart from looking after Gran's rescue animals and catching up on my lessons. When I open the kitchen door, Gran's putting on her sheepskin jacket to go out. Sometimes I wonder if it bothers the sheep. Do they recognise it? Do they ask themselves why Gran looks after them like pets, but wears one of their own? Maybe they're just like humans, happy to turn a blind eye when it suits them.

"I'm off to town, Ian." Gran studies my face. She can always tell when something's wrong. "Want to come?"

When I can feel a bad patch coming, I want to hide from everyone, even Gran. "No thanks. I've got math to do. Maybe watch a DVD. I'll fix dinner."

"You okay?"

"Yeah. Sure."

"Anything you want me to fetch back?"

I get through a lot of movies on our DVD player. We've even got old video tapes. Gran doesn't trust cable and satellite companies, like she doesn't trust banks, credit cards, and the internet. The only phone we've got is an unregistered cell, a really old one without any fancy features.

"If you're passing the thrift store, could you see if they've got any movies, please? Or documentaries."

"Which war?"

"World War One. I haven't got many on that."

Gran nods, looking off to one side for a second like she's running through a mental database of movie titles. "Okay, checklist time. Keys?"

"Gun locker, ammo store, truck." I count them off on the rack on the kitchen wall. It's our drill every time she leaves the ranch. She says Mount St. Helens made her jumpy and now she's always ready to run. "Safe. Desk."

"Folder?"

"Locked in the desk. Open it if you're not back in four hours, and follow the instructions inside."

"Emergency supplies and grab bag?"

"In the hall closet." It's like reciting my times tables, an automatic stream of sound. "And I call Joe if I need to move the animals."

"Good. We're all square, then. See you later."

Athel Ridge isn't far to drive, but it might as well be Outer Mongolia. Our nearest neighbours are a couple of miles away — Joe and a bunch of other folks who live off the grid as well. We avoid the town because every move gets seen and recorded somewhere, according to Gran. She's careful about that sort of thing. Government agencies and big business are all the same species of bastard who spy on you all the time, she says, and she said so years before everyone else found out it was all true.

But I always knew she wasn't crazy. Unusual, maybe, but not *crazy*. I know what crazy is.

I finish my chores and choose a DVD from the tight-packed bookcase. The photo of Great-Grandad — David Dunlop, Huey pilot, the guy who did his duty in Vietnam — sits on the shelf at eye height, a reminder of what I've got in me somewhere. I never knew him. But then I never knew my parents, either. Gran never talks about them. She just says Mom was a waster, and that she doesn't know who my father was. The fact that she tells me everything about her dad and nothing about Mom says it all.

Great-Grandad's the guy I need to take after. He's the one to emulate. I don't want to be a waster like my mom.

But I'm sixteen next birthday. I should be thinking about what I'm going to do with my life. One thing's for sure: the Army doesn't take crazy people.

Knowing what I see isn't real doesn't help. It's enough to fuck up your whole life. Gran says I'd end up on the streets or worse if I tried to cope in the outside world, so I'm better off on the ranch, miles from anywhere, home-schooled and out of the reach of well-meaning doctors and do-gooders from social services.

For once, I can't even wrap myself up in the movie. All I can see is David Dunlop, a man who did amazing things and put his life on the line for his buddies. Forget your flag and country, Gran says. People spat on Great-Grandad when he came home from 'Nam. So much for a grateful nation. War brings out the best and the worst in people, she says, and the best of it is a pretty good example of how to live your life. I've only got to watch the news to see what the worst is like, or think of Great-Grandad Dunlop coming home and wondering what the hell it was all for.

It was for his buddies. That was reason enough for him. I can see that in the movies. It's the one truth that shines out of all of them.

One of Gran's greyhounds, Oatie, jumps on the sofa and puts his head in my lap. It's enough to distract me. My focus shifts from the photo to the TV screen for a second, and — damn, it's another mirror. I don't normally see the TV that way, but the light from the window's at the wrong angle. Before I can shake it off, I see myself.

Did my nose look like that yesterday? Does my hair seem lighter?

It's not real, any of it. But if you know you're nuts, does that mean you're not? If I *was* crazy, I'd think it was real, right?

Maybe I'll grow out of it. Maybe I'll get sane. And maybe I won't, and this is how I'll spend the rest of my life. I don't know what I look like, I don't know much about where I came from, and I don't know where I'm going.

But there's Great-Grandad. Something of him must be in me, something that made him fly that Huey into enemy fire time after time because guys were depending on him for their lives.

I just have to look for it. It's got to be there.

ONE

In my capacity as Career Manager, I write to notify you that with regret, I must issue you with 12 months' notice of termination. This notification can now be treated as an executive order to start planning and make use of the resettlement package available to you.

UK Ministry of Defence notice of compulsory redundancy, issued to Sgt Rob Rennie, Royal Marines.

NAZANI, EAST AFRICA: 48 HOURS BEFORE THE END OF THE NPROFOR/ AFRICAN UNION PEACEKEEPING MISSION.

Time was like falling off a cliff. One second you were alive, and the next you weren't: one minute you had a good career with a few years left before you had to find a job in Civvy Street, and the next you found yourself out on your ear without so much as a thank-you or a kiss-my-arse.

The e-mail from the company handling the MoD's Dear John letters had arrived two days ago. The services of Sergeant Rob Rennie were no longer required. The timing couldn't have been worse.

You bastards. You binned me.

And short of my pension date. So no lump sum on exit. Fuck you.

Rob fidgeted in the passenger seat of the armoured ACMAT pickup, staring at the bleak prospect of unemployment and an equally grim cluster of ruined buildings in the distance, all that was left of a town called Wadat.

There'd been a lot more of Wadat around on his last deployment, but the place was doing well to cling to the map at all given the pounding it had taken. A cluster of shell-shattered, abandoned buildings refused to give up. In a saner world, Nazani could have been a resort for trendy adventure tourists playing at roughing it, but this was Rob's world, the real one, greedy and destructive, another angry, broken place where schoolboys were waiting to kill him.

One of them was loafing in a derelict shop doorway with a scabby ginger dog as the ACMAT passed. The kid couldn't have been more than twelve, smoking with all the weary assurance of a forty-a-day man while he drummed one heel against the shuttered door. Rob couldn't work out whether he was a lookout or a decoy. He didn't seem to have a phone in his hand. Either way, he wasn't waiting for the shop to open so he could go in and buy a Mars Bar.

Sam Obado drummed his fingers on the steering wheel and gave him a quick glance. He must have seen Rob's eyes lock on to the kid.

"He's not a lookout, Robert." Sam was an accomplished mind-reader. "Relax."

Rob craned his neck and didn't take his eyes off the boy until he was completely out of sight. It didn't make sense for anyone to harass patrols when the peacekeepers were pulling out, but the end of deployments was a favourite time to pick off tired foreign troops with home on their minds. He'd be out of here soon along with the rest of the peacekeeping force, and then it would be someone else's problem. Rob had enough of his own to worry about now.

How am I going to top up Tom's university fund now?

I was counting on that fucking money.

He'd thought he'd have a few more years to get things sorted before he had to face Civvy Street for the first time in his adult life. But he'd thought wrong. He had a year to find a new job in a world that didn't have much use for what he did best.

Private security, maybe. Yeah, me and a few thousand other blokes. Not so easy to get your foot in the door now.

Sod it. I'll think of something. I'm thirty-seven. I'm not washed up yet.

If they'd just let him see out his twenty-two years, he could have picked up a tidy lump sum when he left. Now he'd have to wait another twenty-odd years for it, way too late to help Tom when he really needed it.

Bastards. Just to save a few quid on this year's budget. What do I get? A resettlement grant. Ten grand or whatever.

Rob opened the window a couple of inches, letting in air that now smelled of damp earth instead of lightly-toasted war zone. A zebra-striped bird with a rusty pink crest stabbed its long beak into the grass verge like a man searching for land mines. Somewhere a few miles north, a vehicle carrying aid workers and their mobile security guy — no confirmed number or nationalities yet — had missed its last radio check. Rob and Sam headed down the route the party should have taken, expecting to find them trying to repair a broken-down SUV.

It didn't explain why they hadn't called in, though. Rob checked his watch again.

"Be nice to them when we find them, Robert," Sam said.

"I'm charm personified. I don't have any problem with security blokes."

"I meant the aid workers."

Rob realised he'd griped about NGOs more than he thought. "Yeah. One minute we're compromising their precious neutrality. Then it all goes to rat shit and they want us to rescue them."

"At least we have the moral high ground."

"I'll treasure that if I get my arse shot off saving them."

Sam steered through a slalom course of potholes. Shallow mortar craters were mixed with puddles of overnight rain, each one still a potential IED as far as Rob was concerned. Roads had long since ceased to be paths from A to B. Even back in the UK, he was a jumpy passenger. He fidgeted, trying to find a position to keep his boots off the floor, ready for a shockwave from below that could break his back. Sam should have let him drive. He was happier when he was in control.

"Don't worry," Sam said. "You'll find work. Your son will go to college. And the floor won't deform if we hit anything."

"I'm really obvious, aren't I?" Rob studied himself in the wing mirror again to check that he still looked fine for a man who was knocking on the door of middle age. "I just haven't got the civvy skills they want these days."

"You have time to acquire some."

"Not without a brain transplant."

"Try maritime security. You could call at Morrigan's office in Mombasa before you go home."

Bev would have called that mercenary work, but she'd given up having a say in Rob's life when she left him. He had to focus on Tom now. Maybe getting binned was Nature's way of telling him he'd done his duty and now it was Rob Time.

"Yeah, you're right." Rob tried to sound upbeat. No wrapping or whingeing, that was the rule: no giving up and no complaining. However bad things got, a Marine just cracked on with it. "I'll end up guarding luxury yachts. Sorted."

The ACMAT passed a couple of African Union Humvees with Senegalese and Kenyan markings, parked about twenty meters from the tarmac. Sam acknowledged one of the guys on the Miniguns with a discreetly raised forefinger. Then something bounced against the underside of the pickup with a loud clunk, probably just a chunk of concrete, but Rob still held his breath and waited for the bang that never came. It was enough to take his mind off his money worries.

"Relax." Sam read his mind again, not that it was hard. "Morrigan cleared the road this morning. Did you hear they lost another man last week?"

"Course not. Contractors are even lower on the food chain than us." Rob stopped himself mid-whinge. *Cheerful in adversity.* It was such a central part of being a Royal Marine that it was specified in the recruiting leaflet. "That'll be me this time next year."

The radio interrupted. "*Echo Two Three Bravo, this is Zero — confirming three Dutch, one French NGO personnel, plus one US mobile asset, armed. Nothing heard for thirty minutes now, over.*"

Rob adjusted his headset. So that was four aid workers and their American minder, what the civvies would have called their bodyguard, and he had a weapon. No problem there, then.

"Zero, this is Echo Two Three Bravo, any UAVs to give us eyes on, over?"

"*None available yet, over.*"

"Understood. Estimate, fifteen minutes to the Gibure road. Roger out."

Technology was never there when he bloody needed it. Never mind: they had a Mk 48 machine gun and a few hundred-round belts in the back, plus an HK69 grenade launcher to hand, useful both for smoke and giving someone an emphatic hello. In the end, it was reliable kit and basic soldiering skills that would get him out of trouble. Control could keep their toy planes.

"Step on it, Sam. Can't afford to misplace a Septic." Rob slapped the dashboard. "Too much diplomatic fallout. One Yank equals twenty Brits equals a hundred of you."

Sam did one of his terrific belly laughs. "Don't tell them that. They want to be loved."

"What, aid workers or Septics?"

"You always make me laugh, Robert. I shall miss you."

Sam pulled over to the side of the road to let a wide-load convoy pass. It was heading south from Gibure, a mix of tankers and trucks with Morrigan logos on their mud-flecked doors. Rob noted the security escort manned by hairy-arsed, unsmiling, sunglassed white blokes in black T-shirts and body armour, and wondered if contractors ever worked together long enough to feel like family in the same way the Corps did.

And that's my future. Okay. Can do.

"I'll miss you too, mate," Rob said.

He watched the convoy shrink and vanish in the wing mirror. This was how governments liked their overseas wars now — local troops to do the heavy lifting, a lot of Western hired help, and a handful of uniformed blokes like him as "advisers." They called it *scalable* and *flexible.* Rob translated that as *cheaper* and *no visible body bags to upset the voters.*

Sam was about to turn off towards Pelayi when HQ came on the radio again.

"*Echo Two Three Bravo, this is Zero — NGO confirms their vehicle's being held on the south side of the Pelayi river crossing by unidentified locals in three technicals, minimum six crew. No injuries. The US mobile asset's employed by Esselby. The locals want payment for using the road, over.*"

At least the aid party had been able to call in. "Zero, is this a hostage situation, over?"

"*Negative, treat as a bribe, over.*"

Rob ignored that and planned for a rescue anyway. There was looking on the positive side, and then there was being bloody stupid. The crossing on the sat map looked like the kind of spot he'd have picked for an ambush, a choke point overlooked by a hill, with tree cover one side for fire support elements. Sam glanced at it and tutted to himself. He obviously saw it the same way. It was an armed toll bridge by any other name.

"Roger that, Zero," Rob said. "Difficult location. We could use some support, over."

"*On its way. Two AU patrols about ten minutes behind you. Zero out.*"

Rob checked his pouches for the US dollars and local shillings that he took on patrols for those occasions when cigarettes, a watch, or a throwaway mobile phone weren't enough to placate the locals. He kept the cash with his combat trauma kit. That was the measure of its life-saving abilities.

"I'm going to pull up there," Sam said, tapping the dashboard screen at a point fifty meters from the crossing. "That looks like trouble."

"Too right, mate."

The Pelayi road deteriorated gradually from crumbling tarmac to a broad dirt track. Sam kept checking in with the Humvees a few klicks behind, chattering away in French to the Senegalese unit like Jean Paul Sartre on speed.

He looked happier for the chat. "They've split up to approach the crossing on both flanks to give us cover."

"Cracking. Better safe than sorry." Rob counted the dollar bills. This was probably just a last-minute rush to squeeze some income out of foreigners before they abandoned Nazani. "I'm good at sweet-talking the local delinquents. Bung them some cash and we'll be home for tea."

Rob scanned the slopes to the right, looking for signs of activity in the tree line. There would probably be more blokes behind cover somewhere. He was looking for three "technicals", then, the makeshift gun trucks that every dodgy armed gang seemed to tool around in. According to the sat map, there was no useful cover near the road if things went pear-shaped. The left side of the road was flat for about fifty meters, a handy spot to lay mines to stop anyone skirting the control point. There was so much ordnance washing around the bazaars these days that he always assumed the worst.

"No cover," Rob said. "Sam, stand by to put some smoke down if we have problems. I don't like the look of the trees."

Trouble. Check weapons, comms, cam.

Rob adjusted the microcam clipped to his radio headband in case he needed to prove he'd handed over cash. When the road straightened out of a blind bend, he could see a knot of vehicles blocking the road seventy meters ahead. It resolved into a battered

SUV hemmed in by the technicals, three Toyota pickups with Russian RPKs mounted on the back.

Two of the technicals were parked with their guns aimed down the road. The third faced the opposite direction, giving them a 360 degree arc of fire. These blokes weren't amateurs.

Rob counted heads while he went through his ritual again, touching rifle, sidearm, and ammo to remind his hands what might be needed. There were eight local lads on and around the Toyotas, all under thirty, five nursing AK-47s and three manning the guns. Next to the SUV, five white civvies — three men, two women — stood in a tidy line that said they'd been ordered not to move.

Sam brought the ACMAT to a halt at an angle so that Rob was facing the roadblock sideways. At least Sam could get out of the vehicle with the engine block for cover. He was also in position to make a fast exit.

"That must be the American," Sam said, doing a discreet nod.

The bloke stood out like the Eddystone lighthouse. He was big and blonde, much taller than the civvies, wearing the unofficial uniform of black T-shirt and desert camo pants that a lot of contractors seemed to wear. No body armour, though, and no weapon: the Nazani lads must have taken them. He looked like the business, but Rob took nothing on trust.

"When Yanks are good," Rob said, "they're *very* good. But when they're not, they're a fucking liability."

Sam fiddled with his headset. "We can rely on your persuasive powers, Robert. And dollars. The Humvees will be in position in a few minutes."

"Okay, cover the gunner on the left, just in case. Some bastard in the trees has probably got me lined up, but I'll take the other bloke if anything goes wrong. Toss a coin for the third one."

Rob adjusted his beret and slid out to start the lonely walk to the checkpoint, rifle slung to make it clear he wouldn't take any shit. He glanced at the American, working out whether he was going to help or hinder if things didn't go to plan. Their eyes met for a moment. Rob decided he fell into the Good rather than Liability category. Maybe it was the way he held himself, but Rob just *knew* the bloke would do what was needed, weapon or no weapon. They stopped short of nodding to each other in silent agreement.

"Hi. I'm Sergeant Rob Rennie, En-Pro-For," he said. "Call me

Rob. Everyone okay? Who's in charge here?"

A guy loafing in the back of one the technicals jumped down and ambled into the open ground. If he hadn't been carrying an AK-47 and festooned with ammo belts like a terrorist from Central Casting, Rob would have taken him for a distance runner. He didn't have an ounce of fat on him.

"I'm Tariq." He sized up Rob's weapon. Behind him, one of the technical gunners looked up as if he'd heard something. "You're a Brit. My brother drives a taxi in Manchester. My family, we all learn English."

Well, that was a good start. Tariq didn't sound like a jihadist, but he didn't have to be to cause problems. Rob treated it like the road toll extortion that it appeared to be.

"Yeah, I'm English. Good to meet you, Tariq." Rob nudged the conversation closer to the real question. "Okay, what do you want? US dollars? Shillings?"

"Dollars." Tariq looked past Rob as if he was watching Sam. Rob didn't risk taking his eyes off him. "And we keep the car for our trouble. We like it."

If the NGO wanted to argue about rusty tin, they could take it up with NPROFOR later. Rob nodded. "Fine. No problem."

Rob reached into his pouch one-handed and pulled out the dollars. Tariq's gaze strayed past him again for a second, probably watching Sam. If Sam was following the drill, he'd be behind the ACMAT's door with the Mk48 just out of sight.

The Nazani manning the north-facing gun was still looking up at the sky. Fine — he'd lose a second if he swung around, but Rob was more worried about what was making him jumpy. Jumpy wasn't good when you were negotiating. He hoped it was just the sound of Humvees in the distance. Maybe realising that Rob had backup would make them keener to take the money and go, though. It was hard to tell.

"Okay, here you go, mate." Rob couldn't count out the dollars without taking both hands off his weapon, so he held out the roll to Tariq, clocking as much in his peripheral vision as he could without looking away from the south-facing gun. Tariq was conveniently lined up with the gunner. That would give Rob another second's edge if he needed it. "All yours when you let the civvies go."

The guy on the north-facing gun said something to his mate on the ground and pointed down the road. They had their backs to Rob now, murmuring in increasingly urgent tones. Tariq didn't even look around. He just beckoned, confident that someone was waiting to do his bidding. One of his minions herded the two women aid workers out of the group and gestured to them to go. As they made their way towards the ACMAT, they gave Rob a nervous glance.

Tariq counted the notes, head down. Rob could see him glancing to the side, a bit edgy, so maybe he wasn't as cocky as he seemed. Rob concentrated on not spooking him. *He just wants cash. If he'd wanted hostages, we wouldn't be here now.* Then his radio earpiece clicked and he heard one of the Kenyan Humvee drivers.

"We're covering the road and the hill — up to twenty contacts in the tree line to your right. We'll deal with them, out."

It was always much more complicated when civvies were involved. Dead civvies caught in crossfire made bad headlines.

Hurry up, for Chrissakes, Tariq.

Tariq finally seemed satisfied and stuck the money in his back pocket. But all his bagman did was separate the two NGO guys from the American to send them across to Sam. So things weren't going to go so smoothly after all, then. Rob bought time fumbling for the wad of shilling notes and caught the American's eye. They both knew the score.

Rob had come to retrieve five people, and five he'd bloody well have. He knew these bastards. Whatever the country and whatever they called themselves, the Yank would end up sold on to some other bunch of scumbags, handcuffed to a radiator in a shitty basement for the next few years. Nobody sent in a SEAL team to rescue contractors, not even American ones.

"Okay, Tariq, how about him, then? Is he extra?" Rob looked past him at the American. "What's your name, mate?"

"Mike," he said. Mike held himself like he'd spent time in uniform. Rob knew instinctively that he'd get on with him just fine. "Mike Brayne."

"Okay, Mike, let's see what you're worth." Rob held up the wad of shillings to get Tariq's attention. If that wasn't enough, he had about fifty quid in sterling. It all hung on whether Tariq stood to make more from selling Mike on, though, and then things could get awkward. "You've cleaned me out, Tariq."

Tariq held his hand out to take the banknotes. "And I like your watch."

Rob felt the tide turn. He breathed again. The watch looked very TAG-Heuerish but it had only cost him a tenner, just a cheapo he took on deployment for times like this. This was probably a pissing contest to make Tariq look more butch in front of his mates anyway.

Rob played the haggling game, feigning reluctance for a moment. "He's a very expensive Septic."

"*Septic.* Ha." Tariq nodded. Honour had been satisfied. "Funny. I understand."

Rob was unfastening the strap when one of the gunners yelled something and Tariq looked around. They'd heard the Humvees coming, but maybe they'd decided the vehicles were getting too close. One lad got excited and began gesturing. Then all three swung their RPKs around, following the direction of the sound.

"You set us up?" Tariq wrenched open the door of the nearest truck. His bagman tried to force Mike into the vehicle from the other side. "Bad idea. This American, he's my insurance, you hear? I take him, I go."

Rob had seconds to calm things down. "Whoa, steady on, mate. They're not after you. We're sorted, yeah?"

Then someone yelled out, a bloody lookout, probably with a visual on the AU vehicles. Rob didn't need to speak the language to understand the gist of the warning: "Humvees, Humvees!"

The gunner on one of the other technicals squeezed off a burst of fire. Instantly, rounds punched into his truck from the right-hand slope, and it was too late to talk or think things through. A smoke grenade detonated to Rob's right.

Thanks, Sam.

The world was on autopilot now. Tariq raised his rifle and Rob dropped him, then turned on the gunner right in his eyeline. Mike Brayne swung around. For a moment Rob thought he was punching the skinny little Nazani who was struggling to push him into the truck, but then Rob saw the knife.

Mike must have grabbed it off him. He stabbed the Nazani again, snatched his AK, and put a single round in him before ducking behind one of the trucks to return fire. It couldn't have taken more than seconds.

Okay. He's the Very Good kind, then.

Rob was caught in the open with nowhere to run except the

nearest technical. Smoke grenades were no substitute for solid cover. Mike opened up on the tree line and gave Rob the moments he needed to sprint for the vehicle and skid behind it. Incoming rounds zipped past his head.

It was hard to tell who dropped the third gunner and his mate, but it looked like they were suddenly hit from all directions. Rounds sprayed from both sides of the road. Rob couldn't see a bloody thing. All he could do was return fire in the general direction it came from and rely on the Humvees to finish the job.

They seemed to be doing just that. The fire grew more sporadic. Rob reloaded, looking for movement around the trucks.

Mike called out. "You okay, Marine?"

"Hoofing. Great."

Rob knew he should never have tempted fate. As soon as he said it, an RPG shot through the smoke and hit the technical where Mike was crouched. For a deafening second, the gun truck was lost in a sheet of yellow flame before dirty grey clouds and a rainstorm of shrapnel swallowed it.

"Mike? *Mike*!"

Rob scrambled to his feet and ran for the truck. Time was completely fucked. He knew he wouldn't even remember the order things happened in. But Mike was down, and that was where Rob had to be right now. It was as automatic as breathing. Rob turned him over. Christ, he was a mess. Shrapnel had ripped him open. It was hard to tell if his face was cut or just spattered, but he was conscious. Rob was set on keeping him that way.

"*Man down*." Rob's autopilot did the talking. There was no medic around, just him and Sam. "Zero, Echo Two Three Bravo, one hostage down. Request casevac, out."

"Green beret," Mike mumbled.

"Yeah, a *proper* one," Rob said, breaking out his emergency kit. "It's your lucky day."

VEHICLE CONTROL POINT, SOUTH OF THE PELAYI RIVER.

Mike thought he'd pissed himself, but the wet warmth under him wasn't urine.

It was blood. He could smell it. He put his hand to his chest and his fingers came away sticky. And now he couldn't think straight. He bounced between relief that he hadn't been taken hostage, guilt that he'd leave Livvie to cope alone, and — oddly — curiosity as to which of his senses would be the last to shut down. He'd expected to be alert and focused on his own crisis, buoyed up by adrenaline. Instead, he was watching, detached, as some guy called Mike Brayne was bleeding to death.

So that's my body numbing everything. Making the end easier.

Concussion? Head injury?

Well, shit. I didn't think it'd feel like this.

Gravel dug into his cheek as a weight pressed down on him. It should have hurt more, but the pain seemed to get lost on the way to his brain.

"Down. *Stay down.*" It was Rob, the British guy, shielding him. His weight lifted a little. Mike could barely hear him over the noise of the firefight. "Okay, I've got to move you. Sorry, mate."

Rob rolled him onto his back and dragged him closer to a truck that smelled strongly of gas. Jesus, that felt weird. Mike was sure he was disintegrating and that if he looked back, he'd see lumps of himself strewn in his wake.

Sorry, Livvie. I got myself killed. I won't see you again. That's not fair.

I'm going down. Isn't nature amazing?

The gunfire stopped for a moment. Mike stared up at blue sky, yellowish dust, and a black helicopter way above him like a spider on the ceiling. The temperature dropped as he was drowned in shadow. Rob bent his legs and pushed him into a knees-up position, then cut away his T-shirt. Mike tried to cooperate, but it was too much. He gave up and let Rob manoeuvre him like a side of beef.

"Come on, mate, stay awake." Rob rolled him back to the knees-up position. "Sam, where's that casevac? Yeah, I know. Just fucking get them on task. Fetch me the saline, will you? Steady, Mike. That's it. Talk. Say ouch or something. I'm going to stick a needle in your neck."

It hurt like hell. Mike felt as if he was being strangled, struggling to breathe, and instantly he was ten years old again, floundering in an icy river and grabbing at rocks as the roaring water dragged him under. His friend Nick — also ten, up for any adventure — reached for him, anchored by a thin branch and a second away from drowning with him. Nick took the risk, unafraid. *Grab my hand, Mike. Hang on.* And Mike grabbed it. Despite his father's warnings never to trust anyone, he knew there were people willing to spend their own life to buy another's, and that was humanity's one saving grace.

Mike tried to reach up to test that feeling again, but his hand just flailed above his chest. Rob grabbed it. The crushing grip was the same kind that pulled men from rivers.

"Yeah, I know it hurts, mate, but I need both hands free for this." Rob tapped his radio headband. "You jobbed the bastard, though. Good effort. I might even have it on video."

It was almost a foreign language, but Mike understood. He could see some of the detail on Rob's zap patch — Union Flag, SGT, blood group O positive — and just the first two letters of his service number, RE. He could focus clearly on the flash on his shoulder when he turned, though: ROYAL MARINES COMMANDO.

"Tell Livvie. Call her."

"Louder. Can't hear you."

"Livvie."

"Who's Livvie? Your missus?" Rob glanced away for a moment. A brief frown creased the bridge of his nose. Mike felt a sudden pressure on his guts as if everything was squeezing out somewhere like a ruptured tube of toothpaste. "Yeah, I'll tell her you'll be late for dinner."

"Bad?"

"Don't worry. You've still got all your limbs and your dick. How's the pain? Need a shot?"

Rob held a saline bag in his left hand, and his watch — the watch he was going to add to the ransom — seemed very detailed and hypnotically important. Mike had lost track of how long he'd been lying there. He could hear the helicopter.

Rob gestured up with his forefinger. "Hear that? Helo inbound. Just like MASH. You must owe them money."

"It's Dad."

Rob leaned over him, frowning. "Dead? No, you're not dead. You wouldn't be talking to me if you were browners, would you? Not unless you're a zombie."

"*Dad.* Don't tell him." It was too much effort to explain. If the casevac had turned out from the nearest US base, then they might have found out who his father was. He might actually survive this. He'd see Livvie again. The thought was almost a religious experience. "Thanks, buddy. *Thanks.*"

"Yeah, just put in a good word for me at my court martial."

Then Rob was gone, sudden as a camera shutter snapping from light to total blackness. The next face that leaned over Mike, seconds later, surely no more than that, was female and topped with a US issue helmet.

"We got you, Mike," she said. "Just got to load you on the gurney. It'll hurt. Hang in there."

Something else hurt him instead, a white-hot searing pain in the crook of his elbow. After that came a rapid slide into an odd bliss as if he'd been launched into bright blue space. The last thing he remembered was asking someone to get Rob, but he wasn't sure if any sound came out.

Damn, I hope I don't ramble. I always ramble with anaesthesia.

I'm not dead yet. I'm really not.

What was his name? Rob? Rob what? I can't remember.

Mike let himself drift, reassured that he'd open his eyes again. From time to time he was aware of lights being shone in his face, but it was brief and sporadic. Eventually, someone tapped the back of his hand, and kept tapping, saying, "Mike, Mike, Mike," over and over. Everywhere was brightly lit and quiet. It took him a few moments to work out that a nurse in green scrubs was trying to wake him.

"You're okay, Mike." It was hard to tell what she looked like. Her features didn't make sense to him, a recognisable face but somehow also a random jumble like a Picasso painting. He was desperate for a mouthful of water. As he fumbled to wipe his nose, the nurse caught his hand. "That's a feeding tube. You've had surgery. Do you know where you are? Camp Shaughnessy. You're Michael Brayne, right?"

Rational thought was returning in chunks, like bricks appearing in a wall that had been nothing but mist seconds before.

"Livvie?" Mike felt for his wedding band. There was surgical tape around it. "Has anyone told her?"

"Your wife? The Esselby guy's taking care of that. The company's contacted her."

"And where's Rob?"

"Who's he?"

"The Brit who brought me in. He patched me up."

The nurse shook her head. "Our dustoff casevacked you here. No Brits."

"No, *Rob.* He saved me. Where's my phone? I need to call Livvie."

"Okay, take it easy. Are you Senator Brayne's son?"

The whole event gradually uncoiled in Mike's head, a strip of frames from a movie, from getting pulled over at Pelayi to squeezing the trigger to when he felt as if his spine had exploded through his back. And he could see Rob's face looming over him — lean and efficient, the kind of face that said everything was under control.

"Yes. Yes, I am." He had to call Livvie. "Can you get me a phone, please?"

The nurse walked away and spoke to someone. Mike caught the magic phrase that opened all doors in officialdom: "Tell them it's for the senator's son."

The senator's son. It was the last label Mike wanted. He had to justify himself all over again.

"Phone, please?"

"We'll get you one, Mike. Now rest."

Livvie would be quietly angry that her worst fears had almost come to pass. And his father would never yell at him, but he'd have that look, that sad disappointment that asked why Mike had to do this goddamned job instead of accepting his political heritage like his sister Charlotte. *I said not to join that outfit, Micko. I know better than anyone. We spend people like you. It was bad enough when you joined the Guard.* There: he didn't even need Dad to be present. He could have the argument entirely on his own.

There was no clock on the wall. What time was it? Which day? Now he was in a different room, dimly lit and quieter, and vaguely aware that he'd lost hours or even days. He reached for the bedside cabinet, hoping to find a phone or at least some notes to tell him what day it was, but tubes seemed to be plugged in everywhere. He accepted defeat.

Damn, he needed to find Rob, too. He couldn't recall the guy's surname, but an incident like that would have been logged. There weren't that many Royal Marines over here to check out. They'd be based in Nairobi or the local AU camp.

I remembered all that. I'm lucid. I know I am.

That was the last thought he had before a noise woke him with a start. Another nurse leaned over him. She held a cell phone where he could see it and made an exaggerated gesture to indicate she'd put it on the bed by his hand.

"Do you need more painkillers?"

"Can I have a glass of milk, please?" Suddenly Mike craved an ice-cold glass. He didn't even like milk. "Or juice."

"Sorry, nil by mouth until the tube comes out tomorrow."

The nurse vanished again. Mike reached for the phone and tried to focus on the display. How long had he been here? Damn, not quite twenty-four hours. There were already messages for him from Livvie and Dad, and from Brad, the program manager at Esselby.

Livvie's simply read: '*Whenever you're ready. Just glad I've still got you.*' He was desperate to hear her voice. If he called, though, he'd sound drugged and hoarse. She'd be upset. He decided to wait until he sounded like his old self, and settled for a text in the meantime.

The painkiller was much more powerful than he'd realised. He tapped out his reply like a man struggling with a new language, but there was no better excuse for being brief. He didn't need to tell her how close a call he'd had, at least not yet.

'Livvie honey — doing fine. Sorry to scare you. Love you.'

And Dad, as always, got right to the point: '*Micko, your guardian angel is Robert Rennie. I called in a favour from the DoD to bypass all the BS. Stand by for a visit. We'll reward him properly in due course. You're coming home. We love you.*'

Mike felt the relief of something achieved. He typed THANKS DAD, LOVE YOU because he'd fumbled the caps lock, then hit send. The effort left him sweating.

Dad was upset. Mike could understand that. He didn't have to be here, and he wasn't defending his country. It was just a compulsion. He didn't know how to settle for doing anything less for the rest of his life.

The nasogastric tube came out the next day. With the tube gone, he felt whole enough to call Livvie and chat for a few minutes until he ran out of energy. He told her everything positive he could remember about the rescue. The grisly detail could wait.

"I'll be home for months," he said, trying to be casual. "We can take all those trips we promised ourselves."

"So this Rob guy. Have you invited him to visit?"

"I haven't seen him yet. But I will, honey. You sure you're not angry with me?"

"No. Upset, naturally." Livvie paused. "But you've got your quest, and if I stop you, then you won't be Mike any more, will you?"

Mike pondered that after she rang off. It wasn't the first time she'd said it, and she was right. He was looking for something. Every time he thought he'd found it, he'd turn it over and it would transform itself from a right and decent thing to a tainted grey area — wars supporting the wrong allies, training foreigners who turned on you in the end, and guarding aid programs that didn't solve a damn thing. It was simple; Mike just wanted to *do good*. But it was getting harder to pin down what good meant in the real world.

He still couldn't think of anything cleaner than being a soldier, whether in national uniform or as a contractor. It was a difference he could see with his own eyes and make with his own hands. The worst thing about wealth was that it left him with no excuses for what he hadn't done with his life, and at thirty-five he still felt he'd done absolutely nothing.

Mike was starting to worry that he'd be flown home before he got to see Rob and thank him, but the guy showed up the next day. He walked in clutching a plastic carrier bag as if it was a routine visit. He looked dauntingly fit in a khaki T-shirt instead of Kevlar plates, and it was now clear how much of Rob was Rob and how much had been armour.

"So there I am, in the boss's tent, getting a bollocking about all the paperwork I've caused," Rob said, launching straight in without an opening hello. "And then he gets a call, and suddenly I'm the man of the match. Any ideas?"

Mike wasn't sure what to say. Thanks seemed remarkably slight. He held out his hand while he tried to think of something appropriate. Rob shook it with the grip of a boa constrictor.

"Ah," Mike said. "That'd be down to Dad. He *knows* people."

"I was having a nice beer with the AU lads at the base when your lot showed up. I thought I was going to end up with a bag over my head en route to a CIA jail in Shittistan."

"Sorry. It's probably because I kept asking for you."

"Well, here I am." Rob gave him a conspiratorial wink. "Why didn't you tell me you were just an ordinary, average billionaire with an ordinary, average billionaire senator dad who's got government ministers on his speed dial?"

"I was kind of disembowelled at the time. It slipped my mind." Mike felt suddenly emotional, a backslapping, tearful kind of relief. "Rob, thank you doesn't begin to cover it. But anyway, thank you."

"So you hung around just to see me? You mad bugger."

"I wouldn't have made it out alive without you." It sounded lame, but anything Mike said that summed up what had happened would sound feeble. *You saved my life. You saved me from being taken hostage. I owe you.* "And I even know what a bollocking is. I lived in England for a while. I read history and politics at Oxford."

"So we civilised you, did we?"

"You sound like you come from somewhere down west."

"Bristol. *Oh-ahh.* And you sound like Katherine Hepburn."

"New Hampshire. Fairly close."

Rob pulled up a chair and sat down at the bedside, unfazed. Up close, his dark hair was flecked with a trace of grey. "So what's Septic nobility like you doing in a mucky job like this? Bored with crashing Ferraris into swimming pools?"

"I spent a few years in the National Guard. I like the life."

"No offence to the Guard, mate, but your knife skills seem a bit too hardcore for that. I bet you could kill a bloke with a teaspoon, couldn't you?"

"I got myself trained privately." Mike made it a rule never to bitch about the Guard, however frustrated he'd been with it. He knew he was talking to a seasoned commando who wouldn't brook any whining. "I joined Esselby as a contractor. You learn a lot there. Not spoons, though."

Rob didn't blink. "Never wanted to join the regular Army? No, I suppose they'd beat the shit out of you for being the crown prince. That's what the lads on the flight over here called you. Very fairy-tale."

"I keep the family connection quiet. People think I'm playing at soldiers because I'm bored. My sister calls me Marie Antoinette."

Rob didn't ask why, but maybe he understood the reference. Mike felt totally and inexplicably at ease with him. Maybe it was because he exuded a solid sense of his own worth, a certainty about his place and purpose in the world. All the revelations that made people fawn over Mike or want to pick a fight — his dynastic wealth, his education, his service — didn't even make Rob blink. Mike didn't have to wonder whether to trust him. Rob had pulled him to safety under fire and shielded him, and that told him everything he needed to know.

"Well, you're not shovelling the thankless shit for the money, obviously," Rob said.

"It's a compromise. My wife sees more of me and I still get to do the kind of things I'm good at."

"Yeah. I didn't quite get my compromise right. Kids?"

It was a far bigger question than Rob could have realised. "Still trying," Mike said. "We've been married thirteen years."

"Stick with it. My mate and his missus had twins two years after they'd given up." Rob rummaged in the grocery bag and fished out a couple of cans of beer carefully wrapped in a T-shirt, presumably to muffle the telltale clanking. "Nurse Ratched's going to go mental if she sees this, so hide it for later, okay? And Sam retrieved your kit. Phone, wallet, the works." He tossed the items onto the bed. "I hope you didn't leave your contacts on your mobile."

"No, I always wipe it." Mike checked his wallet for Livvie's picture first. He hated the idea of some stranger dumping it. Yes, it was still there. "Thanks, Rob. And thank Sam for me. No watch?"

"Missing something diamond-studded?"

"No. Just a service issue timepiece. Three hundred bucks. My lucky watch."

Rob took something out of his pocket and tossed it onto the bedcover. It was the black diver-style watch he'd offered Tariq as an extra bribe. "You better have that instead, then. Ten quid in Argos. Glows in the dark, too. Great story to tell the grandkids."

It was unlikely Mike would ever have any, but it was a kind thought. He strapped on the watch next to his hospital ID bracelet.

"That's lucky enough for me. Thanks."

Rob took out his cell, tapped it a few times, then handed it to Mike with a big grin that completely transformed him. "Look. This is my boy, Tom. I love him to bits and he's going to university next year. Computer science and linguistics."

Tom looked like a teenage version of his father. Rob started chatting, and in minutes Mike was sure he'd known him all his life. They were still talking like long-lost buddies — family, how much England had changed since Mike had been at Oxford, politics, the price of gas — when the nurse interrupted them. She walked in with a diagnostic trolley and an expression that said it was high time that Rob left. Mike checked his new lucky watch. They'd been talking for nearly two hours.

"Rob, give me your contact details," he said. "We've got to stay in touch. There has to be something I can do for you besides shake your damn hand."

Maybe Rob thought Mike was one of those guys who thrust his

business card at people he met on vacation and insisted they look him up sometime without really meaning it. For a moment, Rob hesitated. Then he rummaged in his pockets and produced a pen and a few dog-eared business cards. One was a taxi company's. Mike flipped it over and started writing.

"You hang on to this." Mike handed back the card. "Now you give me yours. You saved my life."

"I think the surgeon did that."

"Yes, but he didn't patch me up under fire when he could have walked away."

"Bugger it, Mike, you're making me sound even more amazing than I already am." Rob glanced at the nurse, who was waiting with silent impatience, and wrote on another card. He got a faint smile from her, though. "Yeah. Let's stay in touch."

"Seriously. What can I give you? What can I do for you?"

Rob shrugged. "If you ever need someone to clean the toilets, let me know."

"Sorry?"

"More bloody defence cuts. Got to get a proper job soon."

Mike panicked for him. "Hey, I can definitely help with that."

"Thanks." Rob looked awkward, breaking eye contact for a moment. "I appreciate it."

"You've got my number. Call me next week. Understand?"

"Thanks."

"I mean it. I'll call you if you don't." Mike was already trying to formulate a rescue plan. It just took money, and that would never be a problem. "That's the kind of thing I'm good at fixing."

Rob finally surrendered to the nurse's time-to-leave stare. "I better be going." Perhaps he didn't want his future fixed for him. "Look after yourself, Mike."

"You too, buddy," Mike said. "Keep in touch. Whatever you need, I'm there."

"Three wishes, too, eh?" Rob winked conspiratorially. "Keep your head down. I won't be around the next time."

Mike watched him go as the nurse moved in with the blood pressure cuff, and felt oddly cheated. But what was his display of gratitude for, to convince the guy that he'd done something life-changing that would never be forgotten, or to make himself feel like a better human being? No, Mike *liked* Rob. It was the same as that instant connection he'd had with Nick nearly thirty years before. Plucked from the river a second time, Mike was determined to value this extra lease of life and the man who had given it to him.

It looked like it was going to be hard to give Rob anything, though. He was visibly self-reliant, the kind of man who'd finish a race on a broken leg rather than ask for help.

But Mike had his own stubborn streak. He could do good, and he would do it for Rob Rennie.

LOCKSWAY SUPERMARKET, BRISTOL, ENGLAND: DECEMBER, ONE YEAR LATER.

In the aisle between the display of eddoes and the stacked boxes of karela, Rob felt like the last Englishman alive.

The store was busy with chattering shoppers. Some conversations made themselves heard above the public address system pushing today's special offers, but none of the languages were his. He thought he could pick out Bengali and Thai, but he couldn't understand any of it.

No, that wasn't strictly true. Sometimes a word that sounded like Pashto jumped out at him. Instantly, he was back on patrol in Helmand, waiting for the worst to happen in a suddenly-deserted street, or wishing he knew more Dari or whatever, so that he could work out whether the dodgy-looking locals were discussing how far the infidel bastard's legs would get blown when he hit the IED at the next corner, or if they were just griping about the price of carrots.

But it was probably Urdu, not Pashto. They had words in common, according to one of his mates, and there were a lot of Pakistanis around here. The realisation did nothing for the knot in his gut or his guilty sense of resentment. He walked on. Sod it, he was store security. He could look at anyone he pleased without needing to feel bad about it.

It's not race. Shit, we had all colours in the Corps. Bloody good blokes. It's the language thing. It's not knowing what they're saying. This is England and we should all be speaking English. It's not knowing what England is these days.

It was also not knowing if Rob Rennie belonged here any longer. He checked the display clock on the wall above the dairy section, a plain, white-faced thing with a jerky second hand that he'd come to see as running parallel with his life. He hated that fucking clock. He hated it more than he hated his job, although he knew that there was nothing particularly wrong with either. The clock simply counted down the remaining hours of his life, unstoppable and implacable.

But this was for Tom, to help him through uni and see him settled with a job and a family. It was the natural order of things: survive, mate, reproduce, die. Rob had seen it on a depressing documentary once. He refused to dwell on how he'd decayed from an experienced and valued NCO — a bit worried about the defence cuts, nothing more, still fit and functional — to scrambling for low-paid jobs with hundreds of other unqualified, middle-aged, working class blokes.

Wind your neck in and crack on with it. The Corps wasn't always a bundle of laughs either. I get paid. I've got all my body parts. I've got a roof over my head. What am I dripping about?

It was three minutes to six. Some iffy-looking teens were hanging around the snack section. His gut said to go and move them on, but for once he decided that it just wasn't important enough. What was the worst that could happen? Locksway would lose a few bags of peanuts. Nobody would die. Nobody would bleed to death or find themselves out of ammo, pinned down and relying on him to make the difference between life and death.

See, that's what's wrong with all this. It doesn't matter. My job doesn't matter. I don't matter.

He headed for the doors marked STAFF ONLY. Beyond the keypad barrier, the noise of the store dropped to a whisper. Sheets of paper pinned to the employee noticeboard shivered in the downdraft of a heating duct. He checked his watch to make sure it was one minute past six, then waved his pass in front of the sensor and went to change into his street clothes. The bloke on the goods-in gate was a former Gurkha, Krish. Locksway had a policy of employing ex-service personnel and made a lot of noise about it in their ads. Rob wondered if Krish also had moments when he wondered what the hell it had all been for.

"'Night, Krish," he said. "See you tomorrow."

Krish gave him a big grin. "You want to come round for a meal next week? The wife, she says you need a proper *dhal bhat.*"

"Love to, mate. Thanks."

Rob zipped up his jacket and headed for the bus stop. Krish

was a good bloke, the best. But being sociable was harder these days because Rob didn't like turning up empty-handed to freeload off kind people, and money was tight. Still, he'd work something out. Every spare penny went into Tom's university fund so that he didn't have to live on beans. Rob would survive and resume his life later, and Tom would graduate and never find out how much of a struggle it had been for his dad.

Rob took out his notebook on the bus journey home to do his sums, working out how much he could put away this month. The street lights became a blur in the corner of his eye as he rested his head against the cold glass of the window. Sod it, he could do this. It was just like a long tour of duty somewhere shitty, or a bit of escape and evasion behind enemy lines. All he had to do was focus on the outcome and the rest would follow just like it had in the Corps. He didn't need a car, he didn't need an expensive phone contract, he didn't need to get rat-arsed down the pub every night, and he didn't need expensive ready-meals. He cooked plain, cheap food and went running in the evening. He borrowed books from the library and watched TV instead of paying for videos. This wouldn't break him. It would only make him fitter and harder, more of himself than ever.

Yeah, he felt fine just being Rob Rennie. No fucker could take that away from him. It was one of those days when he felt murderously bitter about being disposable, and hated whatever this country had become, because it wasn't home and it wasn't his. But the anger passed. At least he hadn't sacrificed his life, his limbs, or his sanity for this fucking government or any other.

And I've got Tom. That's what matters.

The hardest part of the day was opening the door of his flat. The air smelled empty and stale, not poorly cleaned but just devoid of all the things that made places feel homely and lived in: a roast in the oven, Bev's perfume, air freshener, laundry. *Or even coffee, grease, and sweat.* He wasn't used to living alone. He'd spent most of his life cooped up in barracks or camps with other blokes just like himself, or at home with Bev and Tom.

And this wasn't the kind of place to impress a woman. Friday nights brought that home to him more than ever.

I hope my bloody dick's still working by the time Tom graduates.

He bent to pick up the mail scattered on the mat, a pile of pizza delivery fliers and a pale cream envelope of expensive textured paper. He thought it was bad news from officialdom until he turned over the envelope and saw the US stamp and Mike's distinctive, formal handwriting. Americans still learned to do proper joined-up writing. It always looked very foreign.

Rob sawed open the envelope with his forefinger and pulled out a Christmas card, a proper one, not something run off on a home printer. Instead of a generic snow scene, there was a picture of the Brayne family, all wholesome and smiling in front of a huge, log-laden fireplace festooned with red and green swags of ribbon. It was like a team photo of the very rich and powerful: Mike, Livvie, Mike's politician sister Charlotte, her lawyer husband Jonathan and their two kids, plus Leo and Monica — Mike's parents — and their yellow Labrador, Billy, a nice enough dog if you didn't mind his farting and leg-humping. The greeting was about peace and prosperity in this holiday season, as if Christmas wasn't a word you could use in polite society. Inside the card was folded sheet of velvety paper.

'Rob, if you want a break, we'd love to see you again. Livvie wants to know if you can make it for Christmas. Just leave the travel arrangements to me. And Esselby could really use you. Always open. Dad can fix the work permits. Let's talk.'

Mike never gave up. He was a thoroughly decent bloke, no side to him at all, and it was easy to forget that his family was oligarch-grade rich. Rob stared at the card, trying to see the heir and not an earnest, awkward man who didn't seem to have any mates. Mike was an oddball, all right. He'd paid a fortune to go on every elite tactical training course available so he could be a private contractor, when he could have spent his days shagging his way around ski resorts or snorting coke on some tropical beach. But he'd opted for a thankless, invisible, dirty job a long way from home.

Mad as a fucking hatter. God love him.

Rob dithered for a moment. Did Mike mean his own house in Maine, or his dad's place? Maybe Livvie was hosting the whole family this year. Mike's place was big and empty, like he was always waiting for guests who never came, a house that should have been full of kids and dogs. But it was just him and Livvie. It was a bloody shame that they didn't have children. Mike made it clear that it was a big gap in his life.

Rob studied the photo again before placing the card and the

note on the mantelpiece. Mike was still wearing that cheap watch.

Christ, I'd love to be doing something useful again. But I need to be here for Tom.

Okay, he'd call Mike later, just to chat. He had to crack on with his routine: make a pan of chilli, leave it to simmer while he watched the news, then do half an hour with the weights before he had his dinner. A few decent kettlebells worked out cheaper than membership at the local gym. His day, week, and month were now mapped out more or less to the hour, his finances to the last penny.

It's like being in prison. Still, this was what we did back in Afghanistan. No fancy facilities like the big bases.

Rob started calculating how much difference a job with Esselby would make. He'd earn four times what he was making in the supermarket, but then there was tax, insurance, and other self-employed expenses to pay. Maybe it wasn't as lucrative as it looked.

I'd have three months off a year, though, maybe more. And I'd be doing what I do best.

He could usually switch off while he trained and just concentrate on making his body do what he demanded of it, but it was hard to focus with numbers like that in his mind. He jerked the fifteen-kilo kettlebell over his head, feeling the sweat trickle down his back, and wondered what was getting to him most, the lack of cash or simply being nothing for the first time in his adult life.

He was lost in his thoughts when the doorbell rang. He went to the intercom, expecting it to be someone trying to sell him something he didn't want or need, because it wouldn't be a visitor. He made sure none of his mates ever came here.

The voice on the crackly speaker was the last one he expected to hear. "Dad, it's me."

"Christ. Tom? What are you doing here, kiddo? You're supposed to be in Newcastle."

"Well, now I'm here. Can I come in?

Rob held his finger on the button to unlock the hall door, disoriented for a moment, and waited at the top of the stairs. Tom trudged up the steps with a tight-packed holdall and stared at Rob with an expression that said he was trying hide his dismay at finding his father in a dismal place like this. Rob had never let him see the flat. Tom hadn't needed to know.

"It's the end of term, Dad. Remember? I came back a day early.

Sorry I didn't call first."

"Oh. Seen your mum yet?" Rob showed him in and shut the door before giving him a hug. He'd been caught out and he wasn't sure where the conversation was heading. "What's wrong?"

Tom wasn't the sort of lad to forget to call ahead. He was eighteen going on fifty, a man who body-searched every word before he let it pass his lips. "Nothing's wrong," he said. "Not with me, anyway. I just didn't want to give you the chance to fob me off this time. I wanted to see this for myself."

They stood in the cramped hall for a few awkward, silent seconds. Tom looked around. Rob didn't have any excuses ready. He'd expected to show up at Bev's and be nice to her new bloke in exchange for having Christmas with Tom, and never let Tom see how he was actually living. That plan had all gone to rat shit now. All he could do was make his lad feel at home.

"I'd better get you a drink, hadn't I?"

"How about going for a curry? Come on, Dad. My treat."

"Star of Bengal or The Raj?"

"Raj," Tom said. "They do coconut naans."

"Yeuchh."

"Fibre."

"Fibre's the least of your worries after a vindaloo, son. Okay, give me five minutes to clean myself up and turn off the chilli."

Rob had never felt so ashamed in his life. He could feel Tom's distress radiating like sunburn, sorrow that his father lived in this grim, bare cell of a place. When he came out of the bathroom, Tom was studying the solitary Christmas card on the mantelpiece.

"I see Mike sent you a card."

"Yeah, look at all those teeth." Rob zipped up his jacket. "You could make a piano keyboard out of that lot. Put your shades on, son. You don't want any retina damage."

"Even the dog looks rich. You're the only person I know who could have the Brayne family in his debt and not take advantage of it. Didn't you ever see *Androcles and The Lion*?"

"Yeah. It could have done with some car chases."

"Come on. *Leo Brayne.* Technology, comms, mining, charitable foundations."

"I don't want charity."

"That's a load of crap. Mike's your friend." Tom frowned at the picture. "Look, he's still wearing that watch you gave him. His twelve Cartiers must be at the cleaner's."

"It's his lucky charm."

"Is it okay if I read the note?"

Rob nodded. Tom frowned while he read. Sometimes he looked just like his mum, that square tip to his nose and the way he pursed his lips when he was concentrating.

"You're mad," he said, looking up. "Mike keeps offering you work and you don't take it. He keeps inviting you over there. Do it, Dad. He's your mate. He really cares what happens to you."

"Too far." It had to be said. "And I spent too long away while you were growing up. It's time I stuck around."

"But Newcastle's a long way, too. You know they've got planes and the internet in America, don't you? It's ever so modern. They might even have phones by now."

"I've already got a job," Rob said.

"Not quite what you told me, though, is it?" Tom beckoned and headed for the door. "Come and tell me the truth."

They walked to the Raj, a half-hour stroll that gave Rob time to change the subject and talk about how Tom's course was going. Rob realised it was one of those weird conversations where they were discussing one thing while a separate, unspoken argument was running in parallel beneath the surface. The Raj smelled comfortingly of frying onions and lemon air freshener, but the wailing music in the background suddenly reminded him too much of previous deployments. It was probably only Bollywood soundtracks.

"Do you still run?" Tom asked. They settled down to a pile of poppadums while they pored over the menu. "Why aren't you in touch with your old mates?"

"Who says I'm not?"

"Only one Christmas card."

Tom wasn't giving up, then. Rob braced for incoming. "Yes, I still do my phys every day." He stopped short of saying that he didn't want his old oppos to know where he'd ended up. He was ashamed. "But there's no point looking back. I would have had to leave sooner or later."

"Yeah, and we're all going to die eventually, too, but that doesn't mean you lie down in your coffin and wait." Tom started moving the plates to make room for sizzling platters inbound from the left. "You could have been extended to fifty-five. You just got shat on by the government."

Tom didn't meet Rob's eyes. He dug into the chicken vindaloo as if the comment had been a throwaway observation, which it definitely wasn't. So it was gut-spill time, then. Okay, Rob would give in. He needed to. There had to be one person in the world that he didn't have to present with a stiff upper lip.

"Tom, I'm lucky," he said. "I came back with all my limbs and I don't wake up screaming at night. I've got a job. I'm not living on the streets. I've just got to get used to not mattering."

"Christ, Dad, don't say that. Every second of your life matters. That's why I can't stand to see you wasting it. Forget me for a minute. What do you really want to do now?"

Wasting it. Rob had rationalised about missing the Corps and not having those really tight relationships you only had with blokes you served with, but it wasn't his job that didn't matter: it was his life. He hadn't even returned to the real world. He was back in an *un*real existence with make-believe rules and imagined safety, while actual reality — life-or-death decisions, *real* risks, pushing himself to his limits because he had to — was out there in some combat zone. It was one of the few places left where humans lived the way they'd been designed to, and it wasn't as simple or as juvenile as missing the excitement. What he missed was having to push himself every day. Running marathons didn't cut it. He could always stop running and sit down for a rest, but in combat nobody waited while you got your breath back. There was no safety net. It was life at the limits of human capacity and beyond.

"Okay, so I wish I was a Bootneck again," he said. "And I wish I had the stamina I had at twenty, and the looks, and that I healed as fast, but I don't. Things pass."

"You can't go on like this."

"Like what?"

"You thought I wouldn't realise, didn't you?" Tom gestured at him with his fork. "I knew damn well you'd try to pretend everything was fine. That's why you made sure you always met me at Mum's. So I wouldn't see the state you were in. You let her keep everything."

Rob didn't have a good answer. Suddenly the sound of his own chewing deafened him. "Yeah, well, so I did."

"Dad, I can't take any more money from you. I won't have you living like this to subsidize me."

"You can keep me in my old age. Deal?"

"I mean it. I'm going to pay back what you've sent me this term."

"No. You won't."

"*Yes.* I will."

"Tom, I'm your dad. You think I want to see you trying to study and hold down a job too?"

"Americans do it all the time. Ask Mike."

"You're eighteen. You should be enjoying yourself."

"How can I, when I know you have to live like this?" That was Tom all over, always the little man of the house when Rob was away, sensible and responsible. "I'm serious, Dad. You're not making a fortune and you're not having a good time. Stop lying to me."

"I'd never lie to you. You know that."

"Look, I never needed to know what you did in the Marines, but I *do* have a right to know when you're in the shit. You deserve better." Tom went quiet and carried on eating, but he was just changing tack. Rob didn't have an answer. "I always expected you to go into private security work. Counter-piracy, close protection, that kind of thing. The MoD paid for you to do a CP course and all the other stuff before you left."

Tom knew all the correct words. Rob had to choose his own carefully. "Only so they could bin us and still get the job done on the cheap by rehiring us working for PSCs."

"So you wouldn't notice the difference, would you? Except for better conditions."

"Yeah, but I need to be home for a few years."

"Because of me?"

"I'm your *father.* You put your kids first, although fuck knows that's not fashionable these days." The vindaloo was hotter than Rob remembered. He was starting to sweat and a headache was forming like a storm front. He gulped down some raita as an antidote, but it wasn't working. "I was away too often when you were growing up."

"I was really proud of you being a Marine."

"But not a security guard, eh?"

"That's not what I mean and you know it. I'll always be proud of you, whatever you do. But you should call Mike and see what's on offer."

Sometimes talking to Tom was like role reversal. The kid was going to make a great dad one day. He was doing a pretty good job of it right now. "What if I did?"

"I could brag that my dad was a mercenary. Offend the wannabe Che Guevaras on my course and impress women. Okay, I know mercenary isn't accurate. But you know what I mean."

"I don't think Esselby does the full-on dogs of war rent-a-coup shit."

"Yeah, but I don't have to tell women that." Tom forced a smile. "Just come to my graduation ceremony with two days' stubble and a bandolier."

"It's all polo shirts and baseball caps now. How about a gold-plated AK-forty-seven and a sweaty Bruce Willis vest?"

Tom laughed. "Yeah, you could carry that off. Look, Dad, it's more or less the same work. You'll still be yourself."

Rob felt something prick at his eyes. It wasn't the curry. Tom was giving him permission to do what he'd really wanted, trying to make the decision easy for him. It should have been the other way around. If anyone had asked Rob what he was, his instant answer had always been *Royal Marine*, but there was another identity that defined him just as much: he was Tom's dad, and he was even more proud of that.

"Okay. I'll talk to Mike."

He had no illusions. A dead Rob in a Royal Marines uniform would have had a nice funeral with some media coverage of roses being thrown onto his hearse, but a dead Rob on the payroll of Mercs-R-Us would be completely invisible, with no poppies, no Legion standard-bearers, and no angry voters complaining about Our Boys dying for nothing. He knew that. He wasn't stupid. Neither was the government. This was their plan, the chinless lying fuckers, one of the very few they seemed to actually have.

"I wouldn't see any less of you, would I?" Tom said. "I just want a happy dad again."

Rob felt like he'd been recharged after months on fading batteries. Back at the flat, while Tom was out buying groceries from the all-night supermarket, he stared at the phone and felt almost excited, not *whoopee* excited, but the things-might-go-horribly-wrong variety, that fear of having to swim out of his depth but doing it anyway. It was the challenge he needed. *That, and having the money to do right by Tom.* It was an honest job. He wasn't leeching off Mike's generosity.

He tapped Mike's number and waited. "Hi, mate. Merry Christmas. So, this job."

"Brad's always got contracts to fill, buddy, you know that," Mike said. "And there's always Nazani. Come on, we'd make a terrific team."

"Are you going back?"

"Sure. It'd be great to work with you, Rob. We'd be awesome."

Rob had missed it. He missed doing proper work and he'd missed the company of blokes like himself. Tom had already made up his mind for him, but the prospect of working with Mike gave him a brief sensation of being a lad again, up for climbing over security fences and KEEP OUT signs with his mates.

"Yeah, that sounds like a bloody good idea," Rob said. "I'm in."

TWO

I can assure the House that there are no plans to send British troops back to East Africa. In answer to my honourable friend's question, there are no British troops on the ground. This is line with the stance of our allies in the USA, Europe, and the Commonwealth. The security situation is being managed adequately by local forces with support from its advisers.

The Rt. Hon. J. M. Allen, Secretary of State for Defence, in response to Parliamentary questions.

KAJO AIRPORT, NAZANI, EAST AFRICA: JUNE, EIGHTEEN MONTHS LATER.

The workers' bus was late again.

Mike occupied himself by trying to read the news over Rob's shoulder. The company had started changing schedules at the last minute to thwart insider leaks to local gangs about vehicle movements. The recent spate of ambushes wasn't just bad luck.

"Twat," Rob said, not looking up from his phone. One hand rested on the steering wheel as if he couldn't bear to relinquish control of the Chevy Suburban even when it was parked. "Lying twat."

He didn't say who was guilty of twattery today, but it was almost certainly a politician. "I give up," Mike said, turning down the aircon. "Who's a twat?"

Rob handed over the phone to show Mike the headlines. There

were no plans to send troops back to Nazani, some British defence minister had said. It was official. Private contractors didn't count, even if most of them had come straight from the American or UK forces. That was the way of the world now, invisible, tidy little wars with as few official casualties as possible.

Mike could live with that. He was playing his part to bring water to a region that sorely needed it, which fell under his clear-cut heading of Doing Good. He was with his best buddy. And they'd be heading home in two weeks on extended leave. Life was almost the way he wanted it.

The only thing missing was kids, but he and Livvie hadn't given up on treatment yet. He just needed to hear that she was willing to try one more IVF cycle.

"We're nobody's boys, Rob. No yellow ribbons for us." Mike reached across to flick the peak of Rob's baseball cap. "Chin up. The canteen's getting a resupply of pistachio ice cream today."

"So where's this sodding bus? There'll only be vanilla left by the time we get back."

"Yeah. War sure is hell."

They giggled like schoolboys. Rob went on reading the headlines while Mike checked for e-mails, still looking for a message from Livvie. He found nothing and reset his phone to purge his data.

Kajo wasn't so much an airport yet as an airstrip with a growing collection of buildings, razor wire, and Hesco barriers. A few yards away in the security parking area, Teetotal Mackenzie and Jake the Saffa sat in their own Suburban, escorts for the same bus. Teetotal shrugged at Mike and tapped his ear to indicate he was still waiting for someone to radio him.

Mike nudged Rob with his elbow. "Taken your mefloquine today?"

"Yes, Mum." It was part of their buddy routine, the list of daily health checks that a country like this made necessary. "Hydration. Drink some water."

"Okay, glugging now."

Rob went on reading his phone. Mike thought he was catching up with the sports headlines, but he sat back and made a grumbling noise.

"Shit."

"Problem?" Mike asked.

Rob handed over his phone. "Look. Tom's got a summer job. He's not coming to stay."

The message was succinct: *'Dad, I've got a few weeks' work lined up when the term ends but maybe we can get together later. How does that sound?'*

Mike was already calculating. If Tom felt the need to earn money, then there was an instant solution to the problem, even if Rob wouldn't like it.

"He hasn't told you what it is, then."

"No. I bet it's some shit job in a factory or something. I'll make him take some cash. He's bloody stubborn about paying his way."

"Funny. I wonder who he gets that from."

"I'll sort him out."

"Might be a girlfriend involved."

"No, he'd tell me. He always does." Rob had been excited about having Tom to stay. Mike could see his disappointment. "He knows I'll be pissed off, whatever it is."

"His fall term doesn't start until late September. We'll be home for months, at least. Plenty of time to visit."

Mike took out his cell again and mailed his accountant. It really was only money. What was the point of having it if he couldn't spend it on the people he cared about? Fifty thousand in sterling would probably be about right, ample for Tom's needs but just short of Rob's melt-down level. He still hadn't come to terms with the scale of Mike's resources.

"You're not up to anything, are you, Zombie?" Rob asked.

Mike took a mouthful from his water bottle. "Hell, no, Royal."

Rob sat drumming his fingers. A couple of minutes later, airport security radioed to say that the bus — callsign Blue One — was finally moving. Rob hung back to let Teetotal pull out in front of him as the lead car. It was the kind of escort duty they did week in, week out, mostly without incident, but it was always a time to be extra vigilant. The gates opened and a sixty-seat bus rolled out, packed with anxious-looking foreign workers, mostly white and Asian.

"No ladies. Bugger." Rob watched it pass and then pulled in behind it. "I'm going to have to be nicer to Carolyn."

"She'll chew you up and spit out the gristle," Mike said. He thought it was telling that out of four female security operators, Rob picked the one who'd break something if he pushed his luck with her. "She used to be a line MP, remember."

"It's a price worth paying."

Mike had never met Rob's ex-wife. He'd looked for traces of her in Tom, the part that didn't seem to have come from Rob, but it was hard to tell. Tom was the stealth version of his dad, quiet and self-possessed. It was hard for Mike to look at him without imagining what a son of his own would be like.

"You okay, Zombie?" Rob asked.

"Still waiting for Livvie's answer."

"Right." Rob knew what he was talking about and didn't press him. "Stay sharp."

The twenty-mile road to Dibeg was a flat, straight route across a scrubby plain with no cover either side and no choke points. It was safer than a winding route through ambush-friendly terrain, and a combination of mini-drone patrols and tele-controlled unmanned ground vehicles reduced the risk of IEDs. But Mike had known enterprising locals plant explosives again on exactly the same spot within thirty minutes of the first one being cleared. The TUGV couldn't stop mobile attacks on the road itself, either.

Mike could rely on Rob to spot trouble, though. He knew they were looking for the same indicators: disturbed soil, breakdowns minus drivers, odd litter, and even dead animals, anything vaguely off-key. Five miles out, the bus approached the first side road. Teetotal's voice came on the radio.

"*Red One to Red Two, blocking. All yours, Royal.*"

That was Rob's cue to overtake the bus and move into the lead position while Teetotal pulled across the junction to stop any other vehicles separating the bus from its escort. As soon as the bus cleared the junction, Teetotal pulled out again and moved in close behind. The bounding overwatch system was repeated at each junction.

"See, I'd be fine doing close protection if it was all driving," Rob said. "But I'm not carrying shopping for some celeb or picking up their snotty brats from school."

"You just want to do screeching J-turns, don't you?"

"It's my hormones, Zombie."

Small motorcycles passed them in the opposite direction, wobbling under the load of baskets or pillion passengers. Mike watched them carefully with his HK416 by his leg and one hand resting on his sidearm. A bike, side panniers overflowing with vegetables, puttered slowly ahead them. Mike couldn't tell if it was going as fast as it could or trying to make them pass, but it wasn't low enough on its suspension to be laden with explosives. Rob checked the mirror.

"Red Two, passing, clear ahead."

He pulled out to overtake. Mike glanced at the bike just as something green flew into the air and bounced back towards them.

"Shit — "

Rob didn't even have time to swerve. Mike braced for an explosion before the thing splattered on the road in a spray of seeds and juice. It was still a bowel-loosening moment. Rob sucked in a breath.

"Nearly needed a change of boxers there, mate," he said.

"*Red One to Red Two --you okay, Royal?*"

"Red One, no problem. I just shat myself. Flying fruit." Rob drove on, checking the rear-view with a big grin on his face. "Sorry, Zombie."

Mike did this run so often that he could almost set his watch by it: half an hour, maybe forty minutes if there was a slow freight convoy or a stray goat on the road. It wasn't urban-busy, but it wasn't deserted, either.

It was starting to look that way now, though. The traffic thinned out. Then he couldn't see anything coming towards them. If an attack was planned, locals were often warned to stay clear.

Mike got on the radio. "Red One, anything behind you?"

"*Sweet FA,*" Teetotal said. "*Let's start worrying.*"

Rob's scan pattern — rear-view, left mirror, right mirror, rear — speeded up. It didn't matter that Dibeg was just minutes away. It only took seconds to get hit.

Teetotal sounded relaxed, but he always did. "*Red One to Red Two, still nothing behind.*"

Mike was looking for something mobile like a parked truck with a command wire. They were now seven miles from Dibeg. If anything was going to happen, it'd be in the next few minutes.

Then he saw it. It wasn't a truck, and it wasn't parked. It was a small object coming towards them. It hadn't been there a moment ago. It must have turned onto the road from a track further ahead.

Mike reacted even before he'd processed the thought. *Rider and pillion.* "Red One, Blue One, bike at speed, approaching from Dibeg. Stand by."

Rob jerked his head around, looking for a path into the scrub either side of the road. "Here we go. Might be nothing. Red One, Blue One — get ready to put your foot down."

Mike's eye caught a lateral movement.

"RPG," he said. "*RPG.*"

It might just have been the pillion passenger's arm. But he'd seen the movement a hundred times, and his reflexes reacted to anything that looked like it. Was it a tube? *Yes.* At fifty miles an hour there was no time to debate. The bus was now in rocket range whether it kept going or veered off. The only option was to block the bike and take it out, or hope the guy missed. A rocket had a fifty-fifty chance of missing a fast-moving target over 200 yards. Mike lowered the window, steadied himself against the door, and prepared to fire.

If he was wrong, he'd be in deep shit. But he couldn't afford to wait. They were closing at twenty-five yards a second.

Do it.

He fired a long burst. The bike snaked off onto the dirt for a few yards but carried on. Rob floored the Suburban to swerve into its path and Mike lost his shot. The last thing he saw as they hit the motorcycle was a long green tube and a yellow flash that he was sure was coming straight through the windshield. *Bang.* It was an explosion or the impact or both.

The Suburban did a squealing one-eighty turn and stopped dead, throwing Mike against the seat belt. It took him a couple of seconds to unbuckle, jump out, and take cover behind the open door. Smoke rose from a point some way out in the scrubby bush.

"Over there." Rob crouched behind the driver's door, trying to get Mike's attention across the front seats. "Look."

Mike risked sticking his head out. He could see the bike on its side and a mound of debris. "Red Two to Red One, we've hit a bike. Possible RPG. We're checking it out."

Teetotal's vehicle and the bus were long gone. That was the drill — foot to the floor and get out of the kill zone without stopping. There was always the chance of a secondary attack following up behind. But nothing was moving out there. Mike could hear the chatter on his radio.

"*Red Two, we've called it in. Naz army and police on their way.*" That was Jake, Teetotal's South African co-driver. "*Fok it, man, you okay?*"

"Red One, no injuries." Rob edged out of cover. "Well, not us, anyway. We're checking now. Wait, out."

If they'd shot and rammed some unlucky repairman carrying a length of drainage pipe, there'd be hell to pay. War, or whatever fine legal distinction Mike was allowed to use these days, had become a maze of attorneys and office-bound second-guessers. It stopped him firing when he needed to. It got guys killed.

And maybe sixty civilian engineers killed with them. No thanks. Go ahead. Arrest me.

The bike lay at the end of a trail of tyre marks and fluid that turned out to be oil and blood. One guy lay on the ground with his head caved in, limbs bent. Rob covered Mike while he checked the body. The other Nazani guy lay yards away in the dirt. Mike squatted to check for a pulse. Either Rob had rammed the bike harder than Mike had thought or some rounds had hit their mark.

"So where's the rocket?" Mike asked. He'd seen the flash. It *had* to be an RPG. "Where's the tube?"

It took Rob a few minutes to find some debris scattered in the scrub. He brandished a launching tube like a trophy.

"You called it, Zombie. Good effort."

It was a massive relief. Mike had started to doubt himself. They walked back to the Suburban and inspected the damage, noting dents, gouges in the bumper guard, and scratched paint.

"Not bad." Rob nodded approvingly. "Better put some warning triangles down. There'll be traffic through soon."

Rob took out his phone and grabbed some images of the vehicle and the positions of the bodies as if it was just a routine accident that he was going to report to his insurer. By the time the army vehicle arrived, traffic had started again and a small jam had built up. Less patient or curious drivers just drove off the tarmac and skirted the obstruction. A Nazani Defence Force lieutenant poked around in the debris, slung the bodies on the back of their truck, and took Mike's and Rob's details before driving off. He didn't seem all that bothered. It definitely wasn't like a car wreck in Maine.

Mike drove back to the security compound next to the airport while Rob gazed out of the window, apparently content to be a passenger for once.

"Hoofing," he said absently. There was only one higher rank of approval on his Richter scale of excellence, and that was *fucking* hoofing. "I'm glad we disabled the airbags on this bugger."

They dissolved into nervous, shaky laughter. "I must have hit at least one of them," Mike said. "I put down enough fire."

"Either way, it bought a second or two, and that's all you need, isn't it? Shit, that was satisfying. I've never rammed a vehicle for real. Just on the CP course." Rob patted Mike's arm. "Sorry, mate. I could have got you killed."

"What were we going to do, take a vote?"

"You okay?"

Mike tilted his neck left then right to try to ease the pulled muscles. "My neck's screwed. I hope Livvie doesn't notice. If I don't do a video call, she'll know something's happened."

"Just tell her I beat you at arm wrestling."

The security compound housed contractors from other PSCs as well as Esselby, and word of the contact had already gotten around by the time they arrived. They were greeted with good-natured barracking from a few Brits standing outside the admin office.

"Bloody women drivers."

"There goes your no-claims, Ulcers."

Rob gave them a big grin and waved two fingers as he went in. They must have been former Marines: Ulcers was his old Royal Marines nickname, a play on the Rennie heartburn remedy, but Mike rarely heard anyone use it. Rob's callsign was just Royal. Any other former RM on the local radio net who wanted to use the generic nickname was out of luck.

"Is there anything you can't damage, Rob?" The site supervisor took the key to the Suburban and gave Rob a weary look, along with a sheaf of post-contact and damage report forms. "Go on, go see the medic. You as well, Mike. I don't want you two suing us for whiplash. You can't afford the lawyers anyway."

Rob just winked at Mike and took the forms. "Yes, Supe. Can we roster off, then?"

"Away with you," the supervisor said. "Good result, guys."

The supervisor didn't know anything about Mike's family. Few people he worked with ever did. He kept his connections quiet, and Rob, protective as a big brother, maintained the cover of ordinary guy-ness. For the first time since childhood, Mike had a really close buddy, the kind who gave him a nickname, ribbed him fondly in that way British troops called *slagging*, and always had his back. Rob treated him like a fellow grunt who just happened to have a few more bucks to his name. It was enormously liberating.

And we're a team. We stopped a massacre today. We did good.

At least Livvie wouldn't see it on the news. There was a plus side to being invisible.

Mike submitted to the medic and emerged with a packet of painkillers. He found Rob in the social club, a grim-looking demountable unit next to the canteen. Rob took a more home-remedy approach to analgesics. The joint security compound was officially dry, but that never seemed to stop him or anyone else from drinking liquor. He nursed what looked like a cup of coffee while he slumped in an armchair in the TV room, looking a little lost. A Thermos jug sat on the table in front of him.

"Is that decaf?" Mike asked.

Rob held a cup out to him to taste. "Dave's special blend."

Mike sipped it cautiously. It tasted like a half and half mix of brandy. "You know you get giggly and take your pants off after two beers."

"The curse of extreme fitness, Zombie. Come on. Skip the pills and join me."

They clinked cups. "Good day's work there, Royal."

"You too, mate. I didn't even see him raise the bloody launcher."

Mike was now in the pit of an adrenaline dump. As far as his body was concerned, it had been in a car crash and there was no convincing it otherwise. He spent the rest of the afternoon finishing the heavily dosed coffee with Rob, watching the sports channel in near silence.

"Brad keeps asking me to do yacht work," Rob said. "Fancy it?"

Mike shrugged. "I haven't done my maritime courses yet."

"If you're going to be siring Brayne heirs, you need to reduce your risks."

"It never stopped me before."

As soon as Mike said it, he felt guilty about Livvie. IVF treatment was no picnic, physically or psychologically. Did he have any right to keep putting her through this? It would be the thirteenth cycle. It wasn't the unlucky number that troubled him as much as the stress on her. All he had to do was aim into a container. She was the one who had to put up with the hormone treatments and endless tests.

He'd never missed her as much as he did right then. He checked the time.

"I'll be back later," he said, draining his cup. "I need to call her."

It was Mike's daily ritual. He'd prop his tablet on the small desk in his cabin and try to pretend they were having dinner instead of thousands of miles apart. Livvie's auburn hair was a little untidy, as if she'd just untied her pony tail and raked her fingers through it. They chatted aimlessly for a while.

"What's wrong with your neck?"

There was no fooling her. "Oh, rough-housing. So, one more IVF?"

"Do you want to?" She sounded tired. "Tell me straight."

She wasn't keen. He knew it. "Only if you want to."

"Okay, try not to widow me, then."

"I've got Rob watching my back. I can't lose."

The decision was made. Mike changed the subject and they chatted about the garden and plans for homecoming. It occurred to him that he might simply have been holding her up. It was too easy to forget that she had a job and a life while he was away, even if she was stuck on her own in her office. She never complained.

"I'd better go," she said. "I've got a live interpretation for a client in Paris in half an hour."

She lived in a virtual world. After Mike rang off, he struggled to remember the last time they'd actually been to Paris. He reminded himself that this deployment would soon be over, and that military wives coped.

But we don't have to live like this. I don't have to be here. I've never needed to earn a cent.

The worst thing about compulsions was that even the apparently noble ones were no different to a drug habit for the people you loved. Mike couldn't blame his sister for trotting out the same line every time they had a fight — that he was playing at it, Marie Antoinette indulging in a fantasy of being a simple milkmaid while courtiers worked to maintain the illusion around her.

Livvie was chipper again for the rest of the week, but he couldn't shake his guilt. He needed to accept that he couldn't do this forever.

"Did she bollock you?" Rob asked. They were back on escort detail, with plenty of time on their hands to gossip while they sat in the Suburban waiting for trucks and buses. "You've been a sulky sod this week."

"No. I'm just fretting. You know what I'm like."

"Well, I'll bollock you, then." Rob rapped his phone on Mike's forearm. "You did it again, didn't you?"

"Ouch. What?"

"Fifty grand. You sent Tom *fifty grand.*"

"Come on." The easiest way to give Rob or Tom anything was to dump it on them and beg forgiveness later. "My nematode of a brother-in-law spends twice that on a new car every year."

"It's not a book token, Mike." When Rob was serious, it was always *Mike.* He shoved the phone back in his pocket. "It's fucking serious money."

"I'd only spend it on polo ponies, and I can't even ride."

"Sorry, mate. I must sound like an ungrateful bastard. I just don't want Tom to get used to you bailing him out. I'm his dad. It's my job to support him."

"I haven't got any kids of my own to spoil." Mike wished he hadn't said that. It sounded like blackmail. "Humour me, Rob."

"I'll pay you back."

"You don't owe me a damn cent. Neither does Tom. You're family."

It was hard to tell if Rob had given in. He looked embarrassed, chin lowered. "I'd still be your mate if you were living in a cardboard box. You know that."

"Yes, I do. Which is why I do it."

The issue seemed to be settled. But a couple of days later, Rob tapped on Mike's open door and simply handed him his phone again. He didn't say a word. Mike read the message.

'Hi Dad. I've written a thank-you to Mike. But I'm committed to the summer gig now. We'll get together, though. Promise. I've put the money into my house fund.'

Mike didn't know what to say. He'd never seen that look on Rob's face before. It was a mix of pain and bewilderment.

"He's grown up." Rob managed a shrug. "They say it hurts to let go. Yeah, it bloody well does."

Mike still thought of himself and Rob as young men. But it was another reminder of mortality and all the things they might never do, no matter how fit they were, and that even if middle age now started at fifty, forty was still the halfway mark of a guy's allotted span. It was numerical certainty. And it sucked.

He shook off the thought by focusing on the fact that he'd be back home in days. It would strip years off him.

When they finally shipped out, the long flight with all its stopovers eased him gradually back into a world that ran by his rules and where he had everything he wanted. But it was an illusion, and he knew it. Rob never let him forget that anyway.

"Here we go. Through the looking glass." Rob stretched out in his first class seat across the aisle from Mike, unscrewing and sniffing the freebie bottles of toiletries. "See, civvies think they're safe because they've got rules and someone to complain to. But Nazani's the *real* world. Like Afghanistan. It snuffs you out, bang, just like that. No apology, no reason, and no compensation. It doesn't give a shit who you are."

"I wish I hadn't let you read Camus."

"Yeah, it was tough for a colouring book, but I stuck with it."

They managed to laugh. They always could. The alternative was to dwell on pointlessness and absent friends. Dibeg, at least, had some point to it, and there were too many dead to think of futility without feeling blasphemous.

When they landed in Bangor and picked up the rental car, Mike fell automatically into the routine of letting Rob drive. He counted down the familiar road signs and billboards on the route home.

"I'm stopping to for a leak," Rob said. "Coffee?".

"Sure. Let's find a diner."

Diners were comforting, a rare treat for Mike. Dad had always told him that he should never be too proud to eat in one. The diner that Rob stopped at smelled and tasted of Mike's childhood, and some elements even looked the same. A couple of tables away, a little boy was playing quietly with a toy soldier in DPM and body armour, walking the figure along the edge of the table and lost in his own thoughts. It seemed such an ancient, natural instinct for boys. The father was absent-mindedly stroking the child's hair, gazing out of the window at the passing traffic.

Mike nudged Rob. "Did you have one like that as a kid? GI Joe?"

"Yeah." Rob glanced at the boy. "Ours was called Action Man, though. I bet there was an MoD civil servant version called Inaction Man. Real grasping hands and interchangeable shiny arses."

"Is that what made you want to be a Marine?"

"What, to grip Barbie? Pervert."

"Seriously, how do you bring up a child and let them find their own way?"

"They find it whatever you do. You can't steer a kid by deciding whether he should have Action Man or Unshaven Feminist Barbie."

"Give me the benefit of your unedited advice," Mike said. "Am I pushing Livvie on IVF? Should we call it a day?"

"I can't make that decision for you."

"Just talk some sense to me."

"Jesus, look at me. Forty going on sixteen."

"What would *you* do?"

Rob looked away at the kid playing with his toy soldier. "Okay, Livvie's stuck in that big empty house on her own, year in, year out, and when you're home she's on hormones that make her feel like shit. Just give the baby thing a break and focus on her. It's you who wants a kid most." Rob could be brutally frank and kind in the same breath. "You'll drive her away. Don't end up on your own like me. It's fucking grim. "

Mike didn't know if it was what he wanted to hear or not, but it was what he *needed* to hear. His heart deflated slightly and he felt it would never be full again.

Yes, it's me. Might as well face it.

He tried to look away from the little boy. "You're right."

"Think about adoption," Rob said. "You'd have to beat them off with a shitty stick. Even kids with families would run away from home to get a billet at Zombie Towers."

Mike nodded. It felt painfully final, but it was easier to hear it from Rob. "I'd worry that it'd be like buying an accessory. Celeb style."

"Not to the kid you give a home to. It'll be a lifeline. And you'll love them like your own flesh and blood, believe me."

Rob had the ability to switch into profound mode in a heartbeat and pronounce universal truths. It was one of the things that made him so reassuring.

"Come on." Mike put a tip on the table. "Let's go. I'm a weird bastard, aren't I? I'm sorry."

Rob followed him out to the parking lot. "Zombie, humans always want more than they've got. If you've got everything money can buy, and you're smart, you're bound to want things that have meaning instead."

He opened the car door to let the hot air out and start the aircon. Mike tried to imagine Rob forming any kind of friendship with some of the guys he'd known at school. Rob would probably have punched them out within five minutes and not felt remotely minimised by the experience.

Before they drove away, the little boy with his GI Joe came out of the diner ahead of his dad and ran into the arms of a woman who'd just parked. Mike didn't need to know anything about them to put the story together. The little boy was the spitting image of his mom.

But it didn't need to be that way, did it? Rob said so, and Rob was always right.

DUNLOP RANCH, ATHEL RIDGE, WASHINGTON: JUNE.

A FedEx truck trundled up the track, as exotic a visitor as a camel train as far as Ian was concerned. The ranch didn't get many deliveries. He watched from the barn as Gran signed for the package, which was probably more dollar bills.

Last time the money had arrived by DHL, the time before that had been via UPS, and occasionally Gran went to the post office in Athel Ridge to collect it. Whoever sent the payments liked variety. Ian knew enough about the way the outside world ran to realise that things like pensions and donations didn't arrive that way, so while this was regular, it wasn't routine. Gran didn't trust banks. She was strictly cash-only.

"Here, Ian." She sat at the kitchen table, counting banknotes like a teller and bundling them into small wads and rolls with elastic bands. "Stow this away."

It was part of the emergency plan. Gran hid the cash around the ranch in case some disaster stopped them from accessing a central location. Ian had seen enough storms and forest fires on the news to understand how easy it was to lose everything you had in a matter of minutes, so it seemed like a reasonable precaution. He'd given up asking where it came from years ago. Gran said it was all legal, a regular gift from someone she'd done a very big favour.

Well, she knew best. She'd raised him and he thought she'd done a good job. But he was eighteen, and he'd begun to accept that Gran was also getting older and wouldn't be around forever. He couldn't bring himself to talk to her about it. She was fit and well now, perfectly capable of looking after the ranch, but she was in her sixties and her health wouldn't hold out forever. He had to be ready to take care of her. He couldn't think beyond that to a time when he'd be completely on his own.

How will I cope?

Ian felt like two separate creatures, a grown man who was old enough to vote and had girls on his mind most of the time, and a useless, scared little boy who didn't know the first thing about dealing with the wider world. He had to shape up. He wasn't too crazy to shoulder responsibility.

But I don't even have a driver's licence.

Gran went on counting. "We'll have to talk about this and plan for the future," she said, not looking up. "I need to make sure you won't need to worry about money or a roof over your head."

It didn't sound like she meant right now, but at least that opened the door enough for him to feel okay about mentioning it the next time. He took some of the rolls of banknotes and placed them around the ranch — the pantry, the gun locker, the grab bag in the hall, the steel tool cabinet in the barn — and then went to weed and water the vegetable patch at the back. If he kept busy, he wouldn't waste time worrying about things he couldn't even imagine. He needed his routine. It helped him pretend he had things under control.

When he scrubbed up afterwards, he steeled himself to use the mirror that was usually folded out of sight. He ran the clippers through his hair and tried to remember if it was still the same dark brown that it had been three months ago, which might have been the real colour or just his imagination. He had no way of knowing. He kept staring, waiting for the inevitable distortion to kick in, but nothing happened. Even the hair on his forearms stayed the same. He felt quite pleased with himself for braving the reflection.

People learn to cope with mental problems. OCD. Panic attacks. I've seen it on TV. Maybe I'm getting this under control.

But what if it's neurological? Something wired wrong in my brain, like face-blindness. There's nothing I can do to cure that.

Gran had a doctor friend who came to see them every few years, a guy about her age called Charles Kinnery. He'd always check Ian over as a favour, because Gran didn't trust physicians or dentists either. *Yeah, I can ask Kinnery. When's he coming again?* Ian had never had the nerve to ask the guy before, in case Gran hadn't mentioned that he was crazy. Maybe it was time.

He shook the hair from the clippers into the toilet bowl, flushed it, and folded the mirror back against the wall. It hadn't felt quite so bad this time. Perhaps he'd been doing this all wrong. Maybe he could teach himself to accept what was really there just by forcing himself to look every day rather than avoiding it. Willing it to stop hadn't worked at all.

When he finished the chores, he settled down to watch TV, his only glimpse of a world he'd probably never be part of. It was also his sole guide to how to behave around the kind of people he'd never met, like girls, police, bullies, and bartenders. Wasn't that how normal people learned to fit in as kids, though, by watching others? Ian rehearsed his lines, mimicking the actor as he offered to buy a woman a drink, right down to matching his accent.

Normal people probably didn't notice that kind of detail. Ian knew he had to soak it up, every bit of it, every pause, every rise in pitch, every mannerism, because he hadn't spent years absorbing it gradually by mixing with others.

"What are you having?" He tried out the words. Maybe everybody needed a script in real life. "What are *you* having? So what can I get you?"

Well, that was how impersonators did it. He'd seen a comedian interviewed about how he got his impressions right by watching videos of celebrities for hours on end, dissecting every blink and syllable. As far as Ian was concerned, there was no difference between working out how to talk like the President and learning how act and sound like a regular guy.

Perhaps he could play the role of a sane person long enough to make something of his life. *This* wasn't a life. Life was the thing he saw on TV. Some of it looked as bad as Gran said it was, but the rest seemed to be the things he wanted, necessary human things — friends, interesting places, movie theatres, ball games, *girls*.

Ian sometimes dared to think about going into Athel Ridge, getting a job, and making friends. But that wouldn't happen unless he could ignore his hallucinations. All he had to do was keep telling himself they weren't real, but if anyone looked at him too closely, he knew he'd wonder if they could see that he wasn't quite right in the head.

They'll know I'm crazy. They'll smell it. People are still animals, deep down.

"You feel like coming into town with me today, Ian?" Gran felt in her pockets. "I need to pick up some gentian spray for the sheep."

Ian found it easier to venture into town in the winter. If he turned up his collar and pulled his beanie down tight, he didn't feel that people were staring at him. Summer was more of a challenge. He relied on sunglasses and a baseball cap. You could buy stuff without needing to say a word, and if you paid cash and got out of the store fast, nobody would even look at you. But today he felt like he had *freak* stamped on his forehead. He wanted to hide.

"I think I'll check the fences," he said, instantly ashamed of chickening out. "Will you explain all the tax stuff to me one day?"

Gran took the truck keys off the hook. "Sure. But it's all written out in the folder for when you need to do it yourself." The folder was almost a person in its own right, a battered manila thing bound with heavy four-way elastic bands that Gran said had come from a lawyer's office. She put her arms around him for a moment. "You're a good boy, Ian. I just wish I could give you a better life. This isn't much fun for a young guy."

"I'm fine. Nobody could do more for me than you have." Ian had worked out years ago that his alternative with a feckless mother would have been life in an institution or worse. Gran had done what was best for him, however lonely he felt. "I know what would have happened to me if you hadn't been around."

Gran swallowed hard. It always upset her, but he needed to talk about it. The older he got, the more it had grown into a vast, silent black cloud that neither of them could really discuss but that was gradually blocking every bit of light from his existence.

"You're different, Ian," she said. "And humans don't like what's different. Animals are a lot more tolerant."

"Is there something I don't know about myself? You'd tell me the truth, wouldn't you? It won't hurt me."

She concentrated on her keys, examining them too carefully and blinking fast. That was her I-have-to-pick-my-words face.

"I think you know yourself pretty well," she said. "You're very self-aware. Not many people are."

"I meant would I know if I was crazy enough to be a danger to people. Do mad people know how sick they are?" Ian watched a lot of news. Sometimes he'd follow murder trials and wonder how serial killers saw the world, whether they knew just how weird they actually were or if they simply thought everyone else was abnormal. "Is that what you try not to tell me?"

Gran shook her head a few times, more like she was trying to stop herself thinking about something than just saying no.

"You're not a danger to anyone," she said. "They're a danger to you. I don't just mean all the assholes waiting to take advantage of you. I mean the do-gooders and government busy-bodies who'd think they knew what was best for you. But I'm going to get things sorted out for you, I promise. Now — key check."

Gran treated a trip into Athel Ridge like being inserted into enemy territory, a country full of people with credit cards and all the other recorded, numbered, cross-checked, and monitored things that tethered their lives to the scrutiny of government and corporations. She always wanted to get in and out as fast as she could. There were probably SEAL teams that didn't plan missions as obsessively as she did. Ian went through the checklist with her as he'd done for as long as he could remember.

Was it really that hostile out there, all surveillance and conspiracies? Sometimes he found it hard to believe, but then he'd switch on the radio or TV again and Gran's diagnosis was confirmed. The world was a rough place that would have no patience with someone like him. The radio was the worst. He could hear the hate spilling out of it. He stuck to NPR these days, where everyone was rational and polite, the way the world probably wished it really was.

"Bye, Gran." Ian waved her off. He didn't usually do that. "I'll fix dinner."

He watched her truck kick up dust down the track until it disappeared from view, then collected his tools and drove up to the boundary to check the fences with Oatie.

The greyhound was a lonely, clingy kind of dog who seemed to need someone to follow. He lay watching while Ian worked, occasionally sitting up and looking around when he heard something beyond the range of human ears. Ian spent an hour or two knocking posts straight with a hammer and fixing wires in place with the staple gun. Eventually Oatie jumped up, ears pricked, and looked towards the house.

That usually meant he could hear Gran's truck. But he didn't go racing down the hill this time. He just stood staring. Ian stopped to listen. The rattle of tyres on gravel carried a long way in the still summer air, and the greyhound's expert assessment was that it wasn't Gran's pickup. It'd be a delivery, then, something Gran hadn't been expecting, a rare event. Ian jumped in the truck and headed back to the house.

It was only when he saw black and white paintwork through the trees and a flash of red as the sun caught a light-bar that he realised it wasn't a delivery truck but the sheriff's cruiser. He'd only ever seen it in town a couple of times over the years. Gran didn't like cops or any kind of government authority. Ian was instantly on his mettle.

The sheriff stood on the porch, hammering on the door in bursts and stepping back to peer through the glass panels at the side. He turned around as Ian pulled up. What did he want? They'd paid their taxes and the trucks were licensed. Maybe he had some dogs in the pound that needed a home. Word got around about Gran's open house policy with animals in need.

Ian climbed out and slammed the truck door. "Can I help you, sir?"

"Sheriff Gaskin." He was middle-aged, grey-haired, and bespectacled, and his voice was a lot quieter than Ian expected for a man doing all that urgent hammering. He held up a small card. It looked like a driving licence. "Are you related to Mrs Dunlop? I need to talk to a relative."

Oh God. "Yeah, I'm Ian. Ian Dunlop. Her grandson. What's she done?"

Gran sometimes came back from trips and told him she'd yelled at someone about the way they treated their animals. Maybe she'd gotten herself arrested. But the look on the sheriff's face said it was something worse than that, and it was starting to dawn on Ian that he was catching on way too slowly.

Sheriff Gaskin tilted his head a little as if he was trying to look past Ian's sunglasses and the peak of his cap. "Your gran collapsed in town," he said at last. "I'm real sorry, son."

It still wasn't sinking in. Ian fell back on what he thought normal people would ask at times like this, just like on TV or in the movies. He stomach rolled. His hair felt like someone was tearing his scalp off.

"Where is she? What's happened to her?"

Gaskin held his arms at his sides as if he didn't know what to do with his hands. "Looks like she had a heart attack, Ian. I'm sorry. They took her to the hospital, but she didn't make it. She 's dead."

The world receded into the distance. Ian could see it and hear it, but he was no longer in it. As to what happened with the next heartbeat, the next breath — he just didn't know. *Dead* didn't make sense.

"Maybe you better leave your truck here," the sheriff said. "I'll drive you to the hospital."

Ian felt he was suffocating, but another part of him took over and recited the words like a well-learned script, in control and remembering what he had to do. He had the folder, the oracle that contained the answers to everything except what the hell he was going to do without the one person who'd always been there for him.

"Is there anyone I can call for you?" Gaskin asked. "Any relatives?"

"It's just me and Gran." Ian couldn't tell the sheriff that he was crazy and that he didn't know how he was going to cope without her. *Man up. Come on, do what you have to.* Guys his age were fighting wars. Gran taught him to be self-reliant and what a man should be, but he'd never had to test it for real. "Are you sure it's her? Are you sure it's not some mistake? Maybe it was someone who stole her purse."

The sheriff gave him a pitying look, like he heard that kind of desperation all the time. Making it feel real and true was still a million miles away. Gaskin nodded towards the car, then stared back at Ian again, frowning and baffled. He shook his head — to himself, not Ian, like a little private doubt of some kind — and took off his glasses to wipe them.

"Damn." It was just a breath, muttering to himself. "Got to get a new pair."

Ian knew what it felt like when you couldn't trust your eyes. Suddenly his craziness seemed like the least important thing in the world.

Gran was gone. What did he do now? The only oracle he could ask for guidance wasn't even a person.

It was a manila folder, one he'd never been tempted to look inside because it was so much a part of an unknown, unknowable future disaster. Ian hadn't fully understood what lonely really meant until now.

FOUR HOURS LATER.

Death was almost anaesthetising. Ian found Gran's blue pickup parked at the farm supply store and drove it away without a second thought, even though he'd never driven in traffic on a public road before.

The visit to the hospital morgue felt like a memory from years ago, not hours. Gran hadn't looked terrible like he'd expected, more a waxwork that resembled her. Staff had given him paperwork and forms. But it had all happened to someone else, to the other Ian who was now following the sheriff's cruiser back to the ranch. He knew he should have been distraught, but something else within him had picked up the reins again.

Was it always going to feel this numb, then, this painless, or was grief going to set in later? He clung to the one focusing thought that silenced all the other clamouring voices in his head. He had to open the folder.

The sheriff hadn't asked to see his driver's licence, and Ian hadn't thought of volunteering the information that he didn't have one. As he parked the truck out front and got out, the ground felt unreal, somewhere between a mattress and the deck of a ship. He wasn't sure where to place his next step.

But I've never been on a ship.

He must have seen it in a movie. Sometimes it was hard to find the line between a dimly-recalled past and something he'd seen, but it didn't make it feel any less real. When he looked back, Sheriff Gaskin had his elbow resting on the open driver's window, one hand on the steering wheel.

"You going to be okay, son? Are you sure there's nobody I can call for you? A neighbour, maybe?"

Ian shook his head. "I'm fine. Gran left me a list. A folder."

"Sure." The sheriff frowned, looking into his face like he didn't understand. But he'd never seen the folder, the big manila survival kit that contained everything that would now shape Ian's life. "You've got all the paperwork you need, yeah? You'll find the funeral home's real helpful."

"I'm okay," Ian said. "I know what I've got to do. Thank you, sir."

Gaskin looked at him for a few seconds too long, still frowning as if none of this made sense, then nodded and swung the cruiser around to head back down the track. As soon as the sound of the engine died away, Ian found himself checking the glass panel next to the front door. It wasn't a clear reflection, but it was bad enough.

Shit. Well, I should have known this would tip me back over the edge.

There was something different about the face that looked back at him. The buzz-cut hair that showed under his cap was still brown but a little darker, and his nose looked thinner. He forced himself to look away. That was why he wore his cap most of the time. It was mainly to stop him from seeing what wasn't really there.

But he had real problems now, not imagined ones. He opened the door and a new kind of emptiness rolled out with the smell of stale coffee. There was a big difference between Gran being out and Gran not being there at all. Oatie trotted up to him, looking bewildered. Ian now struggled to think more than a few moments ahead. Nothing fell into place.

Just do what she told you. Go find the folder.

"She's gone, Oatie." Ian just needed to say it aloud to believe it, even if the dog was the only one listening. "I had to identify her. She didn't look dead. Just ... something was gone, you know?"

Oatie looked up at him, unblinking. Ian had never prepared himself for seeing a body. It hadn't been anything like he'd expected from watching TV. But the sheriff had whisked him through it, probably so used to that kind of thing that he knew how to handle people who'd only ever do it once in their lives. Now Ian wanted to feel something beyond numb confusion.

She's dead. Come on, react. Normal people grieve.

But he wasn't normal. Maybe that was it.

This was why Gran had left the folder. She knew how hard it would be to think clearly. She must have lost someone and had to sort it all out by herself.

The desk was a sycamore roll-top with a hutch on top. When Ian unlocked it and rolled back the tambour, it was like entering a scale model, a cityscape of compartments lined with drawers and slots full of papers, notebooks, and Altoids tins. He could have opened it long ago. The key was always on the hook, and Gran never stopped him from using it, but this was her territory. He respected that just as she'd respected his space.

And what am I going to do without her?

There's nobody else. Just me.

The folder was stuffed with dog-eared paper, envelopes, and a few CDs in grey plastic sleeves. Ian had never known exactly what was in there and dreaded the day he'd need to find out. So this was the vindication of Gran's checklist drill. She'd treated it as a game when he was younger, but as he got older it became deadly serious.

She'd thought of everything. Each envelope was numbered with a neat pound sign, contents labelled. A flow chart paper-clipped to the first envelope showed what he needed to do and which envelope related to it. It was written in a neat and steady hand more like a draughtsman's than an old woman's.

But she wasn't that old — early sixties, he thought, not even retirement age. He'd been sure she wouldn't die for a long time yet. So had she.

'Envelopes 1 through 4 — immediate admin. Do this first. Envelopes 5, 6, and 7 — longer term things, personal instructions that'll be tough going but it's stuff you have to know. Incapacitated by stroke, dementia, or similar: power of attorney pre-signed in envelope 1, with instructions. If dead: proceed to envelope 2 for funeral instructions. Call Joe first and he'll assist. See also pre-filled forms for you to sign to notify agencies of death.'

Gran wouldn't have done any of this electronically. She didn't use e-mail, she didn't send faxes, and she didn't use messaging. She'd even disabled data and GPS on the cell phone. The up side was that her preference for old fashioned paper had saved Ian from a lot of baffling, painful bureaucracy.

Immediate admin stuff, envelope number two. Read first. Okay, Gran. I will.

He checked the forms inside against the list in the leaflet that the hospital had given him. All he had to do was date and sign each one, then mail them. Gran had addressed and stamped the envelopes, and even left a book of extra stamps to cover postage increases. Her will, folded neatly in a cream envelope, was short and straightforward: the ranch and everything else was Ian's, and all he had to do was to get Joe to take him to see the lawyer in Seattle. There were consequences in the outside world resulting from all this, he knew, but he couldn't even begin to think of them. What mattered was that everything was covered, from her prepaid funeral to insurances and taxes. He didn't have to panic about what to do next. A cryptic note about money referred to people to call on the list in envelope 5, but Ian put that to one side for the moment. He had to focus on one task at a time.

A separate note in red ink was clipped to the admin envelope, an odd mix of precise instructions and vague warnings.

'You're going to find it hard to manage the ranch on your own. Joe can take the animals. But make sure you read envelopes 5, 6, and 7 before you make any decisions about selling up or having anyone else come live on the ranch. I'm sorry that there was so much I never told you. Joe can also help you get a driving license.'

None of that made sense right then, but she had a point about the animals. Damn, there was even a cheque book in here, so she did use banks after all. Ian flicked through it. But the stubs showed it had only been used to pay taxes. Cash was paid in and a cheque written right away.

Ian sorted through the keys and opened the safe. It was full of bundles of bank notes, each labelled with the total, but it was already too much to take in. His mind jumped between vague, lonely fear and petty worries. *Groceries.* How was he going to get groceries without driving? *Ask Joe. Get a licence.* How would he earn a living and keep the ranch going? Money would still arrive, Gran had said.

He just had to read all the envelopes.

Ian left the paperwork on the desk and went to find the cell phone. It had none of the fancy features he saw on TV ads. Gran didn't trust smartphones. They gave away too much information about you, she said. They tracked you and spied on you. He stared at the keypad for a long time, trying to work out how to break the news to Joe. How often had he spoken to the guy? Two or three times a year, maybe.

Gran had taught Ian how to make calls in an emergency. He'd called the feed store once and answered a few calls from Joe over the years, but that was about it.

"Joe? Joe, it's Ian." It was like listening to a radio play, not a voice that could possibly have come from his own mouth. He blurted it out. "Gran's had a heart attack. She's dead. I'm going through the official stuff."

For a moment Ian thought he'd lost the signal. Then Joe let out a long breath. It must have shocked him. *What was I thinking?* Of course it did. Joe was Gran's friend, one of a handful of people she let anywhere near her.

"Jeez, Ian, I'm so sorry," Joe said at last. "Don't worry, we'll sort everything out. You just sit tight and I'll be over soon as I can."

"There's no rush. I'm kind of, well, you know. I've got lists of things she left me." Ian tried to put it off, but it had to be done. "Drop by whenever."

"Hell, no. *Today.* Give me an hour. Anything you need right away? Got enough food?"

"I'm okay. Thanks. See you later."

Ian realised he'd made his first phone call without Gran around for backup. It was a watershed. He went outside to feed the other greyhounds, prompted by Oatie's mournful gaze, and checked on the chickens. They were all ex-battery hens rescued by animal welfare folks. It felt kind of fitting to be marooned here with them. They tended to stick together and not roam as far as they could.

But he had to finish reading the contents of the folder before Joe arrived. One part of the hand-written note worried him: '*Personal instructions that'll be tough going.*' He was almost too scared to open the envelope. He'd pieced together enough of Gran's comments over the years to know that his mom had a drug problem and that his dad had never been around, but that was all she'd said. Whatever she regretted not telling him would all come out now. It would probably be about his folks.

Maybe he had more family out there after all. Maybe it would all work out and he wouldn't need to be alone. Was it normal to think this way? Why wasn't he crying yet? He forced himself to concentrate.

'*Envelope 5: a letter to you. I need forgiveness. I did it for your safety and I hope you understand why. Read before opening 6 and 7. Envelope 6: the people you need to contact - trust nobody else. Envelope 7: information you need for insurance, and photos. Bless you, Ian. None of this was intended. I loved you and I was proud to call you my grandson.*'

Ian had been mercifully detached by the shock of the day until he read that. His stomach knotted. Forgiveness? The last line crushed him. Tears pricked at his eyes for the first time. *No, don't start. Keep it together.* Whatever Gran wanted to be forgiven for, it couldn't possibly be that bad.

He scanned the first lines of the letter. It was baffling: '*I'm sorry, Ian, so very sorry.*' Then it plunged into details about genetic engineering which made absolutely no sense at all.

There were names: Project Ringer, and a company called KWA, Kinnery Weaver Associates. What did this have to do with him?

Ian started over, one slow word at a time, unable to relate it to

Gran or to himself until he saw the words *dynamic mimicry, chameleons*, and *cephalopods*. No, that was crazy. He'd misunderstood. He was sure of it. He doubled back and re-read a few lines about enabling undercover agents to disguise themselves at will by changing their appearance. He still couldn't take it in, and stumbled on.

'You were the unplanned outcome of that program. I know it sounds like a movie, but it happened. Charles Kinnery ran the research. I don't know if it was specifically illegal then, but it will be now. It makes you worth a lot to governments and biotech companies, so you have to stay off the radar. He thought you'd be safer with me. I was a stranger who couldn't be tracked down, so I raised you and he sent us money. I'm not your real grandmother. I don't even know who your biological parents were or who the surrogate mother was. Think of yourself as being adopted. Because that was what you were. I could never bring myself to tell you any of this. I let you think you were mentally ill, which was a terrible thing to do. You're not. You're not imagining any of it. You really do change how you look. Every time I wanted to tell you the truth, I'd come back to thinking Charles was right and that it was the lesser of two evils to let you carry on as you were. I didn't want you to be turned into a freak show or a laboratory animal. But it was also cowardice. I couldn't face telling you that I'd let you suffer.'

Ian couldn't see the words on the page now. He was suddenly aware of his breathing, little ragged gasps struggling not to turn into animal sobs of panic. He rubbed his eyes and read the letter again and again, maybe six or seven times, but not a word of it changed. He hadn't misread it.

But it was still garbage; it couldn't possibly be true. That kind of thing *didn't happen*. He knew what reality was and where the line lay between truth and fiction. He read *Scientific American* and watched PBS. Gran had to be the crazy one, not him.

He hated himself for thinking that. She wasn't even laid to rest yet.

Not my grandmother? How can she not *be my grandmother? She raised me. How could she lie like that?*

Ian made himself read it all again, more slowly, heart pounding. Then the rising panic turned into a familiar crawling sensation that crept across his skin and tightened his scalp.

I change.

Every damn word suddenly made sense now. It answered all the questions, gaps, and other inexplicable things that had plagued him all his life and made him think that he was crazy. He'd been created in a lab with weird animal genes that changed his appearance.

Oh God. It's true.

It really is true.

He knew he should have been screaming his head off at the thought that he was an impossible genetic experiment. *I'm a monster. I'm not human.* But the pain that shocked and overwhelmed him most was Gran.

She lied to me.

She lied to me. She was a stranger, not my gran at all.

And now she's gone.

Something within him shut down. He actually felt it, a little splash of spreading darkness in his brain like a drop of ink falling into clear water. The light and heat went out of his pain. His grandmother was both dead and a complete stranger, he was a freak, and everyone had lied to him. Those were just facts, and he could come back to sob and rage about them when everything else was under control.

He read on. His hands had stopped shaking.

'I'm sorry I've left you to struggle alone. Call Charles Kinnery on his private landline — see envelope 7. But if he lets you down, or if he's dead as well by the time you read this, then the only person you can trust is Zoe Murray. She's an investigative journalist based in Seattle. She'll never reveal your identity. But she's insurance to use only if you have to. If she exposes Project Ringer, at least you won't be a secret that anyone can kidnap and hide. Don't bother with other media. They don't have the guts to expose classified material any more. Arrange to meet Zoe and give her the envelope marked MURRAY. It's not the full details of the research but enough for her to understand what you are and who's responsible. (Copy for you in envelope 7.) It's sealed in plastic. Don't touch it without gloves. DNA, okay? I don't think they can use the DNA to clone you, but it can definitely identify you.'

They? Everyone was *they*. Which "they" did she mean? The government?

Ian found himself arranging the envelopes and papers in neat rows on the green leather writing surface, overlapping them like cards in a game of patience. His hands were on autopilot and his mind was completely empty, not a relaxed kind of empty but a void desperate for a rational thought to fill it.

Keep going. Look at everything. Don't panic now.

Envelope 7 contained phone numbers for Kinnery and Zoe on

index cards that were clipped to two envelopes marked MURRAY and COPY OF MURRAY FOR IAN. There was also a folded piece of blue card about the size of a wallet, marked PHOTOGRAPHS. Ian almost expected to see the faces of his parents when he unfolded it.

But Gran had told him his life had begun in a lab. He knew he'd be wrong. He was.

Ten photos, all passport-style and printed on computer photo paper, stared back at him one by one. Some were faded and discoloured with age. The pictures were boys of different ages, and then the penny dropped: this was *him.*

These were all the photos that Gran had taken over the years. He didn't recall any of the faces. There had never been a family album apart from the single photo of David Dunlop, but Gran took pictures occasionally, saying she might need them for permits. He'd never looked at them. He'd certainly never seen them all together.

Not my gran. No, someone else entirely.

She lied. All those years.

What's worse? Not being mad, or not being her real grandson?

Ian searched for some resemblance between the pictures. This was *him*, his changes, the thing he thought he'd imagined. This wasn't the hallucination of the moment. It was something permanent, and preserved, and real.

Unless I'm imagining all this as well.

Ian realised he was looking for refuge in an illness. If he was crazy, then he wasn't a freak. For a moment he wondered if he'd lock the desk, go to bed, and wake up to find Gran alive again because this had all been part of his delusion. Being crazy was the easy option.

What am I? Who *am I?*

Ian really didn't know now. Everything in his world had fallen apart in a single day. He'd never been so scared in his life. Gran had drummed into him that he needed to be wary of the outside world, and now he knew exactly why.

But Joe was on his way here. Would he notice that Ian was this *thing*, this hybrid, this experiment? He waited for the knock at the door, almost unable to breathe.

Joe showed up clutching a cardboard box of groceries. "In case you run out of anything," he said. A half-gallon jug of milk inside it made a buckling, slopping sound. "Damn, I'm so sorry about Maggie. We're going to miss her. Let's sit down and work out what you need to do, son. Once all that officialdom's out of the way, it'll be a lot easier."

"It's all done." Ian was certain that Joe was studying his face, but it might just have been normal concern. He wanted to tell him his shocking, horrible, impossible news. *I'm a monster, and she wasn't my gran.* But he had no idea where to start, and Gran's instructions hadn't said to tell Joe about all that. She'd had her reasons. "Gran set it all up. Even the funeral. I'll show you."

Joe sat down on the sofa. "I'm real sorry we don't visit you more often, Ian. Proves how long it's been. You look different every time I see you."

"It's okay," Ian said. *There. It's definitely true. It's not my imagination. Joe's seen it too.* It was probably why the sheriff had looked baffled. Nobody would think they'd actually seen a guy change. They'd think they were imagining it, just like Ian had. "Look, I don't have a driving license. I'll need to visit people soon. Seattle, probably. Can you give me a ride sometime?"

"Whenever you want. No sweat. You want to come over and stay with us tonight?"

"No, thank you, I'm okay. I need some time to think."

"Okay, I'll check in on you later and help out with the animals. But call me if you need anything, day or night, yeah?"

"Sure. Thanks, Joe."

After Joe left, Ian sat at the kitchen table for hours, unable to face a meal. Another random thought added to the evidence that he really was some kind of monster. He knew he'd had his shots as a kid, but he hadn't seen a doctor or a dentist for as long as he could remember. There was only Kinnery. Ian had thought Gran was just afraid of being put on some official database to be cross-referenced and scrutinised, but now he knew it was more than mistrusting the authorities with personal information.

There was something real to fear if anyone found out what he was. The consequences didn't have a shape or form yet, but one thing he'd learned from Gran at an early age was that companies and governments were never on your side.

And Kinnery had deceived Ian just like Gran had, then.

Ian had to call him. He was the only other person who understood what Ian was, and he had responsibilities. This was all his doing.

A voice at the back of Ian's mind said that men didn't wait for someone else to solve their problems. They took the initiative. But he was trying to get used to too many new and terrible things to think straight yet.

One thing was clear, though. This was a crisis he couldn't escape by grabbing the emergency bag and running. It was part of him, locked into every cell of his body. He'd have to find a way of living with it.

THREE

I know it's none of my business now, but I don't want to switch on the news one day and see you being lynched by a bunch of screaming hysterical foreigners. They're not worth it. No country or company's worth it. It wasn't worth it when you were a Marine, either. I know you love your job, but just because you're willing to die doesn't make it right.

Beverley Harris, formerly Beverley Rennie, in a rare email to ex-husband Rob.

DUNLOP RANCH, ATHEL RIDGE: TWO WEEKS AFTER MAGGIE DUNLOP'S DEATH, EARLY JULY.

"It's okay, Ian." Joe herded the last of the sheep up the ramp into the back of his truck. "If you ever change your mind, I'll bring them straight back."

The chickens and dogs — all except Oatie — had already left for their new home. Oatie refused to be parted from Ian. The dog pressed close to his legs as he stood on the porch.

Every landmark in Ian's life had disappeared: family, identity, and even the fragile future he'd thought he had. The only immediate truth was that he'd struggle to look after the animals on his own. Roger the ram looked back at him with an expression of baffled, slit-eyed betrayal before trudging up the ramp.

Ian held out an envelope of dollar bills. "That's towards their feed," he said. "Thanks, Joe."

"No need." Joe waved the money away. "We're going to be

awash with eggs. Just call me when you need a ride. The bus takes forever."

Ian pressed the envelope into his hand anyway. He wanted Joe gone, not because he didn't like the guy but because the longer he hung around, the more likely Joe was to see him *morph.* There: he'd given it a name now. It seemed as good a word as any. How had he made it through the lonely funeral and scattering of the ashes without morphing? He was sure he hadn't changed again. He needed to understand what caused it.

I change. I really do change.

I'm a freak. And Kinnery designed me that way.

Joe bolted the tailgate and the truck rumbled away, leaking plaintive bleats. Ian watched it out of sight before he turned around and almost tripped over Oatie.

"We'll be fine," he told the dog. "I've just got to get my head straight. Go through Gran's stuff. Okay?"

Oatie's expression said *yeah, and then what?* Ian read the leaflet on bereavement that the funeral home had given him and concentrated on the paragraph that said it was normal to feel confused, angry, and all kinds of strange, unconnected things when someone died. Everything the leaflet described had happened, even the weird bits about sex. In the last few days, Ian had veered from being unable to think about anything else except girls he'd never meet to not caring if he did and then not even eating for a day. He couldn't sleep, either.

He was a mess. Maybe the roller coaster of moods and hormones would start him morphing again, but when he made himself take a look in the bathroom mirror, he didn't seem to be much different to the last time he'd studied his reflection.

She wasn't my real gran.

But she's dead. And I miss her.

What am I going to do when the money runs out? Kinnery won't live forever either.

Ian re-read Gran's letter to convince himself that this wasn't some incredibly detailed hallucination. If it was, at least it was consistent. Not a word in the notes had changed. Oatie leaned against his legs.

"No good looking to me for guidance, buddy," Ian said, rubbing the dog's ears. "I haven't even worked out how to get the bus into town to buy groceries yet."

He left Oatie in the kitchen with a bowl of canned dog food and a packet of cookies to distract him while he carried on clearing the house. The compulsion gripped him. He needed to do something, *anything*, to stop the thoughts bouncing around in his head. Then it became a frenzy, dragging everything out of closets and cupboards, sorting through every piece of paper he could find, and stacking whatever he didn't need to burn later.

His gut kept telling him to run away and find somewhere where nobody knew him, but the voice of common sense reminded him that not only did nobody know him around here anyway, but he also had no plan yet for finding a job and somewhere else to live. He couldn't even risk driving anywhere without a licence. Eventually, traffic cameras would pick him up. Gran had warned him about that.

The voice was still in his head. *Run, Ian. Run. You've got to be ready.*

He was eighteen; he might as well have been eight. The scale of the outside world that he'd have to confront began to crush him. His scalp tightened. He was too scared to go check his reflection this time. He felt like an alien who'd landed on Earth with a knowledge of the language and culture but no idea how to apply it.

If he was going to have any kind of life — even something as simple as buying a pint of milk, let alone getting a girlfriend — then he had to find a way to deal with it. Suddenly he wanted to scream at Gran for keeping it from him all these years, but the anger was replaced instantly by guilt and then the worst sense of loneliness he'd ever experienced. A bottomless pit opened up in his chest and his entire life plunged down it.

He carried on mechanically, hauling garbage bags down the stairs to the back yard ready for burning, but when he went into Gran's room and opened her closet it almost took his legs from under him. He sat on the edge of her bed and tried to cry. All he could manage was dry sobs. Was this normal? Was this what you felt like when you lost someone, or was this peculiar to a monster like him?

If only he could go back to being crazy. Crazy didn't stop him having a photo ID for a driving licence. How could he explain it if he morphed in front of someone? No girl would understand that.

But I never thought I'd have a proper life like everyone else anyway, did I? What difference does it make?

He threw himself back into purging the house. Perhaps he'd find something hidden away, some letter or photo that would suddenly make things all right again. But he knew he wouldn't.

When he went to the bathroom, he checked the mirror. His eyes were slightly different, still a muddy hazel but not quite the same shape.

So what's me? *I had to start from somewhere.*

However hard he worked on clearing the house, he still wasn't exhausted enough to sleep. Oatie crept into his room and lay on the bed next to him, making little whining noises every time he tossed and turned. Eventually Ian gave up and went downstairs to watch a movie.

Films were still his main yardstick for assessing the world beyond the ranch. The plots might have been total fiction, but he knew the attitudes and concerns of the characters were straight out of real life, or else people wouldn't have found them so interesting. And Gran had always said they'd teach him a lot about society's expectations of men. It must have been hard for her to bring up a boy on her own. He was still feeling guilty for being angry with a dead woman who'd spent her life looking after him, liar or not.

He paused halfway along the shelf and pulled out a very old movie called *Scott of the Antarctic*. Gran had said it was a true story.

"Let's try this one, Oatie," Ian said. The dog settled down next to him on the sofa. "Maybe it's got dogs in it."

He put his feet up on the stool. Yes, it did have dogs in it, sled dogs, not that Oatie took any notice, and guys with really weird English accents that Ian was sure no real Brit had these days. But that wasn't what drew him in.

It was about a polar expedition. It was bleak and depressing, but he couldn't stop watching. The grim struggle to be the first to the South Pole, the realisation that the Norwegians had beaten them to it, the awful journey back — it was painful to watch. And then a guy walked out into the snow to die to give his friends a better chance of survival, no fuss or drama, a man called Oates. They just carried on in the face of certain death.

Who was going to rescue them? Ian waited for the upbeat ending.

But there wasn't one. Nobody reached them in the nick of time, nobody at all. They all died, still stoic and writing notes to their families to the very end, and this wasn't just a script. It had actually happened. Tears welled in Ian's eyes.

He sat staring at the screen, disturbed and lost long after the credits had rolled. *That* was what real men were supposed to do. They made sacrifices. They put their friends before themselves. They faced the worst with calm dignity. How many really did that? For some reason, the polite little film hit him even harder than some of the war movies he'd seen.

He still preferred war films to just about anything else, though. It wasn't the action and the thrills. It was the *questions.* Could he do that? Would he have been that courageous? What was it like to feel so much a part of something that you'd risk your life for it, or kill for it?

Ian wanted to think he had it in him. He wondered what Scott or Oates would have made of his situation, and realised that he didn't even know what a problem was compared to what they'd endured. He had food, he had friendly neighbours if he chose to see them, and he wasn't risking a cold and lonely death.

I'm a wimp. A child. I've got to man up and stop feeling sorry for myself.

But Scott and his men knew exactly who and what they were, and that they'd be the same tomorrow. Ian had to come to terms with being unlike any other human on Earth.

Why did Kinnery do this? Who the hell does he think he is?

Ian was angry again. It seemed like a better reaction, though — not self-pity, not fear, not doubt. He might be afraid again when he woke tomorrow, but right now he was fired up and ready to act. It was a movie: it was a TV show. If he thought of it like that, if he put a layer of unreality between himself and the crisis, then it wasn't happening to him and he could play it out any way he pleased. He'd work out his lines so that he'd always know what to say next, and he'd have a character that he could step into so that nobody saw the scared Ian Dunlop underneath.

Yeah, that's how I'll do it.

He picked up the phone and told himself he'd do it on the count of five. He'd call a near-stranger to say that Gran was dead and that she'd told him everything. That was his script. He tapped out Kinnery's number, checking each digit on the note that Gran had left. It was a Canadian area code, Vancouver.

It rang a few times before a voice mail message cut in, asking Ian to speak after the tone. He hadn't been expecting that. He almost blurted it all out, but what if someone else was listening? He needed to speak direct to Kinnery. He'd try again later. It was nearly two in the morning anyway, not a smart time to have a difficult conversation.

Ian woke just after nine the next day, floundering in a few seconds of forgetfulness before he remembered everything anew. Yes, he was frightened again. He was alone, he wasn't completely human, and whatever he was would make people hunt him down. Some scientist had put engineered genes in him, *animal* genes, and that scientist was the man who used to come and visit Gran.

It's his fault. He's got to put this right.

Could Kinnery put him back the way he was? Why hadn't he done that already? Was he still carrying out some study?

Maybe I shouldn't be calling him at all. Maybe he's only doing it for his own ends.

But Gran had left instructions, and despite the angry thoughts that still rattled around between the grief and the confusion, Ian was sure that she'd protected him. She wouldn't have left the note to call Kinnery if she'd had any doubts.

He wasn't so sure about involving this Zoe Murray, though, whatever Gran said. She was a journalist. He was a story. But she was only there as an emergency when he'd run out of options, and that hadn't happened yet.

At 1015 he tried Kinnery's number again and got the same voicemail recording. Maybe Kinnery was as scared of picking up the phone as Ian was of calling. Okay, he'd leave a message.

"Mr Kinnery, this is Ian." Kinnery must have known Gran's number. He certainly knew who Ian was. "Call me back."

Ian settled down to wait for a call. He still had plenty to keep him busy around the house. But Kinnery didn't ring back that evening, or the next day. Ian rang again on Wednesday and the voicemail kicked in again.

Now he was upset and scared. He took a deep breath and tried to put more urgency into it. "It's Ian. You need to call me back. Gran's dead. I know what you've done. You have to call me."

He'd give Kinnery until tomorrow morning. Then what? What if he never called back? Ian sat watching the news about somewhere in Africa having another civil war, but he wasn't taking in any of it. He nursed the cell phone in his lap, willing it to ring.

Perhaps Gran had already had her doubts. She'd come up with a backup plan, after all. Ian studied Zoe Murray's phone number on the card. It seemed crazy to tell anyone else that he existed, but Gran must have known what she was doing, or else Kinnery wouldn't have trusted her in the first place. She'd avoided every situation where Ian could have been exposed, from teaching him at home to skipping hospital visits.

That took some planning. All Ian had to do was to stay as mistrustful as she had been. If he needed to contact this Zoe woman, then, he'd do it anonymously until he was sure she wouldn't expose him.

Kinnery still hadn't called back the next day, or the day after. Ian had expected to hold out for a few more weeks before he started to panic, but now he was in free-fall.

Nobody except Kinnery knows what I am.

Isn't that what I want, the safest option? No. I can't live with a secret that big. It's beyond being alone. It's like being buried alive. I need to talk to someone.

He could have waited, but he had no idea how long was long enough. He could huddle here for months, dreading a knock on the door. He had enough supplies to sit out a siege, but if he didn't take hold of his own life right now, if he didn't force something to happen, he'd be a prisoner here indefinitely. He didn't want to call Zoe on the cell in case she could trace him. If she was in Seattle, he'd get the bus and call her from a public phone there, well away from Athel Ridge.

Sorry, Gran. I'm even more suspicious of the world than you were. Imagine that.

There was a lot that you could learn from movies, whatever people said. He'd made his first smart decision without Gran's folder to guide him.

Now he needed a bus timetable. He'd call the ticket office. While he was searching for a directory, he glanced at the photo of David Dunlop and his helicopter, the essence and personification of the kind of man he wanted to be.

Suddenly that hurt more than anything. Ian wasn't related to him at all. Ian was just a device for courageous men to use, not destined to be one of them. There was no blood of heroes flowing in his veins.

He didn't know whose blood was in them at all. But he needed to.

ATHEL RIDGE: TWO DAYS LATER.

Ian kept thinking of Captain Scott as Joe dropped him at the bus station in Athel Ridge.

"You sure you don't want me to drive you all the way?" Joe asked.

"Thanks, but I need to learn to do this on my own." Ian hid behind his sunglasses and cap, distracted by his teeth for a moment. Did they morph too? He'd never considered it. He tested them with his tongue, but nothing had changed. "And it gives me time to read."

"Well, whatever it is, call me if you decide you need picking up."

Seattle wasn't a war zone. It was just a city. All Ian had to do was to stay calm, get on the right bus, and not draw attention to himself. But it was the first time he'd ever been out among strangers on his own. It was a step beyond picking up the phone and calling Kinnery. He tried to think himself into a role and imagine the lines he'd use, but outside the safety of his own four walls, it didn't seem so easy.

Okay, visualise something else. Imagine I'm the way I was — when I thought I was just crazy, not a monster. Imagine I look normal to everyone else.

He thought that he'd be conspicuous, but there were a couple of other guys his age waiting for buses at other stops, dressed pretty much the same. Nobody was going to even notice him if he just stayed calm. When he caught his reflection in the glass window of the ticket booth he felt that pang again, the need both to look away from it and stare to see what had changed. He boarded the bus and slid down in a seat at the back to read a book.

The vehicle smelled of sweat, perfume, and cleaning fluid. It was the first time he'd travelled on a bus, and the first time he'd ventured off the ranch with the phone switched on. Gran said a cell could give away your location even with the GPS turned off, so she usually took out the battery. If Kinnery rang back, though, Ian couldn't afford to miss the call.

Along the route, a man sat down next to him but didn't make eye contact. It was like Ian wasn't even there. Ian began to learn how people managed to pretend they were alone in a crowd. He could act as if he was engrossed in his book, rummage in his backpack — one of the folding ones that he could empty and shove in his pocket — or keep checking his phone, and nobody expected him to look at them or talk to them. People were the most striking new thing in his world now. Ignoring them seemed impossible, but that was exactly what he had to do.

The everyday world was actually a lot more like TV than Gran had admitted, except there weren't as many good-looking people. Ian noted the bits of reality that matched what he saw on screen and those that didn't fit at all.

And Gran's still Gran. I mustn't think about what she wasn't. Not yet, anyway.

Kinnery still hadn't called by the time Ian arrived at the Stewart Street bus station. Maybe the guy had died and nobody knew Gran was out there waiting to hear from him. Well, Ian was here now, and he had a choice: to go ahead with the plan and call Zoe, or just kill some time getting used to walking around a city, hope that he didn't morph in front of anybody, and take the long ride home.

He picked up a street map from a kiosk. It took him a few minutes to pluck up the courage to walk into the men's room at the bus station, but he was bursting, and all he had to do was find a cubicle the way he'd done a couple of times in Athel Ridge. He shut the door, had a pee, and then sat down on the closed toilet lid to study the map and locate a public phone.

Well, that was simple enough. He managed to get out of the rest room without making eye contact with anybody and found the phone booth. If Zoe wasn't in, he couldn't leave a message asking her to call back, so he might still go home empty-handed today. He set himself a deadline to give up and catch the bus back to Athel Ridge. A plan and a timetable were a good substitute for courage.

But I'm doing fine. Look. I'm in Seattle, tracking down a reporter. On my own. It's just a script, just acting. I can handle this.

As the number rang, he glanced around. Absolutely nobody was looking at him. Then a woman's voice answered and startled him. He didn't catch a name. But he was sure she said *The Slide.*

Deep breath. Don't screw this up.

It came out in a rush, not quite the casual tone he was aiming for. "Are you Zoe Murray?"

"That's me. Who's calling?"

It was a good question. Ian would have given a lot to know the answer. Suddenly it felt too dangerous. No, he wasn't going to say who he was or even mention Gran, not yet.

His tried to slow his breathing. They said it helped calm you down. "I've got some information for you."

There was a few seconds' silence while he fidgeted with the plastic-wrapped envelope in his pocket, rehearsing how he'd hand it over without contaminating it.

"What kind of information?" Zoe asked at last. "Can you e-mail it?"

"No, it's hard copy in a sealed envelope. About a medical research project." Wow, this was harder than he'd thought. Perhaps he should have asked for her address and mailed the package. But this had to be done in person. Gran always said letters could go astray or get intercepted. "Can we meet up?"

"Sure." Zoe didn't ask any questions about the contents, probably because she was worried about being tapped, given her line of work. "You obviously know where I am. Where are you?"

"Seattle."

"Okay, that's easy enough. Meet me outside the conference centre, corner of Eighth and Pike. Half an hour?"

Ian studied his map. "Okay."

"How will I recognise you?"

She couldn't have known how impossible that question was, either. "Navy blue hoodie, jeans, blue cap."

"Okay, look for a woman with short grey hair and a red satchel. I'm easy to spot. See you later."

Ian hadn't even mentioned Gran's name, but Zoe had agreed to meet him for no better reason than the offer of unspecified information. People were too trusting. He put the phone back on the cradle and headed for Pike Street.

Seattle looked like every other city that he'd seen on TV, canyons of glass storefronts and streaming traffic. It could have been anywhere in the country. He merged into the sea of pedestrians, getting more confident as he realised it wasn't hard to adopt the shared pretence of being alone. He slowed to look in a store window.

As he passed the automatic doors, a group of girls in bright T-shirts and jeans ambled out, chattering like parrots and leaving a perfumed wake. He froze. He'd never smelled anything like it in his life. His fragile confidence vanished instantly, and all he could see was the vast gulf between what he was and what he could never have, and a few hypnotic details — a silver necklace, lip gloss, and tanned skin. He wasn't prepared for the impact and what it would do to him.

Not now. Please, not now.

It was just as well he'd worn the hoodie. It was already long, but he thrust his hands deeper into his pockets to make sure it reached almost mid-thigh. He was certain that the entire city would spot his erection. Embarrassment and guilt almost blinded him for a second. Then the girls were gone, lost in the endless stream of shoppers. Ian suddenly couldn't understand why he'd ever thought it was a good idea to come here. Gran was dead, his life had plunged into chaotic shit, he didn't even fully understand what or who he was, and now all he could think about was sex. It overwhelmed him. He had no control over his own body, not even how he looked.

Christ, guys my age are fighting wars, and I can't even handle walking past a few girls on the goddamn street.

The shame of not being heroic focused him instantly. He reached the conference centre and wandered up and down on the opposite side of the road to the main entrance before finding a doorway to stand out of the way. He caught a glimpse of himself in a window, temporarily superimposed on the stream of passers-by. He looked completely average. He wasn't a monster, and he wasn't crazy, and it was obvious that nothing about him seemed odd to anyone else, because nobody even glanced at him.

I don't exist. I can hide in a crowd. That's quite something.

Where would he go once he'd made contact with Zoe? He'd have to talk to her to work out whether Gran was right to trust her. He'd practiced sliding the envelope out of the plastic wrapper by letting it fall under its own weight. Now he wouldn't need to wear gloves when he met Zoe. He could just drop the envelope.

On what? A table. On a table in front of her.

Okay, so they'd have to go to a coffee shop or something. There were plenty of restaurants around. He just had to remember not to use a cup, because it was a great way to harvest someone's DNA. He'd seen that on too many cop shows. He tucked the plastic-wrapped envelope into the outer pocket of his rucksack and carried on watching the conference centre doors. He wasn't the only person apparently waiting for someone. He was just doing the same as everybody else.

His stomach growled and he regretted not buying a sandwich earlier. Maybe he'd missed Zoe. Then he saw a splash of red out of the corner of his eye.

That's her. Got to be.

Zoe was one of those older women who still dressed like a student. He saw the red satchel even before he saw her grey hair, but he waited for her to stop at the entrance and look around first before he was certain enough to cross the road and approach her.

"Zoe?"

She looked him up and down. "You're the guy who phoned, yes? Do I get a name?"

Ian was suddenly so far out of his depth that he gave up trying to swim. It really was like a movie. He had nothing else to guide him.

"Not yet," he said. *Oh God. I'm miles from home and about to tell a total stranger what I am.* "I don't even know how to explain this. Someone said I could trust you."

Zoe was still looking him over. "Okay, you want to go for a coffee and tell me what you can?" She pointed up the road to a restaurant. "If you're trying to avoid being seen, you've been picked up on CCTV cameras already. But at least the place up there bans glassholes."

Ian didn't know what a *glasshole* was, but he got the general idea. He followed her. The cafe had a notice on the door: FOR THE COMFORT AND PRIVACY OF OUR CUSTOMERS — NO LIFEBLOGGING, GLASS, OR OTHER RECORDING ALLOWED ON THE PREMISES.

He hadn't even thought about things like that. He hadn't needed to. As soon as he stepped through the door, a wall of noise hit him from hissing coffee machines, clattering plates, and loud conversations. Zoe pointed to a table.

"Take a seat," she said. "I'll get the drinks."

At least Ian was ready for that. "Nothing for me, thanks."

While he waited, he checked around him. It was as much out of disorientation as caution, because there were a lot of mirrors on the walls and the place was busier than he'd expected, much more daunting than being in the street. He was worried that he'd reach a point where he'd have to turn and run. But he sat down, took out the envelope, and slid it from its wrapper onto the table.

There: he'd done it. It was an irrevocable step into a situation that he wasn't sure he could handle.

Zoe came back with a frothing cup in one hand. "Is that it?" she asked, moving the envelope to put down her coffee. "Can I take a look now?"

It was his last chance to change his mind. He didn't. He couldn't stay in this limbo forever.

"Yes," he said.

Zoe opened the envelope. Ian watched the expression on her face while she read the two typed pages for an agonisingly long couple of minutes. Her frown grew and deepened. Judging by her eye movement, she was re-reading everything. Eventually she stopped and looked at him over the top of the sheet.

"I don't suppose I can ask where you got this."

Ian dodged the question because he couldn't think of a safe answer yet. "Do you understand it?"

"I think so. It's pretty vague in places, but it's very specific about the company, isn't it? You know what's in it, do you?"

He nodded. "Yes."

"Are you the subject?"

She waited for him to answer, but he didn't. He couldn't.

"It's you, isn't it?" she said. She didn't smirk or shake her head. She was taking it seriously, believing it all. "Look, I need to know what you want me to do with this. I mean, it's a hell of a story, and just the kind of issue we want to cover in *The Slide*. And it predates the Chinese claim to the first human-animal hybrid embryo. I'd really like to know who wants it out there and why."

Ian could have told her without giving away enough detail for anyone to find him if she let something slip. But his gut told him not to. There was nothing about her that made him uneasy. He was just losing his nerve. He had no more control over where this would lead than he did over anything else.

But it was too late to roll things back and sit on the secret. He didn't have to mention Gran, though. Zoe might well have known about the ranch. It felt like one risk too many.

"It's insurance," he said, quoting Gran. "Does it look genuine to you?"

"You wouldn't believe the stuff that government agencies get up to." Zoe dropped her voice. She'd been talking very quietly, almost drowned out by the hissing of the espresso machine and the chatter around them, but now Ian had to strain to hear her. "Just tell me. Is it you? Is somebody after you? This must be worth a fortune to someone, so I'm guessing that you're running scared."

Ian wasn't ready for that. He should have done this on the

phone after all. And now he was starting to feel breathless. He should have known that the stress of the trip might make him morph. He was terrified of changing in front of her.

And everyone else.

He couldn't sit here any longer, but he couldn't stand up and run out the door, either.

"Okay, you're giving me this," Zoe said. "So I'll take that to mean you want it investigated. Reported. *Public.* If not, you better say so now."

She still didn't ask his name. He could see the sign to the rest rooms on the wall by the stairs. He just needed to walk away for a moment to get himself under control, then think this through. He needed a breather. He'd say something he'd regret. He'd blurt something out.

"I've got to visit the bathroom." Ian jerked his thumb over his shoulder and picked up his backpack. "Excuse me."

He had to weave his way around tables and customers. He still expected everyone to stare and point at him, but he was so ordinary to them, so unimportant, so *invisible* that he had to squeeze past. He trotted up the stairs and shut himself in the men's toilet, a small room with two cubicles and a wide mirror over the basin. He checked his reflection to make sure nothing had changed, then locked the door.

Shit, this was crazy. Zoe believed him. She hadn't laughed or dismissed it. He had just minutes to sort himself out before he went back downstairs, and then he'd have to tell her more detail. Was it safe to identify Gran and admit what he was? Even if Zoe protected her sources, she'd still know where he lived, and things could go wrong. Gran always said there was no such thing as a secret.

But Gran said I could trust this woman.

Ian couldn't stall any longer. He held his breath for a moment. Okay, he'd go back and tell her about Gran. They must have known each other well enough. But as he slid the lock, he could feel pressure building in his sinuses and that wind-burned feeling creeping across his face. By the time he opened the door, he knew what he was going to see in the mirror. Whatever it was, it wouldn't be the same face he'd come in with.

Shit. I should have known it would happen.

His hair was darker and his features were broader. This time he looked so different that he couldn't go back and sit down in front of Zoe again. This wasn't the marginal kind of change that just made the sheriff think he needed new glasses. Even if Zoe didn't freak out, Ian wouldn't be able to look her in the eye. All he wanted to do was go home, lock the door, and hide. But he had to walk through that cafe and past her to do that.

Maybe he could show her. He might not have to say a word. She'd be the first stranger to know, but he just couldn't predict how she'd react, and they'd have an audience.

Ian realised he didn't count Kinnery as a stranger.

Why didn't you call back, you bastard?

Some guy walked into the bathroom. Ian didn't look around. He just caught the reflection as the man edged past him into a cubicle. Then an idea hit him: if he looked that different, he could use it to walk out.

He took off his jacket and cap and shoved them into the rucksack. It looked different when it was fully packed. Then he took off his T-shirt, turned it inside out so that the striped pattern didn't show, and put it back on.

Just walk out. Just walk down those stairs and keep going.

Run. Run, just like Gran said.

Ian was ashamed of himself for retreating, but he'd tried to do too much too soon. As he left the bathroom, he almost ran into customers coming the other way. The place was really busy now. That would be his salvation. He picked his way between the tables and people standing at the counter, took a careful look in Zoe's direction, and noted that she was re-reading the letter. She kept glancing in the direction of the stairs.

If she'd seen him at all, she hadn't recognised him.

He walked straight out of the cafe and down Pike Street. She didn't come running after him. Even if the CCTV cameras picked him up as he headed for the bus station, they wouldn't identify him as the same guy.

For a moment, Ian felt on top of the world. It was like being the Invisible Man. Whatever else this experiment had condemned him to, he could always hide. But the elation faded fast. It was a useless defence mechanism if he couldn't control it.

He had to go hide for real, the way normal people did. And he had to find another way of getting home from the bus station in Athel Ridge. He couldn't call Joe for a ride now. Joe would notice the changes. It was going to be a long, long walk.

He had to come up with a better plan than this if he was going to survive in the world of normal, unchanging people.

EN ROUTE FROM VANCOUVER INTERNATIONAL AIRPORT: JULY.

Was this it? Was he dying, here and now, in a goddamn taxi, in a traffic jam?

Charles Kinnery gripped his briefcase until his knuckles turned white and waited for the pain to pass or finish him off. It was deep and sharp, a knife from sternum to spine that almost stopped him breathing. He was suddenly terrified, not of death itself but of the paperwork he hadn't destroyed and the possible indignity of being found dead having crapped his pants.

He was a biologist, for Chrissakes. He should have known whether a fatal heart attack caused loss of bowel control. Did it? *Did it?*

The chest pain lasted an agonising fifteen seconds, but he was still breathing. *Reflux. Might just be reflux again.* He'd call his doctor next week and get it checked out. He was more worried these days about what he might leave behind, the unresolved mess of his existence.

His phone chimed with a new e-mail. He flicked his thumb across the icon to clear the notification, but one word from the header jumped out at him, a word that almost put him into cardiac arrest for real: RINGER. The world around him vanished and all he could see was that single word.

Project Ringer. God Almighty, where the hell did that come from?

The corpse had drifted to the surface after all those silent, dark years weighted down at the bottom of the lake. Why did he ever think it wouldn't?

His stomach crawled halfway up his throat. The only people who knew the project's name were those who'd worked on it, and they were well drilled not to use it in headers. They were gone, too, long dispersed to other companies, retired, or dead. The driver couldn't possibly see what he was reading, but Kinnery found himself shielding the phone's screen with his hand like a schoolboy trying to hide his exam answers.

His eyes darted wildly over the text. The message had come

from something called *The Slide*. It took him a few moments of mouth-drying panic to decide whether to take a deep breath and read it or break off to check what *The Slide* was. He settled on the message.

'I understand you led a genetics research program called RINGER, *funded by the US government. I've received some documents that I'd like to discuss with you. You might prefer to call me on the number below. Zoe Murray, Staff Writer, The Slide.'*

It was as bad as it got. "Ah, shit."

Kinnery glanced up, worried that the driver had heard him, but the man was still looking straight ahead as the cab exited the bridge. Whatever documents this woman had seen, she knew the project's name and the source of funding. Kinnery didn't dare phone her. It would be a fishing expedition. A skilled interviewer could work out as much from his silences as from what he said. So what the hell was this document?

No — what was *The Slide*?

Kinnery tapped the link in the signature and was almost relieved to see the home page. It was one of those whistle-blowing conspiracy sites frequented by aging stoners and teens who fancied themselves as anarchists, full of crackpot stories about what the government was really putting in the water supply and why your every phone call was recorded on a giant computer. Damn, that was a bad example. Okay, they got it right sometimes. The rest was bullshit, though.

Ringer. What else has this woman got?

He'd have to warn Maggie right away. Fringe site or not, they'd managed to acquire information that not only named Ringer but identified him as project leader.

That was a heart-stopper. It was bitter-sweet, too, because he'd never been able to stand up and tell the media that the Chinese lab hadn't been the first.

We beat them by years. No, I *beat them by years. And not with goddamn rabbits.*

Maybe this Murray woman had seen a redacted budget report that shouldn't have been let out of the filing cabinet. That might have had only his name and the project ID on it. Genetic research — well, it wouldn't take Einstein to look up the name Charles Kinnery and work out that the program wasn't about better ways to reinforce concrete.

Nothing really major, then. Nothing at all. Because even my team didn't know everything, did they?.

Kinnery told himself optimistic lies and tried to work out which of the team might have been sufficiently disgruntled to dredge this up after so many years. But dredge up what, exactly? All his immediate team knew about was the creation of transgenic embryos that were destroyed in days. It was borderline legal at the time, depending on which lawyer gave an opinion, and proper legislation was years away. But it was classified, and, officially, it had never happened.

Creating a full-term human-animal hybrid was way beyond any grey area, though. And it was certainly illegal now.

A change of labels, a discreet amendment of records, and the rest of his team were none the wiser. If *The Slide* had acquired files from the project, it would be damaging but possibly survivable. KWA had no records that even hinted at Ian's existence.

Kinnery reassured himself that it wasn't as professionally humiliating as research into walking through walls or espionage by psychic map reading. Even if the legality was questioned — how would that happen with a classified military project, anyway? — it would make him eminently employable in Britain and some other parts of Europe.

Not here, though.

If Zoe Murray had identified him, then she'd probably called his old business partner at KWA as well. Shaun Weaver was a devious and patient bastard. Why hadn't he rung yet? Perhaps he was waiting for Kinnery to show his hand.

Perhaps he knows what I did. Did he know all along?

"Here you are, sir. The taxi driver slowed to a crawl. "Which number?"

"Ah, two blocks ahead, please."

I go away for a week or so, and the world caves in. Why? Why now?

Kinnery unlocked his front door and went straight into the study to boot up his computer. A red light was flashing on his desk, the voicemail counter on an old landline phone that had rung only a dozen times in the last five years, telling him that he had messages. The call forwarding to his cell phone hadn't worked. Maybe he'd forgotten to set it. Damn: he'd deal with that later. But he already knew who'd called. There was only one person who had the number.

It would be Maggie Dunlop.

Kinnery plucked up courage to press the play button. If she'd called, it was because she absolutely had to, but if this had something to do with *The Slide* it didn't bear thinking about. Nobody should have known she was there. Nobody knew that she had Ian. Nobody knew Ian existed.

"Jesus, Maggie," he said aloud. "Don't be mad at me."

He hit the play button. "*You have three messages*," it said. "*Message one, Monday, one-thirty-two, a.m.*" Damn, she'd be spitting nails. He heard a few clicks and the sound of someone breathing before putting down the receiver. The second message threw him completely, though. At first he didn't recognise the voice that followed the robotic time-check. "*Monday, ten-fifteen, a.m. — Mr Kinnery, this is Ian. Call me back.*" Then the third message — terse, upset, urgent — tipped him into another heart-pounding moment of panic. "*Wednesday, eleven-thirty-five a.m. — It's Ian. You need to call me back. Gran's dead. I know what you've done. You have to call me.*"

It was now Saturday. Shit, shit, *shit.*

Kinnery found himself reaching for his car keys even before he tried returning the call. It would take him at least seven hours to drive down to Athel Ridge. Dear God, Maggie was *dead.* Ian was there on his own. What was he doing? The boy couldn't possibly cope.

He unlocked his desk and took out the second-hand pre-paid cell he kept for calls that needed to be untraceable. His life had become one of a paranoia that had bleached every scrap of normality from his existence — every job, every relationship, and every moment of quiet contentment. He knew he deserved it. Sometimes he wondered if he'd embraced it as his penance. How often did he think about Ian these days? Sometimes he could almost forget the problem existed for months at a time, but it was always going to land on his doorstep one day. And he still didn't have a solution for it after eighteen years.

He keyed the number, shaking. It rang for a long time but nobody answered.

The number was another unregistered cell. Maggie usually left it in the house or switched it off and took out the battery in case someone was using it to track her. She had more security drills than the goddamn CIA. Maybe Ian had gone out to feed the animals. Kinnery decided to keep ringing until he got an answer, and if he didn't get one in a couple of hours, he'd drive down there and collect the kid.

If someone hasn't beaten me to it. Maggie's dead. No answer from the ranch. Conspiracy theory hacks suddenly calling me about the project after nearly twenty years. It's all blown up. Why now? How's all this connected?

Ian was a string of decisions escalating from bad to catastrophic that Kinnery couldn't go back and put right. He'd had plenty of chances to stop, each one successively harder until everything became irrevocable.

I knew what I was doing, or at least I knew it was wrong. I don't understand why he turned out the way he did, though. Not even with all the advances we've made since then.

And what the hell am I going to do without Maggie?

It was hard to think of her being gone. Kinnery hoped his shock was partly grief and that he still had some semblance of human decency left, but he knew his own capacity to lie to himself. Maggie had been the only person he could turn to when he needed to hide Ian. She ran that ranch like a survivalist camp. It had an independent water supply, enough food stored to wait out a disaster, solar power and biogas, and shotguns she knew how to use. She was the paramilitary wing of the crazy cat ladies. Nobody noticed her and Ian in an invisible society of off-gridders and eccentrics that had swallowed them like quicksand.

Kinnery couldn't recall her being any other way. When everyone else in their college class outgrew idealism and took jobs with big pharmaceutical corporations, Maggie had stayed firmly stuck in her save-the-whale mind-set, unbuyable, uncompromising, and — inevitably — unemployable in her area of expertise.

And now she was gone.

He found it impossible to sit down and wait. He couldn't concentrate enough to check the rest of his mail. If Ringer had finally surfaced to bite him in the ass — and if he was getting chest pains — then disposing of the paperwork was long overdue. There was nobody to put his affairs in order if he died now.

But I did it. I made Ian. I had a transgenic embryo implanted in a girl who needed the money by a doctor who didn't.

He opened the safe set in the study wall. The internal bolt slid back with a *chonk* and the small door swung open, releasing a musty chemical scent of old paper and plastic. The top shelf was packed with notebooks and discs, all that remained of his Ringer data, jammed in so tightly that he scraped his knuckles trying to pull them out.

It had been easy to keep two sets of records. As far as the team was concerned, the embryos were all destroyed by the fourteen-day limit, and the failure rate had been high, averaging only four transgenic embryos out of 28 blastocysts per batch. But there was always someone ready to break the law when it came to trading in children: marginal fertility clinics, persuadable physicians, shady adoption agencies, and desperate would-be parents. There were always women willing to be paid surrogates, too. Kinnery thought he recalled what his motives were at the time, but there was only one that rang true today.

Because I could.

And where does it all start? An infertile couple wants a child. A government wants agents who can instantly blend into the group they're infiltrating. A scientist wants to be the first, the best, the groundbreaker. And the intersection of those desires is Ian.

Kinnery spread the stack of folders on his desk. Paper was a wonderful thing. If you kept a single copy, then one copy was all there would ever be, unless you let it out of your sight or were stupid enough to make copies — and he wasn't. Paper didn't reproduce itself across servers. It didn't get backed up automatically onto mainframes or portable drives, or attached to e-mails and carelessly released into the wild like a pathogen. After paper burned, the secrets written upon it only existed in the memories of those who'd seen it.

And memories, like people, all died eventually.

It was time to burn it all. He'd never work in human-animal chimera research again. He'd certainly never be able to publish his papers, not unless he wanted to spend his remaining years hiding in some third world hell-hole with no US extradition treaty.

Quite a few people spliced genes that they shouldn't have. They still do.

But nobody made it work like I did. And I still don't know how I did it. Ian. Proof of concept, and then some.

Kinnery thumbed through the papers, wondering if a solution would finally leap out at him, but if he hadn't had a breakthrough in eighteen years, then he wouldn't suddenly have one today. Gene expression was far more complex than anyone had known back then. He hadn't even been able to carry out tests on Ian. Maggie made damn sure of that. She never left him alone with the boy.

Burn it.

The few files he thought he might need in an emergency one day — medical reports on Ian's surrogate mother, handwritten information from the clinic that was very obliging with off-the-books work, the few details he had about the donors who might have been anonymous but were probably back-trackable — were scanned to an encrypted USB stick. He dithered. Should he destroy that now as well? No, that might be the only route to finding a solution for Ian one day. He'd give it a temporary reprieve.

He rummaged around in the pantry for some disposable carriers and tried not to think too hard about what he was about to incinerate. His life's most brilliant work could fit in two grocery bags.

At the bottom of the garden there was an old garbage can he'd punched with holes and set on legs to make an impromptu barbecue, another hybrid thing he'd created and that now seemed a reminder of his reckless curiosity. He could burn the papers in that. This was a fire that needed feeding a few sheets at a time. He didn't want half-burned papers drifting on the wind and exposing his crimes.

How much of it will I recall? Names, addresses, the paths I took?

For a moment, he almost lost his nerve. *I did it. I made it work. I just need to understand how.* But he pulled out one of the thinner folders, slim enough to burn easily, and laid it on the barbecue.

The step to striking a match and watching it flare took an eternity. Holding the wavering flame under the corner of the cover to see the smoke curl up took a heartbeat, though, no more. The funeral pyre of Project Ringer was now an unstoppable blaze. It was cathartic. It didn't erase what he'd done, but at least the data couldn't fall into the wrong hands, either to recreate what he'd achieved or to incriminate him.

Kinnery fed in a few more folders, paper fanned out to let the air circulate. Gradually he found an unthinking rhythm like a stoker in an engine room, timing the surge and fall of the flames to decide when to add more paper.

The neighbours might complain about the smoke. Okay, a barbecue that got out of hand. Sorry, folks. Won't happen again.

He watched the last of the paper burn and fade to grey ash, then broke it up with the barbecue tongs to make sure that only dust was left. Now he needed a Scotch. But if he had a long drive ahead of him, he'd have to settle for a coffee. He brewed a pot and sat down at his desk, working out when to call Maggie's number again.

Shape-shifting — dynamic mimicry — was a goddamn stupid idea anyway. It was all about going grey, as the intelligence community called it, making yourself inconspicuous and melting into the background. Some people could do it with clothing and the right body language, but if you were the wrong ethnicity or age for the task in hand, it was a trick that might cost you your life. So a dumb what-if conversation over a beer one day solidified into a crazy project. KWA was cavalier enough to try it.

The money wasn't crazy at all, though. The prospect of exploiting animal genes to cure human defects made it worth swallowing the lunacy to get the funding. The techniques that Kinnery developed during the project were worth a fortune to KWA. And damn it, without him there'd never have been a KWA to start with. Shaun just wasn't good enough to build the company alone.

Kinnery had even thought he might get a Nobel one day. But now he could never go public about what he'd really achieved.

And here I am, teaching college. Lying low. Haven't done any research that important since the day I quit KWA. That's the true meaning of nemesis.

He thought he'd covered his tracks. There was nobody to object, not even that senator who'd been such a pain in the ass about it all. The embryo donors had been anonymized and the record of the original clinic had been erased. The woman who'd been paid as a gestational surrogate was long gone, and neither she nor the doctor who'd carried out the implantation had any idea what the embryo was, or that Kinnery hadn't been a frustrated father with an infertile partner.

Nobody checked. People rarely did. Marginal doctors who bent the rules didn't want to. It was disappointingly easy.

Kinnery had no idea if the scraps of almost-life that he'd worked on were the fruits of musicians, truck drivers, storekeepers, or accountants, with lives and identities that would otherwise have been shaped by knowing those origins. They were simply surplus to requirements. He was always surprised how far some couples would go to produce children in the face of Nature's advice not to.

And who wants to know they were just spares?

He checked his watch. Everything that could identify Ian and link his existence to Project Ringer had ceased to exist except for the encrypted thumb drive.

So when was I supposed to dispose of Ian? Before he turned into a recognisable human, or before I gave him a name? What's the difference? I don't know any more.

Kinnery had reached the conclusion that science's price for answering questions was to pose ever more complex ones, an endlessly expanding list of ethical dilemmas. He checked his watch. It was time to try the number again.

This time, someone picked up.

"Ian? Ian, it's Charles Kinnery. I've been away. I just got back." He paused for breath. "Jesus, I'm so sorry. What happened?"

All he could hear was someone swallowing for a moment.

"Gran collapsed." Yes, it was Ian. "The doctor said she probably died right away. We cremated her."

"We?"

"Joe. Our neighbour. She left instructions. I did exactly what she told me."

"Look, don't worry. Stay where you are and I'll drive down. I can be there by two, three in the morning at the latest."

"No. Don't. It's too late."

"You shouldn't be on your own, Ian." *You need supervision. You need a keeper.* "Not at a time like this."

"Stay away. I know what you did. I know she wasn't my gran."

The room suddenly turned cold. Kinnery couldn't distinguish between the slowly-growing acceptance that Maggie was actually gone and the dread of what was unfolding.

"Ian," he said carefully, "whatever Maggie did, she did it to protect you. She loved you. Look, I know you're angry. And upset." He had to coax more information out of him. "What did she tell you? Did she explain?"

Ian took a few seconds to answer. "She left me a lot of notes. She kept a folder and told me to open it if anything happened to her. So I did."

This was almost as bad as playing the how-much-do-you-know game with a journalist. Maybe Ian *didn't* know every detail. One more misplaced revelation might tip him over the edge. If he panicked and went to ground, Kinnery might never find him.

"You want to tell me about that?"

"You didn't call me back. Gran left a note telling me who else to contact if I needed help."

Christ. Maggie, what were you thinking? "Who?"

"A reporter she trusted."

It was getting worse by the second. Kinnery tried to sound calm. He probably failed. "And what did you tell the reporter?"

"I gave her some notes on Ringer. Just a summary. Gran left lots out."

"Oh, for God's sake."

"But I didn't tell her my name. Or where I lived."

Just my name, then. Great. It fell into place. Kinnery couldn't think of a way to retrieve the situation. "The media aren't your friends, Ian. Believe me." *Christ, what a mess.* "You know what's different about you, then."

"I do now. Why did you do it? Why didn't anyone *tell* me?"

"I didn't plan it that way, Ian. I didn't even know it would have that much effect on you."

"What are they going to do when they find me?"

Ian didn't say who he thought "they" were. It didn't matter. Anybody was bad enough.

"They're not going to find you," Kinnery said. "I'll see to that. But you really need someone with you."

"Stay away from me. I'm just an experiment to you."

"No, Ian, never that."

"I'd be gone before you were halfway down the interstate, and you'd never find me."

"Okay, okay. I understand. I'll leave you alone. Just don't run away. Nobody knows where you are, so you're safer staying there. If you go on the road, the cops might pick you up, and then I can't do anything to save you." *I've got to get down there fast. Damn, has he even got a passport? How am I going to get him back across the border?* "Look, write down my cell number." Kinnery spelled it out slowly. "Got that? Don't open the door to strangers, and call me if anyone tries to get in touch with you."

"Joe can take care of that," Ian said. "Thanks for the money."

The line went dead. Kinnery put down the receiver and stared at the wall for a few seconds, his mind in chaos. He couldn't just wait for the axe to fall. He had to get Ian out somehow.

How? Doesn't matter. It can't wait.

As he switched on the burglar alarm, he considered his sins and realised that reflecting on them was all he ever did. He told himself what a bad boy he'd been, as if that was enough to atone and that the act of self-flagellation would make him virtuous. Now he had to damn well put things right. He backed the car out of the drive to head south, cell docked on the dashboard in case Ian called again.

I didn't do the right thing. I forced a life on him. An unnatural life.

There'd be no right answers or good outcomes in this. Tragedy was guaranteed. Kinnery finally understood the origin of the phrase *unable to think straight* as his thoughts went around in loops, stumbling over the same arguments that he'd had with himself minutes or seconds earlier as if they'd never occurred to him before. There was nothing linear and logical happening. His thoughts were like ricochets.

Why didn't I think about this before? Maggie. That's why. I left it all to her. Send her the money and forget about planning for the worst scenario.

But this wasn't the worst scenario yet, or even close to it. He made a conscious effort to stop the churn of thoughts before he started blaming Maggie for being dead or Ian for being born.

His cell rang a few minutes after he crossed the border via the Peace Arch. He didn't usually give out his personal number because students sometimes had a strange concept of a reasonable time to call. It had to be Ian.

"Charles," a man's voice said, no hint of query in it at all. It certainly wasn't Ian. "It's been some time."

It took Kinnery a few seconds to place it: Shaun Weaver. *That's all I need.* "Hi Shaun." Old business partners never died. They only held off calling until the most inconvenient moment. "How's business?"

Shaun didn't ask if it was a good time to talk, but then he never did. "Fine. Enjoy your trip?"

"I didn't know you had my number."

"I rang the university. They said you'd been away."

"How very security-minded of them to tell you."

"Don't chew them out. I told them it was urgent. I've had a call from a journalist about Ringer. I'm just calling to let you know you might get one too."

Kinnery found it nearly impossible to concentrate on the road for a few seconds. "Give me a clue."

"This hack knew a lot about it, considering it was classified. In fact, she seemed to know more than I did."

Deny all knowledge, or brazen it out? "You're going to have to be specific."

"Charles, is there anything you want to tell me?"

It was all falling apart. "Do you want to tell me what she asked *you*?"

"Is there anything you've let slip that she might have picked up? I know this is ancient history, but she's making some pretty weird allegations about transgenic humans. If there's a grain of truth in this, you need to talk to me."

Kinnery measured his words carefully. He didn't know exactly what Zoe Murray had seen, and he wasn't about to volunteer information that Shaun didn't have.

"Yes, *The Slide* mailed me. I haven't responded. It's a glorified comic, for Chrissakes. You've got all the research documentation. That's about the size of it."

"Okay, Charles. I'm sorry to have to ask. Keep your mind on the road. You know what the highways are like. Safe journey."

Kinnery didn't even hear the call cut off. He was too busy looking in the rear-view mirror, breath suddenly jammed in his throat. Was he being tailed?

Come on. He knows I'm driving because he could hear it on the phone. He knows I'm more likely to be on a highway than not. Pure guesswork to shake me down.

But Shaun had never really believed Kinnery's excuses for leaving. He was still suspicious. Kinnery knew it.

He kept looking in the mirror. There were several cars maintaining a steady distance behind him. It wouldn't take a lot of effort to get a home address for him, and there were plenty of private detectives who'd happily sit and observe until Doomsday if you had the budget to pay for it. KWA probably did. He couldn't risk driving to the ranch now. It was as good as handing Ian over.

Shaun's got enough pieces of the puzzle. He could have me followed. He doesn't need to be the FBI to do it.

Kinnery switched off the satnav and his cell's GPS in case someone had managed to get access. Then he started looking for an off-ramp, thinking panicky, irrational thoughts about whether Shaun had already been keeping tabs on him the last time he'd visited Maggie. No, nobody knew, not then. This was all down to Maggie dying, all down to that stupid goddamn letter, and a phone that didn't forward a call when he most needed it to.

Sorry, Maggie. Jesus, I'm sorry. Why am I blaming you?

Kinnery pulled off and found a restaurant to have a coffee and calm down. When he went out to the parking lot, he made a discreet note of every licence plate and spent a few minutes looking around as casually as he could to make sure nobody was following him. Was he going to have to live the rest of his life like this?

Well, Ian had to, so there was no reason that he shouldn't share that sentence. He got back into the car and headed home, slow and suspicious, checking out every car that didn't pass him fast enough.

The cell rang again. The screen showed number withheld. He didn't assume it was Ian this time. Shaun was probably going to ask him if he'd remembered to switch off the oven.

"Kinnery," he said.

"This is Leo Brayne." It was another voice that Kinnery hadn't heard in a very long time, but one he could never forget. "It's time we had lunch. Next week sometime. Call my office and I'll clear my diary."

"Senator?"

Brayne didn't even wait for a reply. Kinnery had been summoned to Washington by a man he hadn't seen in nearly twenty years. He had no choice. If he didn't go, he was sure things would get worse rather than better.

He didn't need to ask what it was about. When he got back and checked *The Slide* site, it had already been updated. It talked about Ringer, how it had resulted in a live human subject who could change his appearance, and how he was now in hiding.

At least Kinnery wouldn't have to list the main points for Senator Brayne. They were now public knowledge, at least for people who took *The Slide* seriously.

FOUR

Leo, there's no possible way that this is anything more than industrial espionage. If we'd succeeded in making mimicry work in a live subject, don't you think we'd have been pounding on the door for more money? It's potentially damaging for KWA, but there are no security ramifications. I think it's in the interests of everyone to keep this off the law enforcement radar. I'll investigate discreetly.

Shaun Weaver, CEO of KWA, in a call to Leo Brayne.

LLOYD HOUSEHOLD, LANSING, MICHIGAN: JULY.

Something was burning.

Dru dropped her briefcase by the front door, wondering why the smoke alarm hadn't gone off. Clare sat at the kitchen counter, cell in hand, scribbling with her fingertip and apparently oblivious of both her empty plate and the pungent blue haze of smoke.

"For goodness' sake, can't you smell that?" Dru jerked the pan of smoking pancakes from the hotplate and turned off the heat. "Put that phone down right *now*."

Clare didn't even look away from the screen. It was like a cartoon where the character's eyeballs remained glued to an object and stretched like elastic bands as they walked away.

"Uhh ... sorry, Mom. Yeah. Okay."

Enough. Clare hadn't managed to slide fully off the stool before Dru snatched the phone. Their hands collided. It was a harder grab than Dru intended.

"Hey!"

"Don't you dare *hey* me." Dru shoved the cell in her pocket and filled the dish pan. The hot skillet hissed steam as she plunged it into the water. "All you had to do was watch the pancakes. Find your bag and get in the car. I've got to go to work. And make sure you've got your inhaler — you know what happened last time."

"Mom, I need my cell."

"Clare, the only people who *need* cells have jobs that require instant responses. Doctors. CEOs. The Secretary General of the UN. Everyone else just likes having one."

"I can't go to class without it."

"Try. I managed it at your age."

"What if I have an asthma attack in class?"

"Then your tutor can call me. That's why I want you to check you've got your inhaler. Remember how much it cost the last time you ended up in ER."

"Mom — "

"Clare, *no.*"

"Why are you taking it out on me? If your job sucks so much, why don't you just quit? It's not my fault that everyone hates you because you're the office *kapo.*"

Dru tried to leave KWA at the front door, but it was getting harder these days. "I do wish you wouldn't trivialise that word. What are they teaching you?"

"Dad said it was *apt.* He says that HR's only there to protect management from the staff. Not to help employees."

Dru chose not to hear that as Larry's latest retort by proxy, a row conducted one line at a time via Clare like some game of postal chess. "Well, when *Dad* gets a job," Dru said, "*Dad* can comment on how I do mine, can't he?"

Clare was fourteen, metamorphosing into an alien species that Dru didn't recognise or remember ever being part of. *Why do I put up with the job? Because I've got a mortgage and an asthmatic kid and a useless ex-husband who pays when he feels like it.* Larry was still pleading poverty and promising he had a new business in the pipeline.

Kapo. Maybe.

Dru had no illusions about the role of human resources at a time like this. KWA was in merger talks with Halbauer, and that meant doing what-if studies into who had to be culled to guarantee the survival of the herd. If Dru became the downsizing angel of death to look after her own family, she could live with that. Halbauer had its own HR department, a costly duplicate in a merger. She wasn't stupid. There'd be casualties close to home, too, and she didn't plan to be one of them.

"Car," Dru barked. "*Now.*"

Clare stormed out ahead of her and wrenched open the passenger door with a drama queen flourish. Dru had moments of actually hating her, then hating herself for hating her, because there'd been a time when all she'd wanted in life after a string of miscarriages was a baby. Clare hadn't come cheaply, either in terms of the cost or the toll the process had taken. Dru found it hard to cut herself any slack. She didn't want to be the mom that her own mother had been.

I'll sort this out. It's what I do.

Dropping Clare off at summer school meant a five-mile detour, plenty of sulking time in rush-hour traffic. "Mom, I'm sorry," Clare said at last. "Can I have my cell back, please?"

"Try going a day without sharing your every move and thought online. You know how dangerous that is." Sanctions didn't mean anything unless they hurt. Dru had another where-did-I-go-wrong moment. "When you're my age and the dumb things you posted are still there, you'll regret it."

"Only if I don't get murdered before then because I didn't have my cell to call for help."

"Clare, the answer's still no."

"You're so selfish."

Dru braked late and almost rammed the car in front. "You want to see selfish? Who pays your phone bills?"

"Mom — "

"I don't have the energy for this, Clare."

"I wish I'd gone to live with Dad."

"Good plan, except his girlfriend didn't want you living with them. Did she?"

"Mom, why do you hate me so much? Because you're ruining my life."

Teenagers had their script, and moms had theirs. Dru decided not to stick to hers. She pulled up outside the school and parked, silent and unyielding. If she stopped escalating this, Clare would lose interest. It was a variant on handling toddlers. She recalled those days all too well.

Clare tried again. "So do I get my cell back? I said I was sorry."

Somehow she'd picked up the idea that apologising was a special achievement that deserved medals, not the minimum expected in polite society. Dru blamed the school again.

"No," Dru said. *No* was an excellent word. She didn't use it anywhere near enough. "I'll pick you up from Rebecca's tonight. We'll talk over dinner."

Clare opened the passenger door and sat waiting, brows raised a little in that verging-on-tears kind of way. Dru waited too. Clare's face morphed from wounded to sour in an instant.

"No wonder Dad left you," she said. "You're the kapo all day at work and you forget to stop being a bitch when you get home."

Clare scrambled out and slammed the door behind her before Dru could react. Chasing after her and demanding an apology would be handing her the power, though. Dru would deal with her tonight when the heat had gone out of this. As she drove off, she caught a glimpse of herself in the rear-view mirror and felt a pang of dismay as her brain clicked into recognition mode. Yes, that greying, fading creature with shadows under its eyes really was her. And she recognised the description of *bitch,* too. It was true. She wore her work persona home.

KWA's automatic gate let her car in to the parking garage. This was her unthinking daily routine: park in her allocated space, then detour via the maintenance area to check the recycling bins. Someone had dumped a cardboard box without removing the originating company's address and the consignment number. On its own it was innocuous, but there was no point in broadcasting the minutiae of KWA's business, and no way of knowing what jigsaw puzzle of information it might complete. Dru hauled it out and sorted through the rest of the flattened packages, looking for offenders.

"Anything wrong, Mrs Lloyd?" Alex, one of the regular security guards, ambled towards her. "Here, let me take those."

"People aren't removing labels before they dump packaging, Alex," she said, sorting through the cartons like giant index cards. "I'll circulate a memo, but if you catch anyone doing this, let me know, okay?"

"Sure, ma'am. But you make a lot of work for yourself. Who's going to bother collecting all that little detail just in case it comes in handy?"

"People like me, I'm afraid."

Alex laughed to himself and walked to the staff entrance with her. As he reached the small glass-fronted security booth, he held up a finger as a signal to wait and reached under the counter.

"There," he said, handing her a couple of magazines. "Bet you can't do *these.*"

They were puzzle books. Alex had a lot of solitary downtime on his hands in this job, and he'd told her he wasn't planning to get dementia when he retired. The puzzles were fearsome; Dru was addicted. She slipped the magazines into her bag.

"I owe you a bottle of bourbon," she said. "Thank you."

It was a harmless little friendship between an old guy nobody noticed and a woman who didn't have many allies in this place, based on a common love of puzzles. They looked after one another.

As Dru walked out of the elevator on the third floor, heads turned in the cubicle farm. A few office staff stood chatting in a huddle behind the glass wall, but they stopped and gave her a look that made her wonder if she was decked out in a black hood and scythe. Dru didn't need Clare's history teacher to remind her what happened to kapos. You could collaborate with the camp commandant as much as you liked, and send your fellow inmates to their doom for a few extra crumbs, but you knew you'd probably end up sharing their fate sooner or later.

That, or one of the other prisoners stabs you in the back for betraying your own kind.

She'd just have to make herself indispensable. The alternative was to get out, but benefits like KWA's didn't grow on trees. What were her KWA shares worth? Maybe it was time to sell them, just in case.

Bobbie was already at her desk, fingers moving over her keyboard in a blur. The admin assistant seemed to have formed the idea that only the visibly workaholic would survive restructuring.

"Good morning, Dru."

"Hi, Bobbie. No boss yet?"

"Sheelagh's not coming in today, remember? She's taking a family day. Son. Dental appointment. I've forwarded some of her mail to you."

Dru keyed in the code to her door. "Fine."

"Halbauer sent over some encrypted files, too." Maybe Bobbie was fishing. "I think it's the IT staffing details."

"Probably. Thanks."

KWA had already offshored its payroll and accounting to its offices in India. There wasn't a lot left of HR, either. Dru couldn't blame Bobbie for getting jumpy. She logged in and found her inbox full of the usual overnight mail, pitches from training companies, and the feed of industry digests that she shared with PR and Marketing. External hearts and minds were PR's problem, but Dru needed to know if staff were saying anything ill-advised online. Keyword monitoring reports picked up every mention of Kinnery Weaver Associates and permutations of the company name on the internet, as well as references to its areas of interest in social media and forums. Text and sentiment analytics reported back on the public perception of the company and the biotech industry. There was nothing said or thought about the company that didn't eventually find its way back to head office.

One paragraph jumped out from a sea of text in the media monitoring digest. Dru tapped the screen and isolated it.

KEYWORDS: KINNERY (CHARLES KINNERY) OCCURRENCES: 1. LOCATION: THE SLIDE

Slide? She hadn't even heard of it. When she hit the link, it was just an online activist magazine like hundreds of others, just better designed, full of routine conspiracy theory stuff with the usual paranormal nonsense thrown in. She almost missed the reference to Charles Kinnery. All she knew was that he was one of the original partners who'd set up KWA.

DYNAMIC MIMICRY IN HUMANS: DID GENETICISTS BUILD A SHAPE-SHIFTER FOR THE DoD?

It was a bizarre story about creating a human with the ability to alter his appearance for undercover intelligence missions. It was clearly garbage. But Charles Kinnery's name was in there, along with KWA's, so there was the potential for fallout. Dru set the page to alert her on updates and called the PR manager.

"Hi, Dean. Have you picked up the mention of Charles Kinnery on the digest? It's on a site called *The Slide*."

Dean laughed. "Yeah, seen it. They're the high IQ end of *Elvis Ate My Hamster* stories. They left out Jimmy Hoffa and Shergar this time, though."

"No crisis, then."

"They could publish today's date and nobody would believe it."

"Kinnery left years ago. What sparked this?"

"No idea. Maybe they forgot their meds. This is routine dingbattery for *The Slide*, though. The shape-shifter bit should clue you in."

"Okay. But I'll keep an eye on it."

"You don't need to make extra work for yourself."

"What's that supposed to mean?"

"Nothing. I'm on it. Relax."

Dru realised she was letting uncertainty get to her. Everyone was looking over their shoulder these days, but mostly at her.

"Sorry. Rough start to the day. Talk to you later."

So Dean wasn't worried, even though it was an oddly specific reference to a man who hadn't worked here for years. Dru relegated it to a watching brief and forgot about shape-shifting agents to concentrate on how many duplicated IT jobs there'd be if KWA and Halbauer merged. It was looking so depressing that she was relieved when Julianne, Shaun Weaver's secretary, called her to a meeting.

Julianne had mastered the art of corporate mime. When Dru reached Weaver's office, the secretary did her usual elaborate hand signals like a bookie at a race track. *On the phone,* she gestured, left hand miming a handset against her ear before extending and lowering. *Wait.*

Dru took a seat. Weaver was a god, and Dru was a minion. She had to wait for an audience. Eventually the door handle clicked and Weaver stood in the doorway with a bloom of light around him that only added to the sense of being allowed some face time with God.

"How are you, Dru?" He remembered her name. That was something. "Sorry to dump this on you, but Sheelagh's out today. I've had an odd phone call."

She almost called him Shaun in return, but familiarity only worked one way. "How odd?"

"Come in and I'll tell you."

The vertical blinds were drawn even though the office wasn't overlooked. Dru decided this already had the signs of turning into something above her pay grade. She sat down in one of the oversized green leather chairs and almost held her breath. Weaver was a hard man to rattle. A volcano could erupt in his backyard and he'd simply raise his eyebrows. But as he read through the notepad on his desk, he kept rubbing his top lip.

"A paranormal news site's running a line on my old colleague, Charles Kinnery," he said. "Dynamic mimicry for the DoD."

"*The Slide.*" Dru nodded. *Time to look indispensable. Especially with Sheelagh away.* "I saw it on the digest. Crazy stuff."

Weaver frowned as if he'd expected her to do something about it sooner. "One of their people rang me for a comment. Zoe Murray."

Dru waited for him to go on, but he didn't. "She bypassed Dean?"

"Yes. But I don't want this discussed outside this office." Routine jitters about the merger wouldn't normally have ruffled Weaver's calm, let alone an obviously crackpot story. "Not even with Dean."

"It's on the internet, Mr Weaver," Dru said. "Even a take-down order can't erase it completely. It's not true, surely."

"Well, we did do some transgenic research funded by the DoD. But this Murray woman has the actual name. Project Ringer. That means there's been some kind of leak, because it was classified. The name was never made public."

"But no actual shape-shifter."

"Dru, if we'd pulled *that* off, we'd have asked the DoD for a lot more money."

"But they thought it might be feasible."

"You know how these agencies are. Win big or fail big, but at least give it a shot. We introduced engineered animal genes into human embryos. It wasn't illegal back then — nobody had done it yet, officially. But they were all destroyed by fourteen days anyway." Weaver sounded as if he was making a defence case to her. She noticed his blink rate for the first time. "The value to us was the techniques we developed during the project, the spin-offs for therapeutic applications. Which paid off."

"My subject's psychology," Dru said. "I just need to know enough to understand the risk."

"You've seen a squid or an octopus change colour and texture. They do it with structures in their skin. Chameleons use cell signalling. Lots of animals have evolved different methods for fast disguise. Now imagine if a human could change colour and even the shape of his features when he needed to, and then change back again. Life would be a lot easier for covert operators."

"And bank robbers. And hijackers."

"I didn't say it was without a downside."

"Okay, I can see how making some red-haired spy look Middle Eastern would be useful, but what about the other giveaways, like gait? Size? Gender? Voice?"

Weaver nodded as if he was relieved that she'd grasped it without the need to draw pictures. "We only got funding for the initial stages before they decided it was too crazy even for them. But that was all we needed."

Dru could have told DARPA that it was crazy for five bucks. But she still wasn't sure what the immediate problem was — that KWA had a leaky employee somewhere, or that Weaver didn't want KWA tarred with the goat-staring wacko research brush, let alone conducting illegal experiments. But sloppy commercial confidentiality was a killer. Nobody would want to team with a technology company that couldn't keep sensitive information secure.

"So what do you want me to focus on?" she asked.

Weaver clasped his hands on the desk top, stroking one thumb across the other. "Did you ever meet Charles?"

Dru bristled. *How old do you think I am? How old do I* look, *for goodness' sake?* "No, I was still looking for my first job when he was around."

"I'm wondering if this journalist's misunderstood something that might have actually happened."

"I can't guess," Dru said. "You need to spell it out."

"Okay, perhaps Charles walked out of here with material or data, and he's been working on it elsewhere. Maybe he parked some engineered genes in a human volunteer, even *himself.* There's a lot we need to find out."

Dru was instantly out her technical depth. "Why would he need to use a host?"

"He wouldn't. DNA's easy to move around. You can even put a drop of fluid on paper and mail it. Using a live carrier's a good way to hide and transport it, though. It's invisible unless you know it's there and what to look for. Who's going to screen people?"

It was fascinating, but the more Weaver explained, the more bizarre and incomprehensible Dru found it. *Motive.* She was still a psychologist at heart. When people leaked information, there was a reason for the when and the how. It might simply have been a case of very old, inadequately shredded documents that had suddenly been unearthed on a dump, but Weaver seemed to be taking it seriously, and Dru never assumed she was being told the full story.

"If this project started twenty-odd years ago, why raise it now?" she asked.

Weaver shrugged. "Sabotaging the merger?"

"Wouldn't somebody float a smear story that was more credible?"

"I would have thought so."

"And who would do it? Kinnery?"

"Only if he was working for a rival. But he's been in academia for years."

"You said he might have walked off with KWA's property. I thought he was the friend you built the company with."

"Charles had his moments. He just quit out of the blue and sold his stake to me. It was some personal crisis. Maybe drink or gambling, because God knows he had his weaknesses, but he refused to tell me the details. So I'm not ruling anything out."

That was an awfully long time to harbour a suspicion. Dru began to see Weaver in a subtly different light. He'd always seemed unflappable, the man in control of everything, but now that relaxed manner looked like something else — an exceptional patience, the kind that could wait quietly for as long as it took to get what it wanted. It was a sniper's mind-set. It might even have been a vengeful one. This was technology with hugely lucrative patents. Yes, it was probably worth the wait.

"I think this something for the FBI. They handle industrial espionage." Dru didn't want to talk herself out of a job, but this looked way beyond her remit. "Or the FDA, if you think he's breached research regulations."

"Imagine how Halbauer would react if we had government agencies crawling all over us. Think about our share price."

"Understood." Dru nodded, shifting back to sabotage as a motive. Maybe Weaver and Kinnery had parted acrimoniously and Kinnery had picked his moment to cause trouble. But that meant she'd be dealing with not one but two men who could ferment a grudge for decades. It wasn't comforting. "So you want to keep the investigation in house."

"Exactly."

"I still think you should touch base with the DoD. For all we know, this leak might have come from them. It's not exactly unknown."

"I've covered the DoD."

"Do you mind my asking how?"

"I've spoken to a senator who was on the committee when Ringer got its funding. We kind of know one another. Leo Brayne."

"Oh." Dru didn't keep up with politics. The name rang only a faint bell. "And?"

"He said he'd handle the DoD. In the meantime, we start our own investigation. We can't compromise him by telling him what we're doing. You know how they like deniability."

Dru would have been fine with investigating an employee. She knew the process inside out. But Kinnery had severed his links years ago. She didn't even know if they'd kept his HR file.

"How about hiring a private investigator?" she asked.

"It's one more person to tell," Weaver said. "And then it gets harder to sit on. By all means use one for compartmentalised information, but I want this run internally. HR won't blip anyone's radar."

Any half-decent PI would do a search for Kinnery on the internet anyway, so Dru wasn't sure how she'd keep the shape-shifter story from an agency. But it was insane. Maybe it didn't matter. She could simply laugh it off and hint at secret but legitimate reasons easily enough.

"Are you sure about this, Mr Weaver? I'm not head of HR. I'm not even Sheelagh's deputy."

Weaver shrugged, but it wasn't convincing. "She's not here. You are." He started tapping his touchscreen. "Anyway, you're the Olympic champion on detail. Very thorough. I took a look at some of the disciplinary cases and dismissals you've handled. You really leave no stone unturned when you're building a case, do you? You could always dig up some dirt to get rid of hard-to-remove staff."

Dru wasn't sure if that was a compliment or an indictment. "I watched too many re-runs of *The Untouchables* as a kid," she said, embarrassed.

"Sorry?"

"Al Capone. Tax evasion. People who break rules tend to do it across a wide spectrum of activity. You can always find something."

Weaver actually laughed. Dru realised she sounded confident. It was entirely accidental.

"Okay, time's not on our side," he said. "Charles already knows I'll want answers. I need this knocked on the head and buried as soon as possible. We're going to be in negotiations with Halbauer through August, and I don't want any last-minute surprises."

"Do we have any leads at all? The text of the document?"

Weaver shook his head. "If I leaned on this journalist, it'd look like confirmation. I've give you what notes I've got. Kinnery's living in Vancouver, so spend what you have to and pass the receipts through me personally, not Finance. No written reports — verbal only. Discretion, remember. PIs don't need to see the bigger picture to function."

"And what are you going to tell Sheelagh? Because this is going to be time-consuming."

Weaver got up and opened the blinds, standing at the window with the sun on his face. He'd come clean and seemed to want to wash himself in the light. It was interesting to watch his body language. She hoped he wasn't fully aware of that and just doing a clever act.

"This is strictly between you and me," he said. "I'll deal with Sheelagh tomorrow. I'll tell her I need you to collate some background for Halbauer."

Weaver definitely wasn't a spur of the moment man. Dru decided to check the timeline. "Just so I know how much ground I've got to make up, when did *The Slide* call?"

"Yesterday," Weaver said, not even blinking. So he'd waited a day. He could have taken it up with Sheelagh after all. "Just as well you were around today, wasn't it?"

So Sheelagh was never meant to know this was happening. Maybe she was out of favour. Tough luck; this was survival, about keeping a wage coming in, about not ending up like other respectable, responsible, middle class people who suddenly found themselves without a job, then without a house, and finally fell so far that they could never get back up again. Dru wasn't proud of it, but she now saw Sheelagh as collateral damage.

She once wondered how kapos had slept at night. She realised that they were too focused on surviving another day to afford a luxury like pity.

WASHINGTON, D.C.: JULY.

Kinnery realised he wasn't as good as he thought at staying off officialdom's radar as soon as he walked down the steps of the hotel.

He wasn't too worried about his logged, photographed, ticketed, scanned flight from Vancouver. There were a hundred reasons for a man in his position to fly to Washington. But there was a security camera in the hotel lift, another in the lobby, and two looking up and down the street outside. Those were just the privately-operated ones that he could easily see. As soon as he looked up at the office block across the road, he spotted another unblinking glassy eye mounted on a metal rail, which could have been another private camera or a police installation. It didn't matter. Any agency could get access to any footage they wanted, legally or otherwise. He was observed somehow, somewhere, from the moment he closed his front door.

And probably in my own home, if I count my wireless connection, my streamed TV, and my phone.

For a moment, Kinnery saw the world as Maggie had seen it. It was a cold, alien, sinister place. Then he saw himself through her eyes as well, and he was a component of its menace.

If all this monitoring had been in place twenty years ago, could I have created Ian and gotten away with it?

He walked the eight blocks to the restaurant as casually as he could, past tourists openly recording their trip with phone cams, and a bespectacled girl wearing those clunky recording glasses, head moving in that telltale way that suggested she was new to it. He tried not to worry whether this trip would be vacuumed up, analysed, and distilled into the information that Charles Kinnery had come to Washington to lunch with Leo Brayne. He could have caught a bus or a cab, but they had on-board cameras too. Did he ever really say that those with nothing to hide had nothing to fear? He'd forgotten to add the qualifier that it was only true if those doing the watching were benevolent, honest, and competent enough to draw the right conclusions from the data.

He did have something to hide. But it was Ian who had something to fear.

I never even got the chance to test facial recognition on him.

Kinnery didn't have much of a plan for the meeting with Leo Brayne beyond a kind of mutually assured destruction. If Kinnery's sins were made public, Leo might want to avoid being mentioned in the same sentence. He'd opposed Ringer, He hadn't been willing to go to the wall over it, though, and human embryo research, legal or otherwise, was still politically fraught. Kinnery wondered if he could use that lever.

But Leo was one of those staggeringly wealthy men from a bygone era who took their politics as a serious public duty. Kinnery suspected he made no profit from it and wielded more power outside it, and that made him dangerous. People with a sense of mission weren't motivated or scared by the same things as ordinary men.

But this has to be about Ian. I have to make sure this is what's best for him. I'm not just saving my own ass, am I?

Kinnery didn't know. That was the worst of it.

He had to accept that he was already out of his depth, tossed in the deep end by Maggie's goddamn stupid, *stupid* letter. He was left with two options: to cut off all contact with Ian and leave him to fend for himself, because he was the one remaining lead that could enable them to hunt the boy down, or to take a chance on Leo's ability to think a lot further ahead than most politicians.

Nobody else knew where Ian was. If the worst happened, Kinnery would make one call and warn him to go to ground.

Run, Ian. Run and hide.

The restaurant was a haven of smoked glass and discreet signage that was illegible from across the road. When Kinnery put his hand on the door, it opened without any effort and he found himself chest to chest with a member of staff who looked well trained in the art of identifying and ejecting the wrong kind of customer. The hum of the traffic died the moment the door closed. Kinnery was in another world. He almost expected to step into snow. It was that kind of quiet.

Leo, a tall, lean man in an immaculate navy blue suit, sat in a booth inspecting the menu. The years since Kinnery had last seen him in person hadn't treated him too badly. His hair was more grey than brown these days, but he still didn't look his age. Kinnery envied him that.

Kinnery let the waiter take his coat and walked across a carpet so thick that it felt like a sprung dance floor. Leo didn't get up. He shook Kinnery's hand from a seated position.

"Glad you could make it," he said. Kinnery watched him snap a breadstick into three pieces and place two on the plate while he chomped on the third. He wasn't the kind of man to casually nibble the entire stick from one end. Leo broke things, and broke them into the exact size that he wanted. "This is as private as it gets without some curious intern seeing you arrive at my office."

The Jacquard fabric whispered against the seat of Kinnery's pants as he slid into the booth. He glanced up to check for security cameras. He couldn't see any.

"So you heard," Kinnery said.

"I got a call from your former partner. I suppose he was heading off his most likely source of trouble." Leo tapped his breadstick on the side of his plate like a conductor whipping the woodwind section into shape. "Or maybe he just missed our little chats."

Kinnery didn't need reminding. Leo had grilled KWA ferociously. This lunch was starting to give Kinnery that same sensation of waiting for Torquemada to ask him the time.

"Shaun was always more political than me," he said. "With a small P. I hope he doesn't know we're meeting."

"Of course not. But just be aware he's watching you. He's a keep-your-enemies-close kind of man, I think. You probably know that better than me."

You bastard, Shaun. All Kinnery's hopes of finding a way to put some pressure on Leo evaporated. He was hopelessly outgunned, an unarmed child who'd wandered onto a battlefield. He was savvy enough to realise that nobody opened negotiations with a concession, though, least of all a politician. Leo was sharing that information to show Kinnery just how deep in the shit he was.

"So I'm not being paranoid, then," Kinnery said. "It's hard to decide which question to ask first. Okay — how do you know?"

"Well, I'm good at watching people watching others, for the most part, so your surveillance from the airport was spotted. That probably means you've been tracked from Vancouver, which isn't hard. And we'll both keep this meeting private from Shaun, because I don't like *not* being told about things like that. It makes me wonder what else is being kept from me."

"What else is being kept from *me?*"

"I don't know. What have you been keeping from him?"

"Are you willing to tell me what he said?"

"I'd like to hear your side of it first."

"Are you planning to use this to take a shot at the biotech industry?"

"Why would I do that?"

"Apart from the fact that you think it's the work of Beelzebub?"

Leo didn't blink. "Apart from that."

Kinnery had no choice but to bend over and take it. "If this blows up, you're on record as opposing the project. You'll point out that you're the clairvoyant guy who said no good would come of it. So why else would you get involved now, except to hammer us?"

"Mud's indiscriminately adhesive once flung." Leo looked weary for a moment. "But I do have a raw nerve where this is concerned. My son served. A lot of his comrades came back broken or in body bags. I think defence funding's primary purpose is to give our military personnel the best chance of winning and coming home intact, not to create civilian jobs or shareholder dividends. It's good if it does, but it's a bonus, not a reason. So is it true?"

"Which part?"

"The most extreme allegations made by a certain alternative news site."

What have I got to lose? I'm still the only one who knows where Ian is. And Leo's the only person I know with enough real power to salvage something.

"I wouldn't be here if we were just talking about embryos," Kinnery said. "Or if the subject was dead."

Leo carried on chewing the breadstick. There weren't many men who could eat and still maintain an icy dignity, but he was one of them. It didn't humanise him one bit. He took some time to respond.

"Good grief." It was just a rumble in his throat. "Really?"

"I know it takes some believing."

"And is this person in a secure place under your control?"

"No."

"That's unfortunate."

Kinnery was starting to wonder if Leo had dismissed the whole thing as a hoax. "Do you think I'm a sane and rational man?"

"I'll give you a conditional yes."

"Well, I've seen it with my own eyes."

"Do go on."

"I still don't understand how I achieved it. But I've seen him do it. And it isn't going to go away."

Leo nodded. "Pronoun noted."

"What?"

"*I*. All your own genius, then. Did Shaun know? Did he have a hand in the Petri dish?"

Kinnery could have spread the blame, but the denial was out of his mouth before he'd even thought about it. *He'd* achieved this. Nobody else. He was telling the truth but for all the wrong reasons. Where did *that* fall in the moral spectrum?

"No," he said. "Shaun had no idea at all."

"Well, he knows now, even if he doesn't believe most of it. I suspect he thinks you've wandered off with some intellectual property that's his."

A waiter approached silently from the back of the room and hovered at a discreet distance behind Leo. The senator just lifted a casual finger, his arm still resting on the table. He must have had the wraparound vision of a fly to see the man. The waiter took his cue to approach.

"I'll have the *vongole,* please. Charles?"

"Risotto." It was the first thing that came into Kinnery's head, even without looking at the menu. "Mushroom, or whatever's good today. Thank you." The waiter dissolved into the quiet gloom at the back of the restaurant. "I haven't discussed this with anyone. But I'm going to be very surprised if my students and my employers don't get to hear about *The Slide* eventually."

"And you're telling me that there really is a live subject. Where is he?"

"I'd rather we fully explored the consequences of this before I go into detail."

"Is that plea bargaining?"

"This is a human being we're talking about. I don't want any agencies with a fluid sense of legal rights getting involved."

"Quick test," Leo said quietly. "Do you think government is, A, one happy, patriotic family with a common purpose, gladly sharing information for the good of the country? Or is it B, just another sub-set of human society, made up of the inevitable cliques, backstabbing empire builders, conflicting agendas, and petty, mediocre assholes collecting dirt on each other?"

It was odd to hear *assholes* said in that patrician accent. "That's a tough one. Can I phone a friend?"

"I don't care for unelected public servants deciding how we run the country." Leo seemed to be almost relishing this in a quiet, leave-it-to-me kind of way. "So this stays informal for as long as I'm able to keep it so."

He sipped a glass of water in silence. He might even have been growing a smile. It was a little late for Kinnery to scramble for the moral high ground. Leo hadn't asked why he'd done it — perhaps that question would come later — but Kinnery had the feeling that Leo thought he already knew, and had put Kinnery in the file marked *amoral know-it-all with sociopathic or narcissistic tendencies.*

The meal arrived much sooner than Kinnery expected, fragrant and exquisite. He wished he'd had an appetite.

"Assuming that I believe any of this," Leo said, "let's split the problem into two. One is perception, and the other is actuality. I won't say *reality*, because both are real in their own way. Let's take perception first. God bless the internet, Charles. It's all that stands between the powers that be and actual accountability."

"I realise *The Slide* isn't exactly regarded as the organ of record."

"Ah, it goes beyond the site and even the medium. Have you had a call from any other media? I'm guessing not."

"I've not been taking calls."

"Well, I doubt you'll get any. If I do, I'll laugh heartily. Because information has been utterly devalued. Most people neither know nor care what's true now. There's only *opinion.* It's all transmit and no receive, as my son's friend would say." Leo attacked the *vongole* in saffron sauce with the controlled precision of a spear fisher. "Everyone's got a front page via the internet."

"You're not talking about democracy or freedom, I imagine. Whatever that means."

"Charles, when the *Times* or the *Post* broke a scandal in the good old days, it had real consequences, real *resigning* consequences, but now we have a volunteer misinformation army doing the cover-ups by accident. You can upload God's own documented truth about every black ops job we ever pulled, every diplomatic indiscretion, and after a while it just sinks in the sea of apathy. The more it happens, the deeper it sinks. Net change to the way the world runs or who runs it — zero."

Leo had a point and it hurt. People believed what they wanted to believe, and even if they didn't, they'd never been taught how to test what they were told. There was probably more information publicly available than at any time in history. Sifting it to work out what was real got harder every day.

Real. That'd be me, doing illegal research on human embryos. Keeping a child as a lab rat. Kidnap, effectively. Would I turn myself in for that?

Kinnery imagined walking into a police station and asking to confess. He wondered how many minutes it would be before the officer taking his statement started to nod and smile before suggesting he went home, promising that they'd be in touch.

"If nobody believes anything any more," Kinnery said, "why are we sitting here?"

Leo had a way of looking through people with a kind of weary patience, too powerful to bother with the effort of a steely glare to make his point. "Because you involved me the moment that Shaun rang me," he said. "And now I can't walk away."

"That's a generic *you*, I hope."

"If it's something that can save troops' lives, or can be misused against us, then it's not your fifth-grade science project to do with as you please."

"It's not that simple."

"It never is."

Kinnery looked around as discreetly as he could. There were just a few people at other tables and none was close enough to eavesdrop, but he saw spies everywhere. "I don't have a definitive evaluation of how practical this is."

"Very well. Just answer yes or no to my questions." Kinnery had to hand it to Leo. He was completely unflappable. "Is this ability transferrable in any way?"

"If you mean contagious, no. If you mean a source for cloning, no. If you mean heritable, I believe the subject's sterile. If you mean a useful live model to study for further development, yes."

"In its current state, is it capable of being used tactically by us or by others? Forget the economic implications for a moment."

That was the question Kinnery had been dreading, the one he'd tried to avoid asking himself. If Ian was a threat, the best outcome he could hope for would be to spend the rest of his life in confinement. If he was an asset, he'd be exploited relentlessly. Both would mean the same quality of life for him, as leper or lab animal or utility.

Kinnery realised he'd made the worst possible mistake. He should have grabbed Ian and made a run for it, not allowed himself to be summoned to sit within biting distance of a predator at the top of the food chain. This was suicidal.

"It depends what you mean by tactical," Kinnery said at last. He searched for a layman's answer, trying to purge it with euphemism. But he didn't even have the full facts himself. "It's not simply the security angle, or even what an individual subject can do. It's more about the implication for all other transgenic work. It's a spectacular example of exploiting non-human characteristics. I did it first, and others have followed since, but this is an order of magnitude more significant. The potential for new therapies is even greater."

Leo blinked a couple of times, looking slightly past him. "I can imagine the medical implications. I just want to know what it means in terms of its original purpose. If this is real and usable, we don't want it ending up in India or China. Or even Europe. Or anywhere else Shaun does business. Nor do we want to find that your company was doing other high-risk research that we weren't aware of. Who else has this information?"

"Nobody," Kinnery said. "You'd be surprised how easy it is to abuse the system. Poor record-keeping and no enforcement."

"All right, assuming any of this is true, the priority is to secure your subject."

"We need to move him as soon as possible. I used to be sure he was safe where he was, but I have absolutely no idea what else might leak. "

"You can't do it yourself. You'll be followed."

"I realise that."

Leo glanced past Kinnery and nodded. Kinnery's pulse began pounding. Was that the signal to bundle him into a limo with darkened windows? But the nod summoned a waiter who appeared with a dessert menu. Kinnery's heart rate dropped back to as near normal as it could right then.

"I'm not giving you a location," Kinnery said. *Last throw of the dice. Oh God.* "Unless you can offer some protection."

"Until I know what the exact risk is, I won't know what I need to protect him from."

"I don't *know* the exact risk. I wasn't able to carry out even the most basic tests. The woman looking after him wouldn't let me."

"So we both have a lot to discover, then."

Kinnery was floundering. He had nowhere to take this. His only trump card was knowing where Ian was, or at least where he'd been most recently. But he didn't even know what Ian looked like today or what he'd look like tomorrow.

"So what can you offer?" he asked.

Leo carried on reading the menu. He tapped his fingernail next to a line of elegant print as if he'd finally settled on a dessert.

"One thing I have that nobody else does," he said. "A trustworthy security resource."

"No agencies. No."

"I mean someone I can trust personally, and that's a very short list indeed." Leo smiled to himself, no humour or satisfaction, more a bittersweet pain that brought him closer to a frown. It looked like the real thing. "I have people in mind. You give them the location, and they'll extract your subject safely. Then I'll take care of things."

"Take care."

"Literally. I'm not the Russian mafia."

Kinnery realised he was now the one taking an awful lot on trust. No: he was desperate and cornered. Part of him wanted this all to be over with, even if it meant jail. All those murderers who buried their victims in the garden, or dumped them in lakes, and let the passing time gradually reassure them that they were further away from being caught every year — how did they live with that? It was agony. And it was never, ever over.

"I insist on participating in that care," Kinnery said.

"You will." Leo took out his cell. "Make time to come on a trip with me tomorrow or the day after. I assume there's no reason you can't drive."

"None."

"Good. We can share the driving. You can explain the details to me on the way." Leo leaned forward a little as he tapped a number and stared in defocus at the seat-back behind Kinnery. His tone changed when someone picked up. "Hello, my dear. Sorry to trouble you, but I really need to come and see the guys ... I know ... okay ... no, it's not something I can discuss on the phone ... is that okay? I wouldn't ask if it weren't important. I hate interrupting their leave."

Leo seemed to know them well, whoever they were. He made a few noises, then rung off with a few fond words that were definitely addressed to a woman he knew well.

"Personal staff?" Kinnery asked. "Mercenaries?"

"Neither." Leo put three hundred-dollar bills on the table. "And while we're at it, let's not bandy around emotive terms like *mercenary*. That has a strict legal definition. But if you want to use it pejoratively, let's also apply it to scientists who amass fortunes from medical patents, shall we?"

Kinnery tried to imagine who a man like Leo would trust. He wondered if he would want to trust them too. But if he didn't, it was already far too late to change his mind.

If he'd had any doubt that he'd mounted a tiger, he had none now.

THE BRAYNE ESTATE, CHALTON FARM, WESTERHAM FALLS, MAINE: JULY.

Rob had spent nearly two weeks trying to work out why Tom called him every weekday morning at exactly the same time, voice only, with no clue to where he was. The penny finally dropped.

He's signed up. He's doing one of those graduate officer things.

Tom insisted on making the calls. That meant he was on a fixed timetable, something with structure and regulations. It wasn't some shitty menial job at all, then. It was something military.

The realisation left Rob feeling slightly shaky. He didn't regret one second of his time as a Marine, but this was Tom, Little Matey, Kiddo, the focus of his life and still his little boy even if he was now a twenty-year-old man. All Rob could see for a moment was injury, death, and the sort of fear that the average bloke couldn't imagine.

Come on. I loved it, despite the bad days. Tom's going to do fine. I can even help him. Something I can understand for a change.

Rob waited for the call on the veranda of the guest cottage, coffee in hand, phone on the table next to the sun lounger. The cottage was bigger than the first married quarters he'd lived in with Bev, set in wooded grounds the size of bloody Norway. He couldn't even see the main house from here. This wasn't the real world at all. It was Mike's own little kingdom, and it wasn't real for him either. It was Mike's attempt at the simple life.

Three hundred acres. Christ, I could live rough in the woods and nobody would even know I was there. All without stepping outside the boundary.

The phone vibrated on the table right on time, buzzing angrily like a trapped bee. Rob pounced on it.

"Hi kiddo. How's it going?"

"Pretty good, Dad. Got your day planned? Playing polo? Going to the country club to teach them how to light farts?"

"Leo's coming for dinner. Apart from that, another day of sitting on my arse." Rob couldn't avoid it any longer. "Why didn't you tell me you signed up?"

"What?"

"The sponsorship. Some graduate officer entry thing, yeah? So you're on some leadership program now. What is it, Navy? Army?" The silence told Rob nothing. He tried to joke a reaction out of Tom. "Oh my God, is it the Crabs? It's okay. Lots of blokes lead useful lives in the RAF. Did you think I'd object?"

"Sorry, Dad, it's not that at all." Tom sounded a bit crestfallen. "Are you disappointed?"

For a moment Rob wasn't sure. Maybe it was relief. The answer threw him. "No, not at all, kiddo. I just guessed wrong. Sorry."

"I don't want to tell you in case it doesn't work out."

It sounded like something Tom really wanted. "Have you told your mum?"

"No. I don't even mention Mike to her. Well, not who he is, anyway."

"I'm not asking you to lie to her."

"Maybe not, but sometimes you need to keep things from people for their own good. She'd tell Paul. He's all right, but I don't think he needs to know you've got a rich mate."

Tom never called his stepfather *Dad*. He rarely mentioned him at all. The lad was a diplomat. "Okay, I won't keep asking," Rob said. "You can tell me when you're ready. Whatever it is, I'll be proud of you."

"You'll be the first to know. I promise." It sounded like the subject was closed. "Got to go, Dad. Talk to you tomorrow."

What was there to worry about? Tom was Captain Sensible, perfectly capable of making his own decisions. Any other student who got Mike-sized checks would have pissed the money up the wall by now, but Tom was investing it for the future. Rob realised that he was worrying more about how redundant he'd become in his son's life than whether Tom was making the right choices.

But that's the plan. Stash away some money for him, see him settled in a good job, and make sure he's got a roof over his head. Then I can get myself sorted out.

There was still a year to go. That was plenty of time. Rob tidied the cottage like he was preparing for an inspection, an ingrained habit that took over whenever he felt at a loose end. He was running his fingers over the edges of picture frames and the tops of cabinets to check for hidden dust when he heard Mike tap on the open patio door.

"You want me to shoot the cleaning company, or tell them to get down and give me twenty?" Mike wandered in, hands in the pockets of his shorts. "It's safe to come back in the house, you know. Don't be a stranger."

"You should still be on shagging duties, mate."

"That doesn't take all day." He gave Rob his mock-disapproval look. It was a lot like Leo's. "Livvie sent me to corral you for lunch."

"Okay. Do I look presentable?"

"You'll do. How's Tom?"

Rob checked his hair in the mirror above the fireplace. "Not enlisting."

"Oh. You asked him, then."

"I had to. It was driving me up the wall."

"You know he doesn't need to worry about a job. Dad's got enough companies he could work for. Hell, he could buy Tom his own IT firm."

"You're a saint, Zombie, but Tom's an independent little bugger."

"Well, whatever it is, he's thought it through. The guy's a planner." Mike patted Rob's back. "Now try to drag yourself away from that goddamn mirror."

The house loomed out of a screen of rhododendrons as they walked past the indoor firing range and the empty stable block. From the road, the white clapboard frontage just looked like a posh farmhouse, with no hint of the steel doors, ballistic glass, and alarm systems. It was nowhere near as grand as Mike's parents' fort of a place with its high walls and live-in staff. The plot, mostly forest, didn't even have a proper perimeter fence. Mike seemed happy with a network of cameras, motion sensors, and modest five-bar gates at the entrance.

Livvie had a Glock 26, though. Mike had made sure she could use it.

Today her weapon of choice was a blowtorch. When Rob opened the kitchen door, the air was thick with barbecue smells. Livvie was grilling peppers with the flame, blistering and blackening the skins. She was a terrifying cook. Rob had no doubt that she could look after herself.

"Leo just rang," she said. "Ten second call. He'll have someone with him."

Rob watched Mike's face fall. "Who?" Mike asked.

"He wouldn't say. ETA about nineteen-forty-five."

That was a lot of fretting time for Mike. Rob couldn't even begin to guess what was going on. His first thought was a lawyer. Livvie shoved the peppers in a plastic bag and strangled it shut.

"I think that bag's dead, Mrs Mike," Rob said. "Do you want me to check for a pulse?"

"Just tell him, Rob." Livvie took a bottle of dressing from the fridge and shook it ferociously. "He thinks Leo's coming to tell him he's terminally ill. Tell him to stop angsting."

Mike hadn't mentioned that. He didn't have to share his every thought with Rob, but it was rare that he didn't.

"Yeah, if it's that personal, why would Leo want to see me as well?" Rob asked. "He just doesn't trust phones or e-mail to do business these days. Who does?"

"Sure, but driving all this way, while the Senate's sitting?" Mike shook his head. "And remember what business we're in."

"Whatever it is, mate, I've got your back. It's nothing we can't handle."

Livvie patted Rob's head as she passed on her way to the back door, clutching a knife to go lettuce slaying. "Well done. He never listens to me."

Rob could see a lot of Bev in Livvie, mostly the no-nonsense, get-it-done side of her. Wives whose blokes were away a lot were either self-reliant to start with or had to get that way fast. Livvie didn't have to live this way any more than Mike did, though. She could have had a housekeeper and spent her day on charity lunches, shopping, and getting rat-arsed on cocktails. She definitely wasn't a society wife. She hadn't *come from money*, as Mike put it. Rob had worked it all out. They'd probably been blissfully happy in their student days at Oxford, and they tried to recreate that uncomplicated life here. Rob couldn't blame them. He knew he was clinging to the kind of life he'd had as a Marine.

It was a long eight hours to wait for Leo, even with all the distractions available at the house. Rob ended up playing Grand Theft Auto with Livvie in the den long after Mike gave up on it and disappeared into the garage to tinker with something.

"This is going to be our last round of IVF," Livvie said suddenly, not taking her eyes off the screen. "I think it's making Mike extra jumpy about his dad."

Rob felt responsible for that. *Me and my bloody advice.* "It's easier getting shot at than dealing with your nearest and dearest. Are you okay with it?"

"Relieved, actually," she said. "I hate getting his hopes up and dashing them every time."

It was hard to know what to say to that. "Plan B?"

Livvie nodded. "Plan B. Buy one off the peg."

It made Rob wince. But that was Livvie, burying whatever she felt under black humour. He imagined that IVF was like prenatal hospital visits but a hundred times worse, with nothing to show for it at the end. Maybe Livvie couldn't bring herself to say that to Mike.

She carried on playing the game, punching out a mugger and taking his victim's wallet. She had the option of keeping it or handing back to the victim. The green light sat there on the map for a moment, testing her honesty.

"Give it back," Rob said. "You don't need it. You're minted."

"I like to know what it feels like to act without consequences." Livvie finally walked her character over the green dot, making off with the wallet. "Actually, it creeps me out. Because that's how a lot of real people live their lives."

"You're just supposed to blow shit up to let off steam, Mrs Mike."

"But I can do that for real."

The debate was interrupted by the quiet *ding-ding-ding* from the hall as the motion sensors picked up a vehicle on the drive. By the time Rob made it upstairs to the hall, Mike was already standing in the doorway, watching Leo's black BMW pull up at the front of the house. The heavily tinted windows made it hard to see who was driving, but Leo got out of the passenger side, and a grey-haired bloke — sixties, maybe — opened the driver's door and squinted against the low sun. He looked more like a harassed social worker than security. He probably wasn't a lawyer, either, not in that crumpled cotton jacket. Next to Leo, always creaseless and immaculate even in a polo shirt, he looked like a drunk after a night in a shop doorway.

"Close protection isn't as picky as it used to be," Rob murmured. "Long-lost relative?"

Mike didn't take his eyes off the scruffy bloke. "Never seen him before in my life."

"Hi, Micko." Leo strode up to Mike and hugged him, then turned to Rob and did a bit of enthusiastic back-slapping. "Good to see you home, Rob. Apologies for the theatrics. This is Dr Charles Kinnery."

Oh shit. Mike's right. Leo had brought a doctor. He really was ill. Kinnery shook hands, looking awkward. Rob froze for a second, expecting the worst, but Mike plunged straight in.

"Have you come to give me bad news?" he asked.

Leo looked puzzled, then held up both hands, embarrassed. "Oh God, did you think I was sick? I'm sorry. No, I'm fine. So's Mom. Everyone's fine. Charles isn't a physician."

Livvie intercepted them. "Go through to the conservatory," she said. "I'll fetch coffee and a defibrillator, shall I?"

"Sorry, my dear. I didn't mean to scare you." Leo gave her a peck on the cheek. Rob caught Mike's eye and spotted that shaky, deflated look that followed a close call. "We've got an unusual security situation. I could use some professional help."

They sat down facing each other across the pot of white orchids on the coffee table while Rob tried to size up Kinnery, not sure what to make of him. He looked knackered and uncomfortable.

"What do we mean by security here, Dad?" Mike asked. "Are we talking generally, or is this classified? Because I doubt our clearance is as high as yours."

Livvie came in with a tray of coffee and put it on the table. "Okay, I heard the S word, so I'm going to fix dinner. What I don't know, the Feds can't beat out of me."

Kinnery looked as if he wasn't sure whether Livvie was joking. He waited for her to leave, then leaned forward, hands clasped.

"We have a vulnerable young man who's in difficulties," he said. "We need to protect him from interference."

Ah, *bodyguards.* That was easy enough. Rob could finally use the close protection training that the Navy had paid for. He looked at Mike, waiting for the cue to pitch in.

"Is this extraction or protection?" Mike asked.

Leo glanced at Kinnery. "Extraction to a place of safety, I'd say."

"Drugs, alcohol, joy-riding? Cult? Runaway? Relative compromised somehow?"

Kinnery looked confused and opened his mouth to answer, but Leo cut across him.

"I'm going to tell you something that might not sound credible," Leo said. "But it's a situation I can't ignore, and the only people I can trust to do things discreetly and intelligently are you and Rob."

Mike just nodded. "Okay, then, strictly within these four walls."

Leo took a folded sheet of paper from his inside pocket and held it up like an auction bid. "Taken from a website. It might look like the usual internet conspiracy fantasy, but apparently it's true." He put on his reading glasses and unfolded the paper. "*On the subject of fringe research, we have seen written testimony that the Department of Defense sponsored research into dynamic mimicry in human subjects, in other words the ability of an organism to change shape, colour, and form at will. Far from being another waste of taxes on paranormal research, it appears that Project Ringer, led by Charles Kinnery, successfully introduced engineered animal-derived genes into human embryos long before the pioneering hybrid research by China. One of those embryos was brought to term, reached adulthood, and was able to change his appearance.*"

Leo handed the report to Mike to read. Mike scanned it before passing it to Rob. "How did it leak?" Mike asked.

"The kid did it himself." Kinnery kept shutting his eyes and pinching the bridge of his nose, not a happy Hector at all. "Okay, crudely put, we have a young man who's a shape-shifter. I can vouch for that. I made him. Forget all the legal and ethical questions for the moment. Right now, a biotech company called KWA will be looking for him."

"You're right, it *is* unbelievable," Mike said.

Kinnery didn't flinch. "By all means use the term *Frankenstein* if that helps you grasp the size of this. I won't mind."

Rob's first thought was that the lad might have needed protecting from Kinnery, not some biotech firm. "What exactly does *brought to term* mean here?"

"Paid surrogate mother," Kinnery said. "She handed him over at birth."

"Didn't she notice?"

"No. There was nothing to notice back then."

"So he can change into anything, can he?"

"Within fairly narrow human parameters." Kinnery just stared at Rob with a weary expression that said *you ignorant twat.* "He can't mimic objects."

Rob tried to look as if he believed every word. Whether Kinnery was mental or lying wasn't the issue. He just wanted to know why Leo was going along with this crap, because that old bugger was as sane as they came.

"Great," said Mike, straight-faced. "That makes life easier."

Kinnery didn't even blink. "So far, we're the only ones who know the boy's identity and location. We need to get him to a place of safety."

"Which is?"

"I'm working on that."

"And you believe this, Dad?" Mike turned to Leo. "You've seen proof?"

"I haven't seen it," Leo said quietly. "But I really need your help with it."

Rob expected Mike to make some excuse and haul Leo off on his own to have a frank chat out of Kinnery's earshot. He didn't. He just blinked a few times as if he was trying to work out whether to take the request at face value or not. Leo had kicked off the conversation with everyone present, so he must have had his reasons for not briefing Mike separately.

"Look, this is an eighteen-year-old boy brought up by a woman he thought was his grandmother," Kinnery said. "And she's just died. His name's Ian. Ian Dunlop. He thought he was mentally ill because nobody told him what he was until a few weeks ago. He's been isolated for years, so he needs the kind of help and protection that he definitely won't get from a government agency — or from a company that sees him as a billion dollars in research assets. They won't give a damn about his constitutional rights. *You* work it out."

"He's not a minor, then," Mike said, still unmoved.

"No."

"And he hasn't committed a crime."

"No. That'd be me."

"Is he mentally incompetent in some way?"

"No. He's very intelligent. Just zero life experience."

"And you engineered all this."

"Sadly, yes."

Mike did that tight-lipped look that he'd probably have given Himmler. He seemed to be taking the principle seriously now, even if he couldn't possibly believe it. Rob wondered how many minutes he'd give it before he asked Kinnery to drop the subject, fuck off, and forget the conversation ever happened.

"If that's true, then you're a sorry excuse for a human being, sir," Mike said.

"You think I don't know that?"

That shut everyone up. The silence pulsed. Rob gave up trying to work out what the real story was and left it to Mike. Rob would back him up, whatever he decided to do. Mike always made the moral choice.

"I still don't get why this is your problem, Dad."

"Well, I opposed the project," Leo said. "And that was long before I knew about Ian. But now I *do* know, I can't ignore it. Someone has to own this problem. Preferably not an agency."

Rob didn't believe in shape-shifters, but he did believe in the power of money. "I get it," he said. "This lad doesn't actually change into Godzilla. He's just carrying some engineered genes, they're worth a lot of money, and he's holding out for the highest bidder. Yeah?" That sounded much more likely. Companies had legal battles over patents for animals and plants. He'd seen it on the news. "So you need to grab the assets before a rival company or some foreign government gets hold of him."

"No, it's not that at all," Kinnery said. "And I fully understand why you think that. But you've got it all wrong."

"So why haven't *you* retrieved him?" Mike asked. "Is he dangerous?"

"KWA's got me under surveillance. I'd lead them straight to him."

"I hope they haven't tracked you here, then."

Leo shook his head. "Don't worry, Micko. We've been prudent. Hence the car. Father visiting his son after a long absence."

"Anyway, he's warned me not to visit," Kinnery said, "I'd only spook him."

"Is he going to want to come with us?"

"I don't know. He was brought up to be wary of strangers."

"Terrific." Mike made a move to the French windows. He gave

Leo a look as if he wanted to take him to one side, but Leo didn't react. "Excuse us for a moment, will you? Rob and I need to talk."

Rob followed him outside to the rear deck and onto the lawn. Squadrons of mosquitoes had come out for their nightly strafing run, dancing around in the dying sunlight as the mozzie trap lured them across the grass. It didn't look like any of them ever made it back to HQ to warn their mates not to be fooled by the green metal thing. Mike folded his arms and turned his back to the house.

"What the *fuck?*" He rarely swore. "Did we both hear the same thing?"

"It's complete bullshit," Rob said. "You know that. I know that. Your dad knows that. I don't know what Kinnery believes, but I just want to know why your dad's humouring him."

"And you *really* don't believe any of it."

"Of course I don't. I'm just uneducated, not a moron."

"If Dad wasn't involved, I'd hand Kinnery the FBI helpline number and kick his ass out of here."

"But he *is* involved."

"Yes. And he's never asked me for a favour before."

Rob could see Mike groping for a reason not to let his dad down. He obviously thought he was in trouble.

"This sounds like kidnapping," Rob said. "Not an arrest. I'm with you, mate, but let's be clear this might be over the line."

"I don't want you involved. If anyone does it, I will."

"Come on, I'm your mate. Besides, I owe your dad. He's done everything for me. All the paperwork and permits and green card. He's entitled to his money's worth from me."

"This is insane."

"But your dad isn't. And by politician standards, he's clean, isn't he? That's the problem. You're worried that he's done something dodgy, yeah?"

"He'd have a reason." Mike chewed his lip, shaking his head slowly. "Okay, I've got to talk to him on his own. Maybe I can work out what we're really dealing with."

"What will you do if you find out he's been a naughty boy?"

Mike looked stricken for a moment. "It'll be a test of my prissy self-righteousness, then, won't it?"

"Well, there's no harm in doing a recce and reporting back." Rob wasn't sure if there was some test for shape-shifters that didn't involve silver bullets. *Fuck me, this really is mental. This definitely won't end well.* "All we've got right now is the word of a nerd website and a mad scientist."

Mike stared down at his shoes for a moment, then turned around and started walking back to the house. "I'm glad it's not true, because I'd have to shoot that bastard on moral grounds."

He just wanted to be the good American, doing good things and championing noble causes. It wasn't a bad ambition. For a bloke with an Oxford degree and combat experience in some seriously nasty shit-holes, though, it was bloody naive. Maybe he wanted to stay that way. Rob chose his words carefully.

"I didn't think you were religious. Or is this about eggs and embryo stuff?"

"Among other things."

"You just can't trust these fuckers to know when to stop." Rob could imagine how all this was getting stirred into Mike's feelings about IVF. "Are you going to tell Livvie?"

"She needs to know what I'm doing."

"Okay."

"Like I said, you don't have to come with me."

"You know that's the biggest challenge you can give a Bootneck, don't you?" Rob gave him a friendly but pointed shove as they walked. "You seriously think I'm going to be out-machoed by a bloody Septic reservist? You big girl. Stand aside and let a man show you how it's done."

"We can take a look."

"Yeah. We can."

"And I wasn't Reserves."

Rob had no idea if he'd be aiding and abetting some kind of industrial piracy, but the one thing he was sure of was his loyalty and obligation to Mike. If they hit any snags, Leo had the money and clout to make trouble vanish. Besides, they were only doing a recce. There was no law against that.

Mike walked in and stood over Kinnery, staring down his nose at him in a very Leo kind of way. It was always interesting to watch sons turning into their dads.

"Subject to the location, we'll do a recon and take it from there," Mike said. "Dad, can I have a word, please?"

They left Rob alone with Kinnery. The scientist looked at Rob as if he was waiting for him to pull a knife.

"Ian's really into the military," Kinnery said awkwardly. "He'll probably enjoy your war stories."

"How normal is he?" Rob tried to find the right word. It was a pretend conversation, but he intended to be professional about it. "Is he going to huddle in a corner banging his head on the wall or something?"

"Actually, he's more socialised than I realised. He's managed to contact a journalist and handle a funeral, which takes some doing. He watches a lot of TV. I think he mimics what he sees."

"Got a recent photo?" Well, there was no harm in asking. Rob managed to keep a straight face. "I suppose not, eh?"

"If I did, I'd have no idea what he'd look like tomorrow."

"Location?"

"Athel Ridge. Washington."

"Can you draw the layout of the house? Doors, windows, lines of sight?"

"Sure."

"Any neighbours?"

"Not nearby. They're pretty well off the grid. Maggie — Ian's guardian — was paranoid. Rightly so, as it turns out."

"What kind of off-grid? Are we going to need a fifty cal and APCs to go in there?"

"No, not crazy preppers. Hippy greens a couple of miles away."

"Dogs? Firearms?"

"Just greyhounds. Nothing aggressive. Maggie rescued strays."

"But is he armed? I know you lot like to be seriously tooled up. As do I."

"As far as I know, no assault weapons and no handguns. Just a couple of small calibre rifles or shotguns. Farmer variety."

"You know those things can still kill, don't you? Never mind. Body armour's never out of fashion."

And it's all good practice. Staves off skills fade. No different from raiding compounds in Afghanistan.

Rob resisted the temptation to look up the satellite view on his phone. They'd have to use paper maps or offline satnav in case someone could link the web searches to this address. When Mike and Leo came back, it was hard to tell if anything had been thrashed out. Rob would find out later. In the meantime, he'd take the planning seriously. He was a pro. He couldn't think any other way.

"Okay," Leo said. "You take my plane as far as Idaho. Then do the last leg by car to cover the tracks. That minimises the journey time, and Ian doesn't have to mix with the public. And you can transport whatever hardware you need."

Rob loved the way Leo just lobbed in his private jet and threw them the keys like it was the family car. *Hardware. Yeah. Might as well go armed and armoured, just in case.* They ended up in Mike's study, poring over maps. Using Kinnery's floor plan, Rob mapped out lines of sight, identified laying-up positions, and worked out points of entry. It felt just like an exercise: you knew it wasn't real, but you gave it all you had, made it as authentic as you could, and lulled yourself into a temporary state of belief that you were at war. Rob was back doing what he knew best and excelled at. However daft the job sounded, he was looking forward to it.

"Can Ian control these changes?" Mike asked. "Can he use it to evade us?"

Kinnery gave him an odd look. Maybe it hadn't crossed his mind. "Up to a few weeks ago, he thought he was having hallucinations. So I doubt he's worked out how to do that yet. That's assuming he can control it at all."

Leo and Kinnery stayed for a quick dinner and freshened up before heading straight back to Washington. That was a lot of driving for anyone, let alone two older guys, even if they were sharing the load. Mike watched the BMW's tail lights disappear down the drive into the darkness, shaking his head.

"He's crazy," he said. "They're too old to do all that driving."

Rob was waiting for something more informative than that. "Well? What did he say when you got him on his own?"

Mike shook his head again. "That he has to take Kinnery's story at face value. I said that we'd just observe what we could and play it by ear."

"Is that it?"

"Is that what?" Livvie walked up behind Mike. He flinched as if she'd pinched his arse. "Or is this OPSEC that you can't mention?"

"No, I have to tell you, honey," he said, steering her towards the kitchen. "It's just bizarre. Rob and I need to be away for a few days."

Rob was halfway down the hall when he heard Livvie laughing her head off. He took that as a vote for the disbelief camp. He expected Leo to call the next day to apologise and explain that it had all been some complicated sting to get Kinnery to do something. But when the call came, it was just travel arrangements to meet the Gulfstream at the small airfield at Odstock and then collect a car in Idaho.

Rob thought it over as he stood in front of the bathroom mirror, running the clippers through his hair. He couldn't see much grey. He still had time on his side. Once they'd knocked this shit on the head, they could get on with what really mattered — working out what two middle-aged blokes with experience and contacts could do next. They weren't getting any younger, and whether Mike and Livvie had a baby or adopted a kid, Mike's life was going to change more than he could possibly imagine. Nothing could really prepare him for being a dad. Rob was still grappling with it even now.

But they were professional problem-solvers. They'd work something out. Rob was certain of it.

LANSING, MICHIGAN: JULY.

Dru was probably already too late.

The clock was ticking. She tried to think like a man who'd kept a secret for nearly twenty years and had now been exposed. Kinnery would cover his tracks as fast as he could, but the trail had been cold for a long time. Her chances of turning up anything useful on him now were slim.

But I don't have to catch him. I just have to find out what he did when he left. If he did anything, he couldn't have done it alone. But why did it go quiet for so long?

All she had to do to save her job was to keep Weaver happy, but it was going to be hard to prove a negative. She gulped her coffee, impatient to leave for the office. Clare walked into the kitchen, tying her hair back with an elastic band.

"Are you back from Mars yet, Mom?'

"Pardon?"

"You've been really distracted. Is it a new man?"

If only. When was the last time I had a date?

"I've got a big project at work," Dru said. "So don't go telling your father crazy things about men, or it'll be even harder to get any child support out of him."

"Well, whatever it is, I'm glad you're happier."

The job would never be a source of joy and satisfaction, but

Dru felt better for having a goal. This was real investigative work, and she loved a good puzzle. Solving puzzles imposed clarity and order on the chaotic unknown. It gave her control in a world where she felt she had none.

Yes, I know that sums up my neuroses perfectly. But at least I know what they are.

Dru dropped Clare at Rebecca's and headed for the office to carry on sifting through KWA's paper archives while she waited for the Vancouver agency to open. Assembling all the internal documentation on Kinnery had taken a few days because she'd requested files by year to disguise exactly whose data she was looking for. When she walked into her temporary office in the basement, the brown, blue, and red boxes were stacked in front of the desk like a playground fort. They smelled ancient and musty.

Weaver had personally signed out the Ringer files to avoid awkward questions. She opened the first box and fanned out a few folders on the desk. *Should I be looking at classified material? Should KWA have shredded this or handed it to the DoD?* She really wasn't sure. She reassured herself that it was solely between her and Weaver.

Besides, she wasn't interested in scientific data. She was just looking for names and places to map Kinnery's associations.

Who would Kinnery ask to carry genetic material for him?

It wasn't like smuggling drugs. The risks were different, but so was the nature of the trust that Kinnery would have to put in his accomplice. His mule could just walk away with the goods at any time. There wasn't anything that cops would find if they stopped and searched the guy. It was a far cry from someone swallowing heroin-filled rubbers that could burst and kill them if they didn't crap them out in time, or carrying a suitcase full of bagged cocaine.

Dru wrote the growing list of names, companies, and locations on sticky notes so that she could move them around on the desk pad to try different combinations and maybe spot a pattern. None of this could be committed to her computer to leave temporary files or even trackable keystrokes. Weaver had insisted on absolute secrecy. She took the desk pad home each night, and any calls or searches she made were via two unregistered burner cells that she kept for sensitive enquiries.

Who would Kinnery rely on?

You don't pluck the people you really need to trust out of thin air. You already know them. So it's someone Kinnery's sure won't disappear, blab, or sell out to a rival. And someone he can keep tabs on. If he did it, it was probably just before he left KWA.

No, this isn't about who he trusts. It's about who trusts him.

Engineered genes could make unexpected changes to the rest of the body. Who would take that kind of risk for Kinnery? A girlfriend? Even smart women would do anything for the worst son of a bitch. *I wasn't immune, was I?* No, the article said the subject was male, although that was hardly a reliable source, and Dru had no idea about Kinnery's sexual preferences. Maybe it wasn't about trust. It might have been about control, someone he had power and influence over: a student, perhaps.

If it's not devotion, then why would he have that power? Fear. Losing a cut of the profits. Bad grades. If he goes down, everyone goes down.

Kinnery's college class from the 1970s was a logical place to start, the earliest point at which he'd have met like-minded people who also understood the science. But what if this mule didn't know what he or she was being dosed with? It still had to be someone Kinnery could keep tabs on.

Another thought struck her. If this mule existed and was found, how was Weaver going to permanently recover the genes? They'd be embedded at a cellular level, even if they were switched off. They weren't goods that could be seized and impounded; a human couldn't be confiscated like a genetically modified crop or animal. KWA would need to intervene physically to extract tissue samples. That almost certainly meant getting a court order if the mule didn't consent. How the hell was *that* going to be kept quiet?

The idea distracted Dru completely for a few minutes as she worked through scenarios of how someone could take genes out of a human being. It just didn't seem possible without violence or kidnapping. Perhaps there was some advanced technique she wasn't aware of. She wasn't a scientist, after all. She simply didn't know.

Her speculation was cut short when someone rapped on the door. Luis, the facilities manager, wheeled in a sack truck loaded with three more boxes.

"I think this is the last of it." Luis tapped a box. "These are the oldest phone records. Twenty-five years old. Ah, those were the days."

That surprised her. "I didn't know we kept them that long."

"Patents last twenty years, and my predecessor never disposed of anything until someone made him, so this is his legacy."

It was another mountain of work. But as long as Dru was busy, she still had a job. "Thanks. That'll keep me going."

"Are you looking for something specific?"

"Just getting an overview for a report. You know how it is. Halbauer wants to know the history of the world before the wedding can take place."

She closed the door again. A paper investigation wasn't just about leaving no footprint on the system. Looking through the hard copy let her mind take in things she might not consciously notice. Writing down the details and even applying them to maps engaged different parts of her brain. Then the subconscious processing would throw up recurrences and connections, and she'd see patterns that might be worth following up. It looked mind-numbingly dull to most people. But that was why she saw what others missed. To her, this was Aladdin's cave.

The Ringer files were a mix of original documents and computer printouts. She was busy scribbling down names when the Skype tone interrupted, and a glance at her screen confirmed it was the agency in Vancouver. The webcam was disabled. It was mainly to prevent the camera picking up any sensitive detail behind her, but not entirely.

I used to be hot. Well, passable, anyway. Now look at me. Worn out. Greying. So over and done with. Let's preserve the illusion of adequacy.

"Hi, Grant," she said, trying to smile audibly. "How did you get on?"

"Well, the subject flew to Washington on Monday." Grant had a lovely, creamy Canadian voice. He sounded about forty. It gave Dru a brief and completely illogical moment of hope that quickly faded. "D.C., that is. Our affiliate says he walked to a restaurant where they couldn't follow him, but he didn't come out the front door. They picked him up later returning to his hotel, then lost him again until he returned to his hotel again on Wednesday. There's a thirty-six to forty-eight-hour gap to be filled there, I'm afraid"

"And he's home now?"

"He got back to Vancouver late yesterday. I'll send you a full report and images, but those are the headlines. Do you want me to maintain surveillance?"

"Has he called anybody?"

"Well, being able to answer that question — unless an operative was in earshot in a public place — would require an illegal act."

Translated, that meant Grant might be able to get hold of phone logs. Dru tried to keep her answer ambiguous as well. She couldn't openly ask him to do it. In his profession, he was probably used to reading between the lines between the *other* lines.

"Understood," she said. "Yes, please carry on. I'll tell you when to call it off."

"I'll mail you some encrypted stuff. Check your spam trap too. You'll know it when you see it."

Dru was baffled for a moment. It sounded like there were multiple messages. If he was worried about spelling that out on the phone, then it was probably illegal, or at least irregular. She took her burner out of her purse, waiting for the report to land in the mail account that she kept purely for off-the-books stuff.

This was a grey area that she'd found herself edging into a step at a time over the years without really noticing that she'd crossed the line. First she'd prided herself on not breaking the law. After a while, she'd lowered the bar far enough to accept irregularly-obtained intelligence for an informal investigation, because a pointed interview with the erring employee almost always led to the individual admitting what Dru had already worked out via the back door. It was a confession. No harm had been done: her hands were clean. She was simply operating from a position of greater awareness to get an answer. Law enforcement did that all the time. Her job wasn't that different.

Ping. Grant's encrypted e-mail arrived. It wasn't easy to view this on a phone screen. There were long-lens images of Kinnery walking down the road or getting into taxis, and a timed list of his movements. Even if she could have accessed CCTV footage, it probably wouldn't have told her much more.

A second encrypted message headed CANADIAN BARGAIN BREAKS: BOOKING CONFIRMATION arrived about two minutes later, from an e-mail address she didn't recognise. Now Grant's odd comment made sense. This message had to be from him. The attachments were images that took some zooming to work out.

They were pictures of itemised billing records with no name or identification. Grant hadn't added any comments except the labels CELL and LANDLINE, but they had to have come from a phone company employee, photographed and returned to their source with no trackable route out through the telco's e-mail system. It didn't so much give Dru a thrill as a slightly sick feeling in the stomach. She was pretty sure that was illegal at some point along the chain.

The landline print-out was very short, showing fewer than a dozen calls to and from the same number, nothing else. The other list was Kinnery's cell activity over the last two months, and it was easy to see that he wasn't a teenaged girl. He didn't call many people, and not many people called him, but she recognised Weaver's direct line. Now all she had to do was enter the numbers into a reverse look-up application and see what fell out.

If anything.

At least it was a relatively short list. For a wicked, guilty moment, she wondered how long it would take to do the same search on Clare's records, but Clare understood the bill was itemised and that Mom was good at checking that sort of thing if she was given cause to worry.

But then she might just go out and buy a second-hand burner that I'd never know about.

There was no such thing as complete monitoring. Dru got impatient with TV dramas and police documentaries that made it look as if every person could be tracked and found, every clue detected, and every crime solved simply by technology. People believed what they saw on those shows. Families with missing loved ones believed it as well, but they were living proof that people could disappear forever even in a surveillance society and right under the noses of neighbours. And crimes went unsolved every day, no matter how many street cameras, drones, spy satellites, phone taps, and computer snoops there were. On the other hand, old fashioned human intelligence, plus hours of work, could often do what high-tech couldn't.

So what's this phone you only use for one number, Kinnery?

It was like some weird Cold War hotline from the White House to the Kremlin. She liked the thought that it might be a big red phone with a flashing light on it. The number he'd called had a Seattle area code, but Dru couldn't tell if it was a landline or a cell.

It's all about people. Observing human behaviour and association. Breach security by asking someone nicely. Wreck the smartest system in the world by employing the dumbest human. How smart are you, Kinnery?

Dru did a reverse look-up for the Seattle number and found

nothing. She'd have to call it to check who answered, but timing was an issue. How would she know if calling would alert someone too soon? She had no idea what too soon or too late meant when she was dealing with something two decades old. All she could do was collect pieces of the puzzle, each innocuous on its own.

If only she could get hold of the document that *The Slide* had received. She pondered that all the way through to lunch as she cross-checked phone numbers, names, area codes, and locations. The drudgery wasn't mind-numbing at all. It was as soothing as needlepoint. Each stitch, each little curved pillow of yarn placed on the canvas field, and each thread of information would build up into something that she could eventually stand back from and see as a complete picture.

Dru switched between checking the phone numbers in the records and reading the paper documents to extract names and places for the timeline. Doing searches on the burner phone was fiddly and it wasn't perfect security, but it was better than leaving trails on the office network.

Just as she left no footprint, though, she also had no proof of what she'd been asked to do. She hoped she wouldn't need it.

By the end of the day, she'd put more flesh on Kinnery's bones than the personnel file or even Weaver had given him. He'd split up with his wife within a year of leaving KWA, and he'd stopped referring to a partner online. Dru had the names of at least ten other biologists who probably knew him well, plus a selection of forum comments, customer reviews, and other unguarded and innocuous stuff that gave her an idea of where he liked to go for weekend trips, the restaurants he visited, and the movies he regretted paying good money to see. She knew where he'd given talks and presented papers for the last ten years. Eventually, it would all form a tapestry recording as vivid a sequence of events as the one at Bayeux.

Why did smart people reveal all this? *Nothing* was harmless detail.

Not paranoid. Never. Just aware.

Weaver paid her a visit while she was packing up for the day. "Any leads?"

"He went to D.C. for the weekend." Dru didn't even say Kinnery's name aloud in the confines of her office. *Should I mention the Kremlin phone? No, not until I've got something concrete.* "I'm still trying to work out what he was doing there. Might be nothing. Have you had any more media calls?"

"None."

"Can I ask you something?"

"Sure."

"If this mule exists, how are you going to retrieve the genes? It'll be part of his cell structure."

Dru was looking right into Weaver's face when she said it. She saw the microsecond of reaction in his eyes. Either he hadn't thought about it, or else he'd already reached a conclusion that he wasn't keen to share with her.

"We'd be dealing with a criminal," he said carefully. "A thief. A smuggler. Like someone carrying drugs or stolen data through customs."

The thought played out like a movie. Dru could see the green customs channel in her mind and some guy trying to walk through, only to be stopped and asked to step into a side office.

"Yes, but how do you *remove* genes from someone?" she asked. "Perhaps you can switch them off, but how do you get all your property back? How do you do it without attracting attention, too? You can't even take a saliva sample without consent if — "

"We'd think of something." Weaver cut her off and looked at her for a heartbeat too long, as if he was willing her to erase the idea. "Confronting a mule and offering a compromise would probably resolve things. Right now, I just want to know if *The Slide's* story has any basis. I hope it doesn't. I'd always thought Charles would come back one day." Weaver now seemed unusually chatty. It was a diversionary tactic. Embarrassment? Guilt? Dru couldn't tell. "Halbauer would like that, I imagine. You just find whatever's to be found, and I'll worry about the rest."

It was as near to a disturbing conversation as Dru had ever had at KWA. "I'd better get home," she said. "I can't leave my daughter on her own for too long, not if I want to find the house standing when I get back."

"Fifteen? Sixteen?"

"Fourteen."

"We have to trust them sooner or later."

"I just got a new carpet for the living room."

"Maybe not quite yet, then. Goodnight, Dru."

On the drive home, Dru mulled over the practical issues of

retrieving stolen genes. It might have made a good movie, but this was the real world, where reputable biotech firms like KWA worked within a complex framework of regulations and laws. That didn't include grabbing thieves whose haul was now an integral part of their body. She was worrying about nothing. If a mule existed at all, Weaver would simply pay him and make sure the genes were switched off.

But how would he enforce it?

If you could switch a gene off, you could probably switch it on again. And how would that affect the mule's health?

It probably didn't matter. She'd have no say in it. *Only following orders. I'm just a good little kapo. Honest.* By the time she pulled into the drive, she'd reached the conclusion that conscripting a mule was a brilliant idea. Kinnery knew Weaver would have a hell of a job getting at the material, and an even harder one securing it permanently. It would have been even better to carry the genes himself. But if he knew what the genes could do, he might not have wanted to take the risk personally.

Goddamn. This is actually getting scary.

Clare was preparing pizza in the kitchen, or at least removing one from the packaging. Dru's reflex these days was to ask her what she was really after. She stopped herself.

"Ready for dinner?" Clare asked.

"Sorry, I got held up."

"If it's not a man, Mom, is it going to get you promotion?"

"Neither. I'll settle for keeping my job right now. Medical and dental, flex time, and a hundred per cent four-oh-one-K matching. And expenses. You'll sell your soul for that in a few years."

"How about having more fun?" Clare asked. "This is the only life you get."

Clare swung between fourteen, four, and forty. She was a teenager. They did that. Dru realised it wasn't the forty-year-old persona speaking but the fourteen-year-old, telling her mom that she was scared that she might end up like her. That was painful.

"Fun," Dru said. "Yes, I've heard of it."

After dinner she settled on the sofa and tried to think like Kinnery again. What if he didn't have someone bound to him by loyalty or fear? Maybe he'd have to pay his mule for silence and cooperation. *Follow the money.* Kinnery had made a mint by selling his stake in KWA. But how could she examine his finances without referring this to the police? She'd need grounds, and a half-assed allegation about a possible gene-stealing shape-shifter wasn't going to do KWA any favours.

I've talked myself into believing Weaver's theory, haven't I?

The Seattle Kremlin-phone number nagged at her. Maybe it wasn't too early to try calling it. She was almost starting to enjoy the immersion in the puzzle before a sobering thought about retrieval surfaced again.

Do I want to be party to anything illegal or violent?

Then she thought of what she owed Clare — a college fund, good healthcare, a roof over her head — and decided that thieves probably deserved whatever was coming to them.

It was late. She plugged the burner phone into the charger and headed for bed. She'd call the Seattle number tomorrow.

FIVE

Here's what I know about Rob Rennie, Charles. He risked his life to save a stranger who happened to be my son. He's watched over Mike like a brother ever since, and he's never asked for a cent. All he wanted was the chance to find a job. Now that's someone I can respect and trust, and therefore you'll respect and trust him too. Do we understand each other?

Leo Brayne, explaining his conditions to Charles Kinnery.

FLIGHT TO LEWISTON, IDAHO: JULY.

Rob walked backwards out of the Gulfstream G550's lavatory as if he was exiting from an audience with the Pope, then sat down opposite Mike with a big grin. He laid his cell phone on the table between them.

"You videoed the john?" Mike asked.

"Yeah, so Tom can see how Gucci it is. The only time blokes like me usually get on private jets is when we empty the shit tank." Rob craned his neck to look out of the window onto cloud-shadowed ground below. "Sometimes I wonder why you and Livvie don't just spend your time swanning around the world in this thing. I would."

Mike saw his own privilege anew and a little more kindly through the filter of Rob's delight in it. It was like taking Charlotte's kids to the zoo, a way of reminding himself that some things really were amazing and that he didn't have to feel guilty for enjoying them. Dad's jet was a novelty even for him. He didn't use it enough these days to be indifferent to it.

"Shall I ask Dad to send it to pick up Tom when he's ready to visit?"

Rob's grin widened. He seemed particularly cheerful today, probably because he had something challenging to do. Somehow he managed to be both a careful planner and live in the moment. Mike envied that.

"Can you?" Rob said. "He'll be thrilled. And he doesn't thrill easy."

"Sure. A limo to collect him up, too. The works."

"Thanks, mate."

"When are you going to learn to just ask? Whatever you want, you can have."

"You know my brain doesn't work like that."

"I'll just have to think rich for you, then."

Mike went back to studying the paper map of Athel Ridge. It seemed more familiar than his own life right then. His personal landscape had shifted as soon as he and Livvie had finally agreed to adopt after the next round of IVF, which changed a vague *if* — if he would ever be a father, something that had faded into a remote fantasy without too much detailed aftermath — to a definite *when.* Now he'd need to spend more time at home. He wouldn't be able to deploy whenever he wanted.

And there was Rob to worry about. He didn't need Mike to hold his hand on a daily basis, but Mike felt responsible for recruiting him for Esselby and upending his life. He couldn't expect Rob to suddenly ground himself just because Mike liked having him around all the time.

Mike had learned at his father's knee to beware a legion of threats, from gold-diggers to the random jerk waiting to punch him out and teach a rich brat a lesson. *Don't flaunt your privilege, Micko. Don't trust anybody. Be careful who you let into your circle.* But now Mike had a buddy, the kind who'd take a round for him, not some casual acquaintance made over cocktails. He didn't want to lose touch with him in the same way he'd drifted apart from the men he'd served with, or never even got on with in the first place. Rob was unbuyable and irreplaceable.

There were few problems that couldn't be solved with money,

though, even if it did breed dilemmas of its own. Mike would think of a solution.

"We've planned the ass out of this now," he said, refolding the map carefully. This was old-fashioned OPSEC. Maps had to be folded exactly the way they were made, in case an enemy got hold of one and worked out the area of interest from the extra fold lines. Nothing was written on the map itself, only sketched lightly on a sheet of layout paper placed over it. Mike decided that if you acquired a habit, overkill beat cutting corners. "We're only assessing the situation."

"Exactly."

"So why did Dad stick with the story?"

"Not that again, for Chrissakes."

"He knows I can keep my mouth shut." Mike tried to ignore it, but it kept nagging him. "So why not level with me?"

"Look, what's your dad?"

Mike calculated. "Sixty-six next birthday."

"I mean what *word* describes him. He's a *politician*, isn't he? Not some toothless inbred banjo-player. And Kinnery's a boffin with PhDs coming out of his arse. They can't possibly believe this paranormal shit. It's just some kind of manoeuvre."

"Surveys say fifty per cent of the electorate believe in alien abduction. They didn't all marry their cousins."

"Maybe, but your dad's not one of them. He's humouring Kinnery because he needs something from him. Kinnery might be a psychiatric case, or just spinning a dit for some reason, but either way it suits your dad to nod and smile. So he's going to keep that act up in front of you. If he tells you, he's compromised you. *Deniability*. If it all goes tits up, he can say, 'Oh, my son knew nothing.' Has he *ever* let you in on any secret squirrel stuff?"

Mike had to stop and repeat all that to himself. Rob was capable of impressive feats of Byzantine logic, another thing Dad liked about him. Rob leaned back in the beige ostrich leather seat and folded his arms in his argue-with-me-if-you-dare posture.

"Just once," Mike said. "And it freaked me out so much I never wanted to hear it again."

"There you go. He's into something awkward, and he's still totally sane. Are you sure you've got a first in politics?"

"*History* and politics. But there wasn't a lecture on applying theory to your own family."

"Well, whatever it is, we're paying a surprise visit to an armed paranoid. Even if he turns into an aardvark, he'll still be an armed, *jumpy* aardvark. Prioritise the threats, Zombie."

Rob scanned Mike's face as if he was searching for symptoms of rabid superstition and banjo playing. Mike had a strange out-of-body feeling about all this. He was taking something seriously that he didn't actually believe. He wasn't even sure that was psychologically possible, but here he was, doing just that because he trusted his father. They'd brought handguns, stun guns, body armour, short-range radios, and even ballistic helmets. As Rob had pointed out, whatever else Ian Dunlop turned out to be, he was probably armed and scared, and that overrode any other complications.

All they had to do was observe. The chance of anything happening that required their intervention was near zero. Mike went to get coffees from the galley and started refilling the machine. Rob wandered up behind him and leaned against the door frame.

"Have you thought what you're going to do when you're a family man?" Rob asked.

"Is this about the job, or diapers?"

"You'll need to be home more."

"You're right."

"Don't worry about me." Rob knew his every thought. "I can take all the yacht gigs."

"Am I that transparent?"

"Yes."

"I don't want you to think that I pick up and drop people when it suits me."

"Yeah, but you're a big boy now, and you've got a life."

"You know you could retire tomorrow. I could fix all that for you."

"No. I need to work. For the same reasons you do."

Mike said the next thing that came into his head. "We could set up our own security company. We don't need Esselby to do something meaningful. Hell, look at all the companies and consultants who trained me."

Rob squatted to open the fridge and gestured with carton. "You could always *buy* a PSC. Your family picks up companies like pints of milk. 'Ooh, we better get an extra one, just in case, 'cos it's the weekend.'"

"I'll put in the capital. But it'll still be a partnership." Mike was only spitballing, but it was making more sense with every second he thought about it. "Equal shares."

"I'd be okay working *for* you. Really."

"You're my buddy. Not the help."

"Okay, dig out that gold-plated address book, then. You must have made some interesting mates at Oxford. Some of them might be defence ministers by now. Or tinpot dictators."

"Dad thought that when I was President, I could just call up some despot and say 'Hey, Binky, old man, remember our undergrad high jinks? How about not invading your neighbour, just for old time's sake?' And I'd save the world."

"Seriously?"

"I've told you that before, haven't I?"

"Not that he made you go to Oxford so you'd have some dodgy statesmen on your speed dial and save the world, no."

"I'm being glib. He just wanted me to have an international perspective. Not some America-fuck-yeah attitude. The big picture."

"Zombie, it doesn't exist. There's no such thing as the world. Just individuals. And they don't all want the same saving."

"You would have been really scary with an expensive education, you know that?"

Rob squeezed past Mike and took over the coffee, feigning annoyance. "I've never known anyone dick around this long brewing two bloody wets. You'd have made a shit president. The country would be at DEFCON Three and you'd still be pissing around with the coffee machine."

He was back to merciless slagging, so he must have been pleased with the idea. Mike took the coffee back to the table, reassured. His world was tidy again. Now he could spend the rest of the flight focused on the immediate task: Ian Dunlop.

The options were finite. If they found a reclusive teenager instead of some drugs warlord or a heavily-armed cult, then the kid would either want to come with them or he wouldn't. They could try to persuade him, but they wouldn't need to snatch him unless he was in immediate danger.

It was only when Mike played the thought back that he realised how feeble it sounded. He knew how certain agencies worked.

They wouldn't think twice about assassinating inconvenient people, let alone kidnapping them. It was the line between being a soldier and some other creature entirely. He wondered what it would take to make him into one of them.

Rob leaned across him to take one of the maps. "You okay, Zombie?"

"Just over-thinking it."

"It'll be fine. We'll know what to do."

Rob gripped his shoulder and gave it a quick shake. Mike could imagine him talking fierce sense to young Marines under fire. It did the trick. Rob could make him believe anything. He was absolute certainty on two legs, able to instil the same resolve into those around him. Yes, Mike would know what to do when the time came. It would distil itself into something immediate and uncomplicated, and his training would kick in. He put on his ballistic vest and started getting focused.

They landed near the Idaho-Washington border and found the car waiting. It was a suitably anonymous silver-grey Toyota SUV from the fleet of a local firm that was somewhere in the complex maze of Brayne-owned companies. Mike's first task was to plug a GPS blocker into the lighter socket to cover their tracks, just in case the worst happened and the car's route became a jigsaw puzzle piece to compromise them. The zapper knocked out the on-board satnav as well. Rob loaded the bags.

"You can drive the first leg, mate." He settled into the passenger seat and placed a selection of snacks at strategic points in the dashboard for quick access. "I promise I won't freak out."

"You raided the galley."

"Yeah, to avoid getting picked up by CCTV at petrol stations."

"That's pretty paranoid."

"I'm not the one who brought the GPS zapper."

"I didn't say it was a bad thing, did I?"

"Okay. Phones off. Batteries out. Deniability shields on."

"Roger that. We're not here."

"I can't even see you, mate. Whoever you are." Rob gave him a sideways look. "It's an urban myth about phone batteries, right?"

"Not if the software's been infected."

"Fuck me. I hate this modern world."

Apart from getting picked up by traffic cameras, they were now as invisible as they'd ever be. Mike kept an eye open for suspicious vehicles, not that he needed to with Rob in the car. For once, Rob didn't sing along with the radio.

They were now nearly two hours down the road, on schedule to reach Athel Ridge mid-afternoon. Rob opened a packet of cookies and started crunching while he checked directions with the offline satnav maps on his phone.

"Want some biccies?" he mumbled, holding out the packet.

"Sure." Mike grabbed a couple put them within reach on the dashboard. "You're quiet."

"My mouth's busy. Chat away if you like. I'll just nod and spit crumbs."

"I wonder how Mom and Dad are going to react if we adopt."

"They'll be doting grandparents. Your parents love you whether you breed more pedigree Braynes or not. They think you're a cross between Superman and Bertrand Russell."

"Why Bertrand Russell?"

"That's the only philosophy bloke I know. Apart from Camus. Did I pronounce that right?" Rob fidgeted, checking the mirrors. "Anyway, I've just spotted a problem."

Mike's gut flipped. He checked the rear-view. "Where?"

"No, a moral one. If Kinnery's really turned some kid into a freak, he ought to serve time for it. But he'd never be charged, would he? Because then everyone would know about the kid, and then *his* life would be shit."

"But Kinnery didn't manage it."

"Does that matter? He must have tried. Sick twat."

"It was only meant to be an enhancement for consenting spec ops personnel."

"Yeah? Superpowers should stay in the comics, mate."

Mike found it impossibly painful for a moment. He thought of surplus eggs and donor sperm and fertility clinics, and it was all far too close to home again. *What do they really do with ours?* He had to put that out of his mind. It wasn't helping.

"I used to love the Fantastic Four," he said, trying to distract himself with trivia. "Did you ever wonder what it'd be like if you could really do all that? Change shape. Be invisible. Fly."

Rob shrugged, straight-faced. "The costumes put me off, to be honest. Spandex always makes your dick look tiny. Even mine. Did you like Batman?"

"No. He's too messed up."

"What, a billionaire who's obsessed with saving the world, likes fighting, and has an ex-military English butler?" Rob started giggling. It was infectious. "You know that's what Brad calls us, don't you? Bruce and Alfred."

Mike found himself laughing against his will again. "The bastard never says it to my face."

"Anyway, if Kinnery was really, properly, paid-up-mad-professor mad, he'd have tried to cross humans with tigers, or give them lasers for eyes or something. Not squirt ink or change colour. Cuttlefish Man's a bit chad, if you ask me. Now, if he'd tried to cross a human with a giant squid, *that* would be something."

"They don't make mad scientists like they used to."

Rob fiddled with the radio to change stations. "Has your dad said where he's going to stash this Ian if he turns out to be real?"

"No, which kind of confirms he doesn't believe it. It just involves more people. He'd want to talk that through with me if he thought it was a possibility."

"Not if he wants to keep you deniable."

"Well, we'll know by the end of the day, won't we?"

"Christ, listen to us. We're talking ourselves into believing it." Rob let out a long theatrical sigh and went back to checking the map. "Time to do a dog leg, Zombie. Double back."

Mike looked for an exit and turned onto a quiet road to let Rob take the wheel for the next hour. It was a much more tortuous route than they'd planned, with five or six detours to shake off people who weren't even there. Mike figured that if he'd abandoned this much of his sanity, then ditching the rest wasn't going to make things any worse. He made a note of motels along the road where they could stop over if this dragged on overnight for any reason.

Eventually the road signs started showing Athel Ridge. The landscape was hill-fringed pasture and fields purple with lavender crops. When they drove into Athel Ridge itself, it turned out to be little more than a loose collection of stores, bars, and offices strung along the road. Most of the parked vehicles were pickups. It looked even smaller than Mike had expected.

"Cameras?" He needed to know where they were, just in case. "There's one facing the liquor store."

Rob switched off the radio. "Traffic cam at the crossroads."

"Post office, left."

They left Athel Ridge and turned off the main road to head into the hills. Only one other vehicle passed them before Mike spotted the turning to Dunlop Ranch. Rob slowed as he drove past it.

"That's it," he said. "Start looking for an observation point."

Mike craned his neck to see if he could pick out the ranch, checking the position against the map. Distant smoke curled above the tree line. If Kinnery's annotated map was right, that was coming from the neighbours' place.

Rob pulled off the road and parked under the trees. "There it is. But Kinnery didn't allow for the bloody trees being in leaf. Still, at least everything's more or less where he said it was."

Mike scanned with the binoculars and picked up part of a roof. They couldn't carry out surveillance from here. The only way they were going to be able to see anything was to head back down the road and turn into the ranch. Kinnery had said the front of the house was visible from tree cover somewhere along the track.

Rob held out his hand for the binoculars and got out of the SUV. "Okay, let's move in closer and hope Doc Frankenstein didn't forget to tell us Maggie had security cameras." He leaned on the hood to steady his grip. "If anyone challenges us, we say we don't know it's private property and we've stopped for pee break."

"I could use one now."

"And if we don't see any activity, I'll go and knock on the door."

Mike stood twisting his lucky watch around his wrist. He was going to need it today. "Maybe I should do that."

"No, I'm lovable paternal Rob. You sound too posh."

"But if this kid watches a lot of movies, he probably thinks all English are bad guys."

"Yeah, you really should be over your national trauma by now. I'll just explain to him that we only wanted to keep Canada."

It was just a kid up there with a shotgun and some greyhounds, not Mossad. After taking a furtive leak in the undergrowth, Mike got back into the passenger seat and Rob retraced their route. The speed limit sign just before the turning loomed into view.

"Thirty seconds to abort this, Zombie."

Mike couldn't pull the plug now. "Go. Hang a right."

"Starboard ninety. Wheel on."

Rob turned without indicating and drove slowly up the track until a blur of brick-red and white began to show through a screen of trees. Mike tapped the dashboard. Rob steered off into the cover of some birches and came to halt. They could see the ranch now, a two-storey painted timber building with dormer windows and a full-width porch.

"Christ," Rob muttered. "We're storming the Little House on the bloody Prairie."

Mike took out his wallet and put a hundred dollar bill in one of the cup-holders on the dashboard. "A hundred says it's Kinnery's wayward son, rejecting his father's freaky science to join a tree-hugging commune."

Rob fumbled in his jacket and shoved a hundred next to Mike's. "A teen computer nerd who's hacked into some blackmail material or industrial secret and he's holding it to ransom. I mean, why else leak it himself?"

"I think I can see a pickup. Wait one while I take a look."

Mike got out and picked his way from tree to tree to get a better view. He didn't have to move far before he knew they weren't dealing with a pro. Maggie Dunlop might have been good at staying off the grid, but she'd obviously thought in terms of obscuring the ranch from view, not stopping ground assaults. Trees and bushes provided cover within fifty meters of the house, and there was plenty of dead ground. Even the exposed areas had outbuildings and other structures that would shorten the distance to short sprints between cover.

The old white pickup was parked out front in the shade of a tree. That would be useful cover too. If Mike got a chance, he'd remove the plug leads to stop any hasty exits.

Nothing was moving except birds in the branches. He held his breath and listened. There were no voices or sounds of human activity, and no sign of the dogs. He went back to sit on the SUV's bumper.

"Give it an hour," he said.

Rob slid out of the driver's seat and stood looking towards the ranch house. "Maybe he's already made a run for it."

"Well, the pickup's there."

"What if he's not alone? Or he's got another vehicle and he's pissed off in that?"

They waited in complete silence for forty minutes. In all that time, only one vehicle rumbled past on the road behind them. Rob was getting fidgety. He kept moving his hand to his holster, his rehearsal habit.

"Okay, let's go on the intel we have," he said. "Time for the Rennie charm offensive."

"So what are you going to say? 'Hi Ian, you don't know us, but we're private security contractors, we want to know who you're hiding from, and by the way, are you the hideous, unnatural fruit of a monstrous experiment that defied the laws of God and man?'"

Rob adjusted his ballistic vest, unmoved. "Just go around the back and make sure he hasn't got company. Radio check when you're in position, okay?"

Mike was beginning to wonder if he'd imagined his time in the Guard. He was pretty sure he'd breached compounds knowing they were booby-trapped, or that he'd probably be greeted by a burst of fire when the door crashed open. Today wasn't in that league. But this was his own country, and he realised this was probably as close as he'd come to knowing how a cop felt, where any of his neighbours could suddenly decide to finish him off.

Rob put in his radio earpiece and gave Mike a thumbs-up that left no room for failure.

"Let's get this done," he said. "We'll be out of here in an hour. Minus a werewolf."

DUNLOP RANCH, ATHEL RIDGE.

Oatie was restless. He followed Ian around the house, jerking his head up at every sound.

He wasn't even distracted by the contents of the pantry. He sat in the open doorway, watching Ian counting the cans and packets, occasionally standing up and turning around to gaze out into the kitchen with his ears pricked.

"She's not coming back, Oatie." Ian studied the instructions on the cans of dried milk and did a quick calculation. He'd have enough for ten weeks once he'd run out of the frozen supply. Well, that would motivate him to find the guts to take the truck out. "What's wrong?"

Maybe the dog was picking up on his own anxiety. Ian put down the milk and went to the living room window, half-expecting to see the sheriff's cruiser outside, but there was nothing there. He went back to the pantry and finished listing the supplies.

I could always phone the grocery store in town and ask if they deliver.

But that wasn't a plan. He couldn't do that forever. He stepped over Oatie and went upstairs again, lost for something productive to do without the animals to occupy his day, and increasingly conscious of the risk of being found.

What had Zoe done with his story? He didn't have an internet connection. She might have tossed the notes in the garbage. Kinnery hadn't pestered him, anyway. Maybe it had all died down and he'd been forgotten again.

He sat on the edge of Gran's bed, just a mattress and frame now that he'd burned the bedding, and studied his reflection in the mirror on her dressing table. He was pretty sure he hadn't changed again since he'd fled from the coffee shop.

Funny. I hated mirrors before. Now I can't stop looking.

Ian was more than alone. He could never make friends or get to know neighbours because sooner or later, he'd change. Joe might have thought his eyesight or his memory were playing tricks before, but now that he'd spent time with Ian, he'd really notice the changes. He'd know he wasn't imagining it.

It also meant Ian could never go near a woman.

The realisation became the lowest point of his life. It was a death sentence. He stared in the mirror, now able to see himself behind unfamiliar eyes, and tried to recapture the state he'd been in when he morphed in the coffee shop. He knew he'd been agitated, scared, and lost, but he couldn't switch on the emotion to order.

Of course I can't. I'd have to pump out adrenaline. That's what starts this, I'll bet. Maybe it takes a threat to trigger it. But how do I come up with the faces? Did Kinnery ever work that out?

Ian didn't plan to ask him. There might come a time when he'd be forced to beg him for help, but right now that was the last thing he wanted.

It was a nightmare. He couldn't control his own body, even if the morphing reflex had gotten him out of a tight spot. He felt like he was eight years old, a grown man, and an alien all at the same time. He wasn't sure how long he could live with this. He couldn't even let his body get on with the second-by-second business of living without wondering what was happening deep in his cells.

There's got to be the real me under all this. There has to be.

Oatie sat by the bedroom door, tail coiled around his haunches. Morphing had never seemed to bother the dogs. Maybe they trusted their noses when what they smelled didn't match what they saw. Ian held out his hand, but Oatie jumped up and looked down the stairs.

Whatever had distracted him, Ian couldn't hear it. The dog wandered off and Ian went back to the mirror, willing something to change while he watched himself. If he could see it in action, he might work out how to control it. Then he heard an engine rumbling. It was a car. Oatie always heard things long before he did.

Damn. Joe's come to check on me.

It didn't sound like Joe's truck, but who else would drop in? What if it was some official from the county wanting to check paperwork or something?

Ian went to the window and tried to get a look at the vehicle without being spotted. If he stood back far enough and off to one side, he could see the entire gravelled area down to the trees. Sunlight glinted off a silver SUV parked about twenty yards from the door. There was nobody in the driver's seat. Then the doorbell rang. Ian flinched.

If it wasn't Joe, it'd be someone he didn't want to see, maybe even Kinnery. But whoever was down there held their finger on the bell for a determined three or four seconds. Ian tried to remember if he'd locked the back door.

They'll go away if I just stay quiet.

What if this was one of the people Gran had warned him about? The bell rang again, followed by loud knocking. Ian heard a shout.

"Ian?" It was a man. "Ian? My name's Rob. We need to talk, mate. Can I come in?"

He wasn't just a stranger: he was a foreigner. He had an English accent, not the kind Ian was used to hearing on TV, but definitely English. And he'd used Ian's name. Only Joe and Kinnery knew he was here.

Ian did as Gran had taught him. He assumed the worst until proven otherwise. He wasn't going to let this Rob in, but the guy wouldn't give up.

"I'm not from the government, Ian." Rob held his finger on the bell again. "But you need to talk to someone, and it might as well be me."

Ian couldn't even phone Joe for help. He was on his own.

The knocking and ringing stopped and Ian heard a muffled

clunk like someone slamming a car door. He could see Rob now. He was standing on the gravel, looking from window to window. Ian estimated that he was in his late 30s: short dark hair, very upright, very fit. He looked casual in jeans and a zipped jacket, but his posture said something else entirely. It was hard to tell if he was armed. But the way he moved said that he was a physical kind of guy who wouldn't take no for an answer.

"Ian? You need somewhere safe to stay. Come and talk to me. I'm Rob. Rob Rennie."

Ian racked his brains for a movie that had played out something like this, anything that would give him a clue about dealing with this man. *Rob Rennie.* Why would he give Ian his name? Maybe he thought Gran had mentioned him, and that Ian should have known who he was.

Shit. If I don't answer, he'll kick the door down. Or even call for backup. I've got to face him.

He leaned over the banister to check if both hall doors were open, because the daylight from the kitchen would silhouette him through the glass at the front. At least one internal door was shut, though. He crept down the stairs, edged along the wall to the back room, and slipped through into the kitchen. The door was ajar. Oatie was gone.

Ian put on his baseball cap and went to the front door, aware of every sound around him. Should he go get his rifle? If Rob Rennie had been sent to grab him, he'd have a weapon and he'd use it if he thought Ian was armed. If he wanted DNA, Ian didn't have to be alive to give him what he'd come for.

His tried to control his breathing to stop the rising panic. If he was going to morph again, it would be now.

I've got to run. How close is the truck? Can I get past him?

There was no movement or shadow visible through the glass door panels. Ian finally opened the door and found Rob squatting a few yards along the porch, making a fuss of Oatie.

"Can I help you, sir?"

Rob straightened up. "Hi, mate. Sorry for banging the door down. Can we talk?"

He lowered his chin slightly as if he was looking under the peak of Ian's cap. Ian thought he'd morphed again, but Rob couldn't have known what he should have looked like anyway.

"You're British." Ian couldn't think of anything else to say. He felt like an idiot the moment he the words tumbled out. "Are you a cop? A reporter?"

"I'm English. And no, none of the above. I've been sent to look after you."

It was only a few yards to the truck. The silver car blocked the track, a short sprint away for Rob. Ian moved his hand slowly to his pocket to check for his keys. Rob braced. Ian froze.

Oh Christ, he thinks I'm going for a weapon. He's going for his.

Ian lowered his arm. "Why do I need looking after?"

If he went back inside and locked the door, Rob would probably go around the back, and Ian could cut through the cellar and get out through the crawlspace. He'd be in the truck and away while Rob was still searching the house.

"That reporter you spoke to," Rob said. "There's some stuff about you on the internet now, and that means you're probably going to get some unwelcome visitors fairly soon."

"Like you?"

"My job is to take you somewhere safe."

That answered the question about what Zoe had done with his story. It took Ian a couple of seconds to join up the dots. Who else knew about her? *Kinnery.* He felt like he was standing in rising water. It was raw fear. He struggled to keep it under control.

"Did Kinnery send you, sir?"

"Don't worry, mate. I don't work for him. Let's sort out your problem."

Ian couldn't move. Rob *knew*, then. He knew Ian could morph. It was an odd relief to find someone who'd talk to him like a regular guy despite knowing what he was. Rob didn't look disgusted or afraid. He just seemed in a hurry. He held his arms away from his sides.

"I'm not going to hurt you," he said.

Ian tried to buy time. *Step back slowly. Close the door. Lock it, like I'm holing up in here.* Did Rob have anyone with him? He kept saying *I*, not *we.*

"I don't want to see Kinnery," Ian said.

"I know, but I still need to get you away from here."

Ian now had no idea who was on his side and who wasn't. The answer was probably nobody.

Run, Ian. Run.

"I'll be fine here, sir." Ian backed away through the open door.

"But thank you anyway."

He closed the door and locked it. Rob would hear the key turn. Now Ian had seconds to get clear. The grab bag in the hall was too big to drag through the crawl space without slowing him down, so he'd have to leave it. As he opened the cellar door, he almost skidded down the steps in his headlong rush and aimed for the crack of light around the edge of the shutters. If he crawled out through the bushes at the side of the house, nobody would see him until he was a few strides from the truck.

Splinters dug into his hands as he eased the shutters open. He crawled like a frantic animal through the dust and sticky webs and out into bushes that tore his skin, then ran for the truck and jerked the door open. He managed to jam the key into the ignition. There was no sign of Rob.

But the damn truck wouldn't start. It didn't even turn over. It just kept clicking.

Gran's truck. Try Gran's truck.

Ian prayed its battery wasn't flat. He tumbled out of the driver's seat and ran for the back of the barn, not daring to look over his shoulder as he swung open the doors and climbed into the blue pickup. It fired first time. As he backed out, he clipped the door frame, but now he was clear.

How much gas in the tank?

How much cash do I have on me?

Where the hell am I going?

He realised he'd left the cell phone in the kitchen out of habit. He had a few bucks in his back pocket, but the only place he could think of going was Athel Ridge. There'd be people around, people who didn't know him or what he usually looked like, and Rob wouldn't try to kidnap him or shoot him in front of witnesses.

Ian slammed his foot on the gas and swerved around the Toyota to get onto the track. Suddenly there was a man ahead of him to his left, sprinting out of the trees to intercept, a blonde guy in jeans.

Ian's instinct took over. The man stopped dead in the middle of the track, boots planted, and Ian saw his hands come up. His only coherent thought was *gun.* He drove straight at the guy.

Oh God. I'm dead. Or he is.

Ian shut his eyes for a second, waiting for the thump of body against windshield, but the truck careered down the track. He hadn't hit anything.

Movement in the rear-view mirror caught his eye. The silver SUV was now on his tail. The pickup's tyres squealed as he turned hard onto the road and almost lost control but he recovered from the skid and put his foot on the gas.

So much for following Gran's emergency drill, then. His cash, his phone, and everything he needed to escape were still at the ranch, and all he had was half a tank of gas and no plan beyond seeking refuge in Athel Ridge.

It was never like that in the movies.

TEN MILES OUTSIDE ATHEL RIDGE, WASHINGTON.

A car chase wasn't the best time to remember a road safety ad, but Rob couldn't get the bloody line out of his head.

'Only a fool
Breaks the two second rule.'

It was an old public information campaign, and despite its total absence of slickness it had lodged forever in Rob's memory. Well, he was two seconds behind Ian's blue pickup as its tail swung out on corners, and that still felt way too close. The winding road was mostly downhill and punctuated by warning signs about maximum speed on bends, all of which Ian seemed to ignore. What did cops do when a chase was too risky? They just followed and waited. Rob had seen it on those tedious reality TV shows.

And whatever happened to 'we won't force him'?

"Is he drunk?" This wasn't much like the defensive driving course he'd done. Maybe he should have tried overtaking the little bastard and slammed on the brakes while they were still on a deserted road. "He's all over the place."

Mike still had the other pickup's plug leads in his hand, swishing them like a fly whisk. He was angry. "He's not used to fast driving."

"No shit."

"I should have checked the barn. I'm sorry."

"And I should have taken him down as soon as I saw him."

"We said no kidnapping, remember?"

"So what are we doing now? High speed observation?"

"You want to abort?"

"No. I bloody well want to know who he is."

"Where did he exit? A storm shelter or something? Kinnery

never mentioned that."

"He didn't mention the second truck, either."

Mike shook his head. "Christ, he really is just a kid."

"The fuck he is," Rob said. "He nearly ran you down."

"He probably thought I'd drawn a weapon. I just put my hands up to make him stop."

"He can't outrun us. First bloke to stop for petrol loses."

Mike winced as the pickup skidded around the next bend. Kinnery had said Ian was highly intelligent, so maybe he had a plan after all. For all Rob knew, whatever Kinnery or Leo really wanted was still in the ranch house and someone else had already moved in to grab it. But when you didn't have reliable intel, and the briefing sounded like a load of bollocks, you had to pick a fixed point and go for it. Ian was shit-scared and running. Rob was going to stop him. It was the only option.

They were going to hit the main road to Athel Ridge in minutes. Maybe Ian would misjudge the turn or stop for oncoming traffic. The rapid flash of brake lights said he really wasn't confident on bends, and the pickup was probably older than he was. That wasn't a good combination.

"Junction," Mike said.

Rob could see the warning sign. The pickup's brake lights didn't come on. He prepped for Ian to slam on the brakes at the last second and turn either way.

Please let there be some vehicles coming. Slow him down.

"Shall I tail-end him?"

"No." Mike unfastened his seat belt and set off the warning chime. "As soon as he stops, I'm out, and I take him."

"Then what, seeing as he'll drive right over you?"

"I'll be fine. It's all about timing."

The pickup didn't brake soon enough for the junction and screeched to a halt. It was positioned to turn left, but then it whipped right towards Athel Ridge in a brief haze of smoking, squealing tyres. Rob pulled out and shaved within feet of an oncoming truck. Angry horns blared. Mike didn't say a word for a hundred yards.

"Shouldn't have taken your seatbelt off," Rob said.

When Mike finally spoke, it came out in a rush like he'd been holding his breath. "What would you do if you were being chased by someone you couldn't flatten, hide from, or outrun?"

"Get help," Rob said. "Head for a building. Pub. Police station. Somewhere they couldn't touch me."

"You think Ian's worked that out?"

"Christ knows." Rob kept his eyes fixed on the pickup's tailgate. Ian seemed to have maxed out at sixty-five, but then slowed to overtake a tractor. Rob stuck hard on his tail. Did they have traffic drones out here yet? Jesus, that was all they needed. They were now only a few miles from town. "If he keeps going straight, I'd say yes. Where's the next turning?"

"Half a mile on the right." Mike gestured, reading from his phone. "Straight into more farmland. I wouldn't isolate myself like that. It's asking to get rammed or shot."

"I wonder if he's got a phone."

"If he has, he hasn't called for backup. Or it's running late."

"Okay, assuming he carries on through Athel Ridge, what have we got? Where's he going to stop?"

Mike paused, one hand clenched around the handgrip above the door. "First left — repair shop. Houses beyond that. First right — post office. Crossroads — on the right, a parking lot for a farm supplies store, and the sheriff's office. Left — road heading east to Fulton. More stores and bars, then we're out of town again, and it's ten miles to the Wal-Mart."

"Sheriff?" Rob asked.

"Would he risk getting the attention of the law?"

"We should have asked Kinnery a lot more questions."

"Doesn't matter now. We'll know what the kid's doing in a couple of minutes."

Rob could see more vehicles coming the other way. With any luck they were about to hit the Athel Ridge version of a traffic jam. There was a truck in front, a big scarlet and chrome slab that looked the size of a container ship, and a couple of cars between the truck and the pickup. The brake lights came on. Rob was right behind Ian's truck, close enough to see the little sod checking his rear-view mirror.

"If we stop at the lights," Mike said, "I'm going for it."

"What, drag him out?"

"Okay, you can rear-end him. I'll jump out and open his door, concerned passenger and all that, really sorry, etcetera etcetera. Don't worry about damaging this crate."

"I'm glad you're mindlessly rich."

The line of traffic rolled on, slow but not slow enough for Mike to do anything. Rob almost rammed the pickup anyway, just to make certain, but he wasn't sure he could pull it off in a way that wouldn't look conspicuously deliberate if he was caught on camera.

"Have you memorised what he's wearing and what he looks like?" Mike asked. "I took a picture while you were talking to him, but it wasn't full face."

"Don't start, Zombie. He's not a fucking shape-shifter, okay?"

"If he makes a run for it and we lose eyes on, we can't risk bundling the wrong kid into the car."

So it really was a kidnap now. *Fine.* "Okay. Blue cap, beige and green check shirt, jeans, brown boots. Darkish brown hair, I think, but I can't remember the eye colour. Dark-*ish.* Might be dark blue, might be hazel."

Rob watched the silhouette of Ian's head in the truck's rear window, trying to work out which way the kid was looking. The peak of the cap gave it away. He was checking to both sides as they reached the centre of town. He was either preparing to pull out and risk overtaking the truck, or deciding where to turn off.

The lights at the intersection were green. Ian's pickup swung right.

Rob followed, locked on to the target now and determined to get a result. The pickup shot down the road. Instead of carrying on to the sheriff's office, it turned into the car park and pulled into a space right outside the entrance to the feed store, nose in.

That was Rob's cue. He stopped behind it, blocking it in. Ian jumped from of the cab and ran into the store.

Mike slid out. "Stay on the radio."

"I'm going around the back," Rob said. "There has to be a loading bay or a fire exit."

Rob left the SUV locked with the hazard lights flashing and made his way along the side of the store, passing a couple of blokes in overalls. Unless Kinnery had been totally wrong about Ian's social circle and the kid was chummy with someone in the shop, he'd have to stay put and wait it out, or approach someone and ask for help.

There was a loading bay at the rear with a chain link security fence and gates. Rob looked around, trying to work out where Ian could exit. Then his radio earpiece popped. He took out his phone to cover the fact he'd look more suspicious talking to himself and eyeing up the rear of a store.

"He's wandering around the clothing section." Mike's voice was a whisper backed by what sounded like a radio playing in the background. "He's clocked me."

"Not approaching any of the staff?"

"No."

"Is the rear exit signposted?"

"Fire exit." Mike broke off and Rob heard shuffling noises. Mike was moving around. "I'm blocking."

"He's got to make a move. He can't stand there until the store closes. He knows we won't grab him there with security cams around."

"Ten yards away. Unobstructed view."

"He knows we're here. Why doesn't he approach a salesman?"

"Scared." There was more rustling. "Looking at the cashier's desk."

"Here we go."

"No. Changed his mind. Big step for him, obviously."

Rob trotted down the access road at the back and looked to see where Ian might run if he came out that way. Maybe it would be easier if Mike let the kid bolt.

"Mike, you still blocking the rear access?"

"Right in his path."

"Who's he watching?"

"Mainly the clerk. Clerk's looking. Coming across."

"Shit, he probably thinks the kid's shoplifting."

"Okay. I'm improvising. Get around the front and just go with it. I'm on transmit."

Rob jogged back to the front of the building, trying to interpret what he could hear. He was used to a conspicuous PRR headset mike that had to be placed right against his mouth, but they were relying on discreet collar mikes today. Snatches of conversation were Rob's only clue to what he'd be expected to do when he reached the doors.

"*Can I help you?*"

Ian's voice drifted in. "*Just looking.*" Then there was more rustling. Rob got to the doors, heard Mike talking, and realised what was coming next.

"*It's okay, sir, I've got this covered. Ian, you're going to have to come with me —*"

"I haven't done anything. Get off."

"Leave him to me, sir. He's okay. He's not violent."

Mike seemed to be posing as a private detective or a social worker, explaining something about Ian needing his medication. He'd be coming out the front with the kid, then. Shit, this was too visible. They needed to get out fast. Rob debated whether to start the car, but if Ian managed to get away from Mike, he'd have to grab him. He got ready to body-check Ian rugby-style. Rob had no intention of holding back this time.

He peered past the display of tool parts and racks of padded work shirts near the entrance. Then one of the doors swung open and Ian came running out. Rob stepped forward, heavier and harder, an instant brick wall. He took the impact. Ian staggered. Rob reached out to grab him by the collar and looked him in the eye.

"Jesus *Christ.*"

This wasn't the kid he'd talked to on the porch. It just wasn't.

He was dressed the same, but the face was different, the hair was different — *he* was different. Rob had grabbed the wrong bloke. Working clothes all looked the same.

Rob's instinct was to let go. "Sorry — "

"Get off me, you asshole." But the voice was the same. "Leave me alone."

Oh shit, it's Ian. It's him. It's real. He's changed.

For a second everything froze, like the moment on patrol when an Afghan soldier a few yards ahead of Rob stepped on an IED. The instant became a narrow tunnel of infinite, awful detail.

Mike jumped into the driver's seat and Rob's drill kicked in. He shoved Ian into the back of the Toyota, pushing his head down to avoid the roof, and pinned him on the seat as Mike drove off.

For no good reason, Rob was pleased with himself. The manoeuvre was a perfect body cover and remove, bodyguard style. That was reassuring. He was shocked shitless, but he was still functioning.

But it's true. Oh my God. It's all bloody true.

All he could see was Ian's terrified expression. Rob knew what he was looking at, but he still didn't believe it.

Mike glanced over his shoulder. "Rob, is it just me? Can you *see* that?"

"Shit. Yes."

"And?"

"You *saw* him. You followed him." Rob looked up. Mike was heading out of town again. "Jesus Christ."

Ian struggled, gasping. The blood had drained from his face. Rob was scared to loosen his grip in case the kid evaporated and he had nothing to prove that he hadn't imagined the whole thing. No, Ian wasn't drained of colour; he'd changed again. He was paler. His hair was lighter. His eyes were different. And it had taken *seconds*. Rob nearly shat himself.

"You did it again," he said.

"What are you, CIA? DoD?" Ian looked like a terror-stricken animal, eyes staring, but he stood his ground. "Gran warned me what you bastards do. Look what you did to *me*."

Mike cut in. "Ian? Listen to me, Ian. We're not the government and we're not going to hurt you. We didn't believe you were real. I'm sorry. I know we've scared the crap out of you, but it's a shock for us, too."

"You're not one of Kinnery's students, are you?" Rob was surprised that he could form a question. Training was a powerful anchor. "Did he pay you to have an injection or something?"

Ian's frown was instant and genuine. "No. I'm home-schooled. And I don't know what you're talking about."

"You've always been like this, then."

"Am I crazy?" Ian gave him a really weird look that overrode the wide-eyed panic for a moment. "Am I hallucinating all this?"

"Well, if you are, so am I," Rob said.

Mike stopped the car and looked back between the seats again. He seemed to be struggling for something sane to say. It took him a few moments.

"Ian, we didn't believe Kinnery could give you the ability to change how you look," Mike said. He sounded as if he'd hand-picked every word. There was no mention of shape-shifting or freaks. His tone had softened, like he was talking to someone who'd just been told they had months to live and was trying to dress it up with weasel words like *not a good outcome*. "We know what's happened to you. Your gran was right. There really are people after you, but that's not us. Will you just hear us out?"

Rob was getting cramp in his calves from bracing against the door to hold Ian down. His brain kept telling him that he couldn't possibly be seeing what he thought he could see, and that a rational explanation would occur to him soon. The world would revert to normal with companies screwing each other over and everyone lying like a pusser's watch, and there would be absolutely no shape-shifters.

He hoped the feed store hadn't called the sheriff. He also hoped their security cameras hadn't picked up any clear facial images, although Ian still had his cap jammed on his head despite the scuffle.

Ian the shape-shifter. Ian the fucking shape-shifter. Oh my God.

Ian stopped struggling, but he was still gulping air as if he'd run for miles. Rob slackened off to let him breathe.

"What are you going to do with me?"

Mike looked at him for a long time, a good ten seconds. "Why don't we go back to the ranch and talk? No agencies, no police, no Kinnery. If I go pick up your truck, will you promise not to give Rob any trouble? You really need someone on your side right now, and we're probably all there is."

Ian had tensed every muscle. Rob felt him relax a bit. Christ, the kid could have had a knife. Rob hadn't checked. That was sloppy.

"Okay," Ian said.

"Where are your keys?"

"Still in the truck."

"It's okay. I'm Mike, by the way. I'm sorry I treated you like a psychiatric patient in there."

Ian looked at him, then drew back his head a bit to focus on Rob. "So who are you if you're not working for Kinnery?"

"Private security contractors," Rob said.

"Mercenaries?"

"Look, son, if you don't call us mercenaries, we won't call you a werewolf, okay?" It came out harsher than Rob intended. He did his best reassuring smile to take the sting out of it. "We served our countries. We still do."

"Soldiers, then."

Perfect. Gotcha. Rob remembered what Kinnery had said about Ian's fascination with everything military. "Yeah. We'll tell you all about it. Now, are you carrying anything sharp or nasty?" He caught Mike's eye for a moment. *Come on, Zombie. Scared people do bloody stupid things.* "If I'm going to drive you back on my own, I'd rather not have to shoot you."

Ian squirmed into an upright position. "Hunting knife."

"Mind giving it to me until we get back?"

"Okay." It was hard to tell if Ian had given in or if he was biding his time. "I sort of guessed you were armed."

"That's because people try to shoot us. Don't they, Zombie? You'll have to show him your scar."

Mike drove back into Athel Ridge and stopped a block from the store to walk back to the car park. Ian sat in the back of the Toyota, silent, head lowered, while Rob moved up front and watched the rear-view mirror, waiting for Mike's radio signal.

"They don't know you around here, do they?" Rob asked.

"No," Ian said. "How could they?"

Mike's voice interrupted in his earpiece. "Right behind you, Rob."

Now that the initial shock had worn off, Rob's brain was clogging with what-ifs and questions that he really wanted to ask Ian. Suddenly he felt sorry for the poor little sod. How was he ever going to have a normal life? Kinnery deserved a serious kicking. Rob liked the idea of giving it to him. He drove north, checking that Mike was still following.

"I really shocked you, didn't I?" Ian said at last. "Gran was right."

Rob wondered whether to ask what he meant, but thought better of it. "Yeah," he said. "Great party trick, though."

When Rob had set out that morning, he'd thought that finding Ian Dunlop would be the end of the job, and then he and Mike would get on with their plans and forget him. But it wasn't going to be quite that simple.

They'd found a shape-shifter, a real live one. All bets were off.

SIX

Stop crying, Ian. It's just a graze. Look at the TV — look at this guy climbing a mountain. See him? He's a soldier. He hasn't got any legs. A bomb blew him up. He has to use metal ones now, but he still climbs mountains and runs races. He didn't cry, and I bet it hurt him a lot more than a grazed knee.

Maggie Dunlop, to seven-year-old Ian, on taking it like a man.

DUNLOP RANCH, ATHEL RIDGE: JULY.

The real world had come crashing in on Ian with a force he'd never imagined.

He sat in the living room, blinds drawn, ashamed of himself for not fighting back. Rob was talking with Mike in the hall. Ian caught snatches of the conversation, which seemed to be about not telling someone until they knew more.

"You're going to have to call the crew, at least." That was Rob. His accent was deceptively soft for a scary guy. "But I need to see it again."

Mike sounded New England, very upper class, with something else in the mix. "Look, I saw it too. You think this is the power of suggestion? Mass hysteria? We're not medieval peasants."

"I don't think your dad knows what he's let himself in for."

Ah, his dad. Who was Mike's father? Was he Kinnery's son?

Was Kinnery trying to clear up the mess he'd made?

They stopped talking and came back into the living room. Mike leaned against the door frame while Rob sat on the sofa. For a moment, Ian thought Rob was staring him out, but then it dawned on him that Rob was waiting to see him morph again.

I can see it on his face. Now he thinks he's *crazy. He doesn't believe what he saw. He's as scared as I was.*

And that's how everyone's going to look at me.

"Sorry about the rough stuff, mate," Rob said at last. "Are you all right?"

"A bit bruised."

Mike joined in the staring. "I take it you don't drive in traffic often."

"No," Ian said. "Only in emergencies."

"Never mind. It took balls to try."

Ian was worried that he might piss his pants and look like an idiot. These guys weren't like Joe or Kinnery. He'd never had close physical contact with another man before, let alone been knocked flat by someone who was so strong that it hurt. Rob and Mike were another species, muscular and intimidating, and Ian wasn't prepared for how that made him feel: scared, envious, and aggressive, but somehow relieved. They made some awful sense of the world.

"You don't know what to do with me, do you?" Ian said. "Who's your dad? Is it Kinnery?"

"God, no." Mike shook his head. "My father's a politician."

"Forget Kinnery. He can't touch you now." Rob studied Ian's face. "We need to get you out of here. Thanks to Zoe what's-her-face blabbing it all over the internet."

"Gran said it was my insurance."

"Well, it got us here, so maybe she was right."

Mike's brow creased a little. "We're sorry about your gran. You must miss her."

"She wasn't my gran. Not biologically."

"Does that matter?"

"She lied to me. Everyone lies to me. How do I know you're not lying too?" *I'm not mad, Gran. Why did you let me think I was? Didn't you realise it'd end like this anyway?* "I thought I was crazy. But I'm not, am I?"

Mike shook his head. "No, you're not, buddy. It's real. I can understand why you're angry."

"Yeah, we get lied to all the time, so we're not going to lie to you," Rob said. He didn't blink much. "Nobody except nutters believes a word that web site says, but the company that worked on your project probably does. You can either wait here for them to track you down, or come with us. We're your safest bet."

Ian thought it sounded like he had a choice. It was confusing. He had good reason to be scared of these guys, but they also seemed to be trying hard to put him at ease. Mike looked around the room, then stepped back to check up and down the hall.

"There's not a single mirror or reflective surface in this place," he said. "Except the windows."

Ian wondered why he'd spotted that. "Gran tried to make sure I didn't have to see my reflection. Why did you notice?"

"Because we're soldiers. When we clear a building, we check for reflections that could get us killed. Ours or the enemy's."

Soldiers had rules. They had *discipline*. Ian had seen it in the movies. Mike and Rob could have shot him and nobody would have known or cared — well, maybe Joe would have — but they were talking like they were taking him seriously. They'd be just like his great-grandfather, decent guys with a sense of honour who cared about their buddies.

But he wasn't my great-grandfather, either.

Mike lined up his cell phone and took a photo. "There. If you change again, I've got another picture to compare you with. You can't control this, can you?"

"I don't know how." Ian felt like a child again, helpless and pathetic. He wanted Gran to be here. "If I did, I'd stop it."

"Well, now that you know what it is, maybe you can learn."

It was the first encouraging thing anyone had said about his morphing. Mike squatted next to his chair and looked him in the eye.

"I'm giving you my word, Ian." He had intense blue eyes, lighter than Rob's. He seemed really earnest. "I won't let anyone take you or do anything to you against your will. I guarantee that. You don't have to come with us, but if you do, you can stay with me and my wife while we work out how to fix things. You can bring your dog if you like."

Rob made a quick huffing sound as if he didn't approve. "You going to ask her first?"

"I don't recall you standing around debating when I was in the shit, buddy," Mike said. "There's nowhere else I'm willing to take him. I'm responsible for his safety now."

The two of them stared at each other for a couple of seconds. Ian wasn't sure if it was a stand-off or some silent question between them. He considered his choices. If he said no, what was he going to do? He'd be stranded here, waiting for someone else to track him down and knock on the door, someone who probably wouldn't be so concerned about his welfare. And he couldn't get away from Mike and Rob anyway. They wouldn't make the same mistake twice.

I have to trust somebody. I can't hide forever.

"If I come with you," Ian said, "can I bring some of my stuff? Not that I'm saying I will."

"Sure." Mike stood up and studied the CDs, tapes, and DVDs lined up on the bookshelves. He stepped over a couple of boxes. "You look like you're moving out anyway."

"Gran wanted me to burn all her stuff."

Mike carried on looking at the DVDs. "So you watch a lot of movies. Let's see. War movies. Explorers. Biopics. No horror. No alien invasions. What's your favourite?"

"*Ice Cold In Alex*," Ian said. He couldn't think straight now that Mike had asked. "*Scott of the Antarctic.*"

"All stiff upper lip drama, huh?" Mike slid out another plastic case and handed it to Rob, who gazed wistfully at it. "*The Cruel Sea.*"

"Now that was a great film," Rob said. "You like military stuff, then."

"I wanted to join the Army. Fat chance."

Mike picked up the photo of David Dunlop. "Who's this gentleman with the Huey?"

"I thought he was my great-grandfather. Gran's dad."

"Well, blood relative or not, he certainly shaped your life, didn't he?" Mike folded the stand flat against the back of the photo and handed it to Ian as if he expected him to start packing. "We'll show you our pictures. Rob's got some awesome stuff. He was a Royal Marine. I started in the National Guard. We've just come back from Nazani."

For the first time in his life, Ian was having a conversation about morphing, a real, honest *conversation.* It seemed incredibly important. It made it real. And that made all the terrible, uncomfortable things that ate at him somehow reasonable. He wasn't wrong to feel betrayed, scared, or angry. He just needed to find his way out of this tailspin.

"So are you going to come with us? We won't force you." Mike went to the window and tweaked the slats of the blinds apart with his thumb and forefinger. "Where are all your animals?"

Ian's gut was still telling him to run and hide, but another part of him wanted to fit in with these guys and be accepted by them.

"Joe's taking care of them for me. Can I tell him where I'm going?"

"He doesn't know that you change, does he?"

"No. And he won't recognise me now. I'll have to phone him."

"A cap and a pair of sunglasses work wonders."

"I know." Ian had come down from the terrifying adrenaline high and now he felt shaky. He realised he'd slipped from *maybe* to *definite*. "How much stuff can I bring?"

"As much as you can get in the car."

"Where are we going?"

"Maine," Mike said.

"That'll take days."

Rob laughed. "Welcome to Zombie's world, son. He's got a his own private jet."

Ian couldn't tell if Rob was joking. Now that he had some time to think about leaving, not just snatching the grab bag in the hall and running for his life — and that hadn't worked out, had it? — he wasn't sure what mattered to him. He had to collect all the cash he'd stashed around the place, though. He'd need that.

Mike wandered in and out of the kitchen, looking at the walls as if he was thinking of buying the place. "Can I use your cell, please? It's unregistered, isn't it? I need to get a message to my pilot. If I use my own phone, there'll be a record that links me to this location."

Ian nodded and pointed at the counter. "Sure. I'll start packing." Damn, he'd need to collect the cash in the tool locker, too. "I need to get something from the barn first."

Rob stood up. "Come on, then. I hope you're not going to make a run for it."

"I promised," Ian said. "So I won't."

Rob waited at the barn door while Ian unlocked the tool cabinet and slipped the rolls of notes inside his shirt. There was David Dunlop's old woodworking chisel, too. He couldn't leave that any more than he could leave the photo. He carried it out by the blade, just in case Rob thought he was going to stab him with it.

"Great-Grandad's," he said. "Well, whoever he was."

"Do you always keep your savings in the barn?"

"In case the ranch burns down. Or I have to get away fast."

"You'd be right at home in Essex."

Ian didn't know what that meant. Rob took a small packet of cookies out of his pocket and offered it to him as they walked back to the house.

"I've got a son about your age," Rob said. "He's at university. Lots of friends, likes a beer or two, plays football, dates girls. You should be doing all that. Not hiding."

Ian shrugged. That stuff was theoretical, things that he knew existed but didn't think were possible for him, like luxury yachts or being an astronaut. Dating girls was still the most distant prospect of all and the most depressing.

"What am I going to say to Joe?"

"I can make the call for you."

"He'll want to hear it from me, or he'll think you're social services coming to take me away."

Rob chuckled. "Yeah, people always mistake me for a social worker. Look, tell him some friends of your gran's old mate got in touch and you're going to stay with them for a while until you've sorted yourself out. It's almost completely true."

"Which bit isn't?"

"I wouldn't call Kinnery a friend."

"But he knows you're here, yeah?"

"He asked Mike's dad for help to hide you, so we agreed to pick you up." Rob held his hand out for the chisel and examined it. "I'm surprised you're willing to trust us. You were ready to punch the shit out of me earlier. Don't trust everybody, though, will you?"

Ian didn't like the thought of a politician being involved. Gran said they were as bad as any government agency and most of them were corrupt assholes on the take, but he didn't have any choice.

"Well, if you're CIA or something, and I try to get away, you'll shoot me, or worse," Ian said. "But if you're telling the truth, and I don't come with you, then I've lost a chance to be rescued. So going with you makes sense either way."

Rob laughed. "Good logic, son. You'll go far."

"But we're going now, aren't we? Tonight?"

"Ready when you are. We don't want to hang around either."

"Has Mike really got a jet?"

"Absolutely. It's his dad's. They're minted. I mean *megabucks* rich." Rob handed the chisel back to Ian. Maybe that was a test of trust. "Mike's a top bloke. A bit mad, straight as a die, and he'd give you the shirt off his back. Which in his case is a really good deal. Five hundred bucks a pop."

Ian still wasn't sure if he believed a word of that. But if gut instinct was worth anything, he felt safer with these two guys than anywhere else right now. They made him feel that things were somehow okay, and that if they weren't, they'd step in and fix them.

It was just after five in the afternoon. Ian stopped on the porch and looked out over the ranch, suddenly appalled at what he was going to do. He couldn't remember any other home. Now he was going to abandon it at a moment's notice.

But Gran had always said he'd need to run one day. Now was as good a time as any.

DUNLOP RANCH: TWO HOURS LATER.

What else could I do?

Mike stood staring at the shelf of tapes and DVDs. How was he going to break the news to Livvie? Where would he start, with the part about finding a real live shape-shifter, or the fact that he'd promised him that he could stay with them? He'd worked out a plan for every eventuality except one, that Ian Dunlop was exactly what Kinnery said he was.

And I'm really not imagining this. Wow.

Upstairs, Ian was still packing his bags. Mike tried to imagine what it felt like to be that isolated, too scared to even look in a mirror because you thought you were insane. Ian was a mess of problems. It was hard to decide which needed tackling first.

"Poor little sod." Rob walked up behind Mike and jangled some keys. "I've secured the firearms in the car, so we've just got to box up some books and DVDs. Maybe this Joe can take all the food before it goes off. Christ, this is really happening, isn't it?"

"That's what I keep telling myself."

"Kinnery needs garrotting. May I?"

"No, I call dibs on that. That's got to be one damaged kid."

"Actually, he seems pretty sane. And disciplined. Look how tidy this place is." Rob ran the back of his forefinger along the tightly packed DVD cases on the shelf like a pianist doing a glissade. "There it is. Maggie Dunlop's manual for being a real man. This is how she made up for Ian not having a male role model around. Take a look."

Mike looked along the shelves again. Rob had a point. These were more than just war movies. If they were Maggie's choices, then she was big on stoical self-sacrifice and the honourable, responsible, dignified hero with good manners. There wasn't a single macho splatter-fest in there. Did it matter where kids learned their moral lessons? It probably explained why Ian hadn't put up a fight about leaving with them. Soldiers looked familiar to him, a known quantity in a frightening situation.

"Yes, that makes sense." Mike paused to listen. Ian was still opening and closing closet doors upstairs. "This is turning into a can of worms. We can't take him to see a physician without exposing him. We can't take him to a shrink. And then there's getting him some photo ID. You can't take a leak without it."

"Yeah, you Septics do rely on that more than we do."

"I promised him he'd be safe."

"Who from, though?"

"If the changes are a random thing, he's no use to spook-kind. But that wouldn't stop them."

Rob did his bank-note gesture, rubbing his thumb and forefinger together. "I'd be more worried about KWA. Boffins love money too."

"But Ian's still invisible, if everything else Kinnery says is true. No school record, no friends, and no trace of him online."

"Yeah, well, I wouldn't believe that bastard if he told me I had a dick. And if Ian's that far off the radar, it's easy for them to make him disappear with no questions asked."

"Just like we're doing."

"I'm betting your dad didn't war-game this fully." Rob kept looking at his watch. "When are you going to call him?"

"I'll work that out when I hear how Livvie reacts."

"Just as well you've got all those bedrooms. You'll be sleeping on your own when we get back to Zombie Towers."

Problems could always be solved by lobbing dollars at someone or deploying lawyers. But Mike refused to delegate a moral dilemma. He was uniquely placed to save Ian in the same way that Rob had saved him, the right man in the right place at exactly the moment he was most needed. The clarity was like the first blast of a freezing shower. Mike didn't have the slightest doubt about this. He was sure that Livvie wouldn't either, not once she saw for herself what a terrible burden Kinnery had imposed on this kid and what the rest of his life might be like without someone to fight his corner.

"DNA," Rob said suddenly.

"What about it?"

"We'll never remove his DNA from this place without nuking it."

"Do we need to? KWA must already have records or tissue samples anyway. It's the live specimen they'll want."

"Granted, but it's a link in the chain if they're looking for him."

"They'd have to know about the place and then get access." *How the hell does Ian's hair change? Hair's not even live tissue.* Raw curiosity kept distracting Mike from the immediate problem. "Maybe Joe can keep an eye on the place. I'll hire a cleaning company."

"My, we're going to be busy boys, aren't we?"

"No, this is my problem. Not yours."

"Bollocks. I've got an adqual in handling teenage lads, remember."

Ian thudded down the stairs and dumped a couple of zipped holdalls in the hall. He'd razored his hair short, possibly to disguise the change of colour.

"Have you got all your documents and paperwork?" Mike asked.

"This is everything, sir," Ian said. *Sir.* It was rather touching. "What about the rest of the stuff in the house?"

Mike checked his watch. If they took off by midnight, they'd be back home before lunch. "I can get someone to ship it later. There's a lot we've got to work out before then. Are you going to call Joe now?"

Ian put on his sunglasses and cap. There wasn't much hair exposed. He looked like a new recruit after his first brush with the barber. "Am I going to get away with this? You can't see my hair colour's changed. And I always flush the clippings, so don't worry about DNA."

Maggie Dunlop really had drilled him thoroughly, then. Mike had to admire the crazy old bird.

"You'd be surprised what people don't notice, son," Rob said. "Just watch and learn."

Ian picked up his cell from the hall table and looked to Mike for a prompt. Mike was ready to take the phone and do the talking, but Ian proved to be surprisingly good at acting out a role. He sounded suitably stressed on the phone, exactly like someone who'd lost their only relative.

But it's true. His gran's dead. He's alone. He's hurting. Whatever else is going on, he's grieving.

Half an hour later, an old truck rolled up to the front of the house and a burly, greying guy in overalls got out of the cab. So this was Joe. Mike's first thought was that he'd do a good job of dissuading strangers from poking around the ranch. He stared suspiciously at Rob and Mike as they came out onto the porch with Ian, but Rob walked straight up to him in defusing mode and did the introductions with a lot of handshaking and explanations about friends of friends of Maggie Dunlop.

Rob had a gift for it. His body language said he wouldn't take any crap, but it also signalled that he was only pretending to be nice because he thought you were worthy of his performance, and that lesser mortals would just get a smack in the mouth. Joe was added to the list of those neutralised and brought on side in a matter of seconds. He was completely distracted and didn't look too closely at Ian.

Mike also made sure that Ian kept his back to the sun. It was low in the sky, and it was surprising what couldn't be seen in those light conditions.

"So you're going to be away for a while," Joe said to Ian, squinting against the sun. Mike opened the SUV's rear door for Oatie to jump in. He wasn't sure how the dog would cope with the jet, but Dad's Labradors had always slept through the entire flight. "It'll do you good."

"Yeah, a few weeks." Ian handed him a set of keys. "You might as well clear all the food. Gran hated waste. Use the place if you like."

Mike kept an eye on Joe's reaction to Ian. There wasn't the slightest indication that he thought anything was amiss. People usually saw what they expected to see, not because they were stupid or inattentive, but because that was the way the brain ironed out the stream of chaotic, ever-changing raw data from the eyes, doing its own predictions. It was a lesson in how Ian might learn to move unnoticed among people on a regular basis.

Rob scribbled on a card and handed it to Joe. "Here's my number, mate. I'd appreciate it if you kept all this to yourself, though. There might be some con artists showing up to look for Ian. He's come into some money. You know how it is."

Joe nodded. He seemed convinced that Ian was leaving voluntarily with people he trusted. "Sure. If anyone asks questions, they won't get anything out of me."

Ian got into the back seat of the Toyota, hands pressed between his knees, and didn't even look back at the ranch as Rob drove off. By the time they left the Athel Ridge limits, Oatie was stretched out on the rear seat, apparently comatose.

Rob stopped at the lights and turned to look behind him. "Is that dog dead?"

"Greyhounds just slob around," Mike said. "He's saving himself for a big race."

Ian didn't join in. He hardly said a word for the first hour, and Mike began to realise just how different he was. Damaged wasn't quite the right word, though: missing a few components, perhaps. He was smart and articulate, but there was also something upsettingly childlike beneath the shell of maturity. He wasn't confident around people. His body language was huddled and defensive, and he didn't seem to know how to handle a group conversation. He spoke only when spoken to.

But if I'd had all those traumas in a single month, I'd be more than quiet. I'd be cataleptic.

Two hours into the journey, Mike took over the driving. Rob kept glancing over the back of his seat to try to draw Ian into the conversation, but if Rob couldn't get Ian talking, then nobody could. Ian kept rummaging through one of his holdalls. Eventually he leaned forward and stuck his head between the seats.

"Can I ask some questions, please?"

"Go ahead." Rob opened a pack of gum and offered it to him. "Anything you want. Except physics. I was shit at that."

"Why do you call Mike *Zombie*?"

"Because his surname's Brayne. Y'know. *Braiiinss.* And he was convinced he was dead once when he wasn't. But that's a mistake anyone could make."

"Why do you keep looking in the mirrors? Are you worried that we're being followed?"

"Habit. I'm used to places where people blow you up or ambush you."

"And he's staggeringly vain," Mike murmured. "You'll get used to that."

Ian carried on undeterred. He seemed to have a checklist of things that intrigued him. It was breaking the ice. "Where exactly in Maine are we going?"

"Westerham Falls." Rob took out his phone and searched for a photo to show him. "That's Mike's lovely big house. His missus is lovely, too. Livvie. She'll play video games with you."

"What about Kinnery?"

"What about him?"

"Is he going to be there?"

Mike cut in. "No, but if you ever want to talk to him, I'll make sure he shows up. It'll be your call." He tried not to stoke Ian's anxieties. "He's got no say over what happens to you. You're not his property. Okay?"

"Okay."

Maybe it was time to lighten up. Mike started rehearsing how he was going to tell Dad and imagining the response. He was sure his father would be equally angry once he saw Ian.

"You've never flown before, have you?" he said. "Don't worry. The Gulfstream's very comfortable. Galley, divan beds, the works."

"Better let Oatie do his doggie business first, though," Rob said. "It's a long flight."

Ian went quiet again. It was hard to tell what he didn't understand and what he was just mulling over, bombarded by a world that must have seemed like Mars to him. He went back to rummaging in his bag, making little frustrated noises under his breath. He had one holdall on each side, laid at right angles to the seat like arm rests. Mike couldn't see what he was doing, but he heard a symphony of noises — rustling paper, the tap-tap of something metallic, and the rasp of fabric. Then Ian reached forward and shoved a wad of dollar bills at Rob.

And it really was a wad. It was an inch thick, wrapped with a red elastic band.

"What's that for?" Rob asked. The bills plopped into his lap. "Because — Christ, Ian, these are *fifties*."

"I want to pay my way."

Mike glanced at the banknotes. "You ought to invest that. You've got to plan for your future now."

Rob hefted the cash in his palm for a moment, then turned to hand the money back to Ian. Mike tilted the rear-view mirror to check what was happening. One of Ian's holdalls gaped open. All he could see was a layer of bundled bank notes, each tightly bound with elastic bands in an assortment of colours.

"Shitty death." It stunned Rob to a whisper. "You should put that somewhere safe, son. Like a bank. I bet Gran didn't trust banks either, did she?"

Ian shook his head. "Or credit cards. Banks know even more about you than the government does."

"Yeah, I used to have neighbours who were strictly cash." Rob still sounded hoarse. "But they sold stuff in little foil packets, and I don't mean beef jerky."

Ian put the fifties inside his jacket as if he hadn't quite given up the fight to pay, then zipped the holdall shut. Mike decided they were now far enough from Athel Ridge for him to call home and beg forgiveness without worrying about the cell identifying exactly where they'd been. He turned off at a strip mall with a likely-looking run of restaurants.

"So — Chinese, Thai, Mexican, Lebanese?" he asked. "We can reheat it in the galley."

Rob looked back at Ian. "Are you vegetarian, Ian?"

"No. I'll eat most anything."

"We had vegetarian choices in the Marines. Starve, or piss off and starve."

Ian managed half a smile. Things were improving. "Can I try Lebanese? I've never had that."

"Good call," Mike said. "Then I can get some *ma'amoul* to pacify Livvie."

Mike left Rob and Ian in the car and went to order a set menu. It was going to take fifteen minutes, plenty of time to find a quiet corner to make his call. He was relieved that this had to be a cryptic yes or no conversation for security reasons. He still wasn't sure how to word it.

"Hey, sweetie," Livvie said.

Mike took a breath. "We're on our way back, honey. Expect us tomorrow, probably mid-morning."

"Everything okay?"

"Fine." *Here goes.* "We'll have a house guest for a while. I said he could stay with us."

"Oh."

"And his dog. It's okay — it's only a greyhound. They just sit around and sleep. Not like Billy."

"Oh."

"I'm sorry. I didn't have the chance to ask if it was okay."

"So was the good doctor right?"

She'll think I'm crazy. "Yes. Yes, he was."

Livvie went quiet for so long that Mike thought he'd lost the signal.

"Really?" she said at last.

"Really."

"Wow. Are you sure?"

"Ask Rob. Kind of changes the world, doesn't it?"

"Have you called your father?"

"Not yet. I don't know what to say."

"Okay."

"I'm sorry, honey."

"I'll get a room ready."

"He seems like a nice kid."

"Just remember you can't stall your dad forever."

"I know. 'Bye, sweetheart."

Mike couldn't tell if Livvie was just keeping the call short and bland as good OPSEC, if she was giving him the frosty treatment, or if she was just stunned. It was probably a little of each. He didn't want to guess the ratio. He collected the food from the counter, paid cash, and went back to the car.

"Sleeping in the guest room tonight, then?" Rob asked. "Or the garage?"

Mike stowed the food in the trunk. "Not sure yet." A phone started ringing. "Is that yours, Ian?"

"Yes." Ian took his cell out of his pocket, but he didn't answer it. He just stared at the small screen. "Number withheld. That's not Joe, then."

Mike couldn't tell if Ian was too smart to risk answering or just too socially awkward. He shut the tailgate and got into the driver's seat. The phone was still ringing. "Do you get many wrong numbers? Does anyone else have the number?"

"No. Gran never registered it or gave it out. You know that. That's why you used it."

Rob took the phone, but he didn't look convinced. "Maybe it's Kinnery. The daft sod should know better. You want me to answer? I'll put it on the speaker."

Mike nodded. They couldn't ignore it in case it was urgent.

"Hello?" But the voice that emerged from the tinny speaker wasn't Kinnery, or even the pilot. It was a woman's voice, thirties maybe. She paused. Mike listened for noises in the background. "Hello, is that you?"

"Maybe," Rob said. "Who's you?"

"Ah, I have a feeling I've dialled overseas." She didn't sound as if she'd been caught off guard. She sounded like someone who made a lot of business calls. "I'm really sorry."

"No problem, love. Happens to us all."

But she didn't hang up, at least not fast enough. It was just a beat too slow. Nine times out of ten, people who got a wrong number would either bluster in apologetic embarrassment or just ring off abruptly. She hung on, very controlled.

"My bad. Sorry to have troubled you. Goodbye."

Ian didn't say a word. Rob switched off the phone and took out the battery. Mike looked at him, waiting for him to confirm the worst.

"Well? Was that what I think it is?"

"It wasn't a wrong number, mate," Rob said. "I think we've just been dicked."

ODSTOCK, MAINE: 15 MINUTES BEFORE LANDING.

"Wakey wakey, Ian. We're landing soon."

It took a few seconds for Ian to work out where he was. He didn't even remember curling up on the divan. One moment he'd been watching a movie on the bulkhead TV, eating crisp pastries filled with lamb, and the next he was in a blissful semi-doze with the faint, soothing noise of engines in the background. He could hear Rob, but it was like part of the movie soundtrack, something he was vaguely aware of but didn't need to note. He was still waiting for the alarm to wake him to go check on the sheep when someone shook his shoulder.

But the sheep were gone, Gran was dead, and he was thousands of miles from home somewhere in the skies above Maine. Rob loomed over him in the gloom, smelling of coffee, soap, and toothpaste.

"Time to stow this away." Rob raised the blinds on the windows. Daylight stung Ian's eyes for a moment. "The pilot likes everyone buckled in for landing. How do you feel?"

Ian was stiff and bruised. "Fine," he said, nodding. Rob was looking at him as if he wasn't okay. "Have I changed again?"

"No. You just need a shave."

"Sure?"

"Don't look so worried. If there's one person you can trust to keep his word, it's Mike."

Ian craved the peace of being able to trust someone. Suspicion of the world beyond the ranch had been fine when he had an ally in Gran, but the last few lonely weeks had left him exhausted by the effort of being constantly on guard against unseen and unimaginable threats. He needed someone to trust in the same way that Rob trusted Mike. He could see it from the way they leaned in and nudged each other, from their eye contact, from all the small unconscious gestures that said they never doubted they could rely on each other. Ian noted it all. He couldn't resist the compulsion to fit in and be one of the gang. He knew why humans reacted that way, but nothing had prepared him for how strongly his gut insisted on it.

Mike was in the galley, standing over Oatie with his arms folded while the greyhound wolfed down chopped steak and cookies from a porcelain bowl on the deck. Gran always said that animals were good judges of character. Oatie certainly seemed at ease with Mike.

"No puddles at all," Mike said approvingly. "What a pro. You want to hang on to him while we land?"

"Is landing that bad?"

"Course not."

Oatie handled it better than Ian did, curled up under one of the tables. The jet touched down with a bump that Ian wasn't expecting. He coaxed the dog down the steps and looked around the small airfield while the crew helped Mike load the luggage and boxes onto a cart to drive it to the parking lot. A black Mercedes SUV was waiting. Oatie stopped to pee up the tyres.

"You're welcome," Mike said, opening the rear door to transfer the bags. "Better out than in."

Rob started the engine. "Is Livvie going to punch me if I ask her for fried egg sandwiches?"

Mike settled in the back seat and shut his eyes as if he was going to sleep. "You can get away with anything," he said, eyes still closed. "She thinks you're Mr Wonderful. I'm the one who's going to get his ass kicked."

Ian glanced over his shoulder from time to time to check on him. Mike gradually slid down the leather upholstery and started snoring. Rob swore a blue streak when some joker cut him up at an intersection, but Mike still didn't stir. Ian studied the satnav screen, torn between fascination and suspicion.

"What's *dicked*?"

"When the enemy tails you." Rob frowned as if he was trying to remember when he'd said it. "In our case, it's a sort of virtual dicking. Whoever that woman was, she got your number from somewhere."

"I don't always understand what you're saying."

"Sorry, mate. You're not alone. I used to speak pure Bootneck, but it's turned into a sort of multi-service multilingual pidgin since I've been with Esselby. That's who we work for."

"Bootneck. Leatherneck?"

"That's it. Same derivation."

Rob stopped at a red light but he was still doing the constant sweep from mirror to mirror that he'd done on the way from Athel Ridge to the airport. Ian started to feel the same compulsion to check everything around him.

"Just your habit, yeah?"

"Sorry." Rob winked at him. "Situational awareness. You'll need to brush up on that. Welcome to my world. You're one of us now, mate."

One of us. Ian had never been part of anything before. What else was possible? It was the first time he'd felt truly hopeful in years.

Small talk wasn't as easy as it looked, though. He had a list of questions, and Rob had a fascinating answer for every one, but Ian had nothing interesting to tell him in return.

"Here." Rob thumbed his phone's screen and handed it to Ian. "Have a look through the videos. There's stuff of me and my mates. And Tom. Some of it goes back years." Rob called everybody *mate*, a term Ian had already filed for future use. "Tap the small pictures to open them, and pull your finger down the screen to go to the next page."

"I know. I watched you and Mike do it."

It took Ian a few moments to get the hang of it. A lot of the videos showed guys doing crazy things in bars, or sitting around wearing desert camouflage in makeshift camps in desolate, dusty places. Rob kept glancing across to check what he was looking at.

"See him?" The car stopped at the lights. Rob pointed to a guy in a bunch of Marines in T-shirts, doing some drunken dance and enjoying themselves with a kind of unselfconscious abandon that Ian envied. "That's Aggie. Alex Agnew. Poor sod got blown up. Nineteen."

The video took on a new perspective for Ian. Aggie, a year older than him, was instantly a real person, not some two-dimensional stranger on the news, and it felt intrusive to watch him knowing that he was gone. Ian swiped through more images, uncomfortable, and came across a kid who looked just like Rob. That had to be Tom. There were lots of pictures of Tom and Rob together, some of them with a dark-haired woman who was probably Rob's wife. Ian couldn't see much resemblance between her and Tom.

Do I look like my biological parents? What do I really look like anyway?

"Does your wife like it over here?" Ian asked. "That's her, yeah?"

"Yes, that's Bev," Rob said. "But she left me years ago."

Ian wasn't sure what to say to that. He carried on and found a video that could have come straight from a news bulletin, a firefight in a rocky landscape. The camera jerked everywhere and the noise of automatic fire almost drowned out the yelling. Ian had never heard the F word used so much in his life. It was Rob. The footage must have been from his helmet cam. Suddenly the event shifted from newsreel to reality again and became the guy sitting next to him, fighting for his life. Someone was yelling "Man down," and Rob was shouting at a guy to fucking well move, fucking *now*, or else he'd fucking come over there and fucking kick him back behind fucking cover. It was loud, distressing, desperate stuff.

"Sorry about that. Me and my big gob." Rob reached into the door pocket and handed Ian a pair of earphones. "Anyway, that's what me and Mike did. So if we're a bit deaf, you know why. Watch it all and get to know us better."

Rob shifted back into loud cheerfulness and went back to singing along with the radio. Ian plugged in the earphones and worked through clips of interesting wildlife, Marines relieving their boredom doing dumb but funny things, and some really amazing stuff at sea involving fast inflatable boats and helicopters. But a lot of it was confusing, painfully noisy firefights, mortars in and out, and big explosions in dry, hot countries. Ian was struck by how matter-of-fact guys were in the middle of terrifying situations.

Who would want to volunteer to do that?

Me. I do.

By the time they reached Westerham Falls, Ian wanted nothing more than to do that kind of stuff alongside guys like Mike and Rob, however terrible some of it looked. Rob was still singing. From time to time, he injected his own lyrics, most of which Gran would have slapped his ass for saying out loud.

"I don't know what vitamins you're popping, Rob." Mike stretched and yawned. "But pass them around, will you?"

"Just glad to be alive, Zombie." Rob turned right past a small house set back a few yards from the road. He gave it a nod. "That's Mr Andrews, the free site security. God bless nosey neighbours with time on their hands."

The Mercedes swept up a long drive flanked by trees and bushes, grounds that were more like a park than a garden. There was a big white house at the top of the drive and a garage block that could have housed half a dozen cars. A woman was waiting on the porch, arms folded. In her check shirt and pressed slacks, she looked like she'd stepped straight out of the Orvis catalogues that Gran used to bring home.

So that was Livvie. She looked much more glamorous than Rob's ex-wife. It was another facet of life from the TV screen that was mirrored in the real world: rich men had wives befitting their status in life. Ian wondered what kind of girl would be right for someone like him.

Livvie intercepted him as he edged towards the front door and put her arm around his shoulders. He didn't get a chance to work out how he was supposed to shake her hand.

"Make yourself at home, Ian," she said. "I'm very sorry about your gran."

"Thank you for letting me stay, ma'am."

Livvie gave him a pat on the back. Everybody seemed to touch him. "We love having guests," she said. "Plenty of room. And this is Oatie, huh? We'll have to get him a basket."

The house was like a mansion in some glossy magazine, miles of plain maple, slate floors, and grey carpet. It even smelled expensive. Ian's room was a suite with its own sitting room, bathroom, and TV. He couldn't believe how neat and perfect it looked. He was almost too scared to mess it up by breathing.

But it was all mirrors — mirrors on the dressing table, a full- length mirror on a stand in the corner, and a wall of mirrors in the bathroom. A month ago, it would have sent him into a panic. Now he felt he could cope with it.

"Okay, take your time." Rob put the bags by the window. "Come downstairs whenever you're ready. Yell if you need anything."

Ian unpacked and took a quick shower, trying not to let the welter of reflections distract him. He'd never really used a full-length mirror. He'd caught his fleeting reflection in shop windows, but that had been a rare event anyway. He couldn't remember studying the entirety of himself from the outside before.

Damn. I'm skinny. I don't look like Rob or Mike, that's for sure.

Bewildering, painful thoughts sat uncomfortably with a strange sense of excitement: he'd never had the chance to remind Gran how much he loved her, he'd been told lies all his life, he'd been whisked away in a private jet, and he was the guest of complete strangers. And he'd just realised how skinny he was.

And I'm not like any other human in the world.

It was still too much to take in. He put it out of his mind for the moment and went downstairs with Gran's folder, coughing a few times to warn everyone that he was coming. He was uncertain how to intrude politely but he was pretty sure that it didn't play out the way in did on TV, where all the stuff the hero wasn't supposed to know was conveniently revealed to him when he blundered into a conversation.

"It's okay, honey," Livvie was saying. "We can put it on hold. You're home for a few months, so there's no rush."

"Zombie, I can keep him occupied. There's plenty I can do with him."

Ian took a breath and walked in. Everyone looked sheepish and caught in the act, including Oatie, stretched out by the back door on a folded picnic blanket. Livvie poured a coffee.

"Sorry about the mirrors," she said, handing Ian the cup. She didn't explain what they'd had to put on hold, but it was obviously because of him. "I didn't think. There's another suite without mirrors, but it's smaller."

"It's fine," Ian said. Really, it was. He'd just realised that he was skinny, which he knew was a dumb thing to worry about when he could look like a different person every day. "It's a lovely room. Thank you."

Mike pulled up a chair for him. "Let's sort out your documentation. What have you got?"

Ian opened the bulging manila folder and spread the contents on the table. "I don't have a driving licence. Okay, so I broke the law a few times. I've got a social security number. I got my high school diploma at sixteen, too."

Livvie picked up some papers and read them. "Home-schooled. But not totally cut off from the outside world, then."

"No, ma'am. Gran believed in just enough contact with the state to keep them from poking their noses in. Shots and tests, that's what she said."

"Please. Not *ma'am*. Livvie."

"Sorry." Ian knew now that Livvie was the boss. That was the natural order of things. "Okay, Livvie."

Rob leaned on the table and raised his eyebrows at her. "He's carrying more cash than a crack dealer. He needs a safe."

Mike took the Ringer papers out of the envelope and looked through them. He had a habit of chewing his lip when something worried him. Ian had known him less than two full days and he'd already worked out how to read his reactions. Rob was going to take a little longer.

Mike slipped the papers back in the envelope. "Your gran certainly kept thorough notes. Is this a copy of the document you gave Zoe Murray?"

"Yes. Are you going to show it to your dad?"

Mike was still chewing his lip. "He needs to know what's out there."

"He's got to tell the government, though, hasn't he? He *is* the government."

"If he'd wanted to tell anybody, he wouldn't have sent us." Mike stood up, patting his pockets to locate his phone. "I'm going to call him now."

"What are you going to say?"

"That Kinnery was telling the truth. That's all I can say on the phone. He'll want to meet you. Are you okay with that?"

Ian had never been asked to make so many decisions in his life. It was Mike's house: how could he refuse?

"Sure. He didn't believe I was real either, did he?"

"Probably not."

"Who knows about me, then?"

"Me, Rob, Livvie, Kinnery, and Dad." Mike shrugged awkwardly. "Not even my mom. Dad needs to work out his cover story for her."

Everybody lied to their loved ones, then. Gran was no different. But there was no reason for Mrs Brayne to be told, Ian supposed, because he was just another classified government project like a jet or a missile, and she probably didn't get told anything about those, either.

"I ought to walk Oatie," Ian said. "He's used to being loose all day. Is that okay?"

"I'll show you around after I've called Dad. It's a lot of ground to get lost in."

Ian went to gather his cash and counted out five thousand in hundred dollar bills to pack into the inside pockets of his jacket, just in case he needed to run for it again. He took the rest downstairs in a grocery bag. Rob was making sandwiches while Livvie fussed over Oatie.

"We need to get this little guy some toys to make him feel at home," she said. "I'll pick up some stuff at the mall. You want to come, Ian?"

Ian couldn't face another onslaught of strangers just yet. He handed her the bag. "Maybe later. But I can pay."

"Wow." She hefted the bag as if she was weighing it. "All random numbers, huh?"

Rob made a *hah* noise without looking up from the pile of sandwiches. "Kinnery's guilt money. Did your gran keep a little black book?"

"She got regular payments. I never knew where they came from." Now the reality had sunk in, Ian was feeling more hurt than angry about Kinnery. He didn't even want an apology. Just telling him the truth would have been enough. How could anyone live with a lie that big? How could Gran? "She just said someone owed her for a big favour."

"Are you okay, Ian?" Livvie asked.

"I'm fine. Why?"

"You've just gone darker."

Rob paused to look. He didn't seem so surprised this time. Ian was reassured to see them react it to it as if it was just interesting, not something that made them recoil.

"So he has," Rob said. "Fast, isn't it?"

Ian put his hand to his face. He hadn't even felt himself morph. "Is anything else different?"

"No. Just your colouring."

"Okay, here's the plan." Livvie moved on instantly as if it hadn't been a big deal at all. Nothing seemed to faze her. It was almost unnatural. "Mike's going to look after the paperwork. He'll get you an accountant and an attorney so that you're set up properly. Rob's going to put a training schedule together and make you a badass like him. And I'm going to teach you how to control your morphing."

She sounded confident, as if it was just like riding a bike. Ian's disbelief must have shown on his face. She cocked her head to one side.

"You don't think it's doable?" she asked.

"It's not like anyone's ever done it before."

"Come on, people learn to control all kinds of automatic reactions." Livvie made it sound as if everything was possible if you just wanted it to be. "Buddhist monks can lower their heart rate. Sportsmen improve their performance. Patients control their own pain. It's proven. You can learn meditation techniques to control your body."

"There," Rob said, sawing through the stack of sandwiches. "Mrs Mike hath spoken. We'll get you totally sorted. Like one of those makeover shows, but with firearms."

Totally sorted. Ian didn't need that translated. Rob and Mike seemed to be the most sorted guys in the world. Ian was desperate for solid ground in his life, and these people knew exactly where to find it.

Mike wandered back into the kitchen and took a sandwich off Rob's plate. "I wouldn't want to be Kinnery now."

"Leo gone nuclear, eh?"

"Dad's more of an angry glacier. You just hear the gravelly rumble and you've got a million tons of implacable freezing wrath coming your way."

"So he really was giving Kinnery the benefit of the doubt."

"Just like he said." Mike reached out and patted Ian's shoulder. "He's going to call in a favour to identify that withheld number. Then he's going to visit as soon as he can get away."

Mike seemed remarkably forgiving. Twenty-four hours ago, Ian had nearly run him down. Now the guy had given him sanctuary.

"I know I've messed up your schedule," Ian said. "You've had to put something on hold. I'm sorry."

Rob glanced at Mike for a second with an expression Ian couldn't quite pin down. He probably thought that Ian hadn't noticed, but whatever had been postponed seemed to be significant.

"It's nothing that won't wait," Mike said. "Let's get you straight first." He clapped his hands together, making Oatie jump. "Come on, Oatie. Walkies. Rabbits."

Ian went upstairs to get his hiking boots. He hadn't unpacked the boxes yet, but there was something he had to do right away. He needed the comfort of familiar things in this luxurious but strange world.

He dug out the photo of David Dunlop at the door of his Huey, wondered again what the man had been thinking about when the photo was taken, and stood it carefully on the windowsill.

SEVEN

No, Jerry, I don't think anyone believes we really created a military werewolf. But every time we spend taxpayers' money studying how to terminate future rogue androids and God knows what else, I get voters on my back. Someone's talked about Ringer, and you know Ringer went nowhere — like a lot of other projects. Let's change the subject before they start asking what else we burned their dollars on. Maybe it was someone on your side of the fence who talked. Best we all shut up and move on.

Leo Brayne, to a reliable contact in the Department of Defense, on the wisdom of letting sleeping dogs lie.

KWA, LANSING, MICHIGAN: FIRST WEEK OF AUGUST.

Dru couldn't get the voice out of her head.

She pushed the open files across her desk to clear some space and took another look at the burner phone's outgoing call log. She knew exactly what was there, because she'd checked it a dozen times. Now she was starting to doubt herself.

She'd definitely dialled correctly. She took another look at the stolen phone records to confirm it really was the Seattle number that the British guy had answered, a number so important to Kinnery that he kept a phone solely for it.

Why would he bother to keep a dedicated landline?

If he was worried about being tapped by the authorities, it wasn't any more secure than a cell call or an e-mail. Unless he knew he'd be home when it rang, it wasn't a priority number for some urgent message, either. He'd have to forward the number, and that would be another weak link in the security chain.

The only possible answer was that he had to keep the number restricted because he needed to be absolutely certain who he was calling, and who was calling him. Caller ID on another line was no guarantee. Dru would have been prepared to believe it was a text phone for a deaf friend or relative if she hadn't heard that English guy pick up.

Maybe Kinnery's done nothing wrong. Humans find patterns to recognise, even if there isn't one. But the British guy doesn't quite fit.

Had the number been reallocated? No, it didn't happen that fast. Maybe someone had moved out and left the phone line. Dru stirred her coffee while she waited for the next report from Grant. She was so engrossed that she didn't care if it was cold by now.

So who's this Brit?

The guy didn't have any of the British accents she was used to hearing in movies, and he was automatically cagey. Dru's theory was that people over thirty tended to answer a landline in a different way to a cell, and the more she heard, the more she believed it. On a landline, they'd often give a name or a number, maybe because they felt secure in their home or office, but usually because they'd been taught to identify themselves. On a cell phone, though, answered anywhere and often in public, the response to an unidentified caller was usually just "Hello." Maybe this Brit was innocent, simply wary because he'd seen the number was withheld, or maybe the number was a cell.

But the guy revealed nothing, he sounded like a wise-ass, and his tone was all *wrong*. A cell could have been stolen, of course. But the voice — thirties or forties, cocky, controlled — didn't sound the stolen phone type. He wasn't a kid. Dru wondered if he was Kinnery's accomplice or even the mule himself. He sounded too old to be the shape-shifter created for Project Ringer, but a creature like that couldn't exist anyway.

This guy's connected somehow.

Dru tried to fit him and the hotline phone into some sort of scenario. She wrote the words on sticky notes and moved them around her desk, waiting for some connection to strike sparks: Brit, hotline, Kinnery. But no matter how she arranged them, nothing jumped out. She carried on sifting through files until the e-mail arrived from Grant.

This was the legitimately acquired stuff, a list of nearly sixty names and phone numbers. Grant was cryptic and sparing in his notes. He'd added only one comment: '*Graduates, CK's year, from college records and reunion sites. Current contact shown where available.*'

Dru was looking for names that might have had a Seattle connection. But the only way to ring all those numbers without raising suspicion was to have a credible reason for calling. Some of those people might still be in contact and compare notes.

Hi, I'm looking for someone who trusted Charles Kinnery enough to let him shoot them full of stolen genetic material. Would that be you?

She resigned herself to deception again. Lying became easy if you did it often enough, then it became a habit, and then you didn't even know you were doing it. She didn't want to step onto that precarious slope. It wasn't the same as other irregular things, like acquiring call logs she shouldn't have had. That was *outside* of her, illegal but not untrue. But lying was within her skin, an assault on reality that she had to create, a different kind of wrong. It would be polluting, distorting, eventually destroying the anchors and fixed points within her that were the foundations of memory and principle. That was the nature of the human mind, malleable and interested only in recognising patterns that meant survival. All humans lied, whether it was the self-deception of being over-optimistic or outright, full-blown fraud.

Dru reached in her purse for a snack bar. She found her Chanel powder compact instead, the only luxury that she'd treated herself to in years. But fancy compact or not, the mirror could only show her what was actually there, and it showed her forty years.

Forty, Dru. Forty. Greying. Looking old enough to remember Kinnery. Weaver said so, as good as. This is where I disappear. I'll metamorphose into a grey, transparent thing with my mind trapped inside, tapping at the window to try to make someone see that I'm still in there. Who needs private investigators? Just hire a few middle-aged women. We move unseen.

It was an incentive to get on with making the calls. Dru fidgeted with the burner phone and wondered whether to simply call Kinnery and ask to see him. He was probably expecting someone to do just that. But she couldn't short-circuit this yet.

What do I need to ask? I'm looking for someone with a Seattle connection. I don't have a name. If it's a cell, the area code needn't even be where the subscriber lives. It might be forwarded. It might even be spoofed.

But it was all she had to go with, and every day that passed made it potentially harder. She rehearsed her lines, reverse engineering the information she wanted without adding detail that anyone might feel the need to check.

Okay, she was trying to track down someone whose name she didn't know, on behalf of a third party that none of these alumni would know, and who might have a Seattle connection. That didn't sound unreasonable. But who should she claim to be? Officialdom might seem intimidating, and it was too easily checked.

While she psyched herself up to make the first call, she looked through the rest of the list. Grant had cross-checked all the names to see if any had been at conferences or institutions that Kinnery had mentioned in his online biographical details and CV. This was the inevitable nakedness of being an academic. He had to reveal information, because nobody would want to be taught by a man who wouldn't say where he'd studied or worked. There were a couple of names who'd had recent professional contact, but none of the numbers that Grant had turned up matched any of those on Kinnery's recent call log. It didn't rule them out. But if Kinnery had called someone about Project Ringer, then it would have been very recent, triggered by *The Slide*'s article or whatever event had resurrected the whole thing after so many years.

Okay. I'm trying to find someone who might have been at university with you in the early Seventies, maybe someone who moved to the Seattle area, because ...

Dru's momentum stalled. It required an absolute lie and the creation of people who didn't exist. Her first idea was to claim she was tracking down an old friend of her late mother and that she had very few details. Her actual mother was very much alive, though. Dru found she had an uncharacteristically superstitious fear that she'd be punished somehow if she tempted fate that much. And wouldn't she know the gender of the friend, at very least?

Possibly not. Not if I only found a Christmas card with an illegible signature. Okay, if I'm worried about curses and thunderbolts for lying, then I'll make it an aunt. I have no aunts.

There was a line to be drawn. She'd try one call, see how easily it tripped off the tongue, and then decide whether to carry on.

Many of the names on Grant's list had no current details, just last known job or location, and they hadn't thrown up much in searches. This was a generation in its fifties when blogs and social media took off. They didn't post every cough and spit online like Clare did. It was harder to build a picture of their associations and movements.

Dru decided to start with a man called Martin Mancini. She tapped out the number, sucked in a breath to steady her voice, and waited.

"Mancini."

"Hi. Sorry to trouble you." *Oh God, here we go.* Even now, it wasn't irrevocable. The Rubicon would be crossed when she opened her mouth to lie. "My name's Dru. I know this is a long shot, but I'm trying to find someone who knew my late aunt. She studied genetics and cell biology at Lomax in the early seventies. I don't even have a name. All I've got is Seattle." There: easy. She could see why lying was seductive. She decided to push the boundary. "Maybe somewhere else in Washington."

Mancini paused. "Sorry, Washington doesn't ring a bell. What was your aunt's name?"

Dru wasn't prepared. *Why didn't I plan that?* "Gordon," she said, snatching a name from the personnel files in her line of sight. "Jenny Gordon."

"Sorry, I can't help. Have you tried the reunion committee?"

"I'm working through a list of names." *Perfect.* That would cover her if anyone rang around the list to check if they'd had a vague, rambling call from a woman called Dru. *Or Drew. Because I didn't say, did I?* "Thanks. Sorry to have bothered you."

Dru ended the call and rested the cell against her cheek, eyes shut. It was done. And now she could do it again, and again, and again, until she cleared the whole list. The heavens hadn't parted to unleash retribution: nobody had been harmed. She could live with it. She went to get a soda from the vending machine before working through the rest of the list.

By noon, she'd crossed off more names of people who couldn't help. She'd planned to walk around town during lunch, but now she didn't want to stop. It was like feeding coins into a slot machine, thinking that each spin of the reels would be the one that spewed coins into her lap. Some calls led her to other numbers. Some went to voice-mail, and she highlighted those to retry later. Others simply rang out until the time limit cut them off. She marked those as retries as well. By the time her own cell bleeped to remind her it was time to go home, her stomach was growling.

Weaver caught her leaving. "How's it going?"

Dru walked a fine line in what she told him, enough to show she was actually doing something, but not enough to compromise her or tell him more than he wanted to know. She indicated her office with a jerk of her head and unlocked it again. This wasn't a conversation for a corridor.

"I'm working through a list of phone numbers," she said. "I've gone back to his college class, because you don't entrust someone with that kind of material unless you know they're reliable." She wondered again whether to mention the hotline. "There's a possible Seattle connection. I'm approaching it from both ends of the timeline."

"Good."

"Does any of that sound familiar to you?"

"I met him after college. I don't remember any kind of link with Seattle. But Charles obviously plays his cards very close to his chest." Weaver lowered his voice. "If you reach the stage where you think you've found an accomplice, stop and call me. Don't take it any further."

"So you'll refer it to the FBI?" Dru was reassured that he'd seen sense. "Okay."

"No, but you don't know who you might be dealing with. If this rumour has any truth in it, there's a lot of money at stake, and I have no idea who Charles might have gotten himself involved with."

Dru hadn't considered that this might become physically dangerous. People shot each other for small change, though, let alone something potentially worth billions. She should have thought of that.

"Do you know something I don't, Mr Weaver?"

"I don't want you taking personal risks."

"If you genuinely think it's risky, we should let the police deal with it."

"And you know that won't do the company any good right now. It won't do Charles any good, either."

Dru understood the risk to the merger and to KWA, but she couldn't see a reason for worrying about Kinnery's welfare. "You won't be sympathetic if you find he's stolen this company's property."

"It's not sympathy," Weaver said. "If Charles did something stupid, he'd probably prefer to come back to KWA and bring his ill-gotten gains with him than be charged and have his career and reputation destroyed."

Dru thought that over. She had the feeling that she didn't know quite as much as she needed to about the nature of Weaver's relationship with Kinnery.

"Is this just for leverage?" she asked. "Is that all it is?"

"If Charles has anything that's ours, then it's a Pyrrhic victory if prosecuting him damages us as well." Weaver opened the door. "It'd be good for business to have him back here and feeling obliged to behave himself."

Now Dru understood. It was the thinking man's blackmail. If it worked, then it was a tidy solution. "How about his mule, then? If he has one."

Weaver just looked at her. "You know the law won't necessarily do what's right for us. Charles can make his accomplice see sense so we can resolve this without defence lawyers crawling all over us."

Dru had no idea what he meant by that, and she was instantly ashamed of herself for not really wanting to know. He didn't appear to be about to explain anyway.

"I better be going," she said.

Dru drove home, fretting about that unidentified English voice, and preoccupied by what someone prepared to be a gene mule might do when cornered. She still couldn't imagine how Weaver could reclaim KWA's patentable genes.

Actually, she could. She simply didn't want to. *People kill for a few bucks from a liquor store, remember?* She was only doing this to keep her job, not to right wrongs or mete out justice. But there was taking the moral low ground to look after her family, and there was being implicated in something illegal. She'd have to be careful.

"Pizza again," Clare said. She sliced it into wedges and put the plate on the table. "Or I could make noodles. Or stir fry."

"Sorry, sweetheart." Dru wasn't paying attention. "I'm being a lousy mom. I got tied up on my way out. And I've got to make a stack of calls tonight."

"Why won't you tell me what's going on?"

"It's just work. It's tedious."

"Dad called me today."

Normally that would have been enough to herald a crisis summit at the kitchen table. Tonight it just washed over Dru as it should have done every other time.

"What does he want?"

"He asked if I wanted to stay over some time."

Larry had resisted that since they'd split up. Dru tried not to ask why he'd had a change of heart, because if the reason wasn't that his girlfriend had found someone her own age to play with and left him, she'd be disappointed.

"Sure," Dru said. "Why not?"

"Really?"

"I might need to be out of town for a few days for this investigation. So you'd have some company. And I wouldn't have to worry or embarrass you with a babysitter."

"You trust me every day during the school vacation, Mom. I'm fourteen."

"But I'm home every evening. And if the house burns down while you're here on your own, I get charged with neglect."

"Okay." Clare piled pizza on her plate and headed for the stairs. "If you're going to work, I'll go watch a movie."

There were times when Dru thought the teenage storm was coming to an end and they were starting to see one another as people again. God, she hoped so. Fighting sapped her strength. She took her plate of pizza into the living room and resumed the ring-around, trying not to smear tomato sauce on the cell phone.

Ten unsuccessful calls down the list, she realised that she was missing her favourite TV show. And it didn't even matter.

"Dr Missiakos? Hi, sorry to trouble you." Dru had trotted out the line so often that she was word perfect. The biggest risk now was sounding as if she was reading from a call centre script. "My name's Dru. I realise this is a long shot, but I'm trying to find someone who knew my late aunt and was studying genetics and cell biology at Lomax Uni in the seventies. I don't have a name, just that they had a Seattle or Washington connection."

"Would this be a woman?"

"I don't actually know." Dru had her second level response down pat now. "All I have is a Christmas card with initials I can't read."

"You might mean Margaret Dunlop," Missiakos said. "Maggie."

Dru fumbled for a pen. *A woman.* She'd focused on a male

suspect too fast, then. "Dunlop?"

"Her family had a place in Washington. Really remote, as I recall. Something like *Bethel* in the name. Sorry, it's been a long time. I lost touch with her. She was on a different course, I think. I often wonder what happened to her."

"Well, thank you, Doctor. That's an enormous help." If she could tie the phone to that as well, it put her miles ahead. "I really appreciate it."

"You're welcome. If you find her, remember me to her."

"I will. And thank you again."

Dru sat looking at the red CALL ENDED icon and felt a smile creep across her face. She couldn't stop it. Then she chuckled to herself.

"Well, Margaret Dunlop," she said. "I thought you'd be a guy. That'll teach me to stereotype, won't it?"

So how did the Seattle cell fit in with the Brit? She'd either found a link she didn't yet grasp, or she was in danger of being diverted by a random element. Kinnery might have had other secrets to bury, perhaps something as simple as a drug habit or an affair. That might have been behind his decision to quit KWA and his wife's reason for leaving him.

Dru put that on a back burner with her other anxieties and focused on the gleaming gold fragment that had emerged from the pan of gravel she'd shaken so carefully. She needed to find a place called Bethel, and look for a Margaret Dunlop.

Or I could ask Grant, seeing as we're paying him. But that's giving him too much information.

I want to do this myself. I'm getting somewhere.

It thrilled her. She felt victorious and clever, and the small success gave her a renewed appetite for more. She was hugging her knees and wondering whether to open a bottle of wine when Clare came downstairs.

"Mom, you can't keep lying to me," Clare said.

It jerked Dru out of that glowing satisfaction. "Lying? What?"

"It's a man. Isn't it?"

The guilt shattered and vanished. "I wish."

"Well, one of those calls made you very happy."

"Okay, I found someone I'd been trying to contact for the company." She'd have that glass of wine after all. She deserved it. "I've got some research to do, but I might need to take that trip later this month."

"I'll call Dad, then."

"You do that, sweetheart." Dru went into the kitchen and poured herself a glass. "I'll let you know when I've got a schedule."

Dru settled down on the sofa again with her drink and switched on the TV to catch the news before continuing with the search. Damn, she'd missed the bulletin. Was it that late? She'd call it a day, then. There was always tomorrow. It was Saturday, and she hated giving unpaid overtime to KWA, but she really needed to pin this down.

Maggie Dunlop. That might be the puzzle piece that would unlock the rest. Dru ate the last chunk of pizza crust on her plate and raised her glass.

"To lying," she said. "In moderation."

VANCOUVER: FIRST WEEK OF AUGUST.

Kinnery stared at his burner phone on the cafe table, waiting for it to show signs of life.

Leo still hadn't contacted him to say if Ian had been removed or not, and the longer it dragged on, the more Kinnery's imagination filled the gaps with nightmare scenarios. If Mike had gone to Athel Ridge, he would have found Ian by now, if the boy was there to be found.

Maybe something went wrong and Ian used that goddamn rifle

Kinnery people-watched while he took a bite of walnut cake and reached for his cup. Coffee slopped into the saucer. The half-empty cup had somehow magically refilled itself. The waiter must have topped it up, but Kinnery hadn't even noticed him approach, and that was a worrying lapse of concentration. If someone could walk up to his table and spend seconds right under his nose, he didn't stand a chance of spotting someone tailing him.

The burner stayed stubbornly silent, but then the cell in his pocket vibrated. He snatched it out to see NUMBER WITHHELD. He hadn't expected Leo to call him, let alone use this number again, but perhaps he didn't trust even the most bland message to encrypted mail any longer. No: Leo probably didn't trust *him.* He hunched over the table with the phone to his ear, but the caller beat him to the punch.

"Hi Charles. It's Shaun. I just wanted to say sorry for making an asshole of myself the other week. Are you still talking to me?"

Kinnery had a brief, sweaty, heart-pounding moment thinking how close he'd come to saying the name *Leo*. He recovered himself. "Hi Shaun. Obviously I am."

"Bad moment?"

"Cake crumbs." Kinnery tried to focus on the table so his reactions wouldn't be swayed by the thing uppermost in his mind — Ian and the ripples that were now spreading from having to reveal his existence. "They went down the wrong way."

"Ah, the joys of academia."

"We do work in August, you know."

"Talking of work, have you been reading the business pages? I take it you know we're in merger talks with Halbauer."

Kinnery had stopped thinking of KWA as *we* a long time ago. He'd forced himself to unplug from it. But at his core, something still said *mine, mine, mine,* and he knew it. The company was like an ex-lover. Kinnery accepted that they'd parted — that he'd abandoned it — and that it had a right to a life of its own, but it hurt to see it happy without him.

"I know," he said. "I wouldn't recognise the old place, would I?"

Shaun paused for a moment. Kinnery knew that timing all too well. "You could always come back, you know."

For a few moments, Kinnery floundered. It was a complete one-eighty from the call that suggested Shaun thought he was a lying, thieving bastard and that there was no smoke without fire.

"It's been a long hiatus, Shaun."

"You left to get your life straight, you said. By all accounts, you've done that."

No, not even close. "Yes, I suppose I have."

"You'd be a big plus for Halbauer."

"I'm not getting any younger. I've reduced my hours."

"I'm not asking for a factory week. A retainer. A consultancy."

Kinnery tried hard to sift the motives. The Halbauer deal would inject cash into KWA, so Shaun would eat shit if it helped the negotiations. By the same token, any embarrassing news like leaky DoD projects, even historical ones, wouldn't help. Kinnery tested the waters.

"So the CEO of Halbauer doesn't subscribe to *The Slide*, then," he said.

"Oh, that's all gone quiet." Shaun sounded as if he'd dismissed it, but Kinnery knew he'd keep it in his mental pending tray until Hell opened a ski resort. The man could wait forever. "That's the internet for you. The attention span of a three-year-old. Will you think about it?"

"We said some pretty harsh things to each other back then."

"That was a lifetime ago. It'd be good to have you on the team again. Give us a bit more weight. Think it over and call me."

The conversation left Kinnery disoriented. He'd never planned to become an academic; the idea of returning to the cut and thrust of the commercial world felt temptingly like a new lease of life. But he didn't need any extra complications. Shaun wasn't having a sentimental moment and honouring his old partner's contribution to KWA's success, either. This was strictly business.

Kinnery finished his coffee. He should have gone home and waited in the privacy of his study for Leo to make contact, but any conversation would be like divining the various meanings of a haiku. Nothing would be spelled out. He strolled along the Seawall, playing a what-if game in his head about the kind of research he could do in a post-Halbauer world, then went to pick up some groceries before heading home. He was searching through the packets of Michelina's in the freezer section when his burner rang.

He took a breath and willed it to be positive news. "Hi. I'm in a store right now."

There was no greeting or identification. "Someone tried to call your late friend. A woman. She didn't leave a name." It was Leo. Kinnery could almost hear him looking down his nose in disdain. "You might want to wonder how she got that number."

Kinnery re-ran the line in his head to work it out. *Maggie. Oh God.* "Nobody should have it. Any news for me?"

"You're going to be at the conference in Toronto the day after tomorrow, aren't you?"

"Yes." Kinnery knew a summons when he heard one. He couldn't even blame the department secretary for being careless with information, because the list of conference speakers was public. *And I do believe you're keeping tabs on me, Leo.* "Are you passing through?"

"Royal York, PM's suite. Make yourself known at the desk around eight and just exercise some situational awareness. I hope the talk goes well."

The call cut off. Kinnery muttered under his breath, frustrated by the stalling on Ian. "God, you could just say yes or no, couldn't you?"

A woman rummaging through bags of green beans gave him a wary look. Maybe she hadn't seen the phone. He carried on filling his basket, but it was displacement activity now. He was none the wiser about Ian, and he had an extra problem; someone had tried Maggie's number.

Knowing the care that Maggie had taken to keep that out of directories, there were very few ways that someone could acquire it. One occurred to Kinnery as he was heading for the cashier's desk, and it was terrifying. Someone had his phone records for the landline. If they had that, they might have his registered cell records too. He started to unpick the detail as he stood waiting to pay for his groceries.

If Leo knows they're calling the number, then he's got access to the phone. Which means he's got Ian. But who can get hold of phone records? How do reporters hack phones? Can any asshole track a phone's location, or is that just the cops? And they're not all saints — they leak and sell information. No, if anyone could track the location, they'd have Ian by now. And I wouldn't be walking around a supermarket.

It's got to be Shaun. He showed his hand on day one.

Kinnery found himself wondering if the woman buying beans was just a customer after all. *Situational awareness.* Even Leo had subtly warned him that he might be tailed in Toronto. Kinnery had lived in dread for nearly twenty years, a blunt-edged kind of anxiety that could be pushed into the background like a constant low-grade pain, but now things were acquiring a sharper, more threatening focus. He couldn't sit around waiting for the axe to fall.

I could call the cops to check the house and car for devices. It's not as if I haven't had threats from activists in the past. Perfect excuse. It'd be satisfying to see Shaun try to explain that. Well, officer, it's like this. I thought my former business partner had built a shape-shifter. Yes, that's correct, officer. No, not like a werewolf. A polymorph.

Kinnery realised the cashier was staring at him. Maybe he'd been talking to himself. He was mortified. He paid and hurried out, then diverted to a 7-Eleven to pay cash for two SIMs in case his existing burner was somehow already compromised, and topped up the credit at a gas station with cash. Damn: handsets had unique identifiers as well. He ended up searching for another store to buy a couple of cheap SIM-free handsets, again with cash. He was hazy about cell security, but right then he was prepared to take every precaution whether rooted in urban mythology or not.

When he got home, he left the car on the drive with the engine running and walked back to the gates to look up and down the road. He stopped short of raising a finger to the unseen. His neighbours wouldn't like that.

So where would a camera have to be mounted to see him go in and out? KWA had limits: budget, imagination, or the law, or any permutation thereof. His bet was a good old-fashioned guy in a car, time-consuming but legal, with none of the drawbacks of technology like placing cameras or retrieving data. If someone wanted to watch him around the clock, they'd need multiple vehicles and investigators.

That must be costing you a fortune, Shaun. Good.

Kinnery noted of a couple of places where he could put his own cameras to watch the road, then garaged the car. When he shut the door, his defiance gave way to a degree of acceptance that this was his comeuppance for doing the unforgivable. He sat at his desk with a glass of whisky, looking at the small, dead, black webcam eye set in the top of his monitor. He'd never used it. He hated teleconferencing and video calls and all the other intrusions into his sanctuary. He resented the idea of having to worry about what was visible behind him before accepting a call, or even if he looked tidy enough for his caller. Now he wasn't even sure the cam was ever truly switched off. His world and his sense of self had changed completely.

This is my home. This is defended space.

He opened the desk drawer, took out a small ball of Blu Tack, and pressed it over the lens. *Fuck you, whoever you are.* It was insane, but the urge to do it overwhelmed him. The things he'd taken for granted as part of the private fabric of his life — that he was genuinely alone when he closed the front door, that his bedroom, bathroom, and the interior of his car were inviolable spaces in which he could do and say whatever he pleased — had vanished. An invisible observer was a threat, and it had nothing to do with having something to hide. It was the fundamental need of any animal to spot predators and find refuge from them. Now his phone, his computer, his own front door, and every basic utility that he needed had become a potential source of betrayal.

We're all two different people, the public face and the private one. That's what keeps us sane. That's what keeps society stable.

Kinnery finally understood why stars punched paparazzi. It was an animal's natural reaction to being dug out of its lair by men with dogs and bright lights. He went out to the garden a couple of times and walked around, hoping to catch some unlucky PI hiding in the bushes, but he drew a blank.

Damn, this was how paranoia took hold. Maggie had been prophetic about where widespread surveillance and data collation was heading. She could trust nothing; eventually she could trust nobody. He understood now.

Uncertainty and mistrust. That's how you keep people cowed down with minimal effort. But I'm not going to let it paralyze me.

He didn't leave the house the next day. If anyone was keeping watch, then they didn't have to be detectives to work out when he'd be leaving to catch his Toronto flight. He went through every room in the house, opening cupboards and drawers, not sure exactly what he was looking for other than reassurance that everything was where he'd left it and that there were no objects he didn't recognise. How did people cope with having to be alert every waking minute? He wasn't like the Mike Braynes and Rob Rennies of this world. He wasn't used to constant lethal threats. He didn't think to vary his route or keep an eye on everything around him.

I will now, though.

And if I were Ian, I could simply change how I looked and melt into a crowd. I hope he uses that.

Kinnery didn't sleep well that night. He got up a few times to visit the bathroom, then admitted defeat and stayed up. He could nap on the flight. Over the years, he'd honed schedules to a fine art, arriving as late as possible to avoid socialising, then catching the first available flight back. He didn't want to network or reminisce. Secrets were hard work. They sucked him dry and chewed quiet, almost unnoticed holes in everything he did. Only the most superficial working relationships could survive the corrosion of never being able to have a conversation without the censor on duty in his head.

By the time he boarded his flight he was threadbare and irritable, head buzzing with fatigue. He read his notes before settling down to doze, and thought how much more riveting his talk on the social implications of gene therapy would have been if he could have referred to Ian.

Not that I understand why Ian's phenotype changed that much. New structures. He's a research goldmine. Right science. Wrong ethics. Without Maggie's intervention, how far would I have gone? I did it first, though. I got there first.

Knowing that was sometimes a comfort, but sometimes it tore him apart.

The flight landed late and Kinnery arrived at the conference with less preparation time than he'd planned. At a couple of points during his talk, he looked up from the lectern and squinted against the lights, half-expecting to see Ian storming down the centre aisle to denounce him and ask those present if they understood the law of unintended consequences. Somehow Kinnery even had a mental image of how Ian would look now, impossible as that was. But the talk was uneventful, and it was close to the end of the day's program. A large proportion of his audience was getting tired, losing concentration, and thinking about dinner plans. The Q and A session was short and weary.

One of the conference organisers cornered him as he left. "Are you coming for a beer, Charles?"

"Thanks, but I've got an early flight tomorrow." What if he ran into delegates at the Royal York who recognised him, though? *Lie. Like I always do.* "I've got to hit on a sponsor, too. Next time, I promise."

The Royal York was a few blocks from the conference. Kinnery had never been inside before, not even for a drink, and he hoped that his tendency to look over his shoulder didn't make him look suspicious. Maybe KWA had skipped surveillance for this trip because it was public knowledge why he'd come to Toronto. When he gave his name to the reception desk — damn, he really should have arranged an alias — he was escorted to the elevator and taken to an entirely separate part of the hotel with its own lobby.

Even on Kinnery's comfortable budget it was unaffordably luxurious, but it was probably just a make-do late booking for Leo. Kinnery tapped on the door of the suite. He was surprised when Leo opened it himself. He was sure the man had an entourage of vigilant men in suits, the Rob Rennie variety.

"Don't you have security?" Kinnery asked, looking around.

"Not always, and never for something like this. Take a seat." There was a jug of water on the table with a set of glasses. Leo didn't offer him anything stronger. "Let's get this over with."

He handed Kinnery a couple of sheets of paper, typed, unsigned, and double spaced. It took Kinnery a moment to work out what it was: Maggie's whistle-blowing document for *The Slide.* She'd obviously taken careful notes of what he'd discussed with her over the years. She'd described Project Ringer pretty accurately, with terminology, a few dates, and some other specific details, sufficient to prove to anyone involved in the project that she'd had genuine information, but nowhere near enough detail to put in front of a committee or even convince a half-educated layman.

"I'd expected worse," Kinnery said. "So I assume you retrieved Ian. Is he okay?"

"Mike and Livvie are looking after him."

"You've seen him, then."

"Not yet."

"So do I get to see him?"

"He doesn't want visitors. Mike's given him his word that he'll protect him."

Protect him. It was all very noble, but these people really didn't understand how different Ian was. Kinnery expected to be told to drop everything and be available to play physician. Okay, Ian was still upset. It was inevitable after all he'd been through. But he'd settle down in time, and then the Braynes would need expert help. Kinnery could wait.

"So what do you plan to do with him?" Kinnery asked.

"Ensure his privacy, and give him every support to lead as normal a life as he can."

"I'll need biological samples, then." It was the first time that Kinnery would have a chance to test Ian since he'd started morphing. Maggie didn't trust him to go off and do it all again. *At last. Some answers.* He'd have to work out how to get tests analysed without inviting questions, though. "I'll think about what can be done without my being present."

Leo stood up and walked across to the window with his hands in his pockets. He didn't say anything for a few moments, but when he turned around he looked murderous and drained of blood.

"You irresponsible *bastard.*" It was a primal growl, probably as near as he ever came to losing his temper. "You actually *did* it. What standards can we possibly have in common for you to begin to understand what I mean by *wrong*?"

Kinnery reeled for a moment. At first he thought that Leo was just on a slow burn, or that he'd been equally incensed in the restaurant but couldn't bawl him out with waiters around. But he could see that it was actually the shock of discovery; Leo hadn't believed him. He did now.

"But I told you everything," Kinnery said. "I thought you believed me."

Leo covered the distance from the window in three strides and loomed over him. "I didn't believe it was possible, but I suspect it was more that I didn't want to believe anyone with your standing would piss over human decency like that." This wasn't Leo the senator, who had less power than the electorate supposed. This was Leo the billionaire businessman, who could do pretty much as he pleased. "Ian can't control his changes. He'll never have even a semblance of a normal life. He'll never have a wife and children. The only thing that's stopping me from tossing you to the CIA to play with right now is that there's nothing I can do to you that won't cause blowback for that poor goddamn kid."

Kinnery's existence now hung on Leo's whim. All he could do was take the onslaught.

"That's why I'm offering whatever help I can give." Kinnery attempted humility. "I assure you that I put Ian's welfare first. Otherwise I would have profited from this years ago."

"You didn't because you *couldn't*. You couldn't reveal what you'd done. And now neither can I. You get off scot free because you've blighted your victim."

"I realise it's feeble to point out that Ian represents huge potential for relieving human suffering."

"You're right. It's so goddamn feeble that I don't even care how true it is."

"If you had to choose between one person and a cure for diseases that kill millions, I don't think you'd find it easy."

"No, I don't have to choose. And *neither did you*. Spare me the disingenuous claptrap. The choice is between one man's welfare and some pretty nebulous potential discoveries that might or might not be a boon for mankind one day if there's a profit in it."

"Leo — "

"Are we clear on this? Don't even try to justify it. Just tell me how you're going to put it right."

Kinnery had paid for Ian with his marriage, his career, and possibly his sanity. There was a limit to how many times he could apologise. "If I could, I don't know if it would do Ian more harm than good."

"Can't or won't?"

"I can't even begin if I can't have access to his DNA or run tests on him. And I need a lab. I certainly can't use the university's."

Leo backed off a few paces, but only to pour himself a glass of water. He seemed to be regrouping, which probably meant he wasn't sure whether Kinnery was stalling him with fake science.

"Cell number," Leo said, changing tack. "Rob took the call and said it didn't sound like a wrong number. Female, thirties or forties. The phone's not registered, but the call was made somewhere in Lansing. So this is KWA on your ass, Charles."

Kinnery already knew that Shaun was watching him, but this was getting much more serious. He didn't know how Leo had traced the location and he decided not to ask.

"I don't know how the hell they got that number," he said.

"Probably someone working for the telco who's got a sideline providing PIs with records. It happens. It's less trouble than a wiretap."

Kinnery took out his new burner phones. He was carrying so many cells now that he was starting to look like a dealer. "Well, I've got two alternative numbers."

"Just remember they're not completely untraceable. And they'll still identify your location."

"Sure, but Shaun's got to tie me to these numbers first."

"Any more contact from him?"

"He called to ask me to come back and sweeten the merger deal with Halbauer."

"Excellent." Leo just raised an eyebrow. Maybe he knew already. "Take the offer."

Kinnery reeled for a moment. That was out of the question now. "Do you seriously think I'd work with him again knowing he's hacked my phone logs?"

Leo took a card out of his wallet and wrote on it. "Here. If you need to call me, use that number. Now rehearse how you're going to say, 'Thank you, Shaun, I'd love to come back to the fold.'"

"I said I don't plan to go back."

"You don't get it, do you, Charles? That's *exactly* what you're going to do." Leo picked up his glass again. "Shaun's sure you've done something, and if he feels he's contained the threat and got something out of it, he'll back off. But if Ringer ever comes home to roost, you've contaminated KWA by returning. So it'll be in his interests to protect you and keep Ian out of it."

"In other words, Leo, I'm your booby trap."

"Excellent analogy."

"But if he finds out that Ian exists, as in a functioning Ian, he might turn it around and use against me."

"I'm sure I could persuade him it's better for KWA to behave than to have me ask the FDA or the Bureau of Commerce to take a look at the company's activities. Claiming ignorance requires your corroboration."

Kinnery almost admired the tightness of that stitching. He just wished he wasn't being stitched as well. "You're good at this, aren't you?"

"I should damn well hope so. If Shaun's ever in a position to make life difficult for Ian, I'll see he never gets access to him for research. If you think I'm trouble as a politician, remember I have zero constraints as a businessman."

"You're taking this very personally."

"My son's involved. There's nothing I won't do to protect him. How likely would Shaun be to break the law to gain access to Ian?"

"He's already broken the law if he's got my phone records."

"I mean something physical."

"I think that's one degree too extreme for him."

"Intelligence doesn't preclude poor judgement. Or greed."

"So my sentence is ten to life with KWA, keeping an eye on Shaun from the inside."

"We understand each other, then. Good."

Leo drained the glass and checked his watch. Kinnery had no way out. It wasn't his fault that Shaun had dragged Leo into this, but he was the one who'd tried to do the deal with Leo to protect Ian. There really was a kind of mutually assured destruction about it after all. It had simply backfired on him.

"I don't have a choice, do I?" Kinnery said.

"Everyone always has choices, Charles. In your case, you can either be a liability to Ian, KWA, and me — and you know what happens to liabilities — or you can do the right thing for Ian, keep your reputation, and maybe even make your world-changing discoveries legally this time around."

Leo walked him to the door. There was no pretence at sociability, just politeness.

"I'll let you know when I walk the plank, then," Kinnery said. "I won't accept the offer too fast. Shaun might get suspicious."

"I might call him myself in due course and ask if he's had any more nonsense since he last rang me. Who knows what'll tumble out?"

Kinnery took that at face value and tried not to wring other meanings from it on the way downstairs in the elevator. It was a lovely evening to walk through the city and pick a restaurant, but he'd lost his appetite. Maybe he could retain his links with the university and still make the KWA deal work. Maybe he wouldn't have to move house.

Why the hell did I ever do it?

Memory was dangerously rewritable. Trying to recall a motive from years ago was difficult anyway, especially if it had proved hard to live with and had to be airbrushed so that he could cope with it. Had he really been too squeamish to terminate Ian as an embryo as the days dragged on, or had he just gone through with it because he could?

It probably didn't matter any more. Kinnery had been tried and convicted by Leo Brayne, and the sentence was life, just as it was for Ian.

GUEST COTTAGE, CHALTON FARM, WESTERHAM FALLS: NEXT DAY.

What the hell am I going to tell Tom?

Rob showered, contemplating how much his view of the world had shifted in the last few days. If he'd strolled into the pub and found an alien playing darts, he'd have told Tom all about it, because it changed the way the world worked. Where did Ian fit into that? Did seeing him morph qualify as a reality-changing, got-to-tell Tom event, or just another classified detail from an op?

Rob didn't know where to file Ian. At the very least, it would dump knowledge on Tom that he might be better off not knowing. Rob would just have to sit on it for the time being.

I suppose it's no different from getting a tan. Losing weight. Blushing. Plastic surgery. Or a coat of make-up — Christ, I've woken up next to a few nasty surprises the morning after. Ian's changes are just faster, that's all.

Now the shock had worn off, worries had room to flex their muscles. Anything medical that involved a close look at Ian's DNA was a problem. How many thousand genes did a human have? Would anyone even spot the shape-shifting ones unless they were looking for them? Probably not.

And Ian was a teenage lad. Rob remembered being one of those. The only thing on his mind was sex. If Ian got some girl pregnant, would the baby be a shape-shifter too? Did Ian even have the confidence to chat up girls yet?

Christ, when I was his age I thought I was God's gift to women. Okay, first things first — build trust and confidence. Then help him work out how to control the thing. The shape-shifting, anyway. The dick — well, I'm not the right bloke to lecture him on that.

Rob shaved and stood back to study himself in the mirror, wondering what he'd change about himself if he could. No, not one damn thing: he kept himself in terrific shape, his hair wasn't thinning, and he liked his looks. Sod it, he looked *great.* He tilted his head to one side and studied his wedding tackle, then looked down at it to consider another perspective. Well, maybe he could improve on perfection.

An inch more. Maybe an inch and a half. No point overdoing it.

If he wondered whether some magic genes could give him a bigger dick, then so would every other bloke. And women wanted to change every bloody thing about themselves. Where would it stop if people could do that? They'd never be satisfied. Then there'd be all the criminals wanting to disguise themselves, and the spooks, the medical researchers, and the biotech companies.

Poor little sod.

But he's still not on anyone's radar. There's the deeds to the ranch, but it's going to be tough for someone to make that connection.

One objective overrode everything else. Ian had to learn to control his morphing. Without that, there'd never be a driving licence or passport photo that he'd match, and without those, he was fucked. It was hard to operate without photo ID here. He wouldn't even be able to buy a beer.

And if he can't stay looking the same, he'll never have a woman. Well, not more than once, anyway. So there's the perfect incentive. Beer, cars and sex.

Rob put on his running kit while he waited for Tom's call. He could at least mention that Ian existed, even if he had to omit the details. As usual, Tom rang right on time and they exchanged sitreps.

"Mike's got a guest for the summer," Rob said. "Ian. He's a bit younger than you. I'm taking him training every day. He wants to toughen up, so I'm making a Bootneck out of him."

"Christ, Dad, be careful you don't end up injuring him. Yanks sue. It's a reflex. Just how far is this going?"

"Daily phys, fieldcraft, firearms. He might still be here when you visit."

And if he is, he'd better have that morphing shit sorted.

Tom laughed. "Dad, you really need to learn to flop on the sofa and veg out."

"I'm saving that for when you visit, kiddo."

When Tom rang off, Rob felt achingly lonely and lost for a few moments. Sod it, he lived over here now, and Leo had pulled every string to make that happen, so it was time he accepted it and tried putting down roots instead of pretending to himself that he was just visiting. Anyway, he owed the Braynes everything, and Mike really needed him around more than ever. The only way Rob could go was further in. There was no backing out of this. He'd always know what had happened.

You know what would be handy, Kinnery? Invent some amnesia pills.

Rob jogged over to the house and found Ian on the front steps, doing his stretches in a track suit that he'd borrowed from Mike. Oatie sniffed around the bushes. Ian was taking this as seriously as recruit selection.

"Had your breakfast?" Rob asked. "What's the rule?"

"Eat whenever you can, sleep whenever you can."

"Good man. No Mike this morning? Lazy sod."

"He said he's going to see his lawyer and start sorting out Gran's will for me." Ian retied his laces. "I think I need some new kit. These sneakers aren't right for running."

It took a couple of seconds to dawn on Rob. *Kit.* Ian was absorbing his slang. Rob couldn't remember when he'd last said it, but he knew he used the word all the time, and Ian didn't miss a thing. He learned fast.

Rob remembered being sixteen and shit-scared, lying in a bed in a dormitory full of strangers, staring up into the darkness and trying to remember the proper terms for things. *Pouch.* The pockets on your belt, your webbing, were called pouches, and Royal Marines pronounced it *pooches.* Pouch with a W sound was for the

Army, for *Pongos*. Anything disgusting was *gopping*. There was so much to get right. It was all part of the essential ritual of belonging, until it became part of the fabric of him and defined what he was, as natural as breathing. He could see that need to belong in Ian. Everybody had it.

"We can go to the mall later," Rob said. "There's a big sports shop. Nobody's going to stare at you or anything."

"Okay."

"How do you feel?"

"Stiff and tired. But good."

"You're still going to beat yesterday's time, right? All that soft civvy shit's over. You're rebuilding yourself from the ground up."

"Yes, Rob."

"Okay." Rob checked his watch and started running down the drive. "Crack on."

A psychologist probably wouldn't have approved of his methods, but he didn't know what else to do. Tough physical training built self-reliance and mental discipline. As far as Rob was concerned, that was a lot better for Ian than sitting through a load of therapy sessions hugging a teddy and being told how shitty the world had been to him. Anyway, it wasn't as if he was going to have to do half of the rough stuff that Rob had done to get his green beret. Mike didn't have the facilities, and Ian couldn't afford to break a leg and end up hospitalised, tested, and compromised. Rob would just have to keep pushing him past exhaustion and thinking up alternative ways to challenge him.

Ian matched Rob's pace and didn't say a word. They ran along the grass verge of the road for a couple of miles before turning right into the forest and following the trails and firebreaks. Oatie loped beside them, occasionally racing ahead and circling back as if he was making a point about his top speed. Eventually a chain link fence with a private property sign loomed in front of them, marking the turnaround point. Rob slowed to look for a good spot to take a breather as Ian shot past him.

"Whoa, stop," Rob called. "*Stop*."

Ian took a few more yards to get the message and jog back. "I thought it was a test," he panted. "To get me to give up."

Rob had to think about that while he swigged from his water bottle. They shared a bar of chocolate and the sugar rush peeled years off him. "You saw that in a film, yeah?"

"Read it. Book on special forces. You fail selection if you accept a ride they offer you at the end of a long run."

"Bonus points for pushing on, then."

"Did Mike do all this in the Guard?"

"Some, but he paid to do his hardcore training privately before he went contracting. Don't underestimate him. He's nails when he needs to be. Despite the cashmere sweaters."

"Nails," Ian said. "Hard as?"

"Correct."

Ian soaked up everything. It was like watching Tom when he was little, the same way that he found everything fascinating and hung on every word Rob said. They retraced their route — three minutes shaved off, not too shabby — and went to do an hour in the gym before getting down to some rifle practice.

Maggie had done a decent job of teaching Ian muzzle awareness and general firearms safety. He was becoming a pretty good shot with Mike's AR-10, and Rob was struck by his lack of boyish excitement about it all. He seemed to treat weapons as necessities to be slightly mistrusted. Watching endless war movies hadn't made him a gun nut.

"How do I address Senator Brayne?" Ian sat back on his heels and cleared his weapon. "Do I call him sir or Senator?"

"You can't go wrong with *sir*," Rob said.

"What if I morph in front of him?"

"Well, he'll be gobsmacked, but he won't take it personally. Come on. Strip down your weapon, clean, and reassemble. Then I'll introduce you to the Glock. Work hard on both weapons and your fire positions, and we can start doing transitions."

Ian looked him in the eye for a few moments, then got up and walked over to the workbench. "Do you think you're wasting your time? I'm never going be able to enlist."

"No, I don't. Because this'll stand you in good stead whatever you do. Do *you* think you're wasting my time? Or yours?"

"I really, really want to do this. I need to know if I could have made the grade. I'm just asking because you and Mike and Livvie bend over backwards to be kind to me, and I don't want to piss you off."

It was hard to work out if Ian was asking if he was going to be shipped out again or if it was just a statement. Leo's imminent arrival had rattled him. Rob didn't know what was coming next either. But at least they knew that the call to Ian's phone had been made from the Lansing area. If that didn't have KWA's fingerprints all over it, Rob didn't know what did.

"You're not pissing me off," Rob said. "It's doing me good, too. Come on. The sooner you finish, the sooner we can go into town to get you kitted out."

Ian just nodded, but the brief flash of a frown gave him away. Maybe Rob was pushing him too far. He relented.

"You don't have to go if you don't feel ready for it."

Ian's shoulders braced. "I'll bet your training sergeant never said it was okay if you didn't feel like tackling the rope slide. I've got to deal with people sooner or later."

Rob was irrationally proud of him for a moment. He had the right mind-set. For all Rob knew, the kid could have been a serial killer in his spare time and the ranch was full of buried bodies, but all Rob saw was someone who desperately wanted to do well and didn't care how hard he had to work to do it.

"Your call," Rob said.

"It's just a bunch of stores. It's not like the places you and Mike end up in."

"That's the spirit. Because you won't meet any shaggable women if you're a hermit."

Ian actually blushed. He cleaned and reassembled the rifle in silence.

"I haven't morphed since I first came here," he said at last.

"Beer, birds, BMW."

"What's that?"

"If you can stop morphing, you can get a photo ID. Which means a driving licence and a passport. Which means you can go out and meet women. And drink, eventually." Rob leaned in and gave him his kindest we're-all-lads-aren't-we nudge. "Look, if you get a woman's name wrong in bed, you've got some explaining to do. But change colour partway through the job, and you'll never be invited for tea and crumpets again."

Ian nodded, all grim concentration, and handed his rifle back to Rob. "Beer, birds, BMW." The stakes didn't get much higher for an eighteen-year-old lad. "Got it."

Mike still hadn't returned by the time Rob was ready to go. He'd take the Jaguar today, then. He didn't know who needed the treat more, him or Ian. The car was the most expensive thing he'd ever owned, and he rarely drove it because he was terrified that some prick would scratch the paint. Actually, it was the *only* thing he owned. Apart from his clothes and some personal stuff, everything was Mike's — the cottage, the furniture, the lot. Bev got the contents of the house when they'd divorced, and it was married quarters, so there was no money from selling a property. Rob would have given her all of it anyway. It was only fair when she was raising Tom.

So I'm an overgrown teenager living with Mum and Dad. I really need to get my shit together.

Ian studied the Jag's dashboard as they drove off towards Porton, occasionally reaching out to touch the trim. "This is nice."

"Mike and Livvie gave it to me for my birthday. I was expecting a pair of socks."

"Kind of weird how people meet, isn't it? Mike showed me his scar."

"Yeah, his days as a swimwear model are over." It was hard to gauge Ian's sense of humour, but he did seem to smile at the right points. "Get him to show you the video. I had my helmet cam running the whole time."

"Pretty awesome, saving a stranger."

"You'd do the same."

"I really hope I would. My great-grandfather — " Ian stopped dead. "Well, whatever."

Rob couldn't let Ian lose his faith in everything he'd clung to. "The Huey pilot? Yeah, those blokes were mental. Saved a lot of lives. He's someone to be proud of."

"But he was never really related to me."

"I know genes are a big deal, son, but they're not the be-all and end-all." Rob slowed to a halt at the lights, wishing the dickhead behind would back off. "If they were, you'd be in a seafood salad and I'd be in prison."

Ian just looked at him. Rob thought he was going to burst into tears. But eventually he smiled and nodded.

"Yeah," he said. "You've got a point."

The lights changed and Rob accelerated away, trying to imagine the level of shock that Ian was dealing with. Every bloody thing in his life had been a lie. The only thing that had been real and positive was the fact that Maggie had taken him in and devoted her life to him. It explained why he wasn't a complete basket case.

However weird his life had been, he'd grown up knowing he was loved and that he mattered.

I wonder how Kinnery broke the news to Maggie? 'Hi mate, can you look after this for me? It's a baby. I crossed it with a squid.' What a bastard.

Maggie must have been one in a million. Rob didn't even know what she'd looked like. It was a shame he'd never meet her now.

"Why would you be in prison?" Ian asked.

He didn't let things drop. Rob could see a bit of Tom in him. "My dad was prone to nicking things. Mum kicked him out."

"What were you like when you enlisted?"

"Sixteen, skinny, and a right little gobshite. I got it knocked out of me."

"Really? Sixteen? I can't imagine you being skinny."

"You think you can morph, eh? If you promise not to laugh, I'll show you my before and after pictures." Rob turned into the mall and parked well away from the other cars in case someone dinged his beloved Jag. "Here we go. Cap on, shoulders back, and follow my dazzling example."

Rob had to bear in mind that this was a beachhead landing for Ian. He kept him talking as they walked through the automatic doors and explained the layout to him like an operational briefing: sports and leisure shop fifty meters ahead, one stop at a fast food place to collect a late lunch, and out, maximum time one hour. That was something Ian could relate to.

"You'll want to hang out here all day before long," Rob said, nodding in the direction of a couple of girls. Ian kept his head down. "Build up to it in small doses."

He stopped in front of a clothing store and made Ian look at the display. The whole mall was either glass, mirrors, or people. Ian didn't seem bothered by the reflection and studied the jackets and T-shirts with apparent interest.

Rob nudged him. "Okay, in three, two — *go.*"

And they were in. Rob steered Ian between the racks to the sports section and kept him talking while he took likely-looking items off the rails and held them up against him for length and a general impression. It was a lot easier than shopping with Tom. Ian just followed orders and seemed to have no opinion on fashion. They moved from rack to rack, picking up a selection of stuff, then queued at the cash desk to pay.

"See?" Rob said. "Easy."

There were two women on the cash desk, one about twenty and the other more Rob's age. He could see Ian shifting from foot to foot. Then the kid lowered his head and pulled down the peak of his cap. Poor sod. He should have been past the bashful stage ten years ago. He had a lot of catching up to do.

"We'll sort out a new phone for you tomorrow," Rob said, trying to distract him. "What do you fancy for lunch? Noodles?"

Ian nodded without looking up. "Sounds good."

"Are you all right?"

"I need to go outside."

"Okay." Rob moved up in the queue. "Where are you going to be? Right outside the door?"

"Yeah. Sorry, Rob."

"No problem, mate."

Ian walked out, head down, and stood sorting through the contents of his wallet. It was only when Rob got outside and Ian looked up at him that he realised what the problem was.

"Sorry," Ian said. "I usually know when it's going to happen. I get this tight wind-burned feeling. I've done it again, haven't I?"

He looked different, not as different as when Rob simply didn't recognise him in Athel Ridge, but enough to notice. Ian's hair was razored so short that it wasn't immediately obvious that it was slightly lighter. His eyes looked wider-set, too, and more brown than hazel.

Don't spook him. Don't overreact.

"Yeah, I think you have." Rob made his best attempt at a casual inspection. "Not much, though. Any idea what triggered it?"

Ian pulled the peak of his cap down again, obviously embarrassed. "The girl on the cashier's desk."

"Oh, that. It'll sort itself out when you get a bit more confidence." *Christ, I bloody well hope so.* Rob picked every word that followed with the precise care of someone defusing a bomb. He had to make it sound like a skill, even something fun, not a disability. "Of course, there's nothing you can do about what morphs in your pants, but make the most of it. When you're my age, you'll be glad that it can still pay attention."

"It's like I dread morphing and then just thinking about it triggers me."

"Be fair to yourself. It's only been a few weeks since you've found out what you can do. If you'd known years ago, you'd be as irresistibly suave as me now. Come on. Lunch."

It was time to reinforce the idea that everything was possible if you had the right mental attitude. Rob steered Ian to the food court and sat him down at a table, then handed him his phone. He flicked through the photos until he found a folder that he usually kept to himself. It was painful to remember being that spotty little boy. "There. You work out who that oik is, and I'll get lunch."

When he came back with the noodles, Ian was still looking through the photos.

"Was that really you, Rob?" he asked.

"Yeah. When I passed PRMC. Royal Marine selection." Rob put a bowl in front of him and took the phone back for a moment. "And this is me after thirty-two weeks." Rob swiped to the formal picture taken after his passing out parade, his transformed spotless self in a new green beret, packing a lot more muscle and generating a gigawatt of confidence. "You're still only eighteen. Come on. Eat."

Rob stopped at the health store on the way out to the car park and bought Ian a tub of protein powder, more for its psychological value than anything. Before he drove off, he sat explaining to him how it took time to build lean muscle and that he'd fill out naturally, so there was no need to worry. Ian kept glancing in the wing mirror. It took Rob a while to realise that he was checking that he hadn't morphed again, not keeping an eye out for KWA ninjas.

"You know what Livvie said about meditation?" Ian said. "Controlling stress?"

"Yeah. You'll get the hang of it. Early days, mate. Early days."

"But it's more about *not* doing something. More stopping than choosing."

Rob glanced to his left. One bay away from him, a woman driver who'd pulled in gave him a long look and smiled. He smiled back. And there was absolutely nothing he could do to follow up. *Shit.* He went back to the conversation.

"Explain."

"I mean that maybe I should decide what I want to look like, and visualise that," Ian said.

"Do you ever revert to a previous face?"

"I don't know. I never tried, because I didn't think it was real."

"So where do the different faces come from? Something you've seen and remembered?"

"I don't know."

"Does your body change too?"

"Yeah, skin and hair colour. That's about it. As far as I can tell."

Rob didn't know Ian well enough yet to ask the dick question. It occurred to him that investments could go down as well as up, and you could accidentally morph yourself something a lot shorter. Maybe it wasn't such an asset after all.

"Well, I'd visualise what I wanted." Rob said. He glanced to his left again, but the woman driver was gone. "If you're a green chameleon and you end up on a brown tree, then something's got to kick in and make you think, 'Okay, I better match that shade before some bugger eats me.' It's some kind of decision."

Ian looked a bit dejected. He read the label on the protein powder, frowning.

"You'll crack it," Rob said. "Really. You will."

"That woman who was checking you out." Ian really didn't miss a thing. "If I wasn't with you, what would you have done?"

Rob wasn't sure what to say. The question threw him. "Not sure."

"Really? I didn't get in the way or anything?"

"She was probably married with six kids. Or a serial killer. She might even have fancied the Jag instead."

"So what did Livvie have to put on hold because of me?"

Rob knew where this was heading now. "You've got a wide arc of fire today, I see."

"Not really."

"Okay. They've been trying to have a baby for years." There was no point treating Ian like an idiot. He'd just keep asking until he got an answer. "Loads of treatment sessions. But don't go thinking you've screwed things up for them, because it was Mike's decision to bring you back, and I think Livvie needs a break. There. That's the truth."

Ian nodded sagely. "Thank you."

"Home now?"

"Yeah. Thanks."

Ian was more relaxed on the way home. All he seemed to want was a dose of truth, however awkward or embarrassing. Rob was starting to understand how he thought. Everyone needed some benchmark of reality. If everything you'd thought was true had disintegrated in front of you, and you didn't even know what you were supposed to look like, then any truth was solid ground to build on.

"Okay, I might have waited until she came back, and struck up a conversation with her," Rob said, awash with guilt for some reason. "The woman in the car park, I mean."

Ian just nodded. "Maybe there'll be a next time."

"Yeah," Rob said. "There usually is."

EIGHT

Charlie, I'm going to have to take Ian out of school and teach him at home. He's started to change. Are you pleased now? Are you happy that your goddamn experiment worked, you son of a bitch? Is he going to get worse? You don't know, do you? Well, fuck you, Charlie.

Maggie Dunlop in a call to Charles Kinnery, on Ian's first morphing incident, aged seven.

LLOYD HOUSEHOLD, LANSING, MICHIGAN: AUGUST.

Dru stood brushing her teeth, her mind coasting, unable to silence a nagging question that wouldn't shut up and die.

How had Weaver made the jump — a big jump — from conspiracy theory allegations about human chameleons to the theft of KWA's property via a mule?

She rinsed and spat, searching the mirror for new wrinkles. No, maybe that was a perfectly reasonable way to explain how Zoe Murray could have made a werewolf story out of embryo research. Introduce genetic engineering into a discussion, and rationality went out the window. Dru could understand that. Patent disputes, gene therapies going wrong, headline-grabbing luminous cats — it didn't inspire confidence in the layman. They were scared of that kind of thing.

That's me. I'm a layman. I don't really understand this.

But it wasn't her job to understand the science, merely to find out if Kinnery had taken KWA's intellectual property. Now she had leads in Maggie Dunlop and a vague location. She grabbed a plate of cherry muffins from the kitchen and settled down at her desk in the back room, invigorated. The job had suddenly become compelling.

Kinnery. Clever bastard.

Dru picked a whole cherry out of the soft crumb and studied it. It wouldn't be that easy to extract stolen genetic material from a human body. The lawyers could argue about intent and informed consent for months. How did the law treat a thief who couldn't return stolen goods because they were permanently embedded in him?

"Awesome," she said aloud. It didn't resolve the unanswered question about exactly what would happen to the mule, especially if he didn't cooperate, but it was probably all hypothetical anyway. "I should have been a lawyer."

Clare appeared in the doorway, still in her pyjamas. "Mom, it's Saturday. It's six in the morning. Are you talking to yourself? And *working*?"

"I'm on a roll, sweetheart," Dru said. "I have to work while the muse is upon me."

"I don't think there's a muse for stalking."

"I'm not stalking."

"I heard you making those calls. You don't have an aunt."

Dru felt her face flush. *She's caught me lying. God, that's a terrible example to set your kid.* How the hell did she explain or justify that?

"You shouldn't be listening, Clare." Dru tried not to sound pompous. She was on shaky ground. "I'm working on something really sensitive."

"I came downstairs to get a drink. I wasn't eavesdropping."

Clare had transformed into her middle-aged persona, the one who seemed slightly disappointed in Dru but forgave her for falling so short of expectations.

"I'm sorry," Dru said. "I'm not proud of that."

"But you're really good at it."

So I'm an expert liar. There's damnation if ever I heard it.

"I'm trying to find out if someone stole some stuff from the company years ago, that's all," Dru said. "If they have, it's worth an awful lot of money."

Clare just looked at her without the slightest hint of excitement.

It was Dru's mother's expression, the one that glanced at the messy painting brought home from class and forced a smile.

"If you get it back, I hope your boss gives you a raise," Clare said, took a muffin, and wandered off.

Dru wondered whether to go after her and have a timely parental chat about ethics, but that might have made more of it than was healthy. She'd catch her later and discuss it in a chatty way, a *harmless* way, dressing it up as the kind of painstaking, necessary work that police had to do.

Maybe that was the career she should have picked, investigation or research of some kind. She enjoyed digging up fragments and assembling them into a picture of perfect revelation. But she'd chosen wrong. She had to make the best of it.

Larry called it self-pity, but it was more a dread of the abyss. If she looked too hard at the choices she hadn't made, she'd see all the things she could have done and been but now never would. If she gave in to it, there'd only be regret: it was better not to look at all. Nobody wanted to accept that they'd squandered so much of their life on a mistake. It was a big bill to pay for nothing.

She shook it off and settled down at the computer to search for place names. There was a town called Bethel after all. *Well done, Dr Missiakos.* But when she checked the map, it was too close to Seattle and didn't fit the rural backwater he'd described. She browsed the local directories for Bethel and the surrounding area, looking for the name Dunlop. There were some, but the first names didn't tie up.

Okay, Missiakos said he didn't quite remember. What else sounds like Bethel?

Dru began compiling a list of place names in Washington and physically checking the map instead of relying on word searches. There was nothing beginning with B that met the criteria.

How did people remember words, though? It was often the general sound, not the initial letter.

Bethel.

Something-el?

Something-thel?

For all she knew, it could have been an F instead of a TH in the name, or nothing like that at all, simply the name of the house itself, like Bethel Farm. She began searching for farms, sites of scientific interest, meteorological data, and any sites with a state list or a database, reading the names aloud in case one sounded plausible.

Then she saw the name Athel Ridge on a geology site, and it smacked her right in the eye.

Not *Beth*-el something, then: it was *Ath*-el something. It was a natural mistake to make after all those years. Eventually she found it on the map. It looked like a backwater. That was good enough to warrant time spent on more in-depth searches for Maggie Dunlop.

It was hard to believe that there was anyone alive who hadn't left some footprint on the internet, or had someone else leave it for them, but Maggie Dunlop seemed to be that rare animal. She wasn't on the county voter's register, at least not under Dunlop, or even in a phone directory. She'd probably married, though. There was no way to guess her surname if she had.

But it had been her family's place, according to Missiakos. Maybe Dru would find Dunlop somewhere in the county land register records. She clicked on the property search and typed in the surname field.

D,U,N,L,O,P.

And that was when everything started falling into place with an ease that surprised her. The search threw up Dunlop Ranch, Athel Ridge.

Got it. Wow.

It was like finding the Holy Grail on an auction site. She wondered if she was creating false patterns, but Athel Ridge was a small town. The chances of Dunlop Ranch not being connected to Maggie Dunlop looked increasingly small.

The online GIS map of the ranch showed a big plot of woodland and pasture with a stream running through it, some miles from the town itself. Dru opened a satellite map to look at the aerial view.

Does someone do that with my house?

It was an uncomfortable thought. She wasn't sure that she really wanted to know. She'd seen sat maps as a handy way to find a restaurant or parking lot, but now she was spying on someone, even if this wasn't real-time data, and it didn't feel quite so harmless.

She toggled back to the property register results, trying to shake off the thought. The ranch was in the name of Margaret and Ian Dunlop. That was fascinating. Maggie was either married by the time she was at university, or she'd kept her maiden name and the ranch was co-owned with a male relative. It didn't matter. Dru had the lead she needed. The slog through small, tedious detail and an informed guess had paid off. She savoured the moment.

So what's Ian to Maggie? Husband, brother, son?

The satellite view showed just how rural the location was. Asking a PI to keep an eye on Kinnery in a city was one thing, but hiding in a hedge to watch a remote ranch was getting into the realms of FBI skills. Surveillance wasn't the answer, though. She had no idea what the theoretical mule might look like. It would be a case of following Maggie Dunlop's trail to see what lay at the end of it. Grant could get an affiliate to do the leg work, but that meant Dru would need to share more information with more people. She couldn't even give him a description of what he'd be looking for. He could make what he liked out of *The Slide*'s piece, if he'd spotted it, but she couldn't give it credibility or add detail to it.

And she had a deadline. Weaver wanted this resolved or buried by the end of the month.

I'll do it myself, then. I have to. I'm dull and grey. Nobody's going to notice me.

Damn, she actually wanted to. She could do this. It was her investigation. Whenever she'd bitched to Larry about big bikes and midlife crises, she'd been sure that women didn't have them, at least not in the same I-can-still-cut-it kind of way. Female midlife angst was about staring into mirrors and buying face creams that couldn't possibly work, a grudging slide into acceptance that once her power over men had faded — the kind that sprang from the subconscious would-she-let-me-do-her game that went on in both minds — it had to be replaced by the application of financial sanctions and psychological pressure.

Dru e-mailed KWA's travel agency with a request to book her flight and hotel, passing it off with the universal project code that silenced anyone in the company these days: Halbauer. Then she made lunch while Clare phoned Larry to arrange her stay. If the bastard backed out now, Dru would throttle him. But whatever he said had made Clare really happy. She came bouncing into the kitchen, grinning.

"He says I can come over on Monday evening."

"Great." Dru dished up the enchiladas. "Did he ask questions? He always does."

"Not really. I told him you were away on business."

"Gee, thanks."

"Well, you told me not to make him think you had a new man."

"Okay. I concede that point."

"He said he wasn't surprised."

Dru wasn't offended. She preferred Larry as a snarky bastard. If he'd been nice about her, she'd have regretted the divorce, but he wasn't, so the parting of the ways had therefore been necessary and inevitable. All was right with the world again. She had no reason to miss a man like that.

While she did the laundry that afternoon, she rehearsed her plan for Athel Ridge. She visualised herself knocking on the door and introducing herself. What happened after that was the difficult part.

Hello, are you Maggie Dunlop? My name's Dru. I work for KWA.

She was going to ask a total stranger if she'd helped Charles Kinnery steal research and DNA from his former company. It was something that law enforcement and government agents did every day, but she was neither of those no matter how many parallels she drew. Her authority ended at KWA's gates. What the hell was she thinking? However she worded it, however clever her con trick, it was confrontational. She hadn't fully considered that until now. But it was too late to back out. Reality began to sap her bravado.

Maggie would ask why she'd shown up on her doorstep. If she was what Dru suspected she was, someone Kinnery trusted, then she'd tip him off right away, and the only good that might do would be to panic Kinnery into making a mistake. But the mule — if he existed — would go to ground.

Perhaps I should just treat it as a recon and see if it's worth coming back later or trying another tack.

And maybe it won't be Maggie who answers the door. Maybe it'll be that British guy who answered the phone.

Maybe he was Ian Dunlop. If Maggie was in her sixties, then the guy sounded around the right age to be her son, but the nationalities didn't make sense yet.

Kinnery's in Vancouver. Washington's right next door to Canada. A lot of Brits end up in Canada. There could be a loose family connection somehow.

Dru had been thinking in terms of the mule as someone bound by trust, fear, or dependency, not blood. The idea that Kinnery might have parked the engineered genes in a relative was freshly disturbing.

It's never like this on detective shows, is it?

As soon as the thought struck her, she began doubting every connection she'd made. A lot of things that she thought she knew probably weren't true. Like anyone else, her mind was prone to retrieve memories and imagined facts that didn't come from the real world at all, but from something she'd seen on TV or read in a book and then forgotten.

And why did I think I could handle this? Because I've watched it so many times on TV that I think I know how it's done.

Realisation of her limits didn't change a thing, though. Weaver didn't want any official investigation. It was her problem. Everything flowed from that. He'd made it impossible for her to tell anyone else the truth, and deception begat deception. Lies were a lot like cookies. It was hard to stop after just one.

After being lied to for an entire marriage, including the lies she realised she'd told herself, Dru actually craved some truth. She went back to the computer to start a fresh search for names, not confined to Washington. A lot of Ian Dunlops were thrown up but none of them had any relevance to the area. For a mad moment, she considered dialling Kinnery's landline just to see how he reacted.

Idiot.

She could have kicked herself. Instead of trying the Seattle number first, she should have dialled the number it was calling — Kinnery's dedicated line. But he'd be on his guard now if her wrong-number English guy had any connection.

Maybe, if she'd called his landline and said nothing, Kinnery would eventually have asked: "Maggie? Is that you?"

But she hadn't. She had to work it out the hard way now.

CHALTON FARM, WESTERHAM FALLS.

"You look like a man in need of a Scotch," Mike said.

Dad walked into the hall and put his bag down to give him a hug. "I'm sorry that I landed you with this, Micko. How's it going?"

"Well, Livvie's using a beanbag launcher to fire steak across the lawn. For the dog, not for Rob. Everything's peachy."

"You sound like you're enjoying this."

"Yes, I suppose I am." Mike led him into the sitting room and fixed a drink. "Ian's pretty normal considering his background. A little withdrawn and awkward. But he's catching up fast."

Dad frowned as if he still didn't believe sanity was possible. "Any more wrong numbers?"

"No. I disabled the phone and got him another prepaid one. There's nothing to locate him now without the sort of spook tech that KWA won't have." Mike rattled ice in the tumbler and poured, waiting for Dad to indicate a suitable dose had been reached. "Are you sure this is shut down at the DoD end?"

"As sure as I can be. If you get a visit from the proverbial black helicopter, then I'll know they were lying. But they're rushing to cover their asses, which is usually a sign of enthusiasm for avoiding an investigation."

"You said they didn't believe it."

"They don't. But you know how I work, Micko. First strike. If you ask who couldn't keep their department watertight and if they've managed to miss a shape-shifter on the loose for two decades despite their very lavish budgets, they'll opt for the crazy rumour and hope they don't have to investigate. Ringer's old. Nobody's got a career resting on it. So they hope I'll shut up and go away. And I will."

"So it's just KWA we have worry about."

"Kinnery's going back to work for them."

"Seriously?"

"Weaver wants him, allegedly to make the company look prettier in merger talks. Kinnery's not keen."

"So why is he doing it?"

"Because I twisted his arm."

Dad could twist very efficiently. Mike was appalled. "Forgive a political amateur, Dad, but that's asking for trouble. He'll blurt something out."

"On the contrary. The guy's a world-class con artist. He's managed to hide Ian for eighteen years, even from his wife. She left him because she thought all that secrecy was about a mistress, and he never once tried to defend himself. Now *that's* tight-lipped. He ought to be in intelligence."

"I still think it's risky. Weaver must suspect him of something."

"If I were Weaver, I'd keep him inside the tent and make sure he didn't piss in the wrong direction. But once he's in, he's mine. He'll watch, and he'll report, and if Weaver ever finds out about Ian and doesn't behave like a Christian gentleman, then he'll regret it."

There'd been times when Mike hadn't been sure if his father ever strayed across legal lines, and he hadn't wanted to find out. Dad didn't operate in a world where nice guys won on points by the righteousness of their cause. But he did have moral lines, very clear ones, and creating transgenic humans seemed to be one of his many no-go areas. Mike was heartened. He suspected that his great-grandfather, the man who boosted the family from rich to super-rich, would have sold Ian to the highest bidder.

"Okay," Mike said. "I trust your judgement."

"I'll deal with this now. You and Rob have done your bit. Thanks. I won't put you in that position again."

"And what does *deal with* mean?"

"You can't look after Ian forever. He probably needs specialist care."

"But who's going to give it to him? There isn't an expert on what Ian is. Not even Kinnery. And he's not a psychiatric case."

"Micko, I know what you're like. You feel the world's your responsibility."

"I gave him my word that I'd protect him. I can't delegate that."

Dad swirled his Scotch around the glass, staring into it. "You don't know what that might entail." Mike waited for him to launch a counter-argument, but he just shrugged as if he'd decided to fight another day. "You know, Kinnery tried the cancer cure argument on me. Ian's worth the moral cost because of the medical benefit for others."

"This *is* the pharmaceutical industry we're talking about, yes?"

"The irony wasn't lost on me."

"Well, Ian doesn't owe the world anything." Mike's indignation tumbled out. He was getting his case straight for his own position rather than drawing a line for his father. "And the world doesn't need to know about him, any more than it needs to know if someone has epilepsy controlled by drugs. There's no practical military use for morphing. It's all about medical applications, and if we really want to relieve human suffering, giving the Third World clean water and drainage would achieve a lot more."

Dad swirled his glass again and shrugged. "You don't have to persuade me."

"Sorry. I'm in my pulpit again."

"I'll go wash up. Then we can crack a few beers." Dad made an emphatic gesture with his glass in the direction of the doors. "Is

Rob okay?"

"Having a ball. He's turning Ian into a Marine."

"You pick sterling friends, Micko. I can't fault your judgement."

"Quality over quantity, Dad."

Mike wandered down the hall to look across the lawn from the back doors while he waited for Dad. Livvie was playing with Oatie and his new toy, a beanbag launcher that sent the greyhound tearing across the grass in pursuit of flying titbits. Rob and Ian were tending the barbecue. Smoke and luscious smells wafted across the garden. All was right with the world and the house was the way it always should have been, busy with family and friends enjoying a summer day.

Eventually Dad walked up behind him and gripped his shoulder.

"By the way," Dad said, "you need to get your ass home and see your mom. And Charlotte. Otherwise they'll both want to visit."

"What about Ian? I can't leave Rob to hold the fort."

"Ask him."

"I've already screwed his work plans."

"I sent him a payment for retrieving Ian, by the way."

"You know he'll try to give it back."

"The man's entitled to be paid for his professional services."

"Well, I've been thinking about that." Mike decided to blurt out his news while Dad was distracted by the extraordinary spectacle of the world's only shape-shifting human placing steak on the barbecue. He started with the down-page items. He'd ramp up to the adoption issue. "We're going to start our own security company."

"Excellent." Dad slapped him on the back. "You can't dodge RPGs forever. Some niche service, I hope."

"And Livvie and I are going to adopt if the next round of IVF fails. So I need to be home more."

Mike held his breath. He hoped that Rob's prediction was right. Dad paused for a moment before cracking a smile.

"You're too good a guy not be a dad," he said. "Your mom's going to be delighted."

"Are you?"

"Absolutely. How far are the plans advanced, then?"

"Early days." Mike didn't want to spend the day discussing babies in front of Ian. It seemed insensitive. "Come on, then.

Come and meet Ian."

"Has he changed since he's been here?"

Mike wished he'd lied outright from the start and simply told Dad that Ian was an ordinary kid who didn't do tricks, whatever Kinnery claimed. It would have left Mike with a totally different set of problems, but at least it wouldn't have been this one. But lying to Dad didn't come naturally to him. No, he just couldn't do it.

"Here." Mike took out his phone and showed him the photos. "See for yourself. I took these a few hours apart."

The pictures didn't give a clinical comparison, but they were enough to make the point. That simple, reasonable decision felt like standing at the top of a ski-run. Now Mike was about to push himself over, and then he wouldn't be able to stop even if he wanted to.

Dad scrutinised the images, cocking his head slightly as he sipped his Scotch. His expression relaxed into unguarded wonder.

"I'll be damned," he said at last. "That's quite impressive. How long does it take?"

Mike was dismayed by the slight enthusiasm. He wanted it all to be dismissed as an anti-climax.

"It's fast — seconds, maybe minutes," he said. "But it's definitely not enough to be useful for covert ops."

"He can't turn from a small guy into a basketball player, then. This is tinkering around the edges."

"Exactly. And he can't control it. I know it's not easy to take Kinnery at his word, but he did warn us about that."

"So what makes him change?"

"Stress, I think. Sometimes embarrassment." This was the one area where Mike had much more life experience than his father — combat, *real* combat, where the next second could be one he never saw. He could tell Dad the truth and still do right by Ian. "Dad, the last thing you need is kit that fails specifically when your adrenaline's pumping. Imagine your cover disappearing in the middle of a mission. Suddenly you're the only Nordic blonde in a crowd debating the best way to behead a filthy infidel. Even the CIA piss their pants sometimes."

"I once saw something like that in a comedy," Dad said, opening the doors. "But context is everything." He strode across the patio with his hand held out to for a meet-and-greet. "Ian. It's good to meet you at last. How are you, my boy?"

Ian shook his hand, the perfect gentleman. "Hello, sir. I'm very well."

Mike wondered how much was Maggie's drill and how much had been gleaned from movies. "Call me Leo," Dad said, and walked Ian across the lawn to the circle of loungers under the trees.

Rob prodded the steaks and burgers, passing no comment while Mike filled him in on Kinnery's enforced return to KWA. Mike couldn't even read his expression. Rob just went on moving the meat around, listening patiently.

"Well?" Mike prodded him. "Say something."

"Trust your dad. He didn't get where he is today by giving people the benefit of the doubt. And find the buns. I'm ready to plate up."

"You don't think it's risky sticking Kinnery back in KWA?"

"Letting him carry on breathing's risky. But he does have a track record in keeping his mouth shut. Did your dad ask him what incriminating evidence he's holding in reserve?"

"Dad says he told him that he burned his notes."

"I bet he kept something. Unfortunately, the only way to guarantee that he keeps it zipped is something that involves a deserted building site and a lot of wet concrete. We just have to live with it." Rob gave Mike a pointed look and spread his arms. "Come on, where's my bloody buns?"

Rob was better at dealing with one problem at a time and making the others wait their turn. Mike ended up spinning plates trying to resolve everything at once. He had to see this for what it was, an impossible situation that his money could improve but never fully resolve.

Like trying to have a baby. Some punches you have to ride.

Mike and Rob ferried the plates over to the table and topped up the drinks. Leo was getting on with Ian like a house on fire. They were talking about sheep and Livvie's meditation coaching. Livvie sat back in her lounger, drink in hand, and winked at Mike. She looked happier than he'd seen her in years.

"Where's the dog?" Mike asked. "I hope he's left room for his burger."

Ian jumped up. "I better go find him. Excuse me."

Dad watched him go, eyes slightly narrowed in appraisal. "I wouldn't have known there was anything unusual about him at all," he said. "That's truly remarkable. A very pleasant young man."

"I'd like him to stay with us until he can cope for himself," Livvie said suddenly. "He's no trouble at all."

Leo held up his hands in mock submission. "I know when I've been out-voted."

"I mean it," she said. "I'm fond of him."

Mike had thought she was being the loyal, supportive wife, always tolerant of his behaviour no matter how hare-brained or selfish it was. But she was starting to drive this. He went with it.

"What if he can *never* cope?" Dad asked. "How does that fit in with your family plans?"

"He's coping now, actually."

"You don't have a rehoming duty. I didn't ask Micko to do this with the expectation that it would become a commitment."

"Where else can he go, Dad?" Mike asked. "An institution? That's just more people who'll know what he is. If we don't step up for him, who will?"

Dad didn't even blink. Perhaps it actually seemed like a good plan to him now. At least he'd know where Ian was. "You sure you're okay with that, Livvie?"

"Yes. And we're not dumping this on Rob, either." She wagged a finger at Mike. "Let's see how it goes. Ian might have plans of his own before long, and then what are we going to do? Stand back and respect them? He's an adult."

Rob opened another beer. "I don't mind. It's been ages since I played dad."

"You've already got a terrific son," Mike said. "Don't hog them all."

There was a short, embarrassed pause before Rob laughed. "Okay, your turn to play surrogate dad, then," he said. "We'll take it in shifts. It's bloody hard work teaching a lad to drink and chase women."

Mike cringed. *Damn, why did I say that? Am I that broody?*

He suddenly remembered the cats at Livvie's lodgings in Oxford. One of them had a litter, and another cat was desperate to mother them. She'd carry off the kittens and spit fury at the real mom when she came to reclaim them. Mike found it heartbreaking to watch. But animals did that. It was an overwhelming instinct, and he was just another animal, subject to all the hard-wired instincts of the wild. Sometimes it bubbled up and there was nothing he could do to stop it.

"Ian's picking up Rob's accent," Livvie said, changing the subject. "He's actually a very good mimic. He really listens."

"Well, my accent's part of my gorgeousness," Rob said. "But I think Ian's going to be better off talking proper posh like Mike. It's better for his prospects."

Dad reached for one of the jugs of Livvie's special mimosa mix. Mike could see Ian jogging back with Oatie at his heels.

"If he's not going back to the ranch," Dad said, "we'd better get that property disposed of and set up accounts for him."

Mike nodded. "I've started that."

"Are you staying tonight, Leo?" Rob asked.

"I certainly am. I've got drinking to do."

"Good. Before we get too hand-carted, let's go down the range and I'll show you how well Ian's doing." Rob stood up and gestured to Ian. "Come and show Leo your marksmanship."

Ian would do whatever Sergeant Rennie told him. Dad fell into line too, probably because he realised that Rob was dragging them off to give Mike some talking time with Livvie. Oatie watched with his ears pricked as they disappeared behind the house, then flopped down next to Livvie as if he knew they were going to do that noisy thing again and didn't want any part of it. Livvie lay back, eyes shut, basking in the sun slanting through the branches.

"Are you asleep?" Mike said.

"No." She reached out and picked up her glass. "Just feeling mellow."

"So you want Ian to stay around."

"Like you said, who else is going to step up for him?"

"I'm sorry I dropped this on you."

"Stop apologising. It's not exactly a scenario anyone could plan for."

"Just bear in mind that he might need to be around for a very long time, and it might be a pain in the ass occasionally."

"That's kids for you, I'm told."

"I'm not asking you to make a substitute family out of him, honey."

Mike hadn't formed a detailed plan beyond not handing Ian over to anyone he didn't want to be handed over to. There were essential milestones, like getting a driving licence and providing for his financial future, but Mike had to consider whether that might turn into a lifetime commitment. What if he developed health issues? Modified animals had problems, and even legitimate gene therapy sometimes went wrong.

The more I read about it, the more I worry. Tumours, rejection, viruses from the original vector. Who knows?

Perhaps every parent worried about their kid's future just like that. Maybe it wasn't Ian who was different, but Mike who was the same as every other anxious dad.

"We could have the barn converted for him," Livvie said. "He'd have his own place, but with security and support next door."

"And how about the IVF?"

Livvie stared into the glass as if she was working up to telling Mike something uncomfortable. "Right now, I'd rather call it a day and go straight to adoption. But let's see how I do with Ian. If I can't cope with a well-behaved adult, I won't be much use with a child."

"Whatever you want," Mike said. Everything seemed to have changed now that a family had shifted from theory to reality. He kept Rob's advice in mind. "As long as we're okay. We *are* okay, aren't we?"

"You had to ask?"

"No. Of course not."

"Mike, this isn't a swipe at you, sweetheart, but I've been stuck on my own in this house for years. You know why I don't drink while you're away? Because I'd get wasted every night. I teach conversational French in town once a year. If I'm lucky, I might see Mr Andrews to wave to a couple of times a week. When you're away, the rest of my social interaction with the outside world is via a video link. I know exactly how Ian feels."

Livvie had never given Mike an ultimatum about his military career, such as it was. He'd dumped it on her early in their marriage and she'd supported him all the way without complaint. But now he realised how long she'd sat on that unhappiness before she felt able to say it. He was mortified.

"I'm a selfish bastard," he said. "I'm so sorry. I know I do this to people. I arrange them."

"No, you're just trying to do the decent thing all the time for *everybody* — serve your country, feed the poor, protect the weak, save the frigging whale, every goddamn thing, and that's spreading yourself too thin. You end up saving nothing at all." She drained the glass in two pulls. "Saving Ian is pretty heroic on its own, Mike.

It's a big ask. Maybe that's enough to keep your karma in the black for the next few years."

"I'll be at home a lot more now we're starting the company," he said. "Life's going to be different, honey, I swear."

"And Rob?" Livvie gestured with her empty glass. "He needs a life too. He's always there for you."

"I know. And I'm there for him. I'm not expecting him to sweep up for me on this."

"We're sorted, then," she said, using Rob's favourite declaration of a situation under control. "So, once the ranch is sold, Ian vanishes completely."

"We'll pass it through a few companies to make sure. And a few bank accounts."

"What if someone gets his social security number, though?"

"They'd have to know he existed before they could even start digging for that," Mike said. "And they don't."

Mike wondered how witness protection actually worked in detail. The people going into hiding almost certainly had much more complex, connected lives to erase than Ian did. They had relatives, employers, all kinds of records like footprints in their wake that had to be swept away and replaced with fake histories. Ian had almost nothing. That, at least, worked in his favour now. The only untidy detail was Kinnery. It was too bad that he'd come to the house, but Dad couldn't have known that the crazy story was completely true.

Ian could be anyone he wanted to be, though, and as long as Kinnery maintained his long silence, nobody would ever know he was here.

EN ROUTE TO DUNLOP RANCH, ATHEL RIDGE.

Dru realised she'd missed the unmarked turning to Dunlop Ranch when she passed a sign welcoming her to Athel Ridge.

A veil of unseasonal chilly drizzle didn't help. She turned the rental car around to retrace her route. Several U-turns later, she found the road and then the ranch's entrance, just a gap in some bushes with no gates, no sign, and an unpaved track leading up a shallow hill. Maybe she had the wrong place.

She checked the sat map. No, this was it.

The track curved across sloping pasture and through trees. A house finally emerged through the foliage, and Dru stopped about fifty yards from it to sit with the engine idling. There were no signs of activity. On a wet day, that didn't necessarily mean nobody was home.

If I can cold-call Kinnery's graduation class, I can knock on that door.

It was another crossroads choice, one path leading to safe failure, the other accelerating her drift into the unknown and possibly indefensible. She started counting. On five, she'd either switch off the engine and get out of the car, or turn around and go home.

One.

Two ... three ... four ...

Five.

Dru pulled up the hood on her jacket and started the long walk to the front door, purse crushed under her arm for reassurance. She was sure Maggie would see her coming and fling open the door.

But it remained resolutely closed. She paused in front of the steps and looked up, trying to catch some movement at the windows, but there was nothing. The only sound was a crow rasping *car-car-car, car-car-car,* in a voice so articulate and human that for a stupid, irrational moment she was ready to believe that the bird was warning someone that a car had arrived. Black shapes flapped out of nearby branches and vanished.

Okay. Knock.

Dru rapped a few times, then spotted the doorbell and gave it a three-second press. Perhaps she'd been optimistic to expect to find anyone at home, but there was no way of checking first. Her only option was to wait and watch. She pressed the bell a few more times but there was still no answer. Birds settled in the branches again. It felt as if the crows were gathering to keep an eye on her.

She rang one more time, then began working her way around the house, first along the porch and then down the side towards the barn. Maybe she'd find someone in there. If Maggie Dunlop was watching her from the house, this might make her come out. Dru made a show of calling out like an innocent visitor genuinely looking for the owner.

"Mrs Dunlop?" Dru pushed the barn door and stuck her head inside. Her voice sounded shaky even to herself. "Mrs Dunlop? Anyone home?"

The barn smelled of farmyard and musty, decaying things that she couldn't identify. Something rustled in the corner. *Calm down. It's just mice. Rats.* Dim light from a couple of small windows showed that the place was empty except for piles of timber. Dru crunched around on the straw-scattered floor, feeling stupid, wishing she'd worn more sensible shoes, and wondering what to do next.

Go into town. Have a coffee and ask at the post office, perhaps. People always help if you ask nicely.

She turned, still trying to compose a cover story, and walked straight into the barrel of a shotgun.

"Jesus *Christ* — "

Her heart beat so hard that she thought it would tear itself loose. But the gun wasn't aimed at her. It was simply all she could focus on. The thickset, curly-haired white guy who was holding it muzzle down looked at her without curiosity, just distrust. He wore faded blue overalls and seemed to be in his fifties, not the age she expected.

"Can I help you, ma'am?"

Well, he wasn't the British guy who'd answered the phone. He sounded local. Adrenaline was worse than alcohol for snatching the reins out of Dru's hands. Her mouth took over. Her rational brain was so slow out of the gate that she was into the next furlong of deception by the time it moved. It was like watching a stranger, a genuine out-of-body experience.

"I'm sorry, are you Ian?" She pushed back her hood and tried to ignore the shotgun. "I'm looking for Maggie Dunlop. Have I got the right address?"

The man just stared into her face for a few seconds. "Why do you want to see her?"

Stick to the story. He might be able to check it with someone.

"My late aunt — she had a college friend, and all I know is that he or she lived in Washington. I don't even have a name, male or female. I got Maggie's name from one of her classmates."

The man wasn't even looking her over. He just focused on her face as if he could stare the truth out of her. "And what's *your* name?"

If Dru got too smartass he might call the police, and she couldn't explain herself without sounding insane, criminal, or both. Now the lies bred. They had to. A fake first name was the easiest way to get tripped up. The only surname that came to mind was her maiden name.

"I'm Dru. Dru Wilson." She held out her hand. "You're Ian, right? Ian, I just came to tell Maggie that my aunt passed on. I couldn't write or phone. Obviously."

Dru thought she was doing okay when Ian took her hand and shook it. But then things started to go downhill.

"That's not my name," he said. "I look after the place."

Now she was stuck. Did he mean Maggie was away, or that he was an employee? She couldn't ask him to clarify without exposing herself to more questions she probably couldn't answer. And she'd blown her one explanation for being here. She couldn't make up another. She either had to walk away or persist.

"Well, can I get a message to Maggie?" *What do I say? People forget who they knew forty years ago. I can brazen this out. Worst case, it's mistaken identity.* "Do I write her, or what?"

"I can pass on a message." He wasn't giving anything away, not even his name. Maybe he didn't believe her. Maybe he shouldn't have been there himself, or perhaps Maggie had warned him to keep an eye out for nosey strangers. "You want to give me your contact details?"

This wasn't how it was supposed to pan out. Even pausing to think of a safe number to give him probably made him more suspicious. Dru rummaged in her purse to buy a few seconds' thinking time and wrote the number of her burner on a paper napkin.

"There." She handed it to him. "I'm going home tomorrow. So if she's available, I'd love to see her."

The guy looked at the number and nodded. "I'll see." It was definitely Dru's cue to go. "Where are you staying?"

"Spokane. Thanks for your help." She decided to risk asking about the Seattle number to see what reaction she got. "Actually, I did call a number from my aunt's address book that I thought might be Maggie's. But I got some British guy."

"I'll pass that on," he said, giving away absolutely nothing. She'd played her last card. "Safe journey."

Dru got back in the car. He'd probably check her cell number, which wouldn't tell him anything, but Maggie Dunlop would probably call Kinnery now — if Dru had connected the pieces correctly.

Damn. What did I say when that Brit answered the call? I didn't mention Maggie. I hadn't even thought up that lie then.

There was still the post office to try. She stopped in Athel Ridge and plucked up courage over a coffee, watching the rain pepper the diner window for half an hour. The town was a couple of bars, an agricultural supplies store, and a garage. More small stores stretched past the crossroads. Eventually, she couldn't spin the coffee out any longer and got up to walk to the post office.

She really did intend to go in. She got to the doors, but the adrenaline ebbed away. This was a small community. If she grilled the USPS staff, the guy at the ranch would probably get to hear. A temporary tactical withdrawal was called for. The trip had been fruitless, unless the man believed her and gave Maggie Dunlop the message.

Dru drove back to Spokane. She'd wait to see what shook out, but meanwhile she'd turn her attention back to Kinnery. Grant was still keeping tabs on him. Sooner or later, Kinnery — a guilty Kinnery, anyway — would slip up. Everyone did.

She already had, after all.

NINE

Here's the thing they never tell you about politics, Micko. There's no such thing as a government. There's a loose gathering of people in the shared business of running a country, but they're just trying to steer their small fiefdom. They're not even steering the same course, or for the same reasons. I don't just mean opposition politics or lobby groups. I'm talking about government departments and agencies too — intra-agency and inter-agency strife. What voters call a government is just a country within a country, in a constant civil war with itself.

Leo Brayne, discussing governance with his son, Thanksgiving 1998.

CHALTON FARM, WESTERHAM FALLS: AUGUST.

Beer, birds, BMW.

Ian stumbled up the slope, sagging under a rucksack packed with six five-pound plates while Rob ran alongside him, yelling and swearing. All he had to do was reach the top of the paddock.

Beer, birds, BMW.

His legs were jelly, but he'd get there if it killed him. He felt like it would. And he'd never been happier.

Phys, as Rob called any kind of fitness training, was now embedded in his routine. *Beer, birds, BMW.* Those were important, yes, but when he was training, his focus was on making himself more like Rob, not just physically but mentally. Rob could take anything. So could Mike, but Rob had made a religion out of it. Rob had so much confidence that it was almost luminous.

"Come on, you slack bugger. Get a fucking move on." Rob yelled right in his ear, point blank and painful. "Move, move, move, move, *move*!"

Ian almost fell a few times, but momentum kept him upright. He was only yards from his goal. The last obstacle was a frame made from a ladder of logs that he had to run up before jumping from the platform at the top. He launched himself off the first log and almost made the second before he slipped and hit one of the verticals as he fell, crashing onto the grass.

It was no great height, but it shook him. Now he couldn't stand up. His rucksack was too heavy. He struggled like a beetle on its back, unable to make his legs obey. Rob reached down to pull him up.

Ian batted his hand away, humiliated. "I can do it."

"Come on. That's what your mates are for."

Rob helped him roll onto all fours and scramble to his feet. He staggered the last few yards and fell against the fence, gasping for breath and hurting everywhere. He'd done it. That was all that mattered.

"Get your Bergen off." Rob lifted the weight of the rucksack. "This is what we brain surgeons call *blood*. Let's have a look."

Ian took a moment to work out what Rob meant. His right sleeve was wet with blood, ripped to the elbow. It was just part of the general pain of exertion, nothing specific yet. Rob peeled back the sleeve and pulled a worried face.

"Normally I'd say it's only pain, mate, but you're a bit complicated, medically speaking. Are your tetanus shots up to date?"

"Kinnery did them when he visited," Ian said. The wound had started to throb but it couldn't be as bad as it looked. "I used to cut myself all the time working on the ranch. It's not serious."

Rob began walking back to the house. "Come on. Better safe than sorry. Is Kinnery licensed to do doctor stuff, then? Well, if he isn't, it's the least of his problems."

"I never asked. Look, I'm okay. Really."

"Let's not push our luck, eh?"

"But I finished, didn't I?"

"You did. Good effort, mate."

Rob took him into the workshop washroom to clean the cut. It was a two-inch rip in the skin, just above the elbow and deep enough to make Ian feel queasy as he watched the blood well out. He didn't dare look away in case Rob thought he was a wimp. Rob had dealt with open abdominal wounds. If he could face that, then Ian had no excuse for being squeamish about a goddamn scratch.

Mike stuck his head around the open door. He must have seen them heading back. "What's wrong?"

"He fell off one of the obstacles. Caught himself on a bolt or something." Rob squirted some gel down the line of the cut. "Make yourself useful, Zombie. Hold the skin together while I tape it, will you?"

"For Chrissakes, Rob. You *know* we've got to be careful with him."

Ian tried to keep the peace. "Mike, it's not serious. I used to snag myself on wire fences all the time on the ranch."

Rob stuck small butterfly sutures along the cut, then covered them with a big strip of waterproof dressing. It was like being mummified a limb at a time.

"We'll keep an eye on it, and if it doesn't look like it's healing normally, we'll have a rethink, okay?" Rob held up a tube from the first aid kit. He looked like he was going to ram it up Mike's nose. "Antiseptics. Antibiotic gel. My first aid genius. And Ian says he's up to date on his tetanus. Sorted."

Mike sucked in a breath. "Ian, we've got a personal physician who makes house calls. He's very discreet. There won't be any tests that you don't want."

"I don't need a doctor," Ian said. "Thanks, but I'm fine."

"Okay, then take it easy for the rest of the day." Mike made it sound like an order, and judging by the look he shot Rob, it applied to him too. "You'll heal faster. Now go clean up."

Ian took a shower, holding his taped elbow out of the water as far as he could. Cuts and bruises were minor scrapes compared to his dented pride. Mike and Rob probably took far worse injuries without stopping, and so would he.

When he checked his face in the mirror, there was no change at all. Adrenaline didn't make him morph every time, then. Okay, it had been worth it. He'd learned something.

Mike and Rob were having an intense conversation in the kitchen when he went downstairs. It sounded close to an argument, and they stopped talking as soon as he walked in. Ian looked from face to face.

"Sorry, mate." Rob's arms were folded across his chest. It was hard to tell if his tight-lipped expression was annoyance or embarrassment. "I'm just getting a bollocking from the boss. He does it so I don't miss the good old days."

Ian couldn't imagine anyone trying to bust Rob's balls, especially not Mike. But the two of them were definitely looking a little tense. Mike carried on as if nothing had happened.

"How are you feeling now?" he asked.

"I'm fine. Really."

"We're going to Porton to pick up something for Rob. Do you want to come? It's time we got you your own laptop."

That wasn't enough to divert Ian. He needed to clear the air first. "Can I say something?"

"Anything you like, buddy."

"Don't blame Rob. I'd do the training even if he wasn't standing over me. I need to know if I could have been good enough."

Mike nodded a few times, chin lowered. "Sorry. I'm being a soccer mom. I haven't been through the parental learning curve of skinned knees like Rob has."

"I'm not handicapped, Mike. Just different. I probably heal faster than you older guys."

Rob chuckled to himself. "There you go, Grandad. You've been told to wind your neck in." He winked at Ian as he walked out, slapping a car key fob against his palm. "See you outside."

Mike waylaid Ian to check that the dressing was firmly in place. Even Gran hadn't been this anxious about accidents when he was little.

"I'm fine," Ian repeated.

Mike did his awkward shrug. "Sorry. Rob's a natural dad and I'm not. He says that kids have to be allowed to take risks. I'll butt out."

"I'm eighteen." Ian said it to make Mike feel better, but he realised it sounded like he was telling him not to be such a nag. "I used to handle sheep. Rams can get cranky and kill you."

"I just don't want anything happening to you on my watch. Not after the start you've had in life."

When Mike and Rob had shown up at the ranch, Ian hadn't known if he was handing himself over to the good guys or his worst nightmare. But Mike had turned out to be the generous, honest, eccentric guy that Rob had said he was. Rob had once taken a chance, just like Ian: he hadn't known that it was worth risking his life for Mike. They were just two strangers who decided to trust each other. Gran had warned Ian what a cruel, selfish, conspiracy-ridden place the outside world was, but she was another honourable stranger who'd taken him in because she felt it was right. Maybe she didn't see that as anything exceptional, any more than Rob thought he'd been a hero for saving Mike. And now Mike and Livvie had taken Ian in without question, just like Gran.

I haven't had a bad start in life at all. I've been lucky every time. Everyone's gone out of their way to keep me safe. Even Kinnery.

If there was a message from fate in there, Ian was happy to take it. He sat in the passenger seat of the Mercedes, wishing again that Gran had still been here to see that things were working out for the best after all, and wondered if he'd have the nerve to access the internet on this promised laptop after all her warnings.

The mall at Porton was still a confusing assault course of noise and mirrors, but Ian found he was more adept at filtering out the clutter with each visit. He was starting to like the place. *Beer, birds, BMW.* There were plenty of girls around, but if he didn't learn to control his morphing, then they'd never be anything more than distant visions that he'd never be able to talk to, let alone touch. He had to learn other skills. He was starting to pick those up from Rob.

He watched while Rob tried on a jacket in a clothes store. Rob was a fit, muscular guy and he must have known that women checked him out, or else he wouldn't have worn those tight T-shirts. The two girls at the cashier's desk kept taking sneaky looks. When he went to pay, they were all giggly with him, and he gave them a big smile, chatting effortlessly. He made it look easy. Maybe it was when you'd been around like Rob had.

There was clearly a different set of rules for married men, though. Mike didn't join in. He rolled his eyes at Rob as they left the store. "You're such a skank, Rennie. You only come here to flaunt your pecs."

"Shall I ask them to guess my inside leg measurement too?"

"Ignore him, Ian." Mike obviously found it funny. "He's a disgraceful role model."

Ian trailed them around the computer store, longing to sit down and rest his arm on something, and tried not to show how much it hurt. It was, as Rob said, only pain. He nodded acceptance of the first laptop that Mike selected for him, bewildered by the choice, and realised again that he wasn't worrying about being conspicuous. It was still a novelty. One day he'd stop morphing, take it for granted, and all things would be possible.

Beer, birds, BMW.

But not an Army career.

The thought still left him hollow with disappointment, but he had choices for the first time, even if he couldn't imagine them yet. He tried his first cup of green tea at an oriental snack bar while Mike bought a box of fortune cookies for Livvie. The tea tasted of grass and seaweed. Ian didn't like it. But it was a novelty, and any new experience was worth having.

Rob sat checking his phone. He was always waiting for messages from his son. Whatever he was reading wasn't good news, though, and he clicked his teeth in annoyance.

"Something wrong?" Mike asked.

"Tom can't make it until later this year," Rob said. "He's working for the rest of the summer now. I'll have go back and see him during term time."

Mike nodded. "Sure. Let me know when you need the jet."

Rob just smiled to himself without actually looking happy and spun the phone around on the table like a party game. He was still fidgeting with the phone when it rang.

"Hello?" He didn't seem to know who it was for a moment. "Yes, Joe, this is Rob ... yeah, sorry, we got him a new phone to stop someone pestering him ... oh Christ, really?"

Rob went quiet, just listening with a defocused look while Mike stared at him. There was only one Joe it could be. Ian's first thought was that the ranch had burned down or something, but Rob felt in his pocket for a pen and wrote some numbers on a napkin. Then he thanked Joe and rang off.

Mike stared at him, head tilted as if he was asking for an explanation. "That doesn't sound good."

"Some woman called at the ranch claiming her aunt was Maggie's old college friend," Rob said. "She knew Ian's name. She didn't seem to know that Maggie had passed on, though. I'm betting that's Mrs Wrong Number from Lansing."

Mike's face fell. "How the hell did that leak? Kinnery?"

Ian felt instantly sick. He needed to focus: he had to stop himself from morphing. He concentrated on his breathing like Livvie had taught him, staring at the detail of pores on the back of his hand to shut out all other thoughts.

It seemed to work. There was no windburn or tightening sensation, and Rob didn't react when he looked at him.

"Don't worry, Joe kept his mouth shut," Rob said. "She called him Ian and he just said it wasn't his name. But she left him with a name and number to pass on."

He held up the napkin with the details written on it. Mike looked at it and shook his head, eyebrows raised.

"Drew Wilson. Description?"

"Thirties, maybe forties, brown hair, smartly dressed, hire car from Ready Rentals. She said she was staying in Spokane for the night. Good bloke, Joe." Rob gestured at Ian. "That's not Zoe the Hack's alias, is it?"

"No." Ian tried to be kind. "She's fifty, grey, and dresses like she's still at college."

Rob put his phone in his pocket. "Well, gents, we've definitely been dicked. Tasks — warn Leo so he can have a word with Kinnery, check out Mrs Wrong Number, and work out how she got the bloody names and address."

"I think it's a good idea to dispose of the ranch right away, Ian," Mike said. "Burn all your connections. Don't worry. Nobody can get anywhere near you."

"What do I do, then?"

"Give me permission to sell, sign a few documents, and I'll take care of the rest." Mike checked his watch. "Let's go home and get things moving. And you need to call Joe and tell him you're okay."

"Which phone?"

"Use mine," Rob said. "It can be tracked to Joe's now anyway. Keep your new number clear of connections to Athel Ridge, just in case."

He was pretty calm about it all. Rob and Mike were completely in control when things went wrong. Ian had absolute faith in them, but was he always going to need protection like some witness in hiding? Sooner or later, he'd have to take responsibility for his own safety. It wasn't fair on others and it made him feel like a useless child. He was eighteen, for Chrissakes. He didn't need to remind himself how he stacked up against the likes of Rob and Mike.

On the drive home, he sat in the back and called Joe while Mike and Rob discussed how Gran's name and address had gotten out. Joe seemed worried.

"Are you sure everything's okay, son?"

"It's a great place. Mike's taking good care of me."

"Do you really want to be there?"

Ian could hear the unspoken question. "Yes, nobody's making me stay. Don't worry. I just need to keep away from people like that woman."

Ian had no idea how to tell Joe that he wasn't coming back now. Gran's note had said not to make any rash decisions, but Drew Wilson had forced one on him. He was surprised how instantly he'd accepted it, but Mike knew what he was doing and could make anything happen if he wanted it to.

So could Livvie. She took the news about Joe's encounter with a faint smile as if she already had the upper hand.

"So this woman stayed in Spokane last night, did she? Okay. So she probably picked up the rental at the airport. Let's get the number." Livvie picked up the cell on the kitchen counter and tapped the screen. "I'm calling the Ready Rentals desk. Mike, see if you can find the number she gave Joe in a directory. It's unlikely, but let's rule out the obvious.

Ian watched her as she walked around the kitchen with the phone to her ear, waiting for someone to pick up. She was just like Mike and Rob in her way. She plunged into situations and took over. Gran would have liked her.

"Hello? This is the accounts office at KWA ... yes, that's right, KWA, Lansing ... I just wanted to confirm that one of our employees dropped off her car today ... I'll hold ... she did? Good ... I can check that off the list, then. Thank you."

Livvie ended the call and turned around to curtsey with a big smile on her face. Ian had no idea she could lie so expertly. It looked as if Mike didn't know, either. He clapped. Rob joined in.

"The prosecution rests," she said. "Ninety-nine-point-nine per cent certain that it was KWA at the ranch. If she hadn't booked via a company account, I would have been screwed, though. But she doesn't know what we know, obviously."

"I'm never going to cheat on you, honey," Mike said. "Ever."

"No hacking, no bugs. Just charm. Easiest way to confirm something is to make a statement and wait for correction. Innocent people do that instinctively."

"We still need to know how Drew Wilson or whatever her real name is managed to locate the ranch, in case we've got an active leak," Mike said. "She only had a Seattle area code. So unless she's got intelligence-level assistance to pull location records to track where that phone's been, she's done some serious digging. Maybe the college connection's real somehow. I'm putting in a call to Dad now. He needs to ask Kinnery."

"But how did she get Ian's name?" Rob asked. "Do you have compulsory electoral registers over here? You know, a public list with the name of every person who lives at an address."

Mike snapped his fingers. "I'd bet it's the property register. Ian's name's on the deeds of the ranch, but she didn't seem to know his age. She thought Joe was Ian."

"Well, whatever she knows about the Washington end, there's no connection for her to follow here. Unless Kinnery's getting careless."

Mike read the number on the napkin again. "I'll be in the study. Don't eat all the fortune cookies."

While Mike made his call, Ian tried to gauge how bad things were by watching Rob's expression, then Livvie's. They seemed mildly irritated rather than anxious. Livvie divided the bag of cookies into four piles and unwrapped one of hers. Ian got up and checked himself in the mirror in the hall.

"It's okay, you haven't morphed," Livvie called out. She must have guessed what was worrying him now. "Well done. Deep breaths. Now come and eat your cookies."

Rob broke a cookie in half and read the message on the crumpled slip. Ian followed suit.

"*Your skill will accomplish what the force of many cannot.*" Rob laughed his head off and put it in his wallet. "Too bloody right, mate. They must have known a Bootneck would be eating that one. What does yours say, Ian?"

Ian thought this was good fun. "*The first step to better times is to imagine them.*"

"There you go. Spooky. How about you, Mrs Mike?"

Livvie's smile spread and turned into a big grin as she read. "*Those who have love have wealth beyond measure.*"

"And those who marry a billionaire's son aren't doing so badly either, eh?" Rob laughed loudly again. "See, that's how horoscopes work, Ian. You can always make any old load of bollocks fit your circumstances.."

Livvie reached across the table and put her hand on Ian's. He'd forgotten how much his arm hurt until she did that.

"Ian, they can't find you here," she said, suddenly serious. "There's no connection for them to find. And even if they did, they've got to get past Mike and Rob."

"Yeah, and *then* they've got to get past Mrs Mike." Rob broke open another cookie. "We'll just find a few bones and a half-eaten handbag."

"If they find me," Ian said, "I've done nothing wrong. But KWA has. They ought to worry about *me* shooting my mouth off."

"That's the spirit. Take the battle to the enemy."

Ian recalled Gran talking about shadowy government agencies making people disappear. He'd had his doubts, but the things he saw on the news now were more like movies than he'd ever imagined. If agencies could kidnap terror suspects on the street and ship them to secret jails, he couldn't take his own safety for granted.

He couldn't expect Mike and Rob to protect him forever, either. He had to be ready to do it himself.

LANSING, MICHIGAN: TWO DAYS LATER.

"You haven't told me what happened yet, Mom."

Clare was loading the washing machine without being asked. Dru almost felt guilty for dropping her T-shirt and underwear in the laundry basket.

"That's because it's company-confidential," Dru said. "And maybe because I've got absolutely no idea what I found."

Clare gave her a theatrical puzzled look as she shut the washer door. "No gold bullion, then. Or secret meth lab."

"A guy with a shotgun."

"Oh wow, Mom."

"A farmer."

"Oh. Not wow, then."

"Okay, I've got to go. Don't burn the house down. If you hang out with Rebecca, make sure you lock up properly before you leave."

Dru resisted the urge to nag, worry, and lecture. She felt she'd turned a corner with Clare and that treating her like an adult would encourage responsible behaviour. When she closed the car door, though, she thought about all those studies that showed how differently teenage brains were wired. She was sure she'd come home to find Clare had succumbed to liquor, drugs, and a boy with a gang tattoo.

And mollycoddling produces entitlement-obsessed brats who never learn to play nicely with others and need some fake syndrome to excuse why they're obnoxious. Jesus, where's the balance? Okay, let her burn the house down. At least I can claim on the insurance.

Dru now carried her bag of paperwork like a diamond courier. She hadn't gone as far as chaining it to her wrist, but she wore the shoulder strap cross-body and used a small suitcase padlock on the main zipper. None of that would have defeated a ten-year-old with a box cutter, but it made her feel she was doing what she could to keep the information secure. Everything was handwritten hard copy. Her bag was getting heavier each week.

Weaver was back from his trip today, Dru's first chance to brief him personally. She passed one of the lab technicians in the parking garage.

"Hi Dru," the guy said. "Haven't seen you for ages. I thought they'd downsized you."

"Oh, I'll be the last out the door." The comment stung, but she felt suddenly bullish. She'd knocked on the door of potential criminals with firearms, after all. "I know where all the bodies are buried."

No, she didn't. The only person with a corpse stashed in the basement was her, thanks to accepting illegally-obtained phone records. She needed to start amassing some insurance in case this blew up in her face.

By the time Weaver was free to see her, she was even less certain about how much to tell him. She met him in his office, her first foray into the Olympus of the third floor in weeks. She had no idea if Sheelagh or anyone else had bought her cover story. It was fine if they hadn't, though, because they'd think she was engaged in some covert downsizing that would affect them, and treat her with appropriate caution.

"So what's come to light?" Weaver asked.

"Some information I can't make sense of. It might mean more to you than it does to me." Dru didn't elaborate. She had no idea if

Weaver was recording this, and she realised what a sorry state her world was in that she even had to consider it. "That Seattle connection I mentioned. I rang the number, and the guy who answered was very cagey. I passed it off as a wrong number."

"Why would that be significant?"

"Because Kinnery has a landline that he appears to keep just for that number."

"I'm not going to want to know where that information came from, am I?"

"I think I'm somewhat hazy about it too, Mr Weaver." *Just listen to me. I lie better each time.* She had to tell him just enough to prove she wasn't just sitting on her ass. "I took *The Slide*'s piece at face value and tried to work out who Kinnery would have trusted with genetic material back then. It would have to be someone who was terrified of him and did whatever he asked, or someone he already trusted implicitly. So I worked back as far as I could — his college class. I mapped his social connections using publicly available data from that point. I follow behavioural patterns, not objects."

Dru paused to make sure Weaver hadn't zoned out. She thought he was staring at the monitor on one side of his desk, but on closer inspection he seemed to be gazing past it at a point in mid-distance as if he was trying to remember something.

"And what did you find?" he asked.

"I contacted people from his college year to look for a Washington or Seattle link, and eventually I got a lead. A classmate who owned a remote property in rural Washington. That seemed to chime with the allegation in *The Slide*."

Weaver turned his head slowly to look at her. It wasn't a relaxed movement. "You're remarkably thorough."

"You asked me to dig, Mr Weaver."

"I realise you're accomplished at discretion, but Kinnery's not going to get to hear about these checks from his old classmates, is he?"

It was an elegant way to be told she was a terrific liar. "No," Dru said. "His name never came up. I found the property, but it looked unoccupied. I left a neighbour with a number to pass on to the owner."

"Not our switchboard, I hope."

"Of course not. Don't worry, there's no audit trail here. Not that we're doing anything illegal." *Well, the private investigator did, but let's bury that.* Dru had an odd detached second as she realised she was lying about lying. "There's something not quite right, which is hardly scientific, but one thing I do know is that humans can be subconsciously aware of real inconsistencies."

"You think this place is significant, then."

"I'll keep an eye on it. The Seattle number certainly is. Keeping a landline solely for one number is odd. Is there anything more you can tell me? Even things that seem apparently unrelated?"

It was a non-threatening way to warn him that she couldn't do much more if he was lying to her about anything. It was up to him now.

"So who's this college friend?" he asked.

Dru wasn't planning to surrender all her cards. "Someone called Maggie. I don't think this is a business rival. It might even be personal. An affair his wife found out about."

"That would explain a lot."

"Okay, seeing as you're talking to him again, why don't you prod him a little and see what falls out?"

"Oh, I'm more than talking to him. He agreed to visit and discuss working with us again."

Dru really hadn't expected Kinnery to want to set foot in the place. Now she wanted to look him in the eye and see if she could tell whether he was lying or not. Even professional interrogators were generally poor at detecting lies from body language, but at least getting him in a room was a good way to pile on the pressure and see if he slipped up. That was probably Weaver's plan. He knew the man better than anybody.

"When is he coming in?"

"End of this week. Do you want to meet him?"

"That depends what you want me to do."

"Observe."

"You really do believe he's stolen something."

"My gut says yes. I'm still working out what he could have taken from Ringer."

"You'd better have a plan in case we find a mule after all, then. You might flush out Kinnery sooner than you expect."

Weaver did his finger meshing gesture as if he was trying on tight gloves, looking at the screen. His focus was all wrong. This wasn't for her benefit. He really was thrashing out something in his mind.

"I'm going to give him the opportunity to come clean with me," Weaver said. "An amnesty. And that could well be the end of it. Neither of us wants bad publicity."

"Before you do, then, we need to know why this leaked when it did, and who leaked it if it wasn't Kinnery. If he wanted to sabotage you, it's a suicide bomber way to do it. He'll take damage too. It's always better to ask questions you already have the answers to."

"Okay," Weaver said. "Carry on, but don't do anything that might force him into a corner before I get a chance to talk with him."

"Understood."

It was the timing that still bothered Dru. Her mind snapped back to those sticky notes that she tried to arrange into a coherent pattern. With the hotline number, the resurrection of a dead project had to be significant.

What haven't I factored in? The times on the phone log. I need to check exactly when those calls were made.

"You missed your vocation, Dru," Weaver said. "You really should have gone into investigation. Good work."

Dru really couldn't read the expression on Weaver's face. She could read the runes, though. He was probably going to lean on Kinnery to do something for KWA to help the merger, and whatever she found would be the blackmail material for that. Weaver had been right. This wasn't a job for Sheelagh. She was risk averse, to put it kindly. Her idea of best practice was not getting sued.

As Dru headed back to the basement, she thought again about the Seattle number. If it was connected to Maggie Dunlop, calling it again might set off a chain of events that would blow whatever game Weaver was playing with Kinnery. But it could also rule out a connection, provided that she was smarter with her response if someone answered. Either way, she couldn't just leave it.

She locked the office door and took out her burner phone. All the cocky confidence built by daring to knock on Maggie Dunlop's door was evaporating again.

Shall I just ask for Maggie? Or Ian? No, that would spook them if there's any truth in this. Weaver wants to confront Kinnery. It's his company, and his property, and if that's how he wants to play it, it's fine by me.

She still wanted to hear who answered, though. They'd have a hard job identifying a withheld number unless they were the police.

She just had to listen. Dru counted to ten before shoving herself over the precipice and keying in the number.

But the call didn't connect. After a delay, an automated message cut in, telling her that the number wasn't available. There was no voicemail option, either. The number was out of service. Either it was a rare coincidence or she'd rattled someone's bars.

Another non-existent pattern? No. I can't ignore everything. This is linked somehow.

Now she had to dig deeper without scaring Kinnery. There were still folders to check and names to add to her paper database. Web searches would now have to wait until she got home.

Kinnery's not innocent. It's just a matter of finding what he's guilty of. Maybe it's an old child support issue and an unhappy ex. In that case — you go, Maggie. You go, girl.

As Dru turned into Ridgeway Drive that evening, her usual line of sight to the house was blocked by a car parked outside the Greggs' entrance, close to the bend. As she passed it, her house loomed into view, still intact with no sign of smoke, firefighters, or teen gangs trashing the front lawn. She found Clare in the back yard, sunning herself.

"Wrinkles," Dru said.

"Sunblock," Clare retorted. "And I'll never get rickets. You know that people in Britain are getting rickets again? It's so *medieval.*"

Dru was starting to like Clare again. It was one thing to love and another entirely to like. Love was wired to all kinds of other compulsions and instincts, but liking had to justify itself. Dru knew she'd stopped liking Larry long before she realised she didn't love him any longer. Clare was actually a smart, curious, sensible kid who was simply growing up, which was a lurching and chaotic process. Nature erased the memory of how extreme and desperate things could feel at fourteen.

I've got a degree in this. You'd think I'd engage that knowledge before I knee-jerk into the Mom from Hell.

Dru got a couple of sodas from the fridge, mindful of the need not to grab a bottle of wine each evening and accidentally teach Clare that alcohol was the antidote for a crappy job. She handed her a can and flopped down on a lounger.

"Thanks, Mom," Clare said. "Any more gun-toting rednecks on your trail?"

The case had started to feel like a shared interest, even if Dru hadn't told Clare the details. It was something to talk about that wasn't centred on battle zones like Larry, the phone, or dating.

"No," she said. "I still can't work out how this employee stole stuff."

"Don't they search your bags or anything?"

"It's not money or paper."

"Oh, it's something on a disc or a card? Well, copy it and e-mail it out."

"What if you can't do that?"

"Swallow it. Or put it — well, you know. People smuggle all kinds of stuff in pretty gross places." Clare pulled a disgusted face. "Did you see the movie about the guy with the chip in his brain? He's on the run with secrets on the chip and the bad guys try to kill him to get it out. I mean, that's asking for trouble. Put it just under the skin, like a microchip on a dog. It's way safer if they catch you."

So what do you do if you're smuggling DNA? They can't cut it out. And you can't just hand it back.

Dru hoped she was simply ignorant of some brilliant new drug that identified specific DNA and flushed it out. She was pretty sure it didn't exist. But Weaver was very good at buying cooperation. He'd managed to get Kinnery to discuss returning, after all. No chips were going to be gouged out of brains or anything distasteful like that.

"Anyway, how was your day?" Dru asked.

"Oh, we went bowling. Rebecca's got a thing for one of the guys there." Clare got up and opened the back door. "Was that blue Kia still parked on the bend when you drove in? Rebecca thought the guy was watching her."

Dru hadn't really noticed colours. She remembered the dumb-ass parking, though. An uncomfortable thought crossed her mind a little too late. She'd set a private investigator on Charles Kinnery. It wasn't impossible to imagine someone doing that back to her.

"Maybe. Hang on."

She walked down the drive to take a look, but the car was gone. Her own guilty conscience was probably making her overreact. Who knew she even existed, let alone where she lived? Kinnery certainly didn't.

"Nobody there now," Dru said. "If the car comes back and I'm not here, call the cops. You know how to do all that. You just need to be situationally aware."

"Oh my God, Mom, have you joined the CIA or something?" Clare burst out laughing. Dru felt like an idiot. The phrase had just slipped out. "We got his licence plate. You think we're dumb? Well, Rebecca's still in ditzy mode, but I know how to take care of myself."

Clare tore a sheet off the notepad by the phone and handed it to Dru. It was a licence number. It might come in handy some day. On the other hand, maybe this was karma. If you spied on others, sooner or later all you did was look over your own shoulder at imagined boogeymen.

"That's my girl," Dru said, pocketing the paper.

VANCOUVER: AUGUST.

Kinnery knew this would be one of the worst decisions of his life. And he had no choice but to obey Leo and make it.

Returning to KWA didn't top the list of disasters, but it was already hurting. The news about the ranch had just cemented it. He knew he'd never let anything slip. He could safely assume they'd acquired the phone numbers illegally, but he hadn't worked out how they were getting the rest of the information.

Who even knew Maggie existed? Shaun must have gone back forty years to dredge this up.

He paced up and down the hall, waiting for the airport taxi and crushed by the prospect of shuttling between Vancouver and Michigan for the foreseeable future. With stopovers, it took longer than a flight to Europe. Jesus H. Christ, he was getting too old for all that.

Then one of his phones rang. He felt in his pockets and took out the burner.

"Glad I caught you," Leo said. "Any progress?"

"No. The source has to be someone who knew Maggie, because her family had that ranch for years, but I can't work out how they identified her in the first place. I agree that the phone number gave them a break. But someone's got more than the call logs."

"Well, they might not have confirmation that there's any connection at all. Play it by ear. You know they've acted illegally. But keep your powder dry. Goodbye."

Leo rang off as abruptly as he'd opened the conversation. It was to reduce the length of the call, Kinnery knew, but he also detected that whiff of disdain. He now had a long flight via Portland and Detroit and an overnight stay to rehearse his responses before he had to face Shaun.

At some point he was going to have to square his exit with the university, too. Automatically, he thought in terms of playing the age card and explaining to the head of the faculty that he simply couldn't cope health-wise. The truth was a theoretically noble thing, but never respected, appreciated, or acted upon: it was lies that kept society stable. Lies were gentler and easier to fit around you. The truth never put anything right, and most people didn't much like it.

So how would I have traced Maggie?

Kinnery put the resignation issue to one side for the journey and spent the next eleven hours working his way through a mental list of everyone he knew who'd also known her. He could only think of friends at Lomax University. If she was in touch with anyone after graduation who also knew him and had left a trail that had persisted for all those years, then she'd never mentioned it, and Maggie was the ultimate destroyer of trails and clues.

That's one of the reasons I chose her.

Kinnery rehearsed every possible confrontation with Shaun, his chest sporadically hollowed by palpitations that made him think the next heartbeat would never come. By the time he arrived in Lansing that evening, he was ready to drop and in no mood to take any crap. But whatever Shaun had unearthed, he'd never find Ian. Kinnery still had the advantage.

Despite that, he woke before five the next morning and paced the floor of his hotel room, trying out different personas — the weary Kinnery, the curious Kinnery, the flattered Kinnery, whatever act was appropriate to explain why he'd decided to take Shaun's invitation seriously after such a long, cold exile. When his taxi dropped him at the KWA building later that morning, he set his shoulders a like a man who had every right to be there.

And I do. I made all this possible. Don't forget that, Shaun.

Coming back to the building felt like returning to high school and finding it was a smaller and meaner stage for life's dramas than it had seemed at the time. Kinnery walked in unrecognised. But the offices were actually much bigger than he remembered, with a couple of extra wings built since his day. The receptionist on the front desk asked him to spell his name.

"Kinnery, as in Kinnery Weaver Associates," he said pointedly. She looked more baffled than impressed.

Shaun came down to greet him. He looked older than Kinnery had expected, but it was probably a mutual assessment.

"You know the way," Shaun said, showing him into the elevator. "You never forget these things."

"Oh, I forget a lot these days." Kinnery walked into Shaun's sumptuous office and looked for the prime seat, the best spot on the fattest sofa, the one he thought Shaun would regard as his territory. The extra creases in the soft leather confirmed his choice. "I'll have a coffee, please."

Shaun pressed the intercom and held down the key. "Cream, no sugar, yes?"

"It's touching that you remember." Kinnery took out his cell and made a show of switching it off. But there was a hair's breadth between disabling the phone and starting a recording for his own insurance. "Any cookies? Chocolate chip?"

Kinnery had thought he'd feel at least awkward about lying on this scale, but now that he was here, he actually felt no shame at all. His brain had done a wondrous thing. The awareness of what he'd created had been sealed behind a bulkhead, quite separate from the game he was playing with KWA, in which he now felt he was the wronged party. What he *knew* and what he *felt* had split off into two equal realities.

It intrigued him, because if he understood it, then he could recreate it whenever he needed to. He'd repeated the lie in his mind so often that his brain had started to airbrush his actual memory. His outright lies had evolved into excuses and finally into valid reasons.

One part of him now believed himself. He'd been minding his own business, nobly serving a virtual life sentence in academia for his hubris, sacrificing a life of wealth to recompense Ian, and his wicked ex-partner had begun spying on him, seeking commercial gain when what mattered was doing the best for the boy. The other part of him, the objective mind, stopped at the top of this deluded hill to look back down the valley at the frightening path he'd taken. Kinnery knew that when the entirety of him believed his cover story, and not just the emotional side that needed to cling to it, he'd be truly dangerous.

"Do you want to clear the air first?" he asked. Someone who'd been wrongly accused would be indignant and want some kind of apology before he was prepared to talk terms. There was a lot to be said for throwing the first punch. "Anything you want to tell me or ask me?"

Shaun didn't blink. He was still standing by the window, seeming lost now that his sofa throne had been taken. He slid into the chair at his desk and settled behind it as if it was a wall of sandbags.

"Come on, Charles, I needed to know if there was even a grain of truth in the story," Shaun said. "I know I've pissed you off, but we're at a delicate stage with Halbauer. It was the last thing I needed. I didn't even know if it was sabotage."

"So I build a functioning shape-shifter, tell nobody for God knows how many years, then suddenly decide to leak it to the lunatic fringe media instead of publishing a paper from the safety of some country that wouldn't extradite me. Does that cover the keynotes?"

Shaun set his elbows on the desk, hands clasped. "Well, that's the full-tar version. Seeing as we're being frank, the thought that struck me was a little less ambitious but equally interesting."

"Do tell."

"That you refined what was needed and made a little progress elsewhere."

"How? Took it down to my dank basement and got out my Big Boy's Chemistry Set and Tesla coil? Please. You're not a layman. I'd have needed the backing of a fairly conspicuous laboratory."

"I would have understood if you'd used a viral vector on yourself."

"Well, I didn't. I'll give you a good portion of buccal cells and hair before I leave so you can check out my DNA to your heart's content."

"Maybe it was a volunteer, though."

Kinnery wasn't sure if Shaun was just fishing or working up to something else. "I'm flattered you think anyone would trust me enough to risk their health for that kind of favour."

"You can see how I could put two and two together and come up with ten. You don't just fall off the edge of the world for no reason."

"I had a lot of personal issues. I needed a gentler pace of life. And Vancouver isn't exactly a wasteland."

"Charles, even if you'd ripped off the research or broken every FDA regulation in the book, I'd still beg you to come back and work with me. Not despite that. *Because* of it. I want to wheel you out to Halbauer and say that you're so keen on the possibilities that you've given up your cosy tenure and lovely Vancouver to work with KWA again."

It was, as someone once said, a trap, and not a very good one. Kinnery knew he was good at his job, but Shaun was trying to keep his enemies close. So it was pure poker, all bluff and counter bluff, neither of them knowing what hand the other held. Kinnery found it thrilling for a moment before it slipped back to a desperate need to call off the dogs once and for all.

"You know how old I am, Shaun."

"Only slightly older than me."

"I want you to be realistic about the useful years you'll get out of me."

"Come on, you're not a bricklayer. We both know people in their eighties who still contribute to the field. Wasted genius is going to feel pretty painful on your deathbed."

Shaun was a lot more adept at twisting the knife than Kinnery remembered, but then he'd had years to polish his technique. Kinnery hoped his cell was picking up all this. Leo would enjoy the finer points. Maybe it wasn't such an inept trap after all.

But that was irrelevant. Kinnery had his orders. "Okay," he said. "Let's talk."

"Do you mind if I bring in my HR adviser?"

"Go ahead." Kinnery reached into his briefcase and took out his notepad. *I'm going to take the offer, so I might as well treat the numbers seriously.* "I'll have to run it past my attorney, obviously."

Shaun went to the door and gestured to his secretary rather than using the intercom. The coffee finally appeared, minus cookies. Kinnery was stirring the cream and making idle chat with Shaun about property prices in Vancouver when the door opened again and a woman walked in: fortyish, business suit and name badge, one of many who wouldn't stand out in a crowd.

"Charles, this is Dru Lloyd from HR," Shaun said.

Kinnery could just about read her badge from where he was sitting. *Dru.* How many Drews or Drus were there generally, let alone working for KWA? Suddenly she wasn't forgettable at all. If this was the woman who'd shown up at the ranch, she knew she'd given at least part of a real name to Maggie's neighbour, and she'd be expecting Kinnery to hear about that pretty damn fast if he and Maggie were connected. She'd be looking for a reaction. He wasn't sure if he'd given her one.

You bastard, Shaun. You brought her in here to shake me down.

Well, my phone's still recording. I'll pick this over later. And you still won't find Ian.

"Nice to meet you, Dru," Kinnery said. "How's my KWA pension fund doing?"

She gave him a look he couldn't fathom, but it didn't matter. This had to be the same woman. Maybe Rob Rennie could identify the voice and confirm what Kinnery was already sure he knew.

"I think it's doing very well, Dr Kinnery," Dru said. "I'll just take notes to make sure Mr Weaver's giving you accurate information about benefits packages."

They talked about time commitments and retainers and shares, but Kinnery wasn't concentrating. He was waiting for the sting. Dru — and probably Shaun — must have known that he realised his phone records had been accessed. They were probably still guessing about Maggie, but the phone was a known quantity, and the poker game was back on. If he said nothing, then they knew he was playing too.

Leo had told him to keep his powder dry. Kinnery knew better this time. He waited until they'd wrapped up the details — in principle, subject to legal advice, and all the usual bullshit caveats — then turned to Dru. Now he'd to push his luck and embroider a story he hadn't planned.

Keep it simple, though. Stuff that I can remember.

"This is going to sound a tad churlish," Kinnery said, "but seeing as you haven't mentioned it, I feel I must."

Shaun was watching intently. Dru cocked her head. "Yes?"

"When a close protection officer gets a so-called wrong number on a dedicated line that only I call, he worries about that and tells me," Kinnery said. Actually, that was exactly what had happened, minus a few key facts such as Rob being someone else's bodyguard at the time. The truth was a wonderfully flexible thing. "I can't discuss my personal security arrangements, but I've got good reason to think one of your employees acquired my phone records improperly and rang the number."

Dru didn't even blink. She frowned the frown of the disinterested pretending to be shocked and concerned. "That's a pretty serious accusation."

"Well, I'll be very pissed off if it was KWA, but at least I'll know it's not pro-life or animal rights activists coming after me for my sins. I've spent too many years checking under my car."

Jesus, what am I doing? No, I'll be fine. I've taken far bigger risks.

Shaun sat tapping his forefinger against his lips. "You actually employ a bodyguard."

Don't overplay it. Stay vague. Tell a dilute version of the truth, even.

"I have security consultants, yes. I'd be surprised if you don't."

"Okay." Shaun looked put out. It was impossible to tell if he didn't know about the hacking. "I can only apologise if that was us."

"Shaun, find out and let me know. If it was your people, just man up and admit it, and I won't take legal action. I just need to know that I'm not going to start the car one day and say goodbye to my legs."

Kinnery's mouth was dry despite the coffee. It was an awful, awkward moment, just as it would have been if that had been the truth. *Maybe I've called their bluff. And maybe I haven't.* He gave Dru a withering look, fed by real resentment, because being too forgiving right then wouldn't have been convincing.

"I'll deal with it and get back to you," Shaun said. "Are you staying for dinner tonight?"

"I'd love to," Kinnery said. "But I've got to get home in time to see the powers that be at the university and extract myself from my contract."

He stood up to leave and shook Dru's hand. Eye contact with her didn't tell him much. She had to know that her card had been marked.

The floor layout had changed little since his day, but he headed back to the elevator lobby on an autopilot setting he'd long forgotten. On balance, he felt he'd won. Shaun looked marginally less cocky than he had when Kinnery had first walked in.

"If it was us, it won't happen again, Charles," Shaun said, leaning on the bronze panel next to the elevator. "I'll get back to you as soon as I can."

The elevator doors parted. "Thanks. Let me know if Halbauer

want to talk to me."

A cab was waiting outside when he reached the reception. He gazed out of the window as the taxi headed back to his hotel, trying to remember what had changed around town, and then he remembered his phone was still recording. He switched the mike off.

Did Shaun believe me? Does it matter? They still won't find Ian.

And Leo was right. They're looking for a mule.

Kinnery decided to eat at the airport and explore Lansing some other time. He was sitting at the gate waiting for his flight to board when his phone bleeped with an incoming text. It was his official phone: not Leo, then. He looked down at the screen and unlocked it. The message was from Shaun.

CHARLES, DON'T WORRY ABOUT PROTESTERS. IT WON'T HAPPEN AGAIN. SORRY.

Kinnery almost allowed himself a smile. He still didn't know if Shaun believed the bodyguard story, but he did know one thing. KWA would think twice before spying on him again.

TEN

I did what I thought best. I don't know if they believe me or not, but now I've confronted KWA on hacking my phone records, I think that's pretty well put Shaun in a place where he can't move. And I don't have to wait for the other shoe to fall.

Charles Kinnery, in conversation with Leo Brayne, explaining his reasons for not sticking with the plan.

KWA, LANSING, MICHIGAN: AUGUST.

When Dru unlocked her office, the first thing that struck her was a heady, clove-like fragrance, the second was realising someone had been in the room overnight, and the third was the lavish bouquet of Asian lilies in a vase on her desk.

Now she knew she didn't have a life. The thought of an intrusion had kicked the surprise gift into third place. Anyone else would have wondered who their admirer was.

Only the security desk would have had access overnight, not even the cleaners. There was no message on the desk. Maybe it was still tucked into the arrangement of pink and white lilies. As Dru moved the stems to check, she remembered the messy orange pollen a moment too late and snatched her hand away to check her blouse for stains. But a closer inspection showed that someone had clipped out the stamens. Now *that* was attention to detail. She respected that.

The flowers had to be a mistake, though. It wasn't her birthday, and nothing happening at work warranted a bouquet.

Larry? No, he'd only send me flowers if he'd been arrested and needed me to post bail. And if he needed that, he'd probably phone in the middle of the night.

She called the security desk to put herself out of her misery. It wasn't Alex today. A younger male voice answered.

"Did you let someone into my office overnight?" she asked.

"Yes, ma'am," the guard said. "Mr Weaver had something he wanted to leave personally."

"Oh." Somehow that wasn't reassuring. "Okay. Thank you."

Dru stood studying the flowers, trying to work out why Weaver would want to pacify her. Perhaps Kinnery was going to make a complaint about the phone records after all, and Weaver needed her to cover for him. *But I'm the only one in the frame on that, aren't I?* How did cross-border cases like that work? She moved the vase to a filing cabinet and wiped her desk with a tissue.

So Weaver got what he wanted. I just damn well hope I do.

Well, she was burned now. Kinnery had seen her and heard her voice. She could be identified. That ruled out any more personal investigations. The worst of it was that Kinnery's explanation made perfect sense, but then so did the theory of the mule.

And he didn't mention the visit to the ranch. Just the phone. So there might be no connection to Maggie Dunlop at all. On the other hand ... if there was, he wouldn't want to fill in the gaps for me, would he?

Every scenario could make sense if she stared at it long enough. This was getting her nowhere.

Dru took another look at the hotline phone log. The incoming calls — July, nothing since January — had clustered just before the date of *The Slide*'s article. How did that fit Kinnery's claim? If Zoe Murray had called him for a comment before publication, then he might have warned his security people, but Dru would have expected to see outgoing calls rather than inbound ones lasting a few seconds.

Got it. Kinnery calls from another number, and this is someone trying to get back to him. Leaving messages, maybe.

But if the calls were from Maggie Dunlop, they might have been warning him about something. Both explanations still made some kind of sense. The unanswered question was why *now* after so many years. Maybe Kinnery had skipped a payment, and because this was an ongoing silence that needed to be enforced, the mule decided to put pressure on him.

Dru realised it didn't feel like work any longer, something that she could forget for a weekend. It had become the single thought she drifted back to when she wasn't worrying about Clare or paying bills.

She logged on to the network to catch up with the web digests. The fringe sites seemed to have lost interest in the DoD shape-shifter and had veered off into debates about government agents who could live right next door to you, even in your own home, and you'd never know they weren't your Uncle Bob, nice Mrs Jones, or the mailman until a big black car with tinted windows turned up and you were bundled inside to disappear forever. Dru despaired. The same psychology underpinned myths throughout human history. A few thousand years ago, it was Zeus who showed up in disguise. Now it was aliens. Seeing that history repeating itself in the twenty-first century exhausted her.

Anyway, wasn't that Invasion of the Body Snatchers? *Or was that* The Thing? *I forget.*

There was even a radio phone-in podcast in the media digest. "*And we have Jason from Sacramento on the line ... so, Jason, you say your neighbour's been disguising his true form for twenty years, and he's in fact an alien observer ...*" The radio host delivered it all with the calm, unsurprised, non-judgemental tone of a news anchor. So did Jason. What made it so disturbing was how sane and rational they sounded.

A knock on the door interrupted the playback. She paused it as Weaver walked in and glanced at the lilies.

"That's for handling the problem," he said, not specifying which part of the Kinnery situation he meant. "You're not buying his story, are you?"

Dru shrugged. "I've still got a lot of unanswered questions."

"Me too."

"But you got him to do whatever you were angling for."

"Exactly. Doesn't that worry you?"

"I don't know him well enough to judge. You've offered him a lot of money for very little effort. Most people would sell their grandmothers for that."

"Ah, not Charles. The Charles I know would have beaten me over the head with moral indignation and lawyered up by now.

Coming here at all is out of character. He likes to summon people to his throne. I can't believe that the worship of students in his own little kingdom has mellowed him any."

"He wants this allegation to go away as well. He doesn't want to be a laughing stock."

"No. He's done something. He can't call the police because he doesn't know what else we have on him. But we'd look crazy if we cite *The Slide* as our defence for illegal access to data. So, one way or another, Charles and I have a mutual grip on one other's throats."

Dru wasn't sure if that was a statement, a question, or an instruction to carry on digging. "So?"

"What still bothers you?"

"Timing. Why now? And the number of elements in *The Slide*'s story that already fit, although they could be coincidence. Plus the Seattle number."

"What about it?"

Dru still had to keep some cards in reserve. "I tried it again and got an out of service message. Which is odd if that's Kinnery's bodyguard. Although the guy who answered it the first time did sound like security. Maybe they just changed phones because I had the number."

Weaver nodded slowly. "I'd go with my instinct."

"Is that an instruction to keep looking?"

"Yes, but with extreme caution. Charles is going to be working here by the end of the year. I need to maintain diplomatic relations. Passive sonar, I think the Navy calls it. Don't ping him — listen for his noise."

Dru wanted some reassurance. She'd done this to secure her job. Even a kapo needed to know that their rations were intact.

"Level with me, Mr Weaver," she said. "The whole point of this exercise was to smooth things over so they didn't derail the merger. Do you feel that's been achieved?"

"Yes, I do," Weaver said. He didn't even pause. "Hence the lilies. I do value your work, Dru. You're thorough. All the technology in the world's no substitute for lateral thinking and the patience to cross-check everything."

Dru already knew her most admirable quality in Shaun's eyes was that she was invisible, a grey shape in grey mist. So now she could add dull, plodding tenacity and a love of drudgery to her résumé.

Special skills: will eat shit for money; can hide resentment well; makes no friends at work, so fully productive during working hours.

"Thank you," she said, demonstrating at least two of those qualities. He might have been bullshitting, of course. He was very good at that. *And damn, you'd think I'd be ready to record things by now.* "I can go ahead and plan for Tiny Tim's Christmas, then."

"And complete your puzzle."

"Sorry?"

"Everyone knows you love puzzles. When you lunch here, you sit in the corner and work on your puzzle book while you eat."

Dru had never thought that anyone gave enough of a damn to watch her until recently. She realised she probably looked standoffish.

"I never leave one unfinished," she said. "My old professor would say it's a sign of insecurity. A need for order and control because my mother was the world's most chaotic and untidy woman."

"And is it?"

"I find comfort in completion."

"There. Even setting bad examples can produce good children."

Weaver did a farewell nod and left before Dru could start to ponder hidden meanings in that. *But I'm as safe as I'll ever be.* And she was still in her little sideline of a project, free of the HR suite. How could she move the investigation forward without being spotted?

Another factor was fuelling her need to keep looking — Weaver's own reaction to Kinnery. People assumed others did what they would do, for the most part. A man who thought that his business partner would steal industrial secrets and even use a human mule had to think in those terms to start with. Shaun wasn't a cop drawing his suspicions from daily contact with the ingenuity of criminals. There might have been precedent for it in KWA.

Forget that. None of my business. Just keep going. What else can I access without making any noise?

Grant was still largely invisible, even if his activity had left awkward footprints. She made a note to call him during her lunch hour. If he'd been able to locate the hotline, he'd have told her. The one tangible pin in the map was Dunlop Ranch, so Dru might at least be able to rule some things out and save herself wasted effort.

She needed to know more about Maggie. She tapped out

Grant's number and waited.

"Hi Grant. Can you do some research on an individual for me, please? Family tree material. I've got a current address."

"I'll start with state records," he said. "Might be very fast, might not. Some states can run record searches in a day or two. Give me what you've got."

Dru repeated Maggie's name and address, but the best she could do for date of birth was guess at anywhere between 1945 and 1955. The woman might have been older than Kinnery, but was unlikely to be a lot younger. All Dru had to go on was that vague comment from Dr Missiakos. She couldn't call him to ask for more information.

"Anything you can steer me on?" Grant asked.

"No, I'm trawling. Anything of note. Any male relatives, possibly called Ian."

It was vague and Dru knew it. She got on with shuffling her paper database, looking for connections between names, places, and dates that might suddenly click and give her another path to explore. Her phone rang about fifteen minutes before she was due to head home.

It was Grant. "I thought I'd share this with you," he said. "Because it's kind of odd."

"You've got a result already?"

"I tried the Washington State Department of Health. I can't request a birth record check without an exact date of birth, and I came up blank on marriage and divorce because I couldn't even guess an approximate year, but I asked for a death certificate search for the hell of it. I started with this year because you might as well work backwards. Believe me, it was a long shot. And guess what."

"She's dead?"

"July."

Dru's gut flipped over. "Before or after the date we hired you?"

"Before. A couple of weeks."

Timing: timing, timing, *timing*. Maggie had died just before *The Slide* had contacted Weaver. It was all too coincidental.

"Anything on an Ian Dunlop?"

"No certificates. Again, I'd need to know the DOB. I checked for a death filed this year, just in case, but there was nothing. That was only my first port of call. I'll carry on with other sources."

"No, hang fire for now." Dru didn't want to create more ripples than she had to. "That's incredibly useful. Thank you."

She phoned Weaver to tell him. It was worth dropping that information on Kinnery to see how he reacted.

"You really think this woman's significant?" Weaver asked.

"It's the activity clustered around July," Dru said. "Look him in the eye when you ask him. If she's involved, then this might well rattle him enough to make him react."

Weaver sounded as if he'd smiled. It shaped all his words. "If I were your husband, I'd never dare cheat on you."

"He did," Dru said. "And I caught him."

It was a reflex answer. Weaver might have known her circumstances, or it might have been an unfortunate joke, but she realised she didn't actually care. This puzzle was doing what puzzles always did, soothing her and convincing her that she could force things to turn out right. She went home that evening feeling triumphant.

She drove down Ridgeway Drive looking for a lurking blue Kia, as she had every day since Clare had mentioned it, but there was nothing to see. It must have been like this on an army patrol, she thought. She couldn't imagine living every day like that. Being watched was bad enough, but if you had to check every shadow in case you got shot or blown up, then it was no wonder so many guys came home in a mess. She could now see how it would never be over for some of them.

The aroma of serious cooking hit her as she opened the front door. There was the smell of a TV dinner reheated, and then there was the complex fragrance of something created in stages that left its sequence of traces on the air. Dru hadn't realised that Clare could do anything like that. She dumped her bag on the chair by the kitchen door and wondered if it was a pre-emptive shot before a revelation about a broken vase or lost piece of jewellery.

"Now what's that?" Dru asked.

Clare fussed with plates. "I made boeuf bourguignon."

"Are we celebrating something?"

"No, I just wanted to be clever."

Dru opened the oven, ashamed of her suspicion. Fragrant steam rolled out. Yes, there was a competently-executed casserole bubbling away. "You know it should have a bottle of red wine in it, don't you?"

"Oh, it's in there." Clare cleared textbooks off the table. "There was some in the pantry."

That bottle was Dru's emergency anaesthetic supply. She couldn't be angry, though. "Good. Otherwise I would have worried about how you acquired it."

She really had to shake this suspicion. She was even second-guessing her own daughter. That was the problem with a job that was about watching people and waiting for them to do something wrong. All you saw in the end was sin, even if it wasn't there at all. And people resented being seen as guilty until proven innocent. The act of surveillance poisoned the whole relationship. Dru knew all this, but it had still crept up on her.

The boeuf bourguignon was pretty good. Dru tried to stand back and see her daughter for what she was, just a kid upset by divorce like any other, getting good grades, doing her chores, not pregnant by some waster, not doing drugs or drinking liquor, not demanding every consumer luxury she saw, and entitled to get things wrong while she learned how to make the transition to adulthood. She wasn't the enemy. She was a fellow inmate.

Is the job making me miserable, or am I colouring the job?

Larry had accused her of being a joyless grey cloud that blocked the sun for him, a phrase that she translated to mean that she'd been unsporting about letting him frolic with twenty-something girls at the marketing agency. Perhaps both meanings were equally true. He'd certainly hit that nail on the head: joyless. But she had a little joy in her now, and it stemmed from stalking prey. It wasn't a great recommendation for her personality.

"Great cooking, sweetheart," she said, having a second helping. "Actually, we do have something to celebrate. I'm probably not going to be laid off when the merger happens. Jobs suck, but not having somewhere to live sucks more. That's being a grown-up, in a nutshell."

"Sad."

"True."

"Have you caught your thief yet?"

"No, but I've seen him face to face now. So he knows what I look like. No more cloak and dagger."

"But you enjoyed that bit."

"Yes." Dru had. She quite enjoyed the thrill of taking the risk. She hadn't admitted it to herself until now. "I did."

"You could always disguise yourself. Change your hair."

It was a thought. If she needed to pay a visit somewhere, it was one of those details that tended to alter an entire description. After dinner, she stood at the bathroom mirror, convincing herself it had to be done.

She was going grey — goddamn *grey*. It wasn't even a stylish Indira Gandhi kind of greying. She had dull brown hair and now she was going dull grey. Everything that she'd looked forward to was now behind her. It was over, capital O.

Bright red or ash blonde? No. Don't be crazy. Who's going to take you seriously then?

Who cares? It's just a disguise.

And then again, maybe that was an excuse to do something frivolous and just a little desperate.

She made a salon appointment the next day for after work. A stylist called Jay ruffled through her hair with his lips pursed, frowning at her in the mirror.

"How about a nice blonde?" he asked. "Nothing brassy. Because you've got a lot of grey. It'll get rid of that awful mousiness. And maybe some texture." He held his hands just under her jaw level. "Take some length off, too. That'll turn back the clock. Yes, blonde. Blondes can get away with anything."

If he'd been a co-worker, she would have punched him out, but a hairdresser had the same immunity as a court jester.

"Do it," she said.

WESTERHAM FALLS, MAINE: TWO WEEKS LATER.

Weeks of intensive training had started to leave their mark on Ian, and he liked it.

He sat on the edge of the bed, inspecting his biceps in the mirror, left then right. He wasn't sure if it was down to more muscle or less body fat, but they looked bigger. He hadn't really noticed the change before the last couple of days. Then — bang — there it was, a transformation that had nothing to do with morphing.

He'd worked for this. He'd earned it in the gym and on dawn runs and by struggling cross-country with a rucksack that was half his own bodyweight. That was what mattered. He'd made it happen himself, and that meant he was in control of his life for the first time. He wanted women to look at him the same way that they looked at Rob. There were probably more important things in the world to aspire to, but right now Ian couldn't think of one.

Rob's right. It's down to me. I've just got to put in the effort.

If Ian could have erased everything in his memory before the day that Mike and Rob crashed into his life, he would have been satisfied with the hand that life had dealt him: no lies, no fears, no loneliness, and no recollection of losing Gran. All he would know was that he was different, but that he could make himself whatever he wanted to be, in every sense of the word.

But I don't have to keep reliving the crap. It doesn't matter where I came from or what I wasn't told.

This was probably what Gran had wanted for him, even if she couldn't possibly have imagined how it would happen. Did he need to find out who his biological parents were? They didn't even know he existed. They might never have met outside of a Petri dish. And then there was the surrogate mother — did he want to find her? He wasn't sure yet. Maybe it was better to keep pretending that David Dunlop was his great-grandfather.

There was no point in looking back, only forward. *Beer, birds, BMW.* All that stood between him and a normal life was a single photograph.

He hadn't morphed noticeably since that day in the sports store. Livvie had taught him a concentration technique that involved thinking about something simple — an apple, a pencil, anything he was familiar with — and imagining every aspect of it from its shape and colour to its smell and how it felt in his hand. It was the hardest thing he'd ever had to do. It seemed impossible to keep his mind on the object and shut out the random thoughts that he usually didn't even notice. He built up his concentration by seconds each time, not minutes. Whenever he had a moment to himself, he practiced.

Today he visualised opening a parcel, hearing the rustle of brown wrapping paper, smelling the musty cardboard, and letting nothing else intrude. He could only manage to immerse for short bursts. But he'd begun to recognise that cut-off sensation that told him he'd disconnected from the world around him and had forced his brain to do something different.

Damn: he'd slipped out of the trance again. He felt like he'd woken from a nap. Next time, he'd memorise his face and try to see every pore, freckle, and hair, and hope that it somehow linked all those weird reactive cells to the map he was forming in his brain.

If I morph, I need to know how to get back to the way I looked before. Everything depends on that.

He poked his biceps again to make sure he wasn't imagining the improvement, then went downstairs. The house was silent except for the faint backdrop of fridge, aircon, and clock noises. It was his turn to clean the kitchen. Chores were part of the natural order of things, something he'd done for as long as he could remember, and even Mike had his cleaning duties. Manual work did you good and kept you grounded, Mike said. Ian scoured the sink and polished the steel surfaces on the range. It didn't matter why chores were good for you. They just had to be done.

"You're going to make some girl a great husband."

Livvie made him jump. He was so engrossed that he didn't hear her walk in. "I thought you were working."

"No, I escaped. I'm going to treat myself to a trip to the garden centre. Coming? We can have a coffee there."

Ian's idea of a garden centre was the feed store in Athel Ridge, and they didn't have a coffee bar, just soda on the cash desk. "Only if I can pay," he said, expecting her to stall him.

Livvie beamed. "That's the best offer I've had all week. Let's go."

Ian was quietly thrilled. He'd been upgraded from problem kid to responsible adult. He transferred some bills to his wallet and prepared to pick up the tab for a woman for the first time in his life. Livvie took the Volvo and drove west through some picture-postcard towns and a beautiful wild landscape.

"Now *that's* why I need to spend less time in the studio," Livvie pulled over to the side of the road and lowered the tinted windows to look out across a valley. "I've had full spectrum light installed to ward off cabin fever, but it's still like working down a mine."

Ian was in awe of her. She had a no-nonsense way about her, very much like Gran. There was probably a more flattering way of saying that but he hadn't worked it out yet.

"You never talk about what you do," he said.

"Well, live interpretation for businesses is pretty dull, and the government work tends to be sensitive material. Mike and Rob do the really interesting stuff."

"Were you angry when I showed up?"

Livvie shrugged and started the car again. "Stunned, but not angry. And you didn't have a choice."

"Mike and Rob can be pretty scary."

"Funny, I still think of Mike as a harmless, over-friendly Labrador. I sleep better knowing Rob's watching his back."

Ian could only see Mike as a soldier, a real man who fought real wars and saved — or took — lives, someone he respected enormously. It was hard to imagine him needing protection.

"Can I ask something personal?"

"Sure."

"When you met Mike, did you know who he was?"

"Did I know he was so rich? Or did I know who his father was? Neither. He didn't tell me for months. I was pretty annoyed when he did. I was only after his body."

Ian's diagnosis of women was confirmed. They were terrifying, powerful, judgemental creatures. They ran the world. He'd never be able to get one to take him seriously.

"He's a really nice guy." Ian searched for a word. "Modest."

"Oh, Leo made sure of that. Mike and Charlotte had a strict upbringing. They had to work for everything and save up from their allowance if they wanted something special. They even had to clean their own rooms and call the staff *sir* and *ma'am*. No cosseting at all. They got a lot of love, but they definitely weren't spoiled. It was all duty and discipline." Livvie was speeding along, obviously happy to talk. "Leo detests rich brats. He thinks they should be sent to gulags until they shape up. Or shot. Or both."

It explained everything about Mike and why he was so anxious to serve. Ian hadn't met Charlotte yet. His only window on her was Mike's occasional comments about the Alien Queen.

"Is that why Mike doesn't have many friends?"

Livvie nodded. "He feels safe with regular people. But when they find out who he is, *they* get scared."

"Rob's not scared of him."

"Ah, Rob operates on another plane of existence." Livvie smiled to herself, all vivid white teeth. "If you want to see how the normal rich live, that'd be Charlotte and Jonathan and their Midwich Cuckoo kids. Mike can't cope with all that. Or Machiavellian politics. He needs everything to be noble, uncomplicated, and transparent."

Gran had always said there was no such thing as a normal

family, just degrees of weirdness. Ian wondered if he was settling into life with the Braynes relatively easily because they were so abnormal that he was just one more detail in a life that was completely off the charts. By the time they reached the garden centre, he and Livvie had discussed everything from Mike's deployment to Iraq to how she hated the hormone treatment she needed for every IVF cycle. It was like she'd been let out of solitary, and now she wanted to talk for the hell of it.

She knew a lot about orchids, too. It was almost magical to see something new through the eyes of a person who was passionate about it. She led him through the house plant section, naming fantastic orchids from purple *Vanda coerulea* that almost glittered in the light to tiny *Masdevallia* with miniature orange blooms like kites. Some had beads of liquid on their stems that looked like water, but sticky to the touch. When Ian licked his fingers, the sap tasted like syrup. He'd only seen pictures of orchids before. Now this whole new world was there to be touched and tasted. This was just a fraction of the things he never thought he'd see and do. Life suddenly felt exciting and rich with promise.

After a couple of hours' browsing and a coffee, they left with a box of orchid plants, a big copper planter, and bags of compost. The sky was heavy with storm clouds and the first spit of rain hit the windshield. Livvie chatted solidly all the way from the garden centre to the Porton exit, about sixty miles' worth of fascinating details about family, work, and the house. Ian watched the rhythmic sweep of the wiper blades as the headlights streamed towards him on the opposite side of the road.

Livvie glanced in her wing mirror, just casually at first, but then it became every few seconds. After driving with Rob, Ian thought that was perfectly normal, and some people were driving too fast and too close in the rain. But Livvie's conversation trailed off. She slowed down and kept checking the rear-view mirror.

"Go on, pass me," she muttered. "You think the outside lane's invitation-only or something?"

Ian tilted his head to check the wing mirror. "What's wrong?"

"Probably nothing." Livvie turned off earlier than he'd expected, ten miles from the Westerham exit. She was still looking in her wing mirror, then the rear-view, and back again. "Keep your head down."

"Livvie, what's *nothing*?"

"Okay, there's an Impala that's been on our ass for too long, and now he's turned off with us."

Ian's stomach knotted. "They can't have found me. Okay, they found the ranch. But they couldn't follow a jet."

"Relax. Nobody's going to get near you. They'll have to go through me first."

Ian had just started to feel okay, and now everything had pounced on him again with a vengeance. He could feel his scalp prickling.

Calm. Relax. Don't morph.

Livvie's jaw was set. "I'm going to stop in the most public place I can find," she said. "If that guy doesn't drive past, I'm calling the cops. Okay? Stand by to get his licence plate."

Ian was suddenly full of angry adrenaline instead of fear, ready to take a swing if anyone tried to lay a finger on Livvie. *She shouldn't have to protect me. I should be looking after her.* A gas station appeared ahead on the right. Livvie indicated to pull in, and a sudden flash of strobing light filled the Volvo's rear window.

Ian took a quick look. It was a dashboard-mounted blue light in the Impala.

"Oh, *damn.*" Livvie sighed. "Unmarked cruiser. Don't worry, he's not after you. Not if he's for real."

She parked away from the pumps and switched off the engine. Ian looked over his shoulder. A state trooper got out of the unmarked car, put on his Smokey Bear hat, and walked towards them.

"If he's bogus, he'd be crazy to try anything here," Livvie said. "Too many cameras."

She lowered the window and put her hands on the steering wheel. Ian could hear the faint chatter of a police radio coming from the cruiser, which sounded real enough. The officer stood looking down at her, then dipped a little to glance at Ian.

"Good afternoon, ma'am. Do you know why I've stopped you?"

Livvie suddenly changed into a meek, polite little housewife that Ian had never seen before. "I'm afraid not, officer."

"You've got one tail light on, which means the other one's out."

Was that all? A tail light? Ian's pulse was pounding in his throat. Livvie shrugged, hands still on the wheel.

"Sorry, I didn't know that. My licence is in my purse, with my concealed carry permit." So that was what you had tell a cop if they stopped you, was it? "I have a Glock Twenty-Six in a carry box under my seat."

Ian knew she had a handgun, but he had no idea that she actually *carried* it. She didn't look at him as she reached for her purse and handed her documents to the trooper. The guy took a step back and checked something on his cell. Ian had never been stopped by a real traffic cop before. It was another element from a TV show that had stepped out of the screen into his real world.

"Reason for the concealed carry, ma'am?" the trooper asked.

"This is going to sound awful."

"No problem. Try me."

"My father-in-law's Senator Brayne. My husband's away frequently on deployment. I'm not saying that in a do-you-know-who-I-am kind of way. I'm just explaining why I feel the need for extra security."

"Very wise, ma'am." The trooper didn't bat an eyelash. "Do you mind if I look in the trunk?"

Livvie popped the lock. "Sure. Go ahead."

The trooper poked around in the back, shifting the box of orchids, then walked back to the driver's door. "Is everything else okay? You slowed down when you saw me behind you. You weren't speeding."

So that was why he was making a big deal of this. She'd triggered some instinct in him to check out the car. Ian's heart rate started to slow down again.

"I didn't know it was a patrol vehicle. I just wanted you to pass me." Livvie voice was a stranger's, small and scared. Ian was fascinated by her alter ego, Mrs Harmless. She was putting on a terrific act. "It's pretty scary for a woman if she thinks she's being followed."

She turned her head to look at Ian as if she was going to refer to him, but for a long heartbeat, she just froze. The look on her face said everything.

He must have morphed again. It was the worst possible moment, but then it always was.

But the cop didn't seem to notice. Maybe he was concentrating on Livvie. It was just like Joe or Sheriff Gaskin, though. If they thought they'd seen Ian change, they simply acted as if they didn't believe it, because things like that just didn't happen in their world.

Livvie recovered instantly. Her voice dropped to an embarrassed whisper.

"Anyway, officer, you can imagine the kind of crazies we have to worry about."

The officer mouthed a silent *ah* and nodded. Ian couldn't decide if it was the Brayne name that had made him back off, but his tone changed.

"Yes, ma'am, I can indeed." He put his cell away. "The lights. It's probably just the fuse."

"I better check that, then."

"Let me do it, ma'am."

"That's very kind of you, officer." Livvie smiled. "Thank you so much."

Ian watched as the trooper fixed the light, sobered by how much there was still to learn about people. Livvie could act, and when she smiled, men obeyed. In five minutes the lights were working again. Livvie drove out of the gas station, giving the officer a little girly wave with fluttering fingers.

They were a hundred yards up the road and heading back towards Westerham Falls before she let out a long breath.

"Well, fuck, Ian, that scared me" Sometimes she swore like a sailor. Now she was Regular Livvie again, in control and tolerating lesser mortals. *And she's carrying a Glock. Oh my God.* "I thought it was KWA. Sorry I scared you."

"I didn't know you had your gun. And you can act."

"No point pissing off the rozzers, as Rob would say. Still, it was nice of him to fix the light." She gave Ian another sideways glance. "I've never actually seen you morph that much before. Do you want to take a look?"

She gave him an odd smile. Ian felt crushed. He'd been sure he'd learned to stop it in its tracks. But he was back to square one, a million miles away from a driving licence and a girlfriend. He reached out and folded down the sun visor.

The small rectangle of inset mirror showed him someone new. He could still see himself behind the eyes, but he was darker, more square-jawed, and even a little older. It was disorienting after a month of stability.

And how long am I going to hang on to this face?

Livvie pulled off the road at a rest area and took out her cell. "Come on, look at me. Look at the lens." The phone made a shutter noise. "There. For the record."

"I don't know what I'm going to do, Livvie."

"Can I make a suggestion?"

"Please."

"You really want to be built like Rob, don't you? You train like crazy and you keep checking your muscles."

That was beyond embarrassing. Ian cringed. "Yes. Sure I do."

"You said that you should focus on what you wanted to look like, not just on stopping changes."

"Yeah, but I don't know what I want. Other than to just stay the same."

"Well, stay like *this*." She held up the phone so he could see the screen. "Take it from a woman. You look really good like that. It's definitely you."

Was that what women liked? "But I couldn't hang on to the last change."

"Seriously." Livvie scanned his face, breaking into a smile. "I think this is what you're meant to look like."

"Really?"

"You study that face, Ian. Make sure you know every contour. Concentrate on how it feels to be in that skin. Whatever else happens, make sure you know how to get back to looking like *that*."

Ian kept the visor mirror in his eyeline all the way home. It was good advice, but there was nothing precise in it, nothing like knowing he had to crank out ten more reps with an extra ten pounds, or check how much protein per pound of bodyweight he'd eaten that day. All he had was Livvie telling him that this look was somehow special. He had to admit that it was great to be admired, even temporarily. He felt good about how he looked right then. Apart from being delighted with his new hard-won muscles, he'd never felt that kind of *happy* before.

He'd remember that feeling every time he looked in the mirror, though.

VANCOUVER, SEPTEMBER: ONE WEEK LATER.

Kinnery peeled the Blu Tack from the beady eye of the webcam and saw himself on his own monitor for the first time in ages.

It was only a test run for one video call. He wasn't going to make a habit of this. The rehearsal was to check what was visible behind him on his study wall and in the bookcases that flanked him, but inevitably the shortcomings of his own appearance dragged him back to his face, and what it revealed to him rather than to the person on the other end.

This wasn't like looking in a mirror, where a benevolent mental filter kicked in. The web cam threw back a stranger's perspective that wasn't moderated by self-image at all.

Kinnery had expected to look old. That didn't surprise him. It was the look of wasted years that made him recoil.

The stark light from the window threw deep shadows. Switching on the desk lamp evened out the illumination and erased some folds and lines, but the miles on his clock still showed, the ones added by waiting to be found out and by wasting the astonishing research potential of Ian Dunlop.

We're back to the punishment cycle of the Greek gods. I get my just desserts before *I go to Hades.*

Kinnery snapped himself out of it and scrutinised everything else in shot. When he watched TV interviews and the backdrop was an interesting bookcase, he found himself trying to check out the titles on the spines, making a judgement about the person who'd collected them. Were there any telltale signs of his wrongdoing behind him? One detail, one single book about child development or something out of character, might stand out in that mass and pique Shaun's curiosity.

Kinnery didn't have time to censor the shelves selectively. He got up and cleared them, stacking the books in piles on the floor and removing photos and certificates from the wall. Then he sat down and adjusted his position to frame up correctly, checking the screen again. His backdrop was now stark emptiness and dark rectangles where the wallpaper had faded around the picture frames. It spoke volumes about him, but in a wholly different way.

He replaced the Blu Tack, incapable of relaxing in front of the webcam even when it was switched off, and went back to clearing his e-mail. Students expressed disappointment that he'd be leaving after the holidays. They seemed to think he was on his last legs. He was only in his sixties. Maybe he'd overplayed the old age card.

Thinking of the Greeks set him off on other belief systems. What would the Egyptian gods have done with him? If they'd weighed his heart against the feather to assess his sins, would it have tipped the scales? He examined those sins for himself. Ian appeared to be thriving, although Kinnery still only had Leo's word for that. He was under the protection of a wealthy family who could make pretty well anything happen for him, right down to buying him his own island if isolation was what he wanted. Maggie might have surrendered her life to some other cause if she hadn't been handed a child nobody else could be trusted to look after. His wife was better off for divorcing him. Maybe his victims had clawed back some benefit, then. He hoped so.

Kinnery checked his watch, peeled the Blu Tack off the webcam, and sat rolling the soft ball between his fingers while he waited. He tested the recording software a few times. He had to remember to click that icon when he picked up the call.

So should I keep sending Ian money? What's the etiquette on reimbursing billionaires?

Shaun's call came in just after eleven, local time. Kinnery was pretty sure they'd never return to the days when they'd been best friends, excited about the future and how they could shape it. But he could at least try to be civilised. He hit the recording icon and then clicked to answer.

"Hi Charles," Shaun said. "How's it going?"

Shaun always looked relaxed, but today he seemed to have something else about him. Maybe it was the webcam. Kinnery wasn't used to seeing him from the low angle of a laptop.

"I think I can agree a January start date," Kinnery said. "I'm going to be looking for real estate in the area, but in the meantime, I'll plan to stay in Lansing for a few weeks at a time to avoid that god-awful flight."

"Well, the deal with Halbauer was signed two days ago, so it's full steam ahead. It's a new lease of life for both of us, I think."

"So what did you want to discuss today?"

"Strange how the intervening years just vanish, isn't it? I won't say it's like old times. But you know what I mean." Shaun had a vague smile on his face. "Talking of old times, you knew Maggie Dunlop at Lomax, didn't you?"

Kinnery had prepared for this for nearly twenty years. He knew the Maggie question was likely if Dru Lloyd had managed to show up at the ranch. But it still had the impact of a brick being thrown through the window.

Jesus Christ, haven't you got what you wanted, you bastard? You've got some nerve for a man who hacked my phone. Maybe I should kick this into touch and call the cops, just for the fun of seeing you tell a court that you think I made a shape-shifter.

Okay, this stops now.

"I do remember a Maggie," Kinnery said. "Not on my course, though."

"Charles, I know she died in July, which isn't an insignificant date in the scheme of things. I'm not stupid. I know what you did."

I doubt it. Kinnery attempted weary impatience. "Shaun, what did I say last time we touched on this?"

"As I said, if you'd made an actual shape-shifter like they claimed, I'd want your autograph. And I'd want to lock you into sharing the profits with me."

"Exactly." Kinnery was sure that Shaun was recording this too. He'd be naive not to, and Shaun probably hadn't been naive since his first day at kindergarten. "So where is this bullshit going?"

"I don't believe you created a live specimen. You're brilliant, but not *that* brilliant. And it would have taken accomplices and years of staggering track-covering. But I do believe you had a mule, and maybe that mule showed some changes. That's what's worth money, Charles. It's company property, and I'll do whatever it takes to get it back."

So you don't know after all. You're bluffing. Now watch someone who really knows how to lie, you amateur.

Kinnery let himself look cornered. "Okay, just tell me how you identified Maggie." Every word had to be precise now. If he appeared to confess when any sensible person would have assumed the call was being recorded, Shaun wouldn't swallow the lie. It had to *look* deniable. "I hope you didn't harass her."

"Well, once we noticed that lonely Seattle number, we just rang around your old class asking about students who had a Washington connection. Someone remembered Maggie and her folks' ranch. It went from there."

The simplicity of the lead deflated Kinnery. He should have worked that out. Never mind: Shaun had admitted his own sin.

Say it, Shaun. Say it so I can record it again. "You hacked my goddamn phone records."

"I've already apologised for that. I didn't order it."

Gotcha. Thank you. "You're damn well trying to exploit it, though."

"So now I know, tell me. I won't go to the authorities. I'm

compromised by my own employees breaking the law, and if this experiment gets out, it won't do either of us any good. Did the leak to *The Slide* have anything to do with Maggie's death? Was it the gene therapy? Did she even know what you put into her?"

It was the perfect set-up for a neatly-folded, all-encompassing lie, almost too easy, but Kinnery had to remind himself that Shaun had infinite patience. If he still had suspicions, he'd pursue it for another twenty years if he had to.

"Which question do you want me to answer first?"

"I'm not in a hurry, Charles. Feel free to be expansive."

"Okay," Kinnery said. "If you want to keep this fantasy going, here's a hypothetical scenario. Imagine Maggie agreed to be treated, so that someone could either preserve the engineered genes where nobody would be able to look for them, or just test what happened in a live human subject. Let's say she confided in someone she shouldn't have, but swore that person to secrecy. Then she died unexpectedly, natural causes, and that grieving friend, for some dumb reason I can't imagine, decided he couldn't do Maggie any harm by sharing what he thought he remembered with some hack who'd listen to a crazy story. That covers the bases for this fairy tale, I think."

Shaun just sat there, fingers meshed again. "Did Maggie exhibit dynamic mimicry?"

"How could she? It's just a theory to amuse you."

"*The Slide* suggests the subject was a young man."

Goddamn. Kinnery knew he should have been ready for that. It wasn't as if he didn't know that Dru Lloyd had found Ian's name, too. She must have told Weaver. Kinnery had to assume that she had.

"*The Slide* suggested a lot of crazy things, Shaun, but we've never seen their source material, have we?"

"I'd be very keen to recover this material if I thought you'd made those genes express in a human subject."

"Is that an offer?"

"No, but I can recover things discreetly if I have to. Off the books, shall we say. Remove the biohazard to a remote site, for public safety. I'd always know where *you* were, though."

It took Kinnery a few moments to decode that odd turn of phrase. Yes, that was a threat. Shaun never banged tables. *I will hunt down your mule, and if I can't find him, then I'll come after you.* Kinnery understood perfectly.

"Maggie was cremated," Kinnery said. "So whether she was a mule or she turned into the Easter Bunny, there'd still be nothing to recover. You really do believe this crap, don't you?"

"Once I get an idea in my head, I find it hard to shake off. Forgive me. Just a bad habit. I'm sure that if you had anything substantial to show me, you'd do it so we could both take advantage of it without any unfortunate publicity."

And that was another threat, not so oblique this time. Kinnery remembered what Leo had said and turned it back on Shaun.

"Yes, I'm fully aware that I'm working for the old firm again, so any dirt that sticks to me would also stick to you and your nice new company. God forbid that should ever happen." He wasn't sure how far Shaun would go to get his goods back. He had to assume the worst. "Like I say, it didn't happen, but if it had, that's how it might have panned out."

Think what'll happen if you pull the pin, buddy. Think what else you might lose. You don't know if I kept all that research you seem to think I've been doing for someone else, do you?

Shaun smiled almost convincingly. "I believe we have one another's balls in a firm grip, then, Charles."

"Good. I do so like an honest relationship. Are we done now?"

Kinnery wanted agreement that now he'd confessed — after a fashion — the matter would be closed. He'd effectively told Shaun he'd stolen KWA property, but there was now no evidence left to show it had ever happened. He'd salted the lie with enough truth to make it easy to swallow.

"I don't think Zoe Murray's going to pursue it," Shaun said, evasive to the last word. "File it under paranormal bullshit stories. So, January. Are we going to see you before then for the holidays?"

"Why not?" Kinnery said. "It'd be good to catch up."

When Kinnery clicked to end the call, he put the Blu Tack back over the webcam and disabled it. He'd have to send a copy of the call to Leo to cover his ass. But Shaun had been made to understand the situation: he'd done some illegal things, and so had Kinnery, and KWA wouldn't come out of it cleanly if the facts were made public. They were now shackled together in such a way that neither could betray the other, like a couple of unhappy bank robbers.

And I'll just make the best of being back with KWA. At least I can watch Shaun sweat. Happy, Leo?

It was Kinnery's bad luck that this had involved Leo Brayne and not some normal politician who could be bought or blackmailed. The idealistic rich were more dangerous and unpredictable than a terrorist with a nuke. It was just as well that there weren't many of them.

Kinnery encrypted the audio file and mailed it to Leo with a covering note about student gratitude for a scholarship from one of the Brayne foundations. It was probably time to change phones and SIMs again, too. He'd pick something up the next time he travelled out of Vancouver. Security had come to rule his life. What was it Mike Brayne called it, in that Newspeak kind of jargon the military favoured? OPSEC — operational security — and PERSEC, personal security, which boiled down to keeping your mouth shut and looking over your shoulder, *situational awareness* to use another of his phrases. Kinnery replaced the books on the shelves and put the pictures back on the hooks in the wall.

Checking his locked desk drawer to ensure the encrypted thumb drive was still there had become a twice-daily nervous habit. He really couldn't let it go, could he? Shaun knew him too well. There was enough information on there, if anyone could decrypt it, to at least find some clues to Ian's origins, and anyone with time on their hands, anyone tenacious and not too choosy about how they acquired information, could probably even narrow down the range of who might be Ian's biological parents. It was hard to tell if the information would have any bearing on why Ian had turned out the way he did, but someone with plenty of resources might even be able to identify one or both of them.

Dru Lloyd certainly met the tenacity requirement, if she was the one who'd done all the leg work. What galled Kinnery was how low tech all this had been. Except for the call log, everything had been excavated from the dirt of time by phone calls, deduction, and simple human observation. He needn't have worried about being watched and analysed by countless spy cameras at all. Then something drifted back to him.

Damn. Maggie's number. I should have said something to Shaun when he explained how they narrowed down the geographical search. I should have mentioned lucky coincidence. I should have dismissed the connection. Too late. Well, he's got what he wants now, and his worst suspicions have been confirmed. It's done.

And the bastard doesn't believe I could create a human capable of dynamic mimicry. Pity I'll never be able to ram that down his throat.

All Kinnery could do now was get on with his life and wait for Leo's reaction.

He certainly got it. Three hours later, Leo called. They almost had a private language now, a grammar of euphemism and avoidance that made the calls short, impenetrable, and potentially misunderstood.

"I told you to keep your powder dry, didn't I?"

Leo could never manage a "hi." He wasn't a discourteous man. It was almost as if he couldn't trust himself not to say *Charles* as an automatic follow-on and reveal a degree of familiarity if anyone was eavesdropping.

"Shaun's made a few veiled threats about hunting down and exacting revenge, but I think we've reached the point of mutually assured misery," Kinnery said.

"Rash. Very risky."

"No, it's based on time spent watching him. He'll back off."

"Don't get sloppy because you think you know better."

"I'm not the one who leaked it," Kinnery said. *And I was always smarter than him.* "Don't forget that."

"I'll keep a watching brief."

"Give my regards to — well, you know."

"I will."

Kinnery wasn't sure that he'd ever hear from Leo again. There was a sense of finality about this for the first time in nearly twenty years, and it didn't feel quite like the relief he'd always expected. But Ian was in the best place he could be now, and he'd be left in peace. Shaun had too much to lose by digging deeper. Kinnery hoped he realised that.

Sorry, Maggie. Sorry I had to lie about you to do this. Pitiful specimen, aren't I? I even lie about the dead.

She would have understood, though. She might even have approved.

ELEVEN

The real risk in morphing isn't compromising security or even creating new medico-ethical dilemmas. It's about the basic human need to believe what you see. We live in a fearful, paranoid age, for which politicians like me have to accept much of the blame, but once people start thinking their neighbour could be someone else in disguise, a different person from one day to the next, society will change for the worse. The real danger in Ian is simply the idea that he might exist at all.

Leo Brayne, talking to his son.

PORTON, MAINE: END OF SEPTEMBER.

"Have I caught you at a bad time?" Brad asked. "I can call back."

Rob sat watching the office entrance from the comfort of the Mercedes, nursing a latte while he waited for Ian and Mike to emerge. "No, I'm parked up. Mike's with his lawyers."

"No problem, I hope."

"Routine family trust stuff. He just blows a dog whistle and they show up anywhere he wants them to."

"Okay, I know you're not available at the moment, but I just wanted to touch base."

It was time for some pre-emptive stalling. "Sorry, mate. I didn't plan to be out this long. I'll be clearer about my schedule soon."

"If you're still worried about long contracts, remember that a lot of the yacht work is under four weeks."

"Yeah, I'd probably be up for that." There. He'd said it. "But there's family stuff I've got to nail down first."

"Understood. By the way, most of the guys you passed on to me are signing up, so thanks for that. Check your bank for your bonus."

These were his old oppos, blokes he'd served with. If he could put any private work their way, then he did. Rob didn't care about the recruitment bonuses. "Have you given them top rate?"

"Would I short-change your buddies?"

"You're a diamond, Brad. I'll stay in touch. I promise."

"Okay. Give Mike my best."

Rob put his phone back on the dashboard and wondered how long he could kick this down the road before he started to get skills fade and Brad decided he was never available anyway. He had to stay looking employable in case he ever needed to go it alone without Mike's patronage. He knew Mike would never let him down, but it was necessary for his self-respect to know he could survive.

But how long had he been sitting on his arse and gathering dust now? Months. He'd never been completely idle for this long since he was a kid. It felt like the beginning of the big run-down period to oblivion. He was forty, Tom didn't need him any more, and he had none of the things that a bloke his age should have had — a permanent home, a trade, a missus, and, for fuck's sake, an identity. He wasn't a Marine now, no matter how much he'd always think like one. He didn't feel at home in England, but he was never going to be an American, either. In fact, right now he didn't feel like he was *anything*. Some days he wondered if he was just as much of a nothing as he was at the supermarket, except now he had a Rolex, a Jag, and a solid gold safety net.

Jesus Christ. Listen to me. Get a grip, Royal. Stop dripping.

When things settled down with Ian, perhaps he could fit in some proper work without leaving Mike in the lurch. Whatever he was doing for Ian didn't count, because it was just common human decency to do it, and Leo should never have been paying him for it. But Ian hadn't morphed since the traffic stop, and that meant stability and a fairly normal life were within his reach.

Rob also felt better for knowing that Mrs Wrong Number was Dru Lloyd. Kinnery had recorded his meeting at KWA and sent a sound file via Leo. There was no mistaking that voice.

But you can't follow Ian here, love. Good effort, though.

Half an hour later, the glass doors of the office block parted and Mike strolled out with Ian, clutching a tan leather briefcase and looking — well, like someone else. This was the other Mike, the one who did business the way his father had taught him and wore the uniform for the task, a very quiet charcoal suit so well cut from such perfect cloth that Rob was afraid he'd ruin it just by sitting too close. If that had been the Mike he'd first met, he wasn't sure they would even have spoken.

Mike laid his jacket and tie on the back seat beside Ian and pulled on a jumper, transforming himself into good old Zombie again.

"I thought you'd decided to move in," Rob said. "You've been hours."

Mike glanced at his wrist. "One hour forty-five." He still wore his cheapo lucky watch even with his sharp suit. It was quite something to see a bloke who was that far beyond the reach of status symbols. "She's very thorough."

"Scary," Ian said, a timid voice from the back seat. He might have been putting it on, of course. He had a low-key sense of humour. It had taken Rob some time to spot it. "I felt like she was preparing me for a murder trial."

"But you're all sorted now, eh?"

Mike nodded. "We've set up Ian's finances and covered our tracks on the sale of the ranch. If KWA go back and want to trace the new owners, it's not linked to us." He didn't elaborate. "We just need Kinnery to swear an affidavit to supplement the hospital birth certificate so we can get a passport."

"Christ, that sounds risky. Are we still chained to him, then?"

"All he has to do is say that he's known Ian for the requisite period."

"I'm okay with that," Ian said. Rob could see him in the rear-view mirror, chewing his lip. He'd picked up that anxious mannerism from Mike very fast. "I've got to deal with him sooner or later. Whatever he did, he's done everything he can since then to put things right."

Rob didn't feel that gracious. But that was Ian: he was still a naive teen about some things, but very mature indeed on the big philosophical stuff. The kid shut out every negative thought, even when being negative was reasonable, always looking for the up side of every scenario. Rob wondered if he'd overdone the Royal Marines' mantra of cheerfulness in adversity. But it really did seem to be something at the core of Ian's personality.

"Well, it only needs to be done once," Mike said. "We discussed changing Ian's surname to add extra camouflage, but you want time to think that over, don't you, Ian? Anyway, it's something you can do any time. We can just get you new papers later."

"Yeah." Ian nodded, busy reading some document. "We can get the photos done this week."

Rob had waited a long time to hear that. "Beer, birds, BMW."

"Beer, birds, BMW," Ian repeated, sounding like he was mimicking Rob's accent.

"Are you teaching Ian bad ways, Robert?" Mike asked.

"Alliteration. I had to look that up in my pop-up illustrated dictionary."

Mike tapped the dashboard and gave Rob a let's-roll gesture, finger pointed. "Lafite, ladies, Lamborghinis."

"Hasn't got the same ring, has it?"

Rob hit the radio and drove off, singing. Ian joined in and Mike glanced over the back of his seat. "Imagine being stuck on convoy protection with this joker," he said. "They only fired at us to shut him up."

Ian could actually carry a tune. Livvie was teaching him French, and she said he had a great ear for accents as well. Rob wondered if that was a result of being cooped up on his own for so many years, hanging on every word of a movie or TV show.

"I do believe you were taking the piss out of my accent," Rob said, mock-huffy. "I don't know, kids today."

"*Oi durno*," Ian mimicked. "*Moi ahk-sent.*"

Jesus Christ. Do I sound like that? "That was brilliant. What we'd call a proper job where I come from."

"*Prah-per jawb.* You always sound like a pirate. *Oh-ah.*"

"Do I really say that?" Rob asked. "Oh-ah?"

"Occasionally. Mostly it's *eh.*"

Ian had obviously noted it and added it to his mental database. He seemed to be able to separate local dialect from military slang. Rob suspected that he spent ages reading up on all the detail.

Mike laughed. "Awesome."

Rob watched Ian smile to himself and marvelled at how kids could put years of crap behind them so fast when Rob found himself permanently changed by isolated events. Rob hadn't worried much about driving beyond usual vigilance until his first deployment, when his patrol had run into an ambush. After that, every road became the front line. The brain was a strange machine that didn't always trust the world to go back to the way it used to be.

Mike looked back at Ian again. "We need to get you a car. I've got to go through the motions of training you for six months before you can take your test. You want to go look around dealerships?"

He said it innocently. It was just the way he was, carelessly generous. Ian leaned forward between the front seats.

"I kind of miss my old truck," he said.

"Sure, but a guy needs a car too."

Rob caught the look between them. Mike wasn't a hard bloke to read. He was in full paternal mode, fretting about Ian's future. He'd been waiting to be a dad for so long that it was probably too much to resist when Ian needed so much on every level. Rob felt a sudden urge to call Tom for an extra-long chat. He was back at university now, so they weren't limited to snatched calls from wherever he'd been working. When he came to visit, Rob planned to give him the time of his life.

You're right, Mike. It's priceless.

"Okay, anyone got any plans when we get back?" Rob asked.

Mike picked some invisible lint off his cashmere jumper. "I need to take Livvie to the movies. Some quality time. We'll be back for dinner."

"Movies? You unimaginative bugger."

"We're never jaded, and we never run out of thrills."

"You could fly her to Singapore. Paris. Anywhere."

"January," Mike said. "We'll do it in the New Year. We'll all be totally sorted after the holidays."

"Okay, I'm going to do some phys after lunch. Can you spot for me, Ian?"

"Sure. I could do with an extra workout myself."

"Recovery time," Mike said pointedly. "Don't forget to schedule it. Or you'll lose lean mass instead of putting it on."

Mike was getting the hang of teenage psychology. Rob tried not to smile.

While Mike and Livvie were getting ready to go out, Rob

opened the fridge to find a tray of fresh protein shakes with neatly written labels like prescriptions, listing when Ian had to drink them. Livvie seemed to be relishing her trainer role. It was touching. She and Mike had thrown themselves unreservedly into the family thing. Ian was an easy kid to like, but it still took a leap of faith even for a couple who never had to worry about the bills.

"Look at this," Rob said, showing Ian the contents of the fridge. "You're made for life."

Ian treated the shakes like they'd been handed to him specially by some Greek goddess. Rob wasn't sure which goddess was in charge of phys, but he was pretty sure the Greeks would have had one.

"I ought to make these myself," Ian said. "Livvie's got enough to do as it is."

"She loves doing it. She'd buy the ready-made stuff if she didn't."

Ian did his weights session with extra vigour as if he had to justify Livvie's effort, then went on to the punchbag. He could certainly land a punch with plenty of aggression, but he saw it as extra cardio training rather than learning how to hit someone. It was probably a good time to tackle that topic.

"Have you ever been in a fight, mate?" Rob asked. "I'm guessing not."

Ian paused, wiping sweat off his nose with the back of his sparring glove. "Can't remember. But I'd have been knee-high if I had."

Rob had to keep reminding himself what Ian had *not* done in his life, no matter how switched on he seemed. It was the stuff that Rob had taken for granted as part of growing up. Ian hadn't had much contact with other kids, maybe a couple of years at primary school if that. It was pointless teaching him how to transition between weapons and storm a compound if he couldn't look after himself in a bar.

"You need to know you can take a punch and ride it," Rob said. "The first time's always a nasty surprise. Some people swing straight back naturally, but normal instinct makes you curl up if you can't run away. So you need to be trained to handle it. Humans aren't designed to hurt each other unless they can't avoid it, believe it or not."

Ian straightened up. "You did unarmed combat, didn't you?"

"I don't mean commando stuff. This is so you know what it feels like to get hit, so that you don't freeze."

"Did you ever box?".

"And ruin this face? No. But I've been in a few unplanned fights."

Ian took it as a joke and stood back, arms out to his side. "You'll cream me."

"Body blows only." Ian was half Rob's age. Rob knew there was no guarantee he'd be the one doing the creaming. "The head's off limits because we don't have any head or mouth guards."

"I think you're the kind who swings back."

"I grew up on a council estate. What's your word for it? A project. I was a bit of a bugger when I was a kid."

"Okay, let's do it."

"I'm not going to think any less of you if you don't want to."

"No, I'm up for it."

Rob pulled on a pair of gloves. "Remember that it's just about knowing that you can fight hurt. Okay?"

"Okay."

"Body only."

"Okay."

Rob talked Ian through it as they squared up to each other. He remembered getting this far with Tom as a kid and then being completely unable to even prod him. Tom, ten and not sure of his own strength, took it seriously and landed one in Rob's gut. *My baby boy. I can't do this.* Rob had abandoned the plan on the spot and signed Tom up for boxing class at the local club instead.

"That's it, that's it," Rob said. *Thwomp.* Ian jabbed at him and caught him in the ribs as he shielded his face instinctively. The blow was faster and harder than Rob expected. Well, Ian had at least twenty years on him. "Good. Hard as you can."

"Okay."

"Come on." Rob stepped into Ian and punched upward into his chest. It wasn't maximum effort, but it hurt. Rob saw it on his face. "Come on. Back at me."

They threw a few more punches almost politely, concentrating on avoiding each other's heads. But then Ian stepped it up a notch, and so did Rob, and then Rob hit him a little too hard in the upper arm with a quick follow-up in the kidneys as Ian hunched over.

The punch that flew straight back at Rob nearly winded him. It was instant, accurate, and bloody hard. Rob returned it equally hard without thinking. He felt under threat. It was instinct.

Ian was much, *much* better at this than he should have been.

"Fuck," Rob said, taking a step back. Ian kept coming. Rob pushed him back. "Break. Stop."

And then he looked at Ian and his heart sank.

The guy in front of him wasn't Ian. More to the point, he was, but not the same Ian who'd wowed Livvie and that Rob had grown used to over the last few weeks. His hair was mid-brown and his face was rounder, younger, a stranger again, all except the eyes.

"Oh Christ, I'm sorry," Rob said. "I'm so sorry."

Ian stuck one hand under his arm to pull the glove off and felt his face. Rob could see his anguish at losing control. *All my fucking fault.* He took off his gloves and put his hands on Ian's shoulders.

"Deep breaths, kiddo. You can get back to it."

"Okay." Ian used that word a hundred times a day. "I'm okay."

"You're not. Come on. Let's pack this in and go and calm down."

Rob was distraught. After all that time and effort, after Ian was on a steady course and Mike was finally getting his photo documentation in order, Rob had fucked it all up by pushing the kid too far. They were back to square one. Ian went upstairs to shower, leaving Rob sitting on the stairs and wondering how the hell he was going to tell Mike and Livvie.

How was Ian going to cope with this new face?

Rob went upstairs and knocked on the bedroom door. "Ian, are you all right?"

"I can sort this." The water was still running. "It's not your fault, Rob. I'm the only one who can fix myself."

Rob spent the next couple of hours at the kitchen table, trying to work out how to resolve this. They'd have to start the process over again, or Ian would have to get used to the fact that his life would be severely limited by things he'd never be able to do.

When Mike and Livvie got home, Ian was still upstairs with the door slightly ajar. Mike looked at Rob and his face fell. They knew each other too well.

"What's wrong? Is it Ian??"

"He's in his room," Rob said. "We were boxing. He morphed. My fault."

Mike went thudding up the stairs and Rob braced for incoming.

Livvie put her hand on his arm.

"It's nothing we can't handle, Rob."

"No, I ballsed it up. I should have known better."

Livvie followed Mike upstairs. Rob could hear the buzz of voices, and then the thud-thud-thud as Mike raced down to the hall again.

He stalked into the kitchen. "What the fuck were you thinking, Rob? Seriously, what the fuck?"

Rob had rarely seen Mike angry enough to eff and blind before, let alone angry with *him*. What else could he say? Ian wasn't like any other kid, and Rob had ignored that fact, thinking that persistence was the answer to all of life's problems. He was gutted. And the last bloke he wanted to upset was Mike.

"I know what I've done, mate. I'm sorry."

"Jesus Christ, the attorney's *seen* him." Mike leaned over him with one hand on the table. It was an odd kind of anger, very cold and white. "What the hell is he going to do now? Any terrific ideas?"

Rob wasn't used to problems he had no power to solve and that weren't his to learn to live with. "I can't change Ian back, mate. He'll come downstairs when he's ready, and then we can work something out. Meanwhile, I'll piss off so you don't feel obliged to hit me."

He got up and went outside to stand on the rear deck, leaning on the rail to watch the dusk fall. Well, they could always start over with a new lawyer. Mike didn't answer to the hired help. It was the dent to Ian's confidence that was the real problem.

He's got the backbone for a fight, though. I bloody well hurt all over.

Eventually the back door opened and Mike walked up to lean on the rail next to him. Rob was trying to think of a new apology when Mike put his hand on his back.

"Sorry, buddy. What a goddamn drama queen. I apologise."

Rob did a theatrical lip wobble, relieved that he was forgiven. "Our first row. I'm going home to Mother."

"I must be hormonal or something."

"Well, if we can't take a pop at each other now and again and shake hands, we're not real mates, are we?"

"I'm even more invested in Ian than I realised. That's kind of scary."

"I'm not going to fight you for custody."

Mike didn't smile. "Yes, I know what my issues are. I'm that goddamn cat."

"What cat?"

"Oh, a broody cat. Can you call cats broody? Whatever. I just want to make everything right for Ian and I can't. Not even with my resources."

"Welcome to the classic dad experience, Zombie. Okay, I'd better go and talk to him. How pissed off is he with me?"

"Not at all. He always finds a reason not to feel hard done by."

"I'll tell you something," Rob said. "He could punch the shit out of me. And not just because he's younger."

"What do you mean, that this is something linked to his genes?"

"No idea, but you can look at the bruises." Rob straightened up and braced himself to face Ian. "I need to go and unfuck this."

When he tapped on the bedroom door, Ian was reading in the sitting room of his suite. It was actually hard to think of him as Ian for a moment. Rob began to realise just how much of a leper Ian might become. It didn't bode well.

"Hi mate. How are you feeling?"

Ian looked up. His eyes still hadn't changed like the rest of his features. That was something. "Bruised. You?"

"Yeah, I've got some lumps." *I'm going to have be careful with you, son.* "How are we going sort this morphing thing, then?"

"I'm meditating. Not now, obviously. I've got photos of the way I looked before. I'll keep concentrating on them." He was reading something on the tablet that Mike had given him. "I think that really was me, you know."

"Can I do anything? Talk? Sod off?" Rob glanced around the room, which was predictably as clean and tidy as a barracks. The black and white photo of Maggie's dad stood on the windowsill. Rob wandered over to take another look. "Maybe if you stop trying and get an early night, it'll help."

"Maybe."

When Rob picked up the photo, he felt like he was intruding on a private, silent conversation. That picture must have meant the world to Ian. By the look of it, it wasn't a professional job, more like a typical snap taken by a mate, a bit posed and self-conscious with the focus as much on the hardware as the man. But as he studied David Dunlop, he realised what he was drawn to: the man's face, and in particular his eyes. He was clean-shaven with buzz-cut hair that could have been anywhere between brown and mid-blonde — perhaps even ginger. It was hard to tell from a black and white photo. But the eyes were familiar.

If Rob imagined David Dunlop a lot younger and darker, then he'd seen that face before. *Is that wishful thinking? If it's not, then I bet I know how Ian comes up with the faces.* Maybe Ian hadn't realised how he was doing it.

Rob handed him the picture. "Why don't you take a look at that and compare it with your last photo?"

Ian took a few minutes to scrutinise both images. Eventually he shrugged.

"I hadn't noticed before. That's what comes of not believing the mirror for so long."

It certainly couldn't be a family resemblance, but Rob didn't point that out. Ian didn't need any more reminders of what he wasn't. Somehow, though, he'd reproduced some of the features of a man who couldn't have been related to him. He'd made that happen himself. Whatever it took, that ability was still somewhere within Ian. But he was the only one who could find it.

He'd certainly found the ability to punch hard and fast. Rob wondered what else lay within, waiting to be let out.

KWA STAFF RESTAURANT, LANSING: SEPTEMBER.

Optical illusions were a bitch.

This puzzle couldn't be decoded or calculated. Dru would either see the solution, or she wouldn't, and there was no process or knowledge that she could apply to work it out.

She put her sandwich to one side and tried defocusing. No matter how long she stared at the apparently random black and white pattern, her brain still couldn't form an image. How much longer should she give it before turning to the back page for the solution? Her eyes only had one chance to get this. Once the image was revealed, she could never go back to seeing the illusion in its raw, unsolved state. She found it fascinating that a written answer — a description, not an image — could instantly turn the random patches into a clear picture. It said a lot about the way the brain was wired.

Dru hated giving in. If she looked at the answer, she couldn't avoid seeing the other solutions and ruining the rest of the puzzles.

She laid the book face down on the table and took another bite of her sandwich.

It was her first visit to the staff restaurant in a couple of months. When she lunched there, she created her own exclusion zone. She wasn't sure now if nobody tried to sit at her table because she read while she ate, or because she was the corporate Grim Reaper. People took furtive glances at her, probably thinking she knew their fates in the reorganisation.

A shadow fell across her table. Alex was standing over her. He nodded at the puzzle book.

"They're weird, aren't they?"

"Optical illusions? You said it." Dru pushed her chair back a little. Maybe he was going to join her. "It's the black and white ones that get me. I just can't see this one, and I daren't look at the answers and spoil the rest."

"Want to know?"

Dru dithered for a moment. Perhaps she was making a religion of not quitting. Persistence could get out of hand. "Okay."

"It's a horse running through trees."

As soon as she turned the book over and looked again at the black and white pattern, the randomness had vanished and she saw the horse. It would always be a horse now. She could never un-see it or imagine something else.

"Damn," she said. "So it is."

"But there's still no actual horse. That's the crazy thing. You fill in the gaps around a few fixed points that *could* be a horse."

Dru had learned never to underestimate people with no formal education in her field. "Why do we all eventually see the same picture, then?"

"Maybe because we all learn what a horse ought to look like. Generally speaking. The main points. Makes you wonder what someone would see if they didn't know what a horse was."

It had the makings of a great debate. Dru indicated the tubular steel chair next to her. "Are you going to join me?"

"Thanks, ma'am, but I was just passing through and I saw you looking like you were going to pull your hair out. Looks real nice, by the way. I almost didn't recognise you when you first had it done."

Alex gave her a polite nod and went on his way. The brief exchanges she had with him were often the most enlightening.

With the puzzle solved, her thoughts went straight back to Kinnery, and Weaver's apparent acceptance of his confession.

Something still didn't fit.

Weaver had played her the recording of the Skype call about Maggie Dunlop. But no penny dropped. There was no eureka moment when the random patches became the horse. Kinnery's story didn't explain how the leak about Maggie playing the mule — or the guinea pig — became the rumour about a transgenic child. It didn't explain why she'd tell a friend about it. And it didn't explain why Kinnery had sold his share in KWA, no matter how big the bill for his divorce settlement, and moved to a more expensive city in Canada.

It doesn't fit. It doesn't gel. Still too many gaps.

Then there was the one detail that really nagged at her. It certainly didn't explain the Seattle phone number.

That was an open door again, banging in the wind at night and keeping her awake. Kinnery's story about his security adviser almost held water until she heard the Skype recording. He'd just skipped over Weaver's comment about using the Seattle number as a starting point to look for old friends based in Washington. Dru would have expected him to remind Shaun what the Seattle number actually was, and correct him. But he didn't even react.

He's a goddamn liar. If he's lied for years, it's second nature now.

If Weaver didn't have his own doubts, it was because he knew something she didn't, or because he wasn't as smart as she thought.

Or maybe he's got another plan he hasn't shared with me.

Dru finished her sandwich and went back to her office, her old suite on the third floor, not the basement. It was sunlit and felt almost threatening now, an exposed arena with too many people walking in and out of the HR department and too many directions to watch. Knowing how insecurity took hold was no defence against falling prey to it. She got an odd look from Bobbie as she unlocked her door, but she didn't understand why until she logged in and read the e-mail addressed to all HR staff, tagged as confidential and bearing the header HR STAFF CHANGES.

Dru got that shivery, bristling feeling in her scalp as she started to read it.

It'll be me. The bastards. It'll be me. Just try it, Weaver.

But no, it wasn't: the casualty was Sheelagh, her boss.

She was out the door — culled, pink-slipped, surplus to

requirements. Halbauer's head of HR was taking over and Sheelagh Thompson was leaving. Dru could breathe again. When the axe was swung within your own castle walls, you were the last to know, especially if you were the target. But the blade had missed her. That was all she could afford to care about.

Dru could see Bobbie through the frosted glass panel in the door. She tapped to come in.

"You saw the e-mail?" Bobbie asked.

Dru nodded. "Yes. Before you ask, no, I've never met the incoming manager."

"Are they going to honour our vacation arrangements?"

Comradely solidarity was a wonderful thing. Perhaps everyone would sign a nice sorry-to-see-you-go card. "I hope so. I already booked my time off over Thanksgiving."

Dru wondered what this did to the hierarchy in the department, but she was determined not to get involved in jockeying for position. She went back to reading her mail. The thought of Kinnery's patchy story wouldn't let her go. She made an appointment to see Weaver in the morning.

Her paper files from the Ringer investigation were locked away at home. There was nothing on the premises to show that it had ever taken place — not from her end, anyway — and therefore there was nothing for an incoming manager to stumble across. That was the way it had to be.

She didn't need to wait until the next day to see Weaver, though. As she left for the day, she stepped out of the elevator into the parking garage and saw him locking his car, heading into the building.

"Hi Dru," he said. "You heard about Sheelagh, I take it."

"I did. Have you got five minutes?"

"Sure."

"I know you said Kinnery was done and dusted, but I have serious doubts."

Weaver shuffled his briefcase impatiently from hand to hand. He'd obviously rushed back for something important, but she had his attention. "What, the phone number again?"

"Mostly, but there are still other gaps that worry me."

"I'm really hoping I've buried whatever ill-advised actions Charles may have taken. Is there a good reason for disturbing the soil again?"

"Is that an instruction to stop keeping an eye open?"

Weaver tilted his head slightly as if he was considering the implications. "Anything active runs the risk of starting this off again." He lowered his voice. "But you've still got a budget. I don't want PIs hired, people contacted, or anything that'll get noticed. Passive observation only. And if you locate anything, you stop immediately and hand it over to me. That's as far as you need to go."

"Okay." Well, that was a definite order to carry on digging. "Understood."

"Do you mind my asking what you think is still missing?"

"There's a man involved," she said. She still didn't want to mention anything too specific, like names. That just created expectations she might not be able to deliver on. "Maggie might have had a male relative."

"The one *The Slide* mentioned? Well, any gene therapy she underwent wouldn't have been germline, so she couldn't pass it to a son. She'd have been forty-plus at the time anyway. You think Charles had a second subject?"

"The point is that I can't make a son, husband, or grandson fit the story as it stands without finding out more. If the number was Maggie's and not Kinnery's security, then it raises questions about the timing of calls and who had access after her death. We know she's dead. That's *all* we can verify from an independent source. The rest is all Kinnery's word."

"I see what you mean," Weaver said. "But no dramas, okay?"

"Don't worry. My ex-husband never saw it coming either."

Weaver didn't smile. "Keep me posted."

Dru drove home, working out what she could monitor now without needing to tell or involve anyone else. There were keyword alerts and any number of feeds, and she could observe Dunlop Ranch in a roundabout way. Realtors would know if the property was put up for sale. It might have already been sold, and if it hadn't been, a relative or someone close to Maggie now owned it. Trying to get a copy of a will was too risky. Dru would have to approach this sideways.

While Clare was doing her homework, Dru shut herself in her study to set up a watch system of alerts and feeds. She started typing keywords and wildcards.

*Shape-shifter. Shape shifter. Morph. Morph**. *Trickster. Werewolf.* She struggled to think of more terms. *Change form. Changeling. Polymorph. Mimic. Mimic**. Ringer.*

It was probably worth adding surnames and locations as well. *Dunlop Ranch. Athel Ridge. Maggie Dunlop. Ian Dunlop. Charles Kinnery. Shaun Weaver.* Who else? There were a couple of scientists whose names had cropped up in the Ringer files, plus the senator who'd been involved, the one Weaver called to cover his ass. Adding those might at least filter out thousands of irrelevant pages at some stage.

Lawrenson. Dominici. Brayne.

She'd add more as they occurred to her. The next step was to bookmark sites and forums that might discuss shape-shifting. Zoe Murray would have this information network at her fingertips. It was a shame they couldn't collaborate. The realtor sites would probably take more hands-on searching and maybe even some calls, but at least Dru had an automated eye on the places most likely to yield results.

But this could take years. I'm obsessive. It's official. And If I go crazy reading those UFO forums, I'll make a master's thesis out of it.

The timeline of events would be the key. Dru tried to avoid pet theories in case they blinded her to better ones, but the one lead that kept surfacing and waving to her was the significance of the British guy who took that call.

If he wasn't Ian Dunlop, then he probably knew where Ian was.

CHALTON FARM, WESTERHAM FALLS: ONE WEEK LATER.

The old face still hadn't returned.

No amount of meditating, willing, and pleading with whoever might be Up There had changed a thing. Ian psyched himself up in front of the bedroom mirror, torn between accepting this was the look he'd have to hang on to and busting a gut to get back to the way he'd been. Rob had never explained how to tell the difference between giving up too soon and knowing when make the best of a bad job.

But this isn't me. I don't really like this face.

He still had his new muscles, though. That was something.

Livvie said a few months of meditation caused physical changes in the brain that showed up on scans. This stuff was *real.* But it wasn't doing a goddamn thing to turn him back to the way he wanted to be. He kept a split-screen image on his phone, made up of the photo of David Dunlop and the picture that Livvie had taken on the way back from the garden centre, scaled to match. He concentrated on the twin images for hours until it gave him a headache. Something should have triggered whatever it was in his brain that told the various nerves, muscles, and pigment cells to do this or do that.

Perhaps he needed to try something different. When he'd morphed in Livvie's car, the moment had been a real mess of stressful emotions: fear of who was tailing him, anger that they'd dared to, and shame that Livvie felt she had to protect a grown man. If he wanted to recreate those conditions, he'd need to go do something dumb and dangerous.

Yeah, but look what happened when I got worked up in a boxing match. A friendly one that I knew wouldn't really damage me.

I should go out on my own. Test myself a little. Nobody's stopping me.

He couldn't stand in front of the mirror all day feeling sorry for himself. He went to find Mike, intending to go straight to the gym to do some phys, but Mike was in his study with the door open, reading something on his computer.

"Hey Ian. Want to see where your money is now?"

Ian wandered in. "Would I understand it? You're the money expert. I mean, I trust you to know what to do."

"I still need you to know about it. Transparency. Education. Whatever." He beckoned Ian over to the desk and showed him documents on the screen. "That's the proceeds from the sale of the ranch. When we get your ID sorted out, you can open your own checking account, but this is the trust the lawyer set up for you. The money can sit there until we can move it somewhere you can access easily."

Ian felt it was time to ask. "You bought the ranch yourself, didn't you?"

"Yes." Mike shrugged. "We had to hide the ownership from prying KWA eyes as fast as possible."

"It cost you."

"Damn, you're picking up Rob habits. You do realise how much money we have, don't you? And I mean that in a don't-worry kind of way. Not an I'm-loaded kind of way."

Ian hoped that Livvie kept an eye on Mike's generosity. A high

IQ and a good education didn't make a guy sensible, and throwing money away was dumb, no matter how much you had.

"I promise I won't take advantage of you," Ian said.

"I know that."

"What use am I to you, though?"

"You don't have to be useful. Not to me. Not to anybody."

"Okay, I *want* to be useful. How do I earn my keep? Can I do stuff for your new company?"

Mike looked to one side of the monitor as if he was taking the idea seriously. "Well, you could help us brainstorm. We've got to come up with something soon. We're looking at doing security assessments for organisations setting up overseas."

"Sure." Ian had no idea what that entailed, but he he'd make sure he found out. "I just want to be ... well, you know. Make a difference. Even if I can't join the Army."

Mike shook his head slowly, just one side to side movement. "I really do know, buddy. I'm *still* trying to make a difference."

"But you served."

"In the Guard."

"You make it sound like that wasn't real."

"Oh, it was real enough in Iraq. I'm not being disrespectful to all the guys who got killed and injured. They made the same sacrifices as everyone else. I just got frustrated with the organisation. Rob says I'd have felt even worse in the Army."

"Is that why you spent all that time and money on private training?"

Mike didn't talk about it much, but Rob had told Ian all the details. Mike's instructors had been former SEALs, USMC, and Delta guys, even SAS and French Foreign Legion. He'd been trained to do things he wouldn't have experienced even in a full-time infantry career. Ian didn't have a word for it, so he invented one: *hyper-legitimizing*. Mike had to go further and do tougher stuff than anyone else to prove he wasn't playing at it.

"Private contractor work was the only thing left for me when I quit the Guard," Mike said. "I needed the best skills I could get."

It made perfect sense, but Ian could see the same need in Mike that he saw in himself. Rob was different. He had his validation. That green beret told Rob everything he needed to know about himself, and he didn't fret about changing the world. He knew that he'd done his utmost and that he could do nothing more.

"Where's Rob, by the way?" Ian asked.

"He's taken his shoulder to the sports physio. Age, buddy. Everything takes longer to heal. That's you in twenty years. So take a day off."

Ian worried that if he skipped a session he'd lose his self-discipline as well as muscle mass. "Okay. Can you give me ride into Westerham, please? Is that okay? I'd like to wander around on my own."

Mike nodded, but he still looked worried. "Sure."

"If I'm alone, it won't matter if I morph again. Nobody can connect me with you."

"How about I drop you off and park up somewhere? That way you get your privacy but I'll be on hand for close protection."

"KWA's not going to find me here."

"I know." Mike just looked at him, more a plea to be humoured than disapproval. "I worry too much."

"It's okay. We both need to get used to — well, whatever this is. It's only been a few months, right?"

Mike tidied papers into a pile. "And that's awesome progress. Don't forget that. Okay, let's hit Vegas."

If Westerham Falls even had a pool table, Ian would have been surprised. It was as small-town as Athel Ridge, except more picturesque, all chocolate-box houses, stores with "artisan" in their names, and upmarket foreign cars. Ian thought that Mike and Livvie would have more fun in a city penthouse, but they seemed to want to hide, an urge he understood. They were people who'd always be targets because of who they were. They had to lead low-profile, anonymous lives, with few visitors and even fewer friends. Ian had much more in common with them than he'd first thought.

It makes them weird, being so different and so set apart. Just like me.

Mike dropped Ian outside the gas station a hundred yards from the town centre and tapped his watch. "You want to meet back here? Or call me?"

"One hour," Ian said. "Thanks, Mike."

He watched the Mercedes pull away. Mike would probably park in the centre of town to keep an eye on who was coming and going, and probably try out his surveillance skills as well. Ian wondered if this was a test to see if he'd spot Mike tailing him.

He strolled around, checking out stores and planning his

pit-stops. He could have a late breakfast in the French patisserie. Then he could browse in the bookstore, and finally drop in to the posh bakery for a couple of loaves of that walnut bread that Livvie liked. Shopping was a sport here, not a chore to bring back supplies. He'd get used to it.

As he passed windows, he checked his reflection, tilting his head to look under the peak of his cap. He still had the face he didn't want.

Fuck it. I can do this. I had it once. I can have it again.

The bookstore sold what he needed: illustrated guides to anatomy and drawing portraits, a source of detail that might help him learn to look at a face the way an artist or a surgeon would. If a guy could reduce pain in his leg by visualising its blood vessels and nerves relaxing, it had to be worth trying.

Ian found an art book that had anatomical diagrams as well as sketch techniques, then headed for the patisserie to study it over a hot drink. The place was a temple to sensory overload. The woman behind the counter was wrapping something for a customer, tying a candy-striped box with gold ribbon against a backdrop of glittering glass shelves that were laden with multi-coloured cakes and tarts as vivid as jewels. It was a ritual conducted in a haze of vanilla and caramel incense. Ian stepped back to let the other customer leave, then stood at the counter, overwhelmed and slightly queasy. There was just too much choice.

His eyes locked on to a strawberry tart, a pastry case filled with perfect, whole berries under a stained-glass layer of ruby jelly. The hand-written label said *tarte aux fraises.* Thanks to Livvie, he could read most of the French names now.

"One of those to eat in, please," he said. He'd feel like a vandal biting into it. "And a hot chocolate."

The woman nodded. "I'll bring it over."

He felt he had to take his cap off in a place like this. *Well, what the hell.* He picked a table by the window, put his jacket over the chair, and tried to look like he did this all the time. Strange: he could talk to the woman behind the counter without that meltdown sensation that he'd had in the mall a few weeks ago. Okay, she was a lot older than the girl in the clothing store, and not as pretty, but it was more than that. He had nothing to lose. He was so anonymous now that whatever he did didn't matter.

This isn't me. It's a disguise. A mask. A veil.

And he had his script, too. But this wasn't the literal kind that he'd fallen back on when he first went to Seattle. In most social situations now, he could ask himself what Mike or Rob would do. Gran had done her best, but there were some things that only another guy could assure him were normal. It was like growing up backwards. He knew all the theory, but he had to catch up on the basic experiences he'd have had years ago if he'd lived among people.

I morph. That's all that's wrong with me. But that's kind of inconvenient when the world's all about what you see and how people look.

Ian admired the tart for a few moments, then felt he'd paid enough respect to someone's skill and broke off a bite-sized chunk with his fork. It was a fantastic mix of flavours and textures. While he ate, he slid the battery back into his cell and checked for messages before putting it into flight mode. Who was going to message him? Only three other people knew his number. But Rob and Mike said the habit was good PERSEC and worth keeping.

So what would I really do if KWA turned up here right now?

He knew he could throw a few punches. He could get away, or at least cause enough of a ruckus to make someone call 911. He took another mouthful of tart, sipped the chocolate, and scrolled through to the pictures on his phone for another look at David Dunlop. Mike still insisted on referring to him as *your great-grandfather*. Ian couldn't bring himself to do that again, not yet anyway. He had to do something serious with his life before he could even begin to think of claiming a hero's name.

Damn, he really *had* looked like him, hadn't he?

Ian hadn't realised how precious that was. It wasn't just a matter of looking good. It was about looking like what you *were*. He took the book from its plastic bag and studied how an artist built up a face from a few crude geometric shapes into something that looked as detailed as a photo. The anatomical diagrams illustrated which muscles and bones gave faces their shape and expression. It was part medical, part art, and oddly enthralling.

"Excuse me," said a voice behind him. "Is it okay if I close that blind? The sun's in my eyes."

Ian hadn't even noticed the girl when he walked in. He couldn't tell if she worked there and had been in a back room, or if there was a rear entrance and she was another customer who'd just come in. All he knew was that she was now standing right next to him —

pretty, dark-haired, in jeans and a cable sweater, and smelling delicious. It took him a confused second to realise that there were vertical blinds in the bay window that made up most of the front wall of the cafe. The sun in the side panel was reflecting off the glass counter.

Rob was the oracle on women. What would he do? He'd take charge.

"I'll get it." Ian was instantly afraid to even breathe. *Why couldn't I stay looking like I did? Do I smell okay? Too much aftershave?* He reached out and tugged the plastic beaded cord to close the slats. "Is that okay now?"

The vision of loveliness smiled at him. "Thank you. That's great. Can I get you anything else?"

So she worked here. What the hell did he say next? He had no idea how to turn this from buying a snack into chatting her up, as Rob called it. Damn, she probably had a boyfriend who'd kill him anyway. His hopes soared and were shot down in flames within seconds.

But I didn't make a dick of myself. That's something.

"I'll have another hot chocolate, please." He smiled back at her, and that, as Mike would say, was progress. He followed up with the next thing that came into his head. "Are you open every day?"

"Sure." She glanced at the book. "Nine 'til seven, seven days a week. Are you an artist?"

"No, but it would be nice to be able to draw like this." *Shit, what kind of an answer is that?* "Maybe I'll try."

"Well, I hope we see you in here again."

When she came back with his second hot chocolate, he gave her his best smile, hoped it didn't come across as creepy, and decided to quit while he was ahead. It was too soon to try anything advanced. This would require a wash-up and post-contact report with Rob, the expert on such matters.

How did Mike meet Livvie? In a bar. How did Rob meet Bev? He never told me.

Ian went on reading and admiring the illustrations, lost in the book for half an hour before he was snapped out of it by the older woman putting his check on the table. He wasn't sure about tipping and put down two tens to be safe. As he left, he glanced over his shoulder to see the girl give him another smile and a little wave. It was crazy how such small things could make or break his day. He wasn't even looking his best, but he was obviously now so ordinary and so normal that he just looked like any other guy.

Once that was all he'd wanted: to be like everyone else. Now he wanted more. He wanted to choose how he looked.

He checked his watch and realised he had ten minutes to make it to the rendezvous point. That meant a brisk walk to the bakery if he was going to meet Mike on time. He went to buy the bread and then headed for the gas station, looking for the Mercedes. It passed on the other side of the road and did a U-turn to pull up alongside him.

"I bought a book." He put the bag in the back and got in. "And some walnut bread for Livvie."

Mike indicated to pull out. "Always wise to make an offering. Anything else?"

"I talked to the girl in the patisserie and didn't make a complete asshole of myself. Which is right up there with discovering penicillin, I think."

"Amen." Mike nodded approvingly. "I have some awful memories of trying to pick up girls in my teens. Took a lot of mistakes to get it right."

Mike was probably trying to reassure him that even confident warrior-type guys like him and Rob had been through the stage that Ian was struggling with now, the same way that Rob made a point of showing him how he'd looked at sixteen. The difference was that they'd grown into the kind of men that most other guys secretly wanted to be. They didn't have to worry about what they'd turn into in the next minute.

It felt like self-pity. Ian slapped it down hard. No wrapping, whingeing, or dripping, Rob said: no giving up, and no complaining.

For the next few days, Ian spent his downtime with the portrait book and even picked up a pencil to try sketching. He didn't expect to become an artist. He just hoped it would make some connections in his brain in the same way that thinking about making a fist would make the muscles of his hand contract and follow through with the action.

The photo session was now on indefinite hold. After three days of sketching, studying angles, and visualising changes until his jaws ached — he hadn't realised that he ground his teeth so much — he woke to the same face yet again and decided that if the girl in the patisserie hadn't recoiled at the sight of him, then maybe he could live with it.

If I can keep it, that is.

After his morning run, he retreated to his room and took out his pad to sketch. He'd never expected to enjoy drawing, but it made him look outward again instead of inward, and that could only be a good thing. Eventually a tap on the door interrupted him.

Mike stood in the doorway. "I'm going into town to get some groceries. You want to come?"

"Sure."

Mike turned the Mercedes around to head down the drive. Rob was outside the garage, polishing his immaculate white Jaguar and looking a little forlorn. When Ian nodded at him as he went past, he broke into an instant grin. Rob always felt obliged to be cheerful in public.

"He's missing Tom like crazy," Mike murmured, as if he could read Ian's mind. "The sooner he visits, the better. You'll like him." Rain began spitting on the windshield and made the wipers start up. "Looks like a miserable old day coming."

Mike slowed at the bottom of the drive to wave to Mr Andrews, the old guy who lived at the gatehouse, and turned onto the Westerham road. If life in a mansion with a couple of mercenaries and a goddess who could cuss in seven languages was normal, then life was starting to feel routine. They wandered around the grocery store in the centre of town, picking up rosewater and pomegranate molasses for Livvie's latest exotic dish and some dog biscuits for Oatie. It was raining steadily now, hard enough for Ian to turn up his collar and pull down his cap.

"When we get some snow, we'll go skiing," Mike said "Rob can ski. God, he can do everything. Climb mountains, fast-rope from helicopters, operate boats. All kinds of hairy-assed stuff. He claims he can sew, too."

"Didn't you do all that in private tactical training?"

"Yes, but I did hardcore stuff. Needlepoint."

"Can I do some survival training?"

"As long as you promise never to get Rob started about living off the land. If I hear his chicken story one more time, I'm going vegan."

Mike laughed. He did that a lot now, maybe a measure of how confident he felt that Ian was beyond KWA's range. They were heading for the car, heads down against the rain and debating whether Rob should pay Tom a surprise visit, when Ian heard a woman call out. He looked around. Mike turned too.

It was the girl from the patisserie.

She stood outside the shop, no coat or umbrella, waving to get Ian's attention. His heart soared. Not only did she recognise him, she was also braving the rain to talk to him. He waited while she trotted across the road. She had something in her hand.

"I think you've scored," Mike said. "That's her, yes?"

Oh God. "Yes."

Her hair was beaded with rain. "You left your bookstore receipt behind," she said, sidestepping a puddle, still yards away. "I've been waiting to catch you."

Ian was absolutely sure he knew what to do now. But then he felt his scalp prickle and his skin tighten, and although every time felt like the worst possible moment, this one definitely was. He was morphing.

No, not now. It's her. It's my chance.

As the girl stopped in front of him, she looked into his face, eyes narrowed against the rain. Her expression changed instantly into frozen surprise.

"Oh, I'm sorry." She sounded breathless and embarrassed. "I thought you were someone else. You've got the same cap and jacket. Sorry."

Ian wanted the ground to open up and swallow him. He could have said no, it really was him, and there was something he needed to tell her, but he knew he could never do that.

"No problem," he said.

She gave him a nervous little *oops* grin and jogged back to the patisserie, arms folded and head down. He was devastated.

If only he'd managed not to morph, he'd be in with a chance now. He could have been charming and thanked her. He could have introduced himself and asked her if she wanted a coffee when she finished her shift. He could have hit on her in a proper gentlemanly way, Rob-style. But he'd morphed. She was lost to him forever. He didn't even know her name.

He turned to Mike. "This is what the rest of my life's going to be like, isn't it?"

It was hard to read Mike's expression. It was somewhere between embarrassment and well-I'll-be-damned. Whatever Ian had morphed into now, Mike wasn't sure how to tell him, and Ian's first instinct was to look down at his hands in case he'd completely changed colour this time. There was nothing nearby to show him a reflection. It was the first time he could remember being so desperate to look at himself that he cursed the absence of a mirror or a window. Mike steered him into an office doorway.

"Before you kick yourself in the ass," Mike said quietly, "you might want to check this out."

He fiddled with his cell phone and handed it to Ian. For a moment, Ian thought he was looking for some video with an uplifting story behind it, but then he realised exactly what he could see — his own face, picked up by the front-facing camera.

He looked the way he had a week ago. He looked like David Dunlop again. He'd finally done it. It was just terrible, terrible timing.

"I know that hurt, buddy, but concentrate on what you've achieved," Mike said. "You get more control over it every day. Okay, you lost a chance there, but she might well like you all over again. It's not as if she knows who you are, is it?"

Mike had a gift for knowing when Ian needed to go to ground. He steered him back to the car and they sat in silence for a few minutes, watching the rain trickling down the windshield. Mike reached up to the rear-view mirror and angled it for Ian to see his reflection.

"Livvie's going to be thrilled," he said. "You'll probably get a peach margarita out of this. Hell, *I* might even get one."

Ian almost expected the face to evaporate as he stared at it. But it was there, all right. This was what he remembered. This was *him.*

It should have been a triumphant moment. If he could revert to it once, he could revert again. He could decide exactly how he needed to look. For now, though, he'd put all his effort into staying just the way he was.

"Beer, birds, BMW." Ian wasn't sure if he was heartbroken or ecstatically happy. The two could feel equally painful, he realised. "We'd better get those photos done."

TWELVE

There's definitely an eccentricity gene in the Brayne family. Leo donates his Senate salary to charity and covers his own expenses. He says that if he let the federal purse simply not pay him, some bureaucrat would piss the savings down the drain without doing any good. And I hear his son's still serving frontline. They're a hair-shirt kind of dynasty.

One member of Leo Brayne's golf club to another.

CHALTON FARM, WESTERHAM FALLS: MID- OCTOBER.

"What's so funny?" Livvie asked.

Mike slid the breakfast tray onto the nightstand, not realising that he was smiling to himself. "You said having Ian around would be a good test run for adoption, and here we are, waiting for the kids to be out playing before we have sex."

"It's a really big house, Mike." Livvie scrutinised the tray of tea, wholegrain toast, lime marmalade, and slices of Havarti cheese. It was her favourite breakfast when they were at university, too odd for Mike's tastes, but he knew it had the nostalgic power of a long forgotten perfume. "Where's the goddamn single red rose?"

"I didn't need it. You've already succumbed to my charm."

Livvie took a playful swing at him with a pillow. Mike hadn't realised how much pressure he'd put on her in the quest for a baby. It was only looking back on the contrast between what he'd thought was a happy Livvie and the woman he saw now that brought it home to him. *Did I do that to her? How do you end up grinding down someone you love?* Rob had warned him, though. It was easier to see the signs from the outside.

"Go on, eat your freaky breakfast," he said.

"It's no weirder than cheese and chutney." Livvie piled the Havarti on the toast, smeared it with marmalade, and munched contentedly. "So where *are* the kids?"

"In the gym. You had to ask?"

"I'm going to have to get in there more often myself. Ian thrashed me at squash."

"You took him to the sports club? We should have discussed it first."

Livvie gave him a mock-peeved look, lips pursed. "Not the club. We used a wall in the stable block. I got my ass handed to me."

"He's half your age, honey. Suck it up."

"He's never played a racquet sport before. His coordination and reaction times are amazing."

"He's eighteen," Mike said. "It's effortless when you're that age."

"It's time to get him out and about more."

"You're probably right. I'm over-anxious."

"It's not entirely misplaced." Livvie tapped her teacup to indicate that she wanted a refill. Mike poured obediently. "He's so mature that I keep forgetting he never had a normal childhood. But we're part of that abnormality now."

"Because he's still isolated?"

"Because we're reinforcing the war-hero standards Maggie set him. He excels at military skills and he gets approval. The real test will be when he mixes with the civilian world and all the soft, undisciplined, irresponsible assholes out there."

"I don't know what else to do with him, honey. He'll always need to watch his ass twenty-four-seven." Mike's own childhood kept resurfacing lately. Mom and Dad hadn't been smotheringly protective, but he'd been left in no doubt from an early age that his name and wealth meant he had to keep his head down. "We can teach him that everyone's out to get him, which makes him into a scared victim. Or we can do it the Army way and train him to be situationally aware, which gives him control."

"I didn't say it was wrong. Just pointing out that kids get raised by guesswork."

Mike could have bought the world's top specialists, but giving them access to Ian was out of the question. The best that Mike could do, according to the Rob Rennie manual of dealing with young lads, was to give Ian confidence and a strong sense of self reliance.

I really have taken over as a surrogate father. I don't know who needs it more, Ian or me.

Ian was certainly gaining confidence. It was the self-assurance born of pushing his physical limits rather than learning to tell dazzling jokes at parties. He still had that modest yes-ma'am-no-sir manner, but when he had something to say now, he didn't hesitate to say it, and he never griped or refused to do anything. Everything was always "fine": every response was "okay." Mike was struck by his inability to hold grudges. If anyone had lied to Mike on the scale that they'd lied to Ian, he'd have wanted vengeance, and got it.

Perhaps Ian still didn't realise what he'd lost and would never get back. But it might simply have been impossible to deal with, so he'd buried it in order to move on.

A few days later, Ian's passport arrived via overnight delivery. Mike signed for it with a sense of paternal satisfaction. This was Ian's confirmation of freedom. It needed celebrating as a rite of passage. Even if he couldn't drive alone yet and still had to wait a few years to buy a beer, he had his own bank account, and with a passport that meant he could go anywhere he pleased. Mike suspected the driving licence would mean more, but it was good to mark these milestones to show Ian that he was building a new life.

Mike checked his watch. Ian would be in the gym with Rob until eleven. It was worth interrupting the session for this. Rob was watching Ian doing triceps dips on the bars when Mike walked in and held up the envelope.

"Something you've been waiting for, Ian," he said.

Ian was counting under his breath, eyes fixed on the opposite wall. Mike could see his lips moving. *Sixteen, seventeen, eighteen, nineteen.* He didn't look up until he said *twenty* aloud and lowered himself from the bars.

"Wow," he said. "It's real now, isn't it?"

He wiped his hands and paused for a moment before opening the envelope. Then held up the passport to Rob like a detective showing his badge. Rob applauded.

"Now you can visit civilised countries that let young gentlemen drink in bars," Rob said. "Like England."

Mike watched Ian's face for signs of a smile. "What our arts correspondent means is that you can now visit all the great global centres of learning and culture."

"That's what I said, didn't I?" Rob took the passport and scrutinised Ian's photo. "Nobody ever looks like their passport picture anyway. Have you checked your fingerprints, by the way? Do they change?"

"Shit." Mike hadn't thought of that. He couldn't believe he'd overlooked it. "Have you, Ian?"

Ian inspected the pad of his forefinger. "No, but I haven't given any fingerprints yet, so even if they've changed, I'll be okay. Scans are only ninety per cent accurate anyway." It sounded as if he'd already done his homework on that. Mike reminded himself that Ian had been raised by the queen of paranoia. "Thanks, Mike. I'd never have been able to get this without you. I'll go put it in the safe."

He trotted off, looking more stunned than delighted. Maybe he was just starting to realise how much his horizons would change now. Rob wandered over to Mike and leaned in for a discreet chat, arms folded.

"I don't want to scare you," he murmured, "but when did you last train with him?"

"A couple of weeks ago."

"What sort of weight was he pressing?"

"One-ninety, two hundred pounds."

"Were you pushing him? He did two-sixty pretty easily today."

"Christ. Really?"

"I'll show you." Rob waited for Ian to come back. "Ian, can you manage a few more benches? I want to check your max."

Ian took any suggestion as something between an order and a challenge. He shuffled himself into position on the bench underneath the barbell stands. "Okay."

"We'll add ten pounds each rep, and you keep going to failure, yeah?"

"Remember there's no shame in *can't.*" Mike looked down at Ian and ensured he had eye contact to make his point. Ian would injure himself before he'd give in. "You reach your limit, you quit, and we take the bar. Understood?"

"Yes, Mike."

Rob started Ian at two-sixty and went up ten pounds at a time to three hundred. It was a visible effort, but Ian still wasn't struggling enough for Mike to call a halt. Then Ian hit three-ten.

And that's my maximum. Oh boy.

Ian strained to lock out his elbows at three-twenty. "Come on, one more." Rob gave Mike a look as they added two more plates. "Three-thirty. You okay, Ian?"

"Fine."

Ian managed to lock out, but he was starting to wobble. One end of the bar dipped. He made a couple of attempts to lower it before Mike and Rob moved in to take it.

"Good lad. Bloody good effort." Rob threw him his towel. "Grab a shower and don't forget your protein drink."

Ian strode off, flexing his fingers as if they hurt. His build and posture had changed completely since he'd arrived, and it was nothing to do with morphing. Mike raised an eyebrow at Rob.

"I know it was just single reps," Mike said, "but he's beaten my maximum."

Rob nodded. "Mine too. I'm gutted."

"And we've both got twenty-five or thirty pounds on him."

"He's young, he works his arse off, and he's eating right. So he's filling out. Lads do."

"Sure, but without drugs, that's still on the dramatic end of the bell curve."

"What do you think?" Rob asked.

"What do *you* think?"

Rob spread his arms. "Okay, maybe it's a side effect of whatever Kinnery did."

"Morphing involves muscle fibres." Mike tried to recall what he knew about cephalopods, which was mostly what he saw in documentaries. "It's not just pigment."

"He hasn't got superpowers, Zombie. He's just very strong, very coordinated, and very fast."

"So are cephalopods. They're incredibly strong for their size."

"Yeah, I get it."

"And an octopus's nervous system is more like a computer network with a mainframe. Their arms make decisions independently."

"So does my dick, but how does that change anything?"

"I told Dad that morphing was no real use in the field."

"It isn't. Handy for a shoplifter, though."

"How about that level of strength and coordination?"

"The services are full of super-fit blokes already. You told your dad the truth. Stop fretting."

Mike was starting to doubt himself. On the outdoor range, he watched Ian make perfect, confident transitions between weapons and knock down targets with unerring accuracy. He was approaching the stage where he'd need the kind of training facilities that even Mike didn't have.

Should I tell Dad all this?

Ian cleared his pistol, checked it, and took off his ear defenders. "I'm scaring you, aren't I?"

Mike wanted Ian to see himself as talented rather than abnormal. Even in regular people, it amounted to the same thing.

"I'd prefer to say impressed," he said. "You're good. I'm just wondering how much more Rob and I can teach you here."

"I still can't do what you do. All the judgement calls. And I'd probably crap myself when it got rough."

"You want to learn to search and clear buildings?" Mike had seen enough of Ian's reactions to know he'd never back down even if he was pissing his pants. "I can set up the stable block as a house layout. And we can use airsoft or simulated ammo. It still hurts enough to make the point."

Ian nodded. It was real enthusiasm this time. "I'd really like to try that. Thanks."

Mike realised he'd just increased Ian's subconscious expectations. No matter how often Ian said he knew he'd never have a military career, Mike knew it couldn't erase the dream. Ian would become more proficient and watch the gap between his skills and the chance to use them growing wider each day. That was crushing.

I've been there. In the end, your differences make the decision for you.

What was he obliged to do, stop Ian from doing something he loved, and tell him what a fine alternative career he could have in law or accountancy? That would be making decisions for him. It was still early days. There was no telling what Ian could and couldn't do yet.

And that's actually wonderful. Damn, it's fun being a dad.

KWA had now been silent long enough for Mike to feel that he could file them under generic potential threats along with terrorists, armed robbers, and kidnappers. The situation was stable enough to get on with the future. He wasn't much nearer to a firm plan for the company, though. He sat down at his desk and cleared his correspondence like he did every morning, and gave himself until the end of the week to come up with something better than threat evaluation or training expatriate workers to stay out of trouble overseas. He hadn't managed to do it himself, after all.

Rob did a drum roll on the open door with his fingers and ambled in, as near to a muse as Mike was likely to get.

"I'm still kicking ideas around." Mike gestured to the leather armchair. Oatie had staked his claim to the sofa under the window, and he was a very long dog when he stretched out. "The Brayne business gene must be recessive."

Rob snapped his fingers at Oatie and gestured *off* at him. Astonishingly, the greyhound complied. Rob lounged on the sofa with his hands meshed behind his head.

"Your dad's still paying me every month," Rob said. "For training services. He really doesn't have to."

"Does it bother you?"

"It wouldn't, if I was doing anything to earn it."

"But you are. You put your life on hold to sort out Ian."

"It's only been a few months." Rob balled up a piece of paper and lobbed it at him. "Anyway, why are you still fretting?"

"It would kind of help if you narrowed down the questions. Or did subtitles."

"Ian. Have you kept your dad up to date with what he can do now?"

"Not every detail, no."

"And you're feel like you're lying to him."

"I hate secrets. But the more I tell him, the more he's got to worry about."

"Mike, for all we know, Ian's strength isn't linked to Dr Frankentosser at all. But we'll never know because we can't get him tested." Rob sat up, allowing Oatie to tiptoe back and curl up next to him. "All your dad cares about is the security angle. Okay, a medical company would kill to have Ian, but he's not a military game-changer like a foolproof IED detector."

"How much would he have to develop before he was, though?"

"So what? Why did you give him a home in the first place?"

"Because his right to live his life trumps whatever use he is to someone else."

"Exactly. Your dad asked you to get involved because he trusted you to do what's *right*." Rob could always rinse everything in clarity. That wasn't easy where family was involved. "And you did."

"You wouldn't humour me, would you?"

"No, I always call a twat a twat. Even if he's my best mate."

"Okay."

"So if your dad asks, tell him exactly how well Ian's doing. If he doesn't ask, he's decided he doesn't need to know. Which means he's worked it out for himself."

Rob's tangled logic always made sense. "You're my permission to be a bad boy, aren't you?" Mike said. "A weaponised Jiminy Cricket."

"Yeah, like you need it. The first thing I saw you do was gut a bloke with his own knife, take his AK, and put a round through him. And I thought to myself, 'Y'know, I bet we have the same taste in opera as well.'"

Mike laughed, unburdened again. "Bromance at first sight."

"There you go."

"So what am I going to do about Ian? Carry on making a soldier out of him, or talk him into taking a nice law degree?"

"How much plain Rob-talk can you handle in a day?"

"Okay, get it over with."

"Whether you like it or not, you and Livvie are effectively his family now. You can't hand him back. And you can't run his life. The best you can do is whatever feels right on the day. That's all I could do with Tom."

Mike knew that he should have had these conversations with his father long before Ian showed up. But it had felt too much like planning for something that would never happen, and the more detailed a dream became, the harder it was to let go or divert it into something more attainable.

"That doesn't answer my question."

"What feels right?" Rob asked.

"Let him carry on. Let him excel. But that might not make him happy. It might be worse for him than never knowing."

"Well, let's see what he can do, let him do it, and see if he still wants to do it after he's tried it. It's not like we can't create a security job for him. Then he'll be in the same position that we are."

It made perfect sense. Rob always knew when to stop thinking and start doing.

"Come on," Mike said. "Let's check out the stable block and see if we can turn it into a kill house for urban ops."

Rob jumped up. "Hoofing. Even if Ian doesn't enjoy it, I will."

Close quarters battle training really got the adrenaline going. If it made Ian even more certain that he was meant to be a soldier, then Mike knew he had only himself to blame for fanning the flames.

But he had money and influence. One way or another, whatever Ian wanted, Ian would get.

CHALTON FARM, WESTERHAM FALLS: LATE OCTOBER.

Gran had told Ian never to trust any technology that could tell someone where he was. He took that to heart more than ever now.

She stuck to the oldest technology that still worked, and the internet was a forbidden world. The computer kit that Mike kept buying for him was predictably the latest and the best, though. It scared the crap out of him. He didn't download software, he checked every link before he clicked on it, and he stuck to the vaguest search terms. E-mail — he didn't need it. Everyone he needed to speak to was here in person.

And he didn't even want to look at that social networking thing. He knew what it was from Gran's list of things to avoid, but were these guys insane? Why would anyone want to tell strangers that much about themselves? Ian just didn't get it. He imagined what his life would have been like if he'd done that, and it terrified him.

His computer was just a library and a typewriter. That was all he wanted from it, no matter how riveting the idea of porn seemed and how hard it was to keep his mind off girls. He was looking for information on cephalopods. It was a topic he'd been avoiding in case it freaked him out, but he could face it now, and there was no harm in searching online with keywords like *octopus*. It was high school biology, stuff that a million kids would access. Livvie assured him the VPN gateway would stop nosey assholes tracking it to his computer anyway.

It certainly beat books. Once Ian found the general sites about marine biology, he was drawn into the video clips. Reading what these creatures could do with lights, colour, and shape was one thing. Seeing it happen was something else entirely.

Part of him had wished Kinnery had based his experiments on more glamorous animals, but now he was mesmerised. A little mimic octopus not only changed colour and shape, but also *acted* like other things. One moment it disguised itself as drifting weed, then a sea snake, a sole, and even a scorpion fish. A regular octopus, the kind he'd seen in movies, settled on a rock and changed colour and texture to merge perfectly with the algae on it. It became invisible. Ian paused the video and just couldn't see where the octopus ended and the rock began.

It was the most astonishing thing he'd seen. He made a note of the URL so he could show Mike. Eventually he moved on to clips of squid, who were anything but invisible, communicating with each other in lights and colours like some incredibly complex, multi-level Morse code.

Now that's cool. Seriously cool.

Yes, he was okay with having something in common with these creatures. They weren't gross. They were smart and oddly beautiful. Octopuses could even work out how to remove childproof caps on bottles. But the most important thing was that they could work out how to hide. They had to. They didn't have claws or armour to defend themselves.

Ian had never eaten one, and now he never would.

He took stock for a moment. He checked himself in the full length mirror, using his learner's driving permit and passport as a reference. *This* was definitely him. This was the self he'd always see in his mind's eye and that he had to be able to get back to without needing a mirror.

Maybe he should have told Mike that he now practised making himself morph just to make sure he could get back to this face if something went wrong. He just didn't want to worry him.

And the whole thing was kind of personal. Rob had pointed out that morphing while he was fooling around with a girl would be a catastrophe. The only way that Ian had found to test if he could keep from morphing in that kind of situation was way too embarrassing to discuss with anyone, even Rob. But now he could do it.

As long as Ian had an image in his mind, he could make himself change. And he was getting better at resembling whatever picture he chose. He still had no idea where the previous faces had come from, but he'd probably seen them and forgotten, like he hadn't realised how often he'd looked at that photo of David Dunlop. He could have chosen to look any way he wanted, but that was too much pointless choice. Something in him knew that he needed to resemble the man he'd cherished as the great-grandfather he'd never known.

Besides, Livvie had told him this was how he was meant to look.

What could he try next? If he could polish this and mimic a few more faces really well, he'd be ready to handle anything. He'd have complete control of it. It would never catch him out. He'd always be able to vanish, and he'd always be able to cope with a girl.

Sorted.

Ian studied the images on his tablet, mostly pictures that Rob had shared from his own album. He wasn't comfortable using those for practice. They were real people who Rob knew and cared about.

But whose face do I know?

He'd seen a lot of pictures of Tom, even live video. The guy was pretty much the same age as him, too. For a moment, Ian couldn't resist the challenge. He visualised Tom's face and felt the familiar windburn sweep across his skin. Then he looked in the mirror.

No. Stop it.

The resemblance was very, very close. For a couple of seconds, it disoriented him. A stranger's face was fine, but this felt creepy and disloyal. *Wrong, wrong, wrong.* He snapped himself back to normal, switched on the TV, and tried focusing on anonymous guys in adverts instead.

That was better. It felt scientific and impersonal. He sat back in the armchair with a pocket mirror and checked how well he'd done each time he morphed. Yes, he was getting results: not right every time, but often enough, and not perfect, but good enough to pass for the original on a cursory glance. And he could snap back to being himself with minimal effort. The more he did it, the easier it got. He studied his own face in the mirror again.

And to think this used to terrify me.

The only thing that scared Ian now was being alone and not part of this group of family and friends. He was happy here. He belonged.

For a moment, he thought of the octopus blending seamlessly with the rock. Maybe it was time to try breaking down his changes into separate components, into pigment and texture and shape, to see what was possible. Why not? He needed to know as much as possible. He could always get back to being himself again now.

His old work jacket was an Army surplus parka in a camouflage pattern that he was sure they didn't use these days. He put his hand on it and tried to visualise the pattern continuing across the skin. For a few minutes, nothing happened. Then his skin began to look blotchy and uneven, like a few old bruises fading through to yellows and greens.

Ian concentrated as hard as he could. The colours moved slightly, then darkened. He shut his eyes to block out distractions for a moment, saw the DPM fabric in his mind, and opened his eyes again.

It wasn't even close to the perfect, seamless match that the octopus had managed, but the skin on the back of his hand was now patterned like the jacket, except the greens were more an olive-brown and the darkest brown was a little lighter. It was like finally forcing open one door and seeing the rest all burst open at the same time. Whatever he'd activated or learned to use in his nervous system was suddenly doing much more than he'd imagined it could.

Ian visualised a cloth wiping across the back of his hand. The skin snapped back to the light olive tan he now regarded as normal. Just to make sure that he hadn't triggered unexpected changes elsewhere, he opened the desk drawer and took out an ink pad to make another record of his fingerprints. From what he could see of his thumbprint with a magnifying glass, the pattern of swirls hadn't changed since he'd started taking prints. Everything was under control.

You were right not to tell me what I was, Gran.

If he'd known what he could do when he was a child, he'd have treated it as a game, someone would have caught him, and he would have been locked up in a lab for the rest of his life. It was far better to find out after he'd learned to take care of himself, and when he understood what the stakes were. Gran got it right. The lie had hurt, but the truth would have been disastrous.

When Ian headed downstairs, the only sign of life was Rob's cell phone on the kitchen table. Even Oatie was absent. A quick check on the garage and the security camera feeds showed that the Mercedes was gone, too. As Ian filled the coffee maker, he heard water running in the pipes and guessed Rob was in one of the downstairs bathrooms.

Then the phone rang. Ian glanced at the screen and saw the incoming call icon, Tom's picture. They'd spoken a few times, but never via a video call.

Ian wasn't afraid of morphing at the wrong moment any more. He picked up the phone.

"Hi Tom." There. It was that easy. "I think your dad's in the john. I'll go get him."

"Ian? Hi." Tom obviously knew the voice if not the face. "He's let you escape from the gym, then."

Ian heard the rush of water. "I think he's on his way. How's college?"

"I'm working up my special excuses to get time off during term. It's going to be great to see everyone."

Rob walked up behind Ian and peered over his shoulder to take over the conversation. "Sorry, kiddo, I was in the loo," he said to Tom. "So, you're definitely coming over next month, yeah?"

It was Ian's cue to hand over the phone and wander off to the living room with his coffee. Rob came to find him about fifteen minutes later, looking pleased in the way he always did when he'd spoken with Tom.

He patted Ian on the shoulder. "I take it you're feeling confident now."

"Yeah. I can maintain this."

"Well, that opens a lot more doors."

Ian wanted to show Rob what he could do, but it didn't seem like the right moment. "Where's Mike and Livvie?"

"Gone out to buy some airsoft kit."

"Couldn't he order it and get it delivered?"

"Come on, you know Mike. He sees every delivery he doesn't need to have as some potential security breach. And he needs to do everything himself. Y'know, he'd have been really unhappy if he'd ended up in the Army full-time. He'd be a colonel by now. All meetings and memos."

"But he hands stuff over to lawyers and accountants. He's got people for everything."

"Even his people have got people, mate. But there's some

things he just won't delegate. Especially manual labour."

Rob wasn't joking. Mike treated making things like a religion. They walked out to the stables to check the progress of the kill house. Stacks of cut wood — planks, batten, sheets of plywood — stood in the covered yard awaiting construction. Inside, Mike had marked the floor and walls with lines of spray paint and stacked straw bales.

Ian walked up and down the flagstone passage that separated two facing rows of stalls, working out how the place would look when the wood was in position. It seemed a shame to spoil such nice stables, but Mike never had to worry about what someone else would think or if it would affect the value of the house. Ian sometimes caught glimpses of what Mike's wealth really meant, and they were never in the places he expected to see them.

"Are we going to build this?" Ian had helped build the log frames on the makeshift assault course in one of the paddocks. Mike was a competent workman. "What is it, partition walls with windows and swing doors?"

Rob studied something on his phone. "Yeah, Mike's trying to make the space a bit more complex. Otherwise it'd be like clearing a hall in a block of flats, although that's pretty bloody hairy too."

"Any tips?" Ian asked.

"Yeah, don't stand in front of a door to open it. That's where the buggers aim first. Having said that, I've kicked down doors a few times, so what do I know? But to be on the safe side, fire through interior walls before you get to the door. Or toss in a grenade. Preferably both." Rob paced out a line, imagining something. "Provided you're not worried about the paperwork or a court martial, that is. We'd all be speaking German now if we'd had bloody lawyers breathing down our necks in World War Two."

"Wouldn't they have shot all the lawyers, though?"

Rob winked at him. "You always look on the bright side, mate. I admire that."

Mike and Livvie returned with boxes of equipment — authentic-looking carbines, magazines, goggles, all kinds of kit — and laid it out in the stables. Ian sorted through the boxes, slightly baffled. It seemed to take more equipment to pretend to fight a battle than to engage in a real one. Mike picked up a carbine and demonstrated it to Ian.

"You can't exactly shoot locks out with this, but it feels the same weight and you can use proper optics," he said. "Everything fits on your webbing the same way, too, and it'll give you a sense of what it's like when someone shoots back. If it suits you and you want to progress, I'll get you some training at a proper shoot house."

Ian looked at the price tags. "Damn, Mike, some of this stuff costs as much as the real thing."

"You want to try it out, then?"

"Sure."

Rob started walking back towards the house with Livvie. "Call me if you need a target. I'm going to track down some of my old oppos and see where they're working now."

Mike loaded a pistol and squeezed off a few rounds at a bale of straw with a rapid *putt-putt-putt-putt-putt.* Ian decided to risk an opinion.

"Rob's still kind of lost, isn't he?"

"Yeah, he needs goals. But he's running out of them." Mike loaded a carbine and demonstrated the mechanism to Ian without saying a word to explain it. "He always wants to be pushed beyond his limits."

"How about an expedition somewhere remote?"

"No, he'd see that as self-inflicted. You know what he'd love? A post-apocalyptic wasteland. A zombie invasion. Anything where he's got no choice but to make the best of it."

"I thought you both liked challenges."

"Ah, but I can always deploy my rich guy's parachute if things go wrong, even if I don't plan to, so by definition I'm playing at it. I think it's *not* having a choice that hits the spot for Rob." Mike handed Ian the unloaded rifle and a magazine. "Come on. We're freezing our asses off here. Let's armour up and go shoot each other."

They dressed in the indoor range. There was a mirror in the small locker room, and it didn't bother Ian until he caught his reflection. He'd never worn full combat rig with helmet and goggles before. With the rifle, he looked like a real solider, and it was too much for him. He was an imposter. He was no better than those guys he saw on the internet trying to come across as badasses when they were just paintballing, guys who'd never faced what Mike and Rob had. *Or Great-Grandad.* He turned away from the mirror, appalled at himself.

"I swear this isn't as dumb as it looks," Mike said. He'd picked up on Ian's reaction and seemed to think it was because they weren't using live rounds. "It's not so different to the simulated ammo we use in training, except that stuff fits regular weapons. The rounds still hurt like hell."

"Don't worry, I understand." Ian adjusted his helmet, trying to avoid the mirror. "Really."

Mike caught his arm and pulled him back in front of the mirror. "Gap," he said, tugging at Ian's body armour. He treated everything as if it was live fire anyway. "You need that tightened up. You'd be amazed where rounds can sneak in."

Ian couldn't avoid his reflection now. It was a whole different kind of recognition, nothing like seeing the core of himself in a changed face. This was a glimpse of a different state of being. He was confronting a fantasy. He hadn't felt this uncomfortable in a long time.

"Am I playing at it, Mike?"

"No more than anyone else in training. And I'm taking you seriously."

Ian didn't have to explain, then. Mike understood.

They stalked each other in the woods, sprinting from trunk to trunk so Ian could get a feel for snap shooting. But in a matter of minutes, it didn't feel like simulation at all. It became real. Mike stepped out of cover to fire and Ian froze mid-aim. His brain said he couldn't possibly shoot Mike. A round caught him in his left shoulder, but he still couldn't return fire.

Mike took a few more shots from the cover of the tree and Ian fired back seconds later, but that was way too slow. He couldn't steel himself to target Mike until the guy broke cover and closed the gap, firing as he moved. Ian forced himself as Mike came in close to fire at very close range. Yes, those rounds damn well hurt when they hit unprotected flesh.

"You okay?" Mike pushed his goggles up to the top of his helmet. "Problem?"

"It was really hard to shoot you."

"Psychologically, you mean."

"Yeah. I don't mean aim."

Mike gave him a slap on the back. "That's normal. Once you get hit and hurt enough times, you'll start shooting back for sure. Like when you were sparring with Rob. Want to try again?"

Ian indicated an empty magazine. "I'm out. Look, can I ask you some personal stuff? "

"Anything you like." Mike started walking back to the range. It was getting dark. "Are you wondering if you'd be capable of killing someone?"

"Yes. Emotionally capable, I mean. Not skill."

"I think most people can kill. It just depends on what presses their button and how hard it needs to be pressed. Coming under fire for the first time did the job just fine for me."

Ian knew the worst thing to ask a guy like Mike was how it felt to kill and how many times he'd done it. It even sounded creepy coming from an interviewer in a serious documentary. But Mike was the most patient guy Ian could imagine, and he wanted to understand how a capacity for violence could be part of that.

"Ever wished you *hadn't* killed someone?" he asked.

"Not yet. I know some people do when they get older."

"Ever get nightmares?"

"Not many, and not about taking a life."

"Am I prying?"

"No. Not at all. They're sensible questions. You're right to ask them."

They changed out of their kit and cleaned up. Ian sat on the bench next to Mike and polished his boots in silence.

"My sister doesn't understand how confusing combat is and what you don't notice or recall," Mike said suddenly, as if there'd been some argument about it in the past. "You know you're being shot at, so you open fire. No problem. Us or them. But you often can't tell if you fired the shot that killed someone. There's usually too much going on. I killed a guy trying to bundle me into a vehicle, and I still don't know if I remember it accurately. Has Rob told you the story?"

"Depends," Ian said. "I don't know if he thinks he remembers the same parts that *you* think you remember."

Mike nodded. "That sums it up."

"You would have ended up dead. Sooner or later."

"Probably. I didn't think that at the time, because American hostages are worth money. But the guy could have sold me to someone who would have beheaded me for the cameras. So I decided I'd rather die trying to escape than go missing for years or have Livvie see a video of me getting my head hacked off. I couldn't bear thinking what my family would go through. I know it sounds crazy, but if I fought back and got shot, at least they'd have closure and they'd know it was quick."

Ian realised courage wasn't the obvious thing he'd thought it was. It was having bigger fears than saving your own ass. Mike was more afraid for the people he loved.

"Yeah, I get it," Ian said.

"I know you like movies, buddy, but the way they depict combat usually makes it look like you can see everything and take decisions the way you do in an office. But it's not like that. There's so much you can't see or hear. And you can't tell what's reasonable force, whatever the hell that means. Even if you're used to it, the adrenaline's pumping. You don't have a conscious second to rationalize. Your training kicks in and you just react." Mike paused, still working shoe polish into the leather. Ian couldn't tell if he was picking his words or trying to recall detail. "Anyway, I took this guy's knife and stabbed him, then I grabbed his rifle and shot him. I don't even recall his face."

Ian remembered Rob's account of the firefight. They'd been right in the middle of it. They could both have died. Killing an asshole trying to drag you away to an uncertain fate seemed perfectly reasonable, exactly what Ian expected a guy to do.

"Do you feel bad about that, Mike? Because you shouldn't."

"No, I don't. But in my head, I didn't think he was going to kill me right then. And I wasn't thinking about killing him. I was just determined to escape or die, and that was the only way I could do it."

"Self-defence, if you ask me."

"What's clear to regular people is something else when a lawyer decides to argue a case years later. But I'm just telling you why I ended up killing a man, and why I know I'd do it again."

Mike stopped rubbing the brush back and forth across the toecap of his boot. He looked frozen for a moment. Ian didn't know if he'd finished.

"Well, I hope I'd have the balls to fight back," Ian said.

Mike shook his head. "I never told my sister or Mom all the details. If Charlotte started with her legal bullshit about rules of engagement, or her husband gave me his armchair opinion on how he'd have handled it, I'd never be able to speak to her again. And that would be awful for Mom and Dad."

Ian had yet to meet Charlotte. Rob said she was nice enough

but a bit of a know-it-all. "Would she really question it?"

"Well, I think she might. So I never want to know for sure. She's got no idea what it's like to spend every minute among people trying to kill you. And I've got zero patience with someone who can't see how that changes everything."

Everyone lied or hid something, then, even the most honest guys like Mike, and often for the best of reasons. But Ian decided he didn't want to keep anything from him. Mike had trusted him with really painful, personal stuff. It made for powerful bonds.

"Would you rather I didn't tell you about my morphing?" Ian asked.

Mike picked up his other boot and began polishing again. "Would you be happier telling me?"

Ian's pants were a similar DPM pattern to his old jacket. He put his hand flat on his thigh and visualised the skin mottling and darkening to match the camouflage. He almost didn't need to shut his eyes to concentrate now.

"That's a sitrep," he said.

Mike looked at Ian's hand for a while, saying nothing. Ian gave it thirty seconds before fading the skin back to normal, then looked for some reaction on Mike's face. Mike just nodded slowly.

"It's like I said to Dad." Mike slid his clean, shiny boots under the bench and stood up. "It's all under control. Nothing to worry about at all. Right?"

Ian understood completely why people not only needed truth and illusion to be woven together, but why they wanted it to be.

He nodded. "Right."

CEDARS SPORTS CLINIC, PORTON, MAINE: FIRST WEEK OF NOVEMBER.

Rob presented his shoulder to the physiotherapist. "I'm a compliant patient, Ryan. I've been doing my exercises."

Ryan took Rob's arm and eased the joint through its full range of movement. Nothing pulled or grated, but Rob already knew it wouldn't. His rotator cuff problem had cleared up a few weeks ago. Ryan didn't need to know that.

"Your problem's not knowing when to stop," Ryan said.

"That's what they pay me for. It's only pain."

"Well, it seems to be healing fine. Pain's a message, by the way, and it isn't saying push harder."

Rob tried his shoulder again. "I'll be back in the ladies' volleyball team in no time."

He had his reasons for continuing the visits. The primary one walked past the treatment room from time to time: Sarah, brunette, forty-ish and divorced, another physio at the clinic.

The secondary objective was to pick Ryan's brains about the kind of detail that could be detected by an x-ray or scan if Ian ever had some kind of medical emergency. Even Kinnery couldn't get his hands on an MRI scanner without involving too many people who didn't need to know. Rob gathered whatever intelligence he could. The more he learned about genetics, the more he realised how much the experts didn't know. Ian had been lucky that shuffling the pack had even given him a head and limbs in the right places, let alone anything that could pass as normal.

And now he could match his skin to camouflage patterns. *Bloody hell.* That wasn't as useful as it sounded, but it was one more thing that would interest all the wrong people.

"Ryan, can you see nerves on a scan?" Rob asked.

"Yes. They look like white wiring."

"So what *can't* it show you?"

"It really is just a partial tear in the tendon, Rob. But if you want an MR arthrography, we can do that."

"No, I'm just curious."

"An MRI images by density, so it isn't going to find microscopic detail. But it gives you a pretty good look inside the body. And scanning technology's getting better all the time."

Anything that could see nerves was probably a bad idea for Ian. It was a racing certainty that his skin and hair would look weird under a microscope, but not even Kinnery knew what else was in there.

"Isn't science wonderful?" Rob said. "See you in a month, then."

Rob took his time getting dressed and paying his bill in the hope of running into Sarah. She couldn't have missed his name in the appointments diary, so if she didn't pop out of her treatment room to catch him, he'd know that first drink at the bar had been his last chance. Eventually he decided he couldn't loiter any longer. Bugger it, he couldn't wow them all. It was her loss. He was getting into his car when he heard someone calling him.

"Rob?" Sarah trotted across the parking bay, not quite breaking into a run. "Are you all clear now? Shoulder okay?"

"Possibly." Rob perked up. He was still in the game, then. "Do you fancy dinner some time?"

"Sure. Why don't I cook it?"

"That's an offer I can't refuse." *Objective achieved.* He tried not to look too pleased with himself. "Pick a day."

"I'll give you a call when I've fixed my schedule."

She gave him a promising smile and went back inside. A second date meant he'd have to tell her a little more detail about his job than just "security." She knew he'd been a Marine, but while everyone understood more or less what Marines were, regardless of the country they came from, "PMC" or "PSC" didn't provide instant meaning for the average civilian. Rob had spent a couple of years trying to distil the job into a one-liner that he could fire off before someone said *mercenary* and told him what they'd seen in some shitty movie.

No, I don't assassinate people or stage coups. You need to call the CIA for that. Do you want to hear about stopping suicide bombers at checkpoints, though? Escort detail? Close protection? Anti-piracy?

If things worked out with Sarah, he'd fill in the gaps as far as he could. He just hoped that the ones he couldn't fill didn't show too much.

There was a lie at the heart of what he did every day now, something that was changing the way he behaved. It was Ian. Rob had to sidestep so many routine things that he felt furtive, so he was bloody sure that he looked furtive too. And Tom was coming to stay for Thanksgiving. Ian seemed to have his morphing under control, but Rob couldn't rule out accidents. How would Tom take it if Rob hadn't warned him?

Every solution that Rob came up with involved having to answer more awkward questions. Mike had already lied to his mum about not going to the family Thanksgiving with Livvie because Rob had plans for them. Adding any more layers to that lie was asking for trouble. Lies needed too much maintenance.

I'd be shit at intelligence work. What sort of prick actually likes *living a permanent lie? Christ, even Kinnery doesn't enjoy it.*

Livvie intercepted him when he walked into the hall, brandishing a FedEx package.

"Business cards," she said, plucking a few out and handing them to him. They were heavy grey card with black heat-embossed lettering, not a plumber's instant-print variety. "Robert Rennie, security consultant."

"Thank you, Mrs Mike. Now all I need is something to secure. And consult on."

"Can you extract my husband for lunch? I'll pay you in peach margaritas."

"Consider it done, ma'am."

Livvie could tell he was getting restless, then. It wasn't boredom. It felt more like skipping the gym for a few months and then finding he couldn't handle the same weights when he went back, not that he'd ever missed his phys for more than a few days. Mike was in the stables with Ian, working on the kill house. Rob had to hand it to him. If Mike lost his fortune overnight, he could get a job on a construction site the next day. Ian was competent too, but then he'd had to be. Mike hadn't. He surrendered to having contract cleaners and gardeners come in once a month. Rob knew that he would have dispensed with that as well if he could have done.

Just as well, though. How would we explain Ian to a daily housekeeper?

Rob stuck his head through the doors to check it was safe to enter. The whine of a power saw and a thumping hammer drill set his teeth on edge.

"Excuse me, sir," Rob yelled. "Can you remember your wife's name?"

Mike stopped and switched off the saw. "Am I in the doghouse?"

"Unless you want Oatie to have your lunch, shift your arse and get over there. You too, Ian."

Ian stood back to point out some features that hadn't been there before, including an extra set of steps up to the hayloft. "We'll be finished in a few days," he said. "This is going to be great."

Mike beckoned to Rob and loosened his belt. "Look."

"I've seen it before, Zombie. I've got one too."

"I mean this."

Mike turned around and pulled down his waistband on one side. There was a spectacular bruise developing just below his hip.

"He shot me in the goddamn ass. Point blank." He buckled his belt, obviously more amused than hurt. "I've asked Brad to hold a couple of places for us on the next kill house course. You want to make that three, Rob?"

He obviously meant to take Ian. "Okay, I'm in." Rob seized every chance to stay on form. "Lunch. Move it."

Mike and Ian seemed to be enjoying each other's company these days instead of trying to pick their way between pity, responsibility, and gratitude. Rob could see it in the way they stood closer and even horsed around. Mike was the better man for the job. Ian was past the stage of needing someone to give him structure and push him to find his potential. He didn't just need a dad. He needed someone who knew how it felt to have to keep something of himself hidden to pass as a regular human being.

Yeah, I'm not one of life's blender's am I? I'm the bloke with what I am written all over me, and proud of it.

Except that's not what I am now. And I still haven't let go.

Livvie served up lunch, steaming plates of cassoulet with crusty bread. "Get used to it, guys," she said. "This is from the gourmet caterer in town. I'll be back to my normal schedule after Thanksgiving, even if you aren't. You know where the freezer is."

"It'll never be as good as yours, Mrs Mike." Rob checked his phone for messages from Tom or maybe even Sarah. There was a text from Leo instead, straight to the point: ROB, PLEASE NAG YOUR KID BROTHER TO VISIT MOM & CHARL BEFORE THE HOLIDAYS. "But it's still very nice."

Mike stole Rob's crust from his plate. "You're such an ass-kisser, Rennie."

"And your dad says you've got to visit. Come on. Charlotte's almost human when she's had a few martinis."

"Okay. I'll call them and fix something."

If Rob mentally deleted shape-shifting, billionaires, and their respective jobs, it became a normal domestic scene: working mum, convenience meals, family spats, a small business to run, and a dog that needed walking. Mike had achieved his ordinary life, in an exotic kind of way. Livvie seemed happier too.

Ian cleared the table and loaded the dishwasher. "Can you give me a ride to the mall, please?"

"Sure," Mike said. "How about now?"

"Great. Are you coming too, Rob?"

It sounded somewhere between a plea and an invitation. Ian certainly liked the mall. As Rob had predicted, he'd discovered it was the only decent place to check out women if you were still too young to hang around bars.

When did he last mix with girls? He must have been six or something. Jesus, he's going to get a shock when he catches up.

Rob patted his pockets for his wallet. "Yeah, I need to get some stuff for Tom. Only a couple of weeks to go."

Tom still hadn't told him anything about the mystery summer placement. It was harder than Rob expected to let go and keep his nose out of his son's life, but he'd wanted him to be confident and self-reliant, and that was exactly how he'd turned out. Maybe this was guilt. Rob was worrying about Ian when he should have been paying attention to Tom, even if he didn't need it.

Ian was coping, though, and far better than a kid raised like a hermit should have been able to. When they got to the mall, he announced he was going off to buy something and that he'd call them later to meet up. As he walked away, Rob automatically memorised what he was wearing — jeans, cap, navy blue padded jacket, and a grey fleck jumper. It was a habit he'd developed when Tom was little. Mike kept watching until Ian melted into the crowd of shoppers.

"If he's meeting a girl," Mike said, "then I don't know how he hooked up with her. Unless I've missed something, it's not the girl from the patisserie"

Rob steered Mike in the direction of the gadget store. "He's the only lad in creation who doesn't live on his phone, surf porn, and hang out online. Maybe there's a gene for that. It'd sell really well."

"He's going to turn into a normal guy sooner or later. Even I had my wild year. Or two."

"Look, he's not going to run into women living in the middle of nowhere. Maybe I need to take him for a lads' weekend somewhere, just so he learns the basics safely."

It took Mike a couple of seconds to catch on. He looked genuinely shocked. "*Hookers*? Jesus, Rob, are you serious? Would you do that with Tom?"

"Tom's probably getting more action than I am right now. And he wasn't raised by wolves."

"Sure, but *paying* for it?"

"Okay, okay, Mr Squeaky-Clean." Rob didn't think it was such a bad idea. "But it's not as emotionally charged, is it? Ian's not even used to being around girls. What's his first crush going to be like? Or were you counting on introducing him to Felicity Mainwaring-

Chinless at the hunt ball?"

Maybe fifteen years of unusually happy marriage had made Mike forget what it was like to be eighteen and sex-starved. Rob had been thrown back to that desperate teenage state by divorce and upheaval. He knew what underpinned Ian's every waking thought.

"Well, at least I don't have to explain to him where babies come from," Mike said at last.

"Can you tell me, then, Zombie? It's been so bloody long since I got my leg over that I've forgotten."

"But you're on a promise with that physio. Sarah."

"Fingers crossed. She'll probably put my back out."

Mike seemed to be thinking of something else. "We're going to need to move somewhere less isolated. Whether it's for Ian or the kid we end up adopting. Or you, even."

He looked a little shell-shocked as they browsed in the gadget store to find something fun for Tom. Poor sod: he liked his lovely farmhouse. But having kids meant you had to make big changes in your life, and the detail of that never ended.

Mike's phone rang about ten minutes later while Rob was paying at the cash desk. "Ian?" He paused, listening. "Sure, on our way."

Rob followed him out of the shop. "So is it a girl?"

"I don't think so. He just wants us to look at something. He's waiting by the elevator to the food court."

Rob's first thought was that there was a display of some kind that had grabbed Ian's imagination. They worked their way through the busy mall until the crowd thinned out near the lifts. Mirrored doors made the short marbled passage look twice the length.

There was no sign of Ian. Rob knew he was okay, but his stomach still knotted. Suddenly he was back home, looking desperately around a supermarket to find four-year-old Tom, a few minutes of absolute terror of a kind he hadn't felt before or since even on the front line. But Ian was an adult. He'd called them. He was waiting somewhere.

Mike looked behind him. "Where is he?"

A few people were standing around, chatting on their phones or waiting for the lifts. A young bloke in a red padded jacket and carrying a shopping bag walked through the door marked REST ROOMS. Rob still couldn't see Ian anywhere. He took out his phone.

"I'm calling him," he said, thumbing Ian's number.

Rob let it ring a few times, starting to think irrationally worried thoughts about KWA. The restroom door opened. Rob was too busy scanning all the routes leading to the lobby to take much notice until Mike turned and made an *ahhh* sound. Rob could hear Ian's sonar ping ringtone close by. He scanned around him to work out where it was coming from.

Ian stood clutching a carrier bag, looking uncertain rather than smug.

"You walked past me, both of you," he said. "Rob, you looked right at me. Red ski jacket. Does that ring a bell?"

Rob replayed the last few minutes as best he could in his head. Yes, he'd seen a lad in a red jacket, but he hadn't recognised anything about him. He looked at Mike for a reaction in case he'd missed something obvious. Rob knew Ian could get back to his default appearance if something made him morph, but this was a whole new situation.

It wasn't the place to have a debate on it, though. Rob phrased his question cautiously.

"Was that an accident?"

"No, I forced it." Ian held the shopping bag open under Rob's nose. There was a red jacket folded inside. "QED."

For a moment, Rob felt uneasy at being tricked. It was just an instinctive reaction. No animal liked being deceived: in the wild, being fooled often meant getting eaten. But knowing that didn't stop him feeling guilty. He knew exactly what Ian was. He shouldn't have felt uncomfortable about him at this stage of the game.

"Let's leave the discussion for the ride home," Mike said. "Is there anything more we need to buy?"

"No, I'm good."

"Okay, mount up."

Mike held his hand out to Rob for the car key and Ian sat up front next to him. Rob had to do his compulsive observing from the back seat.

"I get the feeling you guys are ticked off with me," Ian said. "I was really careful not to morph where anyone could see me."

Mike reached out and bumped him carefully on the shoulder without taking his eyes off the road. "No, buddy, it's fine. So you can morph at will now? Consistently?"

"Yes."

"That's impressive."

"I had to know that I could always get back to normal if something went wrong." Ian was still busy filling the excuse gap. "The only way was to make myself morph."

"So why the demo?" Rob asked.

Ian didn't have an answer for that, not for a while at least. Rob knew Mike was probably wrestling again with how much to tell his father.

"To show you how effective it is," Ian said at last. "I had to do it where you'd have to spot me among strangers."

Effective was an interesting word to pick. Effective for what? Ian always wanted to pull his weight. Rob had started to think of a few uses for morphing, and he was pretty sure Mike had too.

"It's not a problem," Mike said.

"I didn't want to tell you until I was sure I'd nailed it."

The subject seemed closed. Ian took Oatie for a walk when they got back, and Mike went to ground in his study. Rob couldn't find a single damn thing to do now except stretch out on the sofa in the guest cottage and watch TV.

Tom was right. He really wasn't very good at down time. It was a discipline that had to be drilled and exercised like everything else. Okay, that was it, then. He'd have a compulsory do-fuck-all hour a day, every day, even if he sat there scratching himself for the whole time.

He didn't manage it today, though. He mailed Brad to tell him he'd be free for a maritime gig in January as long as it was only a few weeks. It took him a while to hit SEND. Every time he went to click on the icon, he felt he was abandoning Mike, but Ian was stable, and Mike was settling into being a dad of sorts. Everyone would benefit from a brief change of routine.

And while I'm working, I can keep an eye open for companies that Mike can tap up for business.

"There," Rob said to himself. He sent the message. "Conscience clear. Done."

Now he had to go and tell Mike. Things like that couldn't wait. He put on his jacket and walked up to the house to find Mike still at his desk, shuffling paper.

"Zombie, I've told Brad I'll do a couple of weeks' ship work in

January," Rob said, leaning against the door frame. "But if it turns out that I'm needed here, I'll scrub it."

Mike just looked at him for a moment. "No problem. You always said you needed to keep your hand in."

"It's not like I'm sodding off to Nazani in the middle of a crisis."

"I know. I'm fine with it." Mike wouldn't let on if he was pissed off, but he did seem okay. "This was what we were going to do anyway."

"I'll use it to find some new business."

"Good idea. So you're not changing your mind about that."

"No. Definitely not. I need something solid to plan for."

"You need to put down roots."

"I'm used to moving around."

"Sure, but things change." It was Mike's code for getting older. "You need a house. Quit being so tight-assed and let me set you up properly. We've got three hundred acres. You could build something here. Jesus, how long have I been trying? Don't make me wait until they read my will."

"I'm not ungrateful, mate. You've done everything for me. But how can I decide where to live if you don't even know where *you're* going to be in a couple of years?"

"Okay, in principle, then."

Mike, always after a tidy life for everyone, took it as read that he'd buy Rob a house nearby whenever he moved. Rob still struggled with the money involved. But it kept Mike happy, and Rob accepted that he'd miss the bloke too much if he wasn't a neighbour. Mike was his best mate; Rob would do anything for him. He'd known him for far less time than his mates in the Marines, but a couple of years was a lifetime when you served together. In Civvy Street, you'd only see a bloke's outer shell, and finding out what was underneath took time. But under fire, you discovered the real man inside right away, and all you had to do later was peel back the layers on top that showed how he came to be like that.

"Okay, in principle, yes," Rob said. "Thank you. And I'll add it to the list of things I owe you."

"It's a gift. Not an obligation."

"Look, if I didn't think you were the finest bloke on God's earth, I wouldn't accept it. Because I wouldn't want to be indebted to a wanker."

Mike did his baffled Labrador look for a second, then laughed. "That actually makes sense."

"I always do, Zombie." Rob could put it on the back burner until Tom graduated next year, along with all the other big decisions. "All set for the visit, then?"

"God, three days with Charlotte and Jonathan." Mike raked his fingers through his hair and leaned back in the seat. "Maybe we'll tunnel out and take the kids to the zoo. You're sure you don't mind looking after Ian?"

"He doesn't need looking after. We'll find something to occupy ourselves."

"He'll be nineteen in February. He needs a job."

"I think that's what the morphing demo was about."

"He'd be ideal for surveillance. Detail conscious. And we've seen how he can disappear."

"You mean formally employ him?"

"There's plenty he can do. And he can still study part-time. I can hire tutors. He might even prefer night school, so that he gets out to meet people. *Female* people."

It all sounded so normal and achievable. "When you think about it, then, Project Ringer worked," Rob said. "Okay, not quite what they had in mind, but Ian's probably capable of working under cover."

"Don't say that."

"The sky won't fall in if you tell your dad. It's still not a secret weapon."

"And Kinnery will never know he succeeded. The punishment of Zeus."

"But if the bugger doesn't know he's been punished, does that count as justice?"

Mike stared at the desk, chewing his lip. Then he did a little snort that didn't quite turn into a laugh.

"No idea," he said. "But I think Ian's shifted from being a victim to having the advantage over the rest of us."

Rob knew it didn't take fancy genes to do that. Ian's gift was his attitude, the state of mind that could turn shit to gold.

He would have made a great commando. Maybe a job in the family firm was as good a substitute for that as any.

THIRTEEN

Dear Mr Klein,

Thank you again for the check. You said you can't tell me who sent the money, but please let them know how much this has changed our lives and thank them for us. We won't lose our home now and my husband can train for a new job. Just when you think that people have forgotten disabled veterans, miracles happen.

Yours,

Mrs J. Alvarez

Letter from a veteran's wife to law firm Bentley Staffman Klein, lawyers to Mike Brayne, on receipt of a donation from an anonymous benefactor.

ODSTOCK FLIGHT SCHOOL, MAINE: NOVEMBER.

"Take it easy while we're away, Ian." Livvie closed the Mercedes' tailgate as one of the Gulfstream's crew trotted up to take the bags from Mike. "Have some fun that doesn't involve tearing ligaments."

Ian's idea of fun now was reading everything he could find on the security industry and the basics of running companies. He had a job. It was another ordinary thing that he'd once thought was beyond him. It didn't matter if Mike was just being kind and finding ways to keep him busy. Ian was determined to make it real by doing it well.

"I will, Livvie," he said. "I'll make sure Rob does, too."

Rob fussed over Mike like a trainer sending a boxer into the ring, telling him not to let his brother-in-law wind him up. He was a compulsive checker even when there was nothing he could do. He watched while the Gulfstream taxied, and he didn't turn away and get back in the car until the jet had shrunk to a black speck in the distance. Ian could see it as hypervigilance caused by the stress of fighting wars, or just the sensible caution of a man who knew more than most about how much could go badly wrong in the world. The latter made more sense.

"I had an idea," Rob said, turning on to the main road. "We could search for your great-grandfather's service history online. I bet we could find some vets who served with him. Do you know which squadron or company he was in? Army, yeah? Not USMC."

"Army." Ian allowed himself to think of David Dunlop as a relative again, partly due to Rob's refusal to refer to him as anything else. "You think it's safe to search by name now?"

"There's loads of Dunlops, mate, and nothing to link you to Mike's address."

"But that Lloyd woman found the ranch without much technology. Even though Gran always covered our tracks."

Rob went quiet for a few moments. "He *is* dead, isn't he?"

"Gran said so."

Ian suddenly wondered if that had been another well-meaning lie. He hadn't considered that the man in the photo might not have been Gran's father at all, just a random stranger to flesh out her cover story. But he shot down the thought immediately. Gran had told him too much about her father's experiences and what it was like when he came home. She'd only lied by omission. Every deception was just a big gap that she'd managed to leave and that Ian had either obediently ignored or filled in for himself.

"Sorry," Rob said. "I'll shut up."

"No, it's okay. Maybe I should try to find out about my biological parents as well. But they were anonymous."

"They weren't *parents*, Ian. They were raw materials. Everything you are as a man came from your gran, and her values came from her dad."

Ian was starting to believe that was true and not just something Rob said to make him feel better. "Do you ever watch those shows where famous people research their family trees?"

Rob wrinkled his nose like it was a perversion he couldn't bear to think about. "Load of bollocks. If you went back a billion years, you could prove I was distantly related to Oatie, my nan's psychotic budgie, and a dose of E. coli. Which is fascinating, but no bloody use at all."

Humour was often painful stuff, the unsayable broken glass wrapped tightly in thick paper to stop it from cutting anyone. Ian had learned to look for the serious point in Rob's entertaining comic rants. The message was clear. Ian had nothing to gain by finding his biological parents.

"No bloody use *a'uhll*," Ian mimicked.

Rob laughed his head off. "Cheeky bugger. You're a good impersonator, though. Work on it."

Ian checked out the traffic, honing his observation skills by keeping a mental log of the vehicles around him, how many exits they passed, when they turned off, and when other vehicles joined the road. It needed to become as automatic for him as it was for Rob. He found it helped to imagine that every vehicle was potentially KWA on his tail.

Look, Gran, I'm doing fine. It's all working out. I've even got a job.

Gran hadn't believed in an afterlife, but Ian held out hope for a rational version that would have met her approval, some weird quantum foam where whatever echo was left of her would know that her mission had been accomplished. He'd seen the documentaries. Nobody could rule it out.

"Do you want to pick up anything in town?" Rob asked. The Mercedes rolled past the WELCOME TO WESTERHAM FALLS sign. "You haven't been down there for a while."

"Are you trying to make me go in the patisserie?"

Rob winked. "I hear they have irresistible tarts."

"Yeah, I know. It's dumb." Ian was more worried about blushing than morphing. He didn't even know the girl's name. "I should have learned to do this years ago."

"You can't train for women, mate. I'm still waiting for a bird to call me. *Me*. At forty." Rob parked opposite the patisserie and handed Ian a fifty-dollar bill. "Get some fruit tarts, will you? Anything except pineapple. Take your time. Ask her if she's a pastry chef. Show some interest in how they make those things. You'll think of something. And make a note of where you think the

CCTV cameras are."

Ian crossed the road as casually as he could and took a deep breath before going in. Her In The Shop, as Rob had taken to calling the patisserie assistant, didn't seem to be around today. The older woman was putting éclairs on the shelf. Ian's instant disappointment was washed away almost as quickly by relief that he didn't need to say anything clever, so he just looked around discreetly for the cameras while he waited for the woman to wrap the *tartes aux fruits* in their ritzy ribboned box. If he'd had the nerve, he'd have asked her where her co-worker was today. Maybe he'd have gotten a first name out of the conversation. Or maybe the woman was the girl's mom, and all he'd get would be a kicked ass. He took the box, did his best Rob-inspired smile and thank-you, and retreated to the Mercedes.

"She's not there," he said.

"Never mind. There's always tomorrow. And plenty more women. CCTV cameras?"

"Above the cash register. And outside the bank across the road."

"Good man. You can't avoid being recorded these days. But you can minimise the chance of being noticed. Behaviour and clothing."

Ian swapped his baseball cap for the woollen beanie he kept in his jacket pocket. "This makes a big difference."

"You're learning. So I suppose you want to go to the mall later."

"Are you bored with it?"

"No, never. We're still monkeys at heart. We need to get out on the savannah regularly and see what the rest of the tribe's up to."

It was almost a daily routine. Ian, now seeing the world in more general security terms than just watching his own ass, knew that routine was a bad idea, though. It put you in certain places at regular times and it became carelessly subconscious.

"How about the other malls?" he asked.

"There's the older one on the other side of Porton." Rob's eyes swept from mirror to mirror. "Not much bloke stuff there, though. Mainly women's clothing. But there's an Aldi supermarket next door. It'll remind me of the UK."

"Are you homesick?"

"No. I don't know what Britain is any more. It's not the same place I grew up in, that's for sure."

Ian remembered what Gran had said about her dad returning from Vietnam. Home could morph into a foreign country pretty fast. "Aldi's German, isn't it?"

"Yeah, one World Cup and two world wars." Rob said it like it was a punch line Ian should have known. "The most patriotic thing you can do these days is identify your own little tribe and defend that instead. That's all human brains are built to do anyway."

He didn't say much more on the way home. Ian thought about tribes and realised that his consisted of three other people, maybe four if he counted Mike's dad. It was a very small nation to defend. He hoped he could manage that.

As they turned into Mike's entrance, Mr Andrews was sweeping his path. Rob stopped to lower the window and say hello. He always treated the old man like a five-star general: a friendly observer was worth his weight in gold, he said. Ian hadn't said more than hi to Mr Andrews a couple of times since he'd been here, and the guy never came to the house.

"Does he know who Mike is?" Ian asked.

Rob shook his head. "Unless he's worked it out and hasn't said, he just thinks Mike's in some military job he can't discuss. Mike's the world expert at keeping a low profile."

It had taken Ian a few months to see exactly how true that was. At first he'd been wowed by Chalton Farm, but from the road it looked no grander than some of the other upmarket homes he'd seen around the county. Most of the house wasn't visible to passing traffic. The only security anyone might have spotted on closer inspection was the cameras and alarm boxes, not the ballistic glass windows or steel-reinforced doors.

The cars weren't flashy either. Ian hadn't realised the vehicles had ballistic protection until he'd started his driving lessons in the Mercedes. Mike and Livvie saved any fancy clothes and crazy spending for when they were out of town, and they dressed like successful doctors. Nothing about them said billionaire. They just went grey. They blended into the environment here as seamlessly as that octopus in the video, and they didn't need any special genes to do it. Ian had taken that technique to heart.

Rob parked and went in to switch off the alarms, a custom system with camera feeds and motion and IR sensors. The controls were in a small room off the hall. The set-up could trigger alarms on site or at the security company's control room, depending on how you set it. Ian worried about getting it wrong when he was eventually entrusted with it.

"So what do you want to do now the grown-ups have left us to run riot?" Rob asked.

"I was going to do some reading."

"Are you ever going to have a rebellious phase?"

"Do I need one?"

"No, you can save it for a midlife crisis if you like."

Ian wasn't sure how to run riot even if he'd wanted to. His idea of kicking over the traces was sleeping late, something he hadn't been able to do when he had animals to look after. His dreams had peaked at achieving normality. Now that he almost had it and might even exceed it, his imagination hadn't kept pace. He ended up joining Rob to search for Vietnam veterans' organisations.

"What are you going to do if there's more Dunlop family out there?" Rob asked, tapping away at the keyboard. "Sometimes you find out that stuff from a bloke's mates."

Ian considered it for a moment. It didn't spark any feelings either way.

"They'd ask too many complicated questions," he said. "And if they were real family who mattered, Gran would have mentioned them."

Rob nodded as he scrolled down a page of black and white photos of Hueys. "That sounds very sorted."

So this was what sorted felt like. Ian analysed the moment. It was a reflex that said *this is what you do next*, effortless and automatic, with no doubt that you'd taken the right decision. He felt like he'd grown up without even noticing.

The day before Mike and Livvie were due back, Rob took Ian to the Aldi grocery store near the old mall at Mackay Plaza. It was Ian's chance to try out an ATM to make sure he knew how to access his bank account. He walked up to the console, working out what he had to do. He certainly didn't need to withdraw cash.

"Don't forget the camera on those things," Rob said.

Ian tapped slowly and studied the unfamiliar screen. "Wow. I've been paid."

"Ah, the first pay packet. It's a good feeling."

"I need to feel I've earned it."

"Been there, done that, lost the argument with Mike. Has he ever shown you his finances? Christ, it's like nuclear physics." Rob gripped Ian's arm the way he did with Mike to make a confidential point. "He tried to explain it to me once. Bonds, shares, trusts, rents, investments, all kinds of stuff. Bloody hell, Ian, you're really putting on some solid meat, aren't you?"

Ian retrieved his arm and pressed his finger into his sleeve to check what was insulation and what was him.

"Yeah. I hope so."

"Don't worry." Rob seemed to think it was funny. "They're not going to deflate."

The old mall wasn't as plush as the one Ian was used to, but it had a mezzanine floor with an amphitheatre view of the main shopping area. And there were a lot more women around.

"Good trapping territory, mate," Rob said approvingly, leaning on the rail to scan the shoppers below. "The trick is to get strong without too much bulk, or else you won't look good in normal clothes. Yeah, Mike's right. I'm vain. But any woman who says she prefers the skinny poet type or a cuddly beer gut is a bloody liar."

"Or a realist," Ian said. "Or maybe just kind."

Rob laughed so hard that he started coughing. While they watched people milling around below, Ian noted that guys of his own age appeared to roam around in small packs. That was another stage of life he'd skipped completely.

"I've never socialised with my own age group," he said.

"Don't worry. Mike didn't socialise much either."

"Yeah, but he went to school. I can't even remember the last time I was in a classroom."

"You can practice on Tom. He's very sociable."

Eventually Ian got bored with people-watching and they went downstairs to browse around the stores and the seating areas where people congregated. One spot seemed to be the main place for girls to hang out. They clustered around shopping bags and showed each other what they'd bought. Ian felt like he was watching a wildlife documentary where the cameraman zoomed in on an exotic, brightly-coloured species that he didn't dare approach too closely.

Rob nudged him. "I think you should sit down there and wait for me," he said. "There's nothing that crimps a lad's style as much as having his old man with him, if you see what I mean."

Ian didn't, at least not for a few seconds. "Oh."

"Yeah. All you have to do is strike up a conversation. That's your social confidence objective for tonight. I'll see you back in the car."

Rob gave him a discreet thumbs-up and walked off. Ian was now behind enemy lines, and on his own.

MACKAY MALL: 30 MINUTES LATER.

There was an art to looking casual in a busy mall, and Ian knew he hadn't mastered it yet.

He simply hadn't spent enough time in crowds. Children learned to navigate at an early age, Mike had told him, working out how close to pass and where to stand until it became automatic. Ian ambled around for a while, but there were no empty seats. He was forced to stroll aimlessly.

Sitting was easy. You could find a seat, open a book or take out your phone, and right away you were legitimate and invisible. Where and how you stood around strangers, though, sent out messages that you weren't even conscious of. Ian knew it.

He felt like a house that had been built in reverse, with the roof and a few windows installed first and the foundations laid piecemeal years later. He looked around to see what others were doing. Ah, the universal cloak of invisibility: the cell. He could stand anywhere and mess around with it for ages without looking like a jerk. Ian ignored Gran's warning voice in his head, switched on his phone, and started killing time with a game.

It took five or six minutes for him to glance up and catch a girl looking his way. She was with a friend. The ritual was slowly starting to make sense. *Well, here goes.* Ian smiled and went back to his phone, working out when he could look up again without seeming creepy. Then he got his break. Movement caught his eye, and suddenly there were a couple of spaces on the bench. He made a beeline for it. The girls got there first.

The one he'd smiled at looked up at him. She had frizzy brown hair, but a really nice smile.

And legs. Oh God, Rob, what do I do next?

"I'm sorry, did I take your seat?" she asked.

Ian switched to autopilot. Miraculously, everything he'd picked up watching Rob, and even how Mike behaved with Livvie, slotted into the movies and TV shows he'd watched over the years. He had his instant script.

"No problem," he said. "Is it usually this busy?"

"Yeah, at this time of day. Are you from out of town, then?"

"No. But I normally go to Porton Mall."

So they started talking, pathetically vague stuff about the shops and restaurants, but she was the one doing most of the talking. They hadn't exchanged names yet. *What if she asks me a question? It'll be about jobs, college, or entertainment. New movies. Bands. Stuff I don't know about.* Ian tried to concentrate on what she was saying while he got some stock answers ready. But the most distracting thing was that she looked him up and down in the same way that women checked out Rob: face, groin, upper body, and then face again, over and over. He watched the sweep of her eyes. It was the best moment of his life.

She'd finally moved on to asking him what he was studying at college, probably assuming he looked the right age to be doing a degree, when her friend looked away for a second and said something under her breath.

It sounded like, "Oh, not him." Ian followed her gaze, and that was when a bunch of guys stood out of the general crowd as something he needed to watch.

Poor situational awareness. Oops. Too distracted by sex again.

There were five of them. Three didn't look like they were going to do anything, but two — one dark-haired, one curly blonde — were definitely focused on him and the girls.

"Ignore them," the frizzy girl said. "They're total assholes. We keep telling them they're not our type. Because we prefer our own species."

"Yeah, *humans*," her friend added.

Ian's awareness snapped back to the wider picture reflected in a store window. The contrast between him and the other guys was clear. He looked bigger, older, and harder. It surprised him for a moment. His benchmark was Rob and Mike, not guys his own age. These kids weren't even the same shape as him. He could see from their faces that they were carrying a lot more fat.

Okay, I can understand why they're pissed at me.

The two guys took a step forward. Ian didn't need any experience to grasp that he'd invaded their space and this was now some kind of dominance thing. They looked both scared and angry, as if they'd either run or lash out but weren't sure which.

Ancient instinct told him to stand his ground because he knew he could take them. And if he wanted to talk to these girls, he damn well would, because he was the biggest male. Then his civilised common sense reminded him that he couldn't afford to draw attention to himself. He had to walk away. It rankled.

I really could punch the crap out of those guys. I know I could.

He smiled at the girl. He'd be damned if he was going to scuttle away with his tail between his legs. He delayed just long enough to make it clear that he wasn't retreating out of fear.

"It was nice talking to you," he said, turning to walk away. "Maybe I'll see you here next time."

The two guys were right in his path. It didn't look like they were going to get out of his way, and he wasn't going to walk around them. But they could see that. They lost their nerve and stepped aside at the last second as Ian walked on, quietly seething, and put on his cap again. He checked behind him in the reflections in windows and couldn't see anyone following. His pulse was still pounding — part anger, part something indefinable — but he was still in full control.

Ah, screw it. Live and learn. That's what Rob's going to say. Hey, I got talking to another girl. That was the objective. Sorted.

He headed for the exit via the men's bathroom just inside the doors. While he was washing his hands, he checked his face in the mirror out of habit. Despite the adrenaline, nothing had changed. He really had this thing nailed down now. He opened the door, feeling a lot better about the confrontation.

But he walked straight into the two pissed-off guys. They were waiting for him outside the door.

Shit. Okay. Let's focus.

It was a side exit, not as busy as the main entrance. A few people were hanging around, but Ian was only aware of them in his peripheral vision. He kept his focus on the two guys. He could feel his adrenaline flooding back.

"You think you're fucking tough, don't you?" the dark-haired one said. "You think you can make me look like an asshole and get away with it?"

His blonde buddy shoved Ian in the chest. "You want to take it outside?"

Instantly, Ian needed to punch the shit out of him so badly that it felt like starvation. Anger rose in his throat, a weird saltwater taste with a pounding pressure that seemed to radiate from the back of his palate. But he had to keep a lid on this.

"I'm going now," he said. *I could take them. I know I could.* He was only yards from the exit, but he wasn't sure where the security cameras were. He guessed they were directed at the doors. "Lucky for you."

Ian knew he had to walk straight past them and not back away or look over his shoulder. Those were victim gestures, Rob said. They'd tip the balance with a potential attacker who wasn't sure whether to have a go or not. He had to stay looking like too big a threat. He made his move, aware of people who'd paused to watch, and walked past the two guys.

The doors parted ahead of him. He'd done the sensible thing, however much it choked him. But as he stepped outside, he was almost knocked over by two impacts, one square in the back and one really painful blow to the side of his face.

Everything shrank to a narrow tunnel of critical detail as he spun around. It was instant, faster than thought. His fist landed hard in a face he didn't even see until he felt bone hit bone. His skin tightened for a second.

Shit. I've morphed.

He knew it. He snapped back to himself instantly. He could do that now. For a heartbeat, he stared into the shocked face of the blonde guy. The dark one stumbled like he'd just picked himself up. Then they ran.

There was a lull, probably far shorter than it seemed. Ian knew he was hurt — face, back, knuckles, wrist — but he couldn't process the pain yet. The background that had vanished while his brain zeroed in on the threat faded back in again. A couple who'd been watching at a safe distance hurried over to him in a tap-tap-tap of heels on tiles.

"Oh my, are you all right?" The woman peered into Ian's face, all concern. She seemed completely unaware that he'd morphed in front of her. "Do you want us to call the police?"

"I'm okay, thanks." He had to find Rob. Jesus, how was he going to explain this to him? "It was just a couple of jerks."

He fended her off and made his way along the parking bays in the dark, trying to remember where Rob had left the car. He hadn't even reached it when Rob came up to him out of nowhere and grabbed him by the shoulder.

"Whoa, what happened to you?"

"I'm sorry. I got in a fight. Two guys. I'm okay."

Rob led Ian back to the car and put him in the passenger seat. He was oddly quiet and reassuring, no drama at all.

"Would you recognise them again, mate?"

"Why?"

"Because if they're still around, I'm going to slap the shit out of them." Rob started the Jaguar, backed out of the bay, and drove slowly along the row of cars, looking around. "Tell me what happened."

Ian took a breath. "I was chatting to a couple of girls and some guys didn't like it, so I walked off to avoid trouble. But they followed me. I got jumped outside the men's room. By the exit."

"Injuries?"

"Mine or theirs?"

"Yours."

"Maybe a few bruises." Ian had to tell him. "Rob, I think I morphed for a few seconds. Nobody seemed to notice. Well, not the people watching. Maybe the asshole that I punched did, though."

Rob lowered the window and cruised around the parking lot, scrutinising everyone who was walking through or standing by a car. "Don't worry about it." He was still completely calm, like nothing had happened. "People don't see what's right in front of them."

"But what about the security cameras?"

"Mall security's more worried about shoplifters. Relax."

Rob stopped and looked up a parking lane at a couple of guys with a white Ford, one leaning over the open passenger door where another guy was sitting with his head lowered, hands to his face. The car's interior light was bright enough to see them.

"Is that them?" Rob asked. "The kids in the Ford?"

"Rob, please leave it."

Rob's voice took on an edge. "I said, *is it them?*"

Ian had a very good eye for faces and detail. The blonde guy was standing up, and the dark one was in the passenger seat nursing his nose. He didn't look so full of shit now.

"Yeah." Ian felt like he was pulling the trigger. "That's them."

Rob stopped the car, got out, and walked over to the Ford. The blonde guy must have seen him coming, because he zipped around the front of the car and opened the driver's door like he was going to make a getaway. Ian wasn't sure if he'd connected Rob with Ian. He probably didn't have to. When Rob was bearing down on a target, he looked like a total bastard. The blonde guy was just stepping into the car when Rob slammed the door hard against him and pinned him to the vehicle by his leg and shoulder.

Ian heard the dull thud, the shout of pain, and raised voices. It must have hurt like hell. It was also very hard to see that any violence was being inflicted, nothing as obvious as punching a guy out with cameras everywhere. Rob was damn good at this.

"Hey, we're cool, yeah?" the blonde guy said. The sound carried. "We're sorry, man. Get off, get off — "

"You want a nose to match his?"

"Sorry. Really. Please."

"If you two fuckers ever come near my boy again, I'll fucking break your legs as well. Got it? Now piss off."

Rob was pure cold venom. Astonishingly, he stepped back, took out his cell, and calmly snapped a picture. For a moment Ian wondered what the hell he was doing, but then it dawned on him; he'd taken a photo of the Ford and the licence plate to identify the two guys. It was a silent threat.

The Ford pulled out and roared away. Rob got back into the car as if nothing had happened and drove on. Ian didn't dare say a word. As they approached the exit, they came up on the Ford's tail. It was hard to identify a car behind in the dark with its lights on, but the two guys must have thought it was Rob anyway. They raced off with a screech of tyres. They probably thought he was following them.

Rob turned off for Westerham, apparently unconcerned. He reached out and patted Ian on the shoulder.

"Nice punch, mate." He smiled. Then the smile turned into a broad grin. "I think you broke the bastard's nose."

"Oh, shit."

"It's okay. They're never going to report it to the police, are they? Not if the mall CCTV picked them up attacking you. And even if it didn't, what are they going to do about it?"

"But I *morphed*."

"I think they were too busy shitting themselves to notice." Rob seemed oddly pleased with Ian, not angry at all. "So you had a nice chat with the ladies, then. Objective achieved."

Ian was at the shaky post-adrenaline stage by the time they got back to the house. The first thing he did was check his face in the hall mirror. There was a red, swollen patch on his cheekbone close to his ear.

Rob checked him over in the bathroom. "I can't see any marks on your back. You might have some bruising on your face tomorrow, though." He inspected Ian's right hand. "Your knuckles are going to hurt for a while. If you've broken something, it'll heal on its own, but let's keep an eye on it."

"Why was the punch in the face so painful, then?"

Rob tapped his own jaw to indicate the joint. "These nerves around here. If you hit it hard from the side, it fucking hurts. That's probably what made you morph."

Ian had to learn to take pain better than that. "I'm sorry, Rob. Really."

"No, it's my fault for leaving you to it." Rob took a tube of heparinoid ointment from the bathroom cabinet. "It's a fact of life, mate. You're a good-looking, well-built lad now, and that gets the old rivalry thing going with blokes. There'll always be someone who'll want to take a pop at you if they've got their mates with them. But you know you can kick the shit out of them. Okay?"

"Okay."

"If you hadn't walked away, they'd probably have backed down. But I know why you did it. Just remember that it might be better to be outed than stabbed one day. Which reminds me. It's time we added knife work to your training."

It was a funny sort of reassurance. Rob seemed to think this was a normal rite of passage. He took Ian into the kitchen and sat him down with a beer and an ice compress. Ian rubbed the ointment into his knuckles and held the ice pack on top.

"But what if they've caught me morphing on the security cameras?"

Rob put a drinking straw in the bottle of beer and placed it close enough for Ian to drink. "Look, ma, no hands."

"Seriously."

"It was a second or two, you said."

"Yeah."

"Do you know what you morphed into?"

"No idea."

"Well, nobody's going to believe it," Rob said. "People get fed too many fake videos and pictures. They don't believe a bloody thing they see any more. You should start making the most of that, you know."

He flipped the cap off his beer and clinked the bottle against Ian's. He was right. It was no big deal, just a painful lesson. And if you looked at lessons the right way, they were always worth having.

"Cheers," Ian said. His hand was starting to throb, but pain, like adrenaline, was something you could habituate yourself to, and handle it better every time. He'd have to work on that. "But I think I won."

Rob winked. "You did, mate. You did."

LANSING, MICHIGAN: ONE WEEK LATER, NOVEMBER.

When was it time to quit?

It was just before ten in the evening. and Dru was burning her own time and her own data package on her own computer to do work for goddamn KW-Halbauer. If she'd thought the run-up to the merger was a pain in the ass, it had nothing on what was happening now that the two old companies were trying to rub along as one big happy step-family. HR had a new director who talked about the need to *embrace culture change*, which translated as *you've been doing it all wrong*. Dru hated her guts.

But misery was probably her just desserts for helping wield the axe. Keeping an eye on Kinnery was the only truly interesting task she had left, but she had to do it far from the company network while Weaver maintained the smokescreen to make sure she could continue to access records she might need.

Dru needed a breakthrough. Months of sifting every conceivable lead were starting to mess with her mind, mostly because it had forced her to plumb the depths of voluntary human ignorance in places she would never normally have ventured. Shape-shifters, home-grown and alien, popped up on web pages everywhere. She sipped her soda while she studied an image on her monitor, trying to work out why it seemed familiar.

It was a photo — grainy, poor contrast — of a human-alien hybrid taken in Panama, according to the caption. She really *had* seen this before. It took her ten minutes to find the folder, but there it was: another image that was clearly from that same sequence, and it was obviously a goddamn sloth, except the caption said it was taken in Africa. Christ, these whack-jobs couldn't even collate their own bad data. Dru closed the link and went back to her notes. What hope was there of pointing them tactfully in the direction of the simple explanations of the phenomena they thought they'd captured? *None.* They wanted to believe this bullshit. She wanted *not* to.

The Slide was a lot more professional, though, and it hadn't given up on Weaver. Zoe Murray was either pathologically obsessed or else she had good reason to believe her source.

Since the initial call in July, she'd been in touch with Weaver eight times to show him alleged evidence of morphing humans, all different cases, and ask if it was Kinnery's project. Weaver passed them to Dru for her file. Some had images attached, but they were a testament to the skill of digital artists. Dru allowed herself to be impressed by the quality and added the relevant keywords of names and places to her search field. No, she didn't believe any of it, but the whole point of sifting was to bypass her own biases.

Kinnery's done something. But what?

Dru reminded herself that she was up against a man who'd kept something hidden for nearly twenty years without cracking or letting anything leak. He wasn't careless with information. Somebody else had been, though, and she still found it hard to believe that he was prepared to confess to Weaver on the strength of it. Why bother? Why not just sit tight? And why not build a better lie?

Three theories dug in their heels and refused to go away. The Maggie Dunlop story was a decoy to mop up any information that Kinnery couldn't dismiss; there were too many verifiable details in it for it to be wholly invented; and the triangle — the relationship between the hotline number, the ranch, and whoever had answered that Seattle number — was central to the answer.

It was like watching a TV ad where an actor demonstrated an invisible product, telling the world that nobody would know you were using it. A digital artist had removed the actual product from the video and filled in the textures so that the actor's hands were empty and the effects looked like magic. In the pursuit of Project Ringer, Dru could still see the actors — Kinnery, Weaver, the guy on the phone, the guy at the ranch — but a key element had been digitized out of the scene. Something real had once been there. It was driving her crazy.

Clare called from outside the closed study door. "Mom, are you going to be up all night? I'm going to bed."

"Okay, sweetheart. Goodnight."

"There's no point being blonde if you've got bags under your eyes."

"*Goodnight*, sweetheart."

Dru gave it another hour before she headed for bed. She studied her reflection while she rubbed in her miracle hundred-dollar night cream, noting dark roots that needed attention again. She still wasn't used to being blonde. Most people treated her differently now and she was caught up in the feedback loop of behaving differently in return. If she'd ever doubted that humans ran mostly on instinct, she had her proof.

And the damn face cream still wasn't working. She wasn't much smarter than the morons who believed in alien body snatchers. Everybody needed to cling to some fantasy, even her.

In the morning, she did her weekly check of the property register and realtor sites for Athel Ridge. Nothing had changed. Dunlop Ranch had been sold to a property company, then to another developer, and then to a buyer that appeared to be a regular family. Ian Dunlop had vanished in the chain of transactions.

Dru now had no way of tracing him. She'd checked out the companies involved, but they were exactly what they seemed to be. Ian Dunlop had taken his money and disappeared.

Dunlop. Dunlop. Sells ranch, moves to ... where? Did he even live there?

And why hasn't Weaver tried to fill the holes in Kinnery's story? Does he prefer not to know, or does he know and he just isn't telling me?

It had to be about deniability again. Weaver didn't want to know any more about her activity than he absolutely had to. Dru wondered whether that was trust in her skills or if he had another pair of eyes on this that she didn't know about.

She was back to square one, then. She spent her lunch break in the library for a change of scenery, picking a Washington town at random and going through the directory for Dunlops in the hope that she might strike lucky again. But it was desperate guesswork, and she knew it. There was no geographical connection to give her a steer on where this man might go to ground. If Ian Dunlop was the Brit she spoke to, then he could have been back in England now or anywhere on the goddamn planet. Finding the Maggie Dunlop connection the first time had been an intuitive leap from a scrap of illegally obtained information. If Dru was going to pull that off again, she needed another piece of the puzzle, or the kind of million-to-one luck that won lotteries.

Today's batch of Dunlops was as much of a cold trail as the previous ones. After lunch, she took another look through the old e-mail logs that the system administrator had provided back in July to see if she'd missed anything on her previous sift. The reporting app generated communications flow reports showing who was talking to who and what the headers were, and if she asked nicely, the sysadmin could also produce data by a variety of filters — profanities, internal spam, after-hours activity, data leakage, and even staff looking for new jobs.

But she'd already run all the name searches she could think of, Dunlop included. And Kinnery wouldn't have been dumb enough to leave a trail like that. He seemed to have been acutely aware of the security risks that most people still weren't taking seriously ten or even fifteen years later.

You're a clever bastard, Kinnery. A careful one, too. But somebody outed you, and you've been forced to lie. I'll find out sooner or later.

Just before Dru left for the day, Julianne tapped on the door and placed a sealed white envelope on her desk. Dru stood there in her coat, pointedly doing up the buttons. She was going home on time tonight. Not even Weaver was going to stop her.

"Mr Weaver said someone sent him this and that you needed a copy," Julianne said. It wasn't the first envelope that she'd handed over, almost certainly hard copy of the latest approach from *The Slide*. "He said you'd know the sender."

"Thanks, Julianne." Dru slid it into her bag. It was Zoe Murray, then. "Glad you caught me."

Over dinner, Clare wanted to talk about arrangements for Thanksgiving and whether Larry was coming over or if they were going to eat at his place. He always left his arrangements late these days. Dru was in the mood to maintain radio silence and see if he broke first, but it wasn't fair on Clare. She should have been a non-combatant in this rumbling war.

"Why don't you call your dad and see what he's doing?" Dru said. "We'll try to fit in with whatever he wants."

Dru wondered if that sounded like sarcasm instead of the simplest way to get an answer. She loaded the dishwasher and retreated to the study to put in her daily hour or two of checking feeds and alerts. Then she remembered the envelope. At least she'd have some new data to enter tonight.

It was a printed note from Weaver, with a URL to look at: '*Another video from Murray. She wanted me to comment. Again, I didn't.*'

The alleged shape-shifter footage that Dru had seen ranged from honest idiocy of the kind that mistook domestic cats for panthers to elaborate and rather clever hoaxes. Any amateur could be a special effects artist these days. It was a diversion from the real business of tracing Ian Dunlop and mapping Kinnery's contacts. Dru would give it ten minutes, no more.

The video had an interesting caption, though, misspelled but very specific: '*Guy changes into someone else in mall. Defanitely genuine, not messed with.*'

It was security footage from a camera set too high above an exit to pick up more than a couple of yards outside the doors, and the quality wasn't great. There was no audio. Dru could see three guys in their late teens or early twenties, one wearing a cap. It must have been the end of an argument, because the one with the cap walked through the doors, and the other two — one blonde, one dark — jumped on him and swung punches. The cap guy turned around and knocked the dark-haired kid flat; the blonde one lost his nerve and they both ran off. A woman walked up to the cap guy and said something to him, probably checking if he was injured if his hand gesture was anything to go by. He left and the clip ended.

So there was a squabble in a mall. There were probably dozens of those across the country every day. What was Dru supposed to be looking for? She replayed the footage three or four times to check the individual faces and bodies before she spotted it.

The cap guy's features appeared to change and revert, *snap snap snap*, in no more than a couple of seconds. She had to replay it to make sure.

Ah. That's the shape-shifter element, then.

It looked like one of those adverts that cycled through faces of different races and ages to make the point that a product was suitable for everyone: you could see features change, but it was too fast to focus consciously on the detail. Once Dru spotted it in the video, it was noticeable, but not astonishing. It might even have been a glitch. It certainly wasn't state of the art digital effects. She checked the comments, looking for employee names out of habit, and was amazed at how many people still couldn't spell *hoax*.

She found herself nodding in agreement with the comments that it was a poor effort compared to some of the spoofs out there. They were right. It really did need a wolf or an orc's head to stand a chance in the micro-attention environment of video uploads.

And if anyone at KWA uploaded site security footage like this, they'd be looking for another job, pronto. I hope this mall fires the asshole.

So was this what Zoe did all day, surfing for every line of paranormal crap on the internet?

She's just like me, then. Poor bitch.

Dru wondered why someone would post such shoddy special effects when even Clare, who wasn't particular arty, could edit almost professional-quality footage on her cell phone. The guy could have been an average idiot, of course.

Or he could have posted exactly what had been recorded, and that was why it wasn't anything exotic. It was real.

No, that was insane. But Dru had to stick to her method, however implausible the evidence, and rule it in. She checked the web page for details. The user hadn't even posted a profile she could follow. She could have tried contacting him via the comments, but that was a step too far.

The only clue she had was the camera ident and a fuzzy, indistinct date and time code. Why wasn't the image sharper? Ah, the guy must have videoed an actual screen with his phone rather than try to make a copy. The ident said PORTON MACKAY CAM 65A and the date showed it had been recorded about a week ago. Dru copied the name Porton Mackay into her notebook and added another sticky note to the hard copy chart.

She needed to know what Porton Mackay was. The name of the mall? A store? A town? This was going to take some time. She ran another search for Porton, Mackay, and Mall, and got fewer hits than she expected.

There was one with all three terms that threw up a number of related pages: Mackay Mall, Porton, Askew County, Maine. She found it on a map and checked to see if any of the place names around Porton rang a bell, but it didn't mean a thing. Nothing got ruled out, though. That was the point of this exercise. If there were obvious connections, she'd have found them by now.

It was only when she was searching with the location added to the names on her list that something clicked. She'd included the search terms LEO BRAYNE and BRAYNE. That threw up something she hadn't been expecting: Brayne and Askew County.

But it wasn't Leo Brayne. It was a Michael Brayne from Westerham Falls.

She checked the map again. Westerham Falls was maybe an hour from Porton. The search had picked up an old news release on a National Guard site about troops returning from Iraq, complete with a publicity picture of a group of guys, one of whom was identified as Michael Brayne. She searched again using MICHAEL MIKE LEO BRAYNE to see what fell out.

Dru really hadn't been expecting a result from that, either. But she got a quick match and a photo caption. The picture, taken some years ago, showed Senator Brayne with his son and daughter at a charity event. The senator had endowed some specialist treatment centre for veterans. It wasn't the scale of his generosity that got her attention, though. It was the name of his son: Michael.

She copied the two images to her desktop and compared them. They'd been taken years apart, but the son and the soldier looked like the same guy.

Oh boy.

She reminded herself that humans looked for patterns and imposed meaning on completely random things. Astronomy had its roots in that. It took a hell of an imagination to see constellations, and that was exactly what she was doing with these names and places. But she couldn't ignore the fact that Leo Brayne had a connection to Project Ringer, however far removed, and his son appeared to live within an hour of a mall where a security camera might have picked up someone apparently able to alter his appearance on the spot. Was Mike Brayne in any phone directory? No, he was one of the elite, so he'd be unlisted. But she'd look anyway.

It took her just five minutes to find an entry for M.S. and O. Brayne, 2763 Forest Road. There were no other Braynes with a Westerham Falls address.

Dru hadn't really thought he'd have a listed phone number, but then she didn't know anything about him beyond who his father was. He seemed both remarkably invisible and in plain sight at the same time. It took her some time to find the property on the aerial sat map, but when she did, she was struck by how much of a backwater it was.

Like Dunlop Ranch.

No, stop it. That's a connection that isn't even there.

She found herself piecing together all kinds of scenarios, most of them wild theory that made as much sense as a game of consequences. But she couldn't ignore the timeline. She thought she saw a flow there, the vapour trails of causality.

Okay, go with it. To rule it out. It can't be the way it looks.

Under normal circumstances, she'd have hired a local investigator, but asking someone to check out a senator and his family was far too risky. She couldn't even tell Weaver. He had to be kept in a holy state of plausible deniability, and she didn't want to give him any more rope to hang her with.

Her only option was to check for herself. How much time did she have? If Zoe had sent that video to Kinnery and he had any connection to that boy, he'd be making arrangements to hide him.

It was coming up to the holidays. She'd booked time off. Clare had expectations, but Dru couldn't delay now.

If I went to Maine, though, what would I see? The Braynes might be away for the holiday. These people go to ski resorts and private islands. And the mule might already be in some safe house.

The Braynes couldn't live in a small town without somebody knowing something about them, though. It didn't even have to be anything spectacular. A name would do. The Brayne connection was a piece of the puzzle that Dru couldn't ignore, even if it didn't fit her template of a gene mule and the impossibility of shape-shifting. What she needed most was some breakthrough on Ian Dunlop's identity. It was triangulation. Another data point could answer all her questions, and Weaver's.

And I absolutely have to know if this is real or not. For my own sanity.

She had a feeling that she'd find Ian Dunlop had an English accent, and that he was a lot younger than he sounded. Whether he was a living, breathing example of dynamic mimicry was a question she was almost scared to answer.

She hoped he wasn't. There were some complications the world really didn't need.

FOURTEEN

In World War II, the Germans knew the British could easily transmit bogus messages to Luftwaffe bombers, so pilots were suspicious of any orders they received. In fact, the British never bothered to do it. But the Germans thought that they did because they could, and acted accordingly. The power of suggestion and mistrust is enormous. That's another weapon in Ian's armoury.

Mike Brayne, on the lessons of history.

VANCOUVER: NOVEMBER.

"Well, Zoe," Kinnery said, rubbing his eyes one-handed. "What can I do for you today?"

He found it easier to take *The Slide*'s calls and act the patronising, amused, but honest scientist than to ignore Zoe Murray. After eight or nine conversations, he'd almost built a professional understanding with her. Did she have a bullying, knuckle-dragging news editor standing over her, making her do this? He preferred to think that she did. It took the adversarial sting out of the calls, and if he thought of her sympathetically then he was less likely to sound evasive.

"The usual, Dr Kinnery," Zoe said. "I'm going to send you a link to a video clip and I'd just like a comment."

"I liked the orc. That was really convincing. Not my handiwork, alas, but very clever CGI. I take it you've called KW-Halbauer too."

"I always do, but they never respond. Sending now."

It took Kinnery a few moments to access the web page, and the semi-literate caption told him all he needed to know. It was mall security footage.

"What am I looking for this time?" he asked.

"Check out the young man in the cap."

Kinnery watched a scuffle between three youths at a mall. The boy in the cap got punched but hit back a lot harder. Kinnery was waiting for the boy to turn into something interesting, but he didn't. His attackers ran off.

The guy looked about Ian's age, maybe a little older. Kinnery felt a slight prickle down his spine. But there were millions of young men in that age group. This wasn't the first clip Zoe had shown him with a young guy in it, either.

"I didn't see it," Kinnery said, genuinely puzzled. "Hang on. Let me play it again."

"It's there, I promise. Keep watching the kid in the cap."

This time Kinnery noticed the words PORTON MACKAY on the video, probably the name of the mall. It was hard to see the boy's face under the peak of his cap, but this time Kinnery caught a change.

Immediately after the guy took a punch, his head jerked around and, for a second or two, his cheekbones flared wider and his jaw got bigger. Maybe he'd turned paler, too, but it was hard to be sure. Then he seemed to deflate and darken, and suddenly he was back to how he'd looked a few seconds earlier. Kinnery could have blinked and missed it.

"That was pretty dull," he said. Yes, it was odd, but there might have been an explanation beyond ham-fisted special effects. "Are you sure that wasn't just the light and the effect of being punched? Have you ever seen a boxer take a hard blow to the face?"

"I did wonder. But would it look like that at normal playback speed?"

"It's possible. If it's a spoof, it's pretty unimaginative."

"Well," Zoe said, "it's the fact that it's so marginal that intrigued me. Whoever posted that really believed it."

Kinnery had gotten airy dismissal down to a fine art. "People sincerely believe the most ludicrous things. If I really could build shape-shifters, though, I'd make them a lot more versatile than that. Anything else?"

"Apart from the fact that it probably came from a mall in Maine about a week ago, no."

It took a moment for Kinnery's brain to catch up. He suddenly felt out of control, struggling for air. It could have been a terrible coincidence and the boy in the video probably wasn't Ian at all, but he simply didn't know. He had no idea what Ian looked like now. He had to shrug this off like all the other videos and not let his panic leak into his voice.

"Sorry that I can't be more help," he said.

"You're always remarkably patient, considering that you think this is nonsense, Dr Kinnery."

"It's actually quicker to answer your questions than to try to dodge you." *Am I babbling? Stop it.* "I imagine you're under pressure to deliver stories."

"Well, thank you," Zoe said. "Good afternoon."

After she rang off, Kinnery sat with his hand to his mouth for a few moments before he managed to marshal his thoughts. He needed to know if the boy in the video was Ian. He'd have to call Leo, and the rules of engagement with the senator were strict for both their sakes. Calls were for emergencies only. But that video definitely qualified as one.

It took Kinnery three calls to catch Leo. "I need to forward you a link to a video," he said, lapsing into their private code. "It came from a person with a persistent interest. I can't verify the subject matter."

"Understood," Leo said. "I'll get back to you."

Kinnery put the link in an encrypted attachment, unsure if that was much protection these days even for correspondence with a senior politician, but it made no sense to skip it. If Leo confirmed that was Ian, then there were more calls to be made. Kinnery would have to contact Shaun and find out if Zoe had approached him.

It was no idle fear. Against the odds, Dru Lloyd had eventually identified Maggie and located the ranch. If she was made aware of that video, then she'd find the mall too. She wouldn't know about the Braynes, though.

Leo rang back just over an hour later, again without greeting or preamble.

"I'm confirming," he said. "You have to leave it to me now. Please don't make any further contact for the time being."

So it *was* Ian. Kinnery's chest felt like a collapsing building. "I'll call the company and tell them I'm being pestered by the media," he said. "Just to cover the bases."

"Okay. Goodbye."

Leo ended the call as abruptly as he'd started it. Kinnery had no idea what timetable he might be working on or how far this would go, and if he didn't call Shaun now to say that *The Slide* had been in touch, it would look suspicious.

No, he'd call Dru Lloyd instead. That would be what a man would do if he felt this was a minor annoyance for a minion to deal with. If he took it up with Shaun when he hadn't pursued the other approaches with him, it would simply set alarm bells ringing. If he got Dru to take a video call, though, he could record better images to send them to Mike Brayne for identification purposes in case she showed up.

Jesus, am I really scared of that woman? She's a hundred pounds soaking wet. She's a glorified clerk. I'm treating her like she's a goddamn SEAL.

Kinnery sent her an e-mail to set up a call. If Shaun did things by video, then so would she. She'd probably never work out what he was doing it for. If she made excuses to avoid using a webcam, though, he'd have to assume she was thinking along the same lines as he was, and that wouldn't bode well.

But she seemed happy to take the call. Kinnery practiced recording images a few times and peeled the Blu Tack off the webcam. When she picked up and he saw her for the first time in months, he almost didn't recognise her. She'd changed her hair. Colour and cut shouldn't have made such a difference to someone's face, but it did.

"Hi, Mrs Lloyd." He started the recording. "Are you still getting calls from Zoe Murray?"

Dru paused. "Mr Weaver is, but we're not commenting."

"Well, she just called me again. I'm being as polite as I can, but she doesn't know I'm going be working with you. So I'd appreciate some guidance for the future."

"I'll work out something with our public affairs people."

"Thank you."

"There's such a thing as no comment, you know, Dr Kinnery."

"That just triggers their digging reflex." Kinnery clicked discreetly on the STOP icon and checked he had at least a freeze frame sitting there in the app window. *Got it. Good.* "I was given a tip that the best way to deal with media was to be voluble until they got bored and hung up first."

"Interesting technique, but very hard not to let something slip."

"If you have nothing to let slip, it's perfectly safe." Kinnery surprised himself by coming back with exactly the smart response he needed. "And I haven't."

He looked for some reaction in Dru's face, but he didn't know her well enough yet to read her. All he could do was assume the worst and prepare for it.

Dru shrugged. "They'll always make something out of it, whatever you say. I think it's probably time to become unavailable for comment, though."

After he ended the call, Kinnery tried to divine some meaning from the conversation and gauge what she was up to, but it was impossible. He picked a few stills and the best short clip from the recording and mailed it to Leo. Now he was out of the game.

He tried to imagine what Shaun would do in the unlikely event that they traced Ian to Mike's house, but he simply didn't know. Shaun had never been squeamish about bending rules. The stakes were much higher now.

Kinnery went back to the video from the mall and played it again, looking for reasons not to worry. Now that the initial panic had given way to a quieter anxiety, he focused on what he was actually watching.

This was Ian, his creation and his crime, out in the world on his own for the first time. The Braynes hadn't shared any information about his progress or even his health. It was odd to see him and not be able to recognise anything about him except his ability to morph.

Kinnery replayed the clip five or six times, mesmerised. Was that the limit of Ian's morphing, or was he reining it in? Had he lost control under stress? He seemed to be able to revert to a previous form. It was fascinating. Kinnery knew that it was better if he never found out how far the morphing went, but part of him was consumed by the need. Only one thing mattered, though. Ian looked fit and confident, a strong young man able to take care of himself at last.

Kinnery knew he wasn't entitled to be proud, but despite that, he was.

CHALTON FARM, WESTERHAM FALLS: NEXT MORNING.

Rob wasn't in the guest cottage, and he wasn't answering his phone. His car was still in the garage. If he hadn't gone for a run on his own without leaving a note on the fridge, then Mike had no idea where he was.

Mike checked the security monitors. After a few minutes, the recording light came on and Rob appeared on one of the screens, scarf pulled up over his mouth. He must have been freezing. He was testing the camera by pacing back and forth in front of it.

Livvie walked up behind Mike to watch. "He's a gem."

"He never trusts any kit he hasn't checked himself. Don't worry. Nobody's going to show up with mortars."

"I'm not worried, I'm disappointed." Livvie held out her phone to show him the images of Dru Lloyd that Dad had forwarded. "I expect a wisecracking Lauren Bacall type with a smoky voice, trench coat, and stilettos. She's kind of ... well, *fluffy*."

"She's still purely theoretical. We don't know if she'll ever find us."

Livvie did a few mock right hooks to Mike's chest. "I've got reach and ten pounds on her. I could take her any time."

"Sure, honey. And you get to eat what you kill." Mike tried to keep it light. All this could prove to be an overreaction. "I'm going to catch Rob. Is Ian okay?"

"Still beating himself up over it."

"I'll talk to him."

"I'm doing that." She took Mike's beanie out of his pocket and pulled it down on his head. "Keep your ears warm. I don't care if you look goofy."

Mike estimated Rob's next location in the chain of cameras and set out for the woods on the western boundary. Since Dad had called about the mall video, Mike had built up a head of steam and was now at a steady simmering anger.

You want to come after me and my family? Go ahead. See what happens.

He kicked through the frosted grass, seething. His money and influence couldn't do a damn thing to head this off at the pass. Any action he took would reveal that he knew what was coming, and why. He had to wait for KWA to break cover. Being powerless was an authentic regular-guy experience, the first that he hadn't volunteered for and that he couldn't bypass if it got too tedious.

This was his home, for fuck's sake. He refused to be held under permanent siege by a bunch of glorified pharmacists. If KWA so much as exhaled in the direction of his family, he'd declare war. This was about *tribe*. It was about Dad and Livvie and Rob and Ian, and Ian was the victim in all this. His unique skills, marvellous as they were, had come from a monstrous and illegal act.

Mike walked through the trees, looking for the cameras. How could Dru make a connection between the mall and this house? She'd need a reason to link the Brayne name to the video. That was less likely, but it wasn't impossible if she'd found Maggie by going back forty years to some university yearbook. If she went back to day one of Project Ringer, she might do the same with Dad, and eventually find a link. The security cam ident provided enough information for anyone with time, patience, and investigative skills to find all the Portons in the country and then eventually narrow it down. Finding Mackay Plaza wouldn't be a stretch for her.

We keep a low profile. We don't post anything online. But we're in the phone book. Even if we'd been unlisted, we're on the electoral roll.

Mike scanned the trees for movement and solid outlines. Rob probably wasn't trying to hide, but he'd still minimise himself as a target without even thinking. Eventually Rob's olive green jacket resolved out of the vertical lines of the trees.

"Hey buddy."

Rob wandered up him. "I thought it'd be a good idea to get a security regime going."

"We can't buy in extra help. We're not supposed to know we've got a problem."

"Never mind. We're hairy-arsed enough to do this ourselves."

"That's the question. Do *what* ourselves?"

"It's worse than Afghan ROE, isn't it? Just got to sit and wait for them to start it."

Mike could feel the cold in his teeth. He tucked his chin into his collar. "One — we live permanently under counter-stalker measures. Two — we wait for them to make a mistake and call the cops. Three — we *make* them make a mistake."

Rob nodded. "Forget one and two. I'm all for three. Personally, in a saner world, I'd press option four."

"Would that be your council estate rules of engagement?"

"Yeah. Go after the fuckers and teach them some manners. But I'll settle for option three for the time being."

"Agreed. Anything that enables me to call the police. Then

they've got to explain why they're after us or back off. Either kicks them into touch."

"We'll still have to look over our shoulders for the rest of our lives."

"We do that anyway."

They sat on a wooden gate, all that was left of an old fence that had probably marked a field boundary in the past. It was wonderfully peaceful, a frost-glazed Christmas card of a landscape. Crows rasped in the distance. The early morning sun added gilded highlights. It was incongruously pretty for what was going through Mike's mind right then.

"Oh arr," Rob said, exaggerating his accent. "This makes Oi feel prahper rural, this do."

"You taking bets?"

"A tenner says she locks on to us within a week. She's got Ian's name and she can't fit it into Kinnery's cover story." Rob didn't have to say who *she* was any longer. "And that means they know they've got a working prototype, not just a mule."

"I won't let these bastards intimidate me."

"I'll sort it. It's my fault."

"Here we go again. You want me to hold your coat while you beat yourself up?"

"I brought this trouble to your door, mate. Let me redeem myself."

"Let's get the blame straight here. Kinnery broke every law in the book. Ian's the victim. We're the guys who rescued him. The *good* guys. Got it?"

"Doesn't alter the fact that I pushed him too fast."

"Rob, it was just bad luck."

"Well, we can't piss our pants every time the doorbell rings. So we take the battle to them. The hard bit is doing that without confirming they're on the right track."

"Whatever they do, it won't be legal They can't ask a judge to sign a warrant for a DNA sample."

Rob nodded, squinting into the sun. "And Ian's welded to their property whether he wants it or not. Okay, back to plan A for abduction."

Mike was war-gaming some ugly scenarios involving the kind of guys that Esselby tried not to hire. "I don't even know if they need him alive."

"Even if they do, abductions don't always go as planned, Zombie. Remember?"

"Rings a painful bell, yes."

"So how would *we* do it?"

"Keep the place under surveillance for a few weeks. Identify the best time and place for a snatch and what we'd need to do it cleanly."

"Don't tell me you didn't plot lines of sight when you bought the house."

"Of course I did."

"My hero." Rob slid down from the gate. "I scoped out some observation points this morning. You've got a bloody good arc from the workshop roof, and a good view of the road from the top of the assault course, but not as much cover. So that's two OPs, and we can redirect the cams and sensors accordingly."

"Dru won't have the skills to find an OP in a rural location and lay up for an extended period," Mike said. "Especially in this weather. She hasn't got a uniformed background, according to Kinnery. She's just a desk jockey."

Rob beckoned him to walk on. "No, she'll ask around in Westerham. Intercept a postman and ask innocent questions. Reporter tactics."

"Then what? If it's an abduction, she won't be the one doing it."

"What's your dad thinking?"

"I promised him I'd ask for help if I needed it."

"But you won't."

"I can handle this myself."

"*We* can handle it ourselves." Rob skidded down a steep slope to reach a shallow gully between the trees. "You should have fenced the whole estate and put in point vibration sensors. It'd be worth all the false alarms. I know you don't like to advertise that you're worth raiding, but you can take this ordinary bloke shit too far, you know."

"What are we going to do about Tom?"

Rob went quiet for a while. "You want me to call off the trip?"

"God, no. But he'll notice something's going on, so we need a cover story."

"What? Stalker? Paparazzi?"

"Maybe."

"Look, if it all goes tits up, I can take Ian back to the UK to lie low for a while. I'll introduce him to pubs. Proper football. Women. My old oppos. He'll enjoy it."

"And what happens to your yacht contract? And that physiotherapist of yours?"

"Needs must, Zombie."

"You can't keep putting your life on hold."

"First things first."

"You'll still be saying that when you're sixty."

"Things need doing. I'll do them."

Rob strode ahead, occasionally stopping to take a pair of binoculars from inside his jacket and scope through. He obviously didn't want to discuss it. He checked behind him and pointed through the trees to the road.

"She could park off the road there. She'd have line of sight to the front door." He handed the binoculars to Mike. "But we could block it with a van or something. Come on, let's check it out in a car and get all this onto a map."

Rob went bounding off through the trees towards the house as if he was orienteering. Mike jogged after him. "Ian's going to want to be involved."

"He'll have to sit this out," Rob said. "Let's impress that on him."

Ian was sitting at the kitchen table with Livvie, arms folded, clearly uncomfortable with the situation. He never wanted to be any trouble. He certainly didn't want to be cosseted like a child. Mike decided to sell it to him by treating him like a military VIP, someone who was capable of taking care of himself but who was too strategically important to risk.

"Okay, we need to put a few precautions in place," Mike said. "Ian, you're not to go outside without one of us. We'll put GPS trackers on all the cars, and I want you to carry a personal tracker at all times. I also want you to learn to operate the radios in case we can't use the phones for some reason. I don't want you out of voice or visual contact at any time. Understood? Rob and I need to do a recon and then pick up some stuff from Porton, so it's lockdown until we get back."

Ian shut his eyes for a moment. "I'm sorry about all this."

"Don't worry, we *love* it." Rob made a pot of tea, still bundled up in his jacket. "We haven't had any real work to do for ages. Just remember you're what we call the principal, the bloke we're looking after, and we're the close protection team, the bodyguards, so you need to do exactly what we tell you if the shit hits the fan. If you get bored with it, take notes. Because you'll have to do this for some other lucky bugger one day."

Ian took a notebook out of his back pocket and started writing. He really was taking notes. "I'll be in the gym, then. I assume daily runs outside are off."

"Temporarily," Mike said. "But this is going to end sooner rather than later, I promise."

Nazani had finally come to Westerham. Mike had lost his buffer zone between the front line and home, the portal between the real and the unreal in Rob's cosmology. He refused to let it destroy his sense of sanctuary, but that had been tainted forever simply by thinking what might happen. This was how many of the guys he'd known at school now lived. The world outside their gates was a permanent threat.

Rob drove as far around the estate as public roads could reach, occasionally stopping to walk up tracks to check ease of access. Gradually, Mike built a picture of where Dru would need to position herself or a camera to keep an eye on their movements. If she wanted to watch the entrance, then she didn't have any cover at all: she'd have to park on the road and invite attention. If she drove up the dead-end track on the eastern boundary, then she could conceal a car, but Mike could place a camera and motion sensor to watch the turning.

Her best bet was to leave the car well out of sight and lay up in the woods. She'd need some advanced skills to do that. And she'd still have to run the gauntlet of the security sensors to get close enough to the house to get eyes on Ian.

Rob parked the Mercedes on the grass verge with the engine running and made notes on the plan folded on his knees. "If she shows up, she'd better plan how she's going to take a piss. It's the little details that bugger you up on hard routine."

"Did you know ladies can buy plastic gizmos so they can do a tinkle standing up? It changes the whole battlespace."

"Zombie, don't go there. Please. I don't want my last fragile illusions about women to be shattered. It's a fading memory as it is."

"Just trying to lighten the mood. I've turned this into the siege of Leningrad in less than twelve hours."

"Better that than thinking everything's fine while a Panzer

division rolls into your front garden."

"We're thinking too military. I'm starting to favour your con-man idea. She'll pose as someone to get information so she can PID Ian."

"There's something hilarious about positively identifying a shape-shifter."

"Well, there's no pizza boy to tell her about the folks on Forest Road who always tip big. And even if she turns out to be a badass, any hands-on stuff has to be done by someone like us."

Rob sketched a few more lines on the map. "Might as well plan for everything. I bet she's still carrying that burner phone. You know. The number she gave Joe."

"Maybe."

"It'd be fun to ring that at the right moment."

"Are you enjoying this?"

"No, but I'm good at it. And that makes me feel better." Rob checked over his shoulder before pulling out onto the road again. "Okay, Porton here we come."

Mike bought trackers and SIMs for all the cars, plus a wrist GPS and some extra units in case things panned out as they feared and he got the chance to tag a surveillance vehicle. The magnetic variety had a two-month battery life, ample if the worst happened. When they got home, he made it his first priority to find Ian and make sure his personal tracker was set up properly.

"He's been in the store room all morning updating the inventory," Livvie said. "Don't worry, I checked. He's just staying busy."

Ian, like Rob, always needed to find chores to do. The store room housed steel racks of food, fuel, bottled water, generators, and other survival essentials in case the house was cut off by bad weather and they needed to ride things out for a couple of weeks. Mike walked through the garage and opened the store doors.

"Ian?" Mike couldn't see him for a moment, but the tiled floor was immaculately clean and the items on the shelves were sorted and lined up as neatly as a supermarket display. "I got you a GPS tracker watch. That way you won't forget it."

Mike peered around the first row of shelves. Ian was sitting on a set of steps, looking at the palm of his hand as if he was lost in thought. A gas lighter and a small mirror sat on the shelf next to him.

"Ian? Are you okay?"

He looked slightly embarrassed and put his hands together. Mike wondered what he'd interrupted.

Now there's a fatherhood lesson. Knock and wait. Got it.

"I don't know if you'll understand," Ian said.

Mike wheeled a portable generator into the aisle and sat down on it. "Try me. I used to be eighteen, believe it or not."

Ian looked down awkwardly at his hands. Mike expected him to open up about some crisis of confidence or offer more apologies, but he simply unclasped his hands and turned the left one palm up to show Mike. Perhaps this was some new camouflage trick that hadn't quite gone to plan.

But the thought lasted less than a heartbeat. Ian's left palm was blistered and burned. Mike's gut flipped over.

"What the hell happened?" He leaned forward to inspect the burn, but Ian pulled his hand away. "You had an accident? We need to put a dressing on that."

"Promise you won't be pissed at me."

"Of course I won't." *Am I that censorious? Maybe I worry too loudly.* "Why would I be?"

"I had to do it. In case I fuck things up again." Ian took a breath and picked up the lighter with his right hand. "The last few times that I've morphed accidentally, pain's triggered it. But you learn to handle pain the same way you handle adrenaline. You know. You habituate."

Ian mimed the action of holding his hand over a flame as if he was trying to help Mike understand. Mike realised he was probably staring at Ian like an idiot. It took him a few seconds to put it all together.

"You *burned* yourself? Deliberately? Jesus Christ, why?"

"How else can I reproduce the pain thing? You can't hit yourself that hard. And everything else is *really* dangerous, like blades." Ian let out a long breath. "Sorry. I knew you'd be mad."

Mike wasn't mad. He was upset, helpless, and desperate to put things right for Ian. "No, I just — damn, I just don't know what you go through. I don't know enough to help."

"I'm not made like you, Mike. I need to find my own way of handling all this."

"Sure. Sorry." Mike tried to look more relaxed about it. Recoiling wouldn't help. "But you can't keep doing that, buddy.

Let's treat the burn and have another think. You don't have to tell anyone. I'll just say you touched a hot pipe or something."

"It's okay. It worked. I don't lose control now." Ian stood up and put the mirror in his pocket. There was a resigned necessity about him, as if he accepted all this went with the territory, not a trace of self-pity. "It's the same as sparring. You learn how to take a punch to override your instinct."

It made perfect sense, but that didn't mean Mike felt better about it. His anger towards KWA had settled down to background radiation. Now it flared again.

He felt that breathless, bursting sensation rise in the back of his throat. It was every moment that he'd been shot at or threatened. If anyone laid a finger on Ian, he'd break their goddamn neck. This was the legacy that Kinnery had imposed, the kind of thing the kid had to do to deal with his condition. It was hard to see it as a talent right then.

"Under control, then," Mike said, playing things down.

Ian nodded, studying his palm. "Sorted."

KW-HALBAUER, LANSING: NOVEMBER, ONE WEEK BEFORE THANKSGIVING.

"I *know* Mr Weaver's busy." Dru's you-will-obey voice usually worked a lot better on the phone than in person. "This is urgent. Just walk into the meeting and put the note in front of him. It'll take you twenty seconds, and believe me, that'll be less disruptive to your life than what'll happen if he doesn't get it."

It was harder to get face time with Weaver lately. The new company was spread over almost double the number of locations, and this week he was at the old Halbauer HQ in Minneapolis. Dru was running out of time. If the boy in the video was anything to do with Kinnery, he might already have been moved, but he'd leave a trail that she might be able to follow. She had to make her move now.

"I'm going to keep ringing back," Dru said, "and if you stop taking the calls, then I'll start from the top and work down until somebody obliges me. We're working for the same company, for goodness' sake."

Dru could hear the ice forming on the line. "One moment." There was no *please*. "I'll put you on hold."

"Thank you." But the "you" got cut off, and Dru found herself listening to Vivaldi.

She was pretty sure she used to be more diplomatic on the phone. Bumping up against hard corporate objects over the last few months had added sharp corners to her rather than rounding them off. She'd watched her supposed betters flout the law with the expectation of getting away with it, and now she wondered just how many rules she needed to obey herself. She recalled her first term at college, her behavioural studies class. Imagine, her professor had said, if everyone said screw the law and did as they pleased. There'd be no way of enforcing any rules at all, nowhere near enough police or troops to keep order. Laws only worked because humans generally preferred to fit in and followed the herd norm for good or ill.

Dru just wished that that he'd spent more time teaching the class about the individuals who created the norms. Some days she felt that she only had to push the door a little harder and it would swing open into a world of chaos where she had no limits on her behaviour. It no longer seemed like a bad thing, either.

I can break the rules. And the bigger the rule, the less chance I've got of being punished. That's what I'm seeing every day now.

Vivaldi was suddenly cut off mid-allegro. "Dru, it's Shaun."

"Hi. Can anyone hear you?"

"No, I thought this might be sensitive. I'm in a private office."

"I'll keep it short, Mr Weaver." Dru stuck to the oblique code. "I have a lead on our material that I need to follow up, and it'll mean being out of town. Can you cover my absence with HR? It overlaps with my vacation, but not completely, and it could take a couple of weeks. I'd hate this to founder on over-zealous administration."

Weaver understood the term *material.* "Certainly. You sound like this is significant."

Was he really asking for detail? She picked her way through the recurring minefield of what he might not thank her for being told, and what she needed to conceal for her own sake.

"It's sufficiently striking for me not to ignore, and it's current. I don't even know if I can get a flight this close to the holiday, but I'm going to try."

"How current?"

Now she had to commit herself. *Suspect* was too risky on an unsecured line. "There's a chance I might be able to locate a subject."

"Okay." Weaver got the point. "Dru, if you do locate the material, I want you to call me immediately — any time, on my private cell if need be — and don't take any further action. Just observe. Your task is to find it and give me a location. That's all. If this is what we've been thinking all along, it's going to require specialist handling."

Dru got the feeling that she should have undersold it. It was too late now; she'd stoked him up and there was no point in trying to backtrack. But she was doing what he'd asked — just observing. Nobody had to know, least of all a senator who could probably create ripples the size of a tsunami for small fry like her.

There was something that bothered her, though. Weaver still hadn't said how he planned to extract the stolen material.

Damn, listen to me, I'm all euphemism. But I need to know he's not getting into anything illegal that's going to backfire on me. Specialist handling. Sure. What the hell is that?

She decided to risk asking the question on an unsecured line. "How specialist, Mr Weaver?"

He paused for a few seconds. "Need to know works both ways. For the same reasons."

"Yes, I need to know what I'm letting myself in for."

"You're not at risk. Just call me if you find anything and let me handle the rest."

"Understood."

"If you're that concerned, would it be wiser for me to know where you're going?"

If Weaver had taken any notice of the mall video, he might already have gone through the same steps that Dru had. She dithered. If she found a thief — which was all this would be, no matter how unbelievable the results — then she certainly wasn't going to perform a citizen's arrest. She couldn't detain a grown man, or anybody else for that matter. They might even be armed. She'd *want* to hand over the task.

Who would Weaver trust with the information? Maybe he's decided to call in the FBI after all.

Her biggest fear was that she was wrong, she'd cobbled together totally unrelated facts, and all she'd manage to do would be to upset a powerful politician who could grind her underfoot and

Clare's future with her. But she still needed to know.

"If I were to call you and say I'd found what we were looking for, and exactly where I thought it was, who would *you* call?"

Weaver paused. "The one man who has the ability to resolve this without any embarrassment to anyone. He'd want to be discreetly helpful, believe me."

Kinnery. Weaver's got him by the balls. If I find his mule, then Weaver calls him and says it's all over, so how about bringing the guy in and talking terms. It stays in-house. No police, no FBI, no FDA, no whatever. It has to be that. There's nobody else he could call. He really wouldn't do anything physical. We're not in that kind of business.

It made sense. It was a clean fit with Weaver's motives and methods. It made her feel better. "I might be wrong, Mr Weaver, or it might be a dead end."

"It's a risk we all take. So, where is this?"

"East Coast," Dru couldn't say Maine in case Weaver was on the same page. She'd look insane for believing the video, and if he knew something she didn't, she was only giving him more pieces for his own personal puzzle that might not turn out well for her. "I'll call you right away if I get a result."

"Okay. Safe journey, Dru. And I do appreciate that you're disrupting your holiday plans for this."

After she'd rung off, Dru wished yet again that she'd recorded the conversation, simply to check that she hadn't compromised herself or the company. She was pretty sure she hadn't blown it, though.

What she had blown was family harmony, or as much as existed at this time of the year. Larry had been told to stand by to have Clare for the holidays, but for longer than he'd planned. He wasn't happy. He never was. Clare took it pretty well, but she was at the age where having Mom around wasn't the be-all and end-all of Thanksgiving.

Dru couldn't back out of the trip now. The emotional blackmail from Larry would fall on deaf ears. She managed to book a flight to Bangor for a few days before Thanksgiving, then rented a car and rang around the Westerham area to find a room.

And if I can't get a room, I'll sleep in the goddamn car. Might be good practice for when I get fired for this.

She had to be as near the Braynes' home and neighbourhood as possible to do all that waiting and watching. But she did find a room. Now things were set in concrete. She charged it to her own card to avoid going through the travel agency, temporarily covering her tracks. Now she had to go through with this, if only to claim back the expenses.

Dru dropped Clare off at Larry's the night before the flight and he invited her to stay for supper. That was a bad sign. Usually, he wasn't even chatty. Dru wondered what Clare had been saying. Maybe he'd totally misread her recent makeover as some overture to getting back together. She stood on the doorstep and started edging backwards to indicate she really had to leave.

"Clare's upset that you won't be back before the holiday," he said.

"She's not upset. She's got you to herself. It makes her feel grown-up." Dru took a few more steps backwards. Larry never did take any notice of body language. "Look, I've got an early flight. Non-negotiable. Entertain your daughter, and cherish what time you have with her before she grows up and turns into me."

"It *is* a man, isn't it?" Larry raised his eyes from hers, looking at her hair with disapproval. "I didn't miss the new look, by the way. Is that why you won't tell Clare where you're going?"

"No."

"Really. Suddenly you're the CIA."

"It's only goddamn Maine." Shit, she'd lost her temper and let it slip. *Never mind.* "If I was going to fuck anybody, I'd make him take me somewhere tropical, and anyway, it'd be none of your damn business if I did."

"Who books a business trip right before Thanksgiving?"

"For the last time, Larry, it's not a man. It's *work*. It's god-awful, boring, tedious work, which I have to do because you missed so many child support payments when you went bust."

"Am I allowed to call if Clare gets sick, then?"

Dru didn't want Larry calling her cell at the wrong moment. She tore a sheet out of her notebook and scribbled the hotel number on it. "Okay, here's the hotel. Happy? You can even ask if I've got a man in my room."

"Jesus, Dru, you can take some things too seriously."

"If I told you what the job was, you'd never believe me anyway. If I can make it back earlier, I will, okay?" She peered around him in case Clare had been summoned by the raised voices. "So now you're getting back on your feet again, I expect you to pay your share. I'd prefer Clare not to have to see me take you to court."

"I'm fully aware of my responsibilities, thanks. Enjoy your trip. Remember to bury your parachute when they drop you behind enemy lines."

Dru drove off, trying to think if there was anybody she had a completely cordial, relaxed relationship with these days. It looked like there was just Clare. She was at war, acknowledged or otherwise, with everyone else.

It didn't matter now. If she drew a blank on this trip, she could write it off as a respite that she was long overdue and just enjoy a break somewhere pretty and rural, even if that meant staying in her hotel room with a bottle and the TV for company. A change was as good as a rest.

That evening, she laid out her equipment on the bed before repacking it to make sure she'd covered whatever angles she could. Without someone like Grant to call on, she was relying on her own resources. She had Larry to thank for honing those.

This was the Betrayed Wife's Divorce Kit. The security guys at work had been full of great advice on how to check up on Larry when she first suspected he might be straying. She had his old binoculars, a camera with a good zoom, changes of clothes that made her look different, and a small spy cam that she could stick on doors or use freehand. And she had the burner phones from the office. There were plenty of surveillance devices and software she could have bought online, from phone trackers and bugs to the countermeasures for all of them, but she couldn't afford to have any evidence of purchases like that on her own credit card or KWA's. She had to improvise. It was a sobering moment to realise how much she already owned in one form or another.

Now there were different faces she needed to familiarise herself with. Damn: she'd found Mike Brayne via a search on her own computer. What could be traced back to her if she got caught? Too late, it was already done. She wouldn't be any deeper in the mire if she printed off some images to memorise. She sat studying the faces she needed to know, Brayne and the two versions of the young man she suspected was Ian, and printed an ID-card sized version of each to put in her wallet for quick reference.

If he really was a shape-shifter, he'd change again. I'd never recognise him anyway. But he can't be. There's a rational explanation for all this.

Dru didn't enjoy flying at the best of times, let alone around holidays. When she finally arrived in Bangor and picked up her rental car, she was frayed and irritable. But there was preliminary work to be done before she checked in at the hotel or even got her first glimpse of the Braynes' home. She needed to get a feel for the locations. She also needed some props.

Her first port of call was the mall at Mackay Plaza. She managed to identify the men's room where the shape-shifter footage was taken and stood outside for a while, wishing that psychics were genuine. She could have wheeled a few in, asked them to feel the vibe or the sense the astral or whatever that crap was, and then get an address and a cell number out of it.

But the real world didn't make things that easy. Now she needed to buy her stage props, gift-wrapped boxes of Belgian chocolates. If she was going to cruise around Westerham Falls gazing into driveways, then a pile of gifts on the back seat made everything look seasonally normal. She was just an ordinary housewife going about her business, dropping off gifts but a little lost. And if she drew a blank, she could always eat the chocolates.

Westerham Falls was conspicuously more affluent than Athel Ridge with its feed stores and battered pickups. Dru drove slowly, making a note of the two coffee houses and a French patisserie. It looked like a community of weekend homes.

The hotel was about fifteen miles west of the town itself. She checked in and unpacked, enjoying the modest novelty of sitting back in an overstuffed armchair with an unhurried coffee to watch unfamiliar local TV and work out how to allot her time. When she'd worked up some nerve, she'd do a quick recon of the area and decide if she had a hope in hell of seeing anything of the Braynes.

If they're not already in the Caribbean.

I'm just looking. I'm just checking whether there's anything at all to see. Nothing more.

She drove back to Westerham Falls, now shrouded in afternoon dusk, and tried the French pastry place. If nothing else, she'd have happy memories of the *millefeuille*. It took one to stiffen her resolve to drive north along Forest Road, checking the numbers on the mailboxes until she hit the 2000s some way into the hills. The lights in the gloom grew more scattered before she spotted a small house right on the road, and two more reflective signs standing together, 2762 and 2763. When she slowed and craned her neck to look up the long drive, she could see lights between the trees. The small house looked like it might once have been a lodge for the bigger property up the hill.

If this was 2763, somebody was home even if it was the Braynes' staff.

Dru got out of the car and found a spot where she could see a thin vertical slice of a turning circle at the top of the drive. It was almost dark. She could risk using binoculars. A dark-coloured Mercedes SUV stood out front, either black or blue, picked out by the reflected light from the porch, but she couldn't see the licence plates. She didn't know what she was looking for anyway.

That was enough adventure for one night. She knew where the house was, she knew someone was still at home, and everything else would have to wait until the morning. Her next move would be to find a neighbour to talk to.

And that required acting. *Lying.* She'd found it was getting easier each time, and there was a certain skill to constructing false personas on the fly.

She was adept at it now. Maybe everyone had it in them to be a shape-shifter.

FIFTEEN

Hello, Mr Lloyd. I'm sorry to bother you, but your number's in your ex-wife's HR file as an emergency contact, and I assume you're looking after Clare while she's away. Nothing to worry about — I just wondered if she left you a number for her hotel. My secretary can't find it.

Shaun Weaver, seeking information from Larry Lloyd.

BYWAY HOTEL, NEAR WESTERHAM FALLS, MAINE.

How did you keep an eye on a house if you had nowhere to hide, no idea of its normal routine, and no buddy to share observation duties with you?

Dru was finding out. She was awake before the alarm the next morning, checking the weather and grasping the enormity of her task and how little she knew about her target. *Come on, how could I know what I'd find until I looked? You can't plan everything, not even with street view maps.* But if paparazzi and journalists could stalk their targets, then it didn't take classified technology or military skills. She'd take a look, ask around, and adjust her plan accordingly.

Around half past seven, she drove past the Braynes' house and noted one car out front, a dark blue Volvo crossover. The dark-coloured SUV was either gone or garaged. That meant activity and imminent trips.

She still wasn't sure she had the right house, though. It was secluded and obviously expensive, but relatively ordinary for the super-rich. There were no high, wire-topped walls, patrolling Dobermans, or any of the other precautions that she expected the seriously moneyed to take. She needed to come back and check for cameras, but they were no gauge of wealth either. All her neighbours in Lansing had them front and back.

Dru turned around further up the road and doubled back. This had to be a fast pass. If she slowed enough to get a good look, any cameras would pick her up behaving suspiciously long before she saw them, if she saw them at all.

She also had to get past the little lodge house unseen. It was doing the job it was probably built to do, acting as a guard house simply by its position. If anyone was watching, she'd stand out like a sore thumb on this quiet road.

Assume the worst. Someone might have seen me. The next time I go back, I establish legitimacy. Knock on the door at the lodge house.

Dru did another U-turn and drove into Westerham Falls to kill a couple of hours and buy a few things for Clare as a peace offering. But Clare probably wouldn't need placating. Larry would take her out for fancy meals rather than cook. It wouldn't do him any harm to get used to spending money on his daughter, either. Dru didn't feel too guilty about being absent for once.

Just before eleven, she drove back along Forest Road, working up the courage to stop near the Braynes' drive, and parked close to the neighbour's door so that the gifts on the back seat were visible. She couldn't see any cars outside the house now.

Do it. Go on.

She rang the neighbour's bell, trying not to rehearse her lines for once. Spontaneity worked better face to face. Innocent people generally didn't work out what they were going to say. They just opened their mouths and did the thinking as they went. That showed in the delivery. It looked and sounded honest.

I really wasted my degree. I should have been a con artist. I'd be rich by now.

An elderly man in a thick Fair Isle cardigan opened the door. Dru smiled hopefully.

"Hi," she said. "I'm a little lost. I'm looking for Mike Brayne's house. Is that twenty-seven-sixty-three up the drive?"

"Yes, but you've missed them." The old guy looked her over suspiciously. Maybe she seemed too downmarket to be the kind of visitor the Braynes would get. "They left a couple of hours ago."

They. That sounded hopeful. Dru hadn't even had to lie to get that information, or even ask much. People were helpful when you were nice to them. It was another natural primate reaction.

"Do you know when they'll be back?"

"No, but they're never gone long." His tone changed. He sounded as if he was warning her that if she was up to no good, she'd get caught while she was stealing the family silver, but that might have been her guilty conscience filling in the gaps. The man took a few steps back as if to shut the door, then seemed to think better of it. "Maybe Rob and Ian are in, though."

Ian? *Ian.*

No, that couldn't be a coincidence. It simply could *not.* Ian was a common name, but pieces didn't fall together like that. Dru just didn't know yet how they fitted. She steadied herself and tried to stay casual.

"Sorry, I don't know Rob. Or Ian."

She waited. She hoped he would feel the need to fill the silence if she said nothing, as people usually did. This guy didn't, though.

"Okay," she said. "I'll try again later."

"Want me to tell them you called by?" he asked. "You can go on up to the house, you know. Leave a note in the door if nobody's in."

Yes, and maybe get picked up by cameras. Nice set-up, sir.

She could have carried on talking, but a few more questions after the natural end of the conversation would start to look suspicious.

"No, it's okay. Sorry to have bothered you." She gestured vaguely at the drive. "I'll come back later. Thank you."

She'd said she'd return, so she could drive away without going up to the house and it wouldn't look odd. The last thing she wanted to do was to knock on the door and find herself face to face with Ian or this Rob, whoever he was. She didn't have a plan for that yet.

What am I scared of? Blowing my cover? A hostile reaction? Or looking a shape-shifter in the eye?

As she drove away, a thought struck her. Would the old guy make a note of her car? It was just a silver subcompact like thousands of others, but that didn't mean it wouldn't get noticed if she kept showing up. She'd have to think about an alternative if she was going to hang around.

Okay, go back to the hotel and adjust the plan.

Dru assessed her results. She knew who lived at that house, that they'd still be there at least for today, and that the chances of picking the wrong Mike Brayne were now near zero. That was a *lot* of useful information in a couple of minutes. She'd come back later to get visual confirmation, but first she needed to find a vantage point.

This was the kind of place tourists came to admire spectacular scenery. There'd be somewhere to park. Dru drove slowly, scanning until she spotted a patch of sandy soil at the side of the pavement, and a garbage bin with a twee little sign in antique lettering: PLEASE HELP US KEEP THIS VIEW BEAUTIFUL. She pulled over and checked what she could see without getting out of the car.

The cute little lodge house with the helpful neighbour was out of sight around the bend in the road, but there was a glimpse of the Braynes' house through a gap in the trees, enough to see part of the front door. Dru checked the map on her phone. She needed cover for repeat visits. She zoomed into the satellite image, looking for tracks or picnic areas in the forest, and found some trails marked for hikers with a visitor centre nearby. Now she needed to check that against the GIS map to find the boundaries of Mike Brayne's property. She drove back to the hotel to check it out on her laptop.

The hiking trail ran to within a few hundred yards of the Braynes' property. If she left the car at the visitor centre, she could walk the trail and skirt along the boundary, and maybe find a better observation point, or simply head down the road and approach the house from the front. With a wool hat and walking gear, she'd look anonymous.

All she needed was to see who went in and out of the house. Some video or stills would be a bonus. She probably wouldn't be able to stroll up to the Braynes' front door and walk away unnoticed or unrecorded, though.

I just need to see this Ian to check if he's the kid at the mall. That would be enough. Then I can turn the information over to Weaver and wash my hands of it.

But she needed to hear him speak, too. She had to work out where the guy with the English accent fitted in to all this.

Dru opened the mini-bar and wondered whether to reward herself with a proper drink. No, she might have to drive again today. She settled for a carton of juice and curled up in the chair to watch TV for a while.

So what's Weaver really up to?

Weaver said he knew the way Kinnery thought, and she'd believed that. They'd been very close for years. Now she tried to think like Kinnery again for herself. If she'd had some influence over the mule, or shape-shifter, or whatever Ian Dunlop was, she'd warn him to go to ground. She certainly wouldn't hand over her biggest asset. The mule was her leverage, because Weaver couldn't afford to have officialdom crawling over the company. He had as much if not more to lose than Kinnery did.

So he can't expose Kinnery. Kinnery's the one with all the power.

Dru was pretty sure than a man who could sustain this for nearly twenty years would have thought that through. It was obvious now. It always had been, but she'd persuaded herself that there was some science she wasn't aware of that could resolve the problem of a live human who was also stolen goods.

There wasn't any magic answer. Kinnery wasn't going to be pressured into handing over his mule, and the mule and the genetic material were indivisible. If Weaver wanted the genes, he had to possess the mule too. Unless he was simply going to pay them both a fortune to cooperate and keep their mouths shut — and he'd had plenty of time to make that offer to Kinnery — then the only other method was to abduct the mule and forcibly take or use whatever he was full of.

Oh God. Weaver's going to call someone, all right. But it won't be Kinnery.

It made the hair bristle on her nape. Job or no job, she didn't want to be party to a crime. Even if Weaver got away with it, she'd be implicated and that would hang over her for the rest of her life. Who'd believe that she didn't know?

Did that boy really change on camera?

I've got to know. But do I tell Weaver about it if I think he's going to commit a crime?

Dru was back to square one, to her initial reaction when Weaver first dropped this in her lap. It was industrial espionage. It was a job for the FBI. She didn't know if there was even a law that covered this yet. In the hands of a good defence attorney, the mule wouldn't even be an accomplice to Kinnery's theft, just an innocent who didn't know what was being pumped into him, a victim of malpractice.

Indecision and fresh fear paralyzed her. She broke off to check her mail in the hope that it might contain some new information to make sense of it all.

There was no mail from Clare or Larry, but Weaver had sent a cryptic note: *'I'm sure you'd have called if you had any problems. I hope things are working out and that you're taking care. Call when you can.'*

Dru couldn't call him. If she did, he'd ask where she was. She'd have to lie or refuse to tell him. She couldn't let him work out that she was spying on the Braynes, and she was past the point where she could pull out and pretend it never happened. Unless she falsified receipts, it would all come out when she claimed her expenses anyway, because she didn't have the money to write these things off. It was another small but impossible problem that never happened in the movies.

Stop this. Focus. Think about Ian.

If he turned out to be the boy in the mall footage, he wasn't much older than Clare. Her mental image had become one of a mature, experienced criminal. Maybe Ian was one of Kinnery's students. Dru could imagine an eager undergraduate being talked into self-experimentation, or lured by the thrill of sticking it to a big corporation.

Either way, shape-shifter or plain mule, whoever had those genes was a thief aiding and abetting another thief. The stolen goods just happened to be very unusual.

But what were the Braynes getting out of this? It was a question she should have asked herself as soon as she linked the names. She should have stuck to her own rule of following the money. They were rich, they had vast business interests, and this was technology with a massive potential in medical applications. Even the super-wealthy never thought they were rich enough.

Dru started composing a message to Clare and then realised how hard it was to reveal nothing to her own daughter. It was a long day to kill, even in winter.

As soon as it was dark, she drove down Forest Road again and checked for lights at the Braynes' house. Someone was in, or at least the lights had been left on. She parked at the viewing point to see what she could pick out with binoculars, but after twenty minutes she accepted that she wouldn't see enough detail. Catching sight of this Ian was going to be as much by luck as judgement.

She headed back to the hotel. The Byway was better than she'd expected, the kind of small hotel that she might have chosen if she'd still been able to afford vacations. She treated herself to steak for dinner, and over a medium-rare filet she noted a guy at another table checking her out — tall, forties, dark blonde, with an athletic build that didn't quite gel with his business suit.

Dru risked smiling at him. It was still a novelty to see men who'd have walked straight past her as a mousey brown housewife now at least glance at her as a blonde. Her face was no different, and neither was her body, but it was enough to spark a different chain of behaviour for both the watcher and the watched. He looked slightly embarrassed and smiled back before taking an intense interest in his plate.

She saw him again in the parking lot a few hours later while she was checking that she hadn't left anything in the car overnight. A noise like something sliding on runners made her look around. He was brandishing a remote key fob as he approached a dark blue Chrysler minivan. He had the stride of a man who walked through people, not her type of guy at all. She locked her car and went back to her room.

Maybe he was away from his family at Thanksgiving due to an unreasonable boss, fouled-up plans, or even divorce. Dru reflected on the fact that the most conspicuous thing about both of them was that they were alone at a time when most people congregated even with family that they couldn't stand the sight of.

She hoped Clare was enjoying herself. That was the whole reason Dru had had ended up here, after all: Clare's welfare. She was in the grip of a case that wouldn't let her go, but it had all begun because she needed to keep her job for Clare's sake. If she'd been childless and truly single, answerable to nobody, she wouldn't have stayed with KWA, and she wouldn't be skulking around the Maine countryside when all sane folk were heading home for the holiday.

It was a sacrifice. It was what any decent parent had to do. Larry might have forgotten that, but Dru hadn't.

CHALTON FARM, WESTERHAM FALLS: NEXT MORNING.

"It's just like being back in the supermarket, Mrs Mike." Rob skimmed through the overnight recordings from more than thirty cameras, daylight and infrared. At least he could access the feeds four at a time on his phone from the comfort of the conservatory sofa with bacon sandwiches and a mug of tea to hand. "I bloody hated checking the CCTV. You wouldn't believe where shoplifters hide stuff."

Livvie took one of his sandwiches. "I hope you didn't put the food back on sale."

"If I told you, you'd never eat pork again."

"Don't, Rob, I want to enjoy this sandwich." Livvie had a throaty, dirty laugh that made things sound funnier than they were. "Are you going to do this every day?"

"Until we have a head on a spike, yes." The cams facing the wooded parts of the estate had picked up deer. Most of the sensors on the southern side had been triggered by vehicles on Forest Road. It wasn't a busy route, but there were still a lot of individual sequences to check out. "Deer ... deer ... lorry ... oops... do you like venison?"

Ian wandered into the conservatory and looked over Rob's shoulder. He didn't say anything, but Rob heard the faint change in his breathing. If he'd let that breath out, it would almost have been an oh-dear kind of sigh.

"Let me check all that," Ian said. "Tom's arriving tomorrow. You need to get stuff ready."

Rob craned his head back to look him. "All sorted."

"Don't neglect him to look after me."

Ouch. "Don't worry, I've had years of practice at doing two things at once. Three, even."

Rob carried on checking the footage. It wasn't entirely a matter of luck. The location dictated how KWA tackled this, pros or not. There'd be a vehicle recce to check out the place before any activity on foot, which would probably show up as repeated passes by car or bike on Forest Road. That was the only street access. Rob couldn't see the number plates, so he'd have to compare images. One vehicle stood out from the day before, a small silver car that had not only passed the house a few times but had also parked in the lay-by that he'd identified a few days ago. It seemed to have returned to the lay-by for a second night. He had an infrared image.

"Okay, here's at least one to keep an eye on." Rob opened the file of image captures and compared it. "There. What kind of car is that?"

Livvie took the phone from him to look. "Chevy Sonic, I think."

"Does that look like the same one to you?"

"It does. Is it that simple? Don't you have to spend weeks on this?"

"Not if they're funnelled into specific places. They've got to use the road if they want to observe from a vehicle. Good old low-tech spook tradecraft — the Mark One Eyeball. And there's no hard drive to incriminate them if they get caught."

It occurred to Rob that KWA might not have been looking for the kind of evidence that would stand up in court. But that didn't change how he'd handle it.

"They're not expecting you or Mike," Ian said. "They don't have any idea what you guys can do."

Rob wasn't sure he knew what kind of support KWA could hire, either, but it was a nice vote of confidence.

"Yeah, we fight dirty, mate," he said. "Fork in the eyeball job, that's us. I'd better go and tell Mike."

Mike was pounding the treadmill in the gym, eyes fixed on the wall ahead. Rob held the phone in front of him without saying a word. Mike slowed to a halt and studied the images, wiping beads of sweat off his nose.

His lips compressed. He could normally keep a lid on his reactions, but his expression hardened muscle by muscle from Nice Quiet Zombie to Mr Silent Angry Bastard.

"Well, at least we can still think like the enemy." His nostrils flared slightly as he breathed. He was probably still catching his breath, but combined with the tight-lipped expression, he looked like he was about to erupt. "We need to get a look at the driver."

"Let's talk to Andrews. He might have seen someone hanging around."

"What are we going to tell him?"

"What are we going to tell Tom? We still need to sync our cover story." Rob felt obliged to sort this out himself. "I'll pop down and see the old boy. I'll think of something on the way."

He zipped up his jacket as he walked down the drive, rehearsing stories. Okay, they were avoiding someone. Media? Harmless but annoying stalker? Andrews seemed to think that Mike did something sensitive at the DoD or was still serving, so it was easy enough for Rob to do a need-to-know act about not being able to divulge detail. He rapped on the door. It opened fast for anyone, let alone an old bloke.

"Morning, sir," Rob said, still working it out. "How are you?"

"I'm fine, Rob. Did she catch you?"

Jesus Christ. What was he, clairvoyant? "Who?"

"The woman who called to see Mike yesterday. I told her she'd missed him. She wanted to know when he'd be back."

Rob had guessed this was coming, but his stomach still knotted. He took out his phone and swiped through to the photo of Dru Lloyd.

"Well, she didn't come back," he said. "Did she look like this?"

Andrews studied it, nodding. "I think so. You know her, then?"

"Sort of. What else can you tell me?"

"She was driving a small silver Chevy." Andrews paused for a moment, looking up like he was replaying the conversation. "She asked when Mike would be back, I said I didn't know but soon ... oh, yes, I said you and Ian might be in, but she didn't know who you were. So I said she should go knock on the door or leave a note, because I was getting kind of concerned that she was checking if the house was empty for the holidays. You know how people get burglarised while they're away."

Shit, he'd mentioned Ian by name. She'd know she had the right house, then. Well, it was all academic from the moment that video went public. Rob felt he should have been more surprised, but at least he could predict how she operated. That was something.

"Okay," he said. "If you see her again, can you call us?"

"Did I say something wrong? What is she?"

Rob sidestepped the question. "Nothing wrong at all, sir. It's a big help to know what she's driving."

Andrews held up his forefinger at Rob to wait while he went back up the hall. He returned clutching a sheet from a phone pad.

"Here. This is the licence plate, or most of it."

"Good catch, Mr Andrews." Rob reminded himself never to underestimate old men. "That's very useful. Thank you."

By the time Rob jogged back to the house, Mike was already waiting on the front steps, looking homicidal and more like his dad than ever. Rob held up the note.

"Confirmed," he said. "She tried to check us out with Andrews. Here's her number plate. She got the name Ian out of him, but that'll just make sure she tries harder."

Rob waited for Mike to detonate, but he just took the note and went inside. "Good. That means we can provoke her into doing something dumb. Livvie's locating her."

Rob wasn't sure what he meant. When he followed him to the study, he found Livvie lounging at Mike's desk with the phone to her ear, gazing at the ceiling as if she was waiting for someone to pick up. She looked at Rob, then jerked to attention and put a finger to her lips.

"Really? Okay, my apologies. I must have the wrong hotel." She rang off and looked down at a list on the desk, then tapped out another number and sat waiting for an answer. "I'm trawling through local hotels. There aren't that many. She's got to be staying in the area if she keeps coming back."

"I got her licence plate," Rob said.

"*Sssh* ... hi, can you put me through to Mrs Lloyd, please? She might be under a reservation from her company, KW-Halbauer, or under the name Wilson ... no, I don't have her room number. Thank you." Livvie suddenly brightened up, triumphant, and did a thumbs-up. "Okay, thanks." Then she cut off the call.

"There," she said. "They'll think they lost me when they tried to put me through. She's at the Byway. About ten miles west of us. Forty rooms."

Mike looked at Rob as if he was inviting suggestions. "I say we pay the hotel a visit, find her car, and slap the GPS on it," he said. "We need her to trespass so I can call nine-one-one, and that'll be simpler to set up when we track her routine for a while."

"When do you want to do it?" Rob asked.

"Late tonight. We can move around the parking lot without looking suspicious if we time it for when people leave the bar. About eleven."

"We better take the Jag, then. It's not been out of the garage for over a week. She won't recognise it."

"Fine, but Tom's arriving tomorrow," Livvie said. "Are we seriously going to be doing all this while he's here?"

"We don't have a choice, honey. KWA's set the timetable." Mike stood up and shook his head as if he was disappointed with the state of the world. "I'll keep an eye on the cameras today."

Livvie looked at Rob as Mike left. "You know there's only one thing that'll lure her in here."

"Yeah, and Ian will jump at the chance, but we've not planned this yet."

"What if she's got backup?"

"I'd take a guess that she's operating alone with someone on standby elsewhere. These buggers normally keep an eye on their target for at least a couple of weeks. But even if she's brought the entire North Korean army, there's only me and Mike to deal with it, and you to hold the fort. We'll have to manage."

"True. Are you still planning to move into a guest room while Tom's here?"

"Definitely. It makes it easier to secure the place, too. I'll shift my kit now."

The simple act of moving from the cottage to the house reinforced Rob's sense of preparing to repel an assault. He hoped his mood didn't percolate through to Tom. But he had no idea what was out there, and it was probably sensible to get Tom to wear a ballistic vest when they went out. How the hell would he explain that? The one thing he could never take for granted over here was that people — men, women, any age, any class — weren't armed. He was more worried about a woman who wasn't used to firearms panicking and squeezing one off, not a trained marksman. That was how you got killed.

It spoiled his bloody day, that was for sure. Rob counted down the hours until it was time to go, testing his GPS tagging skills in the garage by seeing how fast he could stick the magnetic unit on the Merc. He found an online workshop manual for the Chevy to identify the best spot to place the magnet fast and in the dark. He was still rehearsing the manoeuvre, checking diagrams on his tablet, when he looked up and saw Ian leaning against the door.

"Need any help?" Ian asked.

"No, I'm sorted."

"It's kind of escalating, isn't it?"

Rob tried to reassure him. "We're just psyching ourselves up, mate. We're only going to visit the hotel and stick a GPS tracker on the car so we know where she is."

"I should come too."

"No. This is just routine."

"If you're going to entrap her, the only lure she'll take is me. I need to be part of this."

"Yeah, I knew you'd say that."

"Don't you think I'm capable?"

"Of course you are."

"You wouldn't be doing this if it wasn't for me."

"Remember what I said about principals and protection officers?"

"Sure. Okay."

"Subject closed. How's your hand?"

Ian looked down at the dressing. Nothing was ever really closed with him, though. He'd circle back later.

"It's fine," he said.

Rob wondered how ordinary people with no self-defence skills or security budget coped with a disgruntled ex or some other bastard lurking in the bushes. If it was getting to him as a professional soldier, then it must have been wearing pretty thin for Ian as well. Livvie seemed to take it as a challenge for her deception skills, though, and wasn't remotely intimidated. Living alone here for months at a time had made her completely nails. She'd probably been pretty tough to start with.

By the time Rob had moved his stuff and had a meal, it was still only 1900 hours. He went looking for Mike and found him sitting in the security room with the doors slightly ajar, watching the monitors. Rob pulled a chair into the small room and sat next to him. Neither of them said a word for nearly an hour. There was occasional traffic, but it was a quiet night even by Westerham standards.

"Bike," Rob said, pointing. "Second time."

"Can't tell if it's the same one." Mike stretched and yawned. "Might just be a return journey."

It was a long half hour before anything else happened. "Van," Rob said.

"Have we seen that before?" Mike swivelled his chair and bent down to check a recording. "Yes. An hour ago."

There was still nothing that warranted immediate attention. Eventually Mike leaned forward and pointed at the feed from the cameras facing the lay-by.

"She's back," he said. The infrared image of the car was clear, but they couldn't see the driver. "I'm going to take a closer look."

Rob got up. "No, I'll do it."

Dru wouldn't keep coming back at night if she was confident doing a recce in daylight. But maybe she had some NV kit they didn't know about.

"Okay, but you're just going to ID her, right?"

"Come on, I know what I'm doing, mate."

Mike looked sheepish. "Sorry."

Rob realised he'd snapped at him. He was back in Afghanistan for a few inexplicable moments, choked with frustration because he could *see* some bastards were up to no good, but he had to wait for permission from up the line to engage them. *Fuck that.* He was never going to let himself be put in that position again.

"Look, we've already got loads of images, plus Andrews to back us up," Rob said. "We could call Maine's finest right now."

"No, I need her to do something that looks more threatening than just parking outside," Mike said. "Okay, stay on the radio. I'll warn Livvie and get up on the roof."

Mike was talking sense. Rob knew it. He made an effort to get his head back in the right place while he kitted up in the utility room. Everything he needed for a night op was in Mike's impressive store at the back of the garage: night vision kit, infrared imaging, camouflage, and radios. He adjusted his earpiece under his wool cap, amused for a moment that the place was so big that he might be out of range at the boundary. If Dru saw him dressed like this, she'd shit a brick.

"Lights," he said. "Give me five minutes."

Mike had to temporarily disable the sensors around the house so that the lights weren't triggered. Rob moved between cover, assuming that whoever was out there might be at least as well equipped as he was.

"In position." Mike's voice was suddenly in his ear. "Glad I wore my thermal lingerie."

He'd reached the roof faster than Rob expected. It was just as well there weren't neighbours overlooking the property. The sight of a bloke perched up there with a sniper scope would have been a bit worrying.

"She's still there, yeah?"

"Confirmed."

Rob skirted the lawns to the west of the house and headed into the trees, working himself from trunk to trunk and eventually along the wire that separated Mike's land from the neighbouring forest. It was the only clear demarcation of Mike's land, and it wouldn't have deterred a one-legged granny with arthritis. Rob stepped across it.

He ended up near the road, looking back towards the lay-by.

"Zombie, I've got eyes on the Sonic." He braced himself against a low branch and took out his NV scope. "Confirm one driver. She's just sitting there."

Rob watched for a few minutes. As far as he could see, Dru wasn't using any optics. She was just watching. He could see her profile.

"Vehicle approaching," Mike said. "Wait."

"Problem?"

"It's slowing ... it's stopped. Fifty, sixty yards west, to your right. Dark-coloured van."

"Seen it before?"

"It might be the same one. Chrysler, I think."

"Has it got line of sight with her?"

"Appears so."

"Can you save the image?"

"Not with this scope. I'll check the recording later."

Rob waited. He was tempted to see how close he could get to the car, but he had no idea what the van was doing. He was depending on Mike to call it.

"The van's not moving," Mike said. "Assume that's her backup."

Rob waited half an hour, completely still and remembering what a cold night patrol felt like. Then the door of the Sonic opened. He saw Dru clearly for the first time as she stepped out and walked around the car to stand on the verge looking back at the house.

Go on. Please. Be a good girl and cross over. Walk onto Mike's land. Then I can grab you and knock this shit on the head once and for all.

But she stayed put with her hands thrust into the pockets of her jacket. Then she walked down the road towards the entrance. Eventually she headed back to the car, sat inside for ten minutes, then started the engine and drove off towards town. Rob waited to see if the van followed.

"The Chrysler's backing up," Mike said. Rob could hear a distant engine. "Turning around in the entrance to the trail."

"So is that her backup or not?"

"I'd say yes. Come on in."

At least Rob had something active to worry about for the next hour or so. He checked the monitors with Mike, occasionally fending off visits from Ian.

"You'll be doing this for months," Ian said.

"KWA hasn't got months." Rob gauged their urgency by how fast they'd cracked on with this. They probably thought Ian was about to do a runner. "They'll make a move soon."

It was more hope than prediction. Rob was still no clearer about the Chrysler's role in this. Eventually they spotted the Sonic passing the drive again, heading in the direction of the hotel.

"There we go," Mike said. "Back on plan. We'll drop by the hotel just after eleven."

There were too many what-ifs for Rob to rule anything out. He could only assume the worst and roll back from there. When it was time to go, he let Mike do the driving for a change. Livvie put the house in lockdown and switched the lights off to let the Jag exit in total darkness.

"Assholes," Mike muttered. "This isn't fair on Livvie. It isn't fair on you, either."

"Come on, if Dru even reaches your front door, Livvie's going to be on her like a coked-up stoat. Your missus is nails. And armed."

"Sorry. I'm out of my operational comfort zone."

"What are you, a traffic warden? Christ, Zombie, we fucking *shoot* people."

"I mean doing this on home turf against civilians."

"Weaver's the one doing the *doing*. Not us. We're just bimbling out on patrol to invite Terry Taliban to take a pop at us. They were civvies too. Fuckers."

"But that's straightforward, and this is Machiavellian and Byzantine and all the doublethink I'm just not good at." Mike paused. "You realise you said Weaver, not Dru or Lloyd?"

Weaver. Yeah, that was who they were dealing with. Rob decided to keep him as the mental picture of the threat, not some little HR drone. "She's just the infantry."

"I know. It's a mental shift I should have made months ago. Maybe Weaver hasn't told her everything."

"She's here because she saw the mall video. Does Weaver believe it? Kinnery said he never knew Ian existed."

"Belief doesn't matter. He knows enough to work out what he might have lost by way of future profits, so it's worth pursuing just to rule it out."

"Zombie, don't mega-rich bastards have off-the-shelf solutions for this? Buy KWA, or whatever they call themselves now, and shut them down. Or have someone ruin Weaver's day."

"Threats need maintenance. They don't erase knowledge or suspicion. Sometimes the rich are as screwed as the rest of — " Mike glanced at Rob just as he almost said *us*. Rob could see his lips forming the shape. That was truly weird. "What makes the moneyed class different is that we can afford to run away or sue people back to the Stone Age. But neither case applies here."

At least he still had some rich brain cells firing, then. "If this Dru was a bloke," Rob said, "we'd just get him in a badly-lit alley and beat some sense into him."

"And then what? There's only one way to ensure permanent silence. And that comes back to bite you in the ass when they find the shallow grave."

"You're not digging it deep enough, then."

"Look, I'm not squeamish."

"You fucking are. You still want to be the good American."

"I'm a soldier, and so are you. Not an assassin."

"Well, I'm glad there's a nice tidy line. Because every situation in combat's always crystal-clear, isn't it? No ambiguity at all, no sir." Rob wondered how the Braynes had ever made their money without bending the rules a bit. He struggled with the idea of people with that much power having to sit back and take this shit. "Has your dad ever had anyone done over?"

"Dad? Hell, no. My great-grandfather, and his father, though — possibly. I'm pretty sure they hired heavies."

"Seriously?"

"I'm not proud of it. You did ask."

"That's normal dispute resolution where I come from. Except the hiring bit. We do our own hand-crafted artisan violence."

"If I can do things by the book, I will."

"Yeah, but if it comes to a choice between compromising our people and hitting a girl, I'm not going to be a gentleman. There's no ROEs here, Zombie. If there are, we'll be the only ones playing by them."

"It needn't come to that."

"I just want you to know where I stand. I'm happy to break a few legs to save you the paperwork and embarrassment."

Rob added a second condition to his belief that you knew everything about a bloke if you fought alongside him. It wasn't until a man went up against a female enemy or a ten-year-old with a rifle that you understood where his taboos and non-negotiable lines lay. Rob knew where his were.

"I think we're going to have to tell Tom more than we intended," Mike said.

"Maybe we can do it without making Ian sound like the Hulk."

"We'll think of something."

"What a team, eh? Nazani looks like a piece of piss compared to this."

The Byway had an open car park that wasn't well lit except for the area right in front of the door. A few people were wandering in and out of the building as Mike drove slowly along the rows like he was looking for a space. Rob recognised the silver Chevrolet Sonic and checked the licence plate.

"That's hers."

Mike stopped right behind its rear bumper. Rob slid out, crouched as if he was checking under the Jag for a radiator leak, and stuck the magnetic unit under the Sonic in one quick movement. He was back in the passenger seat in a matter of seconds, wiping his hands.

"Now where's the Chrysler?"

Mike carried on crawling along. "Can't see anything similar." He pulled into a space near the exit. "Wait here."

He jumped out and jogged towards the hotel entrance. A few minutes later, he came back and drove off, shaking his head.

"What was that about?" Rob asked.

"It might have been dumb, but I asked at the desk if any of the guests had a van because I thought I'd hit its wing mirror earlier, etcetera etcetera. The clerk checked. Nothing. So if it's backup, they're staying somewhere else."

"Or they're local PIs. Your dad got the phone numbers checked, so can he call in a favour for licence plates if we get the van's?"

"That means involving more people. I want Dad kept clear of this until we've nailed Weaver."

Rob had never needed to question Mike's judgement in Nazani, and he had even less reason to question it here. Mike didn't just know the system. His family bloody owned it. But everything depended on whether Weaver would press the button that put Mike into survival mode. Rob wasn't sure he was willing to wait for that.

"How far are you prepared to go?" he asked.

Mike didn't even pause to think. "One step further than they are. Like you said, they probably don't have any rules of engagement."

"Yeah." Rob hoped he meant it. "Me too, mate."

CHALTON FARM, WESTERHAM FALLS: 0630, NEXT DAY.

Ian's leather holdall was sitting under the console table in the hall when Mike got up.

He stared at it for a moment, unprepared for the sense of panic, loss, and failure. *Didn't we make him feel safe? Can't he see that we're here for him?* This was a test of his insistence that Ian had a right to make his own decisions. Suddenly he didn't feel so reasonable about it. He wanted to tell him to unpack that damn thing and not be so dumb, and by the way, was he crazy abandoning his one safe haven? Ian couldn't leave. He damn well *couldn't.* Why was he doing this now, when he always did as he was asked?

Just calm down. No histrionics. It'll only make him feel worse.

He found Ian in the kitchen, cleaning the espresso machine as if nothing had happened.

"I hope that bag doesn't mean what I think it does." Mike took a fresh can of coffee beans from the cupboard and snapped the seal, trying to sound seen-it-all and reassuring. "Because we made plans, you know."

Ian took a few moments to look up from the sink. "I think I should go away for a while. I can see the damage I'm doing."

"Ah, come on."

"Rob can't go back to work. You've put your adoption on hold. Now all this crap's on your doorstep. You can't leave the house without treating it like exiting the Green Zone."

"You've been rehearsing that, haven't you?"

"Mike, whatever you do, it's never going to end. It's always going to be this way. It's going to ruin your lives. Drop me off at the bus station when you collect Tom and I'll lie low somewhere."

"That's not going to solve anything." Poor kid: he was blaming himself, taking responsibility for the sins committed against him. Mike felt that protective anger kick in again. "Just keep your nerve and sit tight."

"Would you sit back while Rob bent himself out of shape protecting you?"

"That's not what's happening here, Ian."

"You've given me everything. You've given me the ability to survive on my own, too, and that's priceless."

Mike didn't want to get into the habit of pressing psychological buttons. Manipulation was what you did to strangers, and he couldn't do that to a kid who needed to be able to trust him. But he found himself grabbing for anything that would persuade Ian to stay.

"Well, unless you're planning to call Dru Lloyd and tell her you won't be here, she'll still be staking us out," he said. "And it's going to be hell on a bus the day before Thanksgiving."

"I'm sorry. I know I've hurt you."

"Hey, you're an adult. The whole point of ..." Mike balked at the word *rescuing.* That sounded like a debt. "The point is that I wanted you to have the freedom to make your own choices. Do you really *want* to leave?"

Ian was starting to look defensive, chin lowered. "Of course I don't."

"Then stay."

Mike judged that was a good time to stop. Dad had always let him make his own decisions even as a child, on the condition that he lived with the consequences and understood that he wouldn't get bailed out. It hadn't felt harsh at all. It had been a privilege, control over his own life and the adult respect of a father he adored. Mike had learned at the age of eight that if he blew his monthly allowance in one go and then decided that he didn't really want that pet rabbit after all, that Mom and Dad would simply ask him how he planned to take care of it. It had been a seminal lesson. He chose what he wanted very carefully after that. He also took good care of the rabbit.

Ian rubbed his eyes as if he'd just woken up. "Sorry. I must seem like an ungrateful asshole."

"Not at all. You've had a tough time. You think this'll be easier on us."

"Why are you so patient with me?"

Mike found it too hard to say *because you're our boy, because we love you.* It might have sounded like pressure. He diluted it. "Because you're a good person. A nice guy. Livvie and I are very fond of you.

Now go put the bag away before Rob sees it, or we'll never hear the end of it."

Ian reassembled the coffee machine and disappeared. Mike heard the rasp of the leather bag as Ian lifted it off the tiles and went upstairs. The crisis had been averted.

I'll tell Livvie later, when Tom's here and everyone's distracted.

Tom was finally arriving this morning after months of on-off arrangements, and Mike didn't want to spoil the reunion for Rob. They'd swing by the hotel on the way to Odstock to check that Dru's car was where it appeared to be on the GPS log, confirm that it hadn't moved all night, and then get on with the holiday. Mike could cover this without Rob.

Persuading Rob to leave it to him wouldn't be easy, though. Mike found him sitting in the Mercedes in the garage, eyes glued to his phone as he watched the auto-tracking sending back data as a moving point on a map.

"Alien," Rob murmured.

"What is?"

"This. Like the movie. The bit where all you see is the monitor with one dot moving towards another dot in the air ducts, so you know the alien finds the bloke and rips his guts out." Rob looked up. "It's okay. She isn't slithering around the ventilation system."

"They claim that thing's accurate to within a few meters."

"Only one way to find out." Rob started the car. "You ready?"

Mike wondered if he should go and tell Livvie about Ian and warn her to keep an eye on him. No, Mike had to trust him. If he'd wanted to sneak out, he would have been gone before Mike got up. "Let's go."

Just after 0830, Rob turned into the Byways parking lot. Mike could see the Sonic, still in the same bay. There was also a dark blue Chrysler van in the next row.

"There you go." Rob nodded in its direction. "There might be another explanation, but I'm buggered if I can think of one."

Mike held his phone as if he was checking for a signal and took pictures of both vehicles with their plates as discreetly as he could. The Sonic was local and probably a rental, but the Chrysler had Massachusetts plates. Slapping the spare GPS unit on it would have been ideal, but there were people around and it was too risky in broad daylight. He didn't know if one of the people in the parking lot was the driver, either.

"Bugger." Rob made an annoyed puffing sound. "We could always come back tonight and tag it. Let's go."

Mike wondered what people thought when they had their car serviced and found a tracker stuck underneath. "I check under our vehicles daily. Especially after the trooper fixed Livvie's light."

"He was real, you know. I check too. Mainly for explosives."

"Damn, life's made us paranoid, hasn't it?"

"And we're still here to tell the tale."

They had forty minutes to kill at the airfield before the Gulfstream was due to land. Rob was still mesmerised by the GPS tracker, but he was drumming one heel on the ground as he sat studying the map, a sign of his impatience to see his son again. Twenty minutes later, he nudged Mike and showed him the phone. The GPS marker was now moving towards Westerham. Mike tapped the map to zoom in for a closer look. He wasn't sure how much to trust the accuracy with a moving vehicle, but the car didn't go to the lay-by as he expected. It turned off onto the scenic trail.

He texted Livvie an update. She'd keep the alarms on and the doors locked anyway. "Dru's decided to recon on foot, then."

"Take the car back and leave me here," Rob said. "One of us should be at the house all the time now. Tom and I can get a taxi."

"No, we'll be home soon enough. They can't get into the house. Let's see what they do today."

Mike thought through the permutations. Livvie hadn't left the house since Dru had shown up, so Dru didn't know she was there. Dru hadn't seen Ian, either. If she'd spotted anyone, it was just himself and Rob. They'd be able to use that to their advantage somehow.

Somehow. We track her and see what shakes out.

But Tom was finally here. The jet landed and he came down the steps with a big grin on his face, looking more like Rob than ever. He was wearing an eye-watering orange mountain jacket that flapped open to reveal an equally searing blue lining. Rob scooped him up in a ferocious hug.

When Tom extricated himself, he stepped back for a moment to take his phone and record some footage of the jet, arm outstretched in that universal stance of someone grabbing a piece of posterity. He turned around, still grinning.

"Mike, that was just the most amazing trip ever," he said. "Thanks. I'm gobsmacked. You're the best."

Mike calculated the correct level of man-hug for an honorary uncle. "Can't have the heir to the Rennie empire traveling with the sweaty peasantry, can we? So, Rob, you want me to brief Tom? Or will you?"

"Yeah, I've got something to tell you, kiddo. I'll explain on the way. Mike's driving." Rob put Tom's bags in the trunk. "Christ, what's that jacket the regulation camo for? Mars?"

They were laughing and nudging each other like kids, and just a little tearful. As Mike drove off, he caught Tom's reflection in the rear-view mirror, looking expectantly at his dad. Mike wasn't sure how much Rob was going to tell him. But there'd be no disguising the fact that the house was on alert.

"I need to brief you as well, Dad," Tom said.

Rob looked over the back of his seat. "You go first."

"Okay. I've been dying to tell you for ages. This work placement." Tom took a breath. "I applied to GCHQ. I got the placement and a sponsorship for my final year."

"Say again, kiddo?"

"GCHQ. Cheltenham. You know. That's what I was doing this summer."

Oh God. Mike felt that awful trickling water sensation down his back. Rob said nothing.

"Are we talking about the same GCHQ I think you mean?" Mike asked. "Signals intelligence?"

"You know that look on your face, Mike? That's why I can only tell close family."

So Tom had been working at the UK's eavesdropping HQ. Mike really hadn't seen that coming at all. Nor had Rob, obviously. His jaw really did drop a little. Dru was forgotten for the moment.

"Bloody hell," Rob said at last. "Did you get extra spook points for not telling your poor old dad?"

Tom took it as a joke, but Mike wasn't too sure. "They're sponsoring my final year," Tom said. "That means I'll probably get a job when I graduate. So I can pay Mike back. Well, eventually. By the next Ice Age."

Mike tried to salvage the conversation. How could they tell him anything at all about Ian now? Tom wouldn't thank them for sharing. He'd grown up knowing how to keep his mouth shut, but it was one thing having a Marine for a father, and another being told about classified military research that had gotten out of hand.

"Hey, that was a gift, okay?" Mike said. "I'll just send your boss a note saying that it's a payment from the CIA and that you did a great job with the electrodes."

Tom laughed. Rob didn't.

"You're going to do *intelligence*?" Rob said, as if he still refused to believe it. "Can I even ask that?"

"No, not an *intelligence officer*." Tom said it slowly. "Just research. Remember I'm doing computing and linguistics. A boffin. Not a spy."

"You mean eavesdropping stuff?"

"Bit of a value judgement there, Dad. I can't say."

"Never mind, I'm bloody proud of you all the same." Rob seemed to be getting his breath back, but Mike could see he was struggling with the idea. He really didn't like anything to do with spooks. "Well done, kiddo. That means they vetted you, PV'd you, yeah? The full monty."

"That's one reason why I took so long to tell you."

"I must have come up clean as well, then."

"Yeah, you did really well to cover up all that kidnap and industrial espionage."

Rob didn't even try to laugh that time. Tom couldn't possibly have known how close he'd come to hitting a major artery.

"Seriously, congratulations, Tom." Mike nodded his approval. "We'll have someone to send our complaints to when the intel comes up as shit again, huh?"

"I'm just the IT guy. Try switching it off and on again."

Mike decided to tackle the subject of Ian himself to save Rob from more agonised squirming. "Okay, here's *our* exciting secret. You'll notice some armoured paranoia when we get back. Security lockdown. Don't lose any sleep over it. Ian has a persistent stalker. Maybe two."

"Oh."

"Nothing serious."

"And there was I thinking you were hiding someone from the Mob." Tom chuckled to himself. "That's a relief. No witness protection, then."

Rob turned in his seat. "Kiddo, you would *not* be here now if I thought there was the slightest risk to you."

"I know, Dad. Do I need to know what this stalker looks like?"

"I'll show you a picture later. Woman, blonde, about forty."

"Jesus, Ian's eighteen, isn't he? Okay, I won't knock it until I've tried it."

Rob managed a smile this time, but the look on his face was still suppressed horror.

"I've never shown you my scar, have I?" Mike said, doing his best to derail the conversation. "It's a work of art. Your dad's the Picasso of giblets."

Rob went back to checking out the road around them. "Yeah, there was some offal left over, but I didn't think Mike would need it. Like when I did that self-assembly wardrobe. Remember, Tom? When I had all those screws left? Your mum went ape-shit."

"Is she armed, this stalker?" Tom just ploughed on with his questions. The banter hadn't distracted him one bit. But he was Rob's son, cut from the same persistent and cautious cloth, and he probably knew that strenuously jokey tone all too well. "I'm including bread knives."

"Probably not," Rob said, serious again. "But I am."

"Christ, Dad, are you armed now?"

"Yes. Don't look at me like that."

"Sorry. But that stuff never came home before."

"It's not an artillery piece, for Chrissakes. It's just a Glock."

"*Just.* Is it gold plated? Did you give it a name?"

"Look, I'm a security contractor. It's all legal." Rob checked the GPS receiver again. "It's days like these when I really miss a fifty cal mounted on the back, Zombie."

"Sorry. The dealership said the option was that or fluffy dice."

"Okay, if she's lurking outside when we get back, I'll have a little chat with her. How does *fuck off* sound? Too formal?"

Tom laughed, then started making tapping noises in the back. He was checking something on his cell or tablet. "You're really worried about this woman, aren't you?"

"You Brits might be catching up on us with serial killers, but we're still the proud champions of the crazy stranger league." Mike needed to tell Tom as much as he could to head off questions later. "Just joking. She's not a psycho. More the private investigator variety. Anyway, we put a GPS tracker on her car, so we know where she is."

"Oh, my God, it's a *movie.*" Tom chuckled. "I didn't know you did all this underhand stuff, Dad. Now who's being sneaky?"

"It just happened." Rob hated deceiving his boy. He was

obviously searching for some way to square his conscience. "I was going to give you some background, but you'll have to trust me that you're better off not knowing. Yes, we're keeping someone off Ian's back. He's done nothing wrong. Mike and I might need to step outside while you're here to give some twat a serious picturising, though. That's about it, really. All legal."

"Understood, Dad."

"And I might ask you to wear a ballistic vest. Humour me."

Tom burst out laughing this time. Rob seemed instantly more relaxed for telling him. He'd done it in a way that hadn't involved any lies or sensitive information, but he'd also let Tom know that things weren't being kept from him for a trivial reason. Honour and loyalty seemed satisfied.

"Okay, Dad, I'll follow your dress code," Tom said. "Do you know where she lives?"

"No," Rob said. "Other than Lansing."

"Detail always comes in handy. Have you got a name?"

Mike wished he'd run searches on her from the start, but they'd never needed to find her. She'd found them fast enough.

"Dru, short for Drusilla, I think, Lloyd," Mike said. "Two Ls. Lansing, Michigan. Might also be under Wilson."

"You know plenty, then. Hang on." There was a rip of Velcro as Tom rummaged in his messenger bag and started tapping again. "Here you go. Drusilla Lloyd. Five-seven-seven Ridgeway Drive. Her home number, too. Not much data, but enough to make life less comfortable."

Rob wrote it down in his notebook. "Any family?"

"Kids put all sorts of insane stuff on social media. They post stuff about other kids, too." Tom tapped again. He took no more than a couple of minutes. "Several Lloyds in the area, so I'm guessing now, but this looks likely — Clare. Fourteen. Birthday — December twelfth. Posted about falling off her bike on Ridgeway Drive three years ago." He paused. "Looks like Dru's divorced. Clare says she's spending Thanksgiving at her dad's place because her mum's *away on business in Maine*. Aww, bless. Don't you just love kids? Her dad bought her the coolest purse, apparently. Twenty minutes ago. And people worry about government surveillance?"

"God made idiots so that people like you always have a job, kiddo," Rob said.

Mike wondered if Dru checked what her daughter was posting. "Wow, your kids really can hang you, can't they?"

Tom leaned forward to show Rob something on the tablet. From a snatched glance, it looked to Mike like a picture of Clare.

"People know it's a risk," Tom said. "But life's not worth living if you have to worry who's watching every harmless thing you do."

"Like GCHQ, you mean?" Rob asked.

"It's really not like that, Dad." Tom went back to his task, apparently unoffended. "Mike, do you know how many pictures there are of you online? National Guard news release. Some really old photos from your Oxford college. See what I mean? Even if you don't post it, other people do it for you, years later sometimes. You'd have to spend your whole life in a cave to avoid it."

Maggie Dunlop and Ian had tried to do just that. Maggie would have had her issues with Tom, Mike decided. "Where's the car now, Rob?"

"Still near the house." Rob looked back at Tom again. "Keep your head down as we drive in, kiddo."

Tom seemed to be taking it in his stride and wrapping it all in a joke. He slid down in the back seat. "Wow, tinted glass and stalkers. It's just like being a celeb. Can I punch a photographer, please?"

Mike thought he saw the Sonic as he drove past the visitor centre, but that didn't tell him where Dru was. When he parked in the garage, he made sure the automatic doors had closed fully before he let Rob and Tom get out. It was like being back on patrol again, alert to threats when dismounting. It reignited his anger from the day before.

Reduced to this. In my own goddamn home.

Livvie intercepted them in the rear hall as they brought in Tom's luggage. She did a credible job of behaving as if nothing serious had happened.

"Tom, sweetheart, you look terrific." She hugged him. "Come and meet Ian."

She whisked Tom away in a flurry of hospitality, leaving Mike and Rob to decompress. They stood in the hall with the bags and looked at each other as if a good idea would materialise any moment now if they stared long enough.

"GCHQ." Rob rubbed his hands over his face and shut his eyes. "Oh, fuck."

"I know you're not crazy about it, but it does prove that Tom's very smart."

"Okay. I'll just have to accept that we'll have blank spots we can't talk about." Rob held his arms out in submission. "All that matters is that he's happy and he's here. Let's crack on. We can still stay vigilant without fucking up the holiday."

"No, *I* stay vigilant. *You* have quality time with your son."

"Yeah. Let's go and see how Ian's getting on"

Tom and Ian were chatting as if they were old buddies. It was quite something to see Ian at ease in a social situation, but he probably felt he knew Tom by proxy, and they had something extra in common now — a lot they needed to keep to themselves. The conversation drifted to Mike and Rob's business plans, building the kill house, and why greyhounds sat on their asses all day. Tom never said a word about Dru Lloyd, though. After lunch, the jet lag took its toll and he drifted off to sleep on the sofa next to Rob, gradually sinking into the upholstery with his head resting against his father's shoulder like a small child.

Rob tidied his hair. Eventually he eased a cushion under Tom's head like a builder propping up a collapsing wall and slid out from under. Oatie crept in and curled up in the warm space Rob had vacated.

"I'll keep an eye on Tom," Livvie whispered. "Go do what you need to."

Mike gestured to Ian to stay put and went out to the hall with Rob. The GPS still showed Dru's car at the top of the scenic trail. She had to collect it sooner or later.

"Better check it out," Mike said.

Rob slid his pistol into his belt and put on his cap. "I'm never going to forgive her for dragging me out in this bloody cold. I don't look irresistible in a beanie."

They made their way through the trees and reached the western boundary of Mike's property just as the sun broke through a heavy layer of cloud. Mike held down the top wire of the half-hearted fence and climbed over.

Now they were on public land, five hundred yards from the trail. They stuck to the tree line until Mike saw the low roof of the visitor centre and a few cars parked nearby. He wouldn't have been surprised to find a discarded GPS unit and an empty space, but the Sonic was still there. Dru still hadn't found the tag.

Rob shivered. "She's persistent, I'll give her that. I'm glad I'm not married to her."

"By the way, Ian wanted to leave this morning to spare us the hassle."

"I thought he might." Rob didn't seem at all surprised. "He always blames himself."

"It'd break my heart to lose him. And Livvie's."

"Yeah, he's an easy kid to get attached to. Don't worry. He's not going anywhere."

Mike checked the camera feeds via his phone again to make sure the Chrysler van wasn't watching the house while they were distracted here. He didn't know if Dru would recognise him from photos, especially wearing a cap, but she wouldn't have been able to run a search for Rob, and she couldn't have gotten a good look at him through the Merc's tinted glass.

They still couldn't confront her yet. If she was burned, she'd just get replaced and they'd have to start over to work out who was watching. Mike had to give her the chance to do something dumb. That wasn't going to be easy, though. She was clearly no fool.

"I'm going in," Rob said.

Mike sat on the bench near the parking area to keep an eye on the other vehicles while Rob went into the visitor centre. Next time, they'd bring Oatie. A dog was an easy way to justify being pretty well anywhere. Rob ambled back a few minutes later with a handful of leaflets.

"She's not in there," he said.

Mike was watching the entrance to the parking area. "Heads up."

The blue Chrysler van pulled in and crawled along the row of cars before parking nose in. Rob squinted as if he was taking a look at the driver.

"Same plate," he said. "Male, white, fortyish, on his own. If that's her backup, they're a getting a bit sloppy. We shouldn't even notice them."

"It's not like tailing someone in a city. There's not enough bodies to hide behind. " Mike waited for the Chrysler to get close enough to the Sonic for him to grab pictures. "I'm just collecting what I can to rule out coincidence. Is he meeting her, or looking for her?"

"We're assuming he's on her side."

"Rival company Kinnery forgot to mention?"

"Are you sure you don't want to run this past your dad? Identify the plate?"

"Deniability, Rob. If it all goes to hell, he's linked to the plate query."

Rob sat down again, head turned to Mike but looking sideways at the Chrysler. "Let's grip this. We keep talking about entrapping her, but all I'm seeing now is a two-vehicle operation. She flushes us out and the bloke or blokes in the Chrysler go after Ian."

Mike hadn't seen a second guy. Nobody on the professional food chain would send one man to do a snatch, though, so there had to be at least one other, or maybe even a third vehicle.

"We can sit tight for as long as it takes," Mike said. "They've got to get Ian outside and separate us from him. How about reversing that?"

Rob was now looking straight at the parked vehicles. "You mean invite her in for tea, whether she wants any or not?"

"If we've got her, they have to abort. KWA doesn't keep guys like us on staff. They'd hire them. What would we do if we knew we were compromised on an illegal job?"

"Thin out bloody fast," Rob said. "Or take a huge risk to pull it off and get paid. But we're good boys."

Mike realised he'd walked himself step by step across the line he didn't want to cross. This was about the way he'd chosen to live his life, his decision that he wasn't above the law or exempt from duty and morality simply because he was rich enough to do as he pleased. The guys he'd been with at prep school would have laughed in disbelief. Laws were for the poor dumb masses, not for the elite.

The law wasn't there for Ian, was it? Is it going to protect him now?

It became instantly clear. Mike could either do good, or be good, but not both.

"Let's do it," he said.

SIXTEEN

Mom's not getting any younger, Mike. You hardly visited before, but where the hell have you been all this year? What can possibly be more important than your own mother? Okay, we've all accepted how you want to live your life. Dad lets you play soldiers and he's bought you your very own little friend to play with. The least you could do is show up and be family occasionally.

Charlotte Brayne Aird, in a call to her brother about his Thanksgiving plans.

BYWAY HOTEL, NEAR WESTERHAM FALLS: THANKSGIVING.

Dru stood looking down at her laptop, fuming.

She checked her mail once a day, but she'd taken her eye off the ball when it came to monitoring what Clare was doing online. Part of the daily routine at home was checking Clare's public pages to make sure she wasn't posting too much personal information or getting into conversations that made Dru uneasy. Dru's biggest fear was that Clare would hand out her phone number to the world and all the perverts within it. She hadn't expected her to hand out information on her mother's activities instead.

Checking more frequently wouldn't have shut this stable door in the wake of the bolting horse, but Dru really wished she'd spotted it sooner.

'Mom's on a business trip to Maine.' Terrific. Thanks. Tell everybody.

It wasn't Clare's fault, though. It was wholly Larry's. He was the only one with the information, and he should have known Dru wanted to keep it quiet or else she'd have told Clare herself. Besides, he had her goddamn hotel number, so why did he need to add detail? He knew where to get hold of her if he needed to.

You still think I'm with some guy, don't you? Because that's how you live your life, and of course everyone lies like you do.

Even Clare understood that Mom couldn't discuss employee information, regardless of whether it was the dull routine stuff or building a legal case. If Dru had levelled with Larry about why this job was sensitive and exactly what she planned to do, it would only have opened the floodgates of accusations of being irresponsible and a bad mother. He didn't need to know.

As if I knew exactly what I was going to do when I got here anyway. Stop panicking. Weaver doesn't hang out on teen sites. He'll probably never see it.

In the scheme of things it was harmless, but that was the trouble with information. It was all about context and how it locked into place with other fragments in the mosaic. Dru shut the laptop. Maybe it didn't matter if Weaver found out where she'd gone. It had taken months of grinding, repetitive drudgery for her to make the Brayne connection, and Weaver definitely didn't have the time and inclination to pick the fly shit from the pepper on the granular scale that she did. That was why he'd chosen her to do this job. She was thorough and security-conscious, or, as Larry usually translated it, obsessive, sneaky, and secretive. She dug up long-dead things.

Dru took the room phone over to the window and dialled Larry's number, half-watching the parking lot below as she waited for him to answer. Her credit card would place her here anyway. She wasn't adding any more to the audit trail than she had already, and if anything went badly wrong — wrong enough to pull phone records and credit card data — everything she'd done was legal, if a little seedy. She wasn't counting Kinnery's phone records.

But she was spying on a senator's family. Legality didn't matter. It was serious trouble waiting to happen.

Someone picked up. "Hey Larry," she said.

"Hi. Want to talk to Clare?"

"I want a word with you first. Did you tell her where I was? No, don't answer that. Who else could? Well, thanks a bunch. She posted it on her page. I was trying to keep that quiet. This is a goddamn staff investigation."

Larry went silent for a moment. "Jesus, Dru, you should have spelled it out."

"Well, it's done now. But I'm going to ask her to delete the entry."

"As if your staff read kids' pages. Anyway, when are you coming back?"

"Not for a few more days."

"Did your boss get hold of you?"

"What?"

"He rang me asking for your contact number. He said he'd lost it."

Dru paused to unpick the detail. Was Larry's cell number still on file as her emergency contact? Damn, it probably was. There was nobody else local to call to pick up Clare if anything happened to her.

But I didn't give Weaver a hotel number.

He wasn't the kind of man to forget whether she had or not. The bastard was checking on her. Dru felt the room shrink to suffocating tightness like one of those horror movie focus effects as the maniac's knife paused above the victim.

"Dru? You still there?"

"You gave him the number?"

"Oh, I got that wrong as well, did I? How the hell was I supposed to know you hadn't told your boss?"

"I didn't tell him for a *reason.*" Larry's carelessness wasn't Dru's main problem now. Weaver didn't trust her. At least it was mutual. "Okay. I'd like to talk to Clare, please."

Dru waited, watching guests in the hotel parking lot. The guy who'd been checking her out in the restaurant registered on her in the near-subconscious way that those primal things did. He climbed into his Chrysler but didn't drive off, then got out again after a few moments. Dru looked away as Clare came on the line.

"Mom? It's me. Did I do something wrong?"

"Hi sweetheart. No, you didn't. Nothing at all." Yelling at her wasn't the answer. "Your dad shouldn't have mentioned Maine to you. If the person I'm checking up on saw that, they'd know I'd found them. Can you delete it? Then they might not see it."

"Sure. Sorry, Mom."

"It's okay." *Well, if I don't get anything else out of this, then at least I've learned not to take things out on my daughter.* "Can you do it right away?"

"I'll do it now."

"Okay, I've got to go, but when I come home, I'll make this up to you. We'll have some fun. Do something really different. I promise."

Dru gave Clare a few minutes before checking the page. The entry was gone. It might have been archived somewhere, but that was only a potential problem that might never happen, not a big here-I-am sign. Now she'd have to come up with a list of standby excuses for Weaver. She was stuck, certain that Ian Dunlop was involved with Kinnery's off-the-books activity, but unsure who he was and whether she wanted to be an accomplice to whatever Weaver was planning.

I could just walk away now and tell him it was a dead end. That's the sensible thing to do. But I still need to know.

Dru braced herself for more freezing cold tedium and went down to the front desk to see if she could borrow a Thermos. A hot drink would make all the difference. *Should have remembered that. It's not like I haven't staked out a house before, is it?* Then there were bathroom breaks. She could only keep watch for as long as her bladder let her. She couldn't recall her favourite detective show ever dealing with the thorny issue of needing to break off surveillance to pee.

While the concierge was busy finding a vacuum flask, Dru chatted to the receptionist. "Have there been any calls for me, by the way? I've been out a lot."

The receptionist disappeared into the back office and came out thumbing through a notepad. "Yes, there *was* a call, and we tried to put it through," she said. "But the caller got cut off. Number withheld. They didn't ring back. I'm sorry."

"No problem." If Weaver had genuinely needed to contact Dru, he'd have tried again or e-mailed. He must have been checking the number to see where the hotel was. Clare's gaffe hadn't made any difference, then. "Thank you."

Her plan for today was to walk around the Braynes' boundary, which would at least keep her warm. Binoculars, a couple of wildlife booklets, and a change of clothing — a gilet over her jacket, a headscarf, brown cords instead of jeans — created the right disguise for prowling around. Before she set off, she studied the pictures of Mike Brayne and the guy who might have been Ian

Dunlop. The more she compared the two versions of his face, the less she trusted her own judgement.

At least it was dry and sunny today. The visitor centre at the top of the trail was busy, with a group of mountain bikers poring over the display map outside the office and ten or eleven cars in the lot. Dru took her GIS map and phone compass and headed down the trail. How hard could it be? She couldn't get lost. After a hundred yards she started looking for a point to turn east through the trees and find the fence that marked the Braynes' property. If her math was right, the boundary was more than three miles long. The estate fanned out from the road like a blunt wedge, extending at least a mile into the woods.

Rob and Ian. Rob and Ian ...

As she walked, she replayed the conversation with the Braynes' neighbour. Another element now bothered her, not a missing piece but one that didn't quite fit the hole she'd shaped for it.

He said Rob and Ian. Like they were always there.

The old man obviously knew them well enough to use first names. How did that fit with the scenario of a gene mule, a smuggler? If this was a safe house, when was Ian moved here? And if he was worth that much to biotech and the Braynes had some financial interest, why was he hanging around like a member of the household? They would just have taken what they needed, paid him, and said goodbye. And if they couldn't trust him to keep his mouth shut about it, wouldn't he be locked away or worse by now? Something still didn't fit.

Dru got to within a few yards of the fence. It was just wire, a token boundary she could have stepped over. But she stuck to public land. She tracked the binoculars along the tree trunks at eye height, occasionally tilting up so that anyone watching would think she was looking for birds. The estate had to be hundreds of acres. The most she could do was work out what was at the back of the house and perhaps find another line of sight. The buildings on the satellite map might have been barns. It was hard to tell from an aerial view.

I could just cross the boundary and see how far I can get.

But Dru lost her nerve. If it was a safe house, they wouldn't give an intruder the benefit of the doubt. Right now, she could still go home and tell Weaver something he didn't know about the existence of Ian Dunlop, if she wasn't worried about being implicated in whatever he did next. She didn't need to do any more.

Just one glimpse, though. For the record. And for my grip on reality, I'd like to see him morph as well.

Dru walked a couple of miles, intending to circle around the perimeter, but the land to the north-east of the boundary was marked as private property. She'd have to retrace her steps and skirt around the front. In a few places, it was hard to tell exactly which side of the line she was. The flimsy fence vanished into undergrowth for long stretches or wasn't there at all. There wasn't even a keep-out sign. Security here was either non-existent or it was some technology she couldn't imagine that had already recorded everything about her down to her shoe size.

Maybe I really do have the wrong guy.

When Dru got back to the visitor centre, there were different cars parked out front and people walking with their kids. She carried on and turned left down Forest Road.

Okay, five hundred yards.

She started counting her steps and eventually drew level with the approximate boundary. She couldn't even see the curve in the road yet, let alone the lodge house. That was the scale of the estate. It was a lot of land to get lost in, or hide a thief.

As she passed the house, she glanced up the drive without slowing, but she couldn't see any cars. The eastern boundary that was marked on the GIS map ran parallel with a rough path, but she couldn't see the house from that side. It was no use as an observation point. All she could do was turn around and retrace her steps.

I'm starving. Damn, it's way past lunchtime.

Dru picked up her pace. A guy walking his dog headed down the road towards her, shoulders slightly hunched and chin buried in the upturned collar of a bright orange ski jacket. He looked as cold as she felt. As he got closer, she dithered over whether to do the usual I-can't-see-you urban stare to avoid eye contact. This was the country. It would be weird to ignore someone in the middle of nowhere, but nodding or saying hi might make her too memorable. She focused on his dog instead, a brindle greyhound. All that registered on her before she looked down at the dog was a dark-haired guy in his late teens or early twenties, just another stranger like the cyclists outside the visitor centre.

A little way down the road, something made her glance over her shoulder. She couldn't see him. Had he turned off? He couldn't possibly have walked around the bend in that time. For a moment, she thought she was losing it. When she reached the lay-by where she kept watch on the house, she wondered if he'd turned straight onto the Braynes' land after he passed her.

No, that was crazy. He must have been walking faster than she'd thought and crossed the road to the woods on the southern side.

This was what low blood sugar did to you. It was nothing that a good lunch wouldn't cure. Then she'd come up with a better plan to grab that single glimpse of Ian Dunlop and end nearly twenty years of Kinnery's lies.

CHALTON FARM, WESTERHAM FALLS: FRIDAY.

At 0430, the house had its own unique soundscape.

Ian concentrated, memorising what was normal ambient sound for the early hours, and tried to stay alert. The faint chattering from the central heating was like a chorus of distant voices, while the security room had its own soundtrack, ranging from a high-pitched tone more like a change in air pressure than a noise to the quiet hum from the power supplies. Oatie added the tapping of nails on tiles. The dog tiptoed into the small room and put his head on Ian's lap, looking reproachful.

"You want to go out?" Ian whispered. "I can't take you. Wait."

Lack of sleep was wearing him down. It was getting harder to focus or even keep his eyes fully open. But Mike and Rob were twice his age, and they were watching security displays or patrolling the grounds around the clock. He had no excuse.

Ian caught a sudden glimpse of Rob as he passed one of the cameras along the driveway. It was no way to spend the holiday. Ian felt terrible.

This wasn't Rob's problem, or Mike's. If anything happened to Rob when he returned to security work, all that Tom would remember was that his last visit with his dad had been ruined by some asshole called Ian and his dumb problems.

Ian thought again about *Scott of the Antarctic*. A man really had taken the hard way out to spare his buddies. But there was a solution for all this that didn't involve anybody dying. There was no need to let this drag on. If Ian didn't morph, nobody would ever be able to prove that he could do it, no matter how many tests and scans they gave him.

All they'd find were the genes. That didn't mean a damn thing, any more than sharing genes with humans let a chimp morph into a man or vice versa. The big problem was working out the safest way to turn himself in. He could walk into a police station and tell them he'd been the victim of an experiment without his consent, and not even mention morphing, and that a concerned senator's family had brought the crime to light. Kinnery would be looking at jail; KWA would take some serious damage. He'd have to persuade the police to run DNA tests, though, and that might take some doing. Whichever way he worded it, explaining that he had animal genes in him sounded kind of crazy.

But the hiding — the real hiding, the truly scared kind — would be over. It would just be the media wanting to take a look. He'd have to go away for a while to give Mike and Livvie some peace, but he could come back when the world had grown bored with a shape-shifter who couldn't morph. It was worth facing temporary harassment to spare his friends a life under siege.

So, call the cops? The media? I could ring Zoe Murray again.

Ian tried to ignore the buzzing in his head, then felt himself fall. But he was still in the chair. Oatie was gone. Shit, he must have nodded off for a few seconds and started dreaming. He dug his nails into his palm a few times to wake himself up and inspected the burn, which was now healing into a tight, itchy red patch. It was another painful thing he'd had to do as a means to a better end.

Okay. Focus. The GPS says Dru's at the hotel. She might come back at any time.

But the security room was too warm and cosy. Ian rubbed his eyes and started to feel the world receding around him like the tide going out.

Come on, come on ...

His eyes wouldn't obey. He was seeing double. Then he couldn't see anything at all.

Bang. He was fully alert again.

"Did I startle you? Sorry, mate." Tom was sitting next to him in a sweatshirt and tracksuit pants, drinking coffee. "You haven't missed anything. I've kept an eye on it. I didn't want to wake you."

"Thanks." Falling asleep on watch was unforgivable. "How long was I out?"

"About twenty minutes."

"You didn't have to do that for me."

Tom tapped his wrist, indicating an absent watch. "No problem. I'm still five hours ahead of you. It's coffee time back home."

"Rob's out patrolling. I'm sorry this is spoiling your visit."

"Not at all. I'm riveted." Tom hadn't asked a single awkward question since he'd arrived. He seemed to take it on trust that not knowing the details was for the best. "I'm good at forgetting to be curious if I need to. But if you want me to do anything, just ask. I must admit it was satisfying to eyeball her yesterday."

"Is Rob still mad at you?"

"Come on, Dad's never angry, not for real. I was wearing a vest like he told me to, wasn't I? I mean, that's an adventure in itself." Tom's eyes flicked from monitor to monitor, back and forth along each row. "Trust me, this beats sightseeing. Anyway, I understand dad's job a bit better, even if I haven't got a clue what's going on."

Ian felt he owed Tom at least a partial explanation. "It's not about what I've done. It's about who I am."

"Whatever it is, if it's okay by Dad, it's okay by me."

"Sure. I just want you to know that if it wasn't for Mike and Rob, something pretty nasty would have happened to me."

Tom turned and winked, just like Rob did. "I knew it would be something like that."

It was hard to tell if Tom thought Ian had been saved from a cult, a gang, an abusive family, retribution of some kind, or even from himself. Ian was used to living with obvious questions that never got discussed. Tom seemed to be the same.

Apart from a few deer and some extra traffic — a couple of trucks, a bike or two, and a few cars — there was nothing special going on outside. Mike came downstairs just after 0630 and stood behind Tom to watch the screens.

"As exciting as a test match, isn't it?" Mike said.

Tom seemed to find that funny. "No sign of the usual suspects."

"Her car's still at the hotel."

"What about the Chrysler?" Ian asked.

"I should have tagged it on Wednesday when I had the chance." He clapped Ian on the shoulder. "Okay, buddy, you're relieved. Go have breakfast."

Ian needed to take a nap first. When he woke, he shaved again, concentrating on the contours of his skin. Individual faces looked so different, yet the variations between them were tiny in the scale of the human body. It seemed a lot of fuss and misery about nothing. A face wasn't the only way to identify someone, and it didn't tell you who was inside the skin, either. But faces ruled people's lives and determined their fate. Ian decided that evolution should have come up with a special kind of freckle or pigment that only appeared in nice people. There would have been some point to that, something concrete to judge strangers by.

But I like looking this way. I'm just as superficial.

When he went downstairs, Rob was standing in the hall, talking on his cell. Ian caught a few snatches of the conversation. Rob wasn't Rob the Marine or Rob the Dad this time. He sounded almost submissive. He was probably talking to that physiotherapist he was trying to date.

"No, I'm not making excuses," Rob said, apologetic. "You knew my boy was coming over ... I wish I could ... yeah, but I don't know when I'm going to finish this job ... yes, I *am* working through the holiday ... fine, okay. You do that."

Rob rung off without saying goodbye and stood with his head lowered for a moment. Then he noticed Ian standing on the stairs and snapped back to being relentlessly cheerful. It was a sobering moment for Ian.

"Women." Rob did a comic shrug. "Ungrateful cow. I'll stick it in someone more appreciative, then."

"Sorry," Ian said. "I couldn't walk past you."

"It's okay." Rob checked the phone as if the call had interrupted something more important. "Just another bird I've failed to impress with my work ethic."

And I'm the job that's got to be finished before you can get on with your life. Sorry, Rob. But this isn't going to go on forever, I promise.

Rob had told him never to let the enemy dictate the time and place for a battle. Ian decided to pick his moment. It wasn't a matter of a few days' lockdown, or even five months under Mike's protection. It was eighteen years of exile from the world. Ian had had enough. All the time and expense that Mike and Rob had invested in him had led up to this moment. They'd given him all the skills he needed to get the job done, and he owed it to them to do it.

Livvie and Tom were having coffee in the kitchen, but there

was no sign of Mike. Rob made a beeline for Tom.

"I know we're all fed up being confined to barracks, but I don't want you going off site on your own again. Not even with a vest." He looked around at Ian. "Where's your GPS watch?"

Ian pushed back his sleeve. "Here."

"Good. As long as I know where everyone is."

"Can I go to the workshop?"

"Only via the rear. Don't wander around. Oatie can go walkies on his own."

Ian took a handful of cookies and went into the workshop. The plan formed itself in a matter of minutes. There was a quick way to end this: he'd confront Dru. He'd walk right up to her and defy her to do something. Then she could either talk sensibly to him, or he'd call the cops and she could explain to them why she thought he was a shape-shifter. He didn't have to prove or disprove a damn thing. He just had to tip this out of stalemate and keep Mike and Rob out of it.

It all made perfect sense now. He should have done it ages ago. He could have marched into KWA's offices with a film crew and blown the whole thing, just like Gran said.

He couldn't assume Dru wouldn't be armed, but he couldn't take a firearm. If he carried one, then he intended to use it, and if he used it, things would get complicated. He'd have to rely on a sharp tool and his hunting knife for self-defence. He picked up a short crowbar and climbed up to the workshop roof to lie prone at the observation point. When Dru showed up, he'd pay her a visit.

I can do this. The hardest thing I ever did was spend eighteen years thinking I was crazy.

Somehow that had sloughed off him in days. Once he accepted his changes were real, he hadn't needed to get used to being sane. He'd had to get used to being lied to.

Eventually he heard the springy creak of the ladder. Mike climbed over the edge of the flat roof and settled down next to him to check out something with a monocular. He didn't say anything for a few minutes.

"Tom's having fun," Mike said at last. "You two seem to be getting on fine."

Ian felt like a traitor for having a plan he wasn't going to share with Mike. But it was better this way. "He's a nice guy."

"You don't have a problem with making friends your own age."

"But it's Tom."

"Sure, but that's no guarantee you'd get on." Mike gave him a thumbs up. "Milestone achieved."

It would have been a really great moment if Ian hadn't been set on his confrontation plan. He felt like an undeserving fraud. But Mike and Rob were planning something too. There was an intense focus about them, not excitement or agitation but a kind of controlled impatience.

"So what are you going to do next?" Ian asked. "Dru's not taking the bait."

"We'll keep looking for the Chrysler and any other vehicles that show up too often. They're just parking at the hotel for a few hours at a time. Maybe they use the restaurant, and that's how they don't draw attention."

"They?"

"It can't be a one-man job. There's got to be at least two. One to cover, one to grab. And maybe more vehicles." Mike pressed himself up from the prone position and knelt back on his heels. "Let's go indoors. I'm freezing."

Ian tried to keep the conversation going while Mike was climbing down the ladder. "You're not going to do anything dumb, are you?"

It took Mike the entire walk from the workshop to the back doors of the kitchen to reply. He ushered Ian indoors. "We never do anything dumb. We just take calculated risks."

"Can't you tell me?"

"Okay, we're going to surprise Dru on one of her visits, then pull her in. That's all you need to know."

It sounded crazy to Ian. Mike and Rob would end up being the ones in trouble. "Isn't that kidnapping?"

"Not by the time we've called the cops. It'll be fearing a robbery or home invasion. 'Well, look, officer, they keep showing up on the security cameras day after day, and she's already tried to con my neighbour for information.'"

"But she'll say she was nowhere near the house."

"We can lie. As long as the police question her, calls get made, and Weaver has to give reasons, I can unleash the lawyers. Weaver can never admit what their accusations really are."

Ian didn't think that would stop KWA for more than a few months. Maybe it was time to tell Mike what he was planning and appeal to his common sense.

"If I'm really worth that much money to them, they'll dump Dru and just try another route at a later date," Ian said.

Mike opened the fridge and rummaged in the shelves, taking his time. Ian wasn't fooled by the apparently casual reaction.

"Weaver would be crazy to do that after a brush with the police," Mike said. "But we'll deal with that if and when it happens."

"Look, if we haven't broken any laws, why don't I come clean? Then it's Kinnery's problem to explain. And Weaver's."

"Your life would be hell, and you know it."

Ian trod as close to the truth as he dared. It was hard to lie to Mike. "But I wouldn't morph. I'd just be a victim of medical malpractice or something."

"If they've got the nerve to take it to court, do you know how many years lawyers can string things out? And how much attention that'd focus on you?"

"Sure, but at least they wouldn't dare abduct me. That's exactly what Gran said. The most they'd win is the right to take a sample."

Mike sat down at the table and began picking at a plate of cold cuts and pickles. He gestured at Ian to join him. "I don't think you can imagine how bad things would get for you."

"But I wouldn't be locked up. Or missing."

"I'm responsible for you, buddy, adult or not." Mike reached out and ruffled his hair. "I know why you want to do it, and it's admirable, but it's not necessary. Besides, if you outed yourself, we'd get the flak too. Imagine the headlines. The Braynes, involved in all this. The media would go into a feeding frenzy."

Ian hadn't factored that in. He felt like an idiot. It was naive to think that there wouldn't be any fallout for Mike. Okay, so there had to be a Plan B. If Mike was going to lie and entrap Dru, then Ian could make it easier. He'd walk up to her, show her exactly what he could do, and lure her onto Mike's land. Maybe she'd even oblige by trying to grab him so he could call the cops himself. And then she'd have the choice of telling the police what she thought she'd seen and sounding like a psychiatric case, or keeping her mouth shut while Mike's lawyers trampled over KWA.

Mike would be angry for a while, but at least he'd never have to live like this again.

"I never get tired of turkey." Mike helped himself to a pickle.

"Want some?"

Ian checked his watch. If Dru stuck to her timetable, she'd be on the move soon. He needed to get to her before Rob did.

"I'll eat later," he said. "I'm not easily distracted."

I'm sorry, Mike. But you're not going to break the law for me. I can sort it myself.

Mike had a way of frowning that left Ian unsure if he was annoyed, hurt, or being sympathetic. The way his eyebrows lifted at the inner ends instead of puckering down sometimes made him hard to read.

"I should have had Dad come and pick you up," he said.

"Isn't that running away? As in not solving anything, just postponing it?"

"Yes. Yes, you're right. It is."

Ian relented on the cold cuts and got himself a plate. A little later, Livvie, Tom, and Rob came crashing back into the kitchen, noisy, breathless, and stoked up on adrenaline. Livvie pounced on Mike and grabbed him from behind his chair to bite his ear.

"Have you guys been in the gym?" he asked.

"Rob's been teaching me to punch." Livvie took a slice of meat off his plate. "Why haven't *you* ever done that?"

"Because I thought I was risking my nuts enough by training you to use firearms, honey. How's she shaping up, Rob?"

"Ready to move on to eye-gouging and use of broken bottles, I think," Rob said. "A natural."

Ian suddenly found it even harder to face what he had to do. It wasn't fear of whatever was going to happen to him. It was the risk of being cut off from these people, his friends, his *family*. But he had to do it. What was the worst that could happen? Dru told her story, the authorities believed her, and Ian was suddenly freak of the week. As long as he didn't morph in front of anyone else, though, the interest would eventually die down and he'd just be the kid with weird genes that didn't do anything. Kinnery and KWA would still be in deep shit. Mike would get some attention he didn't want, but that would die down in time too.

Better make sure I do this right, then. I don't want to put Mike through that.

Ian got up to go back to his room. "I'm going to catch up on some sleep," he said. "So that I'll be some use if you need me later."

"Yeah, too many late nights, mate," Rob said. "We'll wake you up if anything exciting happens."

Ian looked back for a moment to fix the memory of these people being happy together, and hoped that they'd forgive him for wasting the time they put into hiding him. He studied the photo of David Dunlop while he sat on his bed. He didn't feel such a fraud now. He'd inherited Great-Grandad's values, and now he could live up to them. A man didn't shirk his responsibilities.

He left his GPS watch on the nightstand so Mike wouldn't know where he'd gone and logged into the tracking site via his phone. Could Rob or Mike tell he had access now? If they could, maybe they'd think he was just watching. It was early afternoon and Dru's car was still at the hotel. When she moved, she'd head back to one of two places to park — the lay-by or the scenic trail.

So I'll wait in the woods. I can get to either location before Rob can. I can follow her on foot.

Ian knew where all the cameras and sensors were by now, and Rob and Mike had trained him how to move around terrain without being spotted. If you knew a location well, you had the advantage.

I choose the time and the place. That's how you do it.

His camo jacket was folded over the chair. Almost without thinking, he put his hand on it and watched the pigment well up and cluster in patches to match the pattern.

This was his tool now, no more than an actor putting on makeup. He'd walk up to Dru Lloyd and show her something that nobody else would believe.

Shape-shifting was a weapon after all. Ian was confident that he knew how to use it.

FOREST ROAD, EN ROUTE FOR WESTERHAM FOREST VISITOR CENTRE.

Dru had formed more of a plan today than yesterday, but it still fell short of being definitive.

There was no point in freezing her ass off at the side of the road day after day in the hope of getting lucky. So she'd play dumb. She'd park up and walk through the woods with her binoculars, climb over the flimsy fence, and if anyone stopped her, she'd claim she didn't realise she was on private land.

She still had one advantage; Mike Brayne didn't know she was here. If he did, she'd have known by now. Calls would have been made at high levels, Weaver would have been on the phone ordering her to back off, and the Braynes would have set their security on her. That was how these people worked.

As she drove the now familiar route to the forest trail, she was more worried about a biker behind her, drifting in and out of her blind spot as if he was trying to pass. *Moron.* He should have known she couldn't see him. She was tempted to turn left without indicating just to prove the point and see how fast he hit his brakes. *No, too much paperwork. It's a rental. I can't afford the excess.* She'd just slow down to make him pass her. When she took her foot off the gas and let the Sonic drop to under thirty, he swerved to overtake and roared off into the distance.

Yeah, didn't see any lights, did you? Watch the vehicle in front, cretin. There. I feel better now.

Dru carried on at her own pace and turned into the parking area. If any security cameras had picked her up returning each day, she was behaving perfectly normally for someone on vacation in a rural area without much by way of entertainment. For anyone who liked nature, it must have been fascinating. She didn't, and it wasn't. The natural world was best viewed on National Geographic from the vantage point of a comfortable sofa. She zipped her jacket up to her chin, pulled up the hood, and got out.

And there was the damn biker. Was he the same one who'd just tail-gated her? It was hard to tell. The bike — mostly black, nothing bright and showy — hadn't caught her eye. Bikers fell into two categories for her, either shiny and brightly coloured, or dull and dark. He was sitting astride his machine with the stand down while he studied something behind the fairing, probably his satnav. He was wearing a full-face helmet and a scruffy brown leather jacket. She half-expected him to pass a comment about her driving, but he didn't seem to notice her. She walked on.

The trick was to look as if she wasn't going anywhere in particular, just ambling east with the compass on her phone. A straight line looked too deliberate. She walked on a long diagonal, ready to brandish her booklets on identifying local wildlife. Movement caught her eye every few yards, but when she turned to look it was just a bird or a swaying branch.

According to her phone, she was now close to the boundary.

The crunch and snap of twigs nearby made her stop and push back the hood of her jacket to listen. There was definitely something moving around.

Oh God. What does a bear sound like? Do bears come this close to the road? No, it's a deer. It's got to be. I've seen them. I've seen the warning signs along the road. What do I do if it's a bear, though? Run? Freeze? Freeze.

Dru stood absolutely still, trying to scan for movement. Then her phone rang. She jumped.

Her goddamn phone was ringing in the middle of a forest, not her own cell but the burner. Her first thought wasn't who might be calling a number she'd only given out to a private detective and the guy at Dunlop Ranch, but that she had to silence it. She fumbled through her pockets, trying to grip it with gloved fingers, and didn't even get to look at the screen before she was suddenly aware of something moving just a few feet away.

Bear. Oh shit.

She swung around. But it wasn't an animal. It was a young guy in an army surplus jacket and a woollen beanie.

It was the same boy she'd seen walking his dog a day or two earlier. She was sure of it: dark hair and the kind of face that would mature into a good-looking man's as he got older. But she still didn't know how he'd gotten so close without her spotting him.

"Sorry." Dru wasn't sure what she was apologising for. She had to say something, though, and she still didn't know if he'd come from the Braynes' estate. "You startled me. I didn't hear you coming."

"Hi, Mrs Lloyd," he said. "Sorry about the phone. I had to be sure."

Dru's legs almost buckled under her. He stood waiting for a response to a question he hadn't actually asked. She could only blurt out astonished noises that sounded like answers.

"How the hell do you know me?"

"Same way as you know me, probably."

"I saw you out with your dog."

He parted his lips for a moment as if he was going to say something, then shook his head. "No, actually, you didn't."

She stared at him. She was sure she knew his face. It had to be that kid. "Are you Ian Dunlop?"

"That's why you're stalking me, isn't it?"

Dru had to brazen this out. Her pulse was going crazy. She was on her own and he didn't look harmless. Her instincts told her to run, but she had to see this through.

"So you're working with Kinnery." She hoped her voice didn't sound as pathetically afraid to him as it did to her. "How much did he pay you to carry the genes?"

"Ma'am, there's no *with* in this. I'm KWA's lab rat."

"What?"

"You people made me. From an embryo. I didn't volunteer."

He was just churning out *The Slide*'s half-assed story. Dru tried to go on the offensive. "What about the Braynes, then? What's that all about? You did a deal with them instead?"

"There's no deal. Don't you understand?"

"Nobody can create live human hybrids. I'm not stupid."

"Kinnery did. You want your property back, do you? Okay."

He turned around and started walking back towards the boundary. Dru had no idea what to do next. Should she try to stop him? *Photo. Check the photo. What's wrong with me?* She should have known the face in the mall video by now, but suddenly she didn't trust herself. As she fumbled in her purse to find the picture she'd printed, she followed him, afraid to lose him after all these months of chasing.

"Where are you going? Ian? *Ian!*" She picked her way between tree roots. "Hey, you've got stolen property."

He looked back, still walking. "I told you. I'm Kinnery's experiment. I didn't ask for this. You're going to be on my ass forever, so if you want it, ma'am, you come and *take* it."

"You want me to believe that garbage in *The Slide*?" Dru stopped dead. *Clever little asshole.* His buddies were probably lying in wait for her. She wasn't going to take another step. "Prove it."

"Prove what?"

"That you're a freak. A shape-shifter. Because I think you're just part of Kinnery's scam."

Ian stopped to stare at her for a moment, hands in pockets. His expression didn't quite make sense. He looked offended for a second, then disgusted.

"I think you believe it," he said. "Or else you wouldn't have ended up here."

And then he changed. God Almighty, his face *changed.*

His features shifted. His eyes faded to blue and his skin lost some of its tan. Dru couldn't breathe. Even though they were such small, *small* changes, he now looked totally unlike the kid she'd been staring at seconds earlier. *This* was the guy she'd seen yesterday, the one with the greyhound. Now she could see the difference. They were totally different faces.

"God," she said. "Oh my God."

Ian walked back towards her and let her take a closer look. She wasn't imagining it. It wasn't a trick of the light, either. It was so fast and complete that she started to doubt what she'd seen.

"There." He turned to walk off again. "You believe me now."

"We can't have done that. It can't happen." The more Dru blathered, the harder it got. None of the intelligent and necessary things she had to say could reach her mouth. Horrified confusion blocked their way while her shock got its questions in first. "Hey, you come back here."

Ian was about to disappear into the trees. She couldn't let him go now. If nothing else, she had to see him change again to really believe it. She ran after him, falling further behind and with no idea where this was going to end, but she couldn't turn her back on this and pretend nothing had happened.

"Ian, wait," she called. "Ian! You can't hide forever. Talk to me."

Dru snapped twigs and pushed branches aside trying to catch up to him. Then she heard thudding coming up fast behind her. She didn't even have time to turn around. *Bang.* A weight cannoned into her, winding her, and she was instantly on her knees, face almost in the dirt, fighting for breath with a gloved hand clamped over her mouth and her arm twisted up her back.

I'm going to die. I should have known. He's got buddies.

She tried to pull free and scream, but she was pinned. She was past the point of thought. There were just wordless ideas, animal ones, just *hand* and *teeth* and *bite.* She sank her teeth into the glove as hard as she could.

But the guy hung on. Dru found herself curling up instinctively, torn between trying to gulp in air and sinking her teeth in harder, struggling and unable to scream. Then something else crashed into her and the guy suddenly let go with a loud *oof* as the breath was knocked out of him. She gulped in air.

It was Ian. He'd come back for her.

She scrambled to her feet to see him beating the crap out of the guy who'd jumped her, one hand raining punches while the other stabbed with a crowbar in a rapid staccato. It was fast and savage.

The man — taller, broader — looked like he was fighting for his life. Ian reached out to pull off his helmet.

That was when the guy's hand went into his jacket, and Dru saw both the pistol and his shocked face.

The man in the hotel. The Chrysler guy. It's him

Perception was supposed to slow down at times like this. Now things were running too fast for her to take in. Ian grabbed the man's fist, pistol still in his grip, and twisted the wrist outwards without even breaking the rhythm of his punches. It was simultaneous, almost choreographed, as if Ian had rehearsed this all his life. Something black and oblong went flying from the gun into the undergrowth

Dru had never seen a real fight at close quarters. It didn't look at all like the cop show version. She'd always thought she'd pitch in and help, too, but by the time she'd worked out where she could land a blow — it was only seconds, she was sure of that — Ian threw the guy on the ground and started kicking him with the same oddly detached ferocity as he'd punched him. Damn, he was *fast.*

"Come on, move." Ian turned and grabbed her wrist. "I need your keys."

For the first time, she realised he'd changed back to himself. She ran and stumbled, dragged through the trees, dodging branches and with no idea where she was heading.

"How the hell did you *do* that?" She was panting already. "How can you fight like that?

Ian let go of her wrist for a moment. He had the pistol. She hadn't even seen him take it. He dismantled it as he ran, lobbing one part into the forest.

"I released the magazine. Glock. Easy." He hurled another part into the undergrowth and grabbed her arm again. "This is in case he's got a spare. I don't want it found on me."

"Nobody's that fast." It almost took her mind off his shape-shifting. "And you're a hell of a lot stronger than you look."

"I train. *Keys.* Come on." Ian now had the short crowbar in one hand. She hadn't seen where he'd stowed it. He would have made an amazing card sharp. "I'll drive."

Dru ran her guts out and stopped trying to work out how Ian functioned. Everything hurt. She wasn't fit, but her legs pumped regardless and refused to stop. Branches snagged her hair. The only thing in her mind right then was what people would think if they saw her like this. Was she covered in blood? Was Ian?

She could see the trail just ahead. Ian slowed down and looked back for a moment.

"Just walk now," he said. "Nice and calm. We don't want to look conspicuous."

Dru struggled to get her breath. She shook off Ian's hand and felt in her pocket for the key. "Where is he?"

"Not behind us. Come on."

People were coming out of the visitor centre and others were sitting in their cars. If the biker caught up, he couldn't do anything in front of witnesses. *Oh God, is he working for Weaver?* Ian took the key and helped her into the Sonic, then backed the car out of the parking bay and drove off as if nothing had happened. He only picked up speed when he was fifty yards down Forest Road.

"Are you hurt?" he asked.

"I don't know." Dru was still bewildered by his strength and speed. "Are you?"

"I'm fine. Don't worry about me."

The next minute was the worst of her life and somehow the most intense. She wasn't dead. The world was clearer, sharper, *brighter* than it had ever been. And there was no biker behind them. She was sure that weird elation wouldn't last.

"Who's he working for?" Ian asked. "He's been following you every day."

"I wasn't followed." *Oh yes I was. I must have been. It's got to be Weaver.* "Have you been spying on me?"

"That's rich, ma'am. It really is. There was a guy in a blue Chrysler minivan. Is he the biker?"

Dru could hardly think straight. "Yes, I think it's the same guy."

They were already at the entrance to the Braynes' house. It seemed to have taken seconds. Ian turned in and raced up the drive.

"Don't worry, the house is secure," he said. "It's the safest place to be."

Dru could see the front door of the farmhouse and a guy running across the turning circle out front, coming straight for the car. He skidded to a halt in their path and aimed a pistol two-handed right at the windscreen. It didn't take much lip-reading skill to pick out the word *stop*. Then he jerked the pistol upright and swore. *Fuck* was easy to lip-read, too.

Ian slammed on the brakes, stopped dead, and got out. Dru could hear him calming the man down.

"Sorry, Rob. We've got an armed guy after us. Biker. Okay? Sorry."

"Jesus Christ, Ian, I can't see past the bloody reflection on the windscreen. I could have blown your head off."

The guy looked furious. And he was English, with an accent Dru wouldn't forget in a hurry. So this was her mystery phone man. This was Rob.

He stalked around to the passenger door. "Get out and put your hands on the roof, ma'am."

Her legs were shaking so much that it was harder to stand still than she thought. He patted her down while she tried to work out what was happening. Normally she would have been outraged by a strange man touching her, but she was just grateful that he hadn't shot her. She heard running footsteps.

"Everybody okay?" The guy who peered into her face was Mike Brayne. She recognised him. Everything was slotting into place now. "Get inside. Quick."

Rob grabbed Dru's arm and frog-marched her to a side door. "Move the car, Mike. Ian? Are you hurt? What the hell were you thinking?"

Dru couldn't make her legs obey. She almost tripped over the metal frame at the bottom of the door. Shock had set in. If Ian hadn't tackled the biker, she would have been lying injured or dead in the forest, and nobody would have known where she was. No job was worth that.

"He saved me," Dru snapped, suddenly offended. Maybe Rob really was Kinnery's bodyguard. He certainly looked like one. "That asshole out there has a gun."

"Yeah, and you led him here, didn't you, love?" Rob snapped back. "So until you prove otherwise, you're complicit in this. Got a lawyer?"

SEVENTEEN

I'm trying to trace any surviving veterans who served with my great-grandfather. He was a helicopter pilot. I never knew him, but I wish I had. Where do I start? What information do I need to provide?

Ian Dunlop, in an initial letter to a Vietnam veterans' group found on the internet.

CHALTON FARM, WESTERHAM FALLS: 1630 HOURS, FRIDAY, 90 MINUTES AFTER THE ASSAULT.

It had been so long since Mike had yelled at anyone that he couldn't actually remember it.

There was no point in shouting at Ian anyway. Mike had understood how his mind worked since the day he and Rob walked into Dunlop Ranch and saw all those movies on the bookshelves, Maggie Dunlop's definitive illustrated guide to being a Proper Man. Proper Men threw themselves on grenades to save their buddies. Mike should have seen it coming. It was pure Ian. He'd almost warned Mike what he was planning.

And he left his GPS watch as a decoy. I didn't even know he was gone. How can I trust him now?`

Mike examined the Sonic in the garage, groping underneath for the tracker while Ian watched. The damn thing was definitely there. It was still transmitting.

"So she's seen you morph," Mike said. "You think the biker did, too?"

"He must have been following her. So yes."

"No sign of anyone else? No van?"

"I don't think so, sir."

"I'm still *Mike*, buddy. I'm not angry."

"You should be. I didn't see him. I should have."

"I know you did it for us, but you really have to stop and leave it to me now."

"It could have worked."

"Maybe. But we don't quit. We hang in there and we finish the job. And if you're going to work with us on contracts, you follow orders or you'll get us killed. You're suspended until you can show me you can do that. Okay?"

Ian took it calmly. It was strictly commander to subordinate, not a dad grounding a son, a more dignified and adult sentence.

"Yes, Mike."

"Ian, it's not just KWA you have to worry about if you're exposed. You think you wouldn't be useful to anyone else? To another company or country? Most wars are about economics and trade, one way and another. Maybe all of them."

It was hard to tell if Ian realised that. It was better to give him a good reason than to rely on obedience.

"Okay," Ian said. "Fine."

Mike still couldn't find the tracking unit. He slid underneath the vehicle, knocking flecks of dirt and grit into his eyes. It had to be accessible: Rob had slapped it on the car in seconds. Ah, there it was. Mike felt something just under the rear bumper and pulled it off.

But it didn't look like the model he'd bought. He checked again and found his own tracking unit. Someone else was playing the same game, then, probably the biker. Mike almost switched the thing off, but decided to leave it so that it looked like it hadn't been found. The guy on the bike hadn't been on the radar, and Mike still didn't know where the van fitted into this, even if Dru said the biker was the same guy who seemed to own it.

"Okay, she's telling the truth." Mike got to his feet and blew the road dirt off the device. "She didn't know he was tailing her."

Ian examined his right palm, flexing his fingers. "Yeah, she was really scared. She wasn't acting."

"Are you going to tell me exactly what happened?"

"It's like I said. I morphed into Tom in front of her and walked off to make her follow me here so that you could call the police.

But this guy came out of nowhere and grabbed her. So I punched him, hit him with the crowbar, got his pistol off him, and we ran for it."

"Just like that."

"Yeah." Ian probably didn't want to sound like he was boasting. "That's about it."

"I need the detail. Help me work out who we're dealing with."

"Okay, I heard someone go down. That's why I turned around. I think he put his hand over her mouth so she wouldn't scream. There were people out walking, and screams carry." Ian had that defocused look of recall, gazing at the Sonic's hood, then shut his eyes for a moment as if he was trying to concentrate. "I don't know why he didn't just shoot her, but maybe he meant to kill her silently so that I didn't know he was right behind me. I dragged him off her and punched him to keep him busy while I tried to grab the Glock."

"You realise how crazy that was?"

"It's okay, I released the magazine. Well, it was the way I grabbed it. It seemed like a good idea at the time. Don't worry. No fingerprints. I was wearing gloves. I broke it down and scattered the parts anyway." Ian shrugged, suddenly looking like an embarrassed kid. "That's about it."

His matter-of-fact delivery was oddly endearing. Mike wasn't surprised that he'd laid into the guy, but his calm analysis in a split-second crisis was almost breathtaking. If Ian had amazed Mike, he must have been a hell of a shock for an attacker who thought he'd targeted a woman and an average teenager.

"He could have killed you," Mike said.

"Then he'd have done it on the spot. I'm worth more alive. Anyway, I couldn't just stand there and do nothing, could I? I reacted. I was on automatic. Like you and Rob trained me to be."

How did Mike argue with that? Ian didn't panic and he didn't run. He took control of the situation and beat the bastard. This was the guy you'd want beside you on the battlefield. Mike tried to find the balance between telling Ian how proud he was and not encouraging him to take more insane risks.

"This guy either makes mistakes or he didn't want bodies." Mike patted Ian's shoulder. "But for what it's worth, that took serious guts. You were awesome. You're still suspended, though."

Ian nodded. He didn't look pleased with himself at all. He

seemed to be working out how to do things better next time. "Sure. Sorry."

"And don't tell Rob you morphed into Tom. I'll handle that when everyone's calmed down."

"But you know why I did, yeah? She thought I was him. It got her attention."

"I know. But let's forget it for the meantime."

Mike hoped that had taken the sting out of it. He also hoped Dru was suitably grateful for Ian's intervention. That would put her in a more cooperative frame of mind.

This wasn't how Mike had planned it, though. They now had a hostage they really didn't want. Rob was keeping an eye on Dru in the guest cottage, making sure she had no contact with Tom in case she mentioned Ian's morphing. She couldn't go back to the hotel while the biker was still unaccounted for, and Mike couldn't call the police until he was sure she was willing to stick to the script he was going to give her.

Every minute he delayed made it harder to explain why he hadn't called 911 right away. He was probably past the credibility threshold now. It had taken him half an hour to find the spot where Ian said the gunman had been. There wasn't a trace of him.

The good news was that Dru was now Mike's to command, whether she realised it or not. She couldn't go back to KWA after all this. She was a single mom with bills to pay, and he was a man who could pay an awful lot of bills. There was only one sensible way out for her.

"Go sit with Livvie and Tom while I talk to Dru," Mike said. "And you *will* stay put unless I call you. Understood? Or I'll handcuff you to the goddamn furniture."

Ian still looked worried. "Mike, have you ever really lost? Has anything gone so wrong for you that you couldn't put it right?"

Ian's questions weren't usually rhetorical or oblique. If he asked, he wanted a factual answer. *Have I ever lost?* Mike knew life had dealt him every possible winning hand: vast privilege, loving parents, health, looks, intelligence, and the ideal woman he'd only needed to smile at to win over. He had few friends, but both of them had been there for him when his life was on the line. He hadn't been able to have the children he'd wanted, but at the bleakest moment of accepting it, he'd been handed someone else's kid to look after, a boy who needed everything that Mike was uniquely placed to provide. No, either he'd never lost, or he only recalled the upside of whatever happened to him. He wondered how he'd deal with failure. Perhaps he wouldn't even recognise it. Maybe he couldn't see that it had already happened, and Ian had been right about what was necessary.

"I think I have a deal with karma," Mike said. "I try hard not to be the asshole my money could have made of me. It's worked so far."

He felt as if he'd gone through the entire cycle of fatherhood in a few months, from bewilderment at encountering a stranger he had to get to know and look after, through pride at seeing him develop and learn, to struggling with the idea that Ian had a life to lead and a mind of his own to direct him. It was surprisingly painful. He took Ian downstairs to the den and gave Livvie her orders as quietly as he could. Oatie shadowed her like a nervous ghost, pressed close to her legs.

"Ian doesn't leave this room, okay?" Mike said. "If he wants to take a leak, you stand outside the door. I'm going down to the cottage. The alarms are on."

Livvie patted the pocket of her jeans, indicating the outline of her Glock. "Nobody gets in or out. Don't worry."

"I'm so sorry, honey." He put his arms around her and kissed the top of her head. "Things are going to get back to normal, I promise. I'm going to see how hard I need to lean on Dru to shut her up."

"It's her word against Ian's."

"And the other guy's, unfortunately."

"But if Ian won't morph, who can prove he ever did? Tell Weaver he's made a very expensive mistake and sue his company back to a neighbourhood drugstore."

"For what? Assaulting one of his own employees?"

"This is blackmail. Either you face it down or turn it back on them."

Livvie could always cut to the chase. She was right. It was two-way blackmail. Mike reset the alarm as he left the house and jogged down to the cottage. The security light blinded him for a moment. Rob opened the front door to let him in.

"How is she?" Mike asked.

Rob shrugged. "Considering she's been shocked shitless twice in an hour and she can't work out if she's been kidnapped or given a bodyguard, I'd say she's okay. Her mouth's working just fine. Can we worry about the bigger problem, please? The fucker who's stalking all of us now."

"What's she saying, then?"

"Nuremberg defence. Only following orders. She didn't know anything about freaky experiments and doesn't want to go down with the ship. Anyway, I've taken her phones, so she bitched about that. But I think it's dawned on her that she's served her purpose for Weaver and she's now surplus to requirements. A liability, even."

"I found a second tracker on the Sonic. That's got to be his. I'd say she's well out of the loop now. I left it switched on, so as far as he's concerned, we haven't found it."

"But you don't kidnap someone on a bike," Rob said. "He's got to have mates on standby with that van. I'd want at least four to pull off a snatch like this, and a lot more observation time. Is Weaver on a budget or something?"

"Perhaps this guy was just doing recon when he saw Ian morph and decided to go for it. He's got to realise how much that's worth. And he thought he just had to deal with a woman and a kid. Nobody knows how tough Ian is."

"Yeah, but a pro would have slotted Dru right away. It's easier and it makes the other target behave."

"I figured that. Maybe Weaver said no bodies. I'm going with Ian's theory that he thought he could snap Dru's neck and sneak up on Ian. Still risky, though."

"Maybe he's not Weaver's man. We haven't ruled out another company being involved."

"Only KWA knew enough to follow the clues. No, it's got to be Weaver."

Rob kept looking at his watch. "Let's sort out Mrs Gobshite, then, so we can call the cops if we need to. If the biker's still logging that GPS, slap it on my car and I'll tool around to see who shows up."

"Maybe he didn't actually notice Ian morphing. People have missed it plenty of times before."

"I'm not sure if that helps the situation, mate. Whoever this bugger's working for, he's probably already called it in. We could have a dozen more armed bastards out there now."

Mike had to deal with Dru first. She could put Weaver in a

difficult enough spot to finish him off, and maybe that would be enough. "Okay, let me talk to her."

Rob opened the living room door. The floor-length vertical blinds were drawn. Dru sat huddled in the china-blue wing chair, clutching a mug, with a plate of untouched cookies on the coffee table in front of her. Rob was thorough with detainees. Her bag lay on the sofa at the far end of the room along with her coat. She had to get past him to go to the bathroom, and nobody could see her from the outside. It all looked like tea and sympathy, but she was being held in isolation. Mike pulled up a chair to sit facing her while Rob leaned against the kitchen doorframe.

"I'm Mike Brayne," he said. "But you know that. May I call you Dru?"

"Sure, if I can call a lawyer. Or the police."

Mike understood the *Mrs Gobshite* tag now. "Do you need one? I think you'd be better off with an employment attorney to sue KW-Halbauer for nearly getting you killed. I found a tracking device on your car."

Dru's touch-me-if-you-dare expression flickered for a split second. She'd obviously grasped how close she'd come to an unceremonious end.

"You think he was working for my boss, then."

"Would there be a business rival involved?"

"I don't think so."

"Are you sure?"

"As sure as I can be. I'm strict about need-to-know, and not even the people I work for needed to know some of this."

"Then your boss used you as a gun dog to flush out the game for someone else," Mike said. "What a stand-up guy."

"Isn't he just."

"Does he know exactly what Ian is?"

"If he does, he certainly didn't tell me." Dru stopped and looked genuinely awkward for a moment, as if she'd detached from her own predicament to stare at something even worse. "If I'd known that boy was an experiment, I wouldn't have gotten involved. I thought this was just industrial espionage."

Maybe she was indicating that she'd negotiate. The fact that it was a classified project was almost nothing compared to the effect it would have on the company, and Weaver would seize the first scapegoat he could find: Dru. Mike could see that dawning on her.

You've finally realised you can't go back to the office again, haven't you?

"We've tracked you, Dru. From the time you called Rob on an illegally obtained number to the time you checked in at the Byway." Mike tried not to sound hostile. Dru kept glancing at Rob as if she was expecting him to step forward and give her a slap like they were running a good-cop-bad-cop routine. "Has Rob summed this up for you? We're completely legal. You and your company aren't. If you want to make a fight of this, fine. My family has the resources to make Shaun Weaver regret the day he started it. But I'd rather resolve this in a way that lets Ian have a normal life without the media turning it into a circus. Do we understand each other?"

Dru looked resigned. "He's quite a kid. And I don't just mean his skills."

"Exactly. He's a boy. Not a commodity. I don't care how many people could be saved by whatever treatments that kind of biotech might make possible — it won't save *him*. So I need your complete cooperation. Think of Clare. What would you want for her? You don't owe Weaver a damn thing, but you do owe her."

Dru's expression hardened. Maybe Rob hadn't mentioned just how much information they had.

"I bet you're going to offer to help," she said. "And I bet you have a price."

Dad had taught Mike that there were always deals to be done, and the best ones locked people in by giving them what they needed most and couldn't afford to lose. The more mutually beneficial, the more binding the agreement would be. Livvie always told him he was too soft for his own good. This wasn't soft. It was prudent and a lot less trouble than violence. Mike wasn't his great-grandfather.

"You help me kill the rumour for good," Mike said. "You say what I tell you to say, and then you forget you ever saw Ian. All your money worries are solved just by doing the moral thing. If you don't do it, you fall with Weaver."

"Do you even know what money worries are? I'm a single mom with a mortgage, an asthmatic daughter who'll be going to college, and an ex who doesn't keep up his payments."

Maybe Mike hadn't made himself clear, or perhaps she didn't really grasp the kind of resources he had at his disposal.

"You can have a secure job, your mortgage paid off, and a good education and medical care for Clare," he said. "Or you can walk out of here now, ring the police, tell them your side of it, and see what they believe. If Ian won't morph, though, all you'll have is a guy with some odd genes and weird skin cells."

Everyone went quiet. Rob made an annoyed rumble in his throat and went to switch on the kettle. "Tea," he said. "Won the war, that did. Anyone take sugar?"

Dru was now staring into an empty mug. She was either looking for the catch or unable to take in what relative financial freedom meant.

"And how are you going to explain why I'm here in the first place?" she asked.

Mike didn't like the ease with which his lies emerged. "Oh, you were trying to set up a discreet meeting with my father away from D.C. so you could ask him for more names from Ringer to pursue leads. Weaver wouldn't like you troubling senators, so you didn't tell him."

"That simple, huh?"

"Yes. That simple."

"Do I get to see Ian again?"

"Why?"

"To thank him."

"We'll see." Mike didn't have an agreement from her yet. He took out his phone and keyed in the Byway's number, ready to press the call key. "It's not safe for you to go back to the hotel. I'll go pick up your things if you call and let them know I'm stopping by later. You can stay here."

"That's the only contact number my family's got," Dru said.

"You might as well switch on your cell, then." Rob put three cups of tea on the table. Mike couldn't tell if he approved of the deal or not. "It's not as if nobody knows where you are now, is it?"

"I'll pick up the hotel bill," Mike said. Dru opened her mouth, presumably to protest, but he held up his hand. "I'll make the call and you verify it, okay?"

It solved the problem of making the hotel staff suspicious, but it also put Dru firmly on his payroll if anyone checked the records. He wasn't sure if she'd realised that or not.

"Okay," she said.

Mike waited for the Byway to answer. "Hi. I'm calling on behalf of Mrs Lloyd, room thirty-two. Someone's going to collect her belongings and settle her bill later this evening. She needs to check out sooner than expected. I'm going to put you through to her now."

Mike held out the phone. Dru waited a couple of beats, then relented and took it, avoiding his eyes. She made apologetic noises of agreement to the receptionist, explaining that her plans had changed. Then she rang off and handed the phone back to him.

"My daughter used to tell me I was KWA's *kapo*," she said, as if she despised herself for giving in. "Selling out the other camp inmates for crumbs and a few more days of life."

Mike knew that he had her now. To make sure, he'd ask Ian to show her the letter that Maggie Dunlop had left him to explain that he wasn't crazy but that he'd been lied to all his life. It would either demonstrate she was smart to abandon KWA and save herself, or appeal to whatever sense of decency she had. Mike didn't mind which prevailed.

"Actually, you haven't sold out anybody," Mike said. "Ian gets to go free. Now, do we have a deal?"

Dru didn't look at all triumphant. Maybe the thought that Weaver had used her and put her life at risk was poisoning what should have been welcome news.

"We do," she said at last. "Because my kid comes first."

"Good," Mike said. "Because so does mine."

CHALTON FARM: 1655 HOURS.

"I never knew you were such a crafty bastard." Rob sat in the cover of the small propane store at the back of the cottage, watching Mike fiddling with his phone in the dim light from its screen. "You got her to take the Brayne shilling. She'll have a hard job claiming she's not on your payroll."

Mike shrugged. His hands must have been bloody freezing. "I'm not the one who took her wallet, got her bank details, disabled her phones, and shut down the telecom in the cottage, am I?"

"What can I say? I'm a pro."

Mike did a tight little smile to himself, but there was no humour in it. "Well, she can't change her mind. On Monday she'll have a few thousand in her account that she wasn't expecting to see. Let's say it's to show goodwill. People respond better if they don't feel they've been screwed over."

"Goodwill, spelled *f,r,a,m,e,d*."

"Or proof that I keep my word. And when I find her a job in one of our companies, we'll be able to keep an permanent eye on her. She can choose whether she sees that as being compromised or winning the lottery."

Rob was relieved that there was a ruthless streak in Mike after all. He deployed it in the same way he turned from nice guy to knife-wielding bastard when threatened. Still, Dru was doing a lot better out of it than the last Nazani guy who'd pushed his luck with him.

"Good man," Rob said. "A chip off the old block."

"I don't want this scheming to become a habit."

"You realise Saint Michael's already trademarked, don't you?"

Mike managed a smile. "Twat."

"You called me a twat. You *never* say twat. You must be feeling more positive."

"Thanks for not punching me out for ruining Tom's visit."

"I know how crucial this is for you, mate. I can punch you some other time." Sometimes Rob caught glimpses of the other Mike, the one who came from a parallel universe where people did things differently. It wasn't bribery. It was more like a weary realisation that the root of most problems was a need for money, something Mike could fix as easily as other blokes changed a tyre. "Well, we can't sit here like spare pricks all night. We better move her to the house, or else we'll be spread thin covering two locations."

"What about Tom?" Mike asked. "She might blurt it all out."

"I'll hint that you're the lovely bloke who gives her money and I'm the total bastard who'll put one through the back of her head if she says one word out of place."

"I think she believes that already."

"Yeah, I blame all your Septic movies where the Royal Marine's always the psycho. Thanks. We love you too."

"You're kind of intimidating when you put on your war face."

"I'll smile nicely, then. I can always lock her in the staff apartment." Rob checked the camera feeds on his phone again. "Oh, and when you pick up her stuff, check her electronics. Especially her laptop or cameras. You know. Any images we need control of."

"Thought of that."

"Your dad's going to be proud of you. When are you going to

call him?"

"When this is over and deniable."

Rob went back into the cottage. Dru watched him as if she was working out where she'd shove a bread knife if she got the chance.

"I think you'll be safer in the house, love," Rob said, careful not to spoil Mike's hearts and minds job. He hoped she wasn't one of those miserable cows who objected to being called *love* or *sweetheart.* "It's easier for me to secure one location. Just two rules, though."

"Go ahead."

"My son's staying at the house. Tom. Don't mention Ian's morphing in front of him. He doesn't know about it. And keep the blinds drawn in your room. It's ballistic glass throughout, but there's no need to make things easier for that bloke out there, is it?"

Dru nodded, not exactly the picture of gratitude that she should have been for a woman who was still alive and a lot better off. Well, at least she wasn't screaming and whining. Rob admired anyone who could shut up and deal with shit. If this was her first encounter with an armed scumbag, then she was doing well.

"He's very clever, your friend," she said. "He *is* your friend, right? Not your employer."

Rob bristled, not sure if she meant brainy clever or sneaky clever. "No, we're mates. He's got a first from Oxford."

"I always try to understand personal dynamics. I can't guess how you met."

"Not at Oxford, but you probably worked that out." Rob picked up her bag and coat. "Hostage rescue. Africa."

"You really are soldiers, then."

"Private contractors these days. That's what we do." Rob decided to be conciliatory. Dru wasn't really the enemy, and Mike was right; people were more cooperative if they didn't feel they'd been humiliated or fucked over. "Look, you didn't lose, so don't feel bad about it. You did a bloody solid job. We're pros, so we know another pro when we see one. You tracked us down, you didn't make many mistakes, and you didn't burst into tears when things went to rat shit. We respect that."

Dru nodded and picked up her coat. "Thanks. I'll mention that at my next job interview."

Rob and Mike covered her, close protection style, all the way to the house. She looked embarrassed.

"Is this necessary?" she asked. "He's not going to have a sniper position out there."

"Why not?" Mike said. "We've got one on the roof."

Rob couldn't tell if she believed it or not, but she didn't comment. Mike went in to check where everyone was and whisked her through to the living room while Rob corralled Ian and Livvie. They left Tom downstairs, playing a game and under instructions to stay put.

"I've warned her to keep her mouth shut about Ian, Mrs Mike," Rob said. "I don't know how long we're going to have to keep her here, but we'll minimise contact. Can you handle her?"

"I can," Ian said. "Leave her to me."

"What, like you handled her earlier?"

"It worked, didn't it?"

"She didn't need to know you could bloody well morph."

"She wouldn't have followed me otherwise."

Livvie stepped in. "Guys, please. I'll stand by to slug her if her lips start to form the S word in Tom's presence."

"I'll brief him. As far as I can."

Tom didn't seem particularly engrossed in the game when Rob opened the door, but he didn't look up from the controller. He was just avoiding asking questions. It struck Rob that it was always going to be like this now. He sat down on the sofa and ruffled Tom's hair.

"How are you doing, Little Matey?"

"You haven't called me that since I was about ten."

"You'll always be Little Matey to me."

"So what's happening? Okay, you don't have to tell me. Just give me my orders."

"Mike's bought her off," Rob said. "He's going to the hotel to pick up her bags. We've moved her back here so I don't have to run my arse off trying to secure two locations. We'll keep her locked down until we find the other bugger. Or buggers.."

The look on Tom's face asked why anyone had bothered to buy off Dru at all, but he didn't say it. "You're sure there's nothing I can do?"

"You could forgive me for ballsing up your trip."

"I just want to hang out with you. I've really missed you."

Rob's guard was lowered by fatigue, and the one thing in life that could always make him tearful was Tom. "Oh, for Chrissakes. You've made a grown man cry. I miss you too."

"Dad, I don't want to know if this is protecting Ian's identity in some custody battle or inheritance dispute." Tom seemed very specific. It was his way of saying he thought he'd worked out that it was precisely that. "If it helps, why not just wheel me out and say 'Look, this is my son, that's who you saw, now go away'? It's easy to prove who I am. Give her a few hairs from both of us for DNA and tell her to piss off."

"It's not that simple." *To put it mildly.* He couldn't tell Tom that she'd had plenty of time to study Ian's face. "She's met Ian."

"But it might be. There's an experiment where they switched people in the middle of a face-to-face conversation that was interrupted by a guy walking between them with a sheet of wood or something. Half the test subjects didn't even notice that everything about the person they'd been talking to had changed. For a species with so much brain devoted to vision, we're totally crap at noticing real detail. And even if she thinks she knows his face, she saw him under extreme stress. Victims get police line-ups wrong."

"Well, she's not the problem now. To be fair on her, she's just the hired help. It's the guy who came after her that I need to worry about."

"Okay, then give the hair to him."

"He's armed, Tom. This is past the talking stage. And I don't want you handing out your DNA."

"I'm documented like a pedigree bull. So are you. It goes with the territory."

Maybe it really is that simple. But let's see what Weaver does next, before Leo finds out and rips his balls off.

"Come here, kiddo." Rob hugged Tom tightly for a long moment and realised he still had that same wonderful, familiar smell he had as a little kid, a clean skin scent with all the body chemicals that marked him out uniquely as Tom. Humans could still sniff out their kin even if they didn't consciously know it, Livvie claimed. "I love you, son. I'm sorry I had to involve you in this. I'll never forgive myself."

"Come on, Dad, it's bloody brilliant. I'm in a billionaire's house, using his private jet, drinking his cocktails, and having a murder mystery weekend, only it's real. And nobody actually dies. How cool is that?"

Tom was a born diplomat. He wouldn't have said if he was scared or upset. But Rob needed to know the truth.

"Do you feel I'm putting Mike's problems before you?"

"Never. Abso-bloody-lutely never. I know what you've been through to give me all this. I'm more worried about you."

"Kiddo, I promise you it's nothing dodgy."

"And I know you weren't pleased about GCHQ."

"Tom, I'm proud. I swear I am."

"You don't like it."

"It's not a matter of liking. I'm just scared of that kind of stuff."

"Dad, I did it because I can't ever be like you. I'm never going to be Action Man. But I'm good at what I do, and if I do it right, blokes like you won't have to die and lose limbs in foreign shit-holes. And I accept there'll always be things I don't need to know and won't be told."

Rob wasn't sure whether to be mortified or proud to the point of bursting. It was terrible to think he'd shaped Tom's choices that much. He wasn't convinced that they'd make a blind bit of difference to troops on the ground, but he'd die before he told Tom as much.

"This'll be over soon." Rob still had a grip on Tom's hand and couldn't bear to let go. "How about taking the Jag for a spin next week? Mike and Livvie want to buy you a car for Christmas, so start thinking about what you want."

Tom laughed. "This is unreal. I'm glad you and Mike haven't fallen out over this."

That was Tom all over. He didn't miss a thing. He could sense the tension.

Mike left the house at eight and told everyone to start dinner at nine if he wasn't back. Rob had discovered long ago that Livvie's dinners weren't girly domestic duty. She cooked and presided over meals like a cross between a High Court judge and Boadicea, defying those at the table to turn down anything she put before them. It was another expression of her authority, Mike said, and she was exercising that authority now. She called everyone to dinner — her favourite cassoulet, real rib-sticking stuff — and sat Dru next to her, facing Tom.

"This is Tom, Rob's son," Livvie said. "Tom, meet Dru Lloyd."

Rob watched Dru's face as she nodded at Tom and then glanced at Ian with a split second of surprised recognition. Rob braced.

"I saw you out walking the dog," she said. "The greyhound."

It was the look at Ian that did it. Rob would have to ask her later what she'd been thinking, but he could guess. She was doing a comparison. She hadn't said exactly how Ian had changed when he morphed. Rob could work it out for himself now. He certainly didn't want to watch Ian do it, because he'd never see Tom the same way again, and he'd feel totally robbed of a face he loved. He couldn't explain it. He just had to know that Tom was Tom, and no other face would ever remind him of his boy except Bev's.

"Yes, Oatie's very well-behaved," Tom said. "He's Ian's."

Rob almost choked with guilt. He *needed* Tom to keep secrets from him now. He wanted him to even the score. It would make it easier for Rob live with his own secret and compartmentalise it.

Ian joined in the conversation and talked about Oatie being scared of the sheep on the ranch, and Rob came as close to an out-of-body experience as he thought he'd ever get without incurring a head wound. There was no hint at all that this wasn't a normal dinner where people who didn't know each other swapped stories to break the ice. There were no shape-shifters, no wars, no moneyed classes, and no armed kidnappers waiting somewhere in the dark. Mike walked in about ten minutes into the meal and sat down as if it was a normal evening. Rob's surreal meter peaked.

"I put your bags in your room, Dru," Mike said. "No messages at reception, but you might want to call Clare."

Rob had Dru's SIM cards. He slipped out to find her bag and put them back in the phones. When he checked her personal cell, it was showing missed calls.

Mike caught him in the hall. "There's no sign of the bike or the van at the hotel," he said. "We still don't know if we're dealing with a guy who keeps the bike in the van, or two separate units. Anything on her cell?"

"Missed calls," Rob said. "One number withheld."

"Better get her to check it's not Weaver, then."

Rob went back into the kitchen and put the phones on the table in front of Dru. "You want to check that one, just in case? Might be Clare."

There was no way of knowing if the biker had called Weaver and let him know where Dru was. If Rob had been her, he'd have been more worried about her kid, halfway across the country with her ex. She cleared her plate and went out into the hall.

Mike followed. Rob strained to hear, trying not to catch Tom's eye. Livvie, telepathic as well as terrifying, gathered Tom and Ian to usher them out.

"Downstairs, *now*," she said. "I'm going to kick both your asses in the game of your choice. I'll bring the dessert."

Rob followed Mike and Dru into the living room to keep an eye on things while she checked her e-mail. "Yes, I need to reply to Clare," she said. "She might ring back."

"Anything else? No Weaver?"

"There's a withheld number. But he'd usually mail me."

She tapped out a message while Mike watched. Rob wondered how they'd keep her secured here for more than a day or two, because it was clear that it was going to get tedious even in a big house. How long would it be before they could risk sending her home?

She sat looking at the phone for a few minutes, a little lost. Then it rang and she made a disappointed *unnhh* sound.

"It's not Clare," she said. "Local number."

"Give me a couple of seconds and put it on the speaker." Rob held his own phone close enough to record the call. "Go ahead. Answer it."

"Mrs Lloyd?" a man's voice said.

"Yes?"

"We both got a hell of a surprise, didn't we?"

Dru was steady under fire. Rob had to give her that. "I have no idea what you're talking about," she said, expressionless. "Who are you?"

"You don't need a name. Our mutual associate didn't tell either of us what his asset could really do, did he? He certainly didn't tell me, or I'd have renegotiated my terms. So why don't we compare notes? I can find a market that'll pay a lot more than he's paying either of us."

Mike was right in Dru's eyeline now, mouthing prompts at her. She followed them. Rob could only watch.

"I don't know what you mean," Dru said carefully. "Are you the asshole who assaulted me? How did you get my number?"

"You could have cooperated and let me take the kid."

"Why don't I call the police and let them talk to you?"

"Oh, I don't think you want the cops involved. Look, I haven't told anyone yet. It's just you and me for now. Or have you done a deal with your rich buddies instead?"

"Did Weaver give you my number?"

"I know where you are now, and where you live. Think about it. You can't hide him forever."

Mike indicated to cut the call off. Dru showed him the number on the call log.

"Either he's dumb or that's a payphone."

"I'll get the number checked," Mike said.

Dru looked like she'd remembered something unpleasant. "A car was hanging around our street before I left. Clare got the plate. I bet that was someone Weaver sent as well. Like the guy said, he knows where I live."

"She's with your ex, so the urgent question is whether this tosser knows where *he* lives." Rob was impressed by Dru's lack of panic. "Is he going to be any use if this bloke's mates come knocking?"

"Larry's in marketing. He's not even the same species as you guys. I'll ring him now, but he'll do the full drama queen act and call the police."

Mike took over the conversation, all quiet reason. "I'll make a call and get security to watch Larry's home. He needn't even know. Just give me an address."

"Who are you going to call?" Rob asked. "Brad?"

"He's got plenty of contacts. He can always find somebody at short notice."

"That's my *kid*." Dru was getting angry at last. "My daughter. Does that mean anything to you?"

"Nobody's going to lay a finger on Clare or anyone else," Mike said. "Sit tight and let us do our jobs. Larry's address, please. And the car's plate if you've got it."

Rob opened the security room doors and sat down to watch the screens while Mike disappeared to make calls. When Mike came back, he had a couple of extra phones. He put one on the console in front of Rob.

"All done," he said. He was wearing his thin-lipped angry look. "Brad's getting someone out there right away."

"Are these things breeding?" Rob examined the phone. "Burner?"

"I don't want any more activity on our own phones. And that *was* a payphone call, by the way. It's the hotel one. It's even in the directory."

"So this is another scenario we didn't predict."

"What is?"

"That Weaver would send a heavy and not tell him what Ian really was. That's bound to piss a bloke off."

"I don't think Weaver knew he could morph at all. Even Kinnery doesn't know how good he is at it."

"Yeah, but our biker friend won't believe that, will he?"

Mike pulled up a chair. "I'm not sure that call puts Weaver in the frame."

"Does it need to?"

"It would be handy to have something solid to lawyer up with."

"Look, let's worry about Biker Boy first. It's clear he saw Ian morph. He still knows what he knows, even if Weaver calls it off and forgets it. And where's his backup, and that van?"

"If he's keeping this to himself, he might be cutting accomplices out of the deal as well as Weaver," Mike said. "He's been told that Ian's just a mule. He's seen for himself that it's way more than that. There's a market out there and he knows it. It's probably not Weaver we need to worry about. It's whoever else the biker offers Ian to."

"How does he think he's going to get Ian out of here, though? And why call Dru?"

"He must still be watching. He realises we haven't called the police, because he's seen no activity. He knows we don't want attention."

Rob didn't like guessing, but they had nothing else to go on. "He probably thinks we're scared, too, and Dru's a way of testing the water. He's still working out the rest. Just like we are."

"I doubt he's aware of you. He knows I live here, though."

"But if he knows you're minted, he probably thinks you're soft and useless. So he'll underestimate what he's up against."

"He'll still need to make sure I don't have a security detail. If I were him, I'd assume there was one."

Rob watched a deer tiptoeing through the trees to the rear of the house, clear as day in infrared. "He'll need to get close to the house, then."

"So we watch and wait for him to come to us. Because he hasn't got forever, either. He'll watch to see if we try to move Ian. There's only one way out for a vehicle."

"Then what?"

Mike started going back through the day's recordings. He'd made up his mind to do something. Rob knew that look. The only way he could describe it was that Mike looked resigned to being someone else for a while, the Mike he didn't seem to like very much.

"I don't think I'll be buying him off," Mike said.

Rob could only nod in agreement. Whatever Mike had in mind, Rob was now committed to going along with it.

CHALTON FARM, WESTERHAM FALLS: 0155 HOURS, SUNDAY.

It was nearly 0200, and Mike found himself on the point of calling Dad to ask him to bring the full weight of his wrath to bear on Shaun Weaver. The house had been in complete lockdown for nearly 36 hours. He'd had enough.

But the moment passed, and he snapped back to normal. This was the result of his own decisions, and he'd deal with them himself. Beds, once made, had to be laid upon. He'd chosen to give Ian a home and now he had to live with the consequences. It was just fatigue and a disrupted body clock talking, making him cold and hungry despite a warm house and a stomach still full of last night's dinner.

I used to be more resilient than this.

He varied his sweep of the security monitors to keep himself alert: left to right, then up and down, then a diagonal pattern. When he heard quiet footsteps, he looked up expecting to see Ian. But it was Rob. He put two cups of tea on the narrow console.

"We shouldn't both be up, Zombie," he said. "There's nobody to relieve us. Stick to your watch."

"It *is* my watch. You're the one who's up early."

"So I am." Rob produced a packet of cookies. "At very least, he's got to watch the drive to see if we panic and try to move Ian."

"And he knows we've got something to hide and that we're constrained by it. Everything we don't do confirms to him that we can't act."

Rob glanced at his watch. When he didn't have car mirrors to look at, he fell back on checking the time. "Nearly thirty-six hours since the contact. You think he'd be worried that we could play dirtier than him, what with your dad and everything."

"The longer he sees nothing happening, the more sure he is that he's got a chance."

Rob sighed. "He's doing what we're doing, Mike. He can't tell anyone else what he's up to, his plans have gone to rat shit, and he's trying to come up with a new plan on the fly."

The switch from *Zombie* to *Mike* was usually a significant pointer to Rob's mood. Mike couldn't war-game this any longer. They'd just have to assume the worst and react accordingly. But he was sure of the one fixed point the biker had to plan around. If he lost track of Ian, the guy had nothing. So he'd still be watching.

Slip out the back? He knows we don't have a rear vehicle access. It's easy enough to check on a sat map.

Ian came downstairs around 0230 and stood watching the monitors with them for a while. Mike reached behind his chair to prod him.

"Go back to bed, buddy. Nothing to see here."

"I can't sleep."

"Then read. But go back to bed."

Ian trudged off again. Rob drummed his fingers on the console.

"He morphed into Tom, didn't he?"

That explained the use of *Mike*. "Does that piss you off?"

"A bit."

"I'll have a word with him when this is over."

"I'm not knocking him. He's a good lad. He gets stuck into a fight and he keeps his head."

"He's what we made him, Rob."

"And what Maggie made him." Rob fidgeted. "Tom said he only went for the GCHQ thing because he couldn't be like me."

"No shit? Wow."

Maybe that was Rob's real issue. It was a heavy responsibility. Mike knew how it felt to be an adoring son who felt he wasn't capable of following his father.

"If he doesn't like the job, will they let him leave?"

"It's not a life sentence, Rob. Even real spooks get to resign. He's an IT man."

"Just checking."

Mike called up the map of the estate on one of the monitors and re-checked lines of sight to the driveway and front door. He was thinking about the calls he'd have to make on Monday to set up transport, finance, and a new job for Dru when one of the movement sensors blipped. Rob pounced on the camera feeds closest to the sensor and put the images on the screens.

"Wait for it to pass the next one," he said.

It took a few minutes before another sensor was triggered. Mike plotted the camera positions and the direction of movement against the sight lines. The NV filter gave a brief glimpse of a human shape moving, but the infrared showed very little, just the hint of a hot spot at head height. The position was less than a couple of hundred yards away.

"So he can't wait any longer," Rob said. "He's getting in bloody close."

"Can you see a weapon?"

"If he's got anything bigger than a pistol, it's under his jacket. He must have some thermal barrier. It didn't look like a clean outline to me."

"Foil blanket with a cape over the top. I've done that."

They couldn't see anything now. The next camera and set of sensors didn't catch the guy, so he'd either stopped within that area or moved off his predicted path.

"Well, we know roughly where he is," Mike said. "Wait one."

He trotted off to the utility room to pick up his plates, jacket, and radio. His Glock and his AR-10 were already out of the locker and loaded. With NV goggles and handheld thermal imaging, he could move around quietly and easily. When he got back to the security room, Rob was marking up a sheet of paper.

"I think he's in this square," Rob said. "I'm going to kit up now."

Mike checked the camera positions again. "No, keep an eye on the monitors and talk me through it."

"You better leave this to me. Stay here and protect the house in case he's a decoy and he's got mates on standby. He's not going to try again without some extra precautions."

"No. I've got this."

"If anything goes wrong, your dad's going to get the blowback."

"I can buy my way out of anything. But if you get pulled in, then it's still on file and it could catch up with Tom one day."

"Don't make me say that I'm better than you at this shit."

"I don't care if you are. This is my responsibility."

"This isn't about your hang-ups, Mike. It's about getting a fucking result."

"I said you're not doing this."

Rob ignored him and lifted his sweater to tap his ballistic vest. "I've already got my party frock on. Take the roof and watch for backup vehicles."

He got up to go, but Mike blocked his path. "You're not listening to me. My problem. I'll deal with it."

"Come on, stop dicking around, mate." Rob wouldn't listen. "Move it."

He just caught Mike with his shoulder, a friendly shove with a little insistence behind it, nothing he wouldn't have done on deployment. Mike reacted blindly. He pinned Rob flat against the wall. He regretted it instantly.

"Whoa, steady, mate," Rob said. "Relax."

"Sorry." Mike was mortified. He let go, embarrassed. "Leave this to me. Take the roof."

Rob looked bewildered. Mike had never done anything worse than swear at him and then apologise immediately. He didn't even think he had the physical edge to take Rob. If he'd been anyone else, Rob would have flattened him without a second thought.

"Come on, why not just call the cops and get it over with?" Rob asked. "He's on your land. We've got enough."

"No. The bastard's *seen* Ian. I'll deal with it. Stay on the radio and update me. No phones. Got it?"

Rob held his hands up. "Okay, mate. Keep your kecks on."

Mike adjusted his earpiece and slipped out through the side door before putting on his NV goggles. He'd deal with it, all right. This wasn't going to escalate. This wasn't going to continue one more goddamn day. It was going to end here and now.

He had to think what he'd do in this guy's situation. A pro might have the same equipment as him — night vision, thermal imaging, the works — and set up alarm trips to protect his back, even if it was just beer cans. He could have marked an escape path through the trees with IR light sticks. Mike would have to skirt all the way around and approach at an angle from the side to conceal his position, working from tree to tree.

"Got eyes on yet, Rob?"

"Yeah. I keep losing him in the trees, but he's getting bloody close to the power box."

The main power supply came in about a hundred yards from the house. Yes, that was what Mike would have done, cut the power first. The emergency generator would eventually kick in, but the guy wouldn't know about that. Either way, Mike was pretty sure that this was no longer surveillance. The biker was getting ready to break into the house.

Mike paused by one of the security cams and swapped his NV goggles for his hand-held thermal optics to check again for the guy's backup, but there was nothing. He held his breath to listen for movement to make sure.

"I think he's going for the power box, for definite," Rob said. "I would."

Mike switched back to his goggles and kept moving towards the power box one tree at a time. "Stand by to distract him before he cuts the power. Garage doors open, lights on."

"I'll start the Jag on the remote. He'll think we're shifting Ian. I'm moving down now."

Mike still couldn't see the biker. He shifted position using the power box as a reference point and tried the thermal again.

Got him.

A patch was moving slowly between the trees. It was the partial outline of a face. The guy might have had a thermal lining to disguise his outline, but he hadn't used anti-thermal camo cream to obscure exposed skin. The small patch of heat was enough to give him away. Mike could see him in context now, ahead and to his right on a diagonal line from behind, and switched back to his NV goggles to leave his hands free.

He couldn't see a weapon. But he knew from the set of the guy's shoulders that he was holding a rifle.

But I want a reason. I need a reason.

The man was still heading for the power box, stopping intermittently to check out the house. He'd probably cut corners on the anti-thermal cream because he hadn't planned for anything like this. He might have been tasked to just observe for a few days. Then he realised he hadn't been told the whole story. Mike moved forward until he was level with the guy and sighted up from about sixty yards.

The man was checking out the power box with a faint light. It would take him a few minutes to get it open and cut the power without zapping himself. Mike watched him crouch to slip off the cape or whatever he'd draped around his shoulders and ease a daypack off his back.

"Rob, I need a diversion. Whatever you've got, buddy. *Now.*"

Mike aimed the AR-10 and found himself thinking dumb thoughts about the line between self-defence and assault. But he knew he'd pull the trigger the moment he saw a weapon, before his conscious mind even finished processing the image. He wanted this to be clean and unambiguous, *his* version of clean. This wasn't Iraq or Nazani or anywhere he could walk away from and forget. This was his home. It would be tainted forever anyway, but there were degrees of contamination.

He adjusted his aim. His earpiece popped. "In position," Rob said. "Five, four, three, two — *go.*"

The lights flared and the garage doors made a faint whirring sound, then the Jag rumbled into life. The guy jerked his head around to look. Mike saw him stand from a squat and bring up a rifle to aim at the garage in one movement.

Endex, you bastard.

Mike fired, hitting him from the side. The guy spun but didn't fall. Adrenaline kept him going long enough to turn and aim at Mike before two more shots put him down. He dropped to one side and stopped moving. It was over that fast. It didn't take long to change the course of two lives.

Mike paused to check for movement before closing in with his AR-10 trained on the body, looking for the rifle or another weapon.

"Rob, I'm okay. Checking."

He had to sound as if he'd fired in a state of fear, just a homeowner afraid for his family and property. The radio's only security was its short range. His story still had to be watertight. *One down* or *clear* would have sounded a little too much like a planned execution if anyone else out there could hear him.

"Roger that," Rob said. "On my way."

"Do *not* move. Wait, out."

Mike flicked on his tactical light. The man's left arm was flung out to his side and his right was folded back towards his head. The rifle lay a yard away. Mike could see two dark patches of blood, one spreading just below the guy's collarbone and another at the side of his chest below his arm. There was a head wound as well, but it looked like a graze. He squatted to check for a pistol. There was bound to be another one somewhere.

Shit. The bastard was still breathing. His eyes opened.

Fine, Mike had an excuse now for touching the body, and the police wouldn't wonder why he pushed the rifle well out of reach, opened the man's jacket, or patted him down. They'd think he'd tried to give first aid.

Pistol? Check. Plates? Yes. But they don't quite cover every angle, do they, buddy? Phone? Nothing. Where's your damn phone?

Mike stood outside himself for a split second and hated the completely detached, rational, calculating Michael Brayne who crouched over a man who lay dying while he thought through every move and precaution. The guy was struggling for breath, still conscious.

"Who sent you?" Mike wanted to hear the name *Weaver.* He took out his burner and pressed the recording icon. He couldn't hand any admission to the police, but he *had* to hear it and know he hadn't imagined it. "Who's paying you?"

"Bastard," the guy choked. "Saw it."

"Who, me? Weaver?"

"You. Fucking Guard?"

It was an odd answer. The guy was going down fast. Mike had seen it once too often. "Just tell me who sent you."

"Weaver. Asshole. Liar."

"Thank you."

And here I am, thanking the guy. You're right, Rob. I'm weird. I should call the police now. I should be shaking. I shouldn't be focused on getting information I can't use.

But what now? He was bloodied, clutching a phone, and a man was dying in front of him. The guy had seen what Ian was. He'd talk, if not to Weaver then to someone else. Mike had passed the point of doing deals. He should have put a round through the guy's head to save him from gurgling out his last moments like this, but he couldn't pull the trigger. He hoped it was because he couldn't bring himself to do it. But the thought uppermost in his mind was that he had to call the police, and that meant he had to let the injuries take their course.

Look at me. Look at the cold, ruthless, has-to-be-done Mike I've got lurking inside. So much for doing good deeds.

Dying seemed to take forever. Mike stepped back a few paces to wait, appalled at himself but in no doubt what he had to do. Eventually the ragged breathing became a regular, rapid choking noise, then it stopped. Mike squatted again to check for a pulse.

It was over at last. "Rob? Rob, I've shot someone."

Mike waited and switched off the radio. Rob came crashing through the undergrowth, a flashlight beam stabbing ahead of him. He looked down at the body, then angled the light at Mike.

"Is he browners, then?"

"Yes. No pulse."

"Well, forget the shovel and the bag of lime. Before we call the rozzers, let's check. Bruises? Ian punched the shit out of him, remember."

"They won't look fresh," Mike said. "Thirty-six hours. Besides, we don't have marks on our hands, do we?"

"Other suspicious shit?" Rob checked him over with the flashlight. "Okay, let's have your plates and vest and anything that looks more than a basic self-defence set-up. Goggles are normal for Yanks, yeah?"

"Yeah. Good call." Mike fumbled with his jacket. *Would I have thought of all that?* "Thanks."

"That's it. You can call nine-one-one now. Then call your dad. *Carefully*. Like it was public. And let him do the lawyering up."

Mike handed Rob his burner. "Put this in my safe." He took out his registered cell, the one that would now be linked to the 911 call forever. "I'm sorry, buddy."

"No problem, mate. Whatever you do, I've got your back. Just give me my script."

"Tell Livvie I'm okay, will you?"

"Will do."

Mike could now see himself as two personas on a parallel path, the everyday Mike who was disturbed by all this and the fact that Rob was so calm about it, and the necessary Mike who still had things to do to shut this down for good. He wanted Nice Mike to come back, but not just yet. Cold Mike still had work to do. Nice Mike could return when he told Rob the full details, because he was damned sure he'd need to when it all sank in.

"Hello?" Mike took a breath when the dispatcher answered and recited the litany he'd learned as a child, filling in the gaps that had once been about traffic accidents and medical emergencies. "I need police and EMS. I've shot an armed man on my property. My name's Michael Brayne and the location is twenty-seven-sixty-three Forest Road, Westerham Falls. I think the man's dead."

Minutes into the aftermath, Mike was already calculating the lies and omissions he'd need to build and maintain to keep Ian out of this. And he still didn't know who else was out there, waiting.

Ian was right. One way or another, it would never be completely over.

EIGHTEEN

I need to see you, Shaun. I plan to be at your offices in Lansing on Tuesday afternoon. Make yourself available. It won't be a long meeting, but I insist we have it.

Leo Brayne, in a message to Shaun Weaver, KW-Halbauer.

MAINE STATE POLICE BARRACKS, PORTON: SUNDAY, 1430 HOURS.

TV shows always made it look like armed misunderstandings were bagged, tagged, and filed away in an hour, but like everything else on screen, it was a bloody lie.

Rob was still in a quiet office at the cop shop, explaining what he'd seen. Mike was somewhere else with the lawyer summoned by Leo. The Braynes could conjure up a high-powered brief on a Sunday morning, possibly their most impressive superpower.

It was almost like old times, though. Rob was practised in answering questions in the right way and giving a dispassionate account of a hard contact, service style: some iffy-looking vehicles in the days leading up to the incident, alarms tripped, attempts to investigate, firearms brandished, shots fired. And that was how it went down, honest, officer.

Actually, it was. It was all a matter of where you put the emphasis.

"You sure you don't want your lawyer, sir?" the trooper asked. "You don't even have to be here, but if he's around, he's welcome to sit in."

"No need," Rob said. "We just want to get this sorted. It's pretty traumatic for our families. Anyway, Mike's dad called him."

"And you're certain you don't know the man?"

Rob was never sure how good he was at lying these days. There were lies people knew you were telling and that you were expected to tell, like saying you hadn't been deployed somewhere when everyone had seen it on the news. Then the spectrum passed through the borderline lies to full-on grade-A porkies. Cops, like sergeants, always thought they could spot a liar, but tests proved they were no better at it than anyone else. It was just thinking that they might be that made guilty bastards confess.

"Never saw him before today," Rob said.

The trooper kept looking at Rob's hands. "No altercations with anyone in the days before, sir?"

"None." It had to be about the bruises on Biker Boy. Rob's hands were unmarked. "Not even cutting someone up in traffic."

"Just covering all the angles. The deceased was carrying tools that support your fear that he was going to cut the power, so with all the firearms and plastic cuffs it probably was an attempted home invasion. But it's worth ruling out people with grudges. Including business grudges, in your line of work."

"Look, the man's bound to have a phone," Rob said, doing a little fishing. "Can't you check that?"

"We're checking everything, including firearms licenses and fingerprints."

Rob couldn't tell if that was an answer or not. "The only blokes we've offended enough to pay us a personal visit have names like Hussein."

"Well, in the meantime, it's probably wise to maintain your security. If he had accomplices, they might be dumb enough to come back another time." The trooper was a nice enough bloke. If he was baffled by Mike's lifestyle, then he wasn't showing it. "So if you get more problems, call *us*, please. I understand that highly trained guys like yourselves deal with situations automatically, but that's what we're here for."

"Thanks, officer," Rob said. *Should I call him trooper?* "Honestly, Mike's not a Masshole or whatever you Mainers call rich buggers.

He just stays off everyone's radar and tries to be ordinary."

Rob could have sworn the trooper was trying not to smile. "I never use the term myself, Mr Rennie," he said. "But I understand your point."

While Rob waited for Mike, he occupied himself by working through the timetable. The crime scene people would be off-site by the evening, and the post mortem would be done tomorrow, but the follow-up would probably drag on for a bloody long time. That was going to take its toll on everyone

It didn't alter the result, though. Some bastard took his chances against Mike and lost.

Rob looked up as Mike, the laywer, and another trooper came down the passage, talking quietly. Mike could usually slap on a collar and tie and look stylish even with two days' stubble and a hangover, but today he just seemed crushed, as if his supply of idealistic Boy Scout optimism had finally run out. Scott, the legal polecat, fussed around him. He didn't look happy either. Rob's spine stiffened.

"Anytime, officer," Mike was saying. "Just let me know if there's anything else you need."

Scott whisked them out to his car and Mike settled down in the back as if he was planning to doze off. Rob kept an eye on him in the rear-view mirror.

"Any further questions go through *me*, Mike," Scott said, following the signs to Westerham. "Don't agree to an interview without me. Not even a phone call."

"Okay, Scott. I get it."

"You didn't need to volunteer to come down here. And you didn't have to offer them your clothing for forensics."

"They're welcome to look at whatever they want. I just want to get this over with." Mike closed his eyes. "They're not even planning to charge me. Deadly force in self defence. You were there. You heard it all."

"Fine, but when they ID the body, there might be more questions."

"Then I'll answer them."

"Have they found the vehicles?" Rob intervened to draw fire. He couldn't tell if Mike didn't like Scott, his advice, or lawyers generally. Perhaps it felt too much like being told off by his lawyer sister. "He must have driven or ridden something."

"Still looking," Scott said.

The conversation died. Mike was silent all the way home, either staring out the window or eyes shut as if he was asleep. The biker bloke was dead and Dru was stitched up tighter than a kipper's arse, but this definitely didn't feel over. Maybe it never would. Mike should have made Ian change his surname on his official documents right from the start. Clinging to your identity was all very well until it hung you.

When Scott dropped them off at the house, the crime scene people were working in the grounds and a police car was still parked at the end of the drive. Livvie loomed on the doorstep and beckoned Mike with her forefinger.

"*You,*" she said, ushering him upstairs like an angry warrant officer. "Hot bath, Scotch, and then get some sleep."

"And ring your dad," Rob called after them. "No rush."

Now he had the chance to get away for a few hours without feeling he'd abandoned Mike. He'd drop in to talk to Mr Andrews later. The poor old sod must have thought the Martians had landed. Tom was out on the lawn, throwing sticks for Oatie, who really didn't seem to be into retrieving.

"Where's Ian?" Rob asked.

"With Dru. In the conservatory. Is he safe with her?"

"Yeah. She's okay. Livvie's ready to gut her if she steps out of line. Come on, kiddo, let's take the Jag out."

"You sure that's appropriate right now?"

"What, lack of respect for the dead?" Maybe Tom was a bit more shaken than Rob had thought. "I need a change of scenery for a few hours. So do you. Let's go to Westerham. You can drive back."

Rob parked in the square and showed Tom the posh supermarket and bookshop. They ended up having cakes in the French patisserie that Ian was partial to. Rob pointed out the girl behind the counter as Ian's unrequited passion.

"She looks friendly," Tom said.

"Is that a polite word for *old slapper*?"

"No, she just looks approachable. Is Ian too shy to pounce?"

"Something like that." It seemed like a natural time to be nosey. "You never told me if you had a girlfriend. I keep hinting."

"You never told me if *you* did, either."

"Plums, kiddo. Zero. I couldn't get a woman now if I dipped

myself in chocolate. It must be the smell of desperation about me."

"Okay. I'm test-driving a few candidates."

Rob was relieved. All was well in the world. "That's more like it."

"But there's one I really like, and I can't tell her where I was this summer. And there's one I met at you-know-where, and I sort of like her too, but not as much. On the other hand, I don't have to lie to her. And that's suddenly become a big deal."

Tell me about it. Rob tried to remember a time when everyone he knew could tell each other anything and not worry. He wanted to tell Tom that he knew better than he could possibly imagine how that felt.

"If you meet the right girl, you'll be able to tell her eventually," Rob said. "Anyway, she'll guess when you buy a house near you-know-where."

"Mike told me that Livvie went ballistic when she finally found out he was seriously minted."

"Well, 'Hi, I'm a billionaire, fancy a shag?' isn't the most auspicious start to a romance, is it?"

Tom extracted a piece of kiwi from his fruit tart and laid it on the side of the plate. "What do *you* tell women?"

"I struggle, kiddo. I say security and they think mall guard. I say contractor, and they think I'm Bob the Builder. I miss being able to just say *Marine.*"

"You blokes should reclaim the M word among yourselves. Mercenary. Stuff the legal definition. Make it cool again. Like the N word. Or Q word."

"Ah, it all helps people to ignore the body bags, doesn't it?" Rob looked up as Ian's pash came over to clear the cups from their table. She gave Tom a long look. *My boy. He's perfect. You noticed. And you were all over Ian the other week.* He handed Tom the key card. "You want to drive?"

"Ooh. Please."

"Lush, innit?"

"*Nice* motor."

"You could have one. Remember Mike and Livvie want to get you something."

"Yeah, and remember I'd have to park it in Newcastle." Tom looked extra-serious for a moment. "It's a shame Mike's having all this hassle. He's such a nice guy. Am I reading the runes right? Is Ian a permanent fixture now?"

"Pretty well."

"I'm glad. They certainly behave like a family. If it wasn't for the colouring, I'd think he was their biological son." Tom couldn't have known that Ian could match any colour swatch he fancied. "I don't ask questions, but from what Ian hints at, he's had the luckiest dog rescue in history. From whatever freaked him out so much to Mr and Mrs Perfect-Goldenballs."

"There's got to be one happy-ish ending in the world," Rob said. "Let's go, kiddo."

Rob picked up a couple of boxes of pastries to take home and basked in the warmth of Tom's delight at driving the Jag. This was when the trappings of money really mattered. Tom was never going to end up in a poxy bedsit or doing ten-hour shifts in a supermarket. This was what everything had been for.

The police car was still parked up when Tom approached the entrance to the drive. "Pull over, kiddo," Rob said. "Hearts and minds time." He jumped out and handed a box of pastries to the trooper sitting behind the wheel. "There you go, mate. I'll bring down some coffee later. You must be freezing."

He got back in, satisfied that he'd played it right. Tom carried on up the drive.

"You're still a class act, Dad."

"It doesn't do any harm to be affable. And you have to feel sorry for the poor sods on the front line."

"This is the life, though. Preferably minus the homicide team."

"Look, why don't we get hideously drunk tomorrow after Mrs Gobshite's gone home?"

"Dru? Aww. I quite like her. She read psychology. Interesting woman."

I'll bet. "She's had a profitable weekend."

"She's very wary of you."

"I'm losing my touch, then. I hoped she'd be fucking terrified."

They laughed it off and Rob let the subject drop. He felt sorry for Dru, and he had to admire her guts. In different circumstances he might even have sidled up to her in a bar and tried his luck, but he wasn't going to turn his back on her in a hurry now. For the foreseeable future, she was a threat that had to be monitored.

He found Mike looking a lot better than he had earlier. That might have been because he was asleep. He was stretched out on the sofa in the living room with his tie askew, both hands locked around a cut glass tumbler of Scotch balanced on his chest. It looked to be mostly melted ice. Livvie peeled his fingers off the glass and extracted it with slow care. He didn't stir.

"Where's Dru, Mrs Mike?" Rob whispered.

"She's in the den with Ian. He's showing her his gran's letter."

"Oh, Christ. Bad idea."

"No, reinforcement. She's very aware of what he's been through now. Shame can be as powerful as cash."

"But not as powerful as a smack in the mouth."

"True. But now she can't claim ignorance as a defence, either."

"Okay. I'll keep my nose out of it."

"Don't worry, he hasn't told her everything. He's not that naive."

Rob marvelled at how they'd all managed to last a couple of days at close quarters without anything leaking in the wrong direction. He wasn't sure if that degree of secrecy and need-to-know was a healthy sign or not. It was a skill each of them needed to perfect, though.

Mike woke up just before dinner and padded around aimlessly from room to room, looking lost. Eventually he sidled up to Rob and jerked his head in the direction of his study. He wanted to talk. When he shut the door behind them, it was clear that this was going to be raw stuff.

"I could use a confession," he said.

"You haven't discussed whatever this is with Livvie, then."

"No. And it might end up being a burden on you. So I won't be offended if you say no."

"If you can't tell me, who can you tell?" Rob couldn't refuse. He didn't want to, anyway. This was the nuts and bolts of friendship. A bloke had to be prepared to share the load if a mate needed support. "You feel bad about jobbing Biker Boy, don't you? I told you to leave it to me."

"It's more than that. Can I tell you why?"

"Go ahead."

Mike took out his burner. He held it gingerly like it was smeared with nuclear waste and cued something up. "Are you willing to listen to this?"

"Delete it, whatever it is," Rob said. "I'll listen first, though. What is it?"

Mike stopped, really *stopped*. It was the only way Rob could describe it. He just froze. He didn't breathe, he didn't blink, and he didn't even twitch for a few seconds. He was looking past Rob at a point on the carpet as if someone was standing there.

Then he got up and opened the door. He didn't seem to want to hear it again. "I can't. Just play it."

Rob took a few moments to work out that he was listening to ragged breathing and hoarse voices, Mike and the biker talking. The biker sounded as if he'd said *seen it*, which might have been about Ian, and then *fucking guard*, whatever that meant. Maybe he didn't know who Mike was and thought he was security, or maybe he knew a lot and was surprised that a National Guardsman had got the better of him. But he'd finally said *Weaver*. Mike thanked him. The breathing went on for a while, getting more wheezy until it stopped, and then there was a couple of seconds of rustling and clicking before the recording ended.

Evidence. Good work, Zombie. I bet your dad's going use that wisely.

It was never pretty watching someone gasp away the last few moments of their existence, but Mike, all titanium casing with a marshmallow core, must have found it bloody hard to stomach.

Rob stuck his head out of the door. "I'm done. Are you going to give this to your dad? Good insurance."

Mike frowned at him as if he'd played the wrong bit. "What?"

"Okay, it's grim. But clear."

Mike almost pushed him back into the room and shut the door. "Rob, I let a guy bleed out. I stood and watched. I didn't even have the grace to finish him off. And you think I'm going to let my father hear that?"

Mike could be bloody tedious when he was set on blaming himself. It was hard to tell if he was just knackered or on the point of tears. Rob had to let him talk it out.

"How much did you edit this?" Rob asked. "Is this the lot?"

"Yes." Mike shook his head. It was hard to tell what he was rejecting. "I started recording when I went over to check him. Don't you get it? I questioned a guy who was dying, just to hear Weaver named."

"Cops do that."

"*I don't.* I have to be better than that."

Sometimes Mike could be set straight with a pat on the back, but occasionally it took a hard kick up the arse. Rob plugged in his headphones so that Mike didn't have to suffer the audio again and replayed the section to time it. The clock on the screen showed just under two minutes to the point where the bloke sounded like he'd died. Rob had heard the first shots while he was waiting outside the house. The time between then and reaching Mike couldn't have been more than three minutes, maximum. Mike just needed to crunch the numbers and get a grip.

And it was bloody good shooting. Rob decided not to point that out, but he'd managed to target the exposed spots around the body armour.

"Mike, even if you'd had a helo standing by, he wouldn't have made it to a hospital in time," Rob said. "Look at the timings. What does he weigh, twelve stone? More? Say one-seventy pounds. Under tree cover. You pick him up to carry him out to an LZ and get him on the helo, and he's probably dead before they've got a line in him. Two, three minutes. He was as good as dead the moment you pulled the trigger."

Rob was prepared to admit that it was probably tougher from Mike's perspective than his own. Mike didn't look convinced.

"But I couldn't finish him off," he said.

"Course not. A close-range headshot at that angle wouldn't have looked too clever when the cops showed up, would it?"

Rob didn't let himself think what would have happened if the bloke had survived. He hadn't. It was hypothetical, which was another word for unhelpful as far as he was concerned.

Mike nodded and put one hand over his eyes as if he was rubbing them. "That's exactly what I thought at the time. And that's why I fucking hate myself. I went through all this callous calculation about what I could and couldn't do so that I left everything forensically tidy. Neat and tidy. Me and my tidy goddamn life."

"You just won't let yourself win, will you?"

"I went out armed." Mike sat down at his desk and slid back in the big green leather chair. "I executed him."

"You might have missed. There's an element of luck in this."

"I didn't go out thinking I was going to detain him."

Rob had been here before with Mike. It just seemed to be part of his decompression process. "Jesus, Mike, what do you think he'd have done if you hadn't squeezed one off first? He'd have put one through *you*. He had a job to do — get Ian, nothing else. That means you, Livvie, me, Tom, we'd all be collateral damage, and

God only knows where Ian would have ended up. So you think he'd have listened politely to your case and thought, 'What a decent bloke, he saves orphans, he's kind to animals, and he does a lot for charity, so I think I'd better apologise and be on my way.' Really?"

"You know what I mean."

"Would you have fired if you'd been sure he *wasn't* armed?"

"No." Mike's answer was instant. "But I don't know if that's my morality talking, or the fact that it would have been harder to justify to a court."

"As far as he's concerned, it doesn't matter if you blew his lungs out after careful moral deliberation or a negligent discharge. He's still in the morgue."

Rob needed to keep repeating the obvious to Mike until he started to believe it. Mike had shot an armed bastard planning to do harm. People wouldn't ask why he didn't rush to get the bloke medevacked. They'd applaud. All that mattered was that whenever the shit hit the fan, Mike's training always kicked in and he got the job done calmly and competently, even the dirty bits. He saved his angsting for later. It was bound to be harder when the enemy was literally in your back yard, a direct threat to your family, and you had to lie about the root cause of it all. But Mike would see that he'd done the only thing that he could. It would just take time.

Anyway, the biker should have come back another day with a better plan and waited for reinforcements. But he hadn't. Rob might have done the same in his position. It was tough shit, and nothing personal, just the way things were.

"I'm psyching myself up to tell Livvie," Mike said. "We've never had any secrets."

Rob found a decanter of Scotch in the cabinet and poured Mike an extra-large one. "She won't bat an eyelash. Your dad won't either."

"He'll have to filter it for Mom." Mike held the tumbler up to the desk lamp. "Damn, I'm drinking too much these days."

"This is what drink's for, mate."

"You know that four or five months ago, that guy was *us*?"

"I don't recall tooling up to shoot anyone who got in our way and dragging some kid off to a lab to have needles stuck in him."

"Actually, I remember it being pretty ambiguous until we hauled Ian back to the ranch and talked to him."

Rob had run out of things to say for the moment. He poured

himself a drink and sat with Mike to keep him company. Sometimes that was all he needed.

"Call your dad. He needs a sitrep."

"Yes, I have to find out what he wants to do about Weaver."

"I don't think Dru's told him to ram his job yet. Have you got a script for her?"

Mike looked sufficiently distracted from his anxiety to make Rob feel he'd achieved something, even if it was temporary. "She's a good liar, but I don't want to push my luck," he said. "I was thinking of getting her an attorney to do the leg work to extract her pension and so on."

"Does she need it?"

"It's hers. Why shouldn't she have it?"

"Actually, I meant our problem, not hers. You know. Explaining why she came here."

"Oh, right. Dad's best placed to broach the subject with Weaver. Then she can just coast in behind on the shockwave."

"Your dad's got a PhD in Applied Bollocking. What's he going to tell Kinnery?"

"The minimum he needs to stay out of trouble and not drop us in it, I expect."

Mike didn't drain his glass. He stood up, took off his tie, and seemed to notice the creases in his shirt for the first time. "I ought to dress for dinner. I need to lavish attention on my very patient and perfect wife. Any other woman would have left me and dragged me through the courts years ago."

"As long as you remember that, mate. Go and grovel."

Dinner was some of the gourmet freezer lasagne Livvie had stashed away. Rob watched her holding forth at the table, entertaining everybody with stories and generally being a charming hostess while Mike sat and listened, looking distracted. Rob couldn't work out if everyone was secretly relieved but felt guilty for showing it, or if they were quietly horrified by what had gone on a couple of hundred yards from the dinner table and were just trying to put a brave face on it.

Livvie seemed a lot more gregarious than she'd ever admitted. It was clear she liked company. She'd given up that and a hell of a lot more for Mike. Despite the money, it must have been bloody miserable for a clever woman to be holed up here on her own for weeks on end, doing a job she didn't seem to like very much and worrying what was happening to Mike in hostile places.

Now she'd seen for herself some of the things he actually did. Rob couldn't detect any signs of shock. Livvie was definitely nails.

She even managed to get Dru talking about Clare. All the time Dru was talking about her kid, she wasn't in danger of letting Ian's secret slip out, but Rob still had a sense of an anvil dangling on a fraying thread above him.

"You okay, Dad?" Tom asked.

"Hoofing, kiddo. Never better." If anyone had walked in now and tried to guess who was who, and how they'd arrived at this point in life to have a meal together, they wouldn't even have come close to the real answer. "When I've done my errands tomorrow, why don't we hit the cinema in Porton?"

"Good idea," Tom said. "We don't have to watch the security cams all night now."

"Yeah, we've seen that one before."

Rob would still keep an eye on the feeds via his phone, but not obsessively. He'd just make sure he stayed alert. Weaver would find out fairly soon what had happened to his hired help, and there was no way of knowing which way he'd jump when he did.

EN ROUTE TO BANGOR AIRPORT: MONDAY.

"It's not the Gulfstream," Rob said, obviously enjoying the chance to get out in his Jaguar, "but it's better than zoo class on a scheduled flight. No little screaming bastards kicking the back of your seat."

Ian sat in the back, watching Dru's reactions as they headed for the airport. Mike had laid on a private flight and limo back to Lansing for her. It was hard to tell if she was happy with the way things had worked out, or if she was still trying to make sense of the bomb that had shattered her life in the last week. There was nothing left of her old existence except her daughter and her house. Ian knew that roller-coaster all too well.

"Larry's going to be a pain in the ass about this," Dru said. "He always cross-examines me, like he still has a say in my life."

"Just tell him to ram it," Rob said airily, like they were old buddies. This was a conversation they couldn't have in front of Tom. "I don't tell my ex anything since she remarried. Least of all about Mike."

"How does Tom handle being in the middle of that? Larry uses Clare like a proxy message service."

"Tom's a diplomat. He never talks about me to her, and vice versa."

"He's an intelligent guy. You must be very proud of him."

"I am. He's my life. I'd kill for him."

It was just a phrase Rob used a lot. It happened to be true as well, but it probably wasn't what Dru needed to hear right then. Ian thought she seemed uneasy. She'd been paid off; the biker guy was dead. Maybe she was wondering whether it could have been the other way around. Win big or lose big, Mike had said.

Rob carried on, oblivious, reminding Dru to make herself known to the security team who'd keep a discreet eye on her until Mike was sure there were no further problems. In the meantime, Brayne staffers were rebuilding her world around her. Mike was very good at tidying up people's lives.

"You'll get a call in a few days from one of Mike's people," Rob said. "They'll arrange everything for you. Any problems, call Mike or me direct. If your old man starts making trouble — *definitely* call me."

"I know I should sound more grateful, but I'm still reeling from the last few days."

"Well, don't lose your nerve," Rob said. "You're home and dry. Weaver's heading up Shit Creek, though. Just trust Mike and follow the instructions."

"Okay." She managed a smile. "I think Larry would need CPR if you showed up on his doorstep."

Ian thought she was trying really hard with Rob, but he wasn't sure if Rob could tell. By the time they pulled in to the short-term parking at the airport, she seemed to have given up.

"Okay, end of the line," Rob said. "I'll take you through."

Ian felt obliged to say goodbye to her properly and got out of the car. Dru stood in front of him for a moment, shifting from foot to foot as if she was working up to saying something.

"I'm glad we got a chance to talk," she said. "I just want to thank you again. That was incredibly brave."

Ian saw what he'd done more as immediate necessity than courage, but he didn't want to ruin Mike's careful work to make Dru more of an ally than a liability. "You're welcome."

"And thanks for telling me about the Dunlops. I hope you find someone who knew David."

"Yeah, he was the brave one," Ian said. "He made choices. I just cope."

Dru reached out as if she was going to shake his hand, but Rob gave her a withering look. He probably thought she was after some DNA. He still didn't trust this not to go wrong. She settled for giving Ian an embarrassed touch on the shoulder instead.

"Take care of yourself, Ian."

He watched her walk off with Rob, wondering if she found secrets painfully restless things or if she could bury them and forget she even knew them. Ian had surprised himself by being able to befriend Tom without feeling that he was deceiving him. The guy was open about not being able to discuss his own career. They both knew that there were questions about each other that they should leave unasked, and it felt perfectly fine. Ian could probably live with that.

While he waited for Rob to come back, he sat listening to the car stereo. One of Mike's music compilations was already loaded, slightly mournful songs that were hard to sing along to, which explained why Rob didn't play it much.

Ian was worried that Mike would be the one who had to live with the real problems. All kinds of stuff would churn up from the shooting, even if he wasn't going to be charged, and instead of crap following Ian, it would now dog Mike's steps. Was it going to be on some file? What would happen when he and Livvie tried to adopt a baby? Would he look like a murderer to whoever decided these things, a bad choice for a parent? Mike said his money could make things disappear and almost everything had a price tag, but it seemed like a lot to pay to put things right for someone else.

It was some time before Rob returned. He jumped in the driver's seat, bouncing on the leather upholstery with exaggerated relish.

"Peace at last," he said, backing out of the parking bay. "I've got five days left with Tom. If there's anything you want to do now, speak up."

"Are you still pissed at me? On a scale of one to ten."

"I'm back to zero, mate."

"I don't want to fall out with you."

"Look, friends have fights. Even Mike lost it with me yesterday. You laugh about it later and forget it."

"What would you have done?"

"That's a trick question. Look, remember when you thought you wouldn't have the balls to step in and save someone? Well, now you know you have." Rob turned up the volume on the stereo as he hammered along the road. "Oh, bloody hell, not Mike's wrist-slashers' greatest hits, *please.* Find something cheerful, will you? Go on, lift that cover. There's a memory stick in there somewhere. Just plug it in there."

Ian rummaged through the console. "Mike seemed a bit better this morning."

"It's all a bit too close to home for him to shrug it off yet."

"And you criticise me for doing something extreme to draw flak."

"Okay, I admit we all try to out-Oates each other."

"I got that."

"I know."

"It might all be for nothing, though. You don't know what's going to come out of the woodwork now the police are looking."

"Maybe there's a shit volcano about to erupt, too, but I know this — we haven't broken any laws."

Ian wasn't sure how he felt about Mike shooting someone to protect him. He'd never say it, but he knew Mike hadn't opened fire to save his own life. He'd put himself on the line to draw that fire so he could kill the knowledge of what Ian was. Mike would work that out, but Ian didn't know if Mike had admitted it to himself and understood that it was a sacrifice, not a crime.

Ian was still unravelling his own reactions. Now he understood why it rubbed all the awkward nerves that he was afraid to acknowledge. He'd never known a father. The gaps in the sketchy chart of how to be a man had been filled in a textbook kind of way by books and movies, and he understood why Gran had done that, but it wasn't just about what he was supposed to be. He also needed to know where that sense of manhood should have come from.

Mike slotted neatly into place as the source. He was all those things that Gran said made a good man, and therefore a good father. He was also rehearsing his own father stuff for the day that had never come, when he'd have his own kids. Ian's gaps snapped into place with Mike's like puzzle pieces. Ian felt weird about the shooting because a voice inside said the unsayable: *that's how much my dad loves me, that's how far he'd go for me, and I'd do anything for him.* It all made sense now.

The house felt empty when they got home. The cars were still garaged, though, and Oatie was stretched out next to the radiator in the kitchen. Rob looked around the usual places for a message.

"Shit." He pulled a face at a sticky note on the fridge door. "Livvie and Tom are having an airsoft battle in the kill house. Bloody hell. Now who's inappropriate?"

"Where's Mike?" Ian walked up the hall, listening for movement. "I can't see him wanting to join in with that."

The alarms were on, so Mike must have heard the drive's motion sensors activate even if he hadn't heard Rob switch off the alarm panel by the front door. Once the interior doors were closed, most of the rooms were pretty well soundproofed, so Ian had to go looking. Mike's study was empty, door open. He wasn't in the utility room, either. It wasn't until Ian reached the other end of the house that he heard the faint, sporadic plink of piano keys.

Most of the rooms in the house were left furnished but unoccupied, like a museum tableau. The door to the music room, a library with a piano and some frighteningly expensive audio equipment, was ajar. Ian knocked in case he'd caught Mike at a bad moment.

Mike sat at the piano, phone held to his left ear while he tapped one key with his right forefinger. He was listening to some long conversation and punctuating it with grunts and sighs. Ian couldn't guess what was going on at the other end until Mike shut his eyes.

"Oh, for God's sake," he said. "It's not an admission of anything. Just send me the rest of it by e-mail. Goodbye, Scott."

So it was the lawyer. The goodbye sounded weary. Mike stared at the phone for a while, still not acknowledging Ian, and finally looked up.

"Hi, buddy. You shipped her out safely, then?"

Ian sat down in the window seat. He could hear Rob coming, whistling some tune he didn't recognise. "Yeah, she seemed fine. Are you okay?"

"Not really."

"Was that your attorney?"

"He was updating me on the case." Mike looked towards the door as Rob came in, followed by Oatie. "Hi Rob."

"Ooh, I didn't know you could play the piano." Rob stood over

Mike and tapped a few keys. "You've never touched that thing in all the time I've known you."

"I had lessons as a kid. Good discipline, Mom said."

"Well, if contracting goes tits-up, we can open a bar. You can be the pianist and I'll be the bouncer."

Mike looked up at him. "I just heard from Scott. The police have a better lead on the man I killed."

"That's harsh, Zombie. It's okay to say *the dead bloke.*"

"So who is he?" Ian asked.

Mike cupped his hands over his nose for a moment, then folded his arms. "He was an Iraq vet."

"Oh, shit." Rob seemed to know what was coming. "Mike, you didn't kill a puppy, okay? No fucking breast-beating."

"They're checking the Army fingerprint database. The medical examiner found a tattoo that clued him in."

Ian could guess what Mike was going through right then. Being responsible for the death of someone who'd served would hit a very raw nerve, whether the guy was a criminal or not. It was the worst thing he could possibly hear.

Rob didn't fire off a reassurance straight away. He was picking his words.

"There had to be a high chance he'd be one of us," he said. "Who else would you hire? There's lots of blokes like us out there."

"Sure, but I bet that when he was downrange, he didn't think he'd come home to die in a tourist-trap town at the hands of another American."

"He should have thought about that before he took the money to do an armed abduction," Rob said.

"He's probably got a family."

"The worst shit-bag I ever put down probably has a dear old mum in Baghdad who still cries over his photo every day, but it doesn't make him a saint."

"So this guy's service doesn't count for anything?"

"It counts, but he still came to your home with firearms, and he wasn't planning to invite you out for a day's grouse shooting, was he?"

Mike unfolded his arms and did a few more plinks on the keyboard, then managed a chord or two. "Anyway, I mentioned to Scott that if the guy had a family, they might be in real hardship, so I asked if there was a way of helping them out. He lectured me on making it look like an admission of guilt. We didn't agree."

Ian thought it wasn't a great idea either, but he knew it was Mike's reflex to reach for his wallet in a crisis.

"If I was his family, I'd be really upset if someone offered me money," Ian said, trying to talk him out of it. "Blood money. That's how they'd see it."

"They don't have to know it's me. There are always ways to give people things."

"Of course," Rob said, "he might have strangled his wife for the insurance money. Or she might be a drug dealer. Or very rich, like you. Or there might be a bunch of his mates biding their time to come back and finish the job. Who knows?"

"Yes, Rob, I *do* understand the point you're making." Mike read from his phone again. "Scott says the medical examiner decided the bruising developed before the guy died, so they're not going to re-interview me about that."

"He got all that out of them? Seriously?"

"He's good. And they've found a micro SD card in the guy's jacket lining, but no phone yet. Or vehicles. There were images that they want to identify."

Mike held the phone so Rob could see it. Ian had to peer over his shoulder. It was Dru in the woods, apparently with Tom, not a very sharp picture but good enough, and another of Tom walking down the road with Oatie.

Ian knew the one in the woods was him. The one with Oatie was definitely Tom. They were pretty damn close, though. He expected Rob to erupt, but he just let out a breath.

"At a distance, it would have fooled me as well," he said.

Ian knew it would slip out sooner or later. He should have come clean. "I'm sorry, Rob. It just made sense at the time."

"Subject closed."

"Well, they recognised both as Tom," Mike said. "An officer saw him when he called at the house. I'll confirm that's Dru Lloyd and feed them the same story we're giving Weaver about her coming to see us. He'll say neither of them saw the guy taking pictures, which is true up to a point."

"Okay, but I will *not* be fucking happy if my boy's dragged into this," Rob said. "He'll know he wasn't in the woods talking to her."

"Okay, I'll get Scott to answer neutrally for them and confirm who they are. It fits what the police think a whole lot better than the truth, doesn't it? The guy was staking us all out." Mike had slipped back to being in quiet control and telling everyone how things were going to be. "If they find something else that points to a KW-Halbauer link with Dru, we've got our story covered, and it's down to Weaver to explain it. I'd buy tickets for that show. Dad's seeing him tomorrow."

"But the guy didn't get an actual shot of me morphing." Ian tried to recover the situation. He couldn't bear to upset Rob again. "He probably took out his phone because he saw it and wanted proof if I did it again. Except the next time he saw me looking like I do now, I jumped him, which kind of ruled out taking more pictures."

"Well, if has, we can't do anything about it now," Mike said. "So let's just sit tight. Dad's seeing Weaver with Dru, by the way."

Rob puffed out a long breath. "That's suicidal."

"It's Dad's show now." Mike tapped out a scale on the keyboard. "He'll do the final polish. He'll turn Dru from being someone who can't afford to expose us to someone who actually wants to give evidence if Weaver ever ends up in court over this. She's our weapon now."

Rob shrugged as if he wasn't convinced but was deferring to someone who played this kind of political chess for a living. "I'm glad I'm not one of your dad's opponents." He snapped his fingers at Oatie. "Come on, useless. You haven't had your dinner yet."

The dog trotted out after him, head down. Mike looked at Ian and shrugged.

"I know what you're going to say, but Rob's disturbed by the Tom thing." Mike tried a few more chords. It was starting to sound like proper music. "You know, I haven't played in twenty-five years. I quite like struggling with it, though. It takes up all my concentration. Like meditating. Do you still do that?"

"Yeah. It's a habit now." Ian wanted to clear up the tension for good. He didn't feel he could move on until he had. "I'm sorry. I feel stupid about the Tom stuff."

"No need, buddy. You're entitled to get a few things wrong. Nobody wrote the rulebook for this." Mike stood up and closed the keyboard lid. "Okay, until we rule out any accomplices for this guy, I still want to see good security practice."

"Is it safe for me to call Joe?" Ian hadn't spoken to him for ages. That was no way to treat someone who'd stepped in to help with Gran's funeral when Ian didn't know how to handle the outside world. "It can't do any harm now."

Mike ushered him out of the room towards the kitchen. "Go ahead. Pity you can't visit him, though. Unless you remember what you looked like then."

It was bittersweet. The one person Ian could have called a true neighbour couldn't be allowed to see him the way he was now. He wouldn't understand. He wouldn't even recognise him. *Can I morph back to the way I was?* Ian could just about remember how he looked a day or two before he left the ranch for the last time. Joe might not spot the differences after a long separation.

But this was the Ian Dunlop he was now, and unless he had a real need to use his ability, this was how he would stay.

He'd call Joe after dinner. He went to find Tom and Livvie and stayed out of Rob's hair for a while. It was time to be sociable and make up for the disruption to Tom's visit.

In the evening, the mood around the dinner table was more subdued than yesterday, when the shock was still fresh, and Mike had gone back to looking preoccupied.

"Who's the designated worrier tonight?" Rob asked.

Mike looked up. "Warrior?"

"Worry-er. As in he who worries and has to stay sober in case emergency action's required."

"I'll do it. I don't feel like drinking anyway."

Livvie poured a very large peach margarita into a highball glass and put it in front of Rob. He studied the sudden bloom of beaded condensation on the glass for a moment and smiled to himself.

"Right, movie quiz," he said. He ran his finger through the condensation, from rim to base, then downed the drink in one. "Name that film."

"*Ice Cold In Alex*," Ian said. "John Mills."

"Well done." Rob nudged Tom. "Ian's a bit of a movie buff. We've got boxes of his DVDs in the basement. We'll have to watch one later."

Livvie went around the table again with the jug. "Top up, anybody?"

"I'd better get a beer, Mrs Mike. You know what I'm like after a couple of your margaritas."

"Go on, just a splash. It's worth it to see you laughing again. How about a toast?"

Rob allowed her to pour a couple of inches into his glass before he raised it. "To us. There's Us, and there's Them, with capital letters."

It seemed to have some significance for Mike. He gave Rob a funny look and raised his glass of water. "To the tribe of Us, then. Is that traditional?"

"It is now." Rob made a gesture, thumb and forefinger indicating a very small gap. He tipped some of the drink into a saucer and put it down on the floor for Oatie to test it nervously with his tongue. "Remember. Us is just you and me and our nearest and dearest. Everyone else is Them. Wherever They may be."

Mike returned the small gap gesture. "Us."

After dinner, Ian watched Mike while he loaded the dishes in the washer. He reached for the bottle of hand wash next to the sink and turned on the faucet, then touched his wedding band to his lips before taking it off. When he finished washing and drying his hands, he touched the ring to his lips again before sliding it back on his finger. Ian had never seen him do that before.

It didn't surprise him. Mike seemed to find comfort in ritual. It fitted with his insistence on his lucky plastic watch. The things you did when you thought nobody was watching told your whole story, Ian decided.

When everyone was in the den later that evening, watching *The Cruel Sea* and drinking too much beer, he saw Mike slip out. He was gone too long to be taking a leak, so Ian got up to find him. He wasn't in the kitchen or the bathroom. It was just a hunch, but Ian had a good idea where he'd be.

He picked up a pair of NV goggles from the utility room and headed for the woods. It took a while to find the right place, but he'd guessed right.

Mike was squatting among the trees with his back to the house, shoulders hunched against the cold and head bowed, staring down at the spot where the body had been.

Ian felt he had no right to watch, but he couldn't walk away. He waited until Mike finally straightened up, stood to attention, and saluted. It was so private and painful that Ian hated himself for not walking away sooner.

Mike's shoulders relaxed and he turned around. "Goddamn." He almost took a step back. "That's the way to give a guy a heart attack, buddy."

"Sorry." Ian walked back to the house with him. "I thought I knew you well, but now I'm sure."

Mike didn't seem embarrassed or upset at the intrusion. Maybe it was easier for Ian to see it than for Mike to say it.

"He wasn't the enemy," Mike said at last. "Just the guy who got shot. The enemy's the guy who sent him."

So there was Us, and Them, but there was also the tribe in limbo, the people who could end up on either side of a line where hard choices had to be made. Belonging was an imprecise thing, something Ian had longed for without even knowing quite what it was that he'd needed.

Now he knew. It was still hard to define, but it was solid enough to hold and taste, and he knew he belonged to the tribe of Us.

RIDGEWAY DRIVE, LANSING: NEXT MORNING.

"Mom? Aren't you going to work this morning?"

Dru sat at the kitchen counter in sweatpants, with no idea what lay ahead except choices she hadn't had to think about since she was at college. She was so disoriented that she'd entered the wrong banking passcode on her cell and was still trying to get it right when Clare came in to the kitchen.

"Later today, sweetheart." Dru concentrated on the phone, repeating the numbers to herself under her breath. "I'll drop you off, so don't worry."

"Mom, what do you always tell me about being glued to the phone?"

"Sorry. I just need to check my account. I haven't logged in since Friday."

The last few days had been a write-off that she was still struggling to take in, but she couldn't tell Clare about that. She just looked at the balance to make sure it hadn't changed.

"Oh *Christ*," she said.

Dru had never seen that much cash in her checking account in her life. There was an extra thirty grand. It had to be an error. It couldn't be from the Braynes, because she hadn't even had a call from their accountant yet to get her various account numbers. But it was. The details showed a payment from Mike Brayne's personal account. How the hell did he get her bank details?

Rob. The bastard must have rooted through her purse. Just

when she was starting to like the guy for being a devoted father, he scared her again. Her heart rate hiked. She could see the pulse twitching in her wrist. There was no way out of this now, even if she wanted to change her mind. As far as an auditor was concerned — if one were to investigate — she'd taken a big payment from the Braynes. Saying it just popped up there like magic wouldn't convince a jury.

What jury? The phone hacking — that's nothing compared to what I've seen lately. I didn't create Ian or send in the heavies.

Clare helped herself to toast. "Are you going to tell me what's going on? You haven't said much since you got back."

"I really want to, but I can't at the moment."

"Mom, I know you always have confidential stuff, but you're really *weird* now. Who were the guys in the car you were talking to after Dad dropped me off?"

"Security." Dru had to tell Clare that at least, in case she thought the security detail were stalkers or worse. "It's nothing to worry about. You might see them around for a few more days."

"Is this all to do with that ex-employee you were looking for?"

"Something like that."

"You're scaring me now."

Dru had to nip this in the bud. She had enough on her plate today without having to worry about Clare worrying about her and in turn stoking up Larry enough for him to stick his damn nose in. He'd trample all over this. He'd ruin everything.

It's none of his business. I have to make that clear.

"Sweetie, here's my problem," Dru said. "If I tell you, you tell your dad, and he makes my life hell. I'll only tell you if you swear not to tell him. I mean it. You're nearly fifteen. You're not a kid any more. This is for my safety as well as yours."

Clare just stared at her for a few moments, unblinking. "Okay. I promise. But what do you mean by safety?"

If it meant scaring Clare into being careful, it would have to be done. Dru had to level with her.

"I could have been badly hurt this week," she said. The more she repeated it, the less it shocked her. "Someone saved me. That's all I can tell you, but that's how serious this is. I don't want you getting excited and telling Rebecca anything. And this isn't like 'promise me you'll finish your homework' either."

"This isn't some joke, is it?"

"No. It really isn't."

"Mom, I haven't told Rebecca any secrets since she blabbed to everyone in eighth grade that I thought Brent Mulholland was hot," Clare said, as if Dru should have remembered that crisis. "Have you told the police?"

"That's been done." Detail wasn't necessary. This was just reinforcing the need for silence. "My company's into something I don't like, and I can't carry on working for them. I've got a new job."

"Wow, Mom, I never thought you'd quit that place." Clare was at the age where all rebellion was cool. She looked impressed. "So you're a whistle-blower? That's awesome."

"No, I don't have the guts to be a whistle-blower. I'm just a walker-outer."

"So why go to the office, then? I'd hide."

"I'll have someone with me. Look, we'll be fine, better than fine in fact, but it's only going to work if you say absolutely nothing to your father about it. I'll deal with him." It sounded like the kind of thing that a criminal would tell their kid. *I robbed the bank for you, Pumpkin, but now we need to hide out in Mexico.* "If I told you what I'd seen in the last few days, you'd never believe me anyway. And your dad certainly wouldn't."

Clare nodded gravely. Now she didn't seem excited at all. The prospect of being allowed into the adult world for a while was normally something prized, but not this time.

"Is this like witness protection?"

"In a way. You mustn't talk about it with anyone except me."

"You're scared. I can see it. And you're repeating yourself."

"You bet I'm scared. But we'll be okay. If you want to move away from here, we could have a great new life."

Clare thought it over for a few moments. "Could I still visit Dad?"

"Sure. I'm not asking you to decide right now. We don't have to disappear or anything. But I'll understand if you don't want to leave your friends."

Clare chewed her toast, minus the jelly. Either her tastes had changed overnight or it was distraction activity. It was hard to tell if she was sobered by the news or just too scared to argue.

"You decide, Mom," she said at last. "I love Dad, but he can only cope with me in small doses. You've got me every day."

She didn't even mention her friends. It was hard to remember being that age and what had been important. Some days, some things were a matter of life and death. The next day, they weren't. All Dru could do was guess her way through it.

"Okay, let's go," she said. "I'll be out between two and four this afternoon, but I'll be here when you get home."

Clare said little on the drive to school. Dru could almost see her working out something, staring at the dashboard but not really seeing it. It might have been about who she'd have to give up seeing: it might have been about disruption before exams. No, those were adult concerns. Dru would have to stop guessing and just ask, but not right away. Clare needed time for it to sink in.

And so do I.

"I promise you that this'll be good for both of us in the end," Dru said. "We've just got to be willing to take a chance on new things."

"I think I told you to do that ages ago, Mom."

Clare was in forty-year-old mode today. And she was right.

Dru drove back from the school, rehearsing what she'd say to Larry. She didn't dare tell him she was okay for money, let alone that she might need to sell up. All she could do was pretend everything was normal and not say a word until things were set in concrete.

But first she had to show up at the office with Leo Brayne. This was so far above her pay grade that it was probably pointless trying to grasp it. Leo — he insisted on first names — had rung personally just after she got back, all reasonable, polite graciousness like his son, but it was clear he wasn't so much inviting her to accompany him as telling her that she would.

When she thought about it, it was another lifeline. If you were going to tell your boss to ram it up his ass for sending hit-men to follow you, then it was probably better to do that with the likes of Leo Brayne at your side.

Or maybe in front of me. He's seriously pissed at Weaver. He might want to keep the juicy bits for himself and just toss me a half-chewed ear.

What was she going to say? Weaver must have known his biker guy hadn't made contact for a while, but he hadn't tried to mail or phone her. He could have been anywhere between complete ignorance of what was unfolding, and standing outside her house with an axe because he'd somehow heard every damn word she'd said in the last few days.

Dru took her time choosing the right suit for a showdown. Maybe clothes didn't matter when she'd walk in with the ultimate accessory, a juggernaut of a politician who also happened to be able to buy companies like trinkets. It felt like preparing for a date. She kept redoing her hair and changing her blouse, but that still left her with hours to sit and replay the seismic shift that had hit her over the weekend.

It wasn't just the headline events, her first encounter with real violence and watching a boy alter his features at will — a shape-shifter, a real goddamn *morphing human being* — but also being among thoroughly alien people. She'd never met really powerful families. She didn't know any soldiers, or security operators, or people who couldn't tell her where they worked. It would take her months to chip away at all that and understand it.

But if she stripped away all the otherworldliness of the Braynes and their friends, she was looking at people who enjoyed working and socialising together, a real honest-to-God team. It shone out of them. It was as unlike her own workday experience as she could imagine. She had no friends at work, except maybe Alex. She was the pink-slip kapo. Outside work, she had a hostile ex and no life beyond Clare. The Braynes' tight-knit circle looked like paradise, and it wasn't all about their wealth.

And yet Mike had killed a guy. He'd seemed such a gentleman. You didn't need to be angry or hostile to kill someone, then, simply able to decide that it had to be done.

Dru was pondering on the capacity of nice people to do unpleasant things when an e-mail popped up on her phone. The header said it was from Shaun Weaver. She felt almost sick, but she had to read it.

It turned out to be a simple note asking where she was. Maybe he really didn't know. Should she respond? She had no choice. She tapped out a reply, saying she'd be in the office after lunch. Two minutes later, a reply arrived: '*Then maybe you should see this.*'

It was the long shot of her in the woods with Ian. How did Weaver get that? It must have been taken shortly before the biker jumped her. Maybe the guy had e-mailed the image to get her ID confirmed or to show Weaver that he'd found someone who looked the right age for the mule, a kid in his late teens or early twenties.

But Ian looked like Tom in that shot. If Weaver had real evidence of Ian morphing, she'd have expected him to mail that if he was going to send anything at all. This was something else. Dru stalled him with an ambiguous response while she thought of a way to turn this around.

'That's not a mistake you want to make,' she typed. It was cryptic and true on many levels. *'Trust me on that.'*

That was the last e-mail she was ever going to send him. She'd have to warn Leo Brayne now. Why would Weaver be stupid enough to show her that he'd been in contact with the dead guy? All she had to do was hand that e-mail to the police, and he'd be sunk.

But he probably doesn't know the guy's dead yet. He might not even be aware that anything's wrong if they avoided contacting each other too often.

She forwarded the e-mail to Mike with a carefully worded note: '*You need to be aware of this. Are there any images of Tom on the internet?*'

It took Mike minutes to respond. He checked his cell as obsessively as a teenager. Dru read the reply: '*The police recovered that image from a cell. Rare pic of Tom — see this URL. University soccer. Are you going to show that to my father?*'

She thought it was essential. '*Yes, unless you tell me not to.*'

His reply was short. '*I'll send him my copy.*'

It didn't strike her as odd. Mike probably had secure systems anyway, and she didn't. She opened the link he'd sent her to see a fairly clear image of Tom, identified by name in a soccer match. If she put the images side by side, the real Tom and Ian's version, they looked pretty much the same person: with the picture quality and the distortion of angle, shadow, and expression, they seemed to be the same guy. Weaver could suck on that. She'd confront him with it, taking Leo's lead.

By the time Leo's black limo showed up outside, Dru was vacillating between bullish aggression and wanting to lock herself in the bathroom. She had her short, bland letter of resignation in her purse. She psyched herself up by remembering how she'd sunk her teeth into that guy's glove and how she'd thought the next second would be her last. She didn't care if Weaver hadn't known how far things would go or if he'd blessed it. It was his doing. Now she was mad as hell. She needed to stay that way for a couple of hours.

"Hello, Dru." Leo shook her hand when she got into the back seat. "How are you feeling now?"

"I'm fine. Really. Thank you."

"Dreadful weekend for all, I think."

She'd seen Leo's picture, but that was no guide to the physical reality. Old money oozed from his polished voice, just like Mike's, and he had the same blue eyes. The back seat was separated from the driver by a glass partition.

Chin up. Don't lose your nerve.

"I don't think Weaver knows I'm coming with you," she said. "But I told him I'd see him."

"It'll be even briefer than he expects, then." Leo nodded to the driver and the car pulled away. "My legal team developed instant ulcers when I said I was doing this, but I'm going to make it very, very short. I'm simply showing up in person because it tends to focus people more effectively than a letter or an e-mail."

I can see why. "You've seen the image he sent me."

"Yes."

Dru took out her phone and showed him the photo of Tom playing soccer. "Subject to your guidance, I'll show him this if he starts making allegations about mules and shape-shifters. It's pretty compelling."

Leo just looked at her. It was hard to tell what he was thinking.

"Works for me." He put on his glasses and checked his phone. "Mike told me nothing about this until after it was over. He didn't want to worry me. That's why I'm here in person, because I won't tolerate anyone distressing my son. You're a parent. You understand."

Dru wasn't sure if that was a statement or a subtle warning, but it hit both spots. While the traffic held them up, Leo chatted about bringing up children and how he and his wife had never employed a nanny for Mike and his sister. Dru couldn't resist looking for the roots of Mike's attitude in his father. It was there, all right, just writ larger in the son.

It was harder than she expected to walk into the KWA offices. As she went up to the reception desk with Leo, the looks started. She could see it out of the corner of her eye. Passing staff did a double take. The bush telegraph would relay the news halfway around the building before she got to the third floor. Even if they didn't recognise Leo, they could certainly see that he wasn't the janitor. Weaver's secretary, Julianne, showed them straight in.

"I wasn't expecting you, Dru," she whispered.

"I know," Dru said. "But I'm here now."

Weaver kept a commendably inscrutable face for a man who'd been ordered back to base to make himself available. He indicated the big green sofa.

"Please, take a seat, Leo," he said. "I wasn't expecting to see Mrs Lloyd with you, though. How can I help?"

Leo sat back, giving it a few beats before he spoke. "Shaun, I'm going to explain something informally before my lawyers contact you. I always find it aids clarity."

"I'm listening."

"You will *not* go near my son, his family, or his friends. You will *not* instruct anyone else to go near them, either. There's no *again*, or *if*, or any condition in there. You simply will not do it. Do we understand each other?"

Dru's stomach was knotted so tightly that it hurt. It was like watching violence. even though nobody made physical contact or even raised their voices. Leo was all the more terrifying for being calm.

"I'm not sure I've understood you." Weaver did a credible impersonation of bewilderment. "Are you accusing me of something?"

"Yes. I am. Harassing my family."

"I assume you can substantiate that, Senator."

"I believe you did that yourself, when you sent Mrs Lloyd a photograph earlier today."

Weaver didn't even start fidgeting. "Very well, since you raised it, perhaps you can tell me what Mrs Lloyd was doing in that photo."

"I'm sure she can tell you herself, but she was trying to arrange a discreet meeting with me at my son's house to go through the original Ringer discussions. She was checking for names or connections she hadn't been made aware of."

"I had no idea. I'd never have authorized her to do that. I do apologise."

Leo didn't blink. "Actually, I was referring to the man you sent after Mrs Lloyd, but I'm afraid my son shot him dead on Sunday, so we can't ask him. It's a police matter now. Never mind."

Dru watched Weaver's face. It was extraordinary to see a man lose all control for a fraction of a second and then pull it all together again, especially someone as laid back as Weaver. It was almost invisible because it was so fast. She couldn't tell whether he was winded by the fact that his guy was dead, or by the revelation that Mike Brayne had shot him. This was heady stuff for a biotech company. Dru would probably never know exactly what instructions Weaver had given and who he'd dealt with, but whatever it was, something had obviously gone wrong.

He carried on without a trace of panic in his voice. "I've no doubt you've told Senator Brayne some story about shape-shifters, Dru."

"No, but I did tell him you suspected Charles Kinnery of parking stolen genes in an accomplice, and that you'd tasked me to find him." She held up her phone to show him the image he'd sent her. "I thought you mailed me this to say you believed I'd found him."

Weaver just looked at her. It was probably easier than looking at Leo. "It's up to you to explain who that boy is, I think, Dru."

He had to know he was screwed, but he was brazening it out. Dru admired his inability to accept defeat, or maybe she'd read this all wrong and he had another much nastier surprise waiting for her at a later date. She opened the image of Tom playing soccer and showed it to him.

"This guy, you mean? That's Tom Rennie. It says so on the caption. He's the son of Mike Brayne's friend. He was over from England for the holidays." Dru held her phone next to print-out of the snatched shot from Westerham so Weaver could compare the two. "I'm sure Tom wouldn't mind providing some DNA so you can look for werewolf genes to your heart's content, though."

Weaver's expression was now locked. Either he knew he'd been manoeuvred into a corner and that she was lying, or he was now having serious doubts way too late. Leo sat swiping through his phone with no real appearance of urgency.

"Here," Leo said. "That's Rob, Tom's father, with Mike, my boy." He held up his phone. It was some photo taken in Africa, with Mike looking suitably military in a dusty landscape, sitting on the tailgate of a vehicle with Rob. "Not that you'd need DNA to see that Rob is Tom's father. Extraordinarily alike, aren't they?" Leo smiled at the picture, which might have been pure theatre or genuine paternal pride, then put the phone back in his pocket. "I think we're done now, Shaun. Just remember that I won't tolerate you or your minions even being in the same time zone as my son or his family."

"Is that a threat, Leo?"

"Let me explain. A threat is when I say that if you do X, then I'll do Y. I'm going to do Y anyway, regardless of whether you do X, so technically, it's advance notice. Y, in this case, is an ongoing police investigation, plus the scrutiny of whichever agency my colleagues might feel is appropriate in the national interest, given the nature of your industry. But I've got people to explain all that to you. I really must be going now." Leo stood up and held his hand out to Dru. "I believe you had some unfinished business, Mrs Lloyd? Letter?"

Leo was skilfully minimising Weaver. Anger was what you showed to people who frustrated you and got under your skin. Disdain was what you showed a minor player. Knowing Weaver, that was probably a more painful way to find out he was going to be turned over by every organisation and committee that Leo could throw at him. Leo's revenge had probably only just begun. He seemed to be a remarkably long-term kind of man for a politician.

Dru placed her resignation on Weaver's desk. "I actually came here to hand in my notice. I completed the investigation. There's no mule and no shape-shifter. And the benefits package just isn't enough to make me forget being staked out like a goat."

Weaver didn't answer. Dru caught Julianne's eye as she left, but there was only surprise there. As she stood in the elevator lobby with Leo, heads popped up over cubicles in nearby offices to gawp. It was far easier to walk away than to walk in. They could keep the remaining candy bars and spare pens in her desk. She'd left nothing here of any consequence.

"How about Kinnery?" Dru asked on the ride home. This didn't feel real yet. She dreaded the moment when it all sank in. "Isn't he a liability now? A weak link?"

"Not really," Leo said. "Who holds all the actual proof of wrong-doing? We do, we being you, me, and Charles. What's Shaun got? Two key personnel — well, one ex-employee and one consultant — who'll throw him under the first available bus, and no proof of the existence of engineered genes at all. Even if he cites Charles's story about Maggie being a volunteer test subject, it can't be proven now, and it's a far less contentious ethical issue anyway. And he really doesn't want the biker linked to him, believe me, so that story dies a death too. Give it six months, and

KW-Halbauer will have airbrushed Shaun Weaver out of the picture and concreted over everything that might come back to embarrass them."

There would be aftershocks from this, Dru knew, but she'd have to handle it. The car drew up outside her house and Leo turned to face her. She was expecting a politician's thank-you-and-goodbye, but she got something else.

"Was that really Tom?" he asked.

It was an odd question. Dru thought he'd understood from the start that it was Ian. She hadn't felt the need to explain it to him. There were things you just didn't spell out in situations like this, where you didn't always know who might be eavesdropping.

"Why do you ask?"

"Because I didn't know."

"Oh." Dru knew thin ice when she felt it underfoot. Had Mike forgotten to brief his father, or had he withheld something? He hadn't given any indication when she'd mailed him earlier. She didn't want to drop Mike in it. "I saw Tom out walking the dog."

It wasn't an answer to any question, and it wasn't a lie, even if it sounded like one. But she was dealing with a politician. She knew she was hopelessly outgunned in the smart answers war.

"You didn't ask what I didn't know, or when," Leo said. "Or answer the question."

"Does it matter now?"

"Not the way you might think it does."

"Well, Weaver still doesn't know Ian exists, and he must know that we'd love to demonstrate that Tom Rennie has no non-human DNA in him. I think Weaver's cornered."

"Well answered," Leo said. "I meant that I hadn't realised just how effectively Ian could morph until I saw that picture today."

Dru felt she'd let Mike down somehow. If he hadn't told his father every detail, that was his business. She did her best to recover the situation.

"I can't see the ability having much military use," she said. "He couldn't pass himself off as me, for example. And he'd still need to work on accents and mannerisms like anyone else."

Was that true? Dru couldn't swear to it, but she knew what she'd seen.

"I don't care what use Ian might be, but *he* would," Leo said. "He'd want to help the DoD. The medical issues aren't even on the table, and never will be."

"I understand."

Leo gave her a proper smile, no show of teeth, but genuinely warm nonetheless. "Dru, I like people who keep their counsel and don't drop my son in the mire. Loyalty's a rare and precious commodity. When I see it, I take good care of it." He took her hand and shook it again. "Take some time off. Don't rush into anything we offer now that you don't have to. Think about what you really want to do."

Dru waved him goodbye, wondering if that was appropriate with senators, and went indoors to kick off her shoes and flop on the sofa. Damn, she was shaking again. It wasn't until she'd made a pot of coffee and was on her second cup that she realised she'd been set a make-or-break test in a few minutes in that limo.

Somehow she'd passed. Leo wanted to be sure she'd back up Mike, and she had. Why wouldn't she? He was her lifeline, and he happened to be doing the moral, decent thing in a world that generally didn't.

She wondered what would have happened if she'd failed that test. If she was careful, she'd never have to find out.

EPILOGUE.

WASHINGTON, D.C.: SEVEN MONTHS LATER, JUNE.

The jeweller unrolled a small black velvet mat on the glass countertop and laid the watch on it with due ceremony. After a brief inspection without touching it, he looked up at Mike.

"This must be of great sentimental value to you, Mr Brayne."

It was a diplomatic way of saying he was stunned that a member of the Brayne family would possess anything so tacky, let alone want it repaired. The last time Mike had visited the store, his impulse purchase had been in the five-figure bracket, a pair of emerald earrings for Livvie. The jeweller knew him as well as he knew Dad. If the man felt his store was being sullied by cheap plastic, he'd never dare say so to his well-heeled customers.

"It's my lucky watch." Mike indicated the small tear in the strap with his forefinger. "You could say it saved my life. Is it possible to fix it?"

The jeweller picked up the watch and looked at it with his loupe. "I'm told the movements in these are surprisingly robust, but I'd have to make enquiries about the strap. You could always have a new one fitted. The case is a separate piece of plastic. But of course, the issue is sourcing it. China, you know."

Mike found himself wondering how much of the watch would have to be replacement parts before it was no longer the same object and its significance had been diluted. He wasn't superstitious enough to think his luck would run out if he didn't wear it, but it was like his wedding band or dog tag, a physical symbol of a state of mind that he wanted to revisit and that required a certain ritual when taken off or put back on again.

"Okay, let me know about a repair," Mike said. He should have left it with the jeweller, but he didn't want to be parted from it for an indefinite period. "I want to keep it as original as possible, no matter what it looks like."

Mike fastened the watch on his wrist again and left to meet Livvie and Ian at the cafe. It was a carefully scheduled trip that required a timetable grid of museum visits, shopping, picking up Rob from the airport, and a charity dinner with Mom and Dad. There were also appointments that they had to keep. One of those was with Charles Kinnery.

Mike had decided to risk meeting him for coffee in a hotel restaurant, somewhere touristy where neither of them would be expected to hang out and where they were unknown faces. Livvie didn't plan to come. Ian was still steeling himself for the event. He hadn't seen Kinnery face to face for some years, and he hadn't even spoken to him on the phone since Maggie's death. It was going to be an awkward reunion.

Livvie sat at a window table with an espresso and her master list in front of her, checking things off. Ian sat opposite her, reading it upside down.

"Is Rob's tux sorted out?" Mike asked, pulling out a chair.

"Yes, they're delivering it to the apartment." Livvie caught the waiter in passing, flashing her best smile to get a coffee for Mike. "But you've got to force him into it this time. I'm not cornering him again. It's like trying to get a cat to swallow tablets."

"Have you tried yours on, Ian?"

"It'll take some getting used to." Ian rattled the ice in his glass of juice. "I don't look like me."

There was a time when that would have meant something very different to Ian, but today he was just passing a comment on how alien formal clothes could seem. Mike took the fact that Ian could even say it without noticing as proof of one task completed.

"So do you want to see Kinnery or not?" Mike asked.

"I thought I'd be okay, but I need some time."

"No pressure. I know it'll be hard, especially in a public place."

"It's not that I don't want to see him. There's just other people I need to talk to first."

Ian went on sipping his drink. The big event for him on this trip wasn't the dinner or the meeting with Kinnery. It was visiting the Vietnam Veterans Memorial. He'd finally tracked down a vet who'd served with David Dunlop, and after a lot of planning and correspondence, he'd arranged to meet him there. It was preoccupying him.

These things could be painfully intense for anyone. Mike knew that it wasn't just meeting the short-lived human bridge between yourself and a lost loved one, which was a gamble in itself. It was the risk of discovering things you didn't expect and weren't prepared for in the reminiscences — things they'd done, people they'd known, and even the small detail of how they'd died, although Ian knew David hadn't been killed in action. The man had come home and rejoined the civilian world, a past that Ian was still hesitant to piece together. He just wanted to flesh out David's Vietnam service for the time being and to try to connect with that. Kinnery was almost a sideshow.

Detail. That's the hard stuff.

Mike knew all the small detail of how an Iraq vet called Ivan Howe had died. He'd avoided looking into the man's service record. Did that make things worse? In a way, he wanted to find that the guy wasn't worthy of respect, but he knew things wouldn't be that tidy. Mike had made a decision that he would have made again today. Now he had to live with it the way his father had taught him.

"Well, if you change your mind, Kinnery's down here every couple of months," Mike said. "We could come back another time. I can ask him the questions for you."

"Thanks. I'm getting a little worked up about this afternoon."

"All set up?" Livvie asked.

"I might need moral support. I've never seen a memorial that big. I can handle the scale of gravestones. But tens of thousands of names, thousands of *people,* is kind of overwhelming."

Ian had quite an ability to imagine how he might feel in a situation simply from examining images. Mike wondered if it was the legacy of the years he'd spent trying to interpret the outside world through a TV screen, but there was also a high level of emotional intelligence at work. Ian was a meticulous observer of the unseen as well as the seen. He'd obviously thought himself into the situation already and knew how painful it might feel.

"I visited the war graves in Normandy, and I wasn't prepared at all," Livvie said. She put her hand on Ian's and squeezed it. "You're right, it's upsetting when it hits you. You'll be glad you talked to this guy, though. You have to seize the chance while people are still around, or else all the personal detail that doesn't reach the history books dies with them."

Mike raised an eyebrow at Livvie. "You're a ray of sunshine today, honey."

"You're the historian. You should know better than anybody."

"I better head out and find Kinnery. I've got to get to the hotel by eleven. Lunch at one-thirty, Dad's favourite Italian. That leaves us plenty of time to get across town to the memorial."

"Done," Livvie said. "Synchronize watches."

"If you want to show up, Ian, please do. You've got the map."

As Mike walked away to find a cab, he reflected on how much Ian had progressed in a year. Nobody would guess that he'd made his first bus trip on his own last July. Now he took a capital city in his stride. The only downside was that Mike couldn't boast about Ian's achievements to any outsider except Kinnery, and even then in a limited way. The fewer people who knew how far Ian had come from that baseline, the better.

It was enjoyable to be alone and anonymous in a city again, observing the world from the back of a taxi. Mike watched how people reacted to him. Today, many of them didn't even seem to see he was there. As he stepped out of the taxi and paused on the sidewalk to put his wallet back in his hip pocket, a woman almost walked into him and looked up as if he'd materialised out of thin air. She didn't know who he was, and she'd forget him in seconds. That was exactly what he wanted.

Kinnery was already in the busy coffee shop jealously guarding a table, almost lost in a sea of tourists.

Mike shook his hand. "How are you doing?"

"I'm good." Kinnery pulled out a chair for him. "No Ian?"

He said it casually, but Mike knew that was his main reason for showing up. "He might stop by later," Mike said. "He's shopping with Livvie. We've got a charity event on Thursday with Rob and my parents. Ian's first black tie dinner."

They sounded as if they were making small talk, but it was an exchange of critical information for two people who couldn't talk on the phone or e-mail each other except in emergencies and via an indirect and tortuous route.

"My God, hobnobbing with the smart set." Kinnery smiled. "He's come a long way. Maggie would be amazed."

"Yes, he's passed his driving test, and he's learning Arabic and Spanish now. He's ready for serious security work."

"Good grief. Really?"

"It's like he was born for it. Just tell me you didn't design that."

"No." Kinnery shook his head. "I think I went quite far enough into the realms of ill-advised fantasy, Mike."

Mike stopped short of telling Kinnery too much about Ian's exceptional physical skills. It was another admission too far. "He's good at it. I'd trust him to work alongside us now."

"Just remember that people could well start looking again one day. They might even be guys like you."

They were, buddy. "What better place to hide him than among contractors, then?"

"Well, he's happy. I'm glad. I really am." Kinnery didn't sound it, though. "Any more problems?"

It was code for uncontrolled morphing. Mike braced to lie unashamedly. "I think you can treat it as shut down now. Well, you'd have guessed that when I asked you for the affidavit for his passport application."

Kinnery nodded, staring across the room as if he'd seen something. Maybe he was trying to spot Ian, thinking this might be some sort of demonstration of his skill. "My offer stands if you need any medical support."

"I don't think he's ready for that yet."

"I've updated the list of tests and procedures I think might be safe to have without causing problems." Kinnery took a folded sheet of paper from his wallet and handed it to Mike. "Do I take it he no longer wants the, ah, problem switched off? Not that I can do that yet."

"No, he's perfectly happy controlling it. He likes the way he looks, and he wants to stay exactly as he is."

"Well, damn. I'd say that's a result." Kinnery steepled his fingers and put them against his lips. "To be honest, I've no idea how much he'd revert to an original phenotype or what it would do to other aspects of his health. When I started this, we didn't even realise that junk DNA wasn't junk."

The conversation faded quietly. Kinnery kept scanning the diners. Mike looked around for Ian, but he couldn't see him at all.

Was he the guy reading a map at the far table, or the one over there struggling to take the lid off his coffee? If he'd come in, he'd morphed radically and changed his clothes. Mike had an odd moment of disorientation. Ian could still walk past him unnoticed unless Mike was looking for giveaways like gait and body language, and Ian was getting more adept at disguising those simply by acting.

They fell silent for a while. There wasn't much else to talk about safely.

"How's Livvie?" Kinnery asked.

"Fantastic."

"And Rob?"

"Due back from Kenya tomorrow. We do hostage and kidnap awareness training now. It's always a good sales pitch when you explain how it happened to you." *Or how we did it to others.* Mike scanned the coffee shop for Ian again. "Dare I ask how things are at your end?"

"Well, I'm okay, but Shaun's had seven months of hell. The board will force him out. Your father really can bury someone, can't he?"

"So I gathered."

"Shaun never forgets, though, and he never quits. Just be aware of that. He'll be a bitter man with a lot of money. Well, not by your standards, but enough to bankroll some trouble."

"Dad doesn't forget, either. He's not a spiteful man. Just robustly protective. And so am I."

"And Dru?" Kinnery changed tack, looking as if he'd taken that to heart. He must have heard about the shooting by now. "How's she doing?"

"She's settled in a new job."

"You keep an eye on her, then."

"Of course. It's one of our companies. Rob calls her every week to make sure she's okay." Mike checked his watch. Ian was now twenty minutes late and he hadn't called. Mike had to assume he wasn't coming. He was scrupulously punctual. "I'm sorry, I think Ian's been held up. I'm sure he'll make it another time."

Kinnery looked around the coffee shop. He seemed genuinely forlorn. "I don't know why I expected him to want to talk to me after what I've done."

"I don't think he's snubbing you," Mike said. "He's just getting his head straight about Maggie and her father."

"So does he want to know his real history?"

"Depends what you call real. That would be his grandmother's family."

Kinnery fished in his pants pocket and handed Mike a metallic green USB drive. "You better have this. I don't think it's beyond you to find out more from the information in here. In theory, if you trace the clinic, it should have records to narrow it down. God knows how you'd get them released or explain it to a court, but you seem to have some fascinatingly irregular resources at your disposal."

Mike turned the drive over in his palm. "What is this, exactly?"

"All that's left of my notes from a certain project."

"I hope it's secure."

"Don't worry, the entire drive's encrypted. The password's on that list of procedures, along with a link for downloading the software, so I'd transfer that information and destroy the original right away if I were you."

There was no reason not to take it. It wouldn't eat or drink anything, as Rob was fond of saying, so Ian could decide for himself one day. The contents were probably classified. But so was some of the material in Maggie Dunlop's folder. Mike wouldn't feel extra-guilty for having a few more pages.

"Ian did have something to ask, actually."

"Sure."

"He wants clarification. He needs to know if his embryo was created specifically for the experiment. That's never been clear to him."

"Will it make that much difference?"

"He was very precise about it."

"Well, no, he was a spare," Kinnery said, an oddly mechanical term to Mike. Then Kinnery frowned at him as if a thought he didn't like very much had crossed his mind. "What, you think I had this batch of donor eggs, went to the fridge for a pint of jizz, and thought, what the hell, why not give it the personal touch?"

"I could recite a long list of eminent scientists who were into self-experimentation," Mike said. "But I won't deny I used to wonder if the bond was more than guilt."

"Well, he's not mine." Kinnery was still looking around the coffee shop every so often. "Don't worry, we worked with a reputable IVF clinic. You sometimes end up with embryos you can't implant immediately for various reasons, so they're frozen, and eventually the parents have to decide what to do with the ones that aren't implanted — give them up to another couple, dispose of them, or donate them for research."

Mike couldn't remember if Dad had ever told Kinnery about his infertility situation or not. But he had to say something. "I know. Livvie and I went through a lot of IVF cycles before we gave up."

"Christ, I'm sorry." Kinnery shut his eyes for a moment as if he didn't dare say another word for fear of picking the wrong one. "Shall I just shut up? Look, if Ian's worried about inherited problems, he's not the offspring of diseased inbred deadbeats who sold their genetic material for crack. Whoever donated him wasn't short of a few bucks. Even his surrogate was off her habit and well looked after for the duration of the pregnancy."

"That's all he wants to know, I think." It was hard to keep the conversation going much longer. Mike was already taking a risk meeting Kinnery anyway, but there was nothing more they could discuss. "I'd better go. I'll try to get him down here next month. Take care of yourself, Charles."

"And you, Mike. Give my best to your family. It'd be nice to see Ian again."

Mike read Kinnery's list in the taxi on his way to the restaurant. Well, he already had the encryption software, so Ian could look through the data whenever he liked. Then a random thought distracted him. Family: Kinnery might well have felt that Ian had been taken from him, that Mike had walked in and snatched the kitten from the basket like that unhappy would-be mother cat. Mike had been sure that he'd think it served the bastard right for a sustained deceit at the expense of another human being. But he didn't, not then anyway. It was rather sad.

But I found Ian. I rescued him. He's mine, and I'm keeping him.

Mike accepted that he liked it when strangers took Ian for his son. Mothering was a word that implied devoted care, but fathering had come to mean insemination and little else to follow, when it should have meant teaching, looking out for, taking pride in, providing for. It mattered.

I don't have to be ashamed of that. I ought to like myself more for feeling that way. I did right. This time, I really know that I did right in the world.

He wondered how Ian would feel when they adopted a baby.

Dad had always joked that Charlotte had been furious when Mom had told her she was going to have a little brother or sister. She still was, it seemed.

Could I ever tell a child that their brother's a shape-shifter? Another secret. Well, all families have them.

The restaurant was the one where Kinnery had first told Dad that Ian was more than a crazy rumour. Mike wasn't sure if Ian knew. It didn't seem the right moment to tell him and risk spoiling the day.

"Ian, I did ask Charles," Mike said. It was all code again. It wasn't a bad habit to maintain. "He says you were a *spare*."

Ian nodded, chewing a section of breadstick. He broke them into equal lengths first, just like Dad did.

"Good. So he saved me."

"Sorry?"

"I would have been flushed away otherwise. Or whatever they do. He gave me a lifeline."

Livvie didn't flinch. Mike did, somewhere inside. Lifelines were Nick hauling Mike from the raging water and Rob stemming the life bleeding out of him, not some lottery of which experiment would make it far enough to risk taking it further.

Am I jealous? Am I expecting Ian to be perpetually grateful that I took him in and protected him? Am I hurt that he equates Kinnery's goddamn whim with that?

Mike shook himself out of it. Ian just had a talent for embracing whatever crap life threw at him and turning it into laurels.

"That's very gracious, Ian," Livvie said.

"No, it's just easier than feeling hard done by." Ian was always frank about his emotions. Mike once thought he was being philosophical, but he'd come to understand that Ian was literal. "Blame's hard work. I'd hate to feel that I needed to get my own back unless I really had to. If there's an up side, then I don't."

Livvie studied the dessert menu as if it was an exam paper she'd just turned over. Mike couldn't tell whether she was trying not to smile or if her eyes were brimming.

"Pistachio," she said. "They've got pistachio ice cream today. And no Rob to eat it."

After lunch, they went back to Dad's apartment to freshen up and change for the afternoon ahead. It was Dad's base when he was in town, a home from home that was large enough for family gatherings as well. Ian was fretting over his shirt in the mirror when Mike decided to bring up the subject of the data Kinnery had given him. He held up the USB drive.

"From Kinnery," he said. "It's the last of his Project Ringer data. He wanted you to have it. In case you ever needed the research." He took a breath. "Or if you wanted to use the information in it to track down your biological parents. You don't have to look at it yet."

Ian examined the drive for a few moments as if he was trying to divine what was on it without plugging it in.

"Password?" He expected security on everything. "Can I use your laptop?"

"Sure. I'll show you how to use the portable decryption so you don't leave traces."

Mike hadn't expected him to be so keen to start. It hurt. He hoped it was more scientific interest in the project than a need to find two people who didn't even know he existed. Ian sat down at the desk in the living room, booted up the laptop, and looked at the password on the paper Mike handed him.

"You really want to open it now?" Mike asked.

"No, I want to erase it securely. If I do it now, I can forget it ever existed. Is that okay? I know it can take hours to do that. I could leave it running while we're out."

Mike was caught out by Ian's reaction. "You don't have to do that. I know you worry about security, but there's no rush."

"It's not about security, Mike. I just don't need to know who they were. I know who *I* am, I know who *you* are, and I'm going to find out what kind of guy my great-grandfather was. Nothing else is relevant."

Mike could only nod. He hadn't expected to feel so choked up by the comment. Ian inserted the drive, tapped away at the keyboard, and decrypted the volume. Everything now hung on a few seconds and a couple of clicks.

"Is this right?" Ian asked, frowning at the screen.

"That's it. That security level there — that'll overwrite it a few times."

"Got it."

"Now it'll ask you if you're sure you want to erase."

"I'm sure."

Ian clicked. The progress bar at the bottom of the window

showed several hours to run.

"There you go," Ian said, getting up from the desk. "I feel better now. When it's done, I'll destroy the drive as well."

"It'll be wiped clean anyway."

"You know how you hang on to your lucky watch?" Ian said. "Well, I need that drive to *not* hang on to. I need to make a point of destroying it."

Livvie walked up behind them and put her hand on Ian's shoulder. "I'm going to stay here. I'll monitor it for you. Go on. Get ready."

Mike retreated to the bathroom to shave again, making a mental list of all the things he'd have to chew over with Rob when he got back. He wanted to get thoroughly drunk and emotional with him. He'd pick his brains on the art of coping with the curve balls that kids threw you, and remind him what a solid, unflinching, always-there friend — what a great *brother* — he was.

Livvie looked Mike over while he dressed. "You look dashing. Very yacht club."

"I don't want to let Ian down." Mike adjusted his collar. The visit to the memorial was a formal blazer and tie event as far as he was concerned, no matter how hot it was today. "Some things have to be done right."

"I know. I'll visit the memorial with him before we go home. Just so he knows I'm there for him as much as you are."

Mike wasn't sure who was more nervous about the visit, him or Ian. When Dad's driver dropped them off at the memorial, it was a real effort for Mike to walk along the polished black granite wall and all those tight-packed, never-forgotten names without feeling that he was intruding. It was simply impossible to speak. He should have had something profound to say to Ian, but nothing would come out, and Ian didn't comment or ask questions. The silence itself was the conversation that passed between them. This time, it was Ian who put his hand on Mike's back as they walked.

"There he is," Ian said. An elderly man in a Panama hat and check shirt was waiting with a sheaf of paper in his hand. "That's Mr Kovac. He was a door gunner. He sent me his picture so I'd recognise him. I didn't send him mine, though. Just in case."

A photo didn't seem necessary, though.

Mike saw the look on Kovac's face as he caught sight of Ian, a flash of the brows and the start of a smile as if he'd recognised an old friend, followed immediately by a slow, sad frown as common sense killed the reflex.

Kovac stepped forward and reached for Ian's hand without any introduction. "Damn, for a second I thought you were him. Crazy, huh? You're so much like Davey it's scary." He shook Ian's hand, then grabbed Mike's. "You must be Ian's dad. It's good to meet you both."

Explanation would have felt like disowning Ian. Mike tried the assumption on for size again, and liked the comfort and weight of it. He decided to keep it.

"Let's find somewhere to have a coffee, sir," Mike said. "We don't know much about David. You know how complicated families can be."

"Ah, you'd have loved the guy." Kovac smiled to himself. "Real quiet. Just melted into the background until there was a tough job to be done, then he'd be the first in. Insisted on it."

Mike couldn't stop himself from patting Ian's shoulder as they walked. "I think that runs in the family," he said.

The story continues in
BLACK RUN
Book 2 in the Ringer series.

ABOUT THE AUTHOR

Karen Traviss is the author of a dozen New York Times bestsellers, and her critically-acclaimed Wess'har books have been finalists five times for the Campbell and Philip K. Dick awards. She also writes comics and games with military and political themes. A former defence correspondent, newspaper reporter, and TV journalist, she lives in Wiltshire, England.

WANT TO READ MORE?

For more information, visit karentraviss.com, where you can sign up for news and exclusive previews of forthcoming books. You can also follow Karen on Twitter via @karentraviss or at Facebook.com/KarenTravissAuthor

ALSO BY KAREN TRAVISS

RINGER

Black Run (Book 2)

WESS'HAR

City of Pearl
Crossing the Line
The World Before
Matriarch
Ally
Judge

COLLECTED SHORT STORIES

View Of A Remote Country

HALO

Glasslands
The Thursday War
Mortal Dictata

GEARS OF WAR

Aspho Fields
Jacinto's Remnant
Anvil Gate
Coalition's End
The Slab

STAR WARS: REPUBLIC COMMANDO

Hard Contact
Triple Zero
True Colors
Order 66
Imperial Commando: 501st

STAR WARS

Bloodlines
Sacrifice
Revelation
The Clone Wars
No Prisoners

CPSIA information can be obtained
at www.ICGtesting.com
Printed in the USA
LVHW03s1918140818
586956LV00013B/1212/P